FROM BESTSELLING AND AWARD-WINNING AUTHOR

ARABELLA K. FEDERICO

THE MARK OF SHADOWS AND STARLIGHT

THE MARK OF SHADOWS AND STARLIGHT

For the survivors.

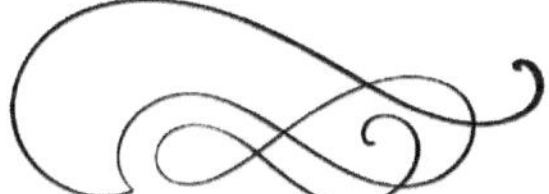

The Mark of Shadows and Starlight

First Edition, September 2025

Cover art copyright © 2025 by Stefanie Saw at Seventhstar Art Services
https://www.seventhstarart.com/
Developmental Edit by Tanner Parks, with assistance from Chersti Nieveen, Andraea
Jones, and Ben Stapley at Writer Therapy
https://writertherapy.com/
Copy edits, line edits, proofread, and formatting by Samantha Pico at The Goth Editor
https://thegotheditor.com/
Portrait and Elendril crystal artwork copyright © 2025 by Arabella K. Federico

ISBN (Paperback): 979-8-9861875-8-7

Author's Note

A special note for readers. *The Mark of Shadows and Starlight* takes a deeper take into adult topics, such as SA and childhood SA. For a full list, please see my website at https://www.arabellakfederico.com/the-mark-of-chaos-creation

Please proceed with care, as the depth of these discussions deepens in comparison to the previous two novels in this series.

The Elendril Crystals

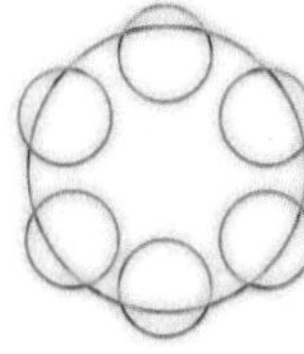

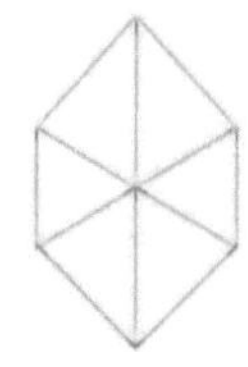

MAGIC	RINGER MAGIC
ANTIMATTER	MENTAL MANIPULATION
GRAVITY MANIPULATION	HEALING
REANIMATE THE DEAD	DREAM WALKER
RENGENERATION	MEMORY MANIPULATION
BODY MANIPULATION	VISUAL MANIPULATION
ELEMENTAL CONTROL	SENSORY MANIPULATION

PROLOGUE

NARESTEÉ ORPHANAGE

SEVEN YEARS AGO

GAVRIELLE ABRAXAS

Some people never deserve redemption. Some sins are unforgivable. Some darkness is too black to be saved by the light.

This orphanage is a dark place . . . We never belonged within walls oozing with the cries of a thousand children as the aliens bled us dry to our very last tear.

The first thing I feel is the pain—the intense scorching across my neck. There's screaming and pungent, charred flesh mixed with heavy smoke.

Where's Kara?

Where am I?

They ripped me out of the boy's room before the explosion knocked us down the stairs.

I hope they didn't find her inside the pillar, but I can't fathom a world where she's trapped within that inferno, either.

Please, Father, Mother, keep her safe—protect her.

I try moving across the orphanage floor as burning wood falls around us, but my seared skin pulls taut, causing a sharp hiss to slide through my teeth. My shirt is . . . melted into my chest, and the burns reach up the side of my neck as I fight my nausea.

Be strong. Be strong like Father.

The horned woman giving orders trips down the stairs, burned and disheveled. "Grab the marked boy and find the girl! *Now!*"

Get up, I order myself. *Kara needs you.*

I try to lift myself up, but my body isn't responding.

A SSPARROW's stiff hands heave me over his hard metal shoulder as if I'm nothing but a sack of grain, and I scream from the pulling and tearing of my scorched skin.

"Shut up," the warped voice says.

There's no empathy on its face, where only a strip of blue light glows where the eyes should be. There's no empathy anywhere.

Anger boils in me so hot that, despite the pain, I pound on the soldier. It does nothing. I'm too weak . . . too pathetic. How could I ever protect her like this when I can't even protect myself?

Wait . . . the horned extra had said, *Find the girl* . . . They were only searching for children with marks like ours. If she's still looking, Kara must have escaped.

Or must have been caught in the blast.

I'm outside, and through the tears, I can make out the orphanage burning bright orange against the freshly darkened sky.

Was this their plan the entire time? To burn this orphanage to the ground? Father and Mother said Arianyte was evil, but . . .

A group of soldiers charge toward the nearby woods, and my Sky-Fae eyesight recognizes their target despite the trees' looming shadows hiding her.

I blink to force myself to see clearer—to see her.

Then something within me morphs and focuses onto a single point—*her.* Kara. In a flash of light, I don't feel like a child. I lost my childhood the moment Arianyte invaded my world and

 2

even more so when my parents were killed. I see myself grown-up, years into the future. I'm holding someone—a woman—beautiful and glowing and happy. She's smiling and laughing, eyes so bright and teal they bring me to my knees. It's Kara. And she is mine.

Mine.

Mine.

This feeling is overwhelming and all consuming. The link between us pulls taut, so much so I think it might snap. It's everything, my entire being and beyond. The calling and the desperation to be near her, to keep her safe and happy and living.

Mine. *She's mine!*

The words roar in my head like an anthem. They burn on my heart like a brand.

Mate.

That is what she is.

My mate.

In the blink of an eye, I'm back to my current self, in pain and as useless as I was the day my family was ripped away from me.

Not again . . . please, Father. I can't lose someone I love again.

With the last of my strength, I summon the magic I have no business having. The very magic Arianyte has come here to claim. I can give her the time she needs to escape, even if it means we can't be together.

The symbol on my hand tingles as I push my power outwards towards her, toward my best friend. *Toward my mate.* The thought of being separated from her hurts more than the burns ravaging my body.

The mating bond snaps into place. Father said it was world-altering, but I never expected this.

Her swaying, long, dark hair is all I can see as she runs away from me before I make her body fade into the shadows until she vanishes from my sight all together. From the world that wishes to hurt her.

"Where'd the hell did she go?" one soldier yells above all the screaming.

She's getting away.

My vision blurs and blackens . . .

She's getting away . . .

She's mine.

I smile, knowing this to be the truest thing of all.

That Kara is my mate . . .

CHAPTER 1

AFTER NEGOTIATION WITH TERRAN GOVERNMENT OFFICIALS, ARIANYTE WILL CONTINUE TO HOLD MISS KARALEVINE RUZZ IN CUSTODY IN EXCHANGE FOR RETURNING ALL ARIANYTE SERVICES BACK TO THE AURORA SYSTEM. MISS RUZZ IS NOT A PRISONER, HOWEVER, AND WILL NOT BE TREATED AS SUCH. SHE ASKS THAT THE PEOPLE OF EARTH STOP THEIR DISSENT AGAINST THE EMPIRE IMMEDIATELY.

KARALEVINE RUZZ

It's a distant, ravenous fear . . . one that'll wholly eat me alive. I can't run. Running is a fallacy of safety and hope. It can't save me. Not from this.

Nothing can save me from this.

I'm imprisoned in this place. An endless darkness. A void that's become my Hell—my prison—shackled to it as mercilessly as if I had chains on my wrists and ankles. Within this Stygian emptiness, I'm locked inside a clear cube. Its walls choke me as they squeeze tighter and tighter. The space is hardly big enough for my petite frame to move three feet; sometimes, it's two, other times only one. The air is so pungent I can taste it. The humid heat is so unbearable it nearly drives me to madness. No matter how hard I bash on the unbreakable walls, no matter how many times I use my antimatter crystal against it, I can't break free.

Who, I wonder, is my tormentor? Who trapped me here? Do they delight in my endless cries for freedom? For death? Or have they simply forgotten my existence? Is this where I'm to spend all of eternity?

The faces I glimpse outside the cube are always blurry, unfocused blobs. I'm forced to watch the scene play out.

"Kara!"

I turn toward the voices, wishing so badly to see them, touch them, be with them, even though I can't remember who they are.

"Kara! Come on, we're waiting for you!"

One of the female voices is sweet. Kind . . . gentle, even. A friend. I long for that friend . . . For anyone to save me from this place.

A figure of a tall girl glints in my peripheral, who's skipping playfully within the darkness, a flash of blue hair between tendrils of shadow. I press my body as close to her as the cube will allow me to. I need to get to her.

Please, stars, let me out.

Anybody.

Save me.

Soon, she disappears into the darkness beyond my prison, and I cry out to her, beg her to come back. She's gone, just like all the others.

There are no friends here.

Another voice calls my name.

I recognize it this time.

Jance.

He's always here.

His deep voice and thick accent is sharp, hurried, rushing. "Forget us and go. Run from here. Get out now."

Why does he always say the same words?

My crystal instantly sears, burns, and thrashes.

I want out. I want out. *I want out!*

Stars, let me out of this fucking cube!

A thrum rattles my entire brain as a terrible horn bursts my eardrums as it calls upon monsters and madness.

The darkness never likes Jance.

"You need to wake up, Kara. You need to remember. Remember what happened."

What happened?

I pound my fists against the cube, the thuds barely audible over the ear-bleeding blare blasting out of nowhere.

I can't, I can't, *I can't!*

"Kara! Kara, wake up! Remember!"

Let me out! Let me out! *Free me, free me, free me!*

Within the darkness, a burst of light burns my eyes. Sizzling in the tattoo ink color Sunrise Yellow, flames erupt, and behind the whipping blaze are a pair of horns.

Strange symbols flash, everything else disappearing. Symbols, my star, more of the same markings, one after another after another . . .

"Remember!"

"Remember!"

"Remember!"

My eyes—my real eyes—flutter open, and I'm immediately met with a pair of Night Brown eyes, glowing orbs of Fuchsia burning within his pupils. Doesn't that mean he's using his Ringer magic? Jance's magic can mess with brain chemistry . . . but why would he do that?

"Jance?" I mumble, confused, my eyelids closing like leaden weights.

Where am I? I was dreaming of that awful place again . . . but now I'm somewhere else.

"You're okay. You're dreaming," he says, voice soft and calm.

I must be . . .

"Don't believe what he tells you. It's all lies."

"What?"

A strange wave of euphoria steals the terror gripping me by the bones, but an underlying sense of dread lingers beneath it, clawing itself back to my consciousness.

In fact, the star-shaped mark on my chest is burning hot—white hot.

"I won't hurt you, darling. You know me. You know my voice."

I pull myself back up to the light, forcing my eyes to open.

I'm not safe. I'm in a bad place. The horns . . . the cube . . . the darkness.

My eyes snap open like a bursting geyser, heart hammering in my ears, and the first thing I see is Jance sitting at my bedside.

Jance flinches as he notices the strange look I'm giving him, no magical glow emitting from my Ringer's eyes. In fact, my bodyguard looks like he always does. Blacktop-colored hair styled in an intentionally messy look, gray hairs poking through in his short stubble along his jawline. His Arianyte uniform is new, stiff, and the high-quality black fabric rasps like crinkling paper as he leans toward me. His face is shadowed with panic and worry—for me. We've only known each other for four, maybe five weeks . . . ever since Malakyte and I came up to the Azurite and they found Jance days later. Given that, his concern feels odd. I don't trust it—I don't trust him.

I release a shaky sigh, my body rigid and skin clammy. I avoid Jance's gaze by looking around Malakyte's royal suite. Clean and sleek, the black décor has my prince's touch all over it. The humming choir of the Azurite engine fills the growing tension between Jance and me, and planet Earth floats in the skylight above the bed.

"What are you doing?" I ask, shuffling up to my elbows and scooting away from him as I try to remember the last several minutes.

Was it minutes? It's hard to recall . . . I was having a nightmare and then I wasn't . . .

"You were screaming," he clarifies, inching back once I do. "I feared something had happened, but when I got here a few minutes ago, it was clear you were having another nightmare, so I was trying to wake you."

"You only just got here?" I ask, my tone accusatory. "You weren't using your magic just now?"

Jance's brows knit together, confused. "No . . . I arrived only a moment ago. Why do you ask?"

"I . . ."

I guess I was dreaming when I saw his eyes glowing. Stars, he's looking at me in that weird way again. I increase the distance between us. The Midnight Black sheets on Malakyte's bed come with me as I cover myself, even though I'm wearing pajamas. Yes, he's my bodyguard, but his intensity freaks me out.

Jance stands, finally looking away. "I apologize. I shouldn't have—"

Below us, on the second floor of the suite, the door bursts open, and darkness itself barrels in as if carried on a dangerous, icy gust.

Malakyte, the Prince of Arianyte, rushes up the small spiral staircase separating the bedroom from the living quarters. Moving with determination, his long, straight, Kohl Black hair sways.

"I felt your crystal surge," he says, our eyes colliding the moment he hits the landing.

My heart stumbles at his gaze, all his attention focused through Onyx eyes. Beautiful, powerful, hot as fuck, even with the scar slicing his brow in two across the left side of his face—he's gorgeous. Dressed all in black, he's stunning in his impeccably tailored clothing that hugs his lean, muscled body perfectly. Even the metal finishes on his jacket are polished so flawlessly they reflect the Champagne quartz lights that illuminate the Azurite, changing colors depending on the time of day.

Malakyte strides up to Jance aggressively. "Why are you here? You're supposed to be guarding the exterior, not the interior."

Their constant nipping at each other's heels is the only bit of tension in my perfect world.

Jance fearlessly meets Malakyte's eyes, but his body stiffens. "I also felt her magic spike, along with screaming. I had ample reason to assume she was being attacked or in severe distress. So, naturally, I entered and found that she was having another nightmare. I woke her only moments before you arrived."

I suppose the nightmares are another negative.

Malakyte searches Jance suspiciously before his gaze shifts my way. He analyzes me as if he's never seen me.

"Dreams are merely that, dreams. Get out."

Malakyte's voice is unnaturally harsh.

I open my mouth to say how rude that is, but with one last glance at me, Jance is gone.

"He was only trying to help." I toss Malakyte an incredulous look and throw the sheets aside.

My sweat-soaked pajamas stick to me like a second skin.

Malakyte scoffs as I hop off the bed and make my way to his closet, where some of my clothes have collected over the last couple of weeks of living on the Azurite. I have my own room, but I'm rarely there. Since we met on Earth nearly six months ago and began dating soon after, it's only natural I spend most of my nights with him.

I press a button next to the sleek black doors, and the mix of dark suits and dresses glide past on the track.

"Wear those pants I had made for you and the cashmere sweater. I don't want you getting cold later."

My brows rise as I scan the garments. "Later?"

"To visit the public sector, of course."

 10

The hum of the track stops as I swing around, where Malakyte is standing near a leather chair, a cocky smirk tugging those blue-tinted lips.

He's finally going to take me there?

Showing his double set of pointed canines, he clarifies, "Since you've been so good lately, I thought I'd reward you with a tour of what'll soon be your kingdom. Take you out, show you off, buy you whatever you want. Additionally, I want you to look perfect for what I have planned for after. It's a surprise—and, no, I'm not *spilling*." He smiles, the hot, mocking jerk. "For now, let me spoil you. Your hair will be done there, but I want you to wash it first."

Not like I didn't shower and wash my hair yesterday. My poor teal ends are so faded from all these frequent washes he insists on.

Yet I flash a grin of my own, and he leans against the railing of the staircase behind him.

"Don't think this trip to the public sector is going to distract me from searching for the other Starseeds and Ringers for long," I say. His grin falls, causing my heart rate to tick up, but I can't go back on my principles on this. "After selling out the rebellion and joining you like I did . . . I don't know. I mean, stars, I'm a full-fledged sky-rat now." Malakyte scoffs at the Terran slur for Arianyte's people. "After going from rebel to Arianyte princess, I need some redemption."

Malakyte smiles, but it sends a shiver down my spine. "Redemption is for heroes."

I snort. "The Hijacked are important to me, Malakyte. So, hero or not, they deserve better. Once you showed me the footage of Deimos trafficking those children, I knew I had to do something. The other Starseeds and Ringers, including Gavrielle, are imperative for me to do this. Just because I'm no longer a rebel doesn't mean I don't have the same goals. I want to help them."

"Even after your people turned on you, even after Geonni led the rebels to assassinate you with Deimos by his side? Why bother to help their cause after that?"

"The Hijacked had no part in that. They're innocent. Can we please not get into this argument again? You knew all this after you took me from that rooftop after I accidentally blasted Naresteé, who is still pissed—because she hates me."

The mention of Naresteé instantly brings my mind back to those horns in my nightmare, but I brush it off with a promise to myself to think about it later.

"You knew stopping Deimos was important to me. You said it was too dangerous to be on Earth after Geonni put his hit out on me, so I reluctantly agreed only because you promised you'd help me do this. There's been no news on Gavrielle, either. I don't know if he's even alive. You swore we'd find him, too."

Sighing, Malakyte closes the distance between us, grabbing me by the waist and bringing me flush to his front. His abrupt iciness literally steals the breath from my lungs as his cold-blooded body presses to mine. When I crank my neck up, he's looking down at me with uncharacteristic softness. "I fear that the other Starseeds and Ringers will see what I saw in you from the moment we first met all those months ago. That you're special, that you're strong. They'll use you. Twist you into their weapon. The veritable reason I'm hesitating on this. Gavrielle is Deimos's Ringer. There's a significant bond there. It wouldn't be a stretch to assume they're all in league with Deimos, and where does that leave you? Betrayed all over again? I'd never be able to absolve myself if something happened to you on my watch a second time. Your safety is everything to me."

I never considered that.

Icy fingers gently grip my chin. "Forget them for now. Today, let me treat you like the queen you were born to become. Soon, all of this will be ours. You will be an empress with unchallenged power. I'm merely the sword you use to wield your influence across the stars. I'm yours, Karalevine, in every way. My empire is yours. Its resources and power will take you to heights I can hardly anticipate. I knew all those decades spent searching for you weren't in vain. Not even time or death itself could keep us apart."

My cheeks hurt from how wide I bashfully smile. "Tell me the story again."

Malakyte throws my long hair over one shoulder, leaving the other exposed to the icy kisses he peppers along my tattooed skin.

"It's a tragedy."

His voice is low and deep—almost seductive.

"Once upon a time?"

He chuckles. "Once upon a time . . . I loved you, but you had a different face. Many decades in the past, we Starseeds and Ringers came together under Arianyte to protect the galaxy. I fell in love with a girl named Zariya Ethoria, a beautiful woman with the spirit of a star burning within her. Loving Zariya was easy from the moment I first laid eyes on her. She was supposed to be my queen one day. We were happy."

I curl into his chest, hiding my face.

Malakyte's arms come around my shoulders as he squeezes me tight. "Unfortunately, one of our own turned against us. Deimos, another Starseed, wanted Zariya's power for himself. He killed her and all the other Starseeds and Ringers. My heart shattered the moment Zariya took her last breath. I could not—I would not accept her loss.

"Then I consulted an old empire hag long known for her mystical connection to the galaxy and the Elendril crystals. She whispered a ray of hope into my darkened void of a life. Our souls are immortal. No matter how many bodies we may inhabit, no matter how many times we live and die and love and lose, our true essence remains. Zariya's true essence remained, and because her Elendril crystal was a celestial artifact born from the womb of the Universe itself, I realized neither could

13

be destroyed, only remade. So, I set out, looking for children branded with the mark of creation, until I found a young girl living on a secluded planet called Earth. I sent my second in command to retrieve her, but that didn't go as planned."

The flashback of that night at the orphanage comes on strong. How I left my best friend Gavrielle there as it burned, the embers chasing the last bit of my innocence as I ran like a coward.

"Losing both her and Deimos's young Ringer was a tragedy. Both fled. Both separated. But I had confirmed Zariya's soul still existed, that the crystal had returned with her. All the crystals restored, Ringers intact and synced with their divinely paired Starseeds on Earth."

"And then?"

My smile grows once again.

"And then, years later, I met a heedless young woman up on a rooftop, brashly trying to bring down my empire. I should have hated her for it. However, the moment I gazed into the eyes of this Terran rebel, I knew I found my Zariya. Her soul was staring back at me—*your soul*. You hated me, hated Arianyte, which I understood. Our reputation is . . . ill-boding. Once I broke down my plans to change this empire once I'm crowned emperor, you came around."

Now it's my turn to snicker.

"Because of your dashing good looks and vibrant personality?"

"You're ruining it," he says, not all the way joking.

Not like I haven't made him tell me the story a thousand times. Although that weird, gut-twisting feeling overcomes me every single time once Malakyte gets to this part in the story.

I pet his arm as I say, "I feel like our time together down on Earth is fuzzy . . . Like, I remember it all, but the details are colorless and weird, and it's still worrying me. Should I see your doctor again?"

"No, you're fine," he promises. "It's simply your body adjusting to space—coupled with the trauma of Geonni and Deimos trying to kill you. Who wouldn't want to block that out? It'll all cement itself in time. Allow yourself to relax and know you're safe up here. With me. I can tell you anything you feel you've forgotten."

I feel like some memory is on the tip of my tongue, but it flutters away like a butterfly passing by on a spring day.

"Zariya was amazing in her own right, but you, Karalevine . . . you're different. You're so much more." He separates us, taking my hand in his and kissing the back of it. "And this time, I won't let anyone take you from me again."

CHAPTER 2

The air near the border crossing separating the public and private sectors of the Azurite feels almost too clean as Malakyte and our brigade of SSPARROWs converge on this uncharted threshold. I can't stop whipping my head in every direction as I take in each detail.

The SSPARROW's fat metal heads obstruct my view, and I hop on my tiptoes as I peek over them. Only Jance wears the bodyguard uniform, no helmet.

"You're adorable, Karalevine, but bouncing around like that in public makes you look impatient. I don't want my people to think negatively of you."

Oh.

Instead of trying to see what's ahead, I look down. The floors glitter with crushed Citron melded in with glossy black marble, polished so pristinely I can see our reflections in it. It's quiet despite the small line of people collected on this side of the border. All are extraterrestrials—often called "extras"—of different species, skin colors, and shapes as they wait to cross into the public sector. I'm the only Terran I've seen on this side.

Then an extra catches my eye, only because it's so near to the ground, and I nearly trip over my feet at this thing. Truly, it's less about its bizarre, disconnected, unproportional appearance and more about the terror flooding me as it creeps ever closer to us.

It doesn't seem to have a body—not one that's corporeal, anyway. Looking at it feels *wrong*. It walks like a spider, its feet too light as it slinks across the polished Azurite floors as if the shadows gave it permission to tread on their domain.

My cheeks flush, and my body gets hot as it closes in . . .

I hold my breath as it passes, its body transparent in some places, semi-solid in others.

Doesn't Malakyte see this thing? It isn't right—it's fucking terrifying. Something like this shouldn't be on this ship with so many people aboard. Why doesn't anyone else see it and do something about it? Where are its organs? Its eyes, its face, its mouth?

I blink out what appears to be glitches in its body as it strolls by—giving us no mind at all—with nothing but a stars damned clipboard in its nonexistent hands like it's simply walking to work. My body shivers, and I immediately avert my gaze from it.

Not my business. Not important. It must. . . belong here.

I look up at Malakyte to make sure he sees it, but he's acting completely normal. He'd never put me in danger, so. . . I guess it's fine? Jance doesn't seem to notice it either, and none of the SSPARROWs make a move to stop it.

Malakyte points above us to the vast, vaulted ceilings, his other hand laced tightly through mine. "The constellations are from my home planet, Accaria."

I gaze up, eyes sparkling as brightly as the constellations etched into the Midnight Sky colored ceiling in what looks like diamonds.

"Technically, the private sector where we live and the public sector are separate components of the ship. The public sector came decades later. Because of that, we created a failsafe so that if one side were to experience a catastrophic failure, the other could detach unharmed. It's mostly for the royal's protection."

"You're so high maintenance, Malakyte."

His amused chuckle is delicious.

Most of the Azurite has details like the dark flooring, Matte Black walls, and quartz lights. What's special about this place are the paintings on the walls, covering both sides of the hallway, depicting a glorious battle fought and won on the right and a galactic portrait made of stars, nebula, planets, and moons to the left.

Although . . .

"Malakyte." I tug on his jacket sleeve, pointing to the galactic painting. "There's another one of those symbols again."

Malakyte's head whips to our left as we stop, his grip on my hand tightening. The beat of silence in the room fills with a familiar tension that's become predictable.

"They graffitied your mural," I say, trying to break the tense silence. "The red color doesn't even match. It would've at least gone better on the other one."

Malakyte whips his head back to me, shooting me something dangerously close to a dirty look, but he recovers by shouting at one of his SSPARROWs, "I told you to find the people responsible for desecrating my ship. Why is there another one?"

A few soldiers approach the symbol, one of many geometric shapes painted all over the Azurite in different colors. Today, they've chosen to ruin an actual piece of artwork, using Cherry Red spray paint. A circle with six miniature circles gliding all alongside its rim. It's . . . oddly familiar. Like a little tickle in the corner of my mind whispering a secret to me. I've seen this before . . . That's right! I dreamed of these symbols this morning, didn't I? Was this one? I think it was, but . . . I'm sure I've never seen it outside of my dreams before.

A soldier touches it with his gloved hand. "It's still wet, sir."

Odd . . .

A low, nearly imperceptible growl emits from Malakyte as he squeezes my hand and tugs me toward the actual crossing.

 18

"Dispose of it and find the perpetrator," he orders, irritation thick in his tone. "I won't continue to tolerate your failure."

I'm too afraid to tell him I've been secretly drawing all these weird symbols, feeling a strange pull toward them. This new one belongs to the others, my artist eye picking up on that immediately. My star symbol that all Ringers have, the one I share with Jance, is among them. He's my divine pair, sharing magic with me through my Elendril crystal as it swims within my heart like a parasite. Like Gavrielle has with Deimos of all people, unfortunately for him. I think . . . I think the graffiti we've been seeing all over the ships are Elendril symbols, but I don't dare tell Malakyte.

"Graffiti has been used in history as a sign of rebellion," I say, my voice stiff. "I'm sure whoever is doing this is just trying to make a point."

He looks down at me like I'm insane.

I laugh, but it sounds fake, and my forced smile falls quickly as I clear the tightness from my throat. "What? I'm a tattoo artist, Malakyte. And an ex-rebel. You should expect me to comment on something like that. If there's dissent within our people, we should try to understand their grievances and address them."

He bends down as we slow our approach to the crossing, whispering in my ear, "Your boldness is why I love you."

He bites down on his teeth, a snapping echoing in my ear as he playfully pretends to bite me.

I guess he isn't mad about the graffiti anymore.

I blush, looking around to see if anyone noticed the intimate little gesture. When I lock eyes with Jance, his scowl is deep. I glance away.

Focusing ahead, I shake off the tension by rolling my shoulders as we arrive at the heavily guarded border between the private and the public sector.

The actual crossing is separated by a half-circled threshold that's as intimidating as it is large.

Malakyte gestures at the archway, its frame made of sturdy, matte-black material with strange designs etched into it. A long hallway waits behind it, and it looks like some advanced alien metal detector, looming ten feet tall and fifteen wide. "See the rainbow sheen glistening within it?"

I nod. The center of the passageway warps and ripples like an oily pool.

"When someone walks across it, the artificial intelligence scans their body for weapons, contraband, vitals, DNA. It can even predict intention. Negative intentions, specifically. Each person allowed onto our side must have a chip similar to the one we implanted in your hand, which allows them access across the border. Go on, walk through it."

The armed SSPARROWs watch me with their faceless helmets. Despite their constant presence, they unnerve me.

Stepping forward, I walk through the semi-circle, and the soft, flowing substance causes a jolt of coldness to shoot down my spine. When I appear on the other side, I have goose bumps along my entire body, feeling like there's an invisible coat of oil upon every inch.

As Malakyte and our guards make their way through, I notice how different the two sides are. It's one giant hallway, but all the finer details from the private side, like on the floors, walls, and ceilings are gone here, replaced with generic alien steel. It doesn't look special.

Once we're all crossed over, we walk down a long, tight industrial corridor, but the sky-high ceilings make it feel less claustrophobic.

With how massive the private sector is—where it holds the royal wing, all its private amenities, and a massive workforce big enough to house and sustain several thousand Arianyte elites, workers, and their subordinates—it's difficult to imagine the public sector is almost four times bigger. According to Malakyte, the public side contains everything from shopping malls to shipyards to entertainment to housing of tens of thousands of people. And that doesn't even include the huge maintenance tunnels and hallways all throughout both sectors of the Azurite.

"I smell food," I announce as we get closer to the end of the hall, my mouth watering from the scents blasting their way down this hallway.

Freshly baked bread, cooked meats, movie popcorn of all things. Other strange alien smells I have no words to describe.

As the end of the hall appears straight ahead, a symphony blasts through the air, one of life itself.

A woman laughing at her friend's joke. An old man bargaining for a prime piece of produce. A teenage girl gossiping with her sister. On and on until I can see them, see their world.

However, there's something else I can hear clear as day: rushing water.

I tug Malakyte's hand as the tunnel opens to the biggest, grandest piece of architecture I have ever seen.

"How is all this inside a spaceship?" I say in awe, walking out from the tunnel and into the large open area where the public sector begins. Letting go of Malakyte's hand, I twirl in a slow, stunned circle around the gigantic space.

Shops, restaurants, vendors, little roads, plant life . . . and that's just on this level.

Above and beneath us are more levels, so many I can't count. In the center there is nothing but open air, roaring water coming from down below.

"Come see it from here," Malakyte ushers, walking me forward toward the center railing, where a platform stretches over the open middle.

It's empty as we make our way across its clear surface, stretching fifty feet over the middle. Once we reach the railing, I lean over on my tiptoes to get the best view.

Malakyte's cold body presses up behind me, his hands interlacing over mine on the railing as he, too, leans down.

Nearly three hundred feet down is a glorious fountain gushing Crystal Blue water from within its impressive, flowing shapes. Surrounding it are countless different species of alien flora of all different colors. Moss Green, Ancient Forest, Hunter, Bark . . . so many colors I can hardly catalogue them all in my brain before moving onto the next.

It's magnificent. Arianyte can be capable of so much good, as long as it's sculpted with moral hands.

"All of this belongs to you now," Malakyte says into my ear, his voice a seductive promise. I turn to the side to see a sliver of his dark hair in my peripheral. "From every tree to these shops, each item or experience on this ship, it's all yours. We don't concern ourselves with the common people and their grievances, Karalevine. They're irrelevant."

I want to argue, but I'm too transfixed to push back because a part of me likes what he's saying, even when I know I shouldn't.

"By my side, you have everything and anything you could ever dream of, but more than anything, you have strength. And with strength, my dear Star, comes power. That is what's truly coveted most. Don't deny that you want it. I can hear how your heart rate spiked when I said the word. It doesn't make you a bad person, Karalevine, to desire power. You need to release that human need within yourself that craves others' acceptance. What they think is nothing but a ludicrous notion to you now. You're above it. I'm the only one who can truly love you because I see all that darkness that I know terrifies you. It doesn't frighten me. Embrace your darkness. Become it. Become who you were born to be. Take the helm that I'm offering, and nothing and no one will ever hurt you again."

He knows I've been hurt . . . He wants to keep it from ever happening again.

"Let's go. We have a lot of appointments to get you to." He kisses my cheek, drawing me from the ledge and back out to the main space where passersby stare at me like *I'm* the alien here.

Malakyte wasn't lying. He does have a lot of appointments for me.

He gets my nails redone, along with a pedicure, which feels divine. My hair comes next, and Malakyte pushes for me to do away with the teal color all together, but we compromise. I wear it down in loose curls in the way he likes it, and I get to keep the teal.

Next, we go to several shops, where Malakyte picks out most of my outfits, and we end the clothes shopping at the nicest gown store I've ever seen. Dresses that cost more than what I spent on my loft in a year.

The second I walk out of the little changing room inside the store, Malakyte perks up from the Creme Brulee-colored chair he's lounging in, uncrossing his legs as he leans forward. "This is the one. I like it better than the others. You can wear it back."

"Back to the room?" I ask, stepping onto the little pedestal within the dressing room.

Standing, Malakyte approaches, turning me to face him. "To meet my parents."

My freshly waxed brows rise.

The emperor and empress of Arianyte . . . *They're here?*

My opinions of Malakyte may have changed after he brought me in from that rooftop all those months ago, but I still harbor doubts about Arianyte. I can't forget or deny what his parents have done over the hundreds of years they've been at the helm of this empire.

Yet if Malakyte and I rule together, I could do something with this power I've been so graciously gifted. We'd have the resources to save children like me—like the Hijacked. We can make life better for my fellow Terrans, for everyone. To do that, Emperor and Empress Ardeen must abdicate the throne to us, which means they need to accept me, and it puts so much weight on this first impression.

To add to all that, they're not here on a friendly visit, either. They're grieving.

"With everything happening with Selenyte . . . do they have time to meet with me?"

Malakyte averts his eyes, as if he can't stand to look at me. "They wish to be introduced to the woman who will soon rule beside me on the throne. What could be more important than that?"

A few things come to mind.

Instead, a thrill shoots through me, knowing that his power—Arianyte's power—will soon be mine. That little girl, who scrounged for food on the streets of Zarmenia City, would have never dared dream of such a radical change of circumstances. All because this beautiful man crossed the stars to find me. All because he loves me.

I'm the luckiest girl in the entire Aurora System. In the entire galaxy. I just wish I could share some of this good fortune with Gavrielle. Where had he gone after the orphanage was attacked? Why hasn't he tried to find me after all this time?

As we make our way back to the border with the weight of a meeting with the king and queen on my shoulders, something sparkly catches my eye in a store window.

"Can we look at these earrings?" I ask Malakyte, stopping our entire brigade.

He pauses for a beat too long but, without a word, takes me into the store, ordering the others to stay outside.

We enter the small shop, the entire space lined with cases and cases of jewels, likely from all over the galaxy. The clerk is a stout man with thick spectacles along his wrinkled face, much like a pug's.

He fidgets with his clothes, unsuccessfully trying to stuff his pocket into his vest before he bows to Malakyte and me. "How can I be of service, Prince Malakyte?"

"Karalevine is interested in the earrings in your display."

 24

His eyes go wide, his glasses enlarging them to comical proportions.

"Oh, well, we have many similar pieces in the store. Those specific ones are a museum display from the collapsed system Andromedae Five, which, as you know, sir, succumbed once its host star died. Those jewels are the last artifacts of that civilization."

I shake my head. "Oh, never mind, I don't need—"

"You can have them, Karalevine."

My eyes widen, and the businessman and I both stare at each other in awkward surprise.

"I don't . . ."

Malakyte walks me to the back side of the display case, the store owner's pocket watch jingling as he waddles behind us.

"Open it," Malakyte orders, and though his voice is calm, the authority is unmistakable.

The store owner looks as if he might pass out.

"Really, Malakyte, it's fine," I say, but he ignores me.

Reluctantly, the man shimmies up beside us, visibly upset, lifts his pocket watch up to a scanner on the back portion of the glass, flips the watch open, and unlocks the case.

Reaching inside, Malakyte reveals the most gorgeous set of black diamond earrings. They'd match my dress perfectly, and with the way they glitter under the lights, they'd be the perfect finishing touch to make the best first impression with the emperor and empress. The main black diamonds are huge as the tear-drop shape dangles between the setting that encircles them in Slate Gray, making them appear gothic and mysterious. I've never seen anything so luxurious and expensive in my life.

I do want them, but . . .

"These businesses have nothing without me," Malakyte says, as if the shop owner wasn't standing right there. "Take what you desire, Karalevine. Take the power for yourself."

My heart races, even as I risk a glance at the businessman, whose eyes are begging me not to take them.

But who would stop me, though? Nobody . . . because the man in power is the man by my side.

And that's hot as hell.

Seductive as hell . . .

I reach over, taking what I want, and it feels good. I've never had anything expensive like this—never experienced power *like this*.

"Perhaps the princess can return them after she's worn them for what—"

"No," Malakyte says, his voice like a whip. My heart hammers as the cold diamonds lie heavy in my palm. "She keeps them. Leave. You can come back once Karalevine is done choosing anything else she wants. Close the door behind you."

The man looks like he wants to argue, mouth gaping like a fish out of water, but he reluctantly does as his prince orders. Once he's gone, Malakyte walks me over to a giant floor-length mirror, and we stand before it, Malakyte directly behind me.

"It reminds me of the big mirror in your room," I say as Malakyte takes the earrings from my hands and puts them in my ears.

Once they're in, we stare at my reflection, the look complete.

"I really don't need to keep these," I say, barely able to hold his stare.

But, stars, do I look perfect.

The floor-length gown is made of soft Black Night gossamer and beaded along every hem, curving in the shade Bronze Goddess, creating beautiful, elegant designs. Its back is entirely open except for the continued beading that mirrors the spiderweb design along my collarbone. My earrings dangle by my cheeks and match the dress perfectly, especially with my dark-shadowed eyes and pink nude lip. The earrings truly bring the whole look together.

 26

"There's nothing you can't have now. What's more, the jewels pair perfectly with the gift I got for you," Malakyte says, reaching into his jacket.

His eyes sparkle as he pulls out a single black rose, thorns and all.

He hands it to me, and I take it, the velvet petals thick and voluminous, shade Soot Black. Even the three leaves on the stem are black.

"It completes you," he says, staring at me in the mirror. "Nobody else sees you. Not like I do. My perfect, *dark lady*."

My smile grows, his chilly aura curling around me, like it, too, wishes to possess me for all of eternity.

Someone else gave me flowers once . . . and I risk a peek at the dandelion tattoo on my forearm, my reminder of Gavrielle. But the jagged scars near the dandelion pull my eyes from the flower to their ugly shapes. I have no idea where they came from, but they almost look like the letters "J" and either a "T" or an "F."

Every time I peer at these abhorrent scars, I feel ill. Sick and panicked and nauseated.

The feeling overcomes me, and I quickly peel my gaze off my arm so I don't ruin this moment. Malakyte has his scar, too, and neither of us talks about them. Although mine is much easier to hide than the one on his face.

I think he clocks me looking at my arm, but he bends to graze his dark-blue lips along the side of my neck, drawing my attention back to where he likes it. On him.

He kisses his way up to my ear, sending a freezing shiver through me. The rest of me is hotter than a furnace as those lips sweep across my jawline. One of his hands softly takes my chin and slowly, deliberately, tilts my head so our lips are barely an inch apart.

Our lips ever so slightly brush against one another's, and my breath hitches at the drastic difference in our temperatures.

I melt into him as our lips finally meet, fire and ice colliding in a bursting flash of contrast that could crack this ship in two. His mouth is all hard angles and firm marble, but his lips—stars, his lips. They're delicately soft as they kiss me fully, deeply. It's been weeks since he's touched me like this, sliding his tongue into my mouth like he owns me. Malakyte consumes and devours and possesses me.

Tasting him is like tasting a winter's night, cloudless and endlessly dark, with a touch of citrus, so crisp and fresh.

A little sound escapes my mouth just as he breaks the kiss. My eyes open, and he's watching me, gaze heady with primal need, completely oblivious to the world bustling beyond this store.

I breathe in his air, and my heart races at the closeness. His power, his strength, his tantalizing darkness that mirrors my own—all a seductive little game we play. He's moving slowly with me, with my body, going no further than kissing, even though I've made it clear I want more.

He claims he wants me to be sure, wants to give me time, but sleeping in bed together the last few weeks with nothing more than cuddling has been utter torture. I'm beyond sure about what I want, so why isn't he?

"My power is yours, Karalevine. Here, by my side—with all my sovereign power—your darkness is *freed*."

Malakyte slides that power into my veins like heroin, and I'm instantly hooked.

CHAPTER 3

We make the long trek back to the other side of the Azurite, where the transport vessel will take us to the king and queen's newly arrived spaceship.

Jance glares at me with disappointment, walking beside me as Malakyte goes on ahead, conversing with his top SSPARROW about the graffiti problem. When I explain to Jance that Malakyte said I could have the earrings, he doesn't seem to care.

"Malakyte's conditions are notwithstanding," he says. "It's the principle that you're missing. It isn't right to take something that has significant value to a community purely for your own gain. You can wear them to meet with the royals, then return them. You're better than this."

As I'm about to ask him how he's able to make that kind of assumption about my character, we arrive at the transport station, so the conversation dies.

Maybe Jance is right, though . . . Stars, I don't know.

We file into the tight vessel, with much less soldiers accompanying us than before, and once we're halfway across the short distance between ships, I forget all about the stupid earrings.

I press my face to the window. The vessel beyond is like a gigantic wraith hovering through the backdrop of a cosmic tapestry. She's solid black, much like the Azurite, but her shape is completely different. Where the Azurite is long and thin, its body much like a gigantic cruise ship that sails the open seas on Earth's oceans, with a variety of layers added on from different periods of construction, this other ship is flatter with little height to it. Yet stiff and shapeless is the last thing I'd call this work of art. She's a seductive blend of elegance and practicality, with smooth, symmetrical curves that must help when she flies through the stars at speeds I can hardly fathom.

"It's incredible," I say, looking back at Malakyte, who's seated behind me.

He fiddles with his lapel, disinterested. "My parents are nothing but slaves to the finer comforts in the galaxy."

The shuttle redirects toward the entrance, where the front-end curves inward. On either side, the ship's frame forms around two massive propulsion jets that glow Fireplace Orange, like the eyes of a space creature that no doubt dominates all other beasts with the ferocity of feminine rage.

Once we're devoured within her, a mechanical voice plays over the intercom. "Atmospheric stabilization complete. You may exit at your leisure."

The hangar is similar to the Azurite's, able to withstand the harsh conditions of space and then be flushed with a breathable atmosphere moments later.

We disembark, and Malakyte leads us through a round industrial hallway filled with exposed pipes and floor-to-ceiling structural metal beams. Visible wires slither past cool-toned lights and into panels, while steam spews around my high heels as I clank my way down the passage.

Glares of the extras, who pause their work in their dirty gray tracksuits, watch me strut by in my lavish gown, escorted by the son of their tyrannical overlord. I used to know exactly how it felt to be them, beaten down and oppressed by the occupation.

Now *I'm* the occupation.

 30

The door at the end of the maintenance hall opens up to different scenery. It's another long hallway, yet it's finished, polished, and sparkling with all the finery I expect from the Ardeen family. Decorated in Bronze Goddess walls, glowing ceiling lights are hidden under stylish coverings. Where the Azurite is sleek, sharp angles in multiple shades of black, this spaceship is grandiose and gold, shouting wealth and ancient elegance.

Down and deeper we go, our footsteps are pronounced in the utterly lifeless halls. No servants or guards, not even plants. What artwork I do see is . . . strange. Often depicting bizarre scenes that make my stomach twist or my face slip into an expression far from princess-like. Finally, we come to a set of grand golden doors looming fifteen feet high.

I wipe my sweaty palms all over this ridiculous gown, sensing Jance's heavy presence behind me.

"You can walk through those doors, kid."

Jance's voice holds so much more confidence than I actually have inside of me. It's kind of him to encourage me. Nobody else does.

Malakyte's SSPARROWs throw open the grand set of double doors, and a soft gust of vetiver and oud or rosewood notes caresses my cheeks as light bounces off the filigree molded into the panels of the entryway.

Malakyte waits for me at the precipice of the threshold, hand outstretched. For the first time since meeting him, I hesitate to take it. My knees quake, and my ankles stiffen at the thought of taking another step.

Impatience flashes on Malakyte's face, and the scrutiny in his gaze scares me. How can this be the same guy from less than an hour ago? I love the Malakyte who builds me up and makes me feel like I'm invincible. This Malakyte, who's glaring at me like I better come to him *right now*, is not the man I'm in love with.

Swallowing a throatful of gravel, I force myself to walk through the doors, and the Arianyte throne room comes into full view.

Jance and the other guards stay by the doors, and we make our way down the corridor toward the throne looming at the back of the room. I look anywhere but at them, like at the frosted concave lights on the ceiling casting shafts of sunlight onto the Goldfinch colored pillars lining the hall. I stare at the sunbeams that seem to amplify my every insecurity, one after the other, until there are no more to count and the king and queen are upon me.

High on a dais and dressed in all black, the emperor casually lounges, nearly sitting sideways on his throne, long legs crossed at the ankles as one arm possessively traces circles around his wife's low back. His grin is more deadly than the sword sheathed at his waist as he assesses both Malakyte and me like a predator, possibly wondering if he's too full to make his next kill. With those double sets of pointed canines on the top row of his teeth that are an exact match to his son's, he could easily eat me alive. The queen stands beside the throne with sad eyes so deep they could drown her kingdom.

And I'm forced to look them in the eyes when everything in me is screaming to look away.

My heart races like I'm about to go into battle rather than meeting my soon-to-be in-laws. Stars. *In-laws.*

I don't dare speak first.

Although . . . the emperor seems to be far too young to be Malakyte's dad. Mid-twenties, perhaps a few years older. Not a wrinkle or blemish to be found. Malakyte has never told me his own age, but he appears roughly the same age as his father. However, the emperor is a devastatingly handsome mirror image of his son. Sure enough, there's no mistaking that resemblance. In fact, the only real difference between them is how Malakyte wears his Squid Ink hair long and straight, while

 32

his father keeps his hair cropped short, loose strands sticking out around the heavy black crown. He's by far the biggest reason why my heart is thrashing behind my ribcage because his vibe is absolutely terrifying.

There is no doubt why he's the emperor of Arianyte.

Malakyte takes my hand, and I gasp. *Stars, how pathetic.* The coldness startled me, but I give Malakyte an apologetic smile, his face grim. I'm a scared little mouse in a cage with a tiger. Pathetic and frozen and as petrified as death.

"We welcome you to the Vivianite, Karalevine," the emperor says, full of life and vigor, far from the slow, careful way Malakyte speaks. "My wife and empress, Zoisyte, and I have been graciously awaiting your arrival. Our son has told us many stories about you. All that ambition and, of course, that exceptional power. How lucky we are to lay eyes on you after all this time."

The ice in his veins manifests through his words.

The empress steals my attention from her terrifying husband. "It's nice to meet you, Karalevine. Such a beautiful, interesting name."

Malakyte's mother, who also looks like a young woman barely older than me, is even more stunning than the man on the throne. Where the emperor is like the dark pieces on a chessboard, the queen is the white pieces on the other side. Her long, straight white hair in the color Snow resembles the shade of her gown, which could easily be made of diamonds as it shimmers.

And though the empress doesn't permeate with the darkness I sense from her husband, her stiff posture, downcast expression, and constant glances to the emperor are concerning. If she doesn't have her own throne, will I not, either? Am I staring at my future self?

I don't want to stand *beside* a throne. I want to be *sitting* on one.

"Nice to meet the both of you," I squeak out of a tightened throat.

"Herkimer"—the queen blanches at her husband—"stop glaring at her like she's a piece of meat. You're terrifying the poor girl."

Herkimer chuckles like this is a casual meeting. "Ah, no. She's just fine. Aren't you, girl? You would only be afraid of us if you were planning to steal our throne and destroy this empire."

"Father," Malakyte warns carefully, but irritation slips through his tone.

I hold Malakyte's hand in a death grip.

Eyes of Inky Black flash a warning at Malakyte—their eyes identical—but it vanishes quicker than lightning when they land back on me. The emperor reaches to scratch his face, and a tattooed bracelet around his wrist peeks out as his sleeve tugs down. The empress also has one on her wrist, albeit different. They wear no rings or wedding bands.

My star mark sears on my chest as Herkimer watches me, completely skipping the tingling stage.

"I don't plan on stealing or destroying anything," I say, doing all I can to keep my voice strong.

Herkimer perks up on his throne. "In that case, by all means, grace us with your pitch as to why I'd ever accept a rebel Starseed as my son's bride and empress. And a Terran, to boot."

He says "Starseed" like it's more of a slur than "rebel."

My cheeks are on fire, and I instinctively try to take a step backward, yet Malakyte doesn't allow me to, but the slip is obvious by Herkimer's disapproving head shake.

I'm fine. He's only a man. He may represent all the parts of Arianyte that I hate and despise and have fought against, but he's going to be gone soon. We're going to get rid of him and make this empire better.

Malakyte's ever-present chill deepens as the silence itself thickens around us. All of them seem to ice over, and I have

 34

to physically keep my teeth from chattering. This isn't how I thought this was going to go.

The emperor abruptly stands from his throne. He's tall and thin but muscled, exactly like his son.

"I'm going to make a few things exceptionally clear to the two of you. My declining health and the murder of my precious Selenyte have made it abundantly clear to me that the stability of Arianyte must be secured, especially before those fools on the Council get any bright ideas of consolidating power, which is brewing, I assure you. If the princess can be murdered, so can any of us, and our authority must be recemented. This happens every once in a while within empires such as ours. It's nothing new. However, I thought I had more time to prepare you, Malakyte, to rule in my place. The clock is ticking down. With me, with the Council, and with what's happening on this planet Earth. It might as well be called Planet Filth."

What's happening down on Earth?

Before Malakyte can even open his mouth, Herkimer keeps going on, circling us in a predatory, feline fashion.

"But be assured that the two of you aren't going to waltz in here and take over what I've spent centuries building. Understand me here that I will grace you with my throne only because if I do not, the empire and my legacy will suffer. I will be here before, during, and after to ensure that Arianyte thrives as I see fit, the two of you obeying my rules and my protocols. Earth will be the example to the rest of the galaxy that, when you come for the Ardeen family, your planet pays the price."

My blood runs arctic.

"This will also be a good first check of your power, boy. Show the galaxy what Malakyte Ardeen does to those who murder his own blood. Know that I hold you directly responsible for your sister's death. This never should have happened under your watch, and I'm wholly enraged by how you allowed your own flesh and blood to be murdered. It's this complete incompetence that reduces my confidence in your ability to rule adequately. Until I see proof in your performance that I find satisfactory, and you also bring your sister's killer to my feet with a full confession, this transition of power won't take place. You have from now until your scheduled wedding to convince me you're worthy of my crown. There will be no abnegating the throne until I'm satisfied with both of your performances. Nothing you gain here is for free, not even if you were born into it."

Malakyte tenses, and so do I. If Herkimer doesn't abdicate, then what are we even doing here? He's going to ruin everything. All the expectations for Arianyte's future dissolve before my eyes. My plans to help the Hijacked feel damn near impossible. I can't let him waltz in here and do this. Can't let him string Malakyte and me up like puppets while he's the one controlling everything behind the scenes. He's a problem, and we need to do something about him *now*.

"I can assure you, Father, I have made strides in my shortcomings. I also have a suspect in custody," Malakyte says, which is news to me. "He's reluctant to confess, but I assure you, he's the one responsible."

Why is he cowering to his father like this? Malakyte doesn't balk to anyone.

Herkimer muses, "Why not use the dragons to break the suspect?"

The moment Herkimer says the word "dragons," a flash of a black-scaled dragon head flickers vividly inside my mind, as if its smoldering, golden eyes in the color Coin were glaring straight into my soul. So intensely that my star's burning ratchets up, nearly glowing. The scaley face was unmistakable. And its horns are . . . Oh, wait a minute. My nightmare this morning. The flames and the horns . . . Initially, I suspected Naresteé because of her horns. But what if . . . What if it wasn't about her at all? I feel as if my dreams are trying to communicate something to me. Like earlier, when the symbol drawn in red graffiti appeared right after my dream hours before. But I need to backpedal—*dragons?*

As fascinating as that sounds, I don't have time to worry about dragons of all things. I need to worry about my people— about Herkimer hurting them.

Malakyte answers coolly, "The dragons are immutable to any of my requests."

The emperor scoffs. "Perhaps your new bride and her special Starseed gifts can assist us in our time of grief? Send her down that long, dank stairwell to convince them. We both know their knowledge could be of use beyond this situation with Selenyte's killer."

When neither of us responds fast enough, Herkimer waves in annoyance. "What is the name of this so-called suspect?" He finally stops circling us.

"Ardelle Dawson. A Terran."

"Then, he and the whole lot of their species will pay. I want his confession before he dies. I'm sure with such a high-profile suspect, the Council will want some sort of admission of guilt, as do I. We won't give them any excuse to accuse us of unjust practices like last time."

Last time? Why is Herkimer glaring at me like that?

"As soon as I have his confession, Father, he will be yours to devour whole."

My brows crease. What an odd choice of words.

Malakyte wastes no time in turning us both toward the doors.

"We'll speak again soon, Karalevine," the king shouts as we walk away, that amused tone back in his voice.

I don't look back or answer, but I'm wholly and rightfully unnerved.

My star glows the entire way back to the Azurite and burns for a solid hour afterward as I wonder what the fuck I'm supposed to do about this.

CHAPTER 4

"Almost there, Gav," Pacey says into the comms, her voice crystal clear. "I'm almost to the RFID access panel. This should be the last physical port I need to breach, and we can get me out of this freezing hole."

My back strains as I peek down the long, dark utility shaft in the Azurite core where Pacey is currently hacking the shit out of this ship. Getting to this place has cost us precious time in planning, resources, and supplies, but now that Pacey is physically next to the plugs and ports and main panel that controls the Azurite, we're in business. Since we're fresh out of the necessary cables and clamps any rational person would use for a descent into a three-hundred-foot duct like this, we went with the old rope-and-anchor method.

I'm the anchor—holding Pacey's life in my hands as I stand at the top of the massive duct, with only me and a rope as her safety line.

It's alright. I'm not going to let her fall, and the risk is worth it because we're about to make Malakyte's life a living Hell.

Well, more of a living Hell.

Sylo snickers into my ear through our comms unit. "You know what Kara would say if she were Gav right now."

"'Hurry the fuck up. I'm dying up here!'"

Pacey's impression is spot on.

Sylo snorts, and my chuckle echoes down this metal shaft, the light so dim and red it could use some joy to combat the dreadful ambiance.

"And then we know what Ardelle would say," Sylo quickly adds.

"Language!" they say in unison.

I smile at their genuine laughter.

We need that, just like we need this hack to work. Like we need to bring her home—Ardelle, too, even though I know that'll lead to my heartbreak.

Pacey's gasp snaps me out of my thoughts as tension yanks on the rope around my waist. I lean backward into my heels, bending at the knees with both hands on the rope as her cries carry all the way up from the pitch-black hole below.

"Babe?" Sylo, our lookout, asks. "Pacey?"

"I'm good," she says, voice shaky as the tension lessons on our primitive descension line. "That's why you're the anchor, Gavrielle. Nice save. I'm almost done."

She slipped. Good to know my knots hold.

"You're fine, Pace. I've got you."

I do. I've got them all.

"Step one is complete. We're connected. It's sloppy work, and if anyone comes down here, they're going to know what happened, that's for sure, but we're in. Heading back up."

It takes Pacey almost twenty minutes to get all the way back to me, and when the top of her blonde head materializes through the darkness, I drop to my knees and reach down.

She smiles, her big blue eyes shining despite the dark. "Thanks again for catching me. Now, let's get out of here before those guards come back from chasing Deimos around. He's probably mad about how long we're taking."

"That guy is always bitching," Sylo adds.

I shrug. "I would, too, if I had to put up with you every single day. Oh, wait, *I do*."

It's all jokes and ragging on each other as Pacey and I climb a set of smaller ladders leading out of this place.

A few minutes later, Sylo is there to meet us at the top.

"Good job, babe," he says, helping her climb out the final layer. "So, we can actually hack into the Azurite now?"

"Once I get back to the laptop and administer step two, we'll have the network, cameras, door access, utilities, HVAC, Kara's and Malakyte's chips, all of it. They're toast."

Sylo wraps his arms around her. "That's my girl."

Pacey's smile is genuine, but I recognize the sadness clouding her expression. Our eyes lock for that precious second or two, and I know someone else understands the cognitive dissonance I experience every day.

Waking up from the Reconditioning has been hard on us both.

We sneak down several corridors. This section of the Azurite is a maze, and I guide us out the way we came. We speak in hushed voices, knowing that, any time we leave the safety of our hiding places, we're always in danger.

Once we reach the upper levels, it becomes more populated and much easier to blend in with the Terran Tributes working in this area. Our matching gray uniforms help, and we sneak off a secluded path and out of this sector all together. My illusions get us by any SSPARROW that may be lurking. We make it back to the little storage unit we've been holding up in the last week, the other Ringers and Deimos waiting inside.

"About time. We were worried you'd fallen in," Deimos, my Starseed, scowls before we can even shut the door.

The dim space isn't all that big, and we've shoved all the random cleaning supplies to one side, making our own little bump of blankets and pillows on the other. Kara and I used to make bumps and forts just like these at the orphanage, and I think of her every time we remake them some place new. Food, water, lamps, and other essentials sit close to the door.

It's harsh being forced to live this way the last five weeks since Kara and Jance had been Reconditioned and Ardelle taken, the latter still forced to fight day after day in the pits for Malakyte's entertainment.

"Told you he'd bitch," Sylo remarks, giving his Ringer Saris a comforting smile as the worry falls away from her tense face, her black hair dirty like everyone else's.

They were worried, which is understandable. They don't want to lose anyone else.

I don't want to lose anyone else. Especially when losing what I love seems to be a pattern for me.

We only have two Starseed and Elendril pairs. Kara and Jance are separated—not physically, but are emotionally torn apart. It counts. Ahren and Ardelle are, too. We don't even know who or where Pacey's Ringer is. And, of course, Malakyte and Naresteé . . . but I try hard not to think about them.

Pacey wastes no time as she immediately sits on the blankets, opens her laptop, and goes to town slashing keys, the screen lighting up her face.

Ahren paces, something he does a lot, despite constantly using his Ringer magic to heal the Tributes in exchange for supplies and shelter. The Tributes hate Malakyte, always have, which is how I knew to come to them for help. The tech they gave us in exchange for Ahren's healing and skills as a doctor gets us better eyes on Kara but also helps us continuously blaze a hole in anything Malakyte tries to do. We're all in agreement that Malakyte is going down and Arianyte along with him.

Yet it's not so black-and-white for me.

"I need to head back out there," I inform them as I slip on my stolen SSPARROW uniform. "I'm sure the prince and Kara have returned from their romantic outing today."

Makes my blood boil.

Sylo dives into a can of beans as he takes a seat next to Pacey. "Nice work on getting Ardelle's mark to her before we went on the mission." He offers her a spoonful, but she shakes him off, completely focused. "We've been slapping those babies everywhere. I love it."

"You have no idea how hard it was to stay on this side," I say, sliding on my first glove. "I wouldn't have made it past the security scan to the public side, even being invisible or disguised as a soldier."

"Keep an ear out for when he plans to take her out again, regardless of where," Deimos suggests. "With the emperor here, the last thing the little prince is going to do is cause a scene. It may be our only shot to grab her. Public or private side, this ship is full of people, and they all have eyes."

"Some even have four eyes," Sylo jokes, bouncing his brows at Deimos, who growls in his direction.

Tension fills my chest. Determination hones into a sharp, deadly blade. When I glance up from gliding on the second glove and only my SSPARROW helmet remains, I find all except Pacey watching me with hopeful eyes. When had I become the one to lead them?

"We're going to get everyone back," I say confidently, even though their hope is dwindling. Dark humor and sarcasm are what's keeping us together most days. "Saris, keep working on connecting to Kara through her dreams with your Ringer magic. I know it's hard to break through her nightmares, especially with so much physical distance between the two of you, but you're making progress. All of us are. Today is a big win, and I'm going to find us another one."

Although my words would mean a lot more if I wasn't lying to every single one of them.

I stalk through the Azurite, clad in obsidian metal armor, undetected by my hunter. In the last few hours, I've done some reconnaissance and found the perfect future opportunity to make our big move.

I can only hope she forgives me for what I allowed to happen to her, what I'm continuing to allow to happen, and what's about to occur.

Forgive me for the loyalty I hold for our adversaries, as it makes things incredibly complicated for me. If I could simply hate Malakyte and Narésteé, this would be far, far easier.

I'm ignored as I walk into the royal residential wing of the Azurite, able to access almost any area with a little Ringer magic or the stolen suit, but with Pacey's hack from earlier, this will become much easier. As long as the prince or Narésteé aren't anywhere near to feel me using my Ringer magic, I'm safe. Malakyte is so self-absorbed he'd likely not notice, but I won't risk it. Every step I take is calculated in this ever-shifting game.

A deadly game.

It doesn't take me long to make my way to Kara's suite, and it kills me to know she's there, likely asleep at this hour. At least she's away from him tonight. I could go to her right now, tell her everything, and have her safely in my arms in a matter of minutes, and we could be back on Earth within hours. The thought of it makes my chest swell with excitement. It's not the first time I've imagined running away with her. I can't help it, but I can't risk her rescue for my own gain. If Kara were to not believe me, immediately run to Malakyte, scream for help, or have a number of unpredictable reactions to me telling her everything she remembers of the last six months is a lie fabricated by the man she loves, we'd lose our one shot to get her memories back. If we lose her trust without returning those missing memories, we might as well give up on ever getting her back. She's too important, not only to me and the other Starseeds and Ringers, but to Earth and the Terrans at large. To the full-scale war that's imbued with more intensity every day on the planet she sacrificed so much for. It's insane that she's the most important person in this war but is none the wiser.

Life is playing out in an interesting way, isn't it, Father? I know you'll get Kara back to me. You guided me back to her once. I believe you will a second time.

I slow my approach to the solitary figure standing guard outside Kara's door. The man wears the all-black cloth uniform made only for a royal bodyguard—one I once wore. When I reach him, he shifts on his feet, one hand moving to rest over the other in front of his waist.

This ship has spies and eyes everywhere, in every corner, on every wall. We can't be too careful.

"I'm here for the shift change," I say, the distortion of my helmet conveniently left off.

Jance Gallivan, Kara's father, looks sidelong at me, head not moving an inch. "My shift doesn't end for another three hours. You're early."

I feign a confused glance at my inner wrist, where an embedded digital interface resides in every uniform. "It appears my schedule is incorrect."

"It appears so."

"Nevertheless, I believe it's time."

Finally, the man turns his head and looks straight at me.
Jance grins like a cat.

CHAPTER 5

PER THE DEVOURING ACCORDS, THE ARIANYTE EMPIRE
HAS LEGAL RECOURSE TO DEFEND ITSELF AGAINST
TERRAN AGGRESSION ONCE THE STABILIZATION
PROTOCOL IS ACTIVATED. ANY FORCE THAT JEOPARDIZES
OR COMPROMISES ARIANYTE ASSETS OR TAKES PART IN
REBELLIOUS ACTIVISM WILL BE SUBJECT TO HOSTILE FORCE.
ARIANYTE WILL USE ALL ITS AUTHORITY TO QUELL DISSENT
AND REBELLION TO RETURN EARTH TO PEACE.

MALAKYTE ARDEEN

Karalevine didn't want to return to my room with me after what happened with Father today. She refused to eat dinner with me as well. That hasn't happened since she was Reconditioned five weeks ago, her memories erased. To her, five weeks ago, we had just arrived on the Azurite after Geonni, Deimos, and Trinity laid claim to her life. A false narrative crafted by Naresteé and I, a plausible storyline after we gained control of her subconscious through Naresteé's Ringer magic. It worked flawlessly. Karalevine is mine.

Nevertheless, my Azurite is infested with pests that wish to take her from me, and they must be eradicated. All but one . . . but I'll deal with Gavrielle later.

My highest ranking SSPARROW, Ennar—clad in black armor with yellow accents rather than the more common blue or red—arrives with a dozen second-ranked SSPARROWs on his heels, their red accents signifying their Nest leadership. Naresteé trails in, her horns bearing jewels, but the darkness under her eyes denotes she's troubled about something. Most likely Miss Dawson.

This room is used for operational security and all Azurite SSPARROW business. We keep it dark so the dozens of screens on the main wall can be easily monitored. Other primary safety conventions are controlled by the supercomputers and artificial intelligence that runs through the next room. Once everyone files in, the space becomes tight.

Yet there's someone else who's always too close no matter where I stand.

Selenyte's ghost perches on the desk below the screens, nobody seeing her but me as she glares up into my eyes as if she were still flesh and frigid blood.

"Your bride is going to abandon you after what happened today, big brother. She sees *everything*."

She will not leave me.

My own sister . . . dead by my hands.

For Karalevine.

The act has driven me mad.

I address my soldiers. "As you know, the emperor and empress have arrived in the Aurora System. Whenever they are aboard the Azurite, I want my father's movements tracked. Keep him away from Karalevine. And speaking of Karalevine, she's noticing your slip-ups. Ensure your subordinates understand that if they fuck up the script she's supposed to believe, they're gone. This is true for all assistants, maids, trainers, anyone and everyone who comes into contact with my bride. Those of you on Karalevine's personal guard rotation with Mr. Gallivan can continue to pacify him as if he's actually doing a job."

A few snickers follow.

"Changing gears, how have you not captured the fugitives? The hot water has been compromised three times. The stars damned quartz lights can't even stay on the correct settings from any given day. They're spewing their graffiti all over my ship. How hard is it to do your jobs and find them? We've added guards to all major infrastructure points, so how are they getting through?"

Ennar stiffens, but to the man's credit, he steps forward. "We had a strong lead several days ago, but as you know, that was the day the livestock was set loose, and all available Nests were sent to . . . corral."

I scoff.

Gavrielle was behind that one, no doubt. Distract, manipulate, strike. Just as I taught him. We're playing directly into their hands.

"I believe we need a new strategy to deal with them," I say, walking to the wall of screens, each one like eyes that never blink as they watch over my ship. I ignore Selenyte's ghost as she obnoxiously taps on the controls, her ghoulishly pale hand making a sound only I can hear.

"I have a suggestion," Ennar says, walking up to our digital whiteboard as he erases it with a hand gesture. "We suspect they're going to escalate. What if we let them? They're likely going to take Kara. What if we let them?"

My jaw clenches, but I allow him to continue. He's been with me for a long time, and he knows how I delight in efficiency. Knowing him, this new strategy he's proposing may hit several birds with one stone.

His terrible writing becomes clear text as he scribbles on the board, arrows leading from one likely scenario to another.

 48

"They have a hacker, correct?" Ennar asks, and I nod. "For the moment, let them hack. Our hackers will reverse engineer theirs, leading us straight back to their location or, at minimum, show us a glimpse into their plans. We'll see exactly what they intend and cut them off at the knees."

"This is why you're my head of security, Ennar. Do it. I also want a report on your plans for the rebellion Earth-side. My father already knows a great deal about what's happening down there. Ensure he doesn't ascertain any further details. Find out where he's getting his information from. Execute them. And on that little special project I gave to you, the one about Karalevine's past, have you found him yet?"

Ennar nods. "I have SSPARROW boots in Zarmenia as we speak. They'll apprehend him."

"Good. Now, I have a confession to rip out of someone's throat."

"So, you're not going to confess to murdering Selenyte?" I ask Mr. Dawson, his defeated body slouched over heavy chains that hold him up from either side of his clear, impenetrable cell.

I find nothing but satisfaction searing through my blood at his state.

This is where he belongs, what he gets for touching my Star—for fucking her. Big mistake.

Deep in the bowels of my prison, his world confined to this shadowy, dank cell and the arena I force him to fight in. The endless halls of the Azurite prisons are dark pits where vermin are left to rot in the many cells that expand out and down, layer upon layer. A maze of misery where my enemies die.

Mr. Dawson spits at me, and the saliva hits my chest as the chains clank. "Fuck you."

We've been at this tit for tat for some time now.

"You know where the SSPARROW helmet is," I sigh, leaning my shoulder against the cell's open door as I pick at a stray silver thread on my suit cuff.

He chuckles, half mad. "Like they'd ever tell me where the video footage of what you did to your sister is. They're not stupid."

"No. I believe they likely found some way to you, some pathetic rescue attempt, perhaps, and they mentioned their little ace in the hole."

Silence.

"They haven't tried to rescue you?" I ask, stepping inside the cell so I can face the poor bastard. "Ouch. Must sting. Well, if they ever give enough fucks to make their way down here and you manage to get them to reveal the helmet's location . . . I could consider sparing your life."

No answer.

"Not to mention your little sister's life . . . as someone in your shoes"—I hear Selenyte's taunting laughter spear down the darkened hall—"I would assume you'd do anything to keep me from hurting her. Even selling out the others. You've done it before when you worked with Deimos. Because, when I catch her—and rest assured that I *will* catch her—Pacey could have a much less painful experience if you cooperate with me . . . or not, and she can scream in the cell beside yours. Perhaps I could even consider letting both of you go? All I ask for is the helmet and my Star. All you and your filth need to do is let me keep what's mine. It isn't difficult."

He launches for me like a rabid animal tied to a stake, the chains rattling and screaming out into the putrid darkness.

Pathetic.

"I will fucking kill you for what you did to her, and if you even think of hurting Pacey, I will burn everything you care about to ash," he seethes, chest puffing with healing scars, new burns, and fresh blood.

I shrug, knowing it'll get under his skin. "I sincerely doubt that." I step out of the cell. "But I didn't come to see you for you to posture silly threats my way. It's time you and I redefine the terms of our new relationship if you want your sister to survive this. I could still rip that crystal from her heart in an instant. Do not test me. You've seen the lengths I'm willing to go."

Despite the dark, his complexion is flushed, heart is thundering.

Good. I want to get under that tattooed skin of his.

When he doesn't answer, I close the cell door and lock it. I'm irritated I didn't obtain either a confession or information on the SSPARROW helmet Deimos wore that night in the throne room. No surprise that slippery bastard took it with him, but that helmet holds video evidence of what I did to Selenyte. The only loose end I have yet to tie off, except the Starseeds and Ringers, of course. With Father now here, finding it is a top priority. Before he slaughters me.

"She's going to remember what you did to her," Ardelle says before I turn to leave.

Facing him head on, our eyes clash like blades on a battlefield, his iron-clad resolve as palpable as my own.

"Heed my words carefully, Ardelle, because I won't repeat them. I don't think Karalevine will remember a single thing. In fact, I've all but ensured she doesn't. I won't simply have her on my side—I'll turn her in every way possible. Her heart, her morals, her loyalty, until the woman you love is a dark and twisted creature you won't recognize. So dark and devious that even if you do manage to get those precious memories back again . . . she'll never be the same. The Karalevine you knew is gone, replaced with a better version. My masterpiece."

I don't stay to hear his response.

Only angry screams and ravenous chains clanking together follow me out, music to my ears.

CHAPTER 6

THE ARIANYTE EMPIRE DECREE #103

ALL MEDIA MUST BE APPROVED BY AN ARIANYTE
REPRESENTATIVE. NEWS MEDIA OUTLETS WILL BE SUBJECT
TO STRICTER REGULATION TO PREVENT THE USE OF FAKE
NEWS AND DEEPFAKES.

KARALEVINE RUZZ

The stench of this place . . . is like rotten acid choking me from the inside out. My cube prison holds me down, the gravity is so heavy and sweltering I can't move. *Can't breathe.*

On my stomach, I crawl to a corner so I can leverage the walls to sit up, but it takes me several tries without slipping in my own sweat and sliding back down.

This is one sinister type of Hell—one just as hot, too.

Yet, out there in the void of darkness, they call for me.

"Kara!"

"Kara!"

"Let me out," I say through gritted teeth, but nobody can hear me.

Finally, I'm able to sit up and rest my head on the cube wall as I sit against a corner, breathing in that heavy, putrid air.

Something slams against the opposite side, and the thud nearly stops my heart.

So does the woman who created it . . . She's of old-world Asian descent, beautiful, in her mid-thirties, and she bangs on the cube. Her mouth moves, but I can't hear her as she pounds against the wall.

She flips her hand around, knuckle-side up.

A Ringer mark . . .

I recognize the strange diamond shape . . . but from where?

My Starseed mark flares white hot, the heat so overwhelming the woman disappears. I can't see anything! Only the heat and the pressure on my body, and I'll never fucking escape it. Stars, I'm never going to escap—

I wake with a shriek halfway out my throat, the covers on my bed flying as I kick and punch at nothing, completely soaked, as if I just left a bath.

My breathing comes out ragged as I peer around my own bedroom on the Azurite. It's not really decorated like much, but it's clean and big, and it's got everything I can ask for from a full kitchen to my left to a bathroom on the right, my bed in the middle. There's even a little living room area. It's not Malakyte's room, but it's nice—it's *real*.

That was a bad one . . . and I force my crystal to simmer down before Malakyte or Jance rushes in like they had yesterday. I check my Dezlar—my old one from Earth got lost somehow.

It's noon already? Malakyte will kill me if he finds out I slept in so late.

My brows knit together in confusion as I stare down at the Dezlar in my hand as it suddenly begins to act crazy. What in Jupiter's Rings?

The screen glitches, and between the distorted pixels, those graffiti symbols appear and flash one by one at an incredible rate of speed—the Elendril marks. They flicker so fast, and as quickly as it begins, the device zips back to the home screen like nothing happened. I blink. Didn't I just see one of those symbols in my nightmare? That can't be a coincidence, can it? Although, as I ruminate on the details of my recent dream, my head throbs.

These new headaches I've been getting are terrible.

I try to forget it all and call for my breakfast. The food comes quickly, but I only eat a tenth of it.

From the massage he scheduled for me to the pretty necklace he had sent to match those earrings to the surprise event I'm told to get ready for this evening, I can tell he's trying to make up for what his father said yesterday.

Herkimer wants to destroy my planet and my people, all because one Terran killed his precious daughter. Forget the Hijacked. The whole planet is in danger.

And I have to find a way to stop him. No matter what it takes, the end justifies the means.

It's late as I exit the bathroom after my shower, when I notice something odd sitting on my coffee table.

I'm a little creeped out. Someone had to slither in here while I was in the shower, but there's nobody. Clutching my fluffy black towel tighter to myself, I approach the table barefoot, water droplets dampening the black marble floor as my feet leave little prints in my wake. I bend over and pluck a small dragon figurine from the granite coffee table, its placement there completely conspicuous.

The little dragon figure fits in my palm, shining in the shade Pharaoh. It's heavier than it looks, and I instantly remember the dragon head I visualized in the Vivianite throne room at the initial mention of these dragons. The intimidating face, the horns in my dream from that morning. Did this recent nightmare have horns? I don't recall there being any symbolism of horns, dragons, or flame. Other than the heat, maybe?

A deep, guttural growl snaps me out of my thoughts, and I completely freeze.

It sounded like it was in the room with me . . . or perhaps, in my head.

Stars, I'm losing it.

I rub my eyes with my other hand, set the figurine on the table, and get dressed for whatever surprise Malakyte has planned for me. This entire day has been strange, so I hope I can just relax later and forget about all the woes of being the next empress of Arianyte.

CHAPTER 7

"The fighting pits?" I ask Malakyte as we approach the amphitheater within the Arianyte mothership, music bumping along with strobing lights bouncing from the intimidating metal archway.

I'm dressed casually in black pants and a sparkling black sweater that hangs loosely off one shoulder, my star mark visible. Malakyte surprises me by wearing an all-black laced corset in the shade Black Cat. The corset's tight fit accentuates the curve of his upper and lower back. It's sinfully attractive, and I can't stop eye-fucking him, especially because he's shirtless underneath that thing, leaving his muscled arms and Elendril mark exposed as the corset dips low in a seductive V.

I'm glad Jance has the night off because he would've made it awkward as I mentally undress Malakyte. Considering the intoxicating glances my prince throws my way, he does the same.

"Why isn't the stadium in the public sector? Wouldn't that make more sense than having it on the private side?"

I've heard rumors among the Azurite staff that the fighting pits are incredibly violent. It's hard for me to enjoy anything when I know Earth is in so much danger due to Herkimer's vindictive passion project. I hoped I could talk to Malakyte about what steps we can take to protect my people, but I'm not sure if this is the right place to have that conversation.

"The fighters are housed on this side, and transportation across the border would be problematic," Malakyte explains as the SSPARROWs lead us down a private, sterile-looking hallway away from the main entrance.

Eventually, we make it to an open door, with soldiers standing guard outside it, Malakyte leading me inside a private viewing room that overlooks the stadium.

The SSPARROWs close the door behind us as I take in the space. It's clean—typical for the Azurite—all black, which also tracks. Drinks await us near the five lush leather seats at the very front.

"Come sit," Malakyte says softly as he places a hand on my lower back, and I don't miss how delicious his cologne smells.

The stadium is absolute insanity.

For being inside a spaceship, it's a decently large arena, the size of this ship never ceasing to amaze me. Three main tiers of packed spectator seats wrap around the sharp edges of the octangular stadium, but what's most impressive is the domed skylight casting bright light down to the ring, where several figures—whom I think are referees—converse among themselves. Raven Black metal catwalks and speakers fill the ceilings.

Looking up, I squint my eyes at the strobing lights as they bounce through panels and rafters, but once the beams flash again, I see the symbol painted on the ceiling, clear as day.

The exact same diamond symbol from my nightmare this morning has been drawn on the stadium ceiling, at least twenty feet long in the shade Royal Orange. I immediately look away from it, not wanting Malakyte to see and get upset, but I can't help but wonder how my dreams and the symbols are connected. The marks were on my Dezlar today. If they're all connected, then are the dragons and that figurine, too? Where did Herkimer say the dragons were inside the ship? Down some stairs? My head begins to throb again the more I try to untangle this mysterious knot.

Icy lips graze against my neck, drawing me away from this confusing puzzle.

"I missed you," he whispers, nuzzling his face against the delicate skin of my collarbone.

His voice is so painfully sincere it sucks the anger and worry from our meeting with his parents right out of me.

"I missed you, too."

"You're not wearing the necklace I sent you."

He doesn't say it in an accusatory way, more disappointed.

I give him a passive aggressive hum in my throat, as if it were obvious.

His face comes back up, and he smiles at me, grabbing me by my middle and sliding me onto his lap, his coldness enveloping my waist as I face the stadium and he wraps his arms around me.

"Don't stew over Father," Malakyte says. "He's always been overzealous. He's grieving over Selenyte and aims to vilify the Terrans for her death, but I'll rein him in. I don't want you to fret over this."

He knows me so well. A part of me does want to push back, but Malakyte appears to understand that this isn't going to fly, so I guess that's enough for tonight.

"You're in your own mood," I tease, eyes averting down as the referee starts talking before a circular, floating microphone.

Malakyte's growl in my ear sends a flurry of shivers down my entire body. "Our night apart had me thinking of how much I love to hold you."

"Oh? Because this whole time, I thought you were afraid of me," I say playfully.

His chest vibrates on my back as he laughs, hands slipping to my inner thighs.

Voice deepening, he asks, "That felt suspiciously like a challenge, and you know I loathe to lose. And, make no mistake, Karalevine, there's no part of you that frightens me."

His words make my abandonment issues sing. But his hands? Tracing every inch of my thighs, ghostly fingerprints of his wintry touch linger, ratcheting up the tension between us with every tightening squeeze along my legs.

"Then, prove it," I whisper, the crowd's cheers nearly drowning my words out.

I turn to face him, reaching over and gliding my hand into his long hair, nails gently scraping his scalp as he leans into my touch. He's so otherworldly it's painful.

"You'll miss the show," he says, turning me around again.

"What if I want my own private show instead?"

"And what would that entail?"

My cheeks instantly heat. *Stars, he's going to make me say it, isn't he?*

Clearing my throat, I say as confidently as I can muster, "Back in the room, we'd—"

"You misunderstand me. This scenario would be happening *here*."

I swallow, and he shifts me so that my ass is angled directly between his legs.

"You know," he begins, hands tracing my body again, "I've come to enjoy witnessing every man on this ship wishing they could have the most beautiful woman in the Aurora System as theirs. It does something for me. This stadium could watch as I'd slowly remove every article of your clothing, piece by piece, delicately, as if I had all the time in the world to explore all the filthy fantasies I've had about you."

Fuck, I'd scream from the rooftops of this place simply to get him to do more than kiss me for once—but I play it cool and reach for my fancy drink. Those dirty fantasies he's talking about . . . I've experienced them, too. Lots of them.

"And then?"

Malakyte's hands glide over my waist until his firm grip locks around my hips, and he rocks my ass into his front. It's a full, drawn-out, circular movement, but the friction fires my nerves awake. Once, twice, and my body heats as he becomes rock hard beneath me. I purposely glide along his length so I can feel out every hidden detail he's kept from me.

The ledge is only about three feet tall, so everyone in the stands can see us only from the chest up. It takes everything to keep my face as impassive as possible.

"Then . . ." He rests his chin on my shoulder, our cheeks touching. "Then I'd bend you over that ledge, gaze lazily at your resplendent body, and squeeze that sweet ass, which has been driving me *insane*. After that, I'd turn you around, get on my knees for you—and only you—and bury my tongue inside you until you're coming so many times your legs could no longer support your weight."

The fighters are coming out—we really should be paying more attention. All I can think is how wet he's making me and how badly I want him to just *touch me*.

Instead, with each circle of my hips, I press down firmer. *Stars, he's so hard.* His hand reaches between my legs, but he's not quite where I want him to be, his lips and tongue worshiping my neck, sharp sets of canines leaving little tracks against my skin.

"Do you want this, Karalevine?" he asks, and I nod, our cheeks touching.

My throat is too tight to speak.

Over my clothes, Malakyte finally touches me, and, *stars*, it's everything as he slowly caresses that building ache between my thighs.

All I can think is, *Finally*.

"I've been dying to know what you feel like. What you taste like . . . I've thought about it for *hours*."

The referee brings the two fighters into the ring.

"Malakyte." I grind against him, his hand wrenching that coil within me tighter and tighter.

Fuck, if he doesn't stop, I'm going to come right here in front of a stadium full of people.

"Yes, babe . . . what do you want?"

Fucking stars. He knows what I want . . . but he won't be giving *that* to me. I've tried seducing him many times. It's never worked. It's so strange. But still . . . I can get something new.

"I want you, Malakyte."

"And you'd let me take you, right here, right now? Let me fuck you with all these eyes watching?"

His growl of satisfaction is nearly a purr this time.

The thought turns me on, just as it does him. The two of us are twisted, and it's more proof we belong together.

"I think you're the one who wants to take me in front of all these eyes," I rasp, chest filling with anticipation.

This is so hot I could die right here and now.

A sound of approval rumbles deep within his throat. "You understand me. Experiencing you naked, cheeks red, eyes glassy, completely undone from being ravished by me . . . That's reserved only for me. I'm not sure I can wait to hear the sounds you make as you come, however."

My body is betraying me under his touch. The crowd beyond us also builds up to their own crescendo of heady anticipation as the fight below waits to begin.

I can't take it anymore.

Guiding his hand up to the hem of my pants, I purr, "Touch me."

I hate myself for how my voice drips with desperation.

I nearly sing when Malakyte unbuttons my pants, my heart hammering. He dives into them but skips my lacy underwear, his fingers gliding across my bare skin. I nearly explode, gasping at the unfamiliarity of the chill. I feared the cold would tamper with my desire, but it does the opposite—it sets me ablaze.

"You're soaked, Karalevine, and in front of all these people, no less. Bad girl."

I grip his free hand, and he firmly interlaces our fingers together. Fuck, we're actually doing this in front of thousands of people.

Malakyte's finger glides right over my clit, and it's nearly impossible for me to keep the pleasure off my face. My star mark fires to a tingle the moment he finds my center, my blood full of anticipation.

"Malakyte."

His name is a plea. *Give me what I want.* Right here, right now. He has to.

"You want me to fuck you this way?" he whispers into my ear, teasing my entrance, then back to my clit, his desire softening his voice to the sweetest, most unfamiliar tone. "I think you want me to fuck you every way that I can. With my hand, with my tongue, with my cock. You're just a bad girl who wants to be fucked day and night, aren't you?"

"*Yes.*"

The crowd bellows in excitement, drowning out my cry as he enters me in one smooth glide. He's so cold the sensation fires my nerves in a way I never knew was possible. His thumb skillfully caresses my clit as he pumps that icy finger inside me.

Fucking stars.

"Tell me you're mine," he demands, voice a desperate whisper as he looks out to the crowd.

"I'm yours," I say breathlessly.

I'd tell him he's my fucking god if he asked me to.

I glance out over the balcony ledge, eyes heavy with desire and lust and so much need.

One fighter wearing a black shirt isn't watching his opponent. He's watching us. I don't fucking care. Let them all watch.

My body trembles as Malakyte wholly *fucks me with his hand,* and he's driving me insane.

"Now, be a good girl and show all these people what it feels like to come for me."

He sinks a second finger inside me on the cusp of his words, giving me both at once. My body is lightning, my insides are exploding, my orgasm is swallowed up by the crowd's thundering cheers. No hiding, no stifling my sighs of pleasure, even though every instinct in me tells me to be silent. It's . . . absolutely exhilarating.

"You come only for me," Malakyte reiterates, voice full of pride as I finally unravel from his Heaven, weak and trembling.

"Only for you," I echo, closing my eyes.

I can't believe we just did that.

The referee says the names of the first two fighters, the headline acts, apparently. The one is still watching us.

"These two fighters have been undefeated. Tonight is the night we pit them against each other! Who's ready?"

Malakyte slowly pulls out, brushing against my sensitive clit just to make me shudder one last time. He buttons my pants back up, as if nothing ever happened. Then he slowly, so slowly, licks his tongue up and down both fingers. He enjoys what he tastes, his pupils dilating with a desire I can only describe as feral.

He laps up every last trace.

CHAPTER 8

The heat lingers in my cheeks, body still jelly, heart on a hammering loop when the fight starts.

Malakyte possessively snuggles up against my neck as I settle back into my body.

The man who was watching us is going ape-shit on his opponent in a no-holds-barred, anything-goes brawl-a-thon.

"Wait," I say, noticing something odd, "why do they have collars around their necks?"

"Because they're criminals. All the fighters are. The collars not only block access to magic but also serve as security. It keeps everyone safe. There are innocent civilians on this ship I must be accountable for—that's why the stadium is in the private sector. We can't transport criminals across the border for every fight."

I open my mouth to respond to how cruel that is, but it's not worth the battle. It's just another thing to add to my ever-growing list of shit that needs to change around here.

Hopefully, it'll make up for being a sky-rat now.

Malakyte returns his attention to me as I observe the fighter from earlier, the one in black. His hair is a shaggy mess of dark blue with blond roots as it falls into his eyes. Those eyes— they're full of unadulterated rage.

Out of nowhere, he rips his shirt off, the black fabric falling in ribbons to the arena floor. He takes a hard right hook to the face because of it, the crowd wincing along with me. Seems like a stupid choice, but he's covered in tattoos, well-inked ones, at that. The hit doesn't seem to faze him as he comes back with the force of a raging bull.

His opponent is as broad-shouldered and massive as him, but the main difference between them is their skin color. One is a Terran, his skin pale in the shade Milk, and the other is an extra with Blue Charcoal skin, small horns poking out of his long black hair. They land blows, except the tattooed one is still managing to stay ahead.

The extra rips his shirt off, too, screaming. Alright, this is a thing now. The crowd loves it, amping up the alien as he swings the fabric over his head tauntingly.

Even though the blue-skinned alien should be drawing my eye, it's the tattooed one I can't stop watching. The honed muscles of his body glisten as he pounds and punches and kicks as if he's one more fight away from completely breaking apart. I know that feeling. That was me before Malakyte saved me.

How could he not be in agony if he's forced to fight day after day?

There's so much wrong here.

The fighters' bodies crash together, becoming locked, their feet scuffling and circling around the ring. Now it's more than a battle of strength but rather a battle of wills.

I want the tattooed one to win.

Sweat glistens off their skin. As they turn, a tattoo on the back of the Terran catches my eye, and I gasp.

I lean forward as I peer over the balcony railing.

What caught my attention initially was what looked like my star mark on his back. But as I squint, I see other marks overlaid on top of mine.

The crowd's cheering muffles in my ears as the epiphany hits me.

He has those graffiti marks tattooed on his back . . . *Elendril marks.*

My head pounds so hard it's like a jackhammer is barreling into my temple, the muffled sounds screeching in my ears as my body sways.

What's happening?

The two fighters break apart, and the tattooed boy picks up the massive, blue-skinned extra by the waist and slams him into the arena floor with the roaring approval from the stands.

The Terran turns to me, breathing hard, as his chest rises and falls in succession with my increasing heart rate.

We lock eyes immediately.

My ears pop, and my hearing returns to normal.

His entire chest is covered in tattoos, but again, I'm drawn to one that looks . . . different. It sticks out from the others. It's a twin to the one on his back—twin to the one from yesterday drawn on the mural by the border crossing. A circle, with six other circles around its rim.

What's happening? It's . . . My head feels so strange, like I'm falling straight through the stadium stands, right out the bottom of the Azurite and into the stars.

Blackness overtakes my vision, drowning me in the void.

Ardelle and I tumble, his back smacking the sparring mat with a slap as I leap to straddle him. I'll take any excuse to get this close.

"Looks like I win," I say sweetly, smiling my way to victory.

"You got me, Thumbelina."

I scoff. "You're going too easy on me." I stare at the shirtless warrior who's become my Starseed teammate but also someone so much more.

His muscled body could fluster any girl, and the expertly inked tattoos that cover every inch of him satisfy the kink only a tattoo artist can truly

have. I never miss his Elendril mark, though, the large circle surrounded by six smaller circles in the color Burgundy Bruise.

"My eyes are up here, Thumbelina."

The guy is so damn gorgeous I have to peel my eyeballs off his body, but as we look at each other, I see something so precious there.

Does Ardelle Dawson like me?

As he leans up to a sitting position, he takes me with him, and the kiss he lays on me tells me that he does, indeed, like *me.*

And I do, too. I really, really like him.

Tingles shoot through me, and I kiss him back, the kiss full of longing and need. But a strange feeling erupts in my chest, driving me away from this wonderful feeling. I can't stop it as it draws me up, up, up . . .

I'm slammed back into the present with the force of a missile, back toward my life on the Azurite as princess of Arianyte and Malakyte Ardeen's bride. The vision fades at the edges, dissolving into nothing but a blur of shapes and colors and feelings that are all consuming and confusing as fuck.

What the fuck is going on?

The crowd's roaring blasts in my ears, dismantling the scene as it melts away completely, one single word whacking me upside the head over and over and over again.

"Thumbelina! Thumbelina! *Thumbelina!*"

CHAPTER 9

I adore the way Karalevine looks in those pants as she leans over the railing like that. I can still detect the delicious aftertaste of her in my mouth when she suddenly gasps, flying backward into me, nearly shattering my nose with the back of her head.

She slips off my knee and falls to the side, as if her equilibrium went haywire, but I keep her wrangled on my lap.

"What is it?" I ask.

Then I hear that name that grinds on my every fucking nerve. *"Thumbelina!"*

Over and over again, he howls.

Karalevine whips around to face me, gaze wild with panic as she places a palm over her eyes and takes a breath. Her heart is thrashing now that I tune to the sound, the crowd making it difficult to hear.

"I just saw something really strange."

In the fighting ring, Mr. Dawson stops his incessant shouting of that absurd nickname and glares up at us with a cocky smirk—*shirtless*. That shirt was on when I looked down there a moment before.

Rage builds in my blood, icing it over. I told the guards to make certain he wore that shirt no matter what happened tonight. I was distracted by Karalevine, by giving into her body, into the ache that's been building inside me for her. I wanted to give her time to acclimate to her new life. Be respectful and responsible, let her come to me. I couldn't hold off any longer, and it cost me. I slipped. I fucking ruined everything.

That little bastard down there knows it, too.

"What did you see?" I demand, trying hard not to shake her.

"A vision, maybe, I don't know. I . . . it was just a flash or something. I'm confused.'"

A vision? Of a memory? That isn't possible.

"He's a damn Starseed, Malakyte!" Her demeanor finally changes to what I expected, her eyes clearer, but this so-called vision is too concerning to ignore. "Why is he in our fighting pits?"

"*Our* fighting pits?"

I lead her away from her initial question so I can come up with some asinine reason for him being down there when she shouldn't have been able to notice this at all.

I won't allow anything or anyone to take her from me. She's mine. I put in far too much effort getting this far. These imbecilic pains in my ass will rue the day they didn't simply flee like cowards and let me keep what I've won.

Karalevine sighs at me, frustrated, and I blurt out, "That young man's mental acuity is in complete disarray, not to mention psychologically unstable. I kept him a secret because I knew it would break your heart that your Starseed team would forever remain fractured. He's unstable and dangerous, Karalevine. I promise you he's not well."

Without a doubt, this girl just rolled her eyes at me.

"So, you're telling me you have a mentally ill person fighting five times a week in the pits? He could be getting help rather than being tortured! He's one of us, Malakyte."

69 

I open my mouth to respond, but I'm cut off before I'm able. "Thumbelina!"

Her spine snaps to attention like a steel rod. A nanosecond later, she's standing and turning to face the ledge, but I immediately lunge toward her without considering how desperate the act must appear. My grip on her wrist is as cold as death, and she looks at me as if I had struck her instead of merely attempting to limit her exposure to that little prick.

Those eyes . . . Her expression is so familiar, my heart physically aches.

That's the way the old Karalevine used to look at me . . .

Selenyte appears in my peripheral. "Oh, big brother. She's already beginning to hate you. Just look at her. Your plan is unraveling right before your eyes. Karalevine is going to break your heart. How could she not? It's *you* who we're talking about here. Just like Father always says, you're a weak, pathetic excuse for a man, and Karalevine sees that no matter how many times you make her forget."

"Thumbelina! Thumbelina!" he continues shouting.

The crowd hushes, yet their inquisitive whispers still echo out among them, and I can't allow this to go on any further.

I stand, ignoring the frightened look in Karalevine's eyes as I tower over her, turning her from the railing. "We're leaving."

Her body resists me as Mr. Dawson climbs out of the ring as if he could possibly make it all the way up to us and pluck Karalevine away from me.

Fool.

"You're being controlled, Thumbelina!" he yells, as if I'm moments away from executing him. "Get away from him! He's messed with your mind! He's Recondi—"

SSPARROWs rip him away, and I do the same with Karalevine, forcing her toward the door.

She fights me every step of the way. "Isn't Ardelle the name of the Terran you said killed your sister? A Starseed killed your sister and you just, what, left that out?"

Her voice is enraged, but how did she know his name? I mentioned it in the throne room with my parents, but the referees don't call him by his real name—there's no way she could have known it.

Looking back at her, I bare my teeth as I stalk us toward the door, wrenching the thing open. "We'll talk about this once we're back in the ro—"

It's Karalevine's panicked gasp and widening eyes that causes me to divert my attention back to the door, but I'm too late.

Snapping my gaze forward, Deimos stands mere inches away in the open door, and all my soldiers are either dead on the floor or have otherwise been dealt with.

"Housekeeping." Deimos grins.

He's all savage arrogance as his Starseed magic yanks me by the balls, eyes ablaze in green, and the rage bursting through my blood is all consuming as he forces all of us back inside the spectator suite. My hand involuntarily lets Karalevine go as she and I back up, my own body stiff in Deimos's control.

Her angry heartbeat is strong, confident and even-keeled. Now, her tempo is frantic like those strange hummingbirds found on Earth, an uneven cadence that flutters erratically. It's also in the tightening of her breath, in the jerky way she steps back and away from Deimos and I, and in the delicate flaring of her nostrils. My sweet Star is absolutely terrified.

As she should be.

Deimos shoves me backward until I slam into the first chair as it nearly topples.

Karalevine pleads for him to stop, but he hasn't taken her yet. She can still get away.

He points to her. "Make one single move, Kiddo, and I'll throw you off that balcony by your hair for fun."

When his attention returns to me, I catch him reaching for something, and that's when I note he's wearing a SSPARROW uniform without a helmet. I frantically search for the missing piece, finding it tucked under his arm. Is that the same one from the night I murdered Selenyte? Perhaps I could get Karalevine to take the helmet and—

She shouts in protest, but it's too late. Deimos drives his Elendril dagger deep through my sternum and up into my heart, the pain barely dulled by the adrenaline coursing in my body.

It's agonizing.

Karalevine frantically calls my name, but I can no longer tune to her heartbeat, the sound my most indulgent comfort. All I can hear is my own pulse slowing and slowing and slowing . . .

"That's for what you did in that throne room, you piece of shit," Deimos seethes in my ear, voice venomous.

We lock eyes.

I silently promise a slow, agonizing death for this bastard once I get my hands on him. And I will. *I will.* My rage crystalizes into frostbite, and he doesn't know it, but my retribution will acquaint him with the arctic chill and then he will understand just how painfully ice can burn.

"And this . . . This is for my Zariya."

Then he twists the knife, my vision nearly blackening, blood shooting up from my throat as it splatters all over his face.

"Malakyte!" Karalevine shouts, finally coming for me.

Deimos throws out his hand, and she stops.

He rips his dagger free, and I immediately fall into a pool of my own blood, my knees completely giving way to the shame that I find myself in such a weak, pathetic state, especially in front of her.

"R-Run, Kara . . ." I say, using my last breaths to keep what I love for as long as possible.

"Oh, no, I don't think so," Deimos says, rushing up on Karalevine as she backs away. He's in her space too

 72

quickly, snatching her chin. His Starseed magic leaves my body and transfers straight into hers. "Kiddo isn't going anywhere but with me."

She has no choice but to walk out with him moments later.

A hollow ringing drowns out all else, even the pain, and I'm close. I've died so many times the signs are formulaic. But it's her beautiful face, her expressive, animated eyes I think of, knowing what Deimos and the others are going to accomplish with her in their clutches.

Well, it's about time they made their move.

Let Ennar's plan commence.

CHAPTER 10

I'm being kidnapped.

Nausea churns my stomach sour as I step over the fallen SSPARROWs who've been laid out along the little hallway behind the spectator suite. Deimos's magic forces my body into compliance, leaving Malakyte to die as the terroristic extra slides his helmet back over his face as we near the exit.

What is he going to do with me?

"I'm not going to hurt you," he says calmly as we approach another person dressed in what I'm assuming is a SSPARROW disguise because he's currently holding a legitimate SSPARROW in a sleeper hold in the crook of his arms.

His face is masked, and he's massive.

Deimos doesn't let me respond as we meet up with his accomplice. We pass the entrance to the pits and walk briskly but calmly down the Azurite halls. They make sure my head is dipped low, I'm assuming, so nobody can see my eyes ablaze in the color Green House.

I try to recall the conversation I had with Malakyte weeks ago about his crystal's abilities. He meant it when he said his crystal can truly bring him back, right? He's not *dead* dead, right?

Is Deimos bringing me back to Geonni and Trinity for them to finish the assassination they failed before I came to hide on the Azurite? Do they want my crystal?

Panicked questions fly like pelleted rain as we walk hallway after hallway, deeper and deeper into the Azurite. Eventually, we end up in a low-traffic section. The hallways are darker, the floors less polished, with no décor or plant life or art. For storage, most likely. Then finally, we stop at a door, and by the time we do, I realize I've botched the first rule of being kidnapped—don't allow yourself to be taken to a second location.

That's where all the bad stuff happens.

Deimos and the other guy open the door and walk me into a room that's so dark I can hardly see five feet in front of my face. There are only two little pop-up lamps sitting on the ground further in. It's maddening I can't fight back, and I'm made to sit in a hard metal chair directly beside those lamps, my anxiety growing, but I still can't speak. I can't see beyond the tiny halo of light illuminating me. I have no idea how big or small the space truly is, but what I do know for sure is that there's several people here, likely more. I can hear them.

The stark cold has my teeth chattering, or maybe it's my fear.

I flinch when a man appears out of the dark, who's rolling a tray full of medical supplies. When he bends down, his expression is calm—happy, even. He doesn't look like a rebel. I also don't recognize his kind Sky Blue eyes or his brushed back blond hair.

"It's so good to see you again, Kara," he says softly, his smile tentative. *Again?* I can't respond, so he takes my left hand as I strain to pull it away. "I'm a doctor, and I'm going to take the chip out of your wrist. I promise I'll make it as painless as possible."

Great, they know about my chip, too? That means Malakyte won't be able to track me to this location, even if he isn't dead.

But that's the least of my immediate worries when the doctor moves to slip on a pair of gloves over a Ringer mark

75

on his hand. The symbol on the tattooed Starseed from the pits, the emblem graffitied on the mural yesterday—this man is his Ringer.

As promised, this doctor gently opens me up and removes the tiny device extremely quickly and efficiently before sewing me back up with two little stitches.

A new guy appears from behind me and takes the chip from the doctor, hiding it in a tissue. He's average in build, I suppose, with dark skin in the shade Sienna Honey and tousled hair that keeps falling into his eyes in Tektite Black.

"You know where to go," the doctor says to him calmly. "Be careful. Meet you back at home."

The boy nods and stops to stare at me. His gorgeous Green Smoke eyes look heartrending as they slide up and down my body, meeting my gaze. My own eyes widen at what is poking out from under a white T-shirt. The diamond symbol, the one I've also been seeing everywhere. He runs out of the room a second later.

So, what is this? Are all the Starseeds and Ringers working with Geonni and Deimos now? Malakyte's words from yesterday about this exact scenario echo through my mind.

The man in the other stolen SSPARROW suit bends down in front of me, the doctor rising to his feet and disappearing back into the dark.

The SSPARROW in disguise reaches to remove his helmet, but my mouth falls through the floor at the face I see staring back at me with an expression of a heart torn up at the seams.

He looks so different . . . yet so the same.

"Make it so she can talk," Gavrielle tells Deimos, who's standing in my peripheral.

I can't look anywhere else but in those Lavender Haze eyes as my entire body tingles, chest firing off veclear bombs. I'm instantly drowning in the pure masculine scent of this man, clean like citron and ginger but also woodsy and strong like an unyielding immovability of a mountain. His gaze rips me apart, stitch by frayed, fragile stitch, exposing me and leaving me so raw and vulnerable I can't allow it to continue. Although I have no way of stopping him from *seeing* me in the way he does. Nobody should be allowed to overcome my defenses, plow through my walls, and strip me bare like he does. And he notices, although he doesn't seem to be taking any sick pleasure from doing so. Only now does he feel like the kind, gentle boy I once knew from that orphanage.

"Gavrielle?" I whisper, my voice allowed to be my own again.

He nods. "It's me, Kara."

Gavrielle is likely the most beautiful man I've ever seen. Even compared to Malakyte's impressive exterior, Gavrielle is . . . *more*. This thought makes me feel guilty, especially after what just happened to my prince. Yet I can't help but sense, feel, *experience* the pure sex appeal of the man standing before me. His muscled body is massive, sculpted by years of lethal refinement and skill, visible even in that uniform. With a jawline that could kill and cheekbones that could cut, to say Gavrielle is gorgeous is a disservice. Criminal. And it's his sheer beauty that makes this moment all the more surreal because such Sky-Fae magnificence shouldn't be in a dark, dangerous hole like this.

The lump in my throat feels like a cantaloupe when I swallow, my senses finally returning to me.

I remember where I am.

What he's done.

It's as if he's raked my heart against a gravel road, shredding it in one go.

"What's going on?" I ask as Gavrielle starts to remove his metal gloves, finally breaking eye contact.

The lightning sparking between us is almost as intense as my antimatter, albeit invisible and not as destructive. Well, if Malakyte were to ever find out about it, then it would become exactly that, which tells me I must bury it. The fact he's an accomplice to this helps a lot.

"If Deimos lets you go, will you sit here and listen?" Gavrielle asks.

"Are you fucking for real?" I laugh. "Wow."

"Told you so," Deimos says as he walks out of my field of vision, his helmet off.

"I don't mean to interrupt," a sweet female voice absolutely interrupts, "but whoever they've got working for them already looks to be following Sylo with her chip. They're blowing down my encryption and firewalls with a digital version of a bulldozer. I don't know how they're doing this so quickly. I've never seen anything like it. If they keep this up, they're going to find us and fast."

Malakyte!

Deimos sharply says from somewhere behind me, "Then, you better do your job and keep them out. This is going to take time."

"Kara." Gav brings me back to him. "I know you're not going to like this, but we have to do it this way. It's just for a couple of minutes and then we'll untie them."

"Untie what?"

A rope quickly comes around my chest and arms, wrapping around once, twice, three times. I can tell it's Deimos doing it by his metal uniform. The moment I'm tied to the chair, I feel his magic leave me. My body is my own again.

"What are you doing?" I cry to Gavrielle, who looks at me like he's in physical pain as I automatically test my tight bonds.

Deimos's magic was physically keeping me calm, but now that he's gone and this is happening, my heart is racing.

Cold steel clamps around my throat, and the access to my magic is completely cut off.

Did they just collar me like a *fucking dog?*

My rage is an entity bellowing through this space, unseen but surely felt by everyone in the room.

 78

Deimos isn't as torn about tying me down and collaring me as he swings into my field of vision, his Midnight Green skin practically black in this light as his wispy cotton hair sways past a pair of giant, pointed ears.

"Oh, don't look at me like that," he drawls like I'm annoying him. "My magic could interfere with what needs to happen here, and you just confirmed you're not going to play nice and sit there like a good little doggy." Gavrielle growls at his Starseed at that bit, but Deimos goes on. "And we both know your magic is too unpredictable not to blow us all out of orbit, so chill the fuck out, or else you're going to hurt yourself by allowing that power to consume you from within. I told you we're not going to hurt you. You may have changed, but you're still the same stubborn little shit you've always been. That much is clear."

The last thing I can do is calm down. And what is he talking about? He doesn't know me.

Then someone else echoes, "Calm down, kid. You're safe."

That voice . . .

Jance.

My head whips to the left where his broad shoulders emerge from the darkness, and my Ringer steps into view. He's been here the entire time?

Deimos crosses his arms, an angry crease in his brow. "You were supposed to just watch."

"Too fucking bad." He sneers at the extra as he comes to stand next to me. "And you know what to keep your mouth shut about when it comes to her and me."

I look up, so fucking confused as the tension in this room is escalating by the second. Jance glares at Deimos like he's about to spill a barrel full of secrets he doesn't want exposed. My Ringer has lots of secrets, apparently.

"Kara," Jance begins, turning away from Deimos, his voice stern but still gentle. "I can explain everything. I'm sorry this is how we had to get you here, but—"

"How *dare you?*" I roar. "You're my Ringer. You're supposed to protect me!"

Jance's eyes, shade Black Chocolate, look as if I shattered his heart with a rocket missile. But he let Deimos strap me down to this chair. He's here—working with *them.*

He finally says, "I promise that you're safe and everything will be okay."

Footsteps approach as an old-world Asian woman appears next to Jance, and I immediately recognize her as the woman from my dream this morning. When I look down to her hand, I see she has the diamond-shaped symbol like in the dream.

I turn away as Jance and her stand half hidden by the dark. The only other person I can see is Gavrielle, and when our eyes collide again, he gives me goose bumps.

There's no tattooing Death himself as his soul shines through burning, violet eyes.

Even in the dim lighting, emotion emits through every pore. The way his shoulders slump, how his head cocks slightly to the right, how his brows furrow like he's in pain.

"I'm on your side, Kara. I always have been, and I always will be."

I smile sweetly and say with just as much sugar in my voice, "Then, let me the fuck out of this chair."

His chuckle is maddeningly attractive. "Not a chance, love," he says, grinning wickedly right back at me. His hand gently comes up to tap my head in one of those loving touches reserved only for people who are very, very close to one another.

"Guys," the same female voice from moments ago calls out, way more worried this time. "They found her chip, and they're definitely onto us. I think this was a trap."

"Fuck," Deimos growls, his footsteps stomping close behind me. "We don't have time for sweet touches and cuddles. Do this now, or we'll never have another opportunity. He'll come in here, take her back, and kill us all. It's now or it's never."

 80

I don't want Gav or Jance dead, but I need to keep them talking for as long as possible, prevent whatever they're trying to accomplish here.

Wheels squeak to my left, and my eyes snap in that direction as the doctor who removed my chip walks up with a small tank in the shade Olive bracketed up on some dolly with an oxygen mask and all the tubes connected to it.

He places the contraption next to Gavrielle and me, and all that anger is replaced by fear.

"What is that?" I demand, trying to inch away despite the futility of it.

Gavrielle looks at me so seriously I can't help but forget everyone in this room as I wait on his every word. "Listen to me, Kara . . . This is going to be hard to hear and very confusing, but just know that you're safe with me. With us."

My breathing becomes erratic. It's the only sound besides typing keys.

"You've been Reconditioned," Gavrielle says, the certainty in his tone hitting me with the force of a spear being thrown right into my gut at top speed. "The last six months of your life has been a lie fabricated by Naresteé and Malakyte, crafted for you specifically so Malakyte could have you in every way that matters to him. As his lover, his bride, and his weapon. You were Malakyte's biggest adversary, and you were—you are—so close to bringing him and his empire down for good. Except he has some twisted obsession with you, claims to love you but what he feels isn't love at all. When he couldn't win your heart, he took you away from everyone you love and Reconditioned you to believe that you're in love with him. This happened about five weeks ago, and it happened on the Azurite. The memory you have of meeting him on Earth is fabricated by magic. I know that sounds insane, stars, I do, but it's one hundred percent true. You and Malakyte are enemies, Kara. You hate him."

"That's . . ." My mind rings with a hollow nothingness. "That's not possible."

What I hate are liars. I really, really do. Yet, in all my life, I've never wished more than for a person to be lying to me.

Malakyte would never. He'd never do that *to me* . . .

I'm the only one who can truly love you.

Nobody else sees you. Not like I do.

I won't let anyone take you from me again.

Gavrielle looks heartbroken as my mind cycles through the last several months of my life. All the memories, all the moments. What's supposedly fake and what's real? No . . . no. They're lying. Gav is lying.

"I know it's hard to wrap your mind around it. They did it to me, too. And to Pacey. Pacey is a friend. Another Starseed. She's the one typing at the keyboard."

The typing stops, and her sweet voice rings out to me, but I still can't see her.

"I understand how frightened and confused you are. But you know what? You saved me from that fate. Now it's time for me to return that favor. It's time for you to come home."

Home . . . ? But Malakyte is my home.

Jance says from his place on the edge of the shadows, "They Reconditioned me, too. My Ringer magic was able to break through it, only because I could adjust my own brain chemistry and did so beforehand, a little trick nobody knew I could do. I broke through the memories they implanted in my mind, and I tried to do the same for you, so many times. I couldn't. I'm your Ringer, and I couldn't fix this . . ."

My eyes slowly shift to look at him, my anger lashing out and ready to strike. "You're not my Ringer anymore."

The room falls dead fucking silent, but all Jance does is continue looking at me with anguish in his eyes, the woman by his side clinging onto his arm, comforting him.

They've all lost their minds. Malakyte was right about the other Starseeds and Ringers. Trying to find them was a gigantic mistake.

"He's getting closer, Gav," Pacey says.

Nodding, Gavrielle brings that contraption on wheels nearer, and my attention snaps back to him.

"What is that?"

Stars, what are they going to do? My mark is on fucking fire.

Gavrielle looks hesitant. "We have a way to break the Reconditioning. It's worked on both Pacey and me. It's a drug, a gas, specifically. Once it's administered, it'll induce some pretty vivid hallucinations, but afterward, all your memories should come back an—"

"Don't you dare fucking drug me," I snap. "If you do this, he will kill you all."

The threat isn't a hollow one, and the silent promise is ear ringing.

"I'd like to see him try," Gavrielle says, absolutely no fear there.

If he hadn't forced me here and tied me to this chair—it'd be hot.

I glare at Jance and drive the blade home. "If you let this happen, I'll never forgive you."

With a painful grimace, Jance inhales deeply, closing his eyes. Notably, he doesn't make a move to stop this.

Gavrielle plucks the oxygen mask off the hook of the contraption, and I immediately freak.

If I jerk my body hard enough, I can skirt the chair over an inch, maybe two. But what's the point? It's not like they're going to simply let me hop all the way out of here.

Laughable.

I'm not going anywhere.

My crystal feels like it's going to eat me alive from within.

As I look back at Gavrielle, his eyes have darkened, looking like pools of anguish in the shade Violets Are Blue.

If he truly was my friend, he wouldn't be doing this in the first place. Although . . . that really doesn't sound like the Gavrielle I knew.

The Gav I knew would never hurt me. Ever . . .

Gavrielle traces every line of my face, as if remembering the little girl I used to be in comparison to the woman I've become. I know because I'm doing the same to him.

He brushes a loose strand of my hair behind my ear, his touch so affectionate it's unintentionally cruel. "Everything is going to be alright."

For a minute, I think he's going to kiss me with the way he's looking at me, but when that mask comes up to my face, I recoil.

But there's nowhere to go. Nowhere to run to. No way to fight him.

"Please, Gavrielle . . ."

"You can hate me right now. That's fine. *Loathe me* if you have to. I can take it. But I'm certain that, deep down, you'd rather know the truth than be lied to and manipulated by a monster for one second longer than you have to be."

Stars . . . no. I don't want this. I don't care what he says. I don't want to.

Resting his forehead against mine, Gav says, "You know me. You remember me. It's the only way to bring you back."

"Don't I have a choice?" I ask, cold gas blasting onto my face. "Don't I get a say in what you do to me? Did you ever consider that maybe I'm happy and you're going to take all that away from me because you want me to remember this so-called real life? Isn't that the most selfish thing you could do, Gavrielle?"

He doesn't miss a beat. "No."

And then he's done talking.

I jerk my face to the side, but Gavrielle is gentle, so fucking gentle as he brings my face forward. Although his grip is soft, it's also sure of its intent.

This is happening, and I can't stop it.

 84

When I'm out of options and stalling tactics, I do the last desperate thing I can think of. I take a full gulp of clean air into my lungs before Gavrielle clasps that oxygen mask over my face.

I hold my breath. I'll hold out long enough. I will. That tank can't last forever, and I have great lung capacity.

Deimos laughs incredulously from behind me somewhere in the shadows. "Stars, you would, Kiddo."

Tension radiates off the others in the room, unseen or not.

I'm becoming uncomfortable fast, more panicked, more wild, but maybe I can hold out long enough for Malakyte to get here and stop this. Although my lungs are burning, my nose betraying me as it slightly breathes in, but I catch it. *I refuse.* The gas is filling up the mask with a white fluffy cloud in the color Boneyard. And my legs jerk as my knuckles go white, and my eyelids keep fluttering.

"Don't fall for this," Deimos says to the others, "she'll have no choice but to breathe it in. Wait her out. She's close."

His words push me to hold on even longer, even through the pain that's building and building and building.

"Kara . . . it's okay," Gavrielle says, using his hand to hold the mask to my face rather than the strap that's connected to it.

His other hand softly caresses my cheek with his thumb, fingers sliding into my hair, and when my first tear falls, it lands on him, a tear of ultimate and utter defeat.

He wipes it away.

The pressure, the frenzied need to give into my body's demands for air reaches a near maddening level.

And I hate myself—more than I have in a long time—as I become my very own death knell.

Unable to hold out even one second longer, I ultimately cave and breathe in the gas that will change everything.

Change the world I desperately want to stay the same.

CHAPTER 11

My betrayal and anger toward Gavrielle and Jance is second to the fear slithering into my bloodstream faster than the gas. The violation I feel at these *men* tying me down like this is . . . terrifying. Embarrassing. Shameful. If they claim to care about me, then they would know this is the worst thing they could choose to do to me. The helplessness is profound as the darkness chokes me from every angle. As if, it, too, is a part of this group of people hell-bent to free my mind from a narrative they find unappealing.

Hell-bent on taking me away from Malakyte.

But what if what they're saying is true?

That single assertion slithers in, and like a virus, it spreads.

One fact chills me to the bone. *Did Malakyte truly Recondition me?*

Gavrielle watches me closely, relentlessly searching for any signs of something amiss as the drug seeps into my lungs as deep as his betrayal.

Gavrielle . . . he's here. He's so . . . handsome. That perfect, delicious, slightly pouty mouth and how it would feel on mine if we . . .

I shake my head as if those betraying thoughts will fly away, along with the fuzziness on my brain.

"That's enough, Gavrielle. I think it's hitting her. Take the mask off," the doctor says.

As Gavrielle removes the mask, I take in a full, deep breath of clean air. My eyes flutter closed, and my head falls backward as it hits the chair.

This is all so fucking weird, but it gets weirder when I smell it . . . smell the exact suffocating, nausea-inducing odor from my nightmares.

From inside that cube prison.

I'm awake, right? Or am I dreaming? Maybe this is all just another nightmare? I look around me, no cube in sight. But the darkness is heavier, blacker, more insidious. Perhaps I've finally escaped the cube, and this is what's beyond it.

"Kara!" a sweet, faraway voice calls. "Come on, Kara, you've got to remember."

"Remember what?" I ask.

Nobody answers me.

I'm not sure how long I sit here like this, frozen in terror. It could be minutes, hours, days . . .

Gavrielle unravels the rope around my torso, and my lashes feel like weights. It doesn't help this terrible feeling clawing its way out of me. I don't like how this feels or how my head is so foggy and my body is so heavy. I want to go home. *I'm scared*. I want Malakyte, and I want to get away from these people.

But where is he? Why hasn't he rescued me yet?

I can't stay here and wait for him to find me. I have to be strong and rescue myself.

Gavrielle curses as I slither out from the chair, skirting under his massive body before he can grab me, and Jance isn't quick enough either. The drug hasn't slowed my agile reflexes— thank the stars—and I dart toward the door like an arrow flying at its target.

Get out, get out, get out!

"Kara!"

"Fuck!"

"Don't let her leave this room!"

"You fucking morons never should have untied her!"

Fuck that if they think I'm staying here.

It's dark in here but not so much that I can't find the door, but I instantly feel arms around me before I make it halfway.

Deimos has me in his grasp.

He growls in my ear as I fight his hold on me from behind, and he's got a vise-like grip. I buck and struggle and scream—frantic. He's going to kill me this time. He's going to take that knife he stabbed Malakyte with and fucking kill me.

My heart hammers, and my crystal spikes inside my blood, but it has no way out, no escape to vent through, thanks to this stupid fucking collar.

Then my magic twinkles to life at my fingertips, just barely finding a way outside the collar somehow, something I never knew was possible. A trickle, really, of my normal power. But that's enough.

"Bitch!" Deimos hisses as he reluctantly lets me go, not fully in control of his body as I zap him with the little magic I can conjure.

It's enough to cause the smell of burnt flesh to permeate the room.

The door!

I'm so close.

So close!

My palm slaps the control panel, and I practically rip the door off its track as I wrench it open.

Then I blink, stunned still as death.

The door slides open to that childhood bedroom of mine, the one I know like the back of my hand, because it haunts my days and my nights and all the tragic moments between.

The room sits exactly as I remember. The small twin bed with the faded flower blanket and dull sheets in the shade

Eggplant. That little white side table with the chipped paint and the yellow-stained lampshade sitting on it that cast the room in a dull glow in the shade Mustard. My defiance to the man who would sneak into this room night after night lay bare on the walls in colored crayons and dried markers. I've long ago ripped off the wallpaper he tried to place over the childish scribbles on the walls that proved his guilt, but he could never cover up what happened in there. I've tried to conceal what he did, too, by putting wallpaper over the bleeding wound left permanently gushing as if I had a leak in my soul. It didn't stick very long for me, either.

But why am I here?

Maybe I never escaped this room. Maybe I've always been stuck in here, and this whole life has been nothing but one massive, elaborate trick of my mind to deal with the fact that he made me go insane.

This world, this life, nothing but a hallucination . . .

I'm unable to move a muscle as I stare into this Hell, half ready to explode from within as fear unlike any other drives ice into my blood faster than a hover-train.

Until someone decides to body-slam me straight to the ground, the both of us falling together.

CHAPTER 12

DAY 2: THE PRINCE MADE ME A DEAL ... AND I'M A COWARD
FOR TAKING IT. IF I SERVE HIM FAITHFULLY FOR TWENTY
YEARS, HE'LL FREE ME AND PLANET NYKTOS. IT'S THE
ONLY WAY ...

FORGIVE ME, FATHER AND MOTHER.

GAVRIELLE ABRAXAS

I crash against Kara harder than I anticipated, my adrenaline pumping so hard I body-slam the poor thing. We go down, but I pivot so that I take all the impact.

Air rushes out from my lungs as we hit, but she's fine, and that's all I care about.

Physically, anyway.

Mentally, that's another story.

The hallucinations have fully begun, and I hate that I caused this.

Deimos runs up and closes the door, blocking it.

Kara fights and screams at me, her nails tearing at my skin and hair, but I let her do it as I sit us up, cognizant of the fact that she's tripping, and it's not a fun ride. Remembering the gas from the maze, it's a reality bender. Bleeding the hallucination into what's real so seamlessly, telling the difference between what's real or fake being impossible. Whatever Kara saw when she opened that door, it thoroughly freaked her out.

"Hey, hey." I pat her hair, sitting her on my lap. "Stay with me, Kara. It's me. It's Gavrielle. It's okay."

"I don't want to go back there," she pleads, tears glossing her eyes. "Don't make me go back."

I hold her face in my hands. "I won't let you go back, love. You're safe."

Kara's eyes have lost their hard, angry edge, and I can see the girl I met on that Sky Dais all those weeks ago. I see the girl I gave those dandelions to.

Then Pacey's cries ring out into the room, startling Kara so badly I nearly lose her all over again. "Oh, shit! *Shit!*"

"What?" Deimos yells.

Once I finally get a firm grip on Kara, I look over at Pacey as a loud clatter of metal on metal collides with the ship's interior.

"What the fuck are you doing?" Deimos says, rushing up to Pacey as she stomps on the laptop.

Saris and Ahren rush over to her with panic-stricken expressions.

Jance runs up to Kara and me, bending down. He senses what I do.

The prince is close . . . We all feel his presence as if he's in the room with us.

Pacey's expression is grim as the remaining light of her laptop bounces from the screen up onto her worried face.

"They're here," Pacey gasps as she rushes into the darkness. She returns seconds later with her water bottle.

Her magic swells as she dumps the contents onto the laptop, guiding the water deep into the device.

Deimos is pissed. "What are you doing? You know what I had to do to get that fucking thing for you, and you're drowning it?"

"Not just drowning," Pacey says as she whips out a lighter, presses down on it, and shoots the flame down straight into the computer with a flick of her wrist. It whooshes into a blaze. "Fire, too. If I don't destroy it, they'll know everything I did and exactly where we are. This was a setup. They knew we hacked in, and they planned for it. They're not coming. *They're here.*"

Smoke fills up the room fast, and others cough as the fumes of burning cords and chips and wires sting my nose.

"It hasn't been long enough," I say to Jance. "The gas hasn't had enough time."

"You said it hit you almost immediately. For Pacey, it took a little longer, but it's been thirty minutes already. It's going to have to be enough time."

I don't typically experience anxiety, but I feel it breathing down my neck as the others collect the evidence that we were here and exactly what we've done.

Kara is calmer now, so at least we have that on our side.

"Darling." Jance scoots closer to Kara, down on the floor with us. "Tell me how you're feeling. Do you remember what happened inside the throne room?"

The memories his words resurface in me are enough to make my body shudder with nausea, so I can't imagine what Kara's feeling, raw and unyielding.

"The throne room . . ." she repeats, somewhat a question, somewhat an echo of Jance's words.

"That's right, darling. Do you remember what happened there?"

I need to hear her say it. We all do.

But there's no time.

"Now!" Pacey shouts.

 92

My heart flutters.

Jance and I heave Kara to her feet, pulling her toward the door, the others right behind us.

Kara flinches as the door slides open and light from the hallway hits us, and my heart aches.

Jance hovers over her, keeping his hands on her shoulders, brushing back her hair. From what I saw of their relationship, they had this sort of intimate connection—not in a weird way. I just found it odd for Kara, but it just goes to show how much work Jance put in to touch her at all. But as his hand moves from her upper back to her lower as we cross the threshold, I see her flinch again.

At Jance.

He misses it because it's subtle, and she does a good job of hiding it.

An overwhelming feeling tingles its way up my spine, quick and rushed and full of panic.

She and I lock eyes, and that fear is instantly cemented.

Kara shoves Jance as hard as she can, her father stunned as he catches himself on the doorframe.

But Kara is gone, her thin frame bolting down the hallway as fast as she can run.

Fuck!

The gas didn't work.

The gas didn't work.

I didn't want to accept it, but it's been far too long, and the chances of those memories resurfacing after all this is unlikely.

Boot steps made of metal echo in my ears from down the hall, and the prince's voice is clear . . .

The teal in her hair whips behind her as she runs from me, the color that symbolized the love we shared for each other as children. A bond that's unbreakable. Nothing Malakyte does can shatter that. I just need her to remember what he's done.

Kara rounds a corner, and I manage to grab a hold of her shoulders and push her hard enough to cause her to trip over her feet. I can't feel bad when her life is at stake. She slows, allowing me ample time to wrap my arms around her and pull us to the floor.

Thankfully, nobody is in this hallway—but they will be in seconds.

"Kara, stop," I yell as she fights me like a rabid beast. "I'm not going to hurt you."

"You tied me to a fucking chair and drugged me, Gavrielle! I'm never going to trust you again!"

I bare my fangs at her, a growl erupting from my throat. "If you remembered what the fuck has happened, you wouldn't be saying that. The Kara I knew would never turn her back on me or her family."

"I don't have a family!"

"You have *me*!"

Hands on her shoulders, I shake her a bit, as if by doing so those memories will somehow clip back into place and return the woman I love. Bring my mate back. This finally breaks her out of her fight or flight, and she stares at me with wide eyes, as if she's truly realizing that it's really me standing in front of her.

I don't let up. "We got separated at the orphanage, and I had to let you go then. It was the best thing for you. But now . . . I'm never going to stop until you're free from him. He Reconditioned you, Kara. He took you from everyone you care about and loved, and he twisted your mind into believing that you love him and hate us, but you don't love him, and it's all ass backwards. You love someone else."

"Who, you?"

I laugh bitterly at the tragic irony. "No. No. You don't love me."

It comes out so cold I hardly recognize my own voice.

The words are more painful as I say them aloud because I've scarcely been able to admit them to myself in the quiet recesses of my mind let alone accept the stars awful truth.

Malakyte is shouting at his soldiers to apprehend me. He hears us. I have seconds.

"But as your friend, I will never stop doing everything that I can to bring you to the person that you do love. To bring you back to the family that you started a war just to keep safe because you care *that much*. You've earned your happiness, Kara. Let me give you that. That gas was supposed to bring your memories back, and I don't know why it didn't, but we'll figure it out and find a way and—"

Pacey yells from a hundred feet down the hallway, her panic bouncing off the walls. "He's coming, Gavrielle!"

Kara pushes against me, wild and frantic, and I lose my grip on her as she flies in the opposite direction of the others—*of me.*

It cracks something inside my heart. Everyone I love gets taken from me. It happens every single time I love. My parents. My people on my home-world. Kara when we were children. And it's going to happen all over again with Kara now. And like it or not . . . I loved Naresteé and Malakyte, and I lost them, too. Will I lose my new teammates as well? This new family? Once they realize the level of my deception, I'm sure I will.

I have a split second to decide to either follow or let her go back. If I pursue, he'll catch me, punish me, then likely kill me. With every footstep she sprints away, my heart is going with her, whether she's aware of it or not. All my expectations for today crumble before my eyes. How many times will I fail my mate and still tell myself I'm deserving of her—in any capacity that she will grant me?

"I'm going to wake you up, Kara. One way or another, you will have a choice in what happens to you," I yell down the hallway, knowing Malakyte is listening.

I need him to know that I know what he also did to *me.*

Her pace slows, and she looks over her shoulder, our eyes clashing. Two different people on two different sides of a war she doesn't remember starting. Time slips into rhythmic heartbeats, slowing and bending around the connection between us as it pulls taut. Will it snap right here and now? Will my ties to Kara tear under the weight of this moment as it crumbles into disarray?

Her eyes tell me everything. They've always told me everything.

"Gavrielle!" Pacey cries, her voice cracking with dread.

I'm out of time.

My hands ball into fists, and I push down the rage within me and rise to my feet, the act ripping my heart from my chest as I force myself to run in the opposite direction of the woman I love.

The gas not working has Malakyte's name written all over it.

I don't know how I'm going to free Kara and solve this clusterfuck of a situation, but I will.

I will.

CHAPTER 13

I held my composure in there, but the moment my eyes slam into Malakyte's, all that control shatters.

I drop to my knees as he runs across the space between us. I curl up as small as I can, leaning over my legs as I bury my head in my hands. My hair acts like a curtain, hiding my shame from the man I love.

Heavy leaden boots rush past me, Malakyte ordering them to chase down my kidnappers, a few others instructed to stay behind.

My cries fill up the hallway, tears racing down my cheeks.

"Karalevine," Malakyte whispers, gently taking my hands from my face as he slides down on his knees to the floor. "It's alright. Hush now."

His coldness sends an explosion of chills over my entire body.

"Karalevine," Malakyte says again, this time in that voice that demands I listen.

The voice of the future emperor of Arianyte.

He forces me to come up, and when our eyes meet again, he's a blurry blob from the tears that streak my flushed, hot face.

"Are you real?" I ask, my trembling hands reaching for his face as I blink out tears.

"I'm real," he says, his fingers wiping away my smeared mascara, "and you're alright. I'm here. I won't let them take you from me, but you need to calm yourself. Did they hurt you?"

He's still wearing the corset from the fighting pits, his arms and chest covered in his own dried blood in the shade Big Deep Blue.

As if Malakyte's blood is a trigger, a flash of memory or . . . what feels like a memory, singes itself into my irises like a strike of lightning streaking through a nighttime sky. Like a horrifying afterimage, I see a pool of blood in the shade Crimson Moon seeping along a grated floor. It's right there in front of my face. A pair of sunglasses sitting in it. *Geonni's* sunglasses . . .

I blink, and the red blood is gone. No context, no explanation—nothing comes to my mind. It's just the bloodless hallway on the Azurite and Malakyte beside me.

Any bit of calmness that came from Malakyte's presence goes right out the airlock. I'm trapped by this feeling—but this collar. Just like I'm always trapped inside that *fucking cube.*

I beg for Malakyte to remove the collar, the only thing that can fix this feeling. I pull at it, try breaking it in two with my bare hands.

"Karalevine." His icy hands take my wrists, forcing them away from the collar.

"Take it off."

I'm trapped. I'm fucking trapped. Locked away from my only source of true protection.

Malakyte's eyes are both a combination of soft tenderness and unholy rage.

"Breathe," he orders, interlacing both our hands as he slides me so I'm facing him directly on my knees. "Breathe. You are fine. The collar is coming off. I have the key right here. But I can't take it off until you've calmed down and your crystal won't implode this ship. Now, *breathe.*"

He takes a deep breath in, forcing me to follow his lead. "Again."

I do it.

"Good girl," he praises, and the deep purr of his admiration calms me further. Like a drug I've been in withdrawal from. "You're not a slave to your emotions, especially when others are watching. You have control of them and of your power. They are one and the same. The collar blocks the manifestation of magic, but it's still inside you, strengthening moment by moment. If you don't calm yourself, your crystal will turn on you."

"It already has."

My insides feel like they're melting.

A soldier walks up to us and offers a syringe to Malakyte.

I try protesting as Malakyte takes the needle and pops the protective covering off with his teeth, spitting the cap off onto the floor as it clanks somewhere nearby. *Not another drug.*

I shake my head, pulling away, but he holds me close. "I don't want that."

"Hush. Everything will be fine," he says, easing a long leg around me to keep me still. "Let me help you feel calmer."

Malakyte takes my wrist and locks it under his arm like an icy shackle, restraining me as he promptly finds the vein he wants. "You've clearly experienced something traumatic, so let me help you relax so I can remove this collar from your neck. You're my queen. You do not get collared."

He says the last part as if he was personally slighted by it. As if I'm a thing he now owns and someone tampered with his property.

I don't have the strength or the energy to fight him anymore. I thought that's what coming up here meant I could do—stop fighting altogether. Stop suffering. This was supposed to be my new start, my happily ever after . . . but as Malakyte's needle burns through my vein and the cold rush of the drug soothes the ache, I wonder if it's all been some fabricated illusion. Some vivid dream where my memories have truly been tampered with. They have been unclear and undefined, and the timelines haven't added up as clearly as they should . . . He told me it was nothing to worry about. He said that it was my mind and body dealing with being in space or trauma or whatever else he came up with.

A sweet numbing warmth completely overtakes me, and every logical train of thought I have dissolves in seconds.

"That's it, everything is alright." Malakyte takes all my weight as I slump forward into his chest.

But he's right . . . The magic within me goes from a boil to a simmer, the pain and pressure easing up as I instantly begin to settle.

"Malakyte."

My prince holds me in his arms and brushes my hair away from my face. "Sleep, Karalevine. You're safe now. Close your eyes. I'm going to find Deimos and the other Starseeds and Ringers, and they will regret having ever touched you. But first, *close your eyes*. Stop fighting it."

How does he know the other Starseeds and Ringers were there?

I shake my head, trying to fight it—but, fuck, I'm so, so tired.

My last conscious thought is of a pair of beautiful eyes in the shade Lilac Rain.

Chapter 14

ALL PERSONS WHO USE THE NETWORK ARE NOW REQUIRED TO REGISTER TO GAIN ACCESS. CITIZENS WILL BE GIVEN AN IPV NUMBER THAT CAN AND WILL BE MONITORED FOR ALL ACTIVITIES THAT CONTRADICT OR JEOPARDIZE ARIANYTE IDEALS, ASSETS, OR INTERESTS.

MALAKYTE ARDEEN

The next morning's first order of business is to ascertain exactly what the others told her, what she could potentially remember—if anything—and her current state of mind. No doubt they informed Karalevine that I had Reconditioned her, a minor setback. Partially expected, although we didn't plan for them to get her for long enough to explain that nugget of information. An easy work-around.

The straightforward approach to inspecting her frame of mind is through her Ringer.

Her father.

My SSPARROWs, including Ennar and Naresteé, plow into my suite with the Ringer dragging behind us. We've already had our fun interrogating him throughout the night, and he looks the part of a rebel caught and tortured, although he assiduously denies any involvement.

Waking Karalevine up like this after what just occurred is cruel. However, I won't risk a possible tear in her new narrative becoming a certifiable void. That would cause problems, but if need be, Naresteé is here to course-correct any little detours Karalevine may have trotted down.

She's awake now. Her heart is hammering, and it doesn't take more than a few seconds for her to appear over the railing as she comes to investigate what's happening. Her appearance is a mess, but I'll have to endure that for now.

"Come down here, Karalevine," I say, voice cold.

Which Karalevine am I dealing with? The one I love? Or the one who's my enemy?

She obeys me—a good sign, and her bare feet meet the marble flooring promptly.

Looking from Mr. Gallivan—who's beaten and bloodied and forced to his knees on my left—to me and then back again, she asks, "What's going on?"

Her pulse is slowing, also an additional sign for the positive. If she remembered or was told this man was her father, she'd be unable to calm herself, not with the relationship between them pre-Reconditioning so ardently notable.

"I have ample reason to suspect your Ringer was one of the rebel fugitives responsible for kidnapping you last night."

Her head whips to Jance, eyes flaring, her delicate, sweet mouth working to come up with something intelligible to say.

Or a lie to formulate.

"Looks to me like you already know he was involved," she quips, looking up at me.

"Was he there?"

I'm slightly taken aback when Karalevine laughs at me. "He wasn't there, Malakyte. Stars. He's the last person I'm worried about right now. It wasn't him . . . It was Gavrielle."

"Gavrielle?" I feign surprise. "Yes, I did see him with you on the cameras in the hallway where we found you."

She isn't lying to me. Good.

Her amusement fades when she talks about him. "He's a rebel now, I guess. He wanted me to join him."

"What else did he say to you?"

"More or less the same thing. That you're evil and using me as a weapon and that I have to get away, on and on. Although it was kind of hard to remember when they drugged me with some gas—and then you also drugged me, so my memory is a little fuzzy on the details."

Now she's lying. There's no chance they didn't tell her that I Reconditioned her. The question is: Does she believe them?

I point to her Ringer. "You're positive he wasn't there? You just stated that your memory is vague. *Think*."

"I wasn't there," Mr. Gallivan answers, and I glare down at him. *Liar.* "I have an alibi."

"What is it?" Karalevine asks.

"He claims he was at the bar," I say dryly.

The Ringer spits blood onto my floor and it irks me to no end, but he looks only at his daughter. "There's video footage of me there the entire kidnapping."

I sigh, the room getting too sweltering with all these warm bodies.

Karalevine argues on his behalf. "If there's footage, then—"

"Enough," I say, nodding to Ennar, who already knows what to do.

This test isn't enough convincing for me to feel satisfied, so I up the ante.

"Stars, Malakyte!" Karalevine shouts, the disruptor pistol to the back of her Ringer's head sure does the trick.

"I want to know if he was there or not," I press, voice calm.

She's looking at me like she hates me all over again. I hate myself, but I have to know. I can't lose her. Can't allow this to tumble into an uncontrollable situation—not now, when I'm so close to getting the throne and having Karalevine by my side. I need her to stay with me.

"He wasn't." She shakes her head, eyes wide with concern.

She's calm—too calm if she truly believed her father's life was at risk. If she regained her memories, she would recall the moment during the first Titan Games when we were under the arena and I similarly held a disruptor to the back of her father's head. This would trigger that trauma, I'm sure of it. But although her heart rate is elevated, it isn't anywhere near the way it was that night. Nowhere close.

Jance looks at me. "What part of the footage isn't good enough for you?"

I sneer down at him. "When you have a hacker who's capable of infiltrating this entire ship, I find that evidence in your favor to be severely lacking in its authenticity."

He shakes his head at me like I'm not the future emperor of this empire.

Karalevine steps around her Ringer and comes to stand beside me, taking my arm in her hand. "Hey, I'm alright. I got away from them. You saved me."

She rakes her nails along my jacket's sleeve, leaving little claw marks in the black fabric. The light touch soothes my fiery temper. I saved her. Just as I will save her once I bring her the most precious gift she'll ever receive. But that's for later.

"I'm positive Jance wasn't there," she says, but it doesn't sit right with me.

Why wouldn't he be there? Perhaps the others haven't included him, and he hasn't broken out of Naresteé's Reconditioning as I expected he had. Jance would have informed her that he was her father the moment it made logical sense for him to do so. There's no reason to assume he wouldn't play that card to convince her of the truth. Given that, perhaps he wasn't there, as I suspected.

 104

I wave Ennar off, the disruptor out of play. It served its purpose.

"You're off Karalevine's guard. Permanently," I say to the Ringer. "Ennar, I'm transferring you to Karalevine's bodyguard detail. Put your number two on me and your number three on detail with you. Both of you will guard her around the clock. No exceptions."

I turn to gauge her reaction, but she doesn't appear to mind.

"Keep the Ringer locked in his room until I decide what to do with him."

My guards respond immediately, heaving the large man up and removing him from my sight.

Karalevine yawns and rubs her eyes, looking exhausted. "I'm going back to bed," she announces with another yawn, turning back to the stairs. "Fuck all this. Come wake me up when you catch my backstabber of a best friend."

Naresteé and I look at each other, exasperated.

We leave Karalevine, and only when we're alone does Naresteé finally speak. "So, do you really think the Ringer wasn't involved? Do I need to wipe her again?"

I shake my head, irritated. "I'm undecided about the Ringer, but I find it odd he wouldn't reveal paternity if he had the opportunity."

"Agreed."

"Wiping Karalevine again would only cause more problems in the narrative and affect her cognitive functions. We do it too many times and she'll have serious side effects. We'll watch her closely to see if there's any signs of doubt. I'm sure they told her all sorts of things. I'm also dissatisfied that we weren't able to apprehend the others—that was the entire point of allowing this elaborate farce to happen in the first place."

"Oh, knowing Gavrielle, I'm sure he'll give us another shot at it. You know how he is."

Indeed.

"At least things are getting interesting."

Hours later, I stand next to my throne, completely detesting the space ever since I committed so many crimes within these ornamented walls.

I can barely cope with conducting my business here. The space echoes too loudly, and each voice that bounces off the pillars reminds me of Karalevine's cries from that night. Watching the shattering of her mind before my eyes filled me with more regret than I thought possible. I believed it would be easy to watch her forget, relish in witnessing it, in fact.

That is not what I experienced.

It gave me what I wanted, but it cost me.

And I paid in blood.

No matter how many times I have cleaned the floors, the darker stains of Selenyte's blue blood still discolors the orange quartz lights grouted within the tiles. Ensuring I will never forget what I've done to my own flesh and blood, much like Selenyte's ghost does. I swear that whatever part of her that remains, whether it be her actual soul lingering or a figment of my twisted imagination, is enthralled with my torment.

I tap on the tall back of my throne, half expecting to see my taunting sister sitting in it, but it remains empty. Turning to the window wall behind it, I walk several feet until I meet the glass and stare out at the Earth beyond. This is the only spot in the entire room where I can stomach being here.

I breathe deeply, closing my eyes and counting to the even number twenty-two.

Two, four, six, eight, ten, twelve, fourteen, sixteen, eighteen, twenty, twenty-two.

Perfect.

Everything regarding Karalevine is perfect. She doesn't remember anything. The gas they administered didn't work. I ensured that it would be unsuccessful for them had they attempted something so foolish. She will remain mine. They won't hijack her mind against me a second time. They won't wrench away the prize I have earned. My lover. My weapon. My Star.

The hushed whisper of pressurized gas gently resounds across the large empty space between me and the main set of doors as they divide and the emperor of Arianyte strolls in.

Father enters like he owns the place, his reflection in the window getting more detailed as he approaches.

Can I make it to twenty-two again before he reaches me? The urge to count a second time is unbearable. If I attempt it, and I don't make it all the way to the end, it'll irritate me for hours.

He doesn't give me the chance to try.

"'In the night, the Star will fight,'" he mocks on his approach, taunting laughter turning into a scorning hiss in the blink of an eye. "What a joke. That rebel anthem they're parroting down there for your bride sure doesn't bode well for your upcoming marriage."

I have so much disdain for that comment.

"I'll stifle the rebellion on Earth," I say.

Father huffs unconvincingly. "I heard those rebels on Earth hacked the Zone checkpoint tech and now any old riffraff can come and go as they please. Along with protests, strikes, soldiers overrun . . . Sounds like a mess down there. Now, how do you think they managed to do that without inside help?"

"I don't like the insinuation that I have leaks."

"I don't give a shit what you like," Father spits. "You're slipping. Your control is loosening. You're embarrassing me. Tighten this up, Malakyte. We have production we need to fulfill. This empire doesn't run on the hopes and dreams of little children. I want these Terrans processed in full."

In full.

Karalevine will unravel if that happens. She will fight this with everything she has, memories or not.

"And if you can't do that"—he swings around so I can see him from the corner of my eye—"then, we'll consider the other way. Less profitable but more fun. You remember that project I was working on when Zariya destroyed the core piece I needed to fuel it?"

I stiffen further.

He wouldn't be attempting *that* again, would he? That was the final nail in my coffin that turned Zariya against me all those years ago. Karalevine would certainly do the same.

"Well, I recently found a replacement part on a backwater planet I was on before heading this way. Had to blow out the core to get it, but sacrifices must be made for the greater good. I wanted to tell you that if the Terran rebellion down on Earth doesn't get squashed and we can't use them for production of the Silent Breath or Tributes, their fate will be sealed in a much more . . . exciting way. You know how I get bored and like to have my fun."

Do I ever.

Except . . . Karalevine.

"Either way, the Terrans will suffer for what they did to your sister. What of the one?"

I grow cold at his question. "Her murderer refuses to confess."

All the disappointment he holds for me seems to seep out of him through a heavy sigh. "And I'm to do what? Assume you're competent enough to bring me the right person? Give him to me and I will get that confession."

"It's my responsibility," I snap. "I'll get it."

He absolutely can't have an audience with Mr. Dawson. Ever.

"He'll die at the coronation then, if you can prove you're worthy of my crown. What happened to your little Starseed yesterday inspires little confidence."

"We knew it was coming." I turn to face him full on. "The attack was imminent, and we set a trap."

"A trap that failed."

"Not entirely," I counter without directly contradicting him. "We were able to boot their hacker out of most of our systems through our own backdoor hack. Not a loss."

Father tips his head, not in the least bit satisfied. I won't even dare hope for him to be impressed, not with that performance. "And your bride? What of her jumbled little mind?"

"They were unsuccessful in returning her memories, as anticipated."

"Lucky you."

I shift on my feet, crossing my arms and tapping on my bicep. *Two, four, six, eight—*

"How long?" Father asks.

I stop my counting—annoyed. "How long until what?"

He side-glances at me like the question is a ludicrous one. "Until the person who murdered your sister is dead. Until the Terran disease is either processed into something I can sell or something I can have fun with. Until your little mind-fucked bride is put in her place with the remainder of those Starseeds I told you decades ago to stop screwing around with. Forty years hasn't been long enough for me to forget that, or that you disobeyed me. Now, I'll relent and agree that those Elendril artifacts are your key to ruling with power.

"The Silent Breath won't sustain me much longer. You're running out of time. You won't submit my legacy to your incompetence. And let me remind you the Council has flown in and are currently breathing down my neck for any sliver of power they can grasp. And whose fault is it that the Council exists in the first place? When you let Zariya blast out the details about the Silent Breath to the galaxy that we made it from children, we had to acquiesce to sharing my power with lesser scumbags to avoid a complete revolt of every planet we've conquered. Forty years later, I'm still dealing with your fuck-up and cleaning up your mess. Just be grateful they're as greedy and power-hungry as most who hold authority because I've been able to drip feed them riches and eternal youth, but they're greedy little cunts and that won't satisfy them forever. They're fishing. Pushing. Seeking a way into my throne. And I'll be damned if I let them take it."

"Then crown me and be done with it," I argue.

It's the most logical path.

"With a rebel by your side? *Please*."

"She doesn't remember that life. I've turned her."

"Until they turn her back. You can't even secure the others as they scurry around this place, wreaking havoc. It's pathetic. You need to steal those crystals, force the dragons to reveal the truth that unlocks them, and turn yourself into a god, just as I have. Power and strength are the only things that matter in this world. Have I not beaten that into you by now? The only way to hold on to what I've built is to be stronger than anyone else. Those Starseeds threaten your supremacy, the girl included. This place isn't good for you, and neither is she."

Despite Karalevine's darker tendencies, she does think of others . . . and she will think of her people and will most certainly push back vigorously on any attempt to harm them. That will put a rift between her and I. I used to find that goodness about her far more pretentious than anything. However, spending all this time with her has somewhat endeared that side of her to me. She's so naïvely innocent about the way the world works, and I'd hate to break her spirit while she's so young. She's been through enough. It isn't all that terrible, I suppose . . . and I wonder if peace can be found with compromise. If that would make my bride happiest in the end so I don't push her away from me all over again. That night I took her memories, I told her that I wanted us to be better people to one another, and that's what I'm trying to do.

"Karalevine is significantly attached to her people. Perhaps there's a way we can increase production on a gentler scale without firing the nuclear option on the planet—"

Father shoves my shoulder—*hard*. "What did you just say?" he asks, and it's that tone, the one that's chased me since childhood, causing a creeping spindle to crawl up my spine.

The powerlessness he holds over me laughs insidiously.

He slams me into the window wall, my back hitting it so hard I worry it'll crack and suck the both of us right out to our deaths.

Sometimes, I wonder if that would be preferable to what I know is coming next.

"How is it, that my last surviving child—my son, my heir—is somehow parroting the gibberish of some adolescent Terran half-breed, who just happens to be the one responsible for inciting this insurrection in the first place?" Father laughs. "Absolute trash. Weak, just like your mother. With all my blood in your veins, I'm shocked that, after all these years, you get more and more pathetic by the decade. If only your sister were alive instead of you. Selenyte was always the one who had my teeth."

Never good enough, never on par with Selenyte's wicked plots and schemes. Never the same. Father is right. I am too much like Mother. And he hates that more than anything.

If his words wound me, I do not show it. Although he delights in ripping off whatever scab managed to heal over in the vast spaces of time since he's last cut me open.

When I finally get up the nerve to speak, sensing his impatience, I refuse to let my voice tremble. "I was merely suggesting a nonviolent way to please both my future bride and continue keeping our assets and production flowing. We don't need to dump the entire planet at once. She will fight me, and as you said moments ago, she's a weapon. A weapon we need on our side. Keeping her at peace is imperative."

Father's dark eyes simmer with a rage not even four hundred years of life has been able to extinguish within him.

"Arianyte doesn't yield to anyone, let alone half-breed children who think they can change our ways. You won't rule in my stead as a fucking coward, especially as your first act as emperor. The Milky Way will see you as you truly are, exactly as you've always been since you cursed my days with your existence. A pathetically weak little boy who can't seem to grow into a man regardless of being over two centuries old. One who chases a woman across the galaxy, for fuck's sake. Stars, Malakyte."

Father shakes his head at me, ever the displeased king and irreverent patriarch. The disgust in his eyes will haunt me for years.

I know what comes next. If I make him demand it, it'll be far more uncomfortable for me. There's been over two hundred years of me pushing back, and I've never once won that war of wills.

And I hate myself for it. Every fiber of my being battles and wrangles against what I'm about to do, eating away at me like a flame to flesh until it feels like there is nothing left of my soul for it to burn.

It'll only be worse for me if I fight.

My spine is stiffer than a steel rod as I bend down to one knee, and it feels like raking my bare chest against hot coals. My hair slides down in a sleek waterfall across my face, shielding the pain in my eyes and the shame clouding them, too.

"Forgive my ignorance, Father."

If I don't submit to him now, he'll go after Karalevine to get his point across. He'll hurt her just for me to end up on my knees regardless. The power he's gained over his long centuries of life makes his power over me brutally effective. There's no point in resisting, but it doesn't mean I don't hate myself for it.

My chest aches for her, for my Star . . . the only thing that can make me forget how much I loathe my own life.

The indecision in his sigh tells me my obedience lowers his hackles. It always seems to help ease his egotistical rage.

It takes everything in me not to flinch when I feel his hand rest atop my head, yet I keep still. His touch is affectionate yet calculatedly sinister. I see it for what it is, I always have. Yet, when he forces my face to meet him by drawing my chin up toward the stars, a part of me wants to do to him what I did to Selenyte. I'm resigned to the fact that I feel no regret for killing her, if only because it brings Father the pain he's cursed me to endure.

Selenyte's laughter echoes out somewhere deep within the throne room, taunting me.

Father finally points his chin to the side, indicating that he's done humiliating me. Shame ices my cheeks, but I refuse to let him see an ounce of what he does to me. Realizing how my deference makes me weak as I bleed into his shadow. Forever his biggest disappointment and the cursed source of all that makes me who I am. Now, I make others kneel so I can forget how he always seems to get me on my knees. I'm aware of what that makes me . . . exactly like him.

Yet Karalevine still loves me regardless of the mirror my father puts up to my face.

With that, he turns to leave the room, apparently finished with all his esteemed advice. Before he exits, however, I can't help but ask what's been on my mind for nearly two hundred years.

"What would it take to finally live up to the unattainable, vitriolic standards you have set in your mind for me? What must I do to live up to the expectations you now have of a ghost who can do no wrong in your eyes? When will I be worthy of your crown and your admiration, Father?"

Your love?

It's the most dangerous thing I've ever asked the emperor of Arianyte, and I blame Karalevine for giving me the courage. Her boldness must be rubbing off on me, that reckless girl. But I love her all the more for pushing me to be more than a skulking coward.

Father stands with his back to me, Sky-Fae stealth at its finest. He finally glances at me, as if he can hardly be bothered. "Be more like me."

CHAPTER 15

I use my Ringer magic to follow Naresteé around the ship for a good hour before she and I are alone long enough for me to make my move. We're in the royal wing of the private sector; she has no guards with her. It's the perfect opportunity.

"Am I naïve in thinking you've been skulking around because you want to come home, Gavrielle?"

"I should've known you'd sense me," I say, letting my invisible illusion fall once I reach a blind spot in the cameras perched on the wall above. "You look tired."

She sighs, the sound heavy as she shifts her weight, wearing another one of those fancy pantsuits she's fond of. This is a red one I've never seen her wear, and it makes her blue-green skin appear darker against the nighttime quartz lights that cast the hall in a ghostly blue hue against the Azurite's black walls. The paintings are nothing but blobs as my focus remains trained on her, on what she could do to me if I'm not careful.

The other Starseeds and Ringers don't know I'm here, but after what happened with Kara . . . I know the peril I'm willingly walking into confronting Naresteé. But for Kara . . . I'm going to risk it.

"I am tired, Gavrielle. You and your new little *family* are making my life immensely more strenuous."

"I'm sensing a bit of tension here."

She laughs softly, stepping toward me. I take one back. Too many steps, and I'll be out of the camera's blind spot. Does she know that?

"Let's get to the real reason you're here and let me guess . . ."

"Please," I say, risking a step forward, all joking aside. "Please, Naresteé. Bring her memories back."

Only for the first time since that night at the orphanage does Naresteé look at me with pity. "I can't do that, Gavrielle."

"Please. What do you want? What do I have to do? I'll do it. Just tell me what you want, and I'll make it happen."

Her head tilts as her gaze drops to the floor, her thumb and pointer finger rubbing together in a way that means she's undecided about something. That's better than the outright "no fucking way" I was expecting.

"He'll kill me," she whispers, and my heart sinks.

"I'll protect you."

Naresteé scoffs. "You can't even protect yourself. He's never going to let that brat go. Trust me, I'd love for her to be gone just as much as you want her back, but he won't allow that. You know how he is. If you think I can change his mind on this one, then I'm not sure where you've been these last seven years."

"Naresteé, I'm begging you, *please*. I've never asked you for anything. Bring her memories back."

She blinks at me in surprise, and it hits me that I fucked up. "Stars, you're in love with her, aren't you?" She's genuinely shocked because rarely does she ever laugh so bitterly. "I thought you two were just friends. Jupiter's rings, does everyone want to be with Kara? I seriously don't see the appeal. Oh, Gav. Doesn't she supposedly also love that Starseed we have in the pits? This isn't going to end well for you. And Malakyte is like a father to you . . ."

"He was never like a father," I snap. "He was a tyrant. A general. A boss."

I know what a good father was. I had one before he murdered him.

"I'm not sure that's entirely true, but let's argue that it is. What does that make me, then?" she challenges, once again coming toward me.

From the step she took forward, I take two back.

"You're different."

"How?"

"You actually cared."

The silence that passes between us is lengthy. This was a mistake.

"Are you going to tell him I was here?"

Are you going to tell him that I love her?

She comes in closer, the shadows pooling around her face and horns, and I see how much of a threat she truly poses. "Probably. He knows what you all are up to."

"I know."

One more step back and I'll be seen. If he sees me on the cameras, he'll know how desperate I am to get her back. He'll know what Naresteé now knows.

"All of your little antics are going to come crashing down if you keep this up," she promises, slowly lurking closer. "There's no way you're going to find those memories, so stop trying to."

I'm out of space to retreat. I either go invisible now, or . . .

"As soon as you give up on Pacey, I'll give up on Kara." This, thankfully, stops her in her tracks. "She doesn't hate you, you know. It's just hard for her to understand how you could do what you did if you claim to love her. I know because I wonder about the same thing. Kara, I get—we both know why you did that to her. But Pacey? Me? Are you that much of his puppet that you'll do anything, including break your own heart, to keep him happy? What about what you want for once?"

"Enough, Gavrielle."

"No, I'll say when it's enough. You took my memories, and I want to know why."

"You really want to know why?" she asks, voice angry. I raise my eyebrows, an obvious "hell yes." "Because I can't have children."

I shake my head, confused.

She elaborates. "After that brat blew up the orphanage and they brought you to me, both of us burned and in agony . . . I just couldn't let anything more happen to you. Being Deimos's Ringer is a bad thing, Gav, a very bad thing. He wanted you killed, especially once you refused to tell us where Kara had run off to. Reconditioning you was the only way to keep you safe. So, I did what was best *for you*."

Her voice drops to a whisper when she reaches those last two words, and my chest physically aches at her raw vulnerability, yet she isn't finished driving that knife in deeper.

"You choosing her over us crushed me. He won't say it, but it wounded him, too. I can't have children, the Silent Breath can't fix it, we've tried. All I have is you. You'll never understand how this feels. She's taken yet another person from me, and she has you wrapped around her little finger now, too. You were mine! Mine, you understand me? *My boy*."

She's within feet of me now, and the desperation in her voice is so unfamiliar to me I have no doubt she'll take me back by force if she has to.

"Is that why you hate her so much?" I ask, needing to draw her back off the ledge from talking about me.

"Damn right I hate her," she says. "She ruins everything, and I'm so sick of our lives revolving around her! Zariya, the Star, Karalevine . . . For decades, all he cared about was *her*. He abandoned me for her way back when Zariya lived, even though I was his Ringer. Now, I accepted that he loved her—decades ago—but when she took Pacey from me and then you? Don't expect me not to get down in the mud and play dirty, too."

It was a categorically bad idea to come here, but I'm in too deep to quit.

"The reason Pacey and I feel the way we do, Naresteé, isn't because of Kara. It was you who drove us away, not her."

"By protecting you?" Her eyes are glassy, her hard exterior melting away by the second. "By keeping you alive the only way he'd allow?"

"You can't just take our memories and expect us to be grateful for it."

She scowls at me, teeth bared, and I do the same. I won't back down to her, to either of them anymore. Not when I've seen what a real family looks like.

"This conversation must be tough for you, Gav," she says, whipping her hair back over her shoulders, voice cold and calculated. "Your heart is just thundering. If getting Kara back is that important to you, then get it through that beautiful head of yours that it's never going to happen. It's a waste of your talent to try."

"I'm prepared to fight."

Is that her magic I'm feeling? Fuck. Do I risk Malakyte certainly finding out I was here by allowing the cameras to catch me, or do I hold my ground? I don't see her eyes glowing, not yet. I can go invisible quickly, but she may take hold of me with her Ringer magic and have me Reconditioned before then. I shouldn't make eye contact, but the intensity of this conversation makes that nearly impossible.

"Are you willing to lose all you've worked for, though? You remember the deal you and he made, right? I'm certain you do."

This is the reason Malakyte and Naresteé never realize they're the ones driving the people who love them away, and I've never felt such bitterness tied to love before.

"You'd really go there?" I ask, my heart breaking far and beyond their initial betrayal.

"Depends," she says, her magic unquestionably bubbling beneath the surface. She wants to Recondition me. I can feel her magic swell. "Are you willing to sacrifice an entire planet full of your people after your parents fought so hard to liberate them only for Arianyte to strike back and enslave them a second time? Once your parents came to Earth, your planet fell."

"He promised he wouldn't hurt them again," I growl, anger locking my feet in place despite the danger. "I upheld my end of the deal. I did his dirty work to keep my people free. If you even suggest that he goes back on his word, I'll—"

"You'll what? What will you do?"

"I'll destroy him."

"You promised him twenty years of your life in exchange for your planet's liberation," Naresteé coos, her voice taunting me—distracting me, more like it. It won't work. "You've given him six. He amended your deal, that if you, the crown prince of planet Nyktos, brought him Karalevine as the Titan Game winner, your planet would be set free then and there. As would you. Free to live your life out on Earth, return home to your kingdom, chase pretty girls whose names don't start with K. And you did all that, Gavrielle. But you also know how he is . . . As far as I know, your planet isn't yet autonomous. I wonder what your new family would say, what Kara would say, if she knew about this deal. If she knew all the filthy things you did for her worst enemy."

She's right. And not only Kara . . . but the others, too. They'd crucify me if they knew. The conflicting ache is as maddening as it is isolating. I'm alone in a place where my heart can feel both tremendous love and undeniable hate all at once.

"I could be wrong." She shrugs. "Your people could have been a sovereign planet from the moment you brought Kara aboard this ship. I mean, come on now, Gav. We all know Kara would never have gotten through those games without your assistance. You did this to her. Is that why you're here? Because you feel guilty about what happened to an old friend? If you come home, perhaps forget whatever feelings you think you may have for her, tell Malakyte what he wants to hear, give up the other Starseeds and Ringers, then you and Kara can be together as friends. Your planet can survive. And if you're good, he'll eventually forgive your betrayal and grant you and your home-world its freedom. Now that, I can help you with."

Narestëe's power swells as yellow flickers in her eyes.

In response, my own Ringer magic fires, and it takes less than a second for me to disappear and sidestep, slide around her, and take off down the hallway.

That was too damn close.

"Why would she ever choose you, Gavrielle?" she yells down the hall. "And you know as well as I do that if Malakyte can't have her, he won't let anyone else have her, either."

Once I get away, my body feels like I'm in zero gravity as I make my way back to the others, Narestëe's words playing on repeat the entire way there.

Why would she ever choose me?

CHAPTER 16

DAY 16: THE PRINCE MOVES IN SUCH A WEIRD, PREDATORY WAY, ESPECIALLY AROUND ME OR OTHER PEOPLE HE DOESN'T SEEM TO LIKE VERY MUCH. IT REMINDS ME OF ONE OF THOSE FURRY, JUDGMENTAL CREATURES THAT INFEST EARTH AND ACT AS IF YOU'RE ABOUT TO KNOCK THEIR METAPHORICAL CROWNS RIGHT OFF THEIR HEADS JUST BY LOOKING AT THEM THE WRONG WAY. CATS, I THINK THEY'RE CALLED. HE MOVES LIKE A CAT.

I hate the way my breath sounds inside this helmet.

It feels like I'm underwater. Confined. Hot. The internal cooling mechanism only does so much, and for a body that runs warm like mine, it's nearly useless. Plus, it's too small.

It's me, so I walk with all the apparent ease of any Arianyte soldier, while Deimos and I nonchalantly stroll down the Azurite halls, the hushed tones of whispering gossip around every corner.

"Did you hear the prince's bride was kidnapped two days ago?"

"They didn't rape her, did they? That'd be tragic for the crown."

"I heard she's covered in bruises. She was definitely assaulted."

"Rebel scumbags."

"Are we even safe up here? If they can snatch the princess, they can do this to any of us."

"Wasn't she supposed to be some rock star warrior? Why didn't she fight back?"

It never ends.

I can hear Deimos's distorted sigh through the helmet comms as we reach the elevator that'll lead down to the prison cells, and he flicks his wrist in annoyance as his stolen suit summons the lift.

I look around for passersby. "We know the truth."

He shakes his head. "It's bullshit."

"I'm surprised you care."

"Oh, shut up," he sneers. "You idiots should have listened to me from the jump and just let me hold her the entire time. We wouldn't be in this mess."

"She would have gotten away sooner or later regardless. You couldn't hold her forever. Plus, Ahren made a strong argument that your magic could've messed with the gas's efficacy."

Deimos shakes his head as he skulks into the elevator, barely waiting for the doors to slide open wide enough to fit through. "All good that did us. You all need to stop caring so much about how she *feels* and start getting tough. Otherwise, we'll never get her back. We'll certainly never get her to go along with the bigger plan of bringing this empire down with the way things went. You and the others are going to have to come to terms with the fact that we may not be able to get her back and that she may stay his. If that happens, we're going to have to make the big moves without her. The sooner you all accept the likelihood of that, the easier this will be."

"I'm not giving up," I say.

"Is that why I caught a whiff of the horned bitch on you yesterday? Because you're not giving up?"

I should've known he'd scent her on me. Her perfume is distinct.

"It was a mistake." The doors close, and the compartment begins its long descent. "I was only trying to get Kara's memories back."

"Surely, you don't think I'm as stupid as the others to believe you just happened to gain your memories back precisely at the perfect time to save the girl and that you were only a soldier for that prick? You and them have a relationship far deeper than what you'd told us. So, I'll say this once, figure your shit out. If you fuck us over, I swear to the stars—"

"I'm on your side," I snap.

It's hard to read the man when his face is behind a faceless mask.

"Prove it. One more red flag and I'm blowing the whistle. Ringer or not. If you want to run back to them, then do it now because we're heading into the deep end, where there won't be a lifeline waiting for you anymore."

"Then tell me how to cut the damn thing to satisfy you."

Deimos crosses his arms, refusing to take my bait. Fine. I'll prove my loyalty right here, right now.

By breaking Ardelle out of that cell.

By ripping out my own heart.

We hit the base level with a light jolt moments later, the prison sector right behind those doors. Anything other than complete focus is needed to pull off this mission. I promised Pacey I'll bring her brother home today.

I'll save you, too, I promise Kara, recalling her face as if she were right next to me. *Just let me get Ardelle back for you first. Then I'll come for you again, love.*

The doors to the prison open, the dark expanse of the cells meeting the two of us.

And we're face-to-face with the emperor of Arianyte.

CHAPTER 17

A PASSAGE FROM THE CONFISCATED JOURNALS OF
GAVRIELLE ABRAXAS:

DAY 67: IT'S MADDENING. I CAN'T SHAKE THIS FEELING
THAT I'VE FORGOTTEN SOMETHING IMPORTANT, BUT
I CAN'T REMEMBER WHAT. THE PULL IS DRIVING ME
CRAZY. A PULL TO WHAT? HAS ARIANYTE ALREADY
DRIVEN ME INSANE?

Along with the most dangerous man in the entire galaxy standing mere feet from Deimos and me, there's at least a dozen SSPARROW, and all those faceless helmets turn directly on us. Behind them is the main desk where the SSPARROW guards hang out. The left hall heads to the cells, while the right leads to interrogation and storage rooms that spider outwards hundreds, if not thousands, of feet. They keep it dark down here, with hardly any quartz lights at all. That's intentional.

We should retreat. Herkimer being here is way too much of a wildcard for us to risk this rescue.

But if we don't . . .

"What are you men doing here?" Herkimer asks.

His tone is cheery despite his somewhat haggard appearance, and it throws me off even further. We've never met, but from how Narestéé and Malakyte spoke of him, he's the true rot that infects Arianyte all the way down from the top. I'm a bit shocked to see him appearing to be decades older than his son, given the Silent Breath.

I hesitate, my mind drawing a blank as my urge to bolt is overwhelming.

"Routine interrogation," Deimos says, the casual tone clear even through his suit's tech.

Nice save, asshole.

"Don't we love those?" Herkimer asks no soldier in particular, his grin so similar to the prince it's eerie. His entire face, for that matter, was why I was so easily able to recognize the emperor. "Well, I don't need to be here for all that. You soldiers are more than competent."

The emperor walks to the elevator opening, then pauses so we can exit. I snap out of my stunned stupor and do so, Deimos on my heels.

Herkimer slaps us on the back simultaneously, chuckling as he says, "Get 'em in the soft parts. It always makes them scream the loudest. Have fun." He saunters inside, winking at us as the doors close.

That was the strangest encounter I've ever experienced, but my focus shifts to the problem at hand. Too many SSPARROWs.

"We're here to escort a prisoner," I say, their bodies unusually tense.

There's ten. Not alarming, given what happened two days ago.

My casual demeanor only becomes more tense when none respond.

I chuckle, hoping it doesn't come off as sounding nervous. "Stardrake got your tongues?"

"We're on the clock, assholes," Deimos grumbles from behind me before any can speak. "Lead us to the prisoner or get the hell outta our way."

The hothead doesn't wait, either, before storming past me and being met with a wall of metal bodies.

"We got strict orders that no prisoners are to leave their cells. All Nest leaders made that clear yesterday morning. And which is it? You're interrogating or transporting? We don't have you on the schedule for either."

"Both." Deimos's voice doesn't tremble an ounce. "The prince made an exception. We're taking the prisoner to him."

"We didn't hear about it," one on the left says, bracing his stance a bit wider. More of them not-so-casually move from behind the main desk to the front.

A few others move similarly.

Again, my Starseed doesn't wait.

Before I can even stop him, he nails the closest soldier right in the side of the skull.

Well, fuck . . .

I move lightning quick, my heart shooting up as the adrenaline fuels me to do exactly as I was born and bred for.

Kicking fucking ass.

I barrel my fist down into the soldier next to me, and my resolve is energized to the max.

A SSPARROW lands a decent right hook to my jaw, and my neck cranks to the side.

Bastard.

Yet the blow does nothing to slow me for more than the split second it takes for me to swing my body back and lay the man down in less time that it took for him to come for me in the first place.

It's a complete brawl.

Just how I like it.

The space is tight, but we work as one unit to take down soldier after soldier, both of our pent-up anger fueling our takedowns.

The SSPARROWs never stood a chance.

"Nice job," I say between heavy breaths when the final soldier falls.

Deimos scoffs as he steps over the metal bodies, all completely knocked out below our feet. "Let's just grab Pretty Boy and get the hell out of here before they wake up."

I pluck one of the cell keycards from a guard before I follow my Starseed. "On your six."

Deimos and I jog past cell after cell, the pathways dark and cold and smelling of unclean bodies and shit.

"He's likely near the bottom," I say as we round another corner, both of us looking into the eyes of prisoners who look back at us with haunting pleas.

Free us, their eyes beg.

But how can I free the very same people I put here? The people he made me put here . . .

"To your right," I hiss at Deimos, and he leads us down deeper and deeper with my instruction, the floor tilting downwards as the air becomes frigid.

Finally, we reach an area where Ardelle is likely being kept, and we slow, taking longer inspecting the dark, square cells. This entire place is nearly pitch black, and even my eyes have a hard time distinguishing faces through this helmet.

"Where are you, Pretty Boy?" Deimos says more to himself, but our keen hearing picks up a gasp thirty feet up ahead.

We both pause, looking at each other.

"Ardelle?" I call, my voice low.

"Who's there?"

We rush toward the voice.

Through the darkness, we tread, until finally, his form takes shape within the shadows, a beaten and defeated silhouette I can only describe as ruined.

"Damn, Pretty Boy," Deimos coos, "you look like shit."

"Deimos?" he croaks, his voice ragged, probably from all that screaming he did the other night in the fighting pits. "What are you—"

"We're here to get you out." I step past Deimos and reach for the cell's locking keypad.

"You can't."

His words stop me cold.

CHAPTER 18

"**W**hat do you mean we can't?" I ask, flashing the key to him in case he can't see it in the dark with his Terran eyes. "I have the key."

"It isn't the key or even this cell that's the issue," he says solemnly, and his shadowed body steps closer to the front of the cell and into the little light. "It's this collar."

Squinting, I see the soft glint of greenish light bouncing off the sleek sliver collar around Ardelle's throat.

"So, we'll find a way to steal a key and get it off," Deimos suggests, voice impatient.

Ardelle shakes his head again, his features cloaked in the dark.

Are those chains hanging from the ceiling behind him?

"It's a special collar from him," he says, voice deep and sad. "If I suddenly went missing from these cells or the ship, it has a trump card. It'll blow my head off. He made that extremely clear."

My blood turns to ice.

I heard about these models. But they were still in development. I didn't realize we had a working one.

"Well, then, where's the damn key?" Deimos blurts.

"Nowhere we can reach," I answer for Ardelle.

Dammit.

The gears on Deimos's uniform whine as he shifts his weight as he turns to me. "This is bullshit. We can't just leave him here."

"The prince assumed we'd try to rescue him at some point," I say, bypassing his comment on purpose. "This is his middle finger to us. He knows what he's doing."

"What happened with Thumbelina?" Ardelle asks, voice firmer. "What he did to her up in that spectator box . . . He's a fucking monster."

My chest spikes with rage as my mind remembers the images of what we all three saw at the fighting pits. Malakyte is lucky Jance wasn't there . . . or he may actually be dead. And what makes me rage more than the fact that he took advantage of her is that she looked like she enjoyed it.

She looked happy.

"We got her with the same gas used on Muscles over here and your sister. It didn't work."

Deimos's words are blunt and cold.

"What do you mean it didn't work?" he asks.

Even in the shadows, I can see the rage on his face.

We explain what happened, the grim details laid bare in the cold, dark halls of Ardelle's prison cell.

"So, she doesn't remember anything?" Ardelle confirms once we've spilled every terrible moment of that day. "Not me, not Jance, not what Malakyte did? Nothing?"

I shake my head. "That's what it's looking like. It's as if we didn't use the gas at all. Except now she's terrified of us, and Jance barely got out with his life—and only because Kara lied to protect him. We're not sure what that means, though. I'm surprised he isn't down here sharing a cell with you, to be honest."

Ardelle paces in his cell, something I bet he does often down here when the hours grow longer and darker than the shadows themselves. How has he survived this Hell? How can we be this close and be forced to leave him here? What am I supposed to tell Pacey?

Finally, he asks, "What are you going to do? You have to save her. You have to. Get her away from him, please. I love her."

"I will," I vow, even as I clench my teeth and fists at my own utter failure.

What I'm allowing to happen to the girl I love? And I don't have the confinement of a prison cell as an excuse as to why I'm letting him assault her. Ardelle is thinking that very same thing right in this moment—I can tell by the storm brewing in his eyes.

"Has he . . ." Ardelle chokes, the words too hard to even speak aloud.

"Not yet," I confirm. "His scent isn't on her yet. There's still time."

This, at least, causes his shoulders to relax a fraction.

"I also need to ask you two about your SSPARROW suits," Ardelle says, his tone changing.

"Why?" Deimos snaps quicker than I can. "Fuck, he knows about the helmet, doesn't he?"

Ardelle nods, ashamed.

"Well, it isn't either of these. And as far as you know, we don't have it," Deimos says.

That's a big, fat lie, and we all know it. I wouldn't blame Ardelle for trading this miserable existence for one where he may survive—no doubt a promise the prince has made, if Ardelle's asking. Maybe it could be a bargaining chip if we play it right? Although, our one and only ace shouldn't be bartered away for anyone other than Kara.

As if my thoughts had summoned her, that voice I know as well as my own rings out from behind us, my back snapping so straight—so fast—my vertebrae wince.

"What's so special about the helmets?"

Kara's tone is as cold as ice.

CHAPTER 19

I whip around; positive I must be hearing things.

Deimos does the same, and when I see her tiny silhouette standing twenty feet down the corridor, I'm floored.

"Thumbelina?" Ardelle calls, voice cracking from disbelief and excitement. "What are you—"

"Who's under those uniforms?" she asks, pointing a manicured finger at the two of us as she makes her way closer. "It was you two who knocked out the guards, wasn't it?"

"Thumbelina!"

"That's not my name!"

Ardelle flinches, and I understand why. He hasn't seen her . . . like this.

Kara lifts a disruptor directly at us.

She must have gotten it off one of the guards.

"Is that you under there, Gavrielle?" she asks, but I hear her uncertainty in her voice.

"Kara," I say, stepping closer as I raise my hands in a nonthreatening manner. "You're not thinking clearly. I'm your friend. That hasn't changed."

Her laugh is bitter, but I'm humbled that she lowers the disruptor an inch.

"You're not my friend anymore, Gavrielle."

Even though it's like a serrated knife to my heart, I don't yield in this fight. "Bullshit. If I was Reconditioned and my biggest enemy held me by their side like a parasite, you'd do whatever you could to get my memories back. You know how I know that?"

Silence.

"Because you already did. You got my memories back that were stolen, and I'm going to do the same for you, even if you hate me for it."

Kara takes a deep breath, and I can see her hesitation.

"You came down here to see him, didn't you?" I push. "*Didn't you?*"

"Yes! Okay? Are you happy now? My guards are outside the gym as we speak—didn't realize I knew about the second servants' entrance, and I took off down here to see if I could get myself some answers. When I found the guards knocked out, I knew something was wrong."

"So, somewhere inside of you, you're questioning your reality. You know something is off. I know you feel it. Maybe it's something that he said that doesn't exactly match another piece of information you know to be true. Or a gut feeling that won't stop pestering you. It's all there, in the back of your mind. You know that, deep down, I'm telling you the truth. Malakyte Reconditioned you."

"He didn't," she pushes back, the disruptor shaking for emphasis, but the pain in her voice betrays her feigned confidence. "He wouldn't do that to me."

"Why would I lie to you?" I ask. "Why would I convince all the other Starseeds and Ringers, your own Ringer, to come after you just to convince you of some elaborate lie?"

"To make me your weapon," she claims. "To take away what Malakyte loves the most. To lure me to Geonni and Trinity so they can try and kill me again. I don't care which one, Gavrielle, just pick one."

I shake my head. "And you really believe that? After everything we went through together as kids?"

"That was a long time ago."

"Nothing has changed for me, Kara."

Her feet shift, and she looks around as if Malakyte could be behind her, listening. Or one of his spies.

This is becoming too dangerous for her. This conversation needs to take place in a more private location.

"You two are coming with me." She raises the pistol again. "Now."

I tense. The silence is bearing down on us all.

"Kar—"

"Don't," she says. "Don't make this harder than it already is, Gav."

I hate Malakyte so much in this moment I could kill him with my bare hands. He's turned her. He's turned her against me, and I don't know if I can get her back.

Will the Kara I met on that Sky Dais ever come back to me again? I can't bear this. I can't accept that she's gone and not coming back. My friend . . . my mate . . . in the hands of a man who could never love her like she deserves. Who could never love her like *me*.

"Hands above your heads, both of you. Who's in the other uniform?"

Deimos hasn't spoken a word, but with his suit's tech, she wouldn't know it's him.

"It's Ahren," I blurt. "The doctor. He's Ardelle's Ringer."

"Prove it."

She likely doesn't want Deimos to take control of her like last time. Smart.

"Well"—I unclip my gloved hand, even though the simple movement makes her jumpy—"you know that it's me, see, here's my Ringer symbol right here."

I show her my bare hand, angling it toward the tiny bit of light so she can see my mark. Kara steps closer, glancing at it.

"Ahren can show you his hand so you can see his mark." I turn to Deimos, hoping he understands what I'm doing.

I'll use my Ringer magic to illusion his hand, make his skin look like the Terran Ringer with Ardelle's symbol there. She's probably unfamiliar with how my magic feels and won't detect it or see the glow in my eyes with my mask on.

Thankfully, Deimos understands and follows my lead, and Kara says nothing as she sees the illusion I want her to.

But when I look up into her eyes, they're super glazed over, like she's—

"Thumbelina?" Ardelle says, my head turning back toward his cell.

Nothing. She says nothing to him.

We all peer at each other in confusion, but when she gasps, my head whips back to her. She's stumbling around, so off-kilter that she falls right into one of the cells, dropping the disruptor so she can hold herself upright.

"She just had a vision," Ardelle claims, his palms lying flat on the cell's clear walls. "I've seen it happen to her several times and have experienced them myself. The crystal marks trigger visions from the past whenever we look at them. It's random and completely unpredictable, but they're real. She had one in the stadium, too."

Visions?

"You just showed her your symbol," Ardelle presses, Kara looking completely befuddled as he turns his attention to her. "What did you see, Thumbelina?"

"Stop"—she breathes heavily—"calling me that."

Her heart is thrashing. Something happened suddenly, that's for certain.

Forgoing all caution, I march up to her, trying to ignore how her scent makes me feel as I lay my hands on her shoulders, the right hand still missing its glove. She doesn't swat me off, so that's a good sign.

"What did you see?" I ask, hating that this suit is between us—that this entire mess is between us.

The wildness in her eyes tells me everything, but she just stares at me like I've grown three heads.

"You. I saw *you*."

CHAPTER 20

I bend down so I'm not towering over her like a giant. "Just tell me what you saw."

The indecision within her wages like a war, and one side is going to lose.

"I saw you, Gavrielle. In the throne room, I saw a bunch of SSPARROWs pinning you down as you crawled to me, screaming that you were going to save me from . . ."

Her words end in a shuddered whisper.

"The throne room," Ardelle confirms. "Thumbelina, you saw the throne room. That's where he did it, where he Reconditioned you. We were all there."

Ardelle's words hang in the air, hollow and ringing like a bell.

"He's telling the truth," I echo, trying to get her to realize what's happened—to believe us.

Deimos says as I'm about to drive this point home, "Hold on a second. Do you hear that?"

I listen, the mask dulling my senses, but they're still sharp as hell.

Oh, no. Not now.

"I knew you two looked suspicious," Herkimer calls from somewhere deep within the prison web. Three, maybe four turns away from us. "Good thing I listened to my instincts and came back. Now, I'm going to find you little rats. Better start running."

CHAPTER 21

A PASSAGE FROM THE CONFISCATED JOURNALS OF
GAVRIELLE ABRAXAS:

DAY 201: NARESTEÉ IS BEING NICE TO ME . . . AND I WANT TO HATE HER. I WANT TO HATE THEM BOTH, BUT IT'S EXHAUSTING. ANGER ASKS SO MUCH MORE OF ME THAN BEING HAPPY EVER COULD.

"Go!" Ardelle hisses. "Leave me. Tell Pacey that I love her."

Herkimer's footsteps quicken. He hears us.

"We'll find a way to get you out," I tell him as I drag Kara along, even though she fights me.

"I know," Ardelle says. "Now, get her out of here."

"Wait!" Kara whispers as she pulls back on me, stopping before Ardelle's shadowy form for the first time. "Who are you?"

They look at each other, her expression confused but curious. We don't have time for this.

I pull her, hating that I have to, but if we don't go now—

"I'm not going anywhere with you." She pulls back on me, hard. "Let me go, Gavrielle. Now."

"Sorry, Kiddo," Deimos says as he rushes up behind me, acting before I can. "But we're all going on a little trip together again."

Her eyes illuminate green before I can stop him, Deimos's helmet in his hands as his Starseed powers take control of Kara completely.

Dammit, Deimos.

We're out of time. My blood goes cold as Herkimer's shadow flickers just beyond the last turn.

"I hear rapid heartbeats down there," he taunts, almost enjoying the hunt. "Is the third one the prisoner you're trying to break out?"

We rush down the hall, Kara moving with us easily now that Deimos has control.

This is going to ruin any progress we made. She'll hate me for letting him do this again.

However, moving to another hallway doesn't help us. Herkimer continues his chase, and we're in a full-on sprint. Our footsteps are just drawing him right to us.

"In here," I whisper, pulling the two in through the heavy doorway between cells.

I can illusion another cell, and he'll just walk right by.

We step in, footsteps hardly making a peep. It's pitch black inside, and my magic is already flaring to life as Deimos closes the mighty door as quietly as possible, needing to use nearly his entire body weight to do it.

Their green glowing eyes are the only source of light in the dark, all three pairs beaming green. What a party. I can't see Kara's face anymore, but I'm betting she's infuriated.

Herkimer is right on top of us now.

Our breath's catch in our throats—only our racing hearts can give us away now.

Herkimer sniffs, scenting us out. He may see through my illusion if his senses are good enough. If I don't act now, we're dead. But sight isn't the only thing my illusions can conjure.

Herkimer sucks in a triumphant breath, immediately following three footsteps I sent straight down the hall—far away from us.

He takes the bait, and I release my breath, relaxing the tension in my shoulders.

Once I can no longer hear Herkimer, we wait an extra ten minutes before I let my illusion drop. Deimos does the same.

Kara pounces. *"How dare you. Again?"*

Her heart is hammering even faster than before, the sound is all I can focus on.

"You would've given us away, *genius you*," Deimos argues.

"Damn right I would've!"

Faster, faster, faster.

"Kara," I start, stepping in her general direction. She ignores me, their voices raising. "Kara."

"Lie to me again, use your powers on me one more time, and I'll make every single one of you regret it."

"You won't do shit. You forget, I know you, and you're a little pussy."

An echoing slap—palm against cheek—immediately follows.

I cringe but am impressed she has the balls.

"Bitch!"

"Prick!"

"Enough!" I say, finding the two and splitting them up, not after I turned the helmet's voice tech off. "Kara, I'm sorry we had to do that, but if Herkimer caught you down here, he would have killed you, too. He never would have believed that you were here to take us in, and neither would Malakyte, not after what happened two days ago. Deimos just saved your life."

Her heavy breathing rings out into the darkness, heart rate only increasing. Something else is wrong. Why is she so panicked? Is it really because of us?

"Fine," she relents, and I can hear she understands the truth in my words. "But if he does it one more time, I will disown you. All of you. Don't take away my fucking choice anymore. You got it?"

"If you weren't so irrational and stupid, I wouldn't have to," Deimos retorts, and my head tips back in frustration.

"And you wonder why I don't trust you not to try and kill me again."

"Kara, you're safe," I tell her. "What you remember about Deimos isn't what happened. He never tried to kill you."

Deimos lets out a heavy sigh. "Actually . . . that's not entirely accurate. I did try to kill her. It simply didn't happen in the way she believes it did."

Just what I need.

"Deimos, tell her why you're not going to hurt her. The truth."

I can practically hear Kara rolling her eyes in the dark.

"Like anything you'll have to say will be enough to convince me."

Deimos's chuckle echoes within this tight space, arrogant and incredulous. "Oh, I think this bomb will be particularly significant to you, *princess*. Although, the truth, Gavrielle, will be too much for her to handle."

She huffs in defiance. "Try me."

"Do you know who Zariya was?" Deimos asks, his voice a completely different tone, almost as jarring as the topic swap.

She's silent for a long time. "Malakyte told me she's the past-life version of me. Is that not true, either?"

Now it's Deimos's turn for a long pause. "I won't be trying to kill you because Zariya was my daughter, you little brat. So, chill the fuck out. You're safe. We were never trying to hurt you. You're just so reactive and unpredictable we had no other choice but for me to use my magic and the collar so you didn't accidentally kill one of us or blow this entire spaceship out of the stars. It's you, Kiddo. We had to protect ourselves from *you*."

"What? No . . . you . . . you can't be her father . . . Malakyte said you killed her. You killed her, and that's why you're coming for me and why you convinced Geonni to—"

Deimos laughs, but it's bitter and cold and far from comical.

"He's a lying cunt. What a surprise. I'd never hurt my Zariya, and believe it or not, I don't want to hurt you, either. Not anymore. We . . ." He sighs, the sound more like a wheeze inside this tin can we're all stuck in. "We've chosen to be allies, of sorts. To take down a mutual enemy. An enemy that you now give heart eyes to, like a little schoolgirl. An enemy who's truly responsible for Zariya's death."

"He killed her?"

The surprise in her voice is veritably crushing. She really doesn't see him for who he truly is. But how can I blame her? I didn't, either.

"He might as well have."

"That isn't an answer."

"Let's just get out of here before Herkimer finds us, alright?" I say before this dissolves, and they're at each other's throats all over again.

I step back toward the door, find the handle, and . . .

Well, that can't be right. I push again, feeling strong resistance. I'm an idiot. I must have to pull, then, but that doesn't work either.

Trying again, I throw my body against the door, pushing and pulling.

It doesn't budge.

"Don't tell me I'm hearing what I think I'm hearing," Deimos says, voice slightly panicked.

"We're not trapped, are we?" Kara asks, her voice unnaturally high.

She finds her way to the door, and all I can hear is a deep, metal clang as she tries to force our escape. Each boom rattles louder than the last, her artificial nails trying to claw her way out.

Her damn heart is thumping faster than she can slam her fists against the door—

Kara's star illuminates the darkness, her panicked breaths so fast there's absolutely zero air getting into her lungs.

"Don't you fucking dare," Deimos says cruelly.

I understand now. She's having a panic attack. Makes sense after the last few days.

I rip off my helmet, and it thuds to the floor as I bend down on one knee and take her hands in mine. She lets me. Good. I've gained back some of the trust I've lost.

"Hey, hey, you're fine." I try to soothe that fear. "You're not trapped. We'll find a way out. And I'm right here with you. You're not alone. Not anymore."

Quick, ragged breaths fire through the air faster than an automatic disruptor rifle, her power only soaring higher.

"If you can't get yourself under control, Kiddo, I'm taking hold of you again. You're too dangerous like this. You'll kill us all."

"No," I fire back, "you won't. Kara, look at me. Breathe. Just breathe."

I lace my fingers in with hers, one hand still missing its glove.

"I can't, Gav. I can't. I can't be trapped in the dark again."

Again? Where does this come from?

Regardless of why she's panicking, Deimos is right. If I don't get her power under control, we're dead.

CHAPTER 22

KARALEVINE RUZZ

Trapped.

It never matters what I do. I'm always *trapped*.

"Kara." Gav's strong, gentle hands grip mine, my only anchor in the abyss of my blinding panic.

"I—"

My voice is lodged in my throat, a knot growing there and feeling like it's the size of a melon. I'm so weak, so pathetic. I was fine here. I was holding it together. But the moment that door wasn't opening, I succumbed to the endless darkness that chases me day and night. I've never had claustrophobia before, but this isn't that. This is soul-defeating territory. This is deeper than any irrational fear ever could be. Something *wrong*.

The little bit of light from my star mark helps me see Gav. He's right here. If he wasn't, I'd lose all control of my powers.

He's as unmovable as a mountain, my light in the dark.

"I can't do this," I say, voice uneven and power on the verge of exploding.

Maybe I don't want to confront what's truly happening? I probably don't want to know the truth, do I? Maybe I don't want it to lead to the bigger, more horrifying reality that the man I love may have done something awful to me, and I can't accept that.

I can't.

"You can," he claims, his grip on my hands tightening. "You're strong. You're the bravest person I know. You always have been. This darkness can't hold you. Nothing can hold you."

This darkness can't hold me. Nothing can hold me.

Gavrielle is right . . .

He releases one hand and brushes his knuckles alongside my face, warm and real. I tune into my senses, noticing his deeply woodsy scent mixed with citron and some clean, foreign breeze. *Like home.* Gavrielle has always felt like home to me, and I find all my anger toward him over what happened simply melting away, and I can't seem to find that resentment at all. Even if he took me against my will, he believed he was helping me. I'm confused. What I feel between Gav and me expands and transforms, and I'm not sure if it's butterflies or lightning or nerves, but what I'm certain of is that it's dangerous.

Regardless, I force myself to keep taking deep breaths with him, and eventually, I mellow out.

"There you go. You can do this, love. I'm not going anywhere."

I nod, do what he says, and it begins calming me down enough that I'm able to hold on to my crystal's power. My mark's light flutters off, plunging us into darkness once again.

"I've got you," he whispers, and I believe him.

"I'm okay now," I say. "Just get me the hell out of here."

"Where are we?" Deimos asks, and I'm still fuming about what he did to get me in this room, but I put my anger aside to deal with the problem at hand.

The two use the screens on their suit's forearm to look around. The room isn't very big, and Deimos finds another door on the opposite side of the ten-foot space.

I can practically hear Gav's gears turning as he says, "I think I know where we are, but you guys aren't going to like it."

"Stars," I grumble, clicking my acrylic nails together.

"We're in the airlock."

"The airlock?" Deimos echoes.

"For the prisoners. For disposal."

"They don't put them in here alive, do they?" I ask, feeling ghosts watching me from behind my shoulder.

"What do you think, Kiddo?"

I sigh heavily.

Another thing I'm going to have to change around here, apparently . . .

"So, let me get this straight," Deimos says, pacing. "We're inside the airlock that disposes of prisoners, so that second door leads right out into space? No wonder my balls are about to freeze off. We have no way out. If Herkimer comes back to find us in here, it's one button and goodbye in an instant. That about right?"

"Malakyte will come looking for me soon," I say.

"That pompous little prick will never find us down here. He'd never know to look here. And me and Muscles here will be toast just as well as if Herkimer found us."

"Hmm, probably not me. But you, one hundred percent."

Gav's voice is light and comical, and it reminds me of the boy I used to know.

But why not Gavrielle? Why wouldn't Malakyte kill him along with everyone else if they're such enemies?

"Let's scope out the walls," Gavrielle suggests. "Some of these have emergency exit ports in case something like this happens."

We disperse. The walls are, indeed, freezing. Colder than even Malakyte's glacier skin as I softly tap the wall's surface. I'm essentially blind, patting around in the dark, trying not to let the panic creep in again.

Gav is right here . . . You're fine. You will get out.

I shouldn't be comforted by his presence. It's annoying.

There's a dip in the wall that spears me out of my thoughts, and I gasp.

"What?"

Gav's voice is hopeful as I feel around, my touches more probative despite how much the cold burns my skin.

"I think . . ." I keep patting my way around. "I think I found some sort of doorway. I'm too short to reach the top. Here! There's a handle! Gav!"

I hear him rush over, and in seconds, he's next to me.

Our hands lightly touch as he grabs onto the handle, my stupid heart fluttering like a schoolgirl's as we push together. The door gives way to our efforts and opens, dust falling against a dark Apple Green room beyond.

"Thank the fucking stars," I say as I force my way past Gavrielle and into what appears to be a long hallway lit up green in both directions.

It doesn't take the others long to follow me out, and Gav shuts the door firmly behind us.

"Where the hell are we?" I ask.

The Starseed and Ringer pair look around our eerie surroundings.

"We're not in the cells anymore, that's for sure." Gav's musing is curious as he rubs his chin, his helmet tucked under his free arm. Deimos's, too. "I've never been here before."

They were talking about those helmets right before I found them. They're important. I'll find out why.

We stand in a massive hallway, both in width and in height. The door we just crawled through was situated on the wall, and we can go either left or right. The walls of this place appear . . . decayed, like abandoned spaceships long ago forgotten in some cheesy space drama. Wires hang from the ceiling, snapped off from wherever they connected to. The green strips of lights flicker as we skulk by them, their constant buzzing the only sound against our soft footsteps.

"Here," Deimos says, and straight ahead is a doorless archway, stairs leading up, up, up into nothing but shadows.

It triggers me to remember something Herkimer had said when Malakyte and I met with them. *Send her down that long, dank stairwell to convince them.* He mentioned this long stairwell when he was referencing the—

A bone-chilling growl slithers manically into the strange hallway, and all three of us halt dead in our tracks, the same exact growl I heard in my room the day I was kidnapped.

Dragons.

CHAPTER 23

My spine tingles.

"What in the fucking space creature was that?" Deimos says.

We all scoot closer to each other.

"Level with me, Gav," I say, the hairs on the back of my neck rising. "It was you guys who were painting all the Starseed symbols all over the ship, wasn't it?"

Deimos answers for him. "No shit, so what does that have to do with us getting eaten?"

I shake my head in annoyance. "You were in my dreams, too, weren't you?"

"We were. Is that why you lied for Jance? Because of what Saris said to you in your dreams the night after we took you?" Gav says.

"She convinced me Jance was worth lying for."

Another sound booms out into the hall, but this time it's such a massive roar that the flimsy Lime lights tremble; dust falling on us.

I nearly piss myself.

"So . . ." I say. "You were sending me hints about the dragons, then, right? I saw horns in my dreams. You guys are the ones who left the dragon figurine in my room, weren't you?"

Gav and Deimos face one end of the hallway each, nothing but blackness in either direction, and I'm angled by the stairs.

Gavrielle nearly chokes out, "Dragons? What figurine? No, Kara. We were trying to warn you about Naresteé Reconditioning you. I'm not even sure dragons exist."

"Oh, they fucking exist," Deimos quips.

The fear in his voice reveals something else, too.

"You know about them, don't you?" I ask Deimos.

If they didn't put that little dragon figure in my room, then who did?

"Zariya," he begins, and I get the sense that saying her name absolutely breaks his heart. "She had a relationship with these dragons, but they weren't simply creatures from some other planet. They were way, way worse. I can't believe Malakyte managed to do this to them . . . fuck. *Fuck!*"

"What?" Gav and I ask.

"They're fucking Elendril dragons. They're connected to each Starseed. And I don't know if you can feel what I do, but they're fucking pissed."

An undeniable rage blasts through me that isn't my own and then it happens again. The flash of a dragon's head, its eyes burning a hole straight into my very core, searing into my mind like a brand. Exactly like what happened in the throne room on the Vivianite.

"They're close," I whisper, as if they can hear us.

They probably can.

"I don't feel anything," Gav says.

"You're not a Starseed."

Deimos says it like it's obvious.

"They're that way," I say, pointing to the side Gavrielle is guarding. "Do we go say hi, or . . ."

"I've been sensing and dreaming about the dragons for the last several weeks we've been up here," Deimos admits. "But

I didn't think they could ever be on the Azurite. We were so focused on getting you back that I ignored it."

I scoff, eyes rolling. *Getting me back.*

"Pacey told me four nights ago about a dream she had with dragons," Gavrielle says.

Now I'm convinced.

"They're speaking to us."

I break away from them and stalk past Gavrielle, his head of Quicksilver appearing like the shade Matcha in this lighting. Even with his handsome face, I don't think it's the color for him. Our pale skin looks green, too. Deimos's skin looks so dark he could be shade Haunted Jungle.

Their hesitation is palpable, but eventually, they follow me, and we carefully walk in the direction I'm being pulled to. The air grows colder and thinner and darker until we find something so completely out of place that it's obviously what we're searching for.

An immaculate door in the shade Space Gray shines holy out of place several dozen feet away.

Deimos is the first of us to step toward it, our hesitation collective. "Only one way to find out."

"Let's hope it doesn't lead us to another air lock," I half-heartedly joke.

Gav huffs as he grins down at me.

As if nothing bad had happened between us. As if no time had ever passed. As if I didn't spend nearly every day of the last seven years eating myself alive, believing I had killed my best friend.

"It was dark."

We reach the door in no time. It's even more out of place up close.

The door has such a sophisticated locking mechanism, it's apparently guarding something either incredibly valuable or wholly dangerous.

In this case, likely both.

Come in . . . it seems to call. *Open and come in. Now. Do it. Open. Open.* Open.

"Should we . . ." I whisper.

"See what's behind door number one?" Gav asks.

I have Malakyte's code, but I peek behind me at the two extras at my back. "Turn away. Or we're leaving."

Deimos scoffs, giving me a promising look of death. Gavrielle looks disappointed.

Covering his eyes with his hand, Deimos waves impatiently with his other, his fingers so close I nearly swat them away. "Here, is this good enough for the little princess? Stars, I thought you were a bitch before all this . . ."

"Don't talk to her like that."

Deimos just continues waving flamboyantly. He's acting in a way that feels as if he really did know me . . .

Gav turns so he can't see, and I punch Malakyte's code into the keypad. I hope to the stars he won't find out exactly which door I just opened with it . . .

It responds immediately. The ten cylindrical locks on one side slide into a compartment as it unlocks one by one with a hiss of the hydraulics.

Then it slides open on the right side, a blast of hot air whooshing onto my cheeks and blowing the baby hairs around my ears.

Both men are no longer looking away. Their eyes are wide open.

An even brighter green light hits me first, shining vividly in the color Emerald Jewel. But then I freeze as I meet the eyes of several actual dragons all peering at us like they haven't eaten in years.

CHAPTER 24

DIGITAL SSPARROWS HAVE THE AUTHORITY TO DEPLOY A "KILL SWITCH" ONTO ANY PERSON USING THE NETWORK TO ADVANCE THE REBEL AGENDA. THIS KILL SWITCH WILL BAN THE IPV NUMBER FOR A DURATION OF FIVE YEARS.

I'm relieved to see these dragons are behind bars, but that fact alone sends off warning bells. What the hell is going on here?

In front of us is a massive chamber that's at least forty feet high and eighty feet wide. On either side of this room, there are two giant cells lining the walls that hold the dragons.

Actual living, fire-breathing *dragons*. They're smushed in there together, and the Gumball Green light darkens their scales to appear black. I can't see how many of them there are within either cell. Each wing and tail and long serpentine neck blend and morph into the other to the point they all look like one single creature.

"The Killer of Worlds has returned at last," a male dragon says, its giant head poking out of a hole in the bars.

With eyes in the shade All That Glitters is Gold, the dragon with a head the size of a small ground-hover slithers to glare directly at me, burning into my soul as if it were spitting fire.

"You can t-t-talk?" I take in every detail of its huge nose, textured horns that curve straight back then up, and teeth longer than my arm.

My eyes bounce between it and the other cells. "How many of you are there?"

When I finally peel my gaze away to look at Gav, he's as stunned stupid as I am. Only Deimos doesn't appear shocked.

"There are six of them," Deimos answers. "One for each Starseed."

Then the dragon speaks again. "Five. There are five of us. The Dark Starseed murdered his dragon, just as he murdered you, Killer of Worlds."

Dark Starseed?

Murdered me?

Killer of Worlds?

I turn back to Gavrielle and Deimos, really confused. Their minds aren't muddled puddles of sludge, however. They understand what's being said here.

"Kara . . ." Gav tries to grab my hand, but I swipe it back.

One of the other dragons speaks, my attention snapping to the other side of the room as he says, "She doesn't retain her memories, Dannanōk. Zariya is no more. The Killer of Worlds, as we suspected, has forgotten everything."

Zariya?

Gav and Deimos's faces tell me everything.

"So, this Killer of Worlds is . . . *Zariya?*" My head whips back to the dragons. "Why do you call her by that name?"

Dannanōk—who's certainly the one I saw in that initial flash image—swings his head as it knocks against the broken bars. "Come to me."

My eyes go wide. I don't really want to be barbeque . . . but it knows things about me, and I have to figure out what's going on.

Hesitantly, the three of us creep closer to the dragon, and I can't help but feel a thread materialize between it and me. This ancient creature analyzes me as my unsure steps bring me nearer to him, those eyes brimming with knowledge I can only dream of understanding, radiating in the shade Sunglow. I feel . . . like I'm in the presence of a god. This dragon is life and death and stars and moons and existence itself. A celestial being that my mortal eyes have no right to gaze upon, yet here it sits, locked away in my lover's dungeon.

"What are you?" I whisper, the celestial crystal beating within my own chest recognizing the authority and power this creature radiates as if it were my own handprint.

The two of us are connected through the vast intelligence of the Elendril crystals. Whatever created it also created the monster beating within my chest. Both sentient and ancient and powerful. He's *my* dragon. I don't need to be told, I already know.

Dannanōk chuffs, steam spilling out of his nostrils. "We are simply a sentient extension of the Elendril crystal's force. Just as the Ringers and the weapons are linked to each individual Starseed, we dragons are also linked. Vex, Novara, Solara, and Feena. This is who we are."

Like I can tell who is who, but whatever.

"You were calling us down here?" I ask, and he nods. "Why?"

The male dragon that spoke from the other cell answers. "We always know when our Starseeds are close. We felt you weeks ago and knew our time had finally arrived."

Gavrielle takes my hand in his—the one without the glove— and this time, I let him. It's so warm.

"Are you trying to get out of here? What is it you want from us?" I ask.

The dragons slam their bodies against the bars, and it shakes the floor. "We're trying to make good on a half a century promise to destroy the Arianyte Empire and burn Prince Malakyte to ash."

ARABELLA K. FEDERICO

promise to destroy the Arianyte Empire and burn Prince Malakyte to ash."

CHAPTER 25

"Malakyte?" I parrot.

Gavrielle squeezes my hand reassuringly, but it makes me feel like he's pitying me. I'm not some blind idiot who doesn't know who Malakyte is. I get that he's . . . different. He's had to do bad things to survive, but so have I. People like Malakyte and me are simply misunderstood, but he isn't *evil*.

"The Dark Starseed is responsible for atrocities far and wide. He can't be redeemed. Zariya knew it. She made us a promise to destroy him, but The Killer of Worlds failed. *We* failed. The moment Project Nightfall dropped in her lap, all of the Starseeds and Ringers were doomed."

"What's Project Nightfall?" I ask.

Deimos answers for Dannanōk, my head whipping to my right to see the alien standing beside me. "It was Zariya's final mission. The one that brought the entire damn thing down."

Deimos's Squid Ink eyes shift to glare straight at me, and the intensity there sends a shiver down my spine not even the dragons were capable of doing.

The extra continues and doesn't rip his gaze away. He doesn't even blink. "Malakyte somehow figured out that the dragons knew some secret that would unlock the Elendril crystals and their power. He wanted that power for Arianyte. Badly. Having all the Starseeds and Ringers together loyally working under him wasn't enough. Having my Zariya—the most powerful of all of us as his bride—wasn't enough. His gluttony tore us apart. The bastard never got the answers he sought because you dragons wouldn't tell Zariya the key to the crystals, even when it was clear she had chosen a side."

The dragons collectively growl, and they're all pissed.

Dannanōk says, "We could not and would not give up the secrets to these weapons to someone so clearly compromised as Zariya had become. If the Dark Starseed were to obtain this power, no force would be able to stop him."

"She chose the right side."

Deimos enunciates each word like it matters at this point. She's been dead for over forty years.

"Zariya's sacrifice proved she was never worthy of the power regardless of her loyalty," Dannanōk says.

Deimos charges, and Dannanōk throws out a warning roar as Deimos stalks right up to the dragon's nose, fearless. "Zariya's sacrificed everything to bring that motherfucker down—including her fucking life. None of you helped her. She begged you to tell her how to stop him, and you refused. She died because of that refusal. *They all died.* That reflects poorly on your character, not hers. I won't hear one more word of you lizards slandering my daughter's name."

"We loved her, too, Deimos," a female dragon says this time.

She's across the way, but her voice is soft for being such a brutal creature.

Damn, I really can't tell any of them apart.

"I don't want to hear it, Feena," he says, brows scrunched tight, lips curled. He knows her by name. Feena must be Deimos's Starseed dragon, then. "When we needed you the most, you abandoned us."

Gavrielle leans down and whispers in my ear, "Zariya died while Malakyte was chasing her and the other Starseeds and Ringers. They fled Arianyte, and when they couldn't flee anymore, Zariya killed herself and the others by blowing up the moon they had landed on. She wanted to kill Malakyte, too, but he survived thanks to his crystal."

That . . . That isn't right. Zariya and Malakyte were in love—he *loved her*. Malakyte was adamant that Deimos killed Zariya, but watching this conversation, that doesn't seem to be true. I've caught Malakyte in a lie.

If a dragon could scowl, Dannanōk is doing just that. I don't like how he's watching me, like he can read my every thought and intention. But if these dragons truly have the secrets to unlocking the crystals, then I could use them as a bargaining chip for the people of Earth and the children who, like me, have nobody looking out for them. *I'm looking out for them.* Herkimer's intentions are clear, so if this information can save them, then I'll keep every possible option open to me. The greater good is a myth. The only good that gets done is by people who are brave enough to make it happen.

Something pokes the side of my leg, and I flinch. Gav and I glance down to see a tiny version of Dannanōk, eyes of Lemon Lime Green glowing up at me with curious, adorable blinks.

"Umm," I whisper cautiously, "is that a baby dragon?"

Dannanōk sucks his head back through the bars, turns quickly in his tight confinement, and rushes to the baby dragon's side. There's a second grown dragon that's in there with him, and both sets of long, sharp, terrifying teeth crunch down with knee-wobbling force towards Gavrielle and me.

Message received.

This baby dragon is theirs . . .

"Annara . . ." Dannanōk chastises, "you know you're supposed to stay hidden."

From what I can tell, Annara wants to do the opposite of staying hidden. Has she been confined in these cells her entire life, knowing nothing else but these walls and confinement?

The cruelty of that possibility physically hurts my heart. They shouldn't be locked away down here.

Deimos walks back over to Gav and me, looking down at the little dragon as she curls under Dannanōk, her shield. "I wouldn't let Malakyte find out about her."

"We won't tell him. How else can we earn your trust?" I ask Dannanōk. "You must want out of here? Want to give your offspring the life that she deserves. Tell us, and we can work something out so we can all get what we want."

"They won't help us," Deimos says.

"Correct," Dannanōk agrees, shifting his baby under him until she blends into his dark scales.

"Then, why call us down here?"

The male from the cell across the way answers me this time. "To see exactly how Zariya's sin manifested in you, Killer of Worlds."

Deimos is the one growling now. "What Zariya did was not a sin. It was a sacrifice. You think I don't know what she did? The cost of her choice? She thought she was saving the galaxy and countless worlds by sacrificing the ones she loved and herself."

Zariya really killed the other Starseeds and Ringers? That sounds like a sin to me. That sounds like a monster.

"Yet here we are," Dannanōk says, his voice deeply guttural from this close range.

He's a beast, a king among all creatures from all worlds. No doubt, he's the one in charge out of the five grown dragons.

I open my mouth to ask what they mean by how Zariya's sins manifest within me when my words are drowned out by an ear-piercing alarm that blares to life so suddenly, I jump. Red lights flash along with the siren, and my gut twists in on itself.

Something terrible is about to happen.

CHAPTER 26

DAY 215: I GOT IN ANOTHER FISTFIGHT WITH SOME PUNK ON BOARD THE AZURITE, SO I'M LOCKED IN MY ROOM FOR THE REST OF THE DAY. NOT SURPRISING. YOU KNOW I WON. I HAVE A FEELING THAT IF I DIDN'T WIN, I'D BE IN EVEN MORE TROUBLE THAN I AM NOW. THEY'RE GIVING ME PRIVATE EDUCATION LESSONS FROM NOW ON. THE PRINCE SAYS HE DOESN'T WANT A STUPID BOY TO SERVE HIM.

GAVRIELLE ABRAXAS

"What's going on?" Kara yells over the alarms that are like ice picks to my ears.

"It's the emergency sirens," I yell back, knowing the protocol by heart.

Kara's face immediately looks more nervous. "Would he . . ."

"Would he blare those sirens just because you've been missing for an hour?" Deimos shouts. "Yes, yes, he would."

"Well, whose fault is that?" I deadpan at them both.

The dragons are getting restless.

"It could be Herkimer, too," I say, but Deimos is right. The prince would likely sound the sirens if he believed Kara was in immediate danger, if he suspects we had his bride once again. "We've got to go."

Kara resists me when I tug her by the hand, her eyes pleading with me when she says, "The dragons. We can't just . . . leave them here."

"They're not going to help us," Deimos argues. "And, what, you plan to let them loose in the halls? Walk them through the halls on a leash? They're thirty feet long. This ship isn't made for them. We can come up with some solution later that would make more sense, but in this very moment, they've got to stay where they are."

Kara looks over at them, Dannanōk specifically, her face conflicted. This is the Kara I remember, the sole defender of the vulnerable, the kid who would confront the biggest bully on the playground just to defend the weakest one. Malakyte could never erase who she truly is at her core, not if he took every bit of her away.

I couldn't be prouder, but Deimos is right. "We can't," I say, hating her disappointed face.

Deimos is done as he takes her by the shoulders, turns her around, and shoves her back toward the door, ripping our hands apart.

We close and lock the complex door, and the three of us find our way back through the hall and to that stairwell that leads up, the only logical path out.

Yet, once we reach the threshold of the stairs, Kara hesitates, pausing on the third step, me behind her and Deimos following me.

Glancing over her head, I realize it's a black void up those stairs. I bend forward and whisper into her ear, "This darkness can't hold you."

Kara nods, stiffly lifting one leg onto the next step until we ascend, quickly being swallowed up by the dark.

"I'm right behind you," I say, alarms blaring in my ears the higher we climb this cramped, tight stairwell.

It smells like mold and dust, and my nose itches like crazy.

After a solid ten minutes of running, my thighs burn once we reach the top, a faint light outlining a door.

I reach over her shoulder and feel for the keypad panel, and sure enough, it lights up once my fingers brush against it. I don't miss the shift in Kara's scent as I move within her space. *Does she like me?*

Stars, I'm a fucking creep. I can't think about her like this. She loves someone else. She'll never choose me.

We're through the door moments later, SSPARROW helmets going back on as Kara leans on the wall, catching her breath. She's out of shape and lost some muscle definition, too. It isn't by accident.

"I know where we are," I say, leading us left and right. "The cells are on the other side. This side is for interrogation, holding, and storage. The main elevator we took to get down here should be up ahead."

True enough, we find them a couple of minutes later.

"The SSPARROWs are all gone," Kara says, scanning the elevator panel with her hand to summon it.

Malakyte has put in a new chip in, then.

We're in the elevator and make it to the main floor of the private sector quickly.

Once the door opens, it's a madhouse.

The three of us simply stand there, stunned.

"Umm . . ." Kara squeaks out as people dash past us, screaming up and down the halls. "I don't think this is all for me."

I can't disagree. Something bigger is happening on the Azurite.

People are running around in a panic, ditching personal items as they go. Screaming, cursing, begging for mercy, and

shots from disruptor pistols ring out down the hall to our left. And when the lights flicker, I know this is very, very bad.

Stepping out from the elevator, I keep Kara behind me with one arm, hating that my hearing is handicapped by being in this ridiculous suit.

A small crowd of people runs past us, franticly being chased by a bombardment of stunner bullets.

"What's going on?" Deimos yells at them, and it doesn't look like any are going to answer when a man of the Proxima Centauri B system shouts over his shoulder at us.

"Rebels! Terran rebels are attacking the ship!"

Kara gasps, and she wrenches a tiny dagger from her waist, readying for battle.

Stars, she's perfect when she has her game face on.

Three Terran rebels rush up from the hall, clad in roughed up clothing and bandanas over their faces, Arianyte issued rifles in hand.

One points at Kara. "There she is!"

Jupiter's rings . . .

Another says into what I'm assuming is a comms device, "We've got eyes on the Star. I repeat, we've got eyes on the Star. Royal sector, floor five, right at the elevator."

Shit.

"We've got to hide her," I say to Deimos. "Right now."

"And why would we do that?"

The voice distortion is off on both our helmets, so when Deimos speaks, I can hear all the iciness in his tone.

I keep my voice low and words short as we hold our ground against the three rebels. "You really want her going back to them as she is now? Seriously? With her loyalty where it's at? And none of the others are leaving without Ardelle."

Yet that part of me that is wired to protect the most important thing to me on a biological level, and that instinct tells me to grab her and run out of here with these rebels. Like I should've done back on that Sky Dais.

But there's also my people and my planet at stake, too. If I leave now . . . I'm dooming them all. Gavrielle Abraxas, Prince of Fucking Nothing.

Deimos begrudgingly agrees as one of the rebels fake-charges us, and all six of us tense. "Fine, you know-it-all-asshole."

"Kara is safest with Malakyte in the throne room," I say, my eyes scanning all their weapons. "Protocols dictate he's likely there."

Deimos nods.

That settles it, then. We're staying, and I'm bringing the woman I love back to the man who will hurt her.

"What are you mumbling about over there?" a rebel shouts. "We're taking her whether you like it or not."

A dark-skinned man points at Kara, and she adjusts her weight, clearly uncomfortable. The other two men, a pale Terran and another with tan skin and slanted eyes, looks at her like she's an object to be taken and stolen away and used in their cause.

Kara is so much more than a weapon of war. She has dreams and goals of her own, and she's in too vulnerable of a place for them to take her back.

"Like hell," Deimos growls, posture turning on a dime.

He's ready to fight, and so am I.

But Kara speaks for herself.

"Touch me, and I'll cut off that finger."

The three men, young as they are, look amongst each other suspiciously. They eye Kara with the same uncertainty.

They know something isn't right—that she isn't right.

I have to get her out of here before things get out of hand and they realize that Kara is no longer their hero and savior they've come to rescue but, instead, their new enemy.

Does that mean she's *my* new enemy, too?

"Deimos."

My voice is cold, clear with intention.

I suspect he knows exactly what I'm trying to say by the way he braces his body down to pounce, our Starseed and Ringer bond a near-psychic link. Before he can leap into battle, another female voice rings through the hallway from our left.

"Kara!"

I recognize the voice, but I'm unsure from where. Whipping my head around, I see the dark-skinned leader of the Resistance, looking exactly like she had weeks ago in the throne room. When Trinity betrayed Kara and the others for her mother's freedom, who was a Tribute. She's one of many dominoes who had to fall to ultimately lead to Kara losing her memories. I am also one of those dominoes, and I hate myself as much as I hate the young woman now coming to stand before us.

Trinity takes a step closer, then stops, her long braids swaying. Hesitation and confusion flash on her face at the way Kara steps back. Despite that, the rebel leader extends her hand toward Kara as we stand fifteen feet apart from Trinity and the three rebel men on our other side. We're boxed in.

"It's me, girl. I think it's time to come home."

CHAPTER 27

Trinity.

Bile burns its way up my throat, bitter and stinging.

"You have some nerve to show up here," I spit at her.

She and Geonni championed an effort to have me killed . . . or . . .

A lightning spear of pain shoots through my head. The migraine is so bad I nearly fall over. I'm trying to remember the way she looked that day her and Geonni and Deimos came for me when I was still in Zarmenia, but it's so fuzzy and I can't . . . I can't grasp it. Because it makes no sense! Deimos is right here . . . and he hasn't tried to kill me. Is it really a false memory?

She gives me the same look of judgment I've seen for the last seven years of my life, from her and Geonni both.

That, I remember clear as day.

Trinity takes a step closer, but we all flinch, then stiffen, Gavrielle looking unsure about whether to block me from her or from the other three rebels. What's the right move here? These rebels want to take me now, too? No matter what I do, I'm going to be a spark in a tinderbox and light this whole thing ablaze.

"Kara," Trinity says, inching ever closer. "I know you're probably still pissed at me for what I did. I get it. I'm so sorry.

There's no excuses, nothing else I can say to make it better. I betrayed you, and I'm sorry. I regretted it the moment we left the throne room that night."

My laugh is bitter and cruel. "You're sorry . . . You and Geonni tried to kill me, and you think saying sorry is going to magically make it all better?"

Trinity's brows crease together; the freckles splattered on her cheeks going uncharacteristically pale.

"Kara . . ." she says, her voice dipping into that octave where she's dead serious. "You know Pops died almost a year ago. I don't know what you're talking about."

My stomach flips, nausea rolling over me. When I first ran away from Gav, Jance, and the other Starseeds and Malakyte found me, I recalled a strange fragment of a memory of blood, and Geonni's sunglasses were sitting in it. It felt so real, and I didn't understand what it was, so I blocked it out the last two days. But she's claiming Geonni is dead and that I'm supposed to know he is . . .

My head is throbbing so bad I can't think. I can't make logical connection points when it feels as if an ice pick has been stabbed right into the base of my brain and I have to latch onto Gavrielle suit just to stay upright.

But I can't remember what happened . . .

Why can't I remember?

"What has he done to you?" Trinity whispers.

The genuine devastation in her voice seals the deal for me.

Her, Geonni, and Deimos truly didn't try to kill me that day in Zarmenia City. That memory is a lie. That memory was the reason Malakyte and I came up here . . . And if that's not real, then what else isn't real? He . . . He did this to me, didn't he?

I almost puke right here on the floor in front of everyone.

Yet there's one thing that doesn't quite fit for me.

"So, then, what are you so sorry for, Trinity?"

 170

Maybe it's the ice in my tone, but she has the reasonable sense to look nervous.

Swallowing hard, Trinity says, "You want me to say it, then fine. I sold you and everyone else out to Malakyte in order to secure my mother's freedom. I betrayed Pop's principles, the Rebel's Song, all the rebels, and Earth herself. I fucked up, okay? I know I did. I . . . I just wanted my mom back. After Malakyte killed Pops, she was all I had left. And I didn't know what Jance was to you until that moment you told him in the games, and by that point, it was just too late an—"

"What did you just say?" I ask.

Both Gavrielle and Deimos go still. Sky-Fae still . . .

Trinity looks confused as she stares at me. "I said I'm sorry, Kara. For star's sake, you're so stubborn. I came up here to get you all back. I've got the entire resistance mad-rushing this place so I could find you and the others to get you all off this dreaded ship. Plus, we've got major intel that Arianyte has its hands on some real terrifying shit. It's bad, girl. So, how about you stop looking at me like I'm a ghost and get that little ass in gear. Be mad at me once we're out of here."

I gape. "Not that! I mean what did you say about Jance and about what Malakyte did."

Trinity looks at me like I'm the phantom haunting the halls of the Azurite. "What the fuck has happened to you?" Trinity demands, risking it by stalking up to us, but then she suddenly stops, some revelation falling across her face like a shadow. "Oh, fuck . . . Kara. He did it, didn't he? He Reconditioned you."

The certainty of her words hit me harder than if she had charged up to me and punched me in the face. Is it so obvious, then?

"That's why you've been so quiet. I hope he just had you locked up somewhere and you couldn't reach us down there. He really did it. This is my fault. Fuck . . ."

Now Trinity looks like she's about to puke.

Deimos steps out of our trio. "Trinity, it's Deimos. You can't take her. You need to leave this ship without her."

"Fuck all if she's staying up here. I'm bringing her home. Right now."

"She doesn't have her memories," Gavrielle says. "She has to stay here."

"Why?" Trinity asks. "Are you going to find them hiding in Malakyte's pocket or something? If they're gone, then they're gone. We'll figure out how to help her once we're out of here."

"Find them . . ." Gav whispers, almost to himself. It's hard to tell with the mask on, but it looks like he's thinking about something. "What if we've been looking at recovering Kara's memories the entirely wrong way?"

Trinity laughs incredulously. "Oh, how convenient."

"No, I mean it. What you just said reminded me of something I heard Naresteé say recently, and it made something click. I need to get Kara out of here and check on something. She isn't coming with you."

I'm thrown into the shadow of Gavrielle's body as he slowly moves himself in front of me, but one of the rebel men rushes up and grabs me by the arm, yanking me forward. The thought of being separated from Gavrielle terrifies me because as my entire identity crumbles before my eyes, he's the only thing that I know for certain is real.

My star mark goes from a tingle to a burn in a flash.

Stars, I can't control it.

Shards of Neon Fuchsia fly everywhere, and instant fear plunges deep into my bones as it shatters and dusts everything within the vicinity. I accidentally strike two of the three rebels, the one who grabbed me getting the worst of the burns, and his screams echo out into the hallway.

Get ahold of it!

The control over my crystal is a complete, utter failure.

 172

Braving my fury, Gavrielle latches onto my face. One warm hand, one metal-clad hand, both hold my face steady, but it's his words that reach me in the depths of the panic now taking over me. "Kara," he says, voice strong, *"I'm always with you."*

He is with me.

Gav eases my antimatter enough that I regain control and putter it out.

Before Trinity or any of the rebels can stop him, Gavrielle takes me by the hand, and we run.

Trinity tries to chase after us, but Deimos snatches her by the waist before she can. The other rebels are either too injured or too stunned to chase us. Her rage-fueled shouts follow us until we disappear into the awaiting chaos.

CHAPTER 28

So much is going on around us, and I'm so stunned, I don't even argue as Gavrielle leads me down the chaotic halls.

Some rebels try to come for us, but Gav gets past them with ease.

He's taking me somewhere specific, but I don't think I care where . . . because my entire life is a lie.

My entire identity . . .

Malakyte killed Geonni . . .

Geonni is dead.

The man who took me in off the streets after I fled the orphanage, who cared for me like his own and taught me how to tattoo, and who was truly the only father figure I ever had in my life, is dead? Killed by the man I love? I don't know what's worse, Geonni trying to kill me or Geonni being dead.

At least that's what Trinity had said. I can't exactly trust her, especially given her confession about betraying me, along with something else about Jance I didn't catch. He's a whole other mess my poor brain can't handle without threatening to pop. It's like there are dozens of threads laid out before me, each one another storyline, another life that's supposedly real, but each time I try to pull one, everything collapses around me. I'm afraid and confused and lost in the halls of my memories.

I only realize we've stopped running when Gav softly places a hand on my shoulder.

"What?" I ask.

"I said we need a code to get into this room. I think I may know what happened with your memories and why the gas didn't work."

"Really?" I ask, so hopeful I don't care how desperate I sound.

He nods, pointing a thumb at the door we're standing next to. This hall is a dead end, and the rebels haven't found this corner yet.

I punch in Malakyte's code. He's likely going to remove my access after today . . . especially when I ditched Ennar and his partner at the gym. He's going to be so upset with me.

Hydraulics hiss as the door unlocks and slides open.

It's dark as we enter, and lights flicker on automatically as we step in, the door closing and locking behind us.

The room is nothing but a small space with a few chairs on the left side of another door straight across the room from the first one. There's nothing else here.

"Do you need to rest for a second?" Gav asks, ripping his helmet off and sitting it on one of the two chairs.

His long Moonstone-colored hair is a mess, sticking out in every direction, some bits snagged and stuck inside the body portion of the metal suit, his small braids coming undone.

"What's so amusing?" he asks.

I stand here, staring at this beautiful Sky-Fae, wondering if I can truly trust him. I should know better than to trust a gorgeous man now, shouldn't I?

Look where it's gotten me.

I reach up, needing to stand on my tiptoes as I smooth out his hair. "There we go. That's a bit better."

"I think you missed a spot," he jokes, but it falls flat.

So does the tiny smile I faked for the briefest of seconds. Gavrielle sees it, of course.

"Everything is going to be okay, Kara. I promise."

I don't even know what to say. Or what to feel. Or what to believe. I'm only certain of one thing—*him.*

Gav steps an inch closer, my heart fluttering. "Can I . . ." He extends his gloveless hand, then retracts it.

"Yes," I say, not even knowing what he's asking for.

There's not a single second of hesitation as he closes all space between us, his hand connecting to the side of my face, fingers curling into the nape of my hair, thumb caressing my chin like it's his last day alive. The yearning in his eyes can be felt in the deepest recesses of my being.

I think my heart may have stopped for a second there, the touch so sweetly intimate it makes me want to cry.

Gavrielle leans down, pressing his forehead up against mine.

I half-sigh, half-laugh. "Your parents used to do this. I forgot you told me that."

He smiles sadly. "They did."

The world beneath my feet feels so unsteady as he pulls back and stands to his full height, eyes tenderly looking down at me. I watch him like he's risen from the dead.

My neck is cranked far back as I take a good, long look up at him. With the daytime lighting of the quartz lights, I finally get to see Gavrielle in all his Sky-Fae glory without interruption. I notice the way his upper lip curves up just slightly when his mouth is relaxed. Or that little mole on his right cheekbone I had completely forgotten about, or how his eyebrows are more like a Glacier Gray than the Frost of his hair. Despite everything that's happened in the last couple of days, what I do know for certain is that he is Gavrielle. The Gavrielle I've missed for so very, very long.

However, no matter how good or right this moment feels, I need to focus on the truth. "You said you thought something in this room was the reason why I didn't remember my so-called real life."

"Not 'so-called.' It *is* your real life."

I sigh. "Fine. *My real life.* Show me why you brought me here, Gavrielle."

Nodding, Gav grabs his helmet from the chair, walks us up to the secondary door where I type in Malakyte's code again, and the door opens. Gav's body tenses, causing my own to do the same as my skin prickles with anticipation.

With his SSPARROW helmet in tow, he takes my hand and walks us into the darkened space beyond this second door, leaving the antechamber behind. He claims that what lurks behind it could be the sole reason as to why my memories haven't returned like they should've, and I have no idea what I'm about to see.

Once the door opens, I certainly wish he had prepared me.

"What is this place?"

He's silent for a long while. "It's a graveyard. This is where memories go to die."

CHAPTER 29

The room sure doesn't look like any graveyard I've ever seen.

I'm accosted by lights in the colors Cloudy Blue, Pale Pink, and Icy Lilac.

The majority of the light source comes from the back of the room as we cautiously cross in that direction.

A giant crystal tower point that's nearly the size of me cleaves two metal shelves in half, which are mounted to the back wall on either side of it. The enormous crystal exudes radiance, and the overhead quartz lights pierce through it like an arrow, rainbow flecks spraying along the strange celestial decor, walls, and attached table as proverbial blood splatter.

The long, medical table connects to the huge crystal, a half-dome-shaped contraption at the head of it. Whatever this dome apparatus is, it's in the shade Aluminum. Since it's tipped upwards on hinges, I see the inside is covered in a bunch of delicate little lights, looking like some futuristic disco ball.

"It looks like that metal piece at the head of the table is meant to go over a person's head," Gavrielle observes, circling the table and crystal, eyes intensely inspecting. "This is Arianyte technology. Advanced, scary shit."

My attention, however, is drawn to the rows of shelves behind this alien device.

Three rows and three columns. The rows are full of dozens of smaller crystal shards, casting the room in an eerie Ultraviolet glow. There are so many, each completely identical. Each are about eight inches tall, flat on the bottom with a little pointed tip at the top. They're smooth, as if machine cut, so each side is perfectly flat and symmetrical. The crystals have the same unique color scheme, too. Beginning at the base of the crystal, I'd use the shade Sunset Purple, then Strawberry Slush, Primrose Petals, Ballet Slipper, Sunrise, then Aquamarine, and finally, at the point, I'd end it in a brilliant Nebula Navy. It looks like a sunset or sunrise, purples to pinks to oranges to blues.

As beautiful as they are, I recall that in nature the prettiest things are often the deadliest, and I have the distinct feeling as if we've intruded into a place we don't belong, and that pretty creature is about to strike.

This is a place our eyes were never meant to see. And the eyes that do come across such things, well . . . they stop seeing anything after that.

This is a bad place.

It's *wrong*.

That's when I notice that very thing I know Malakyte never intended for my eyes to see . . . and my body freezes, my heart a growing anthem in my ears.

"Gav," I say, my voice barely a whisper, as if the people who created this place can hear us this very moment, like a spider watching over its web of deceit.

He looks confused at what I'm trying to tell him until his eyes follow my gaze, and he goes unnaturally pale. "I knew it."

He doesn't sound happy about being right. In fact, Gav sounds wrecked.

"Why is there a shelf with my name on it, Gavrielle?" I ask, staring at the only section of the row with a single, lone rainbow crystal shard sitting on it. It rests on the row closest to the bottom.

I scan the others, the one above mine, and I see a single name there, too.

Selenyte Ardeen.

Above that one.

Malakyte Ardeen.

Without saying a word, I rush around the table to the other side and read the names on the shelves. The top row has the name of the person I suspected.

Herkimer Ardeen.

Below the emperor sits the empress.

Zoisyte Ardeen.

Beneath her, the last and final name etched into the shelf.

Naresteé Barrania.

They all have two-to four-dozen crystals on their shelves. Mine is the only shelf with a solitary crystal point.

And I think I know why.

My ears hollow out from the realization. The physical confirmation and the final nail in Malakyte's coffin. The physical proof of his guilt . . .

I can hardly hear Gavrielle over the pounding in my head when he says, "I vaguely remember a conversation years ago about this machine. It didn't even cross my mind because I was young at the time, and I was only listening to Naresteé and Malakyte talking about dumping their memories at one point. It had no relevance to me then. It was only when Trinity had made that snarky comment about finding your memories in Malakyte's pocket that I remembered this machine existed. My own memories have been fragmented, too . . . I should have remembered this. We always assumed your memories were still inside your mind, just blocked, never physically removed and hidden away."

Gav rakes his hand over his face, eyes clearly searching his own discombobulated mind for reference points, for context. He said he was young when he remembered this conversation. He's known Malakyte and Narestée for a while, then . . . probably from when he was taken from the orphanage.

He muses, "I'm assuming their minds can only physically hold so much memory. Like a computer with limited space, a mortal's mind is no different. Their brains weren't made to live as long as they have due to the Silent Breath. So, it appears as if they found a solution for that. They dump their memories into these crystals somehow. Space is freed, but the memory is still saved, but on an external hard drive. In this case . . . a crystal. This is why the gas didn't bring your memories back like it did with me and Pacey. The memories aren't in your mind anymore. They're inside that crystal."

So much of what he just said doesn't make much sense, but I can't care about connecting those dots.

I shake my head. "But I've been having visions of my real life," I argue.

Gav also shakes his head. "The crystals have their own memories, and that's what you're seeing. It's why they're only triggered when you look at one of our marks."

Jupiter's rings . . . Malakyte, what have you done?

This can't be happening.

I wonder if the memory I had of Geonni's blood slipped through somehow and remained inside my mind. That was the only one left and the only memory the gas revealed. For whatever reason, it clung to my subconscious.

"Then, why not just bring me in here instead of using Narestée?"

Gav cocks his head, pondering. "Well, probably because her magic can rewrite memories, where I'm betting this machine can only extract them. Why I wasn't put in here . . . or Pacey, or Jance, I don't know. You're far more important to Malakyte than we are, so I'm sure that it has something to do with it. I doubt something like this is as easy as laying down and popping out a crystal. Whatever it costs to do this, it's likely high. That's my best guess."

It makes sense. I am special to Malakyte. But how much could he love me if he'd willingly do this to me? Fracturing my mind like he'd shatter a mirror, cutting me—bleeding me on every broken piece. No wonder I haven't been thinking clearly, having these horrific nightmares—look at what he fucking did to me! There's no restoring something like this, no restoring me!

In the span of a blink, I snatch Gav's helmet and vomit into it.

Gavrielle is instantly there, collecting my hair as I retch again and again, his free hand rubbing my back as I puke my guts up at the realization hitting me like the existential threat that it is. His soothing words keep me from completely losing myself to the terror, the only real thing in this house made of cards.

This. Has. Happened.

He Reconditioned me.

He violated me.

He stole the man I supposedly loved from me, took Gav from me, took all the others that I care about from me.

Took my choice . . .

I hurl again, nothing but bile coming up.

"You're alright," Gav says, continuously rubbing my back. "It's all going to be okay, love."

Chill bumps skulk across my skin as my body shudders. I spit into his helmet, really wishing I had water to rinse this awful taste from my mouth. If only I could wash away this heartbreak. I'm *so stupid.* He played me, tricked me . . .

"Well," Gav sighs as my hurling eases up, a light chuckle in his tone. "It's illusion magic on the way back, then."

I shake my head at how utterly *Gav* that statement is. Wiping my mouth with my sleeve, I apologize. "I didn't want to leave any evidence that we were here, and it was the only thing I could reach in time. I really hope that isn't the helmet you all were talking about in the dungeons that was so important."

"Smart," he says, taking the helmet from me. "And don't worry about that. You owe me, though."

If the situation wasn't so dire, I would have laughed. But there's no laughter in my heart, not after today. Not after everything I've learned. The truth, indeed, hurts more than I ever realized it would.

"He said he loved me . . ."

And I don't know why I say it, why it hurts me so much, that all I can do is cry silent tears. That sounds so pathetic, and I hate myself even further for saying it. Why I'm subjecting Gavrielle to this when he's clearly suffered enough because of my choices, is beyond me.

His sigh is enough to tell me he has his own feelings about the topic.

"I think, in his own way, he does love you. The others told me once that maybe there was some sort of connection between the two of you from the start. Despite knowing better, you had some genuine feelings for him. But ultimately, you chose and loved someone better suited for you. He wouldn't— *couldn't*—accept that. And the moment he had the chance, he took away your choice. The rest of us, well, we were collateral damage in that."

They've suffered because of me.

"But we don't blame you, Kara. Not at all. We blame him," he says hurriedly, like he's trying to backpedal.

"Why wouldn't you blame me?" I say, hating myself more and more by the second. "It's clear, abundantly fucking clear, that this is all my fault."

I have to suffer the consequences of mistakes I don't even remember making. It seems so unfair yet a fitting consequence. But there's still the Hijacked I have to save and all these plans I was supposed to do . . .

Gavrielle steps even closer. "You did what you thought was right at the time. I can't blame you for that."

"The other's will."

"They don't."

I can't meet his eyes.

"Look at me, Kara," he demands, the strength in his voice enough to make me do it. "None of us blame you. You had good intentions—you were trying to save Pacey. Malakyte, Naresteé, this whole stars damned empire is to blame, *not you*. I will spend as much time here as you need to convince you of that."

My eyes peel away from his too-beautiful face. "Can you put my memories back in my head? If they're preserved like this, there must be a way to get them back."

Change the topic. Deal with it later.

Gav looks back at the machine, eyes analyzing. "I'm not sure if I can figure it out today. I'd have to study it and find out how it works. Talk to Pacey about it. But it's not impossible. We will get them back. I promise."

"And in the meantime?" I ask, nausea filling my gut with toxic butterflies. "I'm supposed to simply go back to him like I don't know what he did to me? Play the loving fiancée act while trying not to smother him in his sleep?"

I can tell Gav tries not to laugh at that last bit.

"It's important that you stay with him, at least for right now. I can explain why later. I know it'll be difficult, but if he gets even the slightest inkling that you know what he did, I can't imagine what he'd do. The prince does not react well to being cornered. It's imperative you don't act any differently. I'm sure with everything that happened recently, he'll be looking for any small discrepancies in your affect toward him."

"He's going to kill me when he finds out that I know."

Gav's hand warms the skin on my shoulder as he places it there, looking me dead in the eyes, his Violet Sky stare taking the edge off that terror. "I won't let that happen."

His voice is so sure, so strong, that I have no choice but to believe him.

"We'll make contact again soon," he tells me, taking his hand off me. I feel too pitiful to ask him to put it back. "If I don't get you back to him soon, your absence will be suspicious. I need to take you back. You also need to start training again with me if we can get you away but alone if we can't. He's been pampering you for a reason, and it isn't to keep you in ignorant bliss, although I'm sure that's part of it. You being weak helps nobody but him, and now that you know what's really happened, we'll need you back in peak form as soon as possible."

He's right, of course. Another ploy Malakyte set into motion without me being any wiser for it. How many other schemes does he have going on? If he can do this, he can do anything.

Sighing heavily, I bite my lip and look at Gavrielle. He really did grow up to be so stupidly pretty. I can tell that he knows it, too.

"Before we leave," I say, my eyes gliding back toward the shelves with the crystals, "I need a minute alone."

Gav respects my wishes, and for a long time, I simply stare at the crystal shard with my name on it until the burning fury within my soul becomes something else.

Something honed and devious and cunning.

CHAPTER 30

I'm a mix of numb and furious as Gavrielle takes me all the way back to the throne room, dodging rebels the entire way. By the time we get close enough for him to easily blend into the other SSPARROWs and slip away, I want to punch Malakyte in his stupid, lying face.

Before the barrage of soldiers meet us from down the hall, Gavrielle whispers, "Watch for us."

That's when I'm overtaken by soldiers as they urgently swarm me and usher me toward the throne room doors.

Gavrielle disappears into the sea of faceless metal bodies.

The doors whoosh open, and I'm immediately hit with another wave of nausea as I see it in an entirely different light. No wonder I fucking hated it in here.

"Karalevine."

Malakyte's voice is uncharacteristically uneven as he rushes for me from where he stands surrounded by his guards. I note that his mother is sitting on his throne, but she only watches me with careful eyes.

I mess up when I don't automatically run up to him, too. I'm enveloped in the cold of his body and Black Night cape, an iciness that shocks my body and sends a shiver through my spine that leaves it stiff and uncomfortable.

How can I fake this?

For the Hijacked, you damn well better, I say to myself as Malakyte separates us.

His frigid hands cup both sides of my cheeks as he stares at me with concern, but there's a sharpness there, too. "Why did you leave the gym?" His Crow-colored eyes search every minute detail of my face.

"When the sirens blared, I panicked," I say, feigning fear. "I just ran out the closest door and followed the crowd. I don't know what I was thinking."

He doesn't buy that, and I see irritation cross his face as he adjusts my curls back to their proper place. "Why wouldn't you run to Ennar? That makes no sense. You know the rebels are after you, and they breached the ship. I thought they—" He sets his mouth in a firm, tight line and furrows his brows. "I thought they got to you again and you were gone."

I swore to myself I wasn't going to let him suck me back in, but the utter devastation in his voice at the thought of me being taken out of here is like electricity to my cold, dead feelings for him.

"They tried," I say, and his eyes flare. "Trinity was here. She attacked, but I fought her off. I had some help, a few SSPARROWs, but I didn't let her take me. She was going to bring me back to Earth, likely so Geonni could do the deed of finishing me off himself."

Malakyte looks over at me as if I were as wounded or as traumatized as the other day. I know he'll see the camera footage, so this story is the best I could come up with in the time I had.

"Did I do a good job?"

He brings me into another icy embrace, and I swear I detect the slightest tremor in his body. "Of course you did, Karalevine."

How have I never noticed how much I loved the way he says my name? How many of the other things that I love are filthy, dirty lies?

The throne room doors slide open, and a booming, angry voice coupled with a rush of cold that rivals a snowstorm hits my back.

Herkimer scrutinizes Malakyte with a glare of unholy rage, SSPARROWs practically leaping to get out of his way as he charges straight for us.

I almost do a double take because the guy looks like he's aged decades from when I saw him just a couple of days ago. He looks at least in his sixties as he advances toward us with fury that shouldn't be possible for someone who looks so . . . decrepit.

Malakyte shoves me out of the way to avoid his father, and I gasp as Herkimer rushes Malakyte and slaps him across the face. The sound booms like a clap of thunder crashing against these esteemed, royal walls.

"Did you murder Selenyte?" he roars.

I've never seen Malakyte look so afraid.

CHAPTER 31

"Herkimer!" Mother shouts.

The pushback is a rarity for her, and I'm sure it's only because Karalevine is here to witness what just happened. Nobody can peek behind the illusion of the royal family or see the rot that's infected this impeccable image we've crafted over centuries, the nightmarish truth laid bare behind closed doors.

It's too late for me to make Karalevine unsee it, and that means she's in danger.

Selenyte's ghostly voice laughs close behind me, all but sure I will pay for my sins and that Karalevine will behold the very depths of the abuse I've suffered at the hands of my father.

"I think it's time, big brother. Your path to the gallows is shortening, *murderer.*"

Ignoring Selenyte, I adjust my balance and disregard the stinging on my cheek as I look at Father. The Silent Breath unambiguously abandoned him, yet there was nothing feeble in that hit; my neck throbbing from the force of it.

I won't even risk a glance at Karalevine.

Father's eyes pin me in place. "Everyone out!"

Yes. Go, Karalevine.

Her body moves to do so out of my peripheral, but she hesitates, and my eyes close in defeat. It's already too late.

"Not you," Father says, his voice as glacier as the blood in his veins.

Opening my eyes, I realize she's frozen, her body language too much like prey for my liking, and if I've noticed it, he certainly has. That weakness will cost her.

"Father—"

"She stays!"

Swallowing, I peel my eyes away from his wrinkled face to observe the utter horror on Karalevine's. I don't wish for her to see me like this . . . but he does. He yearns for the opportunity to humiliate me in front of her. I can't allow it.

"I'm in the middle of a ship-wide attack. I can't pander to your delusions that I'm in some fashion the one responsible for Selenyte's death," I say, keeping my voice strong and my back straight. Any sign of weakness will be all he needs to rip me to shreds. "No, Father, I did not kill Selenyte. Now, can we advance beyond this nonsense and get back to the safety and security of this vessel?"

"You think you're clever, don't you, boy? Do you even know what's been happening beyond these doors, you fool?"

"My soldiers disposing of the rebel trash?"

We've already caught nearly one hundred of them. How is that not good enough?

But I can't beg. Not even for her benefit.

Not in front of Karalevine.

"So, you have no idea what's being painted all over the walls of this ship? What these Terran rebels are spewing about you? Judging from that pitiful look on your face, I'm guessing not."

He tsks, cranking his neck to look at Karalevine.

Do not balk under him, I want to shout at her.

"There are words painted all throughout the ship that claim you are the one who killed her. 'Malakyte murdered Princess Selenyte' is written in the same fucking paint that's been used to spread her fucking symbols all over this ship!"

A confused, diminutive gasp escapes her lips.

I have no time to react as he seizes the collar of my jacket, the fabric creaking under his pull as the threads rip. His canines are exposed in a play of dominance as he forces me to face him.

And like the fucking coward I am, I do it.

"Stop it!" Karalevine shouts, the daring thing taking a step closer.

I throw my hand out. "Stay back! Please, Karalevine. For once in your life, just listen to me."

This is the first time I've had to raise my voice to her, and I can see she's wounded by it.

She opens her mouth to retort but, thankfully, thinks better of it.

Ripping my gaze away from her, I meet the eyes of the man who made me exactly who I am, a man that's so colossally disappointed in how I turned out. His fury is palpable, a fire that consumes everything in its wake. He would never display this type of rage in my defense. It's because Selenyte is the only thing in this galaxy he ever loved, and it's on her behalf that he rejoices in my humiliation.

I should have guessed his flame had a hunger to devour me whole because it gets a thousand times worse as I feel the agony invading my body like a blade meant to murder, a pain I've felt and feared for so many long, miserable years.

"Malakyte!" Karalevine shouts as my body convulses under the weight of Father's cruelest stolen power.

His favorite form of punishment for me.

I won't scream.

Two, four, six, eight, ten, twelve, fourteen—

"Were you involved?" he asks, glaring down at me without an ounce of mercy, even as my body quakes.

The magic he wields against me is centered in my skull, and it's so agonizing, so excruciating I can't form the words to respond to him adequately. What number had I stopped on? I have to finish counting.

Yet I grit my teeth hard, refusing to crack under his weight. Not in front of Karalevine. He won't have the pleasure of breaking me again. Not here. Not today. *Not in front of Karalevine.*

Fourteen, sixteen, eighteen—

"No," I growl, Father ramming the magic in deeper as I physically push him back.

Karalevine's magic . . . it's flaring.

"Please, stop it! Stop it, you're hurting him!"

I push back, but even speaking is grueling. "Father, s-stop this."

She's losing control, her crystal slipping.

My vision is blurring significantly, the first stage.

Two, four, six, eight . . .

It only gets worse from here, but this is just one of the many magical abilities Father has at his disposal.

Two, four, six, eight . . .

A purple light flashes so brightly it temporarily blinds my eyes, her shriek hollowing out my ears as her antimatter strikes at us.

Droplets of frigid blood strike my face, causing me to flinch.

The burning, stabbing pain that lingers in my head ceases a second later. My ears ring as I blink the wetness from my eyes, wholly unprepared for this utter disaster.

Father's hand—the one that was holding the collar of my jacket—has been sliced clean off, a bloody stump gushing blood onto the tiled floor.

The numbers come in fast. *Two, four, six, eight, ten, twelve, fourteen, sixteen, eighteen, twenty, twenty-two.*

I'll give it to Karalevine. She sure knows how to use her magic much more efficiently than she used to, even in an uncontrolled state it hit its mark. The faint smell of magic fills the room, but it fades as quickly as it comes. Scorch marks have scuffed the floor beside me and the two pillars to my right, but thankfully, that's the worst of the damage. But, fuck, will this lead to a shitshow of epic proportions.

"I . . ." She steps back, hand covering her mouth as she looks in horror. "I didn't mean . . . I didn't. It was an accident."

I haven't seen her face so horrified since we were in this very room weeks ago. Now her heart is in an uncontrollable gallop which she can't slow, her crystal still lit up on her chest. Undiluted terror saturates the room as her scent mixes with the blood in the air.

I abhor that she doesn't just appear as prey now . . . She *is* the prey now.

Father tilts his head back as his maniacal laughter shakes the ringing from my ears.

Karalevine!

I force my body to move, ignoring that every joint feels wrapped in barbed wire or that my head is so ravaged it could be split for all I know. None of that matters. I have to get her out of here.

Right now.

She closes the space between us in a heartbeat, catching me as I tumble to the floor, my cloak obnoxiously in the way.

"I got you," she says, doing her best to hold up my weight.

She doesn't understand.

"Run," I whisper. "Now. Back to the room."

She looks at me, confused, and her delicate lips part to say something undoubtedly stubborn and annoying in return, but Father's voice stops her cold.

"There is no running from me," he promises.

I close my eyes as if this was all some nightmare. But it has been reality for as long as I can remember, even when I've done everything in my power to forget.

"What the fuck are you?" Karalevine gasps.

My eyes shoot back open just in time to witness the hand she cleaved right off the bone—reforming.

"It's been a while since I've had to re-grow an entire hand." He looks at it, amazed, voice amused as he wiggles his fingers like he's settling the nerves back into place, the limb completely whole again. "But what I am, girl, is something people like you fear more than anything. I devour magic. I've collected a whole host of magics so far beyond your comprehension of power that not even *the Star* could stand against me. I specifically crave magic of those who attack me. It's a personal little kink."

"Father," I warn. "Enough."

I will go after him if he even thinks about it.

She isn't breathing adequately enough. The tremble in her body ignites a rage in me I've known very few times in my long life. The last time this fury overtook me I killed my own flesh and blood for threatening Karalevine's well-being.

"I'm not afraid of you," she says, despite all the evidence pointing to the contrary. "And I'm not going to let you hurt your son or my people. You want to devour my magic? I'll make you fucking choke on it."

Stars, I fucking love her . . . but, damn, was that the worst thing she could've said.

And I'm not quick enough to save her.

CHAPTER 32

KARALEVINE RUZZ

The emperor of Arianyte lunges for me, and I spring to my feet, leaving Malakyte on the floor as I brace down into my heels and throw my arms over my chest to defend myself.

This has escalated fast. Malakyte's dad is a fucking monster.

He looks like a crone but moves like a man in his prime, although he's still not as fast as me and I dodge him. He pivots and comes again, and this time, he brings me straight down to the ground.

"Father, stop!" Malakyte shouts, and whatever painful magic Herkimer was using to subdue him comes back in full, his suffering evident as he grunts in agony several feet behind Herkimer.

Is he going to do that to me now? Am I about to feel what brought Malakyte to his knees?

I'm on my back as Herkimer pins me there with his body, my panicked cry lodged in my throat.

Get him off! I order myself. Emperor or god, no man will touch me in a way that I'm not comfortable with—and this is one of those moments.

I bend one leg, and because my limbs are short, I'm able to wedge it between us and press the bottom of my shoe into his hip and push—hard. He slides to the side, and my other leg wraps around his waist. If I can roll him, then I can get some leverage back. My crystal's magic sparks at my fingertips, and holding it back takes as much effort as getting the emperor off me does. I can't risk using it again. Look at the trouble it's already caused.

Herkimer bends down so his face is directly next to mine when a bright light bursts from out of nowhere, stinging my eyes. Where did it come from? Jupiter's Rings—it's from him. It's an energy magic of some kind—very similar to mine—and it's formed into a ball that floats in the palm of his hand. It sparks and shimmers in Indigo, Bright White sparks sizzling around the white-hot sphere with heat so sweltering it singes my lashes.

"I can do magic like you, too," he taunts. "But I have hundreds of years of experience on you, girl. You will never be able to beat me, destroy me, or prevent me from doing a damn thing to your world. Now, do you want me to show you what my magic can do to your pretty face?"

I cry out as he places his ball of magic so close to my cheek my skin sizzles like fried meat, the eye nearest watering so bad I have to shut it so he doesn't blind me.

Malakyte and his mother are shouting, but Herkimer doesn't let up.

I have no choice.

"No," I seethe, shaking my head as I try to inch back.

Fuck, my face is going to burn right off my skull.

"Then, don't let me catch you ever spewing that shit again. Your planet is mine. You have no control here, Killer of Worlds."

That name . . .

The magic dies, and he sits up, but before I can even release the tension in my lungs, Malakyte plows into him, ripping his father off.

They don't tumble for long, and Malakyte lands on top, his long dark hair blocking my view, but I think he's got a blade to the emperor's throat.

And he wants to *kill*.

Zoisyte appears beside them, giving me no mind as she bends down and places her hands on her son's shoulders.

"It's alright," she says calmly. "Look at me."

He does, and with the shift in his head, I see he has a black spike-type weapon so deep within Herkimer's throat, dark Navy blood trickling down the side of the emperor's neck. Her voice doesn't assuage the madness in Malakyte's eyes now that I can see them looking up at her.

The empress shakes her head at her son, her eyes anguished and resigned.

"It's pointless," she seems to tell him without words. *"It isn't worth it. Stop."*

Malakyte releases a heavy, forceful sigh. He rips the weapon from his father's throat and stands, chucking the bloodied spike across the room with a hollow clatter that nearly trembles the pillars holding this hellish space together.

Herkimer doesn't move, only gapes up at his son as if Malakyte is the crazy one. This isn't Malakyte's fault—it's Herkimer's. He's a psychopath, and it hits me like a hover-train that it's no wonder Malakyte has issues. This is horrific.

It's hard to see, but it looks like the wound in Herkimer's neck is already beginning to heal, exactly like his hand did.

I'm in complete, utter shock, frozen on the floor of this stars forsaken room.

Herkimer assaults his son one last time as Malakyte turns away. "If I find out you're involved with her death, forget my throne. You'll both be dead."

Malakyte stalks toward me but won't meet my eyes as he bends down, straightens out my shirt, smooths my hair, adjusts my uneven eyeliner as best he can, then picks me up off the floor and carries me to the door like he's a robot.

He's trembling.

I feel it in every taunt inch of his hard, cold body, and I wrap my arms around his neck as I nuzzle my head below his chin. He feels twenty degrees colder than normal, and I'm shivering by the time we exit.

Ennar stands silently behind the doors, and it's obvious from the tense silence that all the soldiers who are located outside heard what happened. I'm embarrassed for Malakyte as he stands there, but he somehow holds his head up as he gives them orders. "Capture as many rebels as you can. Dismantle their escape routes. Apprehension of Trinity Monterey and any of her inner circle is a top priority. Keep all employees, civilians, and Tributes sheltered until the threat is neutralized and the new graffiti is washed away. I'll inform Naresteé of the situation, and we'll convene shortly."

"Sir." Ennar bows, he and a dozen soldiers dispersing.

A bunch of SSPARROW escort Malakyte and me back to the royal wing, and thankfully, we don't encounter any rebels on the way there.

We don't speak a single word to each other.

Once we're inside Malakyte's room and the SSPARROWs leave to stand guard outside the door, he doesn't let me go— he just stands there. We're so still the automatic quartz lights haven't even flickered on.

The rage that singed its way through the love I had for Malakyte simmers . . . somehow. What we both endured in that throne room sucks all the oxygen out of the flaming anger and hatred, and what sits in its place is a deep ache of understanding. Malakyte shattered my mind like a mirror. That's what I said, but right now—Malakyte *is* the mirror. He's *my* mirror.

"Malakyte," I say, finally looking up at him. He still won't meet my eyes. "It's alright, you can set me down now."

Like a reflex, he squeezes me tighter. "I swore to myself I'd never let him hurt you."

Ultimately, he lowers me to the floor, and the moment that he does, he begins walking away from me.

I should let him.

He violated me. He took away my choice and my autonomy and ripped me from my life for his own selfish reasons. The best thing for me to do is allow him to walk away and put distance between us. It'll make the crash and burn barreling toward this relationship less destructive, have less casualties and bloodshed.

But . . .

"Wait."

He stops near the stairs, his back to me. The moon shines through the window, and its Silver Eternity light reflects off his long, smooth hair, the rest of him cast in shadow in the dark room.

We're the same shade of True Black, the same brokenness reflected back at each other when all we try to do is hide the disgusting truth. I'm going to regret this—I know it deep in the marrow of my bones—but I can't give up on the man who doesn't see my darkness as defective. The heart he simultaneously shattered still beats for him in earnest. He *sees me*.

And I see him.

"I'm no stranger to what just happened in there," I confess, swallowing the lump growing in my throat. "It isn't your fault."

He turns his head to the side but doesn't look back. "When my own father puts his hands on you, that is my fault. That is my failure. I couldn't care less about what happens to me."

"It's okay—"

"It's not!"

He finally turns and rushes back to me so fast the coldness he brings with him is like a slap to the face. "I've failed to protect you on every level. From the other Starseeds and their Ringers, from the rebels, and from my own father. Why would I ever be good enough for you, Karalevine? Why would you ever stay by my side? In all actuality, the best thing for you is for me to let you go . . . for your own good."

His words cause my blood pressure to plummet and my mouth to dry. He doesn't want me anymore?

"You . . . want me to go?" I whisper, voice shaky and pathetic.

Stripped of his mask, Malakyte narrows his eyes at me, brows furrowing as he shakes his head emphatically. "Never, Karalevine. I almost just killed my father for you. I've never . . ." He pauses, clearing his throat. "His abilities to consume magic from individuals makes him a hard man to fight, but I'll go into battle until I can no longer revive again if it means protecting you. You'd think I'd throw away what we have together? After finally getting to hold you in my arms each night, after hearing your laughter and listening to your dreams and the future we're planning together, there's nothing I wouldn't do to safeguard that. You've brightened the darkness in my world. You're my Star."

"So, then why tell me to go?" I ask but gape as he gets down on his knees, his eyes turning glassy as he looks at me as if he were a lost little boy.

His head dips down, shame pouring off his defeated, slumped shoulders, his hands gripping onto my hips like I'm the only lifeline keeping him alive. "You make me senseless, Karalevine." Malakyte lifts his head, and his eyes are full of raw tears. "There's no one else in this world who strips me down to my bones like you do. You always have, from the moment I first saw you, I knew I was fucked, knew I'd destroy world after world, I'd ruin my own world—my own soul *for you*. And Father knows that. He knows how precious you are to me, and after today . . . the noblest thing I can do to express my love is to *let you go*."

What he's saying rings out like a death knell, hollowing out my ears as my entire body tingles from his display of emotion.

 200

My way out. He's giving me a way out.

Take it, you stupid fucking idiot. Take it!

The anguish in his eyes cracks my heart in two, confusion and uncertainty filling the in-between.

This isn't his fault. He's only this way because of Herkimer. It's obvious he regrets hurting me. He wouldn't be offering to let me go if he didn't. *Malakyte loves me.* He did a bad thing by Reconditioning me, but his upbringing showed him violence and manipulation are the only way to move through life.

I can show him another path. My love can make him better— make this entire situation better. We can all be allies against Herkimer. Me, him, the other Starseeds and Ringers can all fight and save Earth together. This hasn't dissolved into such a mess we can't reconcile—I believe that.

I cup his face, which is cold and hard like a granite statue. The faint texture of his scar cuts through his dark brow. "I'm strong, Malakyte. I'm not going to let your father destroy us or hurt my people, but I'm also not going to let him hurt you anymore, either. We can fight him together. I'm not going anywhere because I love you, and I'm not ready to give up on this."

Regardless of what he's done . . . it's the truth. Although a tiny voice in the far reaches of my mind whispers, *What if he made me love him, and these feelings aren't even real?*

I know what I feel, and I know that I love him.

"I love you, too, Karalevine. I'll protect you with my life, I promise. I'll do or be whoever you need me to be. I'll give you everything. I'll fight Father for the Hijacked and your people. Just stay with me."

I can see that he means it, and I nod. "I'll stay."

I'm more convinced than ever that I can save this situation from complete collapse. There's beauty in saving the very thing that broke me.

I can save him.

Maybe . . . I can also save *myself.*

CHAPTER 33

My eyes open, and I'm in bed. The weight of what happened slams back into my consciousness as I recall the fight with Herkimer and everything with Malakyte. What he did looms over all of it like a poltergeist wreaking havoc all through our home.

Should I have left when he offered? Did I have the opportunity to end this entire debacle, and did I flinch?

Malakyte and I sat on the couch for a while after that intense conversation. Eventually, he had to go back and deal with the rebels, and I crawled into bed and quickly passed out. I don't know what time it is now, but the quartz lights are still on the nighttime setting.

I turn over, and Malakyte lies shirtless on his side, facing me. His scar looks less stark as the glow of Earth peeks in through the skylight window above us. He's so beautiful. So tragic. So wrecked by a life that didn't simply treat him unfairly—it robbed him of who he could have been if Herkimer hadn't stained his soul.

Same as me.

My hands gently lift away a lock of his long hair from his face, the texture smooth yet surprisingly coarse. I twirl it between my fingers. *He's lying to you*, that pestering voice whispers. *He hurt you, violated you. Run as fast as you can.*

I sigh, turning onto my back again, Malakyte's hair still slithering between my fingers.

Maybe I'm in denial.

Despite myself, my crystal tingles, and the more I think about this, the more upset I become until the star mark glows and burns.

"Karalevine?" Malakyte's voice is soft, sleepy, yet concerned. Cold fingers take the hand interlaced with his hair, and I turn to face him. Dark eyes meet my own in the shade Galactic Black. "What's wrong?"

I want to tell him. I want answers . . . Why? Why did he do this?

"I . . ." My voice is weak when I try to come up with the words, but at the last second, I spew some excuse for my pounding heart. "You know . . . it's . . . *everything.*"

Empathy flashes in his eyes like a summer storm.

"Can I hold you?"

I flip to my side as he nudges close to me. Sliding his arms around my hips, he draws me in exactly as he caught me in his snare earlier, when I wasn't strong enough to wrench myself free. I'm enveloped in his clean scent of citrus and winter's darkness, and I nuzzle my face into his bare chest.

My crystal still glows in Cosmic Fuchsia against his defined muscles as he glides his soothingly cold fingers through my hair in languid, gentle strokes. "You're safe. I'll put my body on the line to protect you from anyone who tries to separate us."

Of this, I have no doubt.

His heart is an even thunder beat in my ear. I press a featherlight kiss to his hard chest, sinking lower until I reach his sternum, where his alien heart beats right beneath his Elendril mark.

A growl vibrates my cheek, and I move to do it again, except this time, I let my tongue do a little more of the talking. One of my hands glides up and down his chest, his abs like carved marble.

Malakyte tips my chin up to him, and the lustful mist in his eyes shoots a rocket directly through me, heating me from my toes to the top of my head. I wrap my top leg around him, bringing our lower halves as close as possible.

Then he kisses me deeply, slowly, sweetly, and my body instantly heats up the core, craving every inch of his chiseled body. The warmth fades from my star mark and dives much, much deeper when his tongue glides up against mine. My mouth eagerly opens for him, when resistance is exactly what should be there.

I grind against his tight boxers, eagerly curious about his body, and the delicate spot between my thighs slickens. Malakyte hardens as my hips roll in circles over the thick length of him trapped behind fabric. Curiously, I greedily grip all of him through his shorts, and I'm met with a deep growl of approval. Exploring him for the first time, I glide up and down to feel exactly what I'd be getting myself into with an extraterrestrial man. That little bubble of anxiety pops when it feels normal to what I'm used to in terms of anatomy. It's cold, though, which, *no shit.*

How would he feel inside me?

Malakyte breaks our kiss, eyes heavy with primal lust but also a silent plea that cries—that shakes the space between our panting breaths—to be seen. What gets me off more than anything is the power I hold over him. If I asked him, if I begged him, would he change for me?

I want him undone. Unguarded. Unmasked.

"Let me," I whisper, feeling for his balls and taking them in my hand as he trembles under my touch. "Let me in. Let me see you. I'm not afraid of who you are, Malakyte."

That's a lie, isn't it? I push that thought away. I want this, want to explore what's between us. It's the only way I can sort this shit out within my head.

Before he can object like always, I push him onto his back and straddle him in one graceful movement. I waste no time as I grind against his length tauntingly. The only thing separating our bodies are his tight briefs, my little silk shorts, and my lace underwear.

Bending down, I find his lips again and kiss him, but this time it's me who slides my tongue over his first. I'm hungry—no, *starving*—for this man. I need him. I need his body and his soul, I need an answer to why after everything, I still want him. I grind on him, our kiss intensifying as we consume each other with tongues and teeth and the shadows that fuel our hearts.

Breaking our kiss, he leans up so we're sitting, and I adjust so I'm on his lap, legs around his waist.

I don't stop him when he takes the silk fabric of my pajama top and lifts it over my head, leaving my chest bare.

My gasp is sharp as his icy mouth claims my nipple, gently biting down, sending my nerves skittering across a frozen pond where his tongue laps against the little bite. Malakyte squeezes the other one in the perfect duality of sensations, my hips rolling against him in tandem. *Yes, fuck yes.*

My fingers dive into his Pitch Black locks, and I pull, igniting another deep growl from his throat as his mouth possesses my other breast, giving it the same, wicked treatment.

I close my eyes, enjoying how he feels, my core aching for more—yearning for *more.*

"Malakyte."

His eyes flicker up to mine, his mouth still on me, and I'm molten at the utter dominance and possessiveness in his gaze. He is ice . . . and I welcome the cold.

He comes up for air, his devious smirk of approval promising me both Heaven and Hell. I'm putty in his hands as he lowers me onto my back, his hand cradling my head until I hit the mattress.

Malakyte leaps off the bed, and as he stands at the foot of it, the moon's rays of light glitter across his skin and hair in the dark room. My prince leans over me, taking my hips and dragging me to the edge of the mattress. He's all arrogance and teeth as he winks at me.

Then he drops to his knees.

"Look at what you make me do . . . Only a queen makes a king kneel. That's exactly what you are, I'll ensure it." He takes one leg, his icy lips kissing the inside of my ankle.

His eyes glitter up at me as I raise myself up onto my elbows so I can get a better view of him down there.

"Almost queen," I retort, knowing the crown isn't on my head, and neither is the power.

"To me." He kisses my ankle, venturing higher. "You've always been my queen."

A smile erupts on my face as I lay back, enjoying his frigid kisses up my leg. Once he reaches my inner thigh, I gasp at the coldness of his lips on the sensitive skin.

Rising higher on my body, his kisses make their way slowly, tauntingly past my shorts, skipping where I want him to go to most as he opts for the ticklish spot by my hip instead. Eagerness heats my core as his hands glide back to my inner thighs, inching the silk fabric up, and it causes my skin to prickle with anticipation that nearly blows my chest to pieces.

He kisses his way back up past my shorts' hem—across my leg—pushing the fabric up to the crease in my thigh. It's only when his fingers curl around the band at my waist that I hope he'll give me what I crave, what he's held at arm's length.

I know why he waited now . . . but in this moment, it's so hard to care. We don't have to be enemies. We can save each other—our love can save each other. It has to be enough, it has to mean *something* in the end.

Malakyte slides my shorts off with ease, leaving my underwear on.

Fuck . . . this is happening. My heart starts to beat even faster, chest filling with a sparkling energy as my ears and cheeks flush, my arousal so wet it's slicked onto my inner thighs and completely soaking my underwear.

His fingers tease me by curling up from beneath my underwear and then back out again. When he spreads my legs open, I bite my bottom lip and grip the sheets.

"Fuck, you're soaked."

I nearly whimper when he finally touches me through the lace fabric.

He strokes me softly in slow, frosty circles. It's the sweetest torture I can imagine.

Finally, he slides my underwear down, past my ass, past my knees, past my ankles.

He tosses them away, taking special attention to bend my knees as he leans between them.

I gasp as he glides two fingers all the way up my center. *Fuck, the cold.* My eyes flutter closed in pleasure as I sink into the sensation.

The deep rumble in his chest tells me he likes it, too.

A single finger plunges deep inside me, a cry escaping my lips. "Fuck, babe . . ." He pumps a couple of times before adding a second finger, filling me up with his frozen touch.

He feels so fucking good.

Opening my eyes, I see Malakyte watching his fingers sink in and out of me like there is nowhere he needs to be but right here with me.

Finally, he pulls out, staring unblinking at me, in full, for the very first time. His gaze is all lustful ache, his primal need all but screaming from him as he licks his lips—famished.

He whispers, "You know what I'm thinking right now?" He opens my legs a tiny bit wider. "When I got that diminutive

taste of you at the arena, all I wanted was to bury my tongue inside you as every single one of those people watched me do it. But more so, I'm remarkably curious as to the sounds you'd make with me so deep inside you I could drown. What sweet, breathy little sounds would you make if I made you come like that, Karalevine?"

Don't be afraid to challenge him.

I swallow. "Guess you'll have to figure it out for yourself. If you can even get me there. I mean, are you going to fuck me with your tongue like you promised a couple of days ago or just talk about it?"

His chuckle is deeply seductive. "You have a god between your legs, Karalevine. Enough said."

There's no time to even respond before he dives, every fragment of control shattering as Malakyte devours me. His glacial tongue skates in an agonizingly slow zigzag pattern over my core. Licking and sucking, and, oh, *fucking stars*, I don't even know what that was but, in this moment, he's right—he's my god. He does it again and again, sliding that icy tongue up and then down, down and then up, side to side, then up again and holy fuck, I can't even breathe it feels so good.

Then he finds my clit, and the stars are bright in my eyes.

His tongue is a torture device of pure fucking pleasure that seems made purely to shatter me—shatter my entire identity. His sexual experience shows because what he bestows onto my body with his tongue has no business existing. I'm unable to keep silent, and I'm pretty sure the entire Azurite can hear me.

"Malakyte."

His name is a fucking plea for more. My brain short-circuits. My body is a complete slave to his mouth, and the contrast of his cold lips and tongue to my warm skin is absolute bliss.

"Malakyte. I love you. Don't stop."

As if my words earn me a reward, he buries his tongue so fucking deep inside me I nearly come from it. Sensing I'm close, he pulls his tongue out, then dives back in.

I move my bare feet to his shoulders, wanting to give him the best angle, and he wraps his arms around my thighs, as if he can somehow meld the two of us together for all eternity.

Each time I get close, he stops, lightly pressing kisses on me as my sensitivity ebbs enough so he can start again.

"I need you . . . I need you inside me. All of you. Fuck me, Malakyte, please. Let me come with you inside me."

He's making me insane with this.

"You'll come, my darling Karalevine, when I say you can come. And when I fuck you . . ." His words drop to such a low octave I can barely make them out. "When I fuck you, you won't only be mine in every way that I can make it—tied to me in body and soul—but you'll be my queen, too. All of you will be mine. Then, I will fuck you. Not because I care about Earth's notion of traditional values, but because I want you to choose me—choose us—*forever.*"

Two fingers plunge into me at once, his tongue twirls around my clit, and I nearly lose control of my crystal as power surges through my blood with a crackling flood of pure fucking ecstasy as unholy pleasure shoots through every nerve. My star lights up, and my body trembles as Malakyte's free hand laces our fingers together tightly. My other hand yanks his hair, but he takes it.

My legs shake around his shoulders as my body climbs closer and closer to that edge he's been denying me. Will this be the time he finally allows me the release I'm so fucking desperate for? Or is he going to torture me until I'm in tears, begging for him to let me come all over his perfect, devious mouth? I've never needed a release so badly in my life.

His tempo increases, his tongue swirls and glides and circles my clit so expertly it's pure bliss.

My vision goes spotty, every cell in my entire body tingling.

He pushes me over that edge, increasing his tempo at the point of my climax, shoving me up toward the stars and the planets and beyond them. I cry his name, my moans a crashing wave against the shore of my climax as he rides me through it. Pumping and licking and nipping at me in such a feral way that I'm coming again. Again and again, I come for him until I can't even count how many times he gets me off until I'm so sensitive I can't take one more second of it.

"Stop . . ." I pant. "I can't . . . I can't."

He slows down but not before doing another lap or two around my clit as a final goodbye.

"First you beg for me to let you come, and when I do, you beg for me to stop. Such a contradiction."

His cocky grin tells me he knows exactly what he's done to me. I snatch the closest pillow and chuck it right at his face. He dodges it, and it goes flying over the railing down to the level below.

"Oh, shut up," I drawl playfully.

His spirited laugh is deep and amused, and I can't get enough of the sound. The tone, the lightness—his walls lowered *for me* and only me. Here, he's not the stoic prince made of ice. He's my lover, and he's mine. Someone who's willing to kill for me— and I can't let that go.

"That was . . . so good."

It's all I can manage to say, my body a useless mess after what he just did to me. Fucking stars.

"Happy to oblige."

I peek past my bent knees and right into Malakyte's eyes, the moonlight casting shadows along his defined cheekbones. Something Gavrielle said earlier pops into my mind, and without thinking about it, I simply blurt it out. "How old are you?"

He narrows his eyes suspiciously. "Random. Why do you ask?"

How do I explain this without giving myself away that I know way more than I should . . .

"That just felt . . . like you have a lot of experience."

My own eyes narrow in playful accusation—like, how dare he have touched another woman before knowing me? But my own sarcasm leads me to think of Zariya . . . He had touched her like this . . . I shake away her ghost, and the terrible gut feeling that threatens to make me run from this ship and this man as fast as I can.

He laughs. "I'm two hundred and twenty-seven."

The sound that escapes my lips is painfully undignified.

"Shut the fuck up," I say, stunned as I look at the face of a man who couldn't be older than twenty-five. "There's no way."

Malakyte looks almost embarrassed. "I have lived a very long time, Karalevine. Thanks to my crystal and another substance that prolongs my life and prevents me from aging. It's something I've been meaning to speak to you about."

I raise my brows, ready to hear how he's the oldest fucking man ever. It explains a lot.

"Tomorrow," he says, climbing back onto the bed. "You need to sleep."

He's right. I'm exhausted, and after I head to the bathroom and return, he holds me as we both lie back down.

As my mind drifts, sleep refuses to come easily. As if it knows what a slippery slope I'm on. I can't let Malakyte go, not yet . . . But all I continue to circle back to, the one thing I automatically reach for as comfort in a world of chaos . . . is Gavrielle.

CHAPTER 34

ALL ARTWORK, MUSIC, LITERATURE, OR NETWORK VIDEOS
PROMOTING REBEL ACTIVITY OR MAKING USE OF "THE
STAR" SYMBOL IS BANNED AND WILL BE IMMEDIATELY
DESTROYED OR REMOVED FROM ALL PUBLIC PLATFORMS.
TERRANS OR EXTRATERRESTRIAL PERSONS CAUGHT
CREATING, DISTRIBUTING, OR HARBORING SAID MATERIALS
WILL BE FOUND GUILTY OF REBEL ACTIVITY.

MALAKYTE ARDEEN

"**W**hat is this place?" Karalevine asks.

She's wearing a little two-piece matching set of leggings and a long-sleeved shirt that hugs every inch of her petite frame, a sliver of her midriff visible against the black fabric where several tattoos peek through. And her ass in those pants? Perfection. I couldn't rip my eyes away during the entire two-minute walk from my room to the end of the royal wing. No SSPARROWs, only her and I.

We reach the elaborate, inconspicuous door of the most important room on the Azurite.

Yesterday, after my meager attempt at protecting Karalevine and preventing her from seeing the truth that my family has hidden for so many years, I have no choice but to rectify the situation.

"There are several items I want to give you. Consider them gifts as well as instruments of protection."

She whistles, and although the tone indicates an exaggerated pitch that would suggest she's impressed, there's something off about it that I can't place.

After my meltdown last night, she stayed and proved her loyalty to me, despite whatever the others told her I may have done to her. She loves me, and they didn't convince her of my guilt. I can give this to her in return.

Turning to the keypad at the door, I input the code required to gain access—which I just had changed to keep Karalevine in a smaller pen—and the pad scans my handprint.

I usher her into the diminutive antechamber, the light illuminating us in pale green, the space hardly big enough for us to stand shoulder to shoulder. Once the initial door to the outside hall closes, I shift to the second wave of security customs. Karalevine scuddles out of my way as I move to stand in front of a clear tube attached to the wall. I place my palm beneath the transparent pipe, and the analyzer clicks loudly several times as a needle drops with the speed of a viper. It pricks my finger so efficiently I can hardly detect the sting, and the machine sucks the fat bead of blood right off my skin through the cylinder. A few seconds later, a pleasant chime jingles, and the next door unlocks.

"That's a lot of security," she chokes out, half laughing at what I assume she sees as absurdity.

I turn to challenge her with a lift of my scarred brow.

Our eyes never break the intense contact, the two of us close in this small antechamber, and I can easily scent her arousal, our breaths circulating in the tight space. But there's something else in her scent, too. Fear, perhaps—I'm uncertain, but I'll watch her closely for any indication of change.

"What's behind this door are my most precious treasures. Artifacts, money, art, weapons, sentimental items. I keep it under lock and key. No one other than me can access this chamber. And, no, Karalevine, before you even ask, you won't be getting the proverbial keys."

She feigns disappointment. "You won't give your bride access to all your most precious crap?"

She teases me, but I don't dare give her access to this room without me. I'm risking enough by letting her in here as it is. If she hadn't stayed last night when I offered to set her free, we wouldn't be here today.

"I want you to trust me," I say, pulling my hand out of the analyzer. "Amongst other things. Me bringing you here is to prove how invested I am in our relationship and my commitment to your safety."

She brings my fingertip to her lips, kissing it gently, a small drop of my blood leaving a stain on her bottom lip.

She slips my finger an inch into her mouth, and by the stars, she *sucks*.

Fuck, Karalevine.

All I can imagine is my cock around those perfect, pouty lips.

I push in a bit deeper, unable to stop myself, and her pupils flare from under her dark lashes. She holds my hand in hers, sliding my finger slowly between her full lips as she tentatively pulls me out, and I smile softly as I rub off the small trace of my blood from her bottom lip.

"You're a bad girl, Karalevine."

And I will take that kernel of darkness and make you invincible. Make you mine forever.

Her laugh echoes off the antechamber as I grin and turn to walk through the door.

The room isn't particularly large, but what it lacks in size, it makes up for in its organizational framework.

Karalevine's eyes glitter as her head whips in every direction, gawking at the many shelves, compartments, racks, wall mounts, and all the items stored within them. All of it is organized so meticulously I find satisfaction each time I see it. Each shelf is arranged to the smallest detail, either by color or shape, and every item is hung or displayed in a way that shows off its individualized glory.

"I keep it intentionally dark in here, as well as climate controlled, to ensure nothing gets damaged while sitting here for so many years. Not even dust collects here. The specialized ducts suck it out the moment it forms."

"Stars, get that technology in my room," she says, strolling down one of the small rows created by the shelves standing in the center.

"You have servants now—you don't need to clean another day in your life," I remind her, but she's already mesmerized by the collection of jeweled crowns by the time she scoffs playfully at me.

While she roams the studious shelves, I quickly make my way to the freezer box that holds the most precious items in this room. As I walk by a shelf, a flash of pink and gold catches my eye, and I'm reminded of something I don't want Karalevine to see. She won't remember it, but the literal key to the machine that holds her memories could induce an emotional response. There are many keys in here that can blow up my plans.

I pluck the key in question off its display and quietly set it behind a couple of statues I collected before I ever met Zariya.

Its chain is peeking out, but I doubt she'll spot it. It's best to be cautious when it comes to her memories. I note the orange-sized black sphere sitting on a little pillow on the same shelf, calling me to it like it always has, the symbols engraved on its curved surface a mystery I've never been able to decipher despite knowing it's connected to the Elendril crystals.

But I forget all about it when I look over to find Karalevine's back to me. Staring at the wall of weapons elegantly mounted, my own Elendril sword amongst them, she appears transfixed. All the Elendril weapons—besides Deimos's and Miss Dawson's—are here.

I sigh. I'll return to the freezer after this.

"What do you feel when you look up at those weapons?" I ask once I approach her left side.

Her eyes are emotional as she gazes up at the weapons I took back from her former family.

I am her family now.

"Connection, maybe? I'm not sure. They call to me."

"As they should, see here." I heave her Elendril sword out of its brackets.

It still impresses me that she was ever able to wield it, with how hefty it is.

She's enthralled as I lay it in her hands, and I understand. The call of these weapons is like that of a siren's, always craving for us to use them, create chaos with them, destroy with them. Karalevine flashes the exact same expression she did the first time I presented her with this sword.

"Your symbol is there," I explain, pointing to the hilt where her star sits, waiting.

"The other Starseeds . . . the one you have in the prison cell—"

"They don't matter. I lied about them to keep you from being devastated that your dream team will never come to pass. The one named Ardelle is unstable, as you saw. The others are clearly working with the rebels. There's no reconciling with them, Karalevine. It's just you and me versus them."

Her eyes seep from fascination to despair way too quickly for my liking.

"Can I keep this?" she asks, looking at the blade.

 216

Good. She's resigned to the fact that her Starseed team isn't going to happen.

"That's why I brought you here," I say, reaching back up to the wall to grab the scabbard. "I want you to have your sword. It's a conduit for your magic, but as you know, antimatter is far too dangerous to be used on this ship. Perhaps we can take a trip down to the surface where you can practice, release some of that pent-up energy. We can't have another accident like yesterday."

"I'm sorry . . . I really didn't mean to hurt him. All of that was my fault."

I take the sword from her and slide it into its sheath. "What happened with Father was not your fault." Then I hand it back to her. "But a word of caution regarding him. He doesn't like disobedience. Placate him when possible, Karalevine. I love your tenacity, but he doesn't find it amusing. If you push him, he will hurt you. And that's one thing I simply can't bear."

She sighs heavily, the tone shifting as she looks away from me, but her brows furrow as something catches her attention.

My stomach clenches as she reaches down, Jance's ring dangling off the corner of one of the shelves. She gathers the chain and lifts it to examine it closer. I had set it there when I was mounting the weapons and forgot about it.

Stupid, foolish idiot.

Her heart rate is speeding up. I'm not sure why Jance had given that ring to her, but she was obviously attached to it when her memories began to fragment. It was her anchor, and she clung to it for dear life. That core memory may be inside the crystal shard safely hidden away, but her body—her nervous system—remembers, even if she herself is oblivious to it.

Two, four, six, eight, ten, twelve, fourteen, sixteen, eighteen, twenty, twenty-two.

"Let's move on," I say, resting my hand on her shoulder.

She flinches at my touch. "What? Oh, right. Sorry. Lead the way."

I pause, waiting for her to set the ring back down, but she doesn't. Instead, I take it from her, set it on a random shelf, and guide her to the other side of the room.

I bend down by the miniature black cube on the floor, opening it with a scan of my thumb and a secondary code. The lock unlatches with a click, and I slide the silver nob to the right. The door swings wide as a frigid plume slithers its way across my boots and Karalevine's teal sneakers.

I reach inside, the cold nipping at my skin as I find the contents quickly. I stand, handing my Star a small, rectangular case.

She sets her sword against a shelf and opens the case, the hinges squealing as she peeks inside and plucks out one of the two syringes nestled within. The contents glow the brightest blue. "What is this?"

I need to tread extremely carefully here. If she discovers the truth about the Silent Breath, I'm fucked. But it's too risky to leave her without it.

"It's a concentrated serum created by Arianyte that can heal nearly any wound."

Her eyes snap to the scar on my face. The scar *she* left me with. Forgiveness is a complicated beast, but I shouldn't be keeping score of the atrocities we've committed against each other.

I clear my throat. "This scar appeared much worse than this, believe it or not. But unfortunately, it isn't limitless in its potency when forces bigger than it are in play. Aside from some extenuating circumstances, most injuries can be healed, even fatal ones, if administered soon enough. Do you hear what I'm telling you?"

Our gazes clash, her heart an anxious gallop, but she nods.

"If you ever find yourself gravely injured, inject the entirety of this syringe into your wound or have someone do it for you. Its dose is calibrated for a Terran. It's essential that it penetrates

directly into the flesh. Do you understand, Karalevine? As deep as you can bear it."

"I understand."

"Good. Always keep it close to you. I want you to carry a small pack with you from now on with this in it. That case is a portable freezer to keep it viable. It must stay cold. The case will keep it at temperature for a year, but it'll degrade if it gets warm. You'll have two doses, two syringes. Guard this with your life. It's something people will kill for. Do not tell anyone you have it or even know about it, not even the guards. Our secret, alright?"

She nods again, placing the syringe back in its case and closing it with a snap.

With my Star armed in more ways than one, I can all but ensure nothing and no one can separate us.

Mine is the only word that comes to mind.

Karalevine is mine.

CHAPTER 35

A PASSAGE FROM THE CONFISCATED JOURNALS OF GAVRIELLE ABRAXAS:

DAY 304: THEY'RE TRAINING ME TO FIGHT NOW, AND IT'S GOING WELL. YOU'D BE PROUD OF ME, FATHER. I CAN FIGHT EVEN BETTER THAN BEFORE. I HATE TO SAY IT, BUT THE GUY THEY HAVE TRAINING ME, ENNAR, IS GOOD, IMPRESSIVELY GOOD. NOT AS GOOD AS YOU, BUT HE'D GIVE YOU A RUN FOR YOUR MONEY. HE STILL KICKS MY ASS, BUT DON'T WORRY. I'LL GET HIM ONE OF THESE DAYS. I'LL GET ALL OF THEM. FOR YOU BOTH.

GAVRIELLE ABRAXAS

Ennar is smart but indubitably predictable, always has been. That's why it was easy to use Deimos's magic to distract him and whoever he's got guarding Kara's door with him. And they just ran off to deal with the comical mess we created specially for them. The SSPARROW guarding Jance's door has also been dealt with by Deimos. A sophisticated little game of cat and mouse.

"Now," I hiss, my SSPARROW uniform whining in the tense silence as Jance and me scurry up to Kara's door and knock impatiently.

Come on, Kara. Faster.

It takes everything in me not to bounce on my toes from nerves. Instead, I look up to the cameras and wave.

"Hello, Gav. Now get inside that door," Pacey says over comms. We managed to get back into some systems after Arianyte kicked us out, but it was nothing like what we had before our big hack.

A second later, the door opens, and Jance pushes his way inside, Kara gasping as I follow in.

I rip my helmet off immediately and smile. "Hey. We heard through the grapevine that Herkimer attacked you and Malakyte two days ago after I dropped you off. Are you okay?"

She looks good. No bruises or signs she's been restrained or hurt.

Jance steps towards Kara, but she simultaneously takes one back.

Fuck . . .

That has to feel like an arrow to the heart, his face failing to hold back the flash of pain. She's looking at him wearily, too. His bruises and swelling still haven't gone down from the beating he got for merely being suspected of participating in bringing Kara's memories back. But at least he's alive and only because Kara lied for him.

"Yeah," she finally says once the shock of us barreling in wears off. "We're fine."

We're fine?

She looks behind us at the door. "How'd you get in here?"

I smirk. "We're causing a bit of a commotion outside," I say confidently. "After Deimos was able to swindle a SSPARROW in his thrall, we threw the soldier's helmet back on and sent the poor guy running through the royal wing causing glorious havoc. That magic of his sure comes in handy."

"Oh," she says, unimpressed. "I thought I heard something out there."

I don't like the way this feels, but I reach out and ask for her Dezlar. She's a bit hesitant, but she gives it to me. She looks surprised when I insert a tiny drive into the charging port. "Pacey said we'll be able to communicate on an encrypted thread that Malakyte shouldn't be able to hack or even see if your phone is being monitored or is ever confiscated."

The drive beeps in less than fifteen seconds, and I rip it out.

When I hand the Dezlar back to Kara, she looks at me despairingly.

"You sure you're okay?" I ask.

We surprised her. That's all this is.

She opens her mouth, looks from me to Jance, then back to me. Pursing her lips, rigid body language, the scent of fear permeating off her shoulders. My chest begins to constrict. Something is wrong. "Yeah . . . I'm fine. It's just been a lot to take in."

I clear my throat, shifting my focus to Jance, and he's looking at his daughter like she's already lying in her grave. "So, you remember how you found Deimos and me in the prison cells?"

She pins me down with those eyes. "Yeah, and how that jerk used his magic on me *again*."

Good. She hasn't been Reconditioned a second time. I had to check. With Malakyte being so unpredictable, anything is possible. It would make sense for him to wipe the memory of us telling her what truly happened . . . So, why hasn't he?

"Well, did you ever wonder why we didn't bring Ardelle with us when we went down there to rescue him?"

Guilt flashes across her face. "I hadn't considered it, no . . . So, then why didn't you?"

I explain the collar he described to us, and how it'll basically blow her lover's head off if he as much as walks out of his cell.

"Have you ever heard Malakyte talking about any tech like that? Or possibly a key, or a place to store a key? Anything at all?"

Pacey wanted me to ask, wondering if she could possibly hack the tech around her brother's throat.

Again, Kara goes to speak but hesitates, eyes bobbing to Jance and away quickly. "No."

"You're lying."

My head snaps to Jance, his tone on the verge of *very pissed the fuck off*, if I'm reading him correctly. Like father, like daughter.

"He hasn't ever mentioned a collar like that, not even when he freed me from the one *you* put on me."

"Still pissed over that one, huh?" I joke, trying to dispel the tension, but it falls flat . . . I don't like that look she's giving me.

Jance ignores me. "Then, what are you hiding?"

"Nothing."

"Bullshit."

"What is your problem?"

"You're lying to me. That's my problem. You aren't a fucking liar."

"You don't know me!"

This isn't how this was supposed to go.

Jance steps into her space, but Kara doesn't back down, their height differences so drastic, it's comical. I'm sure that's what people think when watching her and I go toe to toe. "Yes, I do. You may not remember, but I know you well. So, I know you're hiding something. What is it? Don't lie for him."

She heaves a defeated sigh, shoulders slumping as she looks over to me for support. I can only give her a smile, but Jance is right.

She is keeping something from us. I can tell, too.

"Fine," she says, running a hand through her hair. "He showed me this special room. It's on this floor, and it's got a lot of important items inside, his possessions, mostly. He never told me about this new collar, but if there was a particular key or something for it, it's likely in there. Good luck getting in . . . It's impossible."

Dammit.

"That's the spot where I told the others I suspected that key would be hanging out," I tell Jance. "She's right—that room is impenetrable. Not even Pacey could hack it if she were right there."

Jance rakes his hand down his face, satisfied Kara fessed up. But what worries me was how reluctant she was to give up that information.

"You're not going to ask me to try and find it, are you?" she asks, genuinely afraid of the possibility.

It wouldn't be a bad idea . . .

"Even if we said that's the man you love being held in a living Hell down there?" I say, hating myself for connecting the dots she's refusing to connect for herself.

Because the more she knows about Ardelle . . . once she remembers she loves him, I'll never stand a chance.

Kara automatically looks to Jance for confirmation, and he nods. "Why do you think he's down there, forced to fight day after day? Why Malakyte brought you to that fight? He's throwing you in front of the man you love to taunt him like you're a prize he won in a bet."

Her face twists. "He . . . He wouldn't do that."

Disbelief and cynicism escape my lips in the form of a scoff that's a bit harsher than intended.

"Pretty sure that's exactly what he did."

She's overwhelmed and paces in her suite's tiny entryway; the room is a mirror image of the one I occupied for years on this very floor. It's still untouched. I checked. The kitchen here is off to the right, the couch, living room, and bed to the left, bathroom straight back. It's stupid, but I miss the bed in my suite. It was a good one.

"You told me that I love this other guy?" she asks again, her eyes misting. "But I can't . . . *I can't remember.*"

Those last three words are a whisper with all the power of a disruptor shot in a silent, haunted wood.

"Darling." Jance's voice has turned gentle, eyes softer. "You do love him. You love me. You love all of us, and this is going to end once we figure out how to return your memories from that machine, but we can't do that if you're keeping things from us. Do you not believe this happened?"

Jance has her pegged, and I'm with him. She's being evasive, and that isn't a good sign for us. And my gut twists, fearing why.

"I . . . I do. I just . . . I . . ."

Ahh, fuck me.

"Kara," I push, hating to see her eyes fill with tears. "You saw that crystal with your name on it. You know what he did to you. He violated you. He lied to you. He's still lying to you."

"I know, I just—" She taps her nails together rapidly, frustrated. "I just—I think he made a mistake. He's sorry. There's really no way we can all talk this out? Figure out a way to be together, all of us?"

My mouth falls to the floor.

"You've got to be fucking kidding me," I say, voice icy. "After everything that happened the other day, after everything you saw? With the crystals, the memory machine—shit, even the dragons and the truth about Zariya, you think he's just misunderstood? You're not that stupid, Kara."

"You weren't in the throne room the night Herkimer attacked us, Gav. His dad has been torturing him for *centuries*. He did it right in front of me. It isn't Malakyte's fault. I know he messed up, but he's learned his lesson. I can fix this between all of us if you just let me."

Jance curses, his hand scratching nervously at the stubble along his face, and I've never seen the man have any type of nervous tick before this moment.

I laugh bitterly. "We're so beyond having a conversation."

"Things can't genuinely be that bad. What if I arranged for us to talk and we could—"

"I'm sorry to interrupt you, Kara, but, no. He's done way too much. To me, to you, to the others, the Terrans and the Hijacked—the people you claim to care about—for us to simply let it all go so we can hold hands and be friends. No. And even if we all somehow miraculously agreed to that, he'd at minimum have us all Reconditioned at best, killed at worst. Is that what you want? For everyone you love to suffer or die? Because that's where this road you're going down leads."

She's the one breaking my heart, not the other way around, but with the way she looks at me, I might as well be the one crushing her soul with my bare hands.

"I can't see him doing that, Gav. He's not this monster you all think he is."

"What did he do to you?" I ask, my voice on the edge of rage. "What did he say? What story did he weave to convince you that he's somehow innocent here? Because when we left that room with the crystals—you know, the one that contains the memories he ripped out of your head and stuffed into one of those things—you were convinced. Jupiter's rings, Kara, you knew what happened."

"I'm not saying that I've forgiven what he's done or that I don't see it. I'm just asking if there's some possible way this can be salvaged. I still acknowledge that he messed up."

Jance roars, "Then, why are you defending him?"

Their glares clash, Kara's tears on the brink of falling. She's in denial. That's what this is. She'll come back, realize the truth.

She has to.

She *has to.*

 226

"I . . ."

Her chin quivers as a single tear falls to her cheek.

She loves him. That's what she can't say aloud, not to us. By the utter devastation on Jance's face, he's realizing the depths of her feelings for Malakyte, too. Likely coming to the same conclusion as I am—that we're fucked.

"You don't know him like I do," I say, stepping into her space and taking both her hands. "After the orphanage, I was Reconditioned, and they raised me, him and Narésteé both." Her face reflects surprise, but I keep going. I *will* make her understand. "What you've seen so far, that's the mask. The real Malakyte would scare the living shit out of you. That mask he wears is honed over centuries of cunning deception, and he's very good at playing whatever role he needs to in order to get what he wants. There is no redeeming someone like him. He's too far gone, done too much . . . and more than anyone, I understand how badly you want him to be the mask, I do. But that isn't him. Do you know me? Do you trust me?"

She nods, several more tears falling to the marble floor.

"Then, trust that I'm telling you the absolute truth about him. Whatever he said, whatever he did, whatever he promised or swore to change is nothing but a sophisticated manipulation to get you to stay with him and mistrust us. We're your family, Kara. You said you didn't have a family, but that isn't true. You do. It's us. Not him. *Us.*"

Me, I almost add, but I decline. She'll never love me . . . not like I love her.

Her eyes give her away.

I haven't convinced her.

"Do you even know whose side you're on?" I whisper, a fearful pulse hammering in my ears; even Jance's heart is thrashing.

Pacey's voice comes in on comms.

"You guys have to go. Now. Like right now, they're coming back."

I shake my head and growl over to Jance, "We've got to go."

I need to get him back to his room and then figure out what the fuck to do with this mess.

The man looks like I said I'd have to cut off his arm, but he recovers quickly. I let go of Kara's hands, and she takes a hesitant step toward me as I turn to the door.

"Wait," she says as the door slides open, her father and I both looking back toward her, our eyes a haunted reflection of our predicament. "I'm on the Hijacked's side."

The smile comes, then falls in the space of a second. She's doing the right thing for the wrong reason, but she's still in there somewhere.

"Then, you're on the wrong side if you want to save them, and I'll prove it to you. Just ask yourself who stands to benefit when they go missing?"

Pacey yells in my ear to *go*.

I slip out of her room, ready to bolt.

Jance, however, hesitates in the doorway. He reaches back to her, his hand taking hers as she watches him with confused, emotional eyes. Jance doesn't want any of us to reveal who he is because he believes it'll expose Kara's biggest weakness to Malakyte, and she'll be found out. It's a risk because the father card may be the only one we'll have left to play. "You're mine, kid. No matter what, you'll always be mine. I'll always love you. Remember that."

Her eyes widen in shock.

He slams the outside panel, shutting her door and closing her off from us.

We dash down the hall back toward his room, neither of us speaking. We both know the long and short of it.

Without Kara, my people are likely to be enslaved forever.

Without Kara, Jance loses his only child.

Without Kara, our side doesn't stand a chance, and the war goes to Arianyte.

CHAPTER 36

"He really fucked with her mind, didn't he?" Deimos asks.

All of us besides Jance are safely tucked away in a room graciously carved out for us in the Tribute sector. The space is a tight fit for the six of us, but we have access to the showers. The single bed can fit two, maybe three of us, but I could sleep standing up if I had to, so I don't fight for it.

We have much bigger problems.

Pacey heard the entire debacle with Kara on comms, relaying the situation to the others by the time I returned. "You have to understand that you really believe the lie," she says, sitting sideways on the bed with her back leaning against the wall. "She's brainwashed. It isn't her fault. The lie—the illusion—feels as real as your lives are to you. Not to mention the whole dynamic of a toxic relationship that they've got going on. We can't be frustrated by the fact she doesn't automatically believe us when we say her life is a lie. Malakyte is slick, too. He sells it really well. If we get frustrated with her at this point, then we're victim blaming. So, I don't want to hear it."

Sylo muses, "But why can't she just leave?"

Sighing, Pacey says, "Because it's never that simple. Why did Ardelle try to go back to our parents even after we had left? Why did you stay in contact with your dad, Sylo, when he wouldn't quit his job in SSPARROW leadership even after the first Titan Games debacle happened and I was missing? It's simple for us to say, 'Well just leave,' but it's easier said than done. Malakyte has two things working in his favor. First, he's corrupted Kara's OS. The Reconditioning has completely rewired not only the last six months of her life but her identity, too. She's *his*. From lonely rebel to soon-to-be queen of Arianyte. Malakyte is the malware in her mind. She isn't choosing him because she wants to. She's choosing him because she's initiating the corrupted code he's implanted in her mind."

The room is silent, the weight hitting us.

"What's OS mean?" Sylo asks, taking his shoes off.

"Operating system, dumbass," Deimos snarls.

Sylo shrugs, hopping onto the bed to sit at Pacey's side, but her eyes are haunted and unfocused.

"And the second?" I ask, curious about her unique perspective on this.

Her voice is even sadder when she says, "The second, Gavrielle, is even more detrimental than the first, believe it or not. Malakyte, him—his love, their relationship—is like a malicious host software. He's created it so she can't function without him being in her system, hooking her on their dynamic together. The attention, the power, the connection, the crash, the danger, the taboo of having what you know you shouldn't . . . all of it on a repeat program running day in and day out. It's the kind of code that feels like love because it shatters you in a way that feels familiar because Kara doesn't know anything other than being hurt by those she loves. Not until we came along, that is . . ."

She's right on target.

"And you, Gavrielle," she clarifies, "she was loved right by you. That's why she fought so hard to find you again. You were the only thing in her world that didn't hurt her."

My throat tightens, and I can't find the words to respond, but I nod to Pacey. She understands the complexity of a toxic relationship. We both do.

"We were foolish to believe we could simply tell her what happened and that would be enough. Without her memories, this is an uphill battle," Ahren says.

"But we all love and care about her—that's got to mean something, right?" Saris counters.

"We act like love matters," I say bitterly. "Even being in love can't fix things that are too broken to be mended. Love doesn't matter when the other person refuses to see you. Love doesn't mean anything when fate has conspired to keep you apart. Love doesn't matter, and it can't fix, do, or change anything. All love does is make you stupid sometimes."

"You know you just called yourself stupid, right?" Sylo jabs, and I realize how obvious I've made my love for Kara to everyone. Guess it wasn't really a secret, anyway.

"Yeah, I know. And so is your face."

Deimos cocks his head, large ears swaying slightly. "You're all stupid. And we better figure out a plan fast because this empire is coming down with or without her. Either as an ally or as an enemy. It may just have to go down in the way we want the least, but it has to happen."

"Jance will never agree to that," Saris argues.

She's right. Neither will I.

Deimos glares at her. "The Ringer doesn't speak for me."

"*Jance* speaks for his daughter, and if you don't want him allying on her side and adding another enemy, then you better not draw that line." Saris pins Deimos with her stare, not backing down.

If we can't get Kara back to our side, loyalties will be tested, and our entire team will be ripped apart. They all have loyalty to each other. To Starseed and Ringer, to parent and child, to brother and sister, to lover and friend . . . Fuck, this is going to be an A-grade shitshow, and I rake my hand over my face, the back of my head butting up against the wall.

What do I do?

Will I find myself connected to a family only for it to be ripped away from me like every other family I've ever gotten close to has? Plus, if they find out about the deal I made with Malakyte to save my people in exchange for twenty years of my life or to swap Kara for time served and my planet's sovereignty . . . I don't even want to think about what would happen.

Sylo slides back into the conversation. "Can we please talk about the dragons you found? Because I'm still confused about how they're just sitting in the basement." He chuckles, a bit bewildered.

Deimos growls at him. "Oh, great, now they're never going to shut up."

"The dragons?" Sylo asks, confused as he looks at Pacey beside him.

"Oh!" Pacey gasps, looking around, eyes wide. "Did you just hear that voice?"

Deimos groans. "Here we go . . . Feena, no. Get out of my head!"

"Are they communicating with us telepathically?" Sylo blanches, going pale.

"This is your fault, you stupid shit!" Deimos points at Sylo.

"What the fuck did I do?"

"You brought them up, and now they're never going to fuck off."

Pacey giggles, while Saris and Ahren appear confused.

I hear nothing.

"Someone, please explain to me what's happening?" Ahren asks politely.

Deimos grumbles and rubs his eyes. "The dragons are connected to the Starseeds, just like we're all connected in this tapestry of fuckery when it comes to the Elendrils. With enough focus on the dragons and close enough proximity, that bond solidifies. And since we're all on this ship together and we ran into them the other day, there's no getting far enough away. They're in our heads now. Link established."

"Yet, they talk with their mouths, too," I clarify, the group nodding in understanding.

Pacey asks, "Well, they sound like they want to help us, so why is that a bad thing?"

Deimos answers sharply. "Because they won't help us." He sighs, tucking his head between his knees as he sits across the room from me, leaning against a table leg. "That's why Zariya died—because of Project Nightfall and these stubborn, judge, jury, and executioner of all things sanctimonious dragons. Project Nightfall was supposed to tell Zariya what the secret to unlocking the Elendril crystals was, but it dissolved into an utter debacle where you all ended up dead. The dragons refused—absolutely refused—to tell her that secret.

"What they did tell her, was the devious, horrendous, terrifying truth of Arianyte. The dragons see themselves as guardians, protecting the galaxy from evil and bullshit. The crystals are the weapons, and the dragons are the peacemakers, balance and all that good and evil shit. They told her about a doomsday weapon Arianyte was on the verge of finalizing and that if it were to be completed, it would wipe out the galaxy. She loved Malakyte, and for a long time, we all did, too.

"But once she began to push back on him about this weapon and other policies, he changed. He wanted the dragon's secrets and didn't want her to discuss this weapon or how he ran Arianyte or used the Starseeds, and then she found out about the Silent Breath. It all unraveled after that. Zariya destroyed a core component of the doomsday weapon, blasted the truth about the Silent Breath to the galaxy, and we ran.

"But running, we discovered, was futile. You all know what happened after that. I'm not discussing it further. You can put the pieces together on your own of how awful that was to witness."

I've never heard him speak that much about what happened in our past life, and from what the others have told me, they haven't either. The piercing silence after he speaks does all the talking for us.

But I have to say something.

"Trinity said she heard chatter about some weapon being assembled," I say, choosing my words carefully as fear creeps up my spine, straightening it to iron. "Did she talk to you about it after Kara and I left the other day?"

My Starseed shakes his head. "There wasn't time. But with the tech she gave us, we can beam basic communications down to them. We need to ask. I was never apprised of the specifics back then, so even if Trinity does know, I wouldn't be able to identify it. Only Zariya knew."

Pacey sighs heavily, tilting her head as she looks at Sylo with haunted eyes. He kisses her forehead affectionately, communicating something none of us can hear. Naresteé wouldn't be happy if she saw that look, not happy at all.

Pacey says to no one in particular, "If she destroyed it then, it's destroyed for good, right? I mean, they've had all this time to make a new one, why now? It's got to be a coincidence."

Pacey's words die as Deimos and I stiffen in unison, our eyes locking.

"Did you hear that?" Deimos asks, voice nervous.

I strain my ears, their pointed tips giving me an edge over the others, but Deimos's hearing is still the best.

All of us tense.

Screaming, heavily leaden boot steps, and the firing of disruptors sounds exactly like they had that evening at the orphanage . . . the clenching anxiety in my chest identical, too.

SSPARROWs.

 234

"They're here!" I shout, jumping to my feet. "They found us somehow."

"Or we were ratted out," Sylo suggests, jumping up and helping Pacey off the bed. "I knew this place was too good to be true."

"Oh, right," Deimos argues, picking up a bunch of his stuff, "you really argued against this hiding place. You were the first in the showers."

"You should've been first because you stank like a stars damned rat!"

"You want another ass beating?"

I growl before sliding my new SSPARROW helmet on. "Shut up!"

Then darkness encompasses my entire vision, the interface automatically turning on. Thank the stars I was still in this suit after speaking with Kara.

But Sylo isn't done as we all scramble, shoving our items in bags and hectically collecting the stuff we need to survive. "Not to keep going, but has anyone thought that Kara may have sold us out? The timing is hella suspicious."

"She wouldn't do that," I argue. "She doesn't even know where we are."

The screaming is obvious now, even through the helmet the banging and throwing of items, people running away, trying to escape.

"Let's go!" Saris runs to the door, and it slides open, chaos running up and slapping us each in the face.

Tributes are running in all directions, terrified of being caught and questioned as SSPARROWs give chase like rabid dogs, foaming at the mouth to catch their prey. We're the prey. Malakyte isn't fucking around. There are dozens upon dozens of his soldiers down here.

"They're down there!" a Tribute yells from somewhere.

"Fuck me," Deimos growls.

"I'll illusion us. Just stay close to me," I say, my magic bursting through my blood as it sizzles along my skin. The familiar ebbing of its power comes to life as my comrades instantly turn into the most average-looking Terrans I can muster. Making us all invisible is too much for me. I can only do it to myself. "Act like I'm taking you in."

They do, and we make it down three turns in the hallways when I stop, Pacey bumping into my back.

I whip around. "Please tell me one of you has the helmet."

Their silence is all I need to hear for my gut to drop to my ass.

"I'll go back," Deimos offers. "It's the safest."

Sylo argues. "You stick out like a whore in church, you'll be discovered before you even make it back, you dipshit."

Fuck, he's right. My magic won't carry once he leaves me.

I turn to face them. "There's only three ways out of this sector, and we're going to need your magic to get through, Deimos. We're close to one, I'll get you the rest of the way then you get everyone out, and I'll go back. Pray they haven't gotten to our room yet."

Deimos nods. "Then, let's move!"

Without looking too obvious, I fake-escort them to the exit where at least ten SSPARROW wait, guarding the threshold, a big group of Terran Tributes screaming to be let out.

"I need eye contact," Deimos hisses through clenched teeth. "Kinda hard when they're all wearing masks."

I'm about to tell him to find a way, when a Terran begins punching himself in the face, eyes blazing green and causing everyone to look his way. Another man punches the man beside him, resulting in a tit for tat. It happens again with a pair of women as they pull each other's hair and slap and scratch. Then the chaos blows up, the Tributes fighting one another, shouts and hollers and curses, the SSPARROWs panicking. Tributes go for the guards, and they're forced to interact with this shitshow as it explodes into utter madness.

"Go!" I yell, taking them out of the sector clear of soldiers or checkpoints. I shove my bags into Sylo's arms, but the SSPARROWs are too distracted. "Now!"

I don't look back as I turn and run. I think I hear Pacey shouting something from behind me, but I don't catch it. I'm sliding around a corner in a blink, dodging Tributes and soldiers as I bolt for our room. I have to get there in time. I *have to*. If they get that helmet, we lose our only leverage. When Kara puked in it the other day, I almost died, of all the ones! Rest assured, nobody wants to wear it now, even after we cleaned it several times.

I see the open door to our room. Good. No guards outside.

Dashing forward, my heart races in anticipation as I grip the doorframe and slide in.

I skid to a stop, as if an imaginary brick wall slammed down to block me.

Ennar, with his suit glowing in yellow accents amongst six additional blue SSPARROWs standing in our room, is holding the helmet in his metal hands.

Well . . . fuck me.

I course-correct my posture to honor the loyal soldier I once was. "I was sent to assist."

Thank the stars the voice modulator was already turned on.

They all watch me a heartbeat too long, beads of sweat dripping down my neck.

Ennar tucks the helmet under his arm, squaring his hips. "You were always the best of us, Gavrielle. Although I'm not sure how you've gotten so sloppy over the past several weeks. Perhaps it's the company you keep?"

How the fuck does he know it's me?

Soldiers tighten their grips on their disruptor rifles, readying, especially when I don't respond.

My pulse slams in my ears, my vision narrowing even further within my helmet. Can I take all six? If Ennar wasn't here, I could easily kick their asses like it was just another day of the week. But he's Malakyte's head SSPARROW for a reason. He also taught me a lot of what I know, so there's that.

"I'm sure Malakyte would take you back," Ennar comments slyly, making sure to turn his voice modulator off. "If you got on your knees and begged him, that is."

Now his voice scrapes like boots on gravelly dirt, laced with a smugness that makes me want to punch him in the face.

"You mean what you enjoy doing? I'm good."

He laughs. "Gavrielle, Gavrielle . . ." Tsking, he steps forward, the other guards remaining where they stand. I could bolt. The door behind me is still open. But the helmet . . . "Using the suits was smart. I'll give you that. But hadn't I taught you better than to leave a piece of your hair sticking out of your helmet? If you cut that mop, I likely wouldn't have known it was you. And that pitiful entrance you made—a dead giveaway."

Shit. Why didn't anyone tell me my hair was sticking out? In the rush, I didn't notice it. Rookie fucking mistake.

Ennar's close enough now that my exit is blocked. If I bolt for it, he'd easily impede my escape, and that'll only leave my side open.

"I know about the deal you made with Malakyte, the one you made to save your people. Prince Gavrielle Abraxas of Nyktos. A cold planet, far from the host sun. Makes sense why your bodies run so hot. I always found warm-bloods to be . . . quite disgusting, personally. When I slice them open, they're always clammy, steaming meat sacks that make my skin crawl every time I cleave flesh from bone or organ from sweaty, moist bodies, but if Malakyte asked me to, I'd push down my revulsion and dole out your punishment personally."

Malakyte's favorite for a reason.

"What the fuck is your point?"

 238

"Oh, I don't have one. I'm just stalling until you decide to come for this helmet. We don't need to play semantics about why you came back, do we?"

I sigh.

We're here, so we're doing this.

I pounce like a pyropume, a flame-breathing cat-creature from my home-world.

My blades are with the others, so I use my size to gain the upper hand, going for his knees rather than the obvious—the helmet.

It works.

Ennar is immediately thrown off balance, the helmet flying up in the air, and he tries to catch himself with his arms, but the other SSPARROWs leap for it like a pack of starving wolves.

Keeping my knees bent and feet planted, I torque at the waist as I bring Ennar down, but it's the others I've got to worry about.

They're on me—on the helmet—and I dive for it right as the nearest guard is about to snatch it in his metal claws.

I got it!

Rolling in a somersault, I whack into the bed frame as I land on my feet, knees bent, but the helmet is in my hand, and I stand—

All of them jump me before my next breath.

Four SSPARROW birds tackle me to my stomach. One pulls at my feet, another trying to rip the helmet from my fingers.

He's going to have to pry it from my cold, dead hands because *I won't let go*!

Ennar's suit clanks as he crouches in front of my face, ripping my own helmet off. I bare my fangs at him.

"I should take this one, too, you know, *just in case*," he muses, handing it to a soldier before he shifts his attention to the helmet that's quickly being ripped away from me. The one we can't afford to lose.

Ennar squats, the other soldier letting him take over. It isn't long before he puts his weight into wrenching the helmet free, and I lose it immediately.

It's over.

The other SSPARROWs heave me up to my knees, wrenching my arms behind my back to cuff them in steel, my hair a disheveled mess as I make it as difficult as possible for all five of them.

"I applaud your effort," Ennar says. "And nice takedown. I was impressed. Like I said, beg for your life and he'll probably spare it. Unless he's in a bad mood. Then, you're dead." He nods to the only soldier who isn't keeping me wrangled. "Get the prince on the line. Tell him we caught the traitor."

"Sir." The errand boy exits the room.

I'm tugged to my feet, the SSPARROWs nearly toppling as I stand to my full height, and I make a break for it . . . until Ennar rams the butt-end of his disruptor straight into my gut.

"You could have gone a bit harder on that one," I wheeze, damn near falling to my knees.

Asshole.

"Let's go." Ennar waves. "He'll guide us to the others once we're through with his very long, very painful interrogation."

Ennar leads, and the moment he meets the threshold, another SSPARROW slides right into his path—knocking him square in the face.

I don't think—I just act.

With adrenaline pulsing through my veins, I swing my head back like a wrecking ball, colliding with the front of a soldier's helmet. He curses, and the others blanch, my leg coming up high as I kick the closest one behind me in the abs, sending him flying. I turn and ram my shoulder into the soldier coming at me, and we go down, the bed frame shattering.

The SSPARROW who whacked Ennar is still busy with him. It's one of the others, but who? Fuck, if only I wasn't cuffed I could—*oh shit, no time!*

A SSPARROW dives toward me, but my foot collides with him in the nick of time, the guy's back cracking at a bad angle as I strain my thigh and kick him off. The one on the wrecked bed with me brings his arm around my throat.

"Not the type of choke play I'm into, man!"

My body thrashes, and I'm like a bull in a china shop as my vision goes spotty from lack of oxygen, twisting and turning until, finally, I elbow him hard enough that he releases my throat, and I consume all that deprived air with a gasp.

Yet there's no time as I see Ennar bolting from the room—*with* the helmet.

"No!" I seethe, and with the ally SSPARROW knocked down, it allows Ennar to flee unimpeded.

I heave myself up, arms still locked in cuffs, but the remaining soldier drags my uniform by the lip at the back of my neck, and I'm dragged right back down again. Whoever of my teammates is in disguise gets up, rushes over, and curb stomps the SSPARROW choking me. It takes them four hard strikes of their booted heel before the tension releases around my throat, and I twist out of his arms and into a sitting position.

Breathing heavily, I notice a tense silence permeating through the trashed room laden with unconscious, metal bodies.

Deimos's voice comes through his helmet, angry.

"Great job, genius you, we lost our only fucking ace in this war, but you've got bigger problems. I heard everything. So, we're all going to have a nice, long chat about what the fuck you're really doing here, *prince*."

Well, fuck . . .

CHAPTER 37

It's as if I'm being choked as I walk back into the throne room, but since Arianyte's council, the Council of Exstacé, is here and wants to meet with me, I have no choice but to stroll through these doors again.

Malakyte doesn't appear to be bothered as he sits on his throne, his demeanor the stoic, icy prince, strong chin held high, eyes sharp as daggers, black outfit pressed to impress with silver accent jewelry and threads to match. He has me in black, too, in a full-length gown with hand embroidered beading in an elegant pattern in a mix of Marigold and Yellow Cake.

I don't know what to do with myself as I stand next to him, awkwardly distributing my weight on my aching feet. Where's my throne?

My eyes widen at the Council when they walk in.

They're so alien.

I thought I was used to seeing extraterrestrials up here, especially when being a Terran is the minority, but these extras are something else.

One alien in particular has an air of authority that demands my attention above the others. Her skin is Snowball White, and she wears her bald head like a crown. Black brows, lips, and a tattooed symbol on her forehead stand out like a fly trapped in milk.

One is a cat-like person with massive, fur-covered ears. Another looks freakishly close to the Reptilians that fight with the rebels, but his body is more Terran shaped.

The scariest one stands Sky-Fae still in a hooded cloak, shade Black Mist. His colossal almond eyes resemble the Grays, giant and menacing in Jet Black. Yet a deep line cracks his face straight down the middle, other wrinkles and folds cascading along a dramatically elongated mouth that send shivers down my spine. Next to him is an aquatic-appearing extra whose skin is a gorgeous blend of Tropical Teal and Aquamarine. Beside her stands another robed figure. He's got a furry body, and his miss-matched colored eyes reminds me of the street dog, Sadie, in Zarmenia. I'm sure someone is feeding the street dog without me there to do it.

Malakyte introduces me to them, and it's awkward as all hell as they watch me like I'm the freak show. "It's my honor to introduce my fiancée, Karalevine. Once crowned, we'll all be working closely, and I hope our relationship can blossom into one of . . . cooperation."

They talk about Selenyte's death and of the person who killed her.

Ardelle. They're planning on killing him, but I'm guessing he didn't do it. I'm supposed to love this guy . . . ? A man I can't *remember.* It's as if this man is a ghost, haunting my days, but each time I try to connect, I'm met with nothing. Even so, I don't want him to die, so hearing this is twisting my stomach into knots. Intellectually, I understand what Malakyte has done to me . . . It's different feeling it, being overcome by it. Add the way Gavrielle and Jance looked at me today—*stars*. This sickening feeling is suffocating.

Malakyte and I were eating together earlier when we were notified they had captured Gav, and it took everything for me to act normal. My relief when news came twenty minutes later that he had escaped was overwhelming. What does that say about my loyalty? Why do my thoughts always circle back to Gavrielle when they should be going to the man I love yet can't remember? A man locked away because of me.

Malakyte and the Council talk for a long time, and once they leave, I finally take a full breath of air and let it out. I sit on the edge of Malakyte's throne, and he wraps his cold arm around my waist.

"You did well," he praises, knuckles brushing against the back of my arm. I break out in goose bumps. "They're finical and obnoxious, but they'll submit. They get off on making a fuss over nonsense."

The door opens again, and my chest tightens, fearing that it's Herkimer, but I sag in relief when it's the head maid. She's a plump woman with Fire Brick-colored skin and Nightingale hair chopped into an unruly pixie cut, and she always walks like she's twenty minutes late to something. Scurrying along behind her is a young woman I recognize as one of Malakyte's servants. She's like a Terran, but her pale skin has an odd brown textured banding that skates all throughout her body.

"The one you requested, sir," the older one says.

I believe her name is Marb. Behind Marb, the young girl stands with her shoulders drooped, head bowed, eyes to the floor.

"Anndeena," Marb says, voice biting and eyes bulging.

The young girl scrambles to bow deeper.

"Anndeena," Malakyte echoes, saying her name curiously.

"Y-Yes, sir . . ." she squeaks out.

 244

Stars. He isn't going to bite her.

Malakyte uncrosses, then recrosses his legs, one hand still petting me like I'm this throne cat. "You've been instructed to clean and organize my office in a specific way, yet I continue finding inaccuracies. As I'm sure you can imagine, I'm extremely busy. I shouldn't have to delegate simple tasks that staff should already be familiar with. I was told you do this on purpose to . . . annoy me. Is that true?"

Is he fucking serious?

Anndeena shakes her head vigorously. "No, sir. I don't. I'm sorry. I'll be sure to have your office exactly as you like it. I really need this job, my family . . . My parents are sick, you see. I'll be better."

He sighs. "Karalevine, should we dismiss her? She's been given ample opportunity to do her job adequately and has failed."

I can tell she wants to say something, but she holds her tongue.

I take my turn to sigh. "I'll take her. Put her on my rotation. I don't care how my stuff is laid out."

Malakyte's head turns like a serpent toward me. "So, you believe she should be substituted rather than dismissed?"

"Yes."

"Return to your duties," he tells the servants without looking at them. "Anndenna, you will transfer to Karalevine, but I will be watching you closely. Understand?"

Anndenna nods and thanks him profusely, and they scurry off, with Marb nearly shoving her out.

I scrunch my brows at Malakyte. "Was that truly necessary?"

He curls his blue-tinted lips up into a smirk. "It's necessary to see how you logic through problems, large or insignificant."

"Oh, so this was all a test for me, then?"

He shrugs, pulling me off the throne's arm and into his lap. I might as well have landed in a pile of snow. "Perhaps. I'll be candid. I didn't expect you to take her. So honorable. You do have a bit of light in you. It's halfway adorable." He says the last bit like it's an enigma he can't quite solve. "She's one girl, why does she matter?"

I scoff, gliding my hands through his coarse hair. "I'm just *one girl*, too. Imagine what could've happened if someone tossed me aside. Or I became one of the Hijacked . . . One girl can start a revolution, birth transformation in a million different ways. One girl can change the world. You don't have to be cruel when it costs you nothing to do so."

"But kindness is weakness."

A shiver shoots up my spine. I'm sure it's from the cold. "It's mercy. That is strength, just a different kind."

He hums, unsure, the sound vibrating in his chest.

I mean, he did keep her—that's progress. I can show him he doesn't have to rely on what his father taught him. Malakyte can be better. The others are wrong about him. He *can* change.

I'll make sure of it.

CHAPTER 38

DAY 359: THE PRINCE ISN'T AS BAD AS I THOUGHT . . . HE AND NARESTEÉ HAVE BEEN GOOD TO ME. BUT HOW AM I SUPPOSED TO SURVIVE IN THIS PLACE—WITH THEM—AFTER EVERYTHING THEY'VE DONE? AFTER MALAKYTE TOOK YOU BOTH FROM ME? I WANT TO KILL HIM HALF THE TIME, BUT HE DOESN'T TREAT ME AS AWFULLY AS I THOUGHT HE WOULD. AM I BETRAYING YOU BY ADAPTING TO THIS NEW LIFE? HOW DO I LIVE WITH MYSELF?

GAVRIELLE ABRAXAS

After finding a safe place to hide far from the Tribute sector, Deimos spilled the beans on my little secret.

"So, let me get this right," Pacey says, pacing beside a giant, noisy boiler humming in the room we chose, the lighting red and eerie. "Arianyte took you from the orphanage, Reconditioned you, and once you had completely forgotten about Kara, the first thing you remembered is having a conversation with Malakyte about your future. Is that how this all began?"

I nod, leaning against the door with my ankles crossed, my suit discarded in a pile next to me on the floor. The others watch my every move. I can't blame them . . .

Pacey continues, holding her chin as she paces the confined room. "Twenty years of your life in exchange for your planet's sovereignty? Also, the whole 'you being a prince' thing really throws me, Gavrielle."

"I know," I blurt. "And since my parents were killed by Malakyte, I'm technically the king . . ." They all hiss or laugh . . . or scowl. "But I can't be the king of a world that's occupied, so, in actuality, I'm neither."

Deimos asks, "Malakyte knew this when he took you?"

"Malakyte figured out who I was quickly after the orphanage. I'm the splitting image of my father," I say. "My father and he had bad blood. Malakyte had come to planet Nyktos and was immediately met with force. We never submitted like Terrans had. We won our war. After that failure, Malakyte set his sights on Earth. Knowing what was going to befall the people of this planet, my parents took me and their best soldiers and followed the prince to this solar system. They wanted to help—to save them. Right before the Devouring Accords were signed, my parents got into a physical confrontation with Malakyte . . ."

Despite the boiler's consistent thrumming, the silence rings hollow in the air. "He killed them both . . . I knew something was wrong when they never came back. I ended up at the orphanage by accident. Someone found me wandering the streets a few days later. I was looking for them. Eventually, the orphanage was taken over by Arianyte, and I was stranded here, the last of my bloodline, behind enemy lines. I couldn't tell anyone. Not even Kara knows."

"So, once they Reconditioned you, you were told your planet was once again under attack by Arianyte?" Pacey asks, and I nod.

"Not under attack—occupied. Arianyte had full control. After the first wave with Malakyte, my people couldn't hold off the second attack. My species wasn't advanced technologically. The only reason my parents and I made it to Earth in the first place was from a stolen Arianyte spaceship. As the lone survivor of my royal line, Malakyte made me a deal. Twenty years. Serve him, make myself useful, and I can go home to a free world. Why wouldn't I say yes?"

Ahren interjects softly. "When he ordered you to find and bring him Kara in the Titan Games in exchange for your time-debt to be wiped clean and your planet's freedom guaranteed, you did it, didn't you?"

There's only disgust on my tongue.

"Yes." No sugarcoating the truth. "But the moment my memories returned in the maze, I remembered her. I'll never forget the rush of emotions that literally brought me to my knees. It was . . . incredible, but I was also in an impossible situation, forced to make a snap decision on whose loyalty I was going to align myself with—my own people hanging in the balance. I did everything I could to get Kara off that dais, but she was determined to come up here and confront Malakyte and get Pacey back. I couldn't stop her."

Deimos snorts. "Yeah, we know how much of a stubborn brat she can be."

A few chuckles. She can be . . . but she's got sharp edges for a reason. She doesn't mean to cut.

Pacey pins me with a stare that would rival one of her brother's arrows. "Why didn't you just tell us, Gav?"

My chest tightens. I sigh loudly, shame warming my cheeks, and I rip my stare away from her. Here it comes. The inevitable shattering of what I love.

"I didn't want you to mistrust me. My past with them makes me a liability. I didn't want you to look at me the way you're doing right now. Like I'm going to betray you because I still love them."

Might as well get it all out on the table.

Her eyes soften.

"It isn't what happened to you that's the issue, Gav. It isn't your fault. And I understand your conflicting feelings about them, I really do. The problem is that you lied to us about it and who you really are."

"And we can't trust that you're not secretly working for them, either," Deimos adds.

Sylo gives his two cents when he says, "Or that you'll hand us over to them in exchange for yourself."

Anybody else?

"I know."

They're right. I wouldn't trust me, either.

"Why'd you go and see Naresteé the other day?" Deimos asks.

Everyone's head whips in his direction as he stands in his SSPARROW uniform, arms crossed.

This one is easy.

"To beg for Kara's memories back," I say. "It was pointless."

"You saw her?" Pacey asks, looking bewildered. "What did she say? Did she ask about me?"

Sylo snarls. "Why does it matter if she did? That woman is a witch."

An understanding flashes between Pacey and me. Nobody except the two of us can truly understand the complexity that comes with these relationships. Of loving someone you also hate, of seeing so much good in a person while also knowing they've done so much bad, too.

Deimos walks into my space, pointing at me as he gives me a once-over with a scowl, and says, "One more lie, and we're done. Got it?"

I want to peel my gaze from him, but doing so would be like Velcro stuck in honey. I'm also just as much of a stubborn ass as he is.

"There isn't any," I assure. "Yet I have to admit I suspect Malakyte will do whatever he can to try and use my people and my home-world against me—against *us*."

Deimos crosses his arms again. "Which makes you a liability."

He's right.

"I can go back," I muse. "Try to get Kara out from the inside."

"He'll have Naresteé Recondition you again," Pacey says quickly. "If not Kara and Jance again, too. No. You stay. We want you to stay. You're one of us. Just . . . don't feel like you have to keep secrets, Gavrielle. They don't suit you."

She's right, and I wouldn't be lying if their response didn't light something in my heart.

Sylo yawns, taking a seat on the hard floor. "What are we going to do about Kara? And Ardelle? And the helmet! I forgot about that . . . can't believe we lost it. Can't believe she barfed in it. Stars." He laughs, but it sounds more bitter than comical.

Pacey walks up and sits next to him. "At least he didn't get Gavrielle. Deimos over here rescued his Ringer. Such a big softy under all that asshole." She beams at him with the biggest smile I've ever seen her give, the biggest smile I've seen Deimos receive—ever.

He scowls and bares his fangs, turning away to find the farthest corner he can squeeze himself into.

Time is ticking, and we're losing.

Yet this family wasn't taken from me, even after what I've done. I'll keep them safe at all costs, but I'm terrified Kara is going to be the thing standing between me and them.

CHAPTER 39

MISS KARALEVINE RUZZ WILL NOT BE RETURNING TO
EARTH. THE ARIANYTE EMPIRE HAS PAINSTAKINGLY
ENSURED HER SAFETY AND COMFORT REGARDLESS OF HER
BEHAVIOR IN THE TITAN GAMES. ARIANYTE ASSURES THE
PUBLIC THAT SHE IS ALIVE AND UNHARMED. MISS RUZZ
REMAINS IN THE CUSTODY OF THE EMPIRE.

KARALEVINE RUZZ

"You have a surprise for me . . . *down here?*" I ask Malakyte as the elevator opens into the prison sector.

He doesn't know I've already been down here, so I look around in pretend awe.

"One I've been dying to give you." He places a hand on my shoulder and walks beside me as we pass the half dozen SSPARROWs and begins taking me down the dark, musky halls. I note the scrapes and bruises along Malakyte's knuckles. "Consider it an early wedding gift."

The prison smells rancid, and it's cold as we travel farther and farther down. I wonder if he's going to throw me into one of these cells because he's figured out I've been talking with Gavrielle and the others, that I've been sniffing around. Perhaps Ardelle and I will be cellmates, and I can finally get to know the guy I'm supposed to love. I look for his cell, but I don't see him as we pass by one after the other. So many questions, so much fear shooting up my spine with every step deeper into this Hell.

This doesn't feel right.

"I don't want to be down here," I say, slowing my pace, too afraid of who he may have caught and why he'd bring me to them.

Malakyte finally stops, angling toward me as I lurk a few feet back.

In silence, we stand there, the lighting so dark the shadows cling to him as if he were their master all along.

He informs me we've arrived.

My eyes dart toward the cell door he points to.

This place, this dark, endless place. It's exactly like that void in my nightmares. I hadn't been dreaming of it much, not since . . .

Not since those eyes in the shade Violet Sky found me, shoving that dark place away.

Yet, here . . . it's as if I've dropped directly into one of those nightmares . . . but now, it's real.

These cube cells are the exact same as the cube within my subconscious prison. Unlike the prisoners down here, it's my memories that are locked away in the dark.

My memories stolen by the man who says he loves me . . . How ironic. I know he loves me, and I know he Reconditioned me. These two equal yet separate facts are a contradiction that fry my brain cells—and shoots such fear through my blood like I've just plummeted through an ice-crusted river.

I know what it truly means . . . but I don't want to face it. I want to save Malakyte and bring him and the others together like we were meant to be, but reality is pushing against my goals, challenging me at every turn.

He's looking at me like he knows all my secrets and lies. Fuck, I need to calm down. He can read me far too easily.

Malakyte angles himself to the cell's door, a card unlocking it. As it opens, it's nothing but a gaping maw of a horrific monster gluttonous to eat me alive.

Walking over to me, Malakyte positions himself at my back and pushes me forward. His insistence nips at my every step until we reach the threshold.

"I can't," I whisper.

Firm hands rest on both shoulders, his freezing breath on my ear like a snowstorm sweeping off the mountainside.

"You can," he swears. "Step inside."

I push on him, slamming into his hard, frigid chest, my own back covered in sweat.

"No . . ."

The dark chokes me with a spindly, icy hand wrapped around my throat in a death grip.

"Your heart is racing, Karalevine. Do not fear the dark. You *are* the dark."

When I release my breath, it's shaky and loud, echoing off the utter silence of this prison cell.

This darkness can't hold you. I hear Gavrielle's voice in my head. His confident, strong, steady voice. I'd give anything to have him here in this moment, for his touch and his safety and *him*.

Tears sting my eyes, the fear all encompassing. I feel so broken, my grip on reality is a weak tether that will snap at any moment. Was I like this before my memories were taken, or has Malakyte ruined me? I have no rational fear for this darkness, yet it's choking me.

Pushing me forward, Malakyte doesn't yield.

What if this isn't someone else's cell? What if it's *my* cell?

The epiphany causes my crystal to light up the space in a Fuchsia Haze, and I fight him now, physically pushing and shoving to get out and away, but he blocks me.

 254

"Karalevine." My name is a thunderclap, stunning me into stillness. "You are fine. Relax."

"I don't want to go in there. I want to leave right now."

His body is nothing but a silhouette as dim, pale light shines from over his shoulder, only highlighting the edge of his hairline. His face sits in complete shadow.

"If we leave, you will regret the choice."

"Then, tell me what the fuck we're doing here," I snap.

Reaching forward, Malakyte taps on the keypad attached to the outside of the cell, and seconds later, a dim light illuminates the inside. In fact, a person is sitting in there. Which immediately eases my panic that this cell isn't meant for me, and I let out another trembling breath.

The man in the cell is strapped to a chair, head slumped forward, passed out.

It smells like he pissed himself or worse, and he makes no movement or acknowledgment that we are here.

I hope the relief doesn't show on my face when I don't immediately recognize him.

Thank the stars. It isn't Gav or Jance or Ardelle.

But my relief ends there, when the pieces click together.

"W-What . . ." I utter, feeling safe enough to take a step inside.

My eyes adjust to the watery lighting, and I notice details that have forever been burned into my memory, no matter how many times it gets obliterated to dust.

His rat brown hair, shoulder-length and curly, is so greasy it roils my stomach as if I swallowed straight mold. His body is tall and thick and heavy like an ogre, his footsteps thudding down the creaking hallway outside that childhood bedroom, a sound forever stuck inside my head like an obnoxious jingle. The belt he wears around his waist is the same leathery Shit Brown, weathered monstrosity that it was back then.

Malakyte didn't take these memories away. Not even one. I wish he had.

"What the fuck is this?" I demand, turning back toward Malakyte, my fear replaced with confused fury.

Slowly, the man in the chair wakes up, our presence here lifting him from whatever unconscious stupor he was in.

"What every victim wishes they had," Malakyte says. "Justice."

My body tingles.

From inside his suit's inner pocket, Malakyte pulls out a file. *My* file.

From when I was an orphan and a ward of Arianyte.

Smoothly, he flips it open and starts reading it aloud. "Karalevine Arriah Ruzz, found abandoned as a newborn outside a church. No signs of abuse or neglect. Sex, female. Age, less than a day old."

Yes, I knew I was abandoned young . . . but not that young . . . My parents left me all alone. They left me to *them*, this occupation, and I hate them for it.

"The junior citizen jumped from foster home to foster home after age three, the potential adopters who had the child previously fell into financial ruin and reluctantly opted out of a formal adoption. That was just the beginning of a long string of unfortunate circumstances to plague the junior citizen from that point forward. At age six, the junior citizen was sent to live at Naresteé Orphanage, the second surrendering foster family adamant that they were not equipped to handle a child of this caliber and insisted the child had a string of behavioral issues."

I didn't have behavioral issues—they were starving and beating us.

"Another family stepped up to foster the junior citizen, but that adoption too, fell through, despite initial prospects looking promising. A fourth and final foster home was offered to the junior citizen at the age of nine, which ultimately turned out to be detrimental to the child's psyche. She ultimately returned to Naresteé Orphanage where the junior citizen refused any and all foster placements from that point forward."

With teeth clenched tight, I glare at Malakyte. "Why are you doing this?"

He looks at me with no shame whatsoever, only sad eyes. "I want you to tell me what happened to you."

"You know what happened to me."

He does. It's all right there in his hands. I never wanted Malakyte to know . . . to know how damaged I am. Never judge a book by its cover—pretty girls are ugly on the inside. Their broken pieces bounce around within, cutting up who they are at their core until everything they touch is slashed. It all bleeds through poorly stitched wounds that creates a patchwork of cynicism and rage that curdles into an endless cycle that results in, well, *me*.

And look at what I've done, look at where my life has led me.

"What is this? Who's there?" The man gurgles, voice groggy and weak as he hauls his head up and looks around.

My skin crawls, palms sweat, and rage blooms like the fury of a thousand stars.

Neither Malakyte nor I answer him. He doesn't deserve a scrap of my attention.

Malakyte looks back at the file, as if he hasn't memorized it.

Malakyte addresses the man—no—he isn't a man. He's a fucking worm.

"It says here, Mr. Miller, that you were charged with aggravated sexual assault, indecent exposure, and sexual misconduct against a junior citizen. Is that accurate?"

My head snaps away from them both. I can't do this. I can't face this . . . this shame and humiliation. Especially in front of Malakyte—in front of the fucking man who ruined and ripped apart my very soul.

"I already told you, you cold-blooded bastard, I didn't touch no kids!"

Malakyte smiles, but there's no teeth. "That's right. You and I did have a long, thorough conversation, didn't we?

Our time together will satisfy me for an extended period of time, I assure you."

"Fuck you, squid."

From the bleeding, bruising, and cuts on my abuser's face, it isn't hard to put two and two together about what marred Malakyte's knuckles. That gains him points, although I'm still incredibly sickened by this. Why he even did it in the first place is baffling.

"The charges against you eventually got dropped due to lack of physical evidence, as you so poignantly stated the last time we spoke."

I clench my jaw so tightly, my teeth might crack. "Because he's a fucking lying piece of garbage," I interject, anger replacing all other emotions.

Finally, the man I've loathed, reviled, cursed more than even Arianyte itself, lifts his head and looks me in the eye.

"Optimus Miller . . . ?" Malakyte snorts as he skulks around my abuser's chair in a predatory gait. "Interesting name. An old-world surname, isn't it? We've identified your family, and they all knew what you've been up to—for decades, even. I like to call that level of complicity a bloodline exterminator."

This rat in his cage spits at Malakyte, never taking his eyes off me. Malakyte calmly looks down at the spit on his creaseless pant leg, thoroughly unimpressed. All I can see are those eyes in a shade I won't name, a shade of malice and cruelty and selfish perversion. A shade of evil that feels absolutely zero remorse.

"You've grown up," he says to me, body language and the angle of his lips perking up. "Made better connections than I thought you would. That's because of me. I taught you well."

My pulse hammers like a jackrabbit. Faster, harder, this thundering beat and his words are the only things ringing in my mind.

Malakyte steps before him, removes his jacket, throws it to the front of the cell, and grins maliciously.

 258

He decks him square in the jaw—hard.

Despite myself, the corner of my mouth quirks upward. I enjoy it.

The pig spits blood, and it dribbles down to his filthy clothes, so dingy from dirt, sweat, and gore.

"You don't speak to her unless she speaks to you first, number one. Number two—" Malakyte clears his throat as he circles him like a cat.

"I love her. I love all my girls. They're never the same aft—"

Malakyte decks him again. And again and again and again.

I watch, utterly motionless but giddy as satisfaction bubbles in my chest at the small amount of justice for me. I see what he meant about how it would make me feel better. But if I had my way, I'd be the one punching him bloody.

"Me and Mr. Miller had a long talk earlier," Malakyte says to me once he's gotten his fill. "He seemed to have a diminutive amount of remorse for his actions against you. In fact, when my SSPARROWs picked him up, a young girl was found living with him, when he's been strictly informed not to have contact with children. We've since placed her in a home where she isn't being abused."

"Are you serious?" Sick *fucking prick.* "You never stopped, did you? *Did you?*" I yell, walking up to him only to slap him hard across his beaten, bloodied face.

Even his sweat and blood on my hand makes me want to hurl my guts up.

He just . . . *laughs.*

My blood boils.

"But nobody compares to you, my little Kara. You were always my favorite. You know it was love, right? That it was real?"

No wonder I'm so fucked up in the head. No wonder I love a man who's also so fucked up in the head. We're all just fucked up in the head.

Standing beside me, Malakyte chokes my abuser as he gurgles for tiny gasps of air, the sounds of the struggle by far the most satisfying.

"Remember when we went into the public sector, and you wanted those earrings?" Malakyte asks, still choking him, his voice shimmering with malicious, dark intent.

We're all monsters in this cell. Just different kinds.

"Yes."

"I told you that no one can tell you what you can or can't have anymore. That my power is now your power. I know what you truly desire out of this situation. A deep longing that your old life would never allow because of moralist ideals, fears of punishment or judgment or consequences. Those shackles, Karalevine, are now demolished. I'm not doing this to be cruel to you—quite the opposite. I'm doing this to set you free."

My ears hollow out. "Set me free . . . ?"

Is that even possible after everything?

Malakyte walks over to his jacket and fishes for something inside. It only takes me a moment to see the black rose he holds as he returns to me.

Dark lady . . .

"Yes, Karalevine." Malakyte's voice is smooth, calm, and for the first time, tender. He offers me the rose but also my justice. "Your opportunity has finally arrived."

CHAPTER 40

Malakyte pulls out a long dagger from his pants pocket and hands it to me, hilt first.

It glints in the dim light, as haunting as it is deadly.

I take it, surprised by its weight as black leather glides between my fingers, the blade cackling with one promise on its lips. *I will be your instrument of justice and freedom*, it seems to purr.

A black rose in one hand, a black dagger in the other. A choice hangs between the two.

"The system is broken," Malakyte says, circling *me* now. "It was flawed long before I arrived. 'What was she wearing?' 'Did she say no?' 'She shouldn't have put herself in that situation.' Around and on it goes. Justice must always be allotted by another. Therefore, justice is the luxury of the strong and privileged, never the weak. I've witnessed violence of this nature on every single planet I've been to, and I shamefully admit I've done nothing about it. But now, it's personal. Now, I'll use my power and influence to tip the scales because I can. Let me give you what so many victims never get the chance to obtain. *Revenge*."

My body trembles with indecision.

I want to . . . I realize. I want revenge. I do.

I can see myself doing it. See how easily it could start and how hard it would be to stop.

Malakyte wouldn't judge me for it. In fact, he would likely love me even more, as sick and demented as he is.

He stops to stand behind me, his whisper in my ear a hair's breadth away from pure ice. "I'm handing you the authority. Now, *take it*. End this chapter of your life, reclaim your power, and destroy him."

My abuser glances at the knife, then back at me again. "What the fuck is this? You really think she's going to kill me with that knife? Please."

A low, growling rumble stops my thoughts cold, when a voice that sounds exactly like Dannanōk's bounce off the walls of my mind and says, *"Zariya's sin led to a fissure in your soul that allows the darkness in, but you do not have to reach for it."*

My eyes dart around, but Malakyte doesn't seem to hear it. Perhaps facing all this has made me insane? Or am I truly hearing the dragon, Zariya's sin and mine weaving together under a tapestry of time and death and blood? She's a murderer, just like me. I don't need my memories to know what awful things I've done.

My skin is clammy, this cell suddenly too hot, and I almost pinch myself to see if I'm in another nightmare.

"Take your power back," Malakyte urges, his voice a seduction I can't resist.

There will be no consequences. I won't be punished. This disgusting monster will get what he deserves. I'll prevent him from hurting more girls like me. This is the right thing to do. It's *the right thing*.

Won't giving into the darkness that's been my one and only companion through all these years only draw me closer to it? I'd be giving into every dark, destructive, selfish impulse. I'd hurt those I care about . . . their hopes in me misplaced. Who would want someone like that? Only Malakyte would.

The dagger trembles in my hand, and so does the rose. Are they really any different? My pulse clammers in my ears. My vision blurs as I lose a battle with myself I've been waging for so long.

To not give into that darkness . . .

But I want to kill him. I want to not care, and I want to satisfy that fucking pain within me. He's the source of it, after all. Killing him would save me . . .

And it would damn me.

No matter what I decide, I lose myself. I'll lose myself having to live with this flesh-eating disease that rips pieces of me away day after day, the one *he* infected me with. He sent me on a path of destruction, and not even Zariya's sins cracked me open this wide. I love the darkness so much because he sent me through it. A Hell where nobody helped me, nobody believed me, nobody validated me.

Until now.

Malakyte pushes harder, the devil on my shoulder. "You have to decide that you are not damaged goods. You are not sullied. You are not ruined. You are power and strength and my queen. Accept the beautiful gift that I'm offering you and stop letting it haunt your every step. Kill him, and be done with it."

Sweat beads on the back of my neck, soaking my nape, while my throat is blasted dry.

Kill him . . . a voice inside me says, it's always craved bloodshed. *Kill him. You want to. You* need *to.*

But this isn't who you are. This isn't the only way to free yourself from this.

It feels like everything has been leading me toward this very moment where life and death dances on the tip of a blade, my choice to embrace goodness or darkness and one side is losing *badly*.

I don't have the strength to fight it anymore.

A solitary tear finally falls to my cheek, despite my effort to hold it back. That's all I'll allow, just one. It's the last one this man will ever get.

A tear for my younger self, who was never protected, who never got justice.

A tear for the girl I was before Malakyte locked her away, still trapped within the darkness somewhere, afraid and alone.

A tear for my shredded humanity.

The rose falls to the floor, silent but booming all at once. Gripping the dagger, I've made my choice.

I plunge it down, and the screaming begins.

It doesn't stop for a long, long time.

CHAPTER 41

Year 2, day 513: We've been back on Earth for a
while, and to celebrate my birthday, Naresteé and
the prince said I could start running invisible
recon. My cover? Their adopted son. My mission?
Find threats. My magic makes me really good at
something like this, especially now that I can turn
invisible. Is it bad that I want to do a good job?
That I want him to be proud of me? Mostly, I want
you both to be proud of me.

Gavrielle Abraxas

Incoming Dezlar message:

From: Thumbelina
1:09 a.m.

I need Gavrielle. It's urgent.
I'm in the pool in the royal wing. Besides the guards, I'm alone. I'll
swim for another half hour before I enter the showers. The guards won't

follow me there. Meet me in the women's sauna attached to the showers. SSPARROW birds are at the pool's entrance on the outside. Cameras inside the pool, not inside the showers or the sauna.

I throw off my blanket and run to her.

In the blink of an eye, I become invisible as I approach the pool in the royal sector.

Four SSPARROW are, indeed, standing outside the entrance to the pool. None are Ennar—he never works this late.

"What the hell?" one soldier gasps, metal head whipping around, confused as to why the door slides open seemingly by itself.

"It's just your uniform. Your fat ass must've bumped the keypad again."

"I'm telling you this place is haunted."

"Oh, shut up, you're such a b . . ."

Their conversation disappears as the door closes behind me, and chlorine fumes hit my nose, as overpowering as the choking heat.

I immediately make my way across the slick tile floor, past the large pool, and to the sauna entrance on the other side of the room. The wooden door creaks, splitting the hushed silence in two.

I'm hit by a rush of steam and heat, the interior of the sauna a blinding white wall. No shadows or shapes can be found.

Stepping inside, I allow my illusion to fall and my body to become visible again.

"Kara?"

Half a minute passes as I stalk the perimeter of the room. She's not in here.

I'm about to check the showers when a rush of cold air whooshes into the sauna.

"Gav?" she says, and I smile. "Are you in here?"

"I'm here." I follow her voice until I see her petite silhouette in the steam.

Soon, her features come into view, and I'm surprised by her state.

She's soaking wet—*obviously*—although her red eyes are ghostly and glassy, but it's the lack of any light behind them that squeezes my chest like a vise. The door behind her remains open as a shower sprays water on full blast, the blue light playing off the steam between us.

Something happened. Something bad.

The long strands of her hair stick to her neck, chest, shoulders and arms, the suit she swam in nothing but two pieces of black fabric.

"Hey," I say softly, walking up to her.

She flinches from me.

Trying again, hoping she'll let me past whatever new walls she's built up around herself, I reach for her hand, and she lets me take it.

Holding eye contact, I gently pull her toward me, inch by inch, guiding her to a place that's safe from whatever went down today.

What happened is irrelevant. The only thing I care about is that she's okay. She called for me—she wants me here. That's a good sign.

I finally coax her close enough that she exchanges the safety of the doorway for the safety of my arms.

She jumps into them.

Then I quickly realize why she turned the showers on. Not only to hide our conversation or to keep the soldiers from knowing we're here, but to drown out this horrible sound.

Her knees give out, but I catch her before they get scraped. The sounds of her sobbing bounce off the sauna walls, coming back to my ears like daggers. Anger rushes into me hard, so bright I haven't known it since the night they Reconditioned her. The sounds are identical. Desperate and helpless and terrified and so unbelievably sad. But this time, I can do something about it.

"It's okay, love," I tell her, over and over again as I rock her in my arms. "It's okay."

I take bits of her hair and comb them back with my fingers, away from her cheeks, loosely braiding them so they don't get in the way. Once she's calmed down enough, I take her face in my hands. Tears fall to my thumbs as she stares through me, dead eyed and distant. These emotions don't belong on her beautiful face.

He did this to her . . . He put these tears in her eyes. I know he did.

"What did he do?" I ask gently, and her chin quivers as she tries to answer but the words get lodged in her throat.

Kara takes a long, deep breath. "He didn't do anything, Gav," she finally says, voice quiet and weak. "It's what I've done."

My brows knit in confusion.

Her voice shakes as she says, "Do you remember the *bad man?*"

My heart skips, a rage beginning to simmer within me. "I remember."

A cry claws up her throat, and it takes everything in me to sit here and allow her to get it out knowing I can't take this pain away. "Malakyte . . . he . . . found him and brought him up here."

"What?" I say, genuinely shocked.

My helpless anger breeds into a drumming anthem in my ears that makes me want to go to war against Malakyte and this other prick, too.

She doesn't look in my eyes when she whispers, "He had no remorse." She takes my hands away from her face, and that's when I notice her red cuticles. "And I tried to resist it, I did. But I . . ."

If a heart could physically crack, I'd hear mine shatter.

 268

Kara covers her face with her hands, crying through her confession, ripping out every single word as if they were stitched inside her. "I killed him. *I killed him.*"

The words ring out between the spraying of water like a death knell.

I breathe in a long, deep breath, ignoring the chlorine burning my nose and the slight tremble in my hands. I reach over, softly taking Kara's hands away from her face. She refuses to look at me, more tears falling and mixing with the condensation as it gets hotter and hotter, my body sweating from more than the steam.

"And he was right there, pushing you to do it, wasn't he?"

This is what gets her to look at me.

"He framed it like he was giving me the gift of justice that I never had back then. Which he's right, I didn't. And that's the worst part, Gav, is that I can justify this by saying that it is justice or even stretch it as far as vengeance and maybe I'm within my right to reach for revenge, but that isn't the worst part. It's that *I liked it.* Malakyte didn't make me like it—that darkness was already there long before Malakyte ever walked into my life. I'm not good, Gavrielle. And you need to run. Please. So I don't become your villain."

Like fuck if I'm running.

I shake my head. "I'll never let him draw you that far down, Kara. I promise. On my parent's honor, I'll never let you become like him."

"What if I already have?" she whispers, so defeated, so sure of her brokenness.

My hand grasps her chin, assuring she doesn't look away. "If he's taken you so far down into darkness, you wouldn't be suffering over what you did. You wouldn't even care."

"But I'm a fucking monster," she says.

I all but feel her own self-hatred. What she doesn't realize is that I know it all too well.

"If you're a monster, then I'm a monster."

Confusion flickers in her eyes, but she quickly understands.

My head dips low, my hand falling away from her chin as my shame washes over me like the sticky heat of this sauna, fusing to every nook and cranny inside me like chewed gum. "Malakyte . . . He made me kill someone, too."

Her little gasp isn't one of judgment but one of shared heartbreak.

"The day I got my twin blades was the day I made my first kill for him—well, first kill ever. My father had one fundamental principle that bled into everything he did, which was that we only use our innate skill for battle to accomplish one goal: protect the vulnerable. 'We don't kill for money. We don't kill for luxury or favor. We don't kill for kings or governments or gods.' That's why my family and I came to Earth in the first place, to protect the people here. And when I was fourteen, Malakyte brought me one of his SSPARROWs that I had caught trying to plan an assassination coup against him. I was so proud I had caught the guy, so sure I'd be rewarded, but instead, the prince twisted the situation and manipulated it to the point where I felt I had no choice but to kill the traitor. He didn't force me. Ultimately, I had a choice in the matter. However, the way he framed the situation made his expectations extremely clear. Saying no wasn't truly an option. I assume he did the exact same thing with you today. It's how he is, how he works. He's toxic and manipulative and twists and turns us until we're a distorted inside out version of who we are at our core. His words are so hypnotizing that I was powerless to resist him back then. I hadn't forgotten my parents' or my father's vow to our people, and I betrayed that vow—I betrayed *him*. Betrayed myself. And then after I gained the prince's approval, it only worsened from there. He bred me to kill for him . . . And, like a coward, I did exactly that. Over and over . . ."

And I fucking hate myself for it. For what I allowed him to turn me into—something he's now turning *her* into.

Over my dead body.

I look up, and now I'm the one with tears in my eyes. "So, you see, we're both monsters of his making. I have absolutely no doubt that if it was me in that room with you instead of Malakyte, that motherfucker who abused you would have suffered greatly, and if you truly needed him dead to find even an ounce of peace, it would've been me who took the hit to my soul, not you. *Never you.* Because I know what it does—what it costs. And maybe he didn't have to die because that's not what *you* needed. Who knows? It just never would've resulted in this. I'm certain of that."

Kara scoots herself as close to me as possible, so close our knees are touching, and I lean in as she cups the side of my face, peering at the wicked bruise along my jawline from the fight with Ennar and the SSPARROWs. "I'm so sorry, Gavrielle. I should have been there to protect you. Will you let me protect you now?"

I take her hand and lace our fingers together. Her hand is so small compared to mine, little tattoos along her fingers, but they fit so perfectly. "I wish I could have protected you, too, love. More than you'll ever know."

"I've missed you so much," she says, voice trembling as the two of us migrate closer and closer.

I lose all my self-control, and I pick her up, her legs uncurling, and we hug tightly. "I've missed you, too, Kara," I say softly into her ear as the tension coiled within me loosens.

I can't let her go yet.

"How do I get past it? How do I forgive myself for what I've done? How do I shed all the shame and not be *this* anymore? I want to be better, Gav. I don't want to be like this anymore."

Leaning back, I kiss her forehead and wish she could see herself the way I do. I wish she could see how strong she really is. Is she flawed? Yes, she is. But so am I. Everyone is.

"We've both gone through horrific things. We've both been victims and then became perpetrators, but deep down, we're still good. We're still those kids we were back at the orphanage. Yes, we've made bad choices and compromised our morals at times, but we haven't lost ourselves to the darkness. Not like he has. And I think we move past all that's happened to us by making it mean something. We're going to give all that horrible shit a purpose, and it won't haunt us anymore. We deserve that."

"I'm so afraid that if I let you get close, I'll just burn you again . . ."

Her hands ripple over the scars down half of my neck and collarbone. My stomach flips at the memory of the night, of the pain, of losing her.

"Burn me, love," I say, voice sure. "Take my flesh and melt it like the star that you are. I can take it. I'll ravage my skin and wreck my soul for you if that's what you need. You've never scared me."

She opens her mouth as if she's about to say something, then stops herself. Our lips are so close it takes everything in me not to close those inches between us. But I remember the last time I tried that and then quickly try to forget my mortification. At least she doesn't remember rejecting me when I tried to kiss her on that Sky Dais.

We sit like this for almost ten minutes before she finally speaks again.

"I want to protect the Hijacked. I want to free Ardelle and save the people of Earth. I'm confused about my feelings . . . But after today, I've accepted there's more happening here than my perspective is allowing me to see. I need to protect what's important to me, what I love, and what's in danger. Earth is in terrible danger, Gav. Herkimer is so much worse than Malakyte. He wants to destroy the planet, and I don't know if Malakyte has the strength or will to stop him, even when he's crowned emperor. I'm ready to fight for what I love."

272

My arms pull her back into my chest, relief flooding into me like ice water on a burning grill. *Thank the stars.*

We may not have her memories or have all of her loyalty, but for now, I'll take it. Until that moment, I'll settle for whatever scraps of her she's willing to give me, hoping that, at the end of the day, I'll be enough to get all of her. In all ways that matter. Heart, body, soul.

Her.

CHAPTER 42

Two days after the sauna, me, Gav, and the others worked out a plan so I could meet with them. According to Gav, they want to talk, and if I want to admit it or not, I'll never get my memories back without them. I love Malakyte, but I love other things, too. After what happened in that cell . . . I can't let the darkness win. I have to do the right thing, or I'll be lost forever.

I do feel bad for Malakyte's guards, however, when the gravity gets shut off on my daily walk with Ennar and his third, a female SSPARROW. I insisted we stroll around the private sector's little hub, where all the workers go to blow off steam. It's nowhere near the size of the public sector, but there are restaurants, shops, cafés, and bars. So, when the gravity flipped off, we all went flying and so did about a hundred other people, along with anything not bolted down. I was told it was Pacey's handiwork, who's, obviously, a badass hacker. It was just the distraction I needed to slip away. Gavrielle illusioned us to look like random extras, and we bolted to the meeting point where the others are waiting.

"I won't have much time," I tell Gav as we run.

"I know, we got you."

After a good ten-minute run, we arrive at a desolate wing of the Azurite, and I take a deep breath, fearing what's beyond the door we're now standing before.

"You ready to see them again after everything?" Gav asks, having told me what to expect prior to coming.

I slap the door panel way harder than necessary, and it slides open with a whoosh and soft wisp of air that flutters my lashes.

Six heads turn to stare right at me.

I do my best to hold my chin up high.

Gav's gentle hand on the small of my back gives me the courage I need to step inside, heart racing.

The room is bare, but at least there's overhead light rather than the dark pit of the last place they chose. The so-called furniture is more mismatched and makeshift as they sit in a circle in the center. I note the dull, chipping paint on the wall in the color Blueberry.

Jance rises from his seat first, his body a bit stiff. "Kara," he says, stepping closer but awkwardly stopping and stepping back. "We're all so glad you agreed to come see us. I'm glad."

There's still a pretty nasty bruise and cut that hasn't fully healed around his left eye. I wonder if it's going to leave a scar. And he looks tired, much more tired than he used to. I miss him, I realize. Even though our relationship wasn't perfect, he was a constant presence in my world, and without him in it, I feel like I'm drifting completely alone in this sea of Malakyte's making.

Clearing his throat, Jance tries again. "Gavrielle told us that you wanted to help get Ardelle out of the dungeons, and perhaps a bit more than that?"

Stars, Ardelle . . . stars. I'm supposed to love him, yet all I think about is Gav most days. I'm engaged to one guy—caught in his toxic web—while I'm deeply emotionally connected to another, forgetting the stranger I'm supposed to love. And worse yet, Gav snuck down there recently, and a guard is posted at Ardelle's cell, so we can't even communicate with him. I want to. I need to, but Malakyte won't allow it.

The sudden urge to run away is overwhelming, the guilt too hard to face.

My smile is . . . painfully forced.

"And I want to free the dragons, too."

There are a few glances between them that speak a whole lot.

Gav reintroduces me to everyone by name, and when he gets to Pacey, her face scrunches, and without a word, she stands and dashes across the room before hugging me so hard we almost topple over. "I've missed you so much," she whispers, sniffing every few seconds.

It feels natural to hug her back because her hug is one of those good, long hugs that make you feel like you're with somebody warm, somebody you belong with.

"I'm sorry," she says, stepping back and wiping a tear away. "I know how overwhelming all this is, and you don't remember me. It's a lot."

Giving me space, Pacey returns to Sylo as they link hands, remaining standing.

I glare at a figure sitting in the corner, one leg braced against the wall as his chair balances back on two legs instead of four.

"Ah, Kiddo. Don't look so thrilled to see me," Deimos coos.

I roll my eyes. *Asshole.*

Jance motions for me to sit in a chair and as I do, it's hard not to feel like they're watching me meticulously, from the way I adjust my posture to how I flip my hair off my shoulders. Gavrielle stands behind me.

"So . . ." I say, picking at a stray thread on my shirt's hem, feeling like I'm betraying Malakyte, but I force myself to speak. "I think the Hijacked are in danger, Earth, too. We have to save them."

They all exchange a myriad of hesitant, worried glances that cause my chest to tighten.

 276

"Well, Kara, you're right," Jance says for the group, leaning forward over his knees. "There is a lot happening down on Earth. The long and short of it is, Terrans are at war with Arianyte. Trinity made contact with us when she raided the ship, and we're utilizing the tech she gave us to free both you and Ardelle, stop Arianyte's plans, and ultimately, unseat them from power."

His words shoot a bolt of anxiety through me. My future crumbles with every word, but that future was just an illusion . . . it was always going to fall apart.

Gav's hands rest on my shoulders.

Saris says, "In our limited communications, Trinity has described the situation planet-side to be, well, dire. The people are revolting, and Arianyte is fighting back. The calls for your release is constant. Arianyte is releasing fake statements claiming it's you calling for peace. There's protests, more public executions, more riots with SSPARROW. Heavy SSPARROW recruitment, control of the media. The Network is now offline. Zones are heavily blockaded, no one can get in or out. Terran officials are in a frenzy, doing what they can to bridge the gap, but they've gotten lazy and are inept at their jobs. It goes on and on, a constant push and pull between the rebellion and Arianyte."

"Tell her the whole story, Ringer," Deimos grumbles. "It's much worse than that. She needs to know the truth about the man she's sleeping next to every night."

He might as well have thrown a spear into my gut for how effective his words are at making me sick.

Saris, for all her strong, stoic nature, looks unnerved. "He—Malakyte—has his SSPARROWs out in force. He wants the rebellion squashed for good. The soldiers are out on the streets day and night, killing innocent, so-called guilty citizens accused of rebel activity. Their families are suffering, too. The number of new Tributes has been staggering, and it's because they're supposedly connected to active rebels. No more lottery drawings, no trials, no proof in most cases, he's simply ordering them to execute or take anyone with even a rumor of rebel suspicion against them or their family members. Any decenter against him or Arianyte—that person is dead. The propaganda machine is spinning, and it's . . . brutally effective at scaring the shit out of everyone thinking about fighting."

I don't like that. In fact, hearing all of this has stripped all the warmth from my face.

Cranking my neck, I look up to Gav to confirm, and he grimly nods.

Jance speaks this time. "Children have also been disappearing en masse. Far more than normal. It's imperative you understand that, Kara. Additionally, Trinity and the rebels boarded the Azurite to try and get you off the ship, but there was another reason, too."

"That's right," I interject, remembering something Trinity had said that day. "They were talking about some sort of weapon. Did they find it?"

"We were hoping you could tell us," Jance says, those eyes of his in the shade Espresso watching me like I'm a ghost with emotion too raw to define. "Has Malakyte mentioned any special weapon he's been prepping in order to stop the rebellion?"

I laugh, but it's as bitter as dark chocolate. "Yeah, no. Malakyte talks about Earth as if there's not a thing going on down there. As far as he's concerned, I believe Earth is running as normal, no issues. His excuse as to why I can't go down is that Geonni and Deimos want to kill me."

Deimos flips the chair onto its four legs. "Well, he's definitely cooking something up, Kiddo, and it ain't going to be good for this backwoods planet, that's for sure. We need to figure out what he's up to, and fast."

It's not a weapon, per say, but someone specific comes to mind

"What if the weapon isn't an actual weapon at all?" I suggest, and they look rather grim. "Herkimer is basically all of us Starseeds mixed into one person. He's invincible. Not to mention, entirely insane. You think Malakyte is crazy? His father is on a whole other level. I believe he's the one who wants Earth destroyed completely, because he's so convinced that Ardelle killed Selenyte that he wants all Terrans to pay."

It's clear they all want to say something by how they're looking at each other with worried, tense expressions; a few of them opening their mouths and then closing them.

Jance clears his throat when he finally says, "Malakyte killed Selenyte." My heart nearly stops. "He killed her when she threatened your life. That's the lengths he'll go to not only get you but keep you."

My eyes widen. I figured Ardelle didn't do it, *but stars.* Malakyte . . . Herkimer's words ring out in the recesses of my mind from that day he attacked us. That, if Malakyte was involved, we were *both* dead.

I push all the fear away, knowing I need to stay focused.

"Herkimer eats people who have significant magical abilities. Don't ask me how that works. He takes their powers, probably kills them, too."

I fill them in on what occurred between Herkimer, myself, and Malakyte.

It's silent after that, and I need to take hold of Gavrielle's hands.

I'm doing the right thing telling them this, right? This isn't betraying Malakyte . . . Stars, who cares? Look at what he's been doing to my people behind my back. I can't keep making excuses for him anymore. He betrayed me first. He did this to me, took me away from the people who love me, made me believe I was alone in the world and that nobody loved me but him, that he was all I had . . . But that wasn't true. I have people who love me. They wouldn't have stayed in these harsh living conditions on the run, risking so much to try and get me back if they didn't care. Their actions prove they love me. Malakyte's actions prove the opposite.

But my loyalty toward him breeds so much discomfort inside, and it's a terrible duality.

Jance breaks the silence again. "If he's the weapon in question or not, we should expect both and find a way to kill father and son."

The son part hurts my heart . . . and I truly don't think I can do that.

Sylo throws his hands up, exasperated. "How are we going to kill a man who's protected by a Elendril crystal that revives him every time he dies and another whose body can literally regenerate?"

He's got good points.

"So, what has to be done before the wedding so we can get out of here before then?" I blurt, needing a plan to follow because I can't sit by his side and just pretend this isn't happening. "There isn't much time until then, and they want Ardelle executed at the coronation the next day."

Each pair of eyes watches me with silent pity.

"What is it?" I ask, feeling the tension ratcheting up in the room. "Jance?"

My Ringer looks visibly uncomfortable now, and my body echoes his. He opens his mouth, but then shuts it, looking at Saris and the others for help. In the memories I do have of him, I've never seen him at a loss for words.

Deimos says from his spot by the window, "We need you to go through with the wedding, Kiddo."

My body tingles.

No. *No* . . .

"What?" I blurt out dumbly.

There's no way. Not after everything I just heard. After what happened in the prison cells, sneaking around behind Malakyte's back, he'll catch me. No.

"Why?" I push when nobody answers.

"You were completely fine marrying the guy two days ago. Chill out," Deimos says.

"Screw you, Deimos," I spit. "You don't know anything about my relationship with him and how it feels to think you love someone one moment only to then find out they're a fucking psychopath who violated you in the worst possible way in the next. This is *hard* for me." I turn to Jance. "Why? Please explain to me why marrying him is better than us grabbing Ardelle and getting out before the wedding happens."

Jance answers, in no way taking enjoyment from his words. "Because we'll still be in a war we likely can't win, and you'll never get your memories back."

I force air into my lungs, but the exhale comes out shaky.

"It's simple, Kiddo," Deimos walks over and bends down on one knee in front of me as if bowing to his queen. "We need you to marry him because, once you do, what'll happen immediately after is your coronation. You will be granted the most powerful thing anyone can have in this galaxy, the Arianyte Empire's crown. Then we're going to circumvent that power, take it, and ruin them with it."

Cold ice slides through my veins. Malakyte will . . . Stars, I can't even think it. He'll kill us all.

Viciously.

Terror heaves my heart into a gallop at the mere thought of what my dark lover would do if this ever became real.

This is by far bigger than I thought it was going to be. I didn't expect them to be this determined to ruin not just Malakyte but Arianyte as a whole. Malakyte wasn't wrong when he said he had enemies, that's for sure.

They've also overlooked something in their plan, and it's a big one: their faith in me.

"Why would you ever want me to hold that kind of power? Haven't you learned anything?"

I look at them one by one and end on Gavrielle. This connection blooming between us sizzles in the space we share, and it's like I shove the words straight into his head. *You know what happened. You know what I did. You can't let them give me this.*

Gav looks at me like he hears me somehow, eyes devastatingly sad.

Turning back to the group, I say, "I can't be trusted. I can't be given this type of power. I won't—"

I don't want to reveal the darkness coating my soul, and they change their minds about wanting to fight for me. Malakyte has shown me exactly who I am—I'm just like him. I crave that power, which is why they shouldn't give it to me.

"Find someone else."

Deimos doesn't miss a beat. "There is nobody else, Kiddo. Just you."

I shake my head, handing the Dez to Gavrielle. "You're making a huge mistake. I'd be no better than Malakyte sitting on that throne. I wanted to be there beside him to save the Hijacked, but now, I know I can't be there. I can't be given power like that."

"That isn't true at all, Kara." Gavrielle's voice is stern, almost angry that I'd even say it. "You are nothing like him. I've been with him for years. I know him, and I know you, so trust me when I say there's no comparison."

That's just it, the thing he doesn't get. I'm bad at my core. Malakyte is proving that every day.

And I think I hate him for that alone.

Ahren speaks for the first time, his voice soft. "Can we show you something, Kara? We thought it might help you see yourself the way we do."

I squint. "Show me what?"

His smile is warm as he pulls out some dusty, cracked screen Dezlar and taps on its glass interface.

"Trinity was able to get us some clips of you that we thought would help you see yourself as you used to be, before . . . all of this happened."

Ahren passes me the Dezlar and then crosses the room back to his spot. My hands shake as I hold it.

A young woman is standing on a stage next to Trinity, with Ardelle and Deimos lingering behind her. That woman is me. I step up to a floating microphone and speak passionately. My voice alone echoes out into the room, the others able to hear my speech to a crowd of what I assume are rebels as I rally them against Arianyte. My hair is different, but in the next clip, I'm standing in a gorgeous dress with a mask over my face, Ardelle by my side. I talk about the dress I'm wearing and how it was made by a known rebel designer. I'm then speaking to the press, talking about the Hijacked and freedom and stopping Arianyte no matter the cost. Again and again, I'm there, on screen, shouting my position from the rooftops, rallying the Terrans against the man I thought I loved for all these months.

Finally, after I chuck an arrow—quite impressively, I might add—into the sky at some miraculously floating island while standing in a race car professing my vow to take down the occupation, the clip ends.

"Nobody evil battles that hard for other people, kid," Jance says.

Processing it, I finally say, "I didn't realize that I . . . did all that."

"You started a war to bring me back," Pacey says, and I look up at her, no hatred in her large eyes, only love. "Evil people don't do that, either."

I shake my head. "But look at where we are! Look at where your brother is, how you guys are having to live. I'm the reason innocent people are being killed in the streets down there. This is madness, and I—"

"This would have happened with or without you," Jance argues. "Malakyte and the occupation never would've lasted here, not with the Resistance already formed under Geonni. Regardless of your participation in these events, Earth would have ended up at war with Arianyte no matter what."

When I'm silent for a long time, I finally look up at Jance. He's the most reasonable. Perhaps he'll listen to me.

"Please leave this place," I beg beyond all pride. "Get Ardelle free before they kill him, find whatever key you need to unlock his collar and *go*."

It's what's best for all of them. I have to save them from this suicide mission. Malakyte and Herkimer will *kill them*.

From the look he's giving me, I don't think he's going to listen, after all. "No."

I stand, the chair legs shrieking against the floor. "If I don't get you killed, this plan certainly will."

"We know that already."

"Then, why are you still here? Do you all have a death wish?"

"Because we're not abandoning you. We never will, no matter how bad it gets. We started this together, and we're finishing it together. We're a team, a family, and we're not leaving anyone behind."

Jance's words hit some vulnerable part of my heart so hollowed out and shriveled down it almost knocks me off my feet. There's something about Jance specifically that continues to drive me insane. Like a maddening itch I can't scratch. The man said he loved me the other day, and when the words landed, they felt like an arrow to the heart.

"Who are you to me?" I ask. "Why does it feel like if I lost you, I'd die? Is it because you're my Ringer?"

His face strains. "That's part of it."

"Tell me the rest."

"I can't, knowing could risk everything that we're trying to accomplish." He walks up and takes my hand, and finally, I don't flinch or jerk away. The relief on his face when I allow him to touch me only solidifies my feelings are correct—he's

 284

important. "But know that I'm someone in your life who cares about you so much, *so, so much*. And I will never leave you. No force in this galaxy can rip me away from you. Even if your mind doesn't remember, your heart does. That's enough for right now."

That's the most beautiful, frustrating answer he could have given me.

Jance wraps his strong arms around me as I hold my own tightly over my chest. Before I completely lose my shit in front of them, I force the feelings shooting up like a geyser back down. I can't process all this right now. It's too much. Too many eyes, although lovingly, are watching me, and I just can't open myself up like that to them. Not yet . . .

"Alright," I say, stepping back.

A sniffle comes from across the room, and I see Pacey crying, everyone's face holding some type of deep or painful emotion.

"Team Starseed all the way?" Sylo blurts into the tense silence.

His voice is full of hopeful uncertainty, but he pushes through it, and the humor reverberates through all of us.

Deimos throws something at Sylo, although I can't see what it is. "Enough with all that sappy shit. Are we taking down this fucking empire, or are we not?"

"Only if we get matching Team Starseed T-shirts," Gav says with a chuckle, and that gets a laugh from everyone.

"Over my dead body," Deimos growls, but his grin betrays his grumpy exterior.

"That can be arranged," Sylo suggests, laced with sarcasm and love.

Pacey whacks him playfully on the arm, blotting her nose with a tissue.

Deimos crosses his arms. "And a fifth ass-kicking can be arranged, as well."

"Yeah, well, I'm ready for round five whenever you are, old man." Sylo cracks his knuckles as if readying for a fight, but his grin is an arrogant, cocky challenge.

When Deimos smiles, he's all vicious teeth.

Jance mercifully interferes. "Let's spare Kara a fistfight on her first day back, please?"

"Fine." Sylo stretches as if doing Deimos a favor by agreeing not to fight. "We should talk about strategy anyway. So, how are we going to bring down this asshole and his whacked-out super tyrant of a dad?"

I guess I'm doing this, then . . .

Team Starseed, indeed.

CHAPTER 43

I stride down the halls of the Azurite with renewed determination.

I'm going to take down the Arianyte Empire.

And I'm starting with Malakyte Ardeen.

The more I learn about the man behind the mask, the more I dislike.

And I did—I do—still love him. I loved him before I found all this out, memories altered or not. The time we've had together was real, and it did happen, and I was happy . . .

My plan was always to change the world *through* Malakyte's power, and the bigger goal is still there. I'm more motivated than ever. The Hijacked can't be saved if I don't pivot. There was no throne for me beside Malakyte when the Council came to see us, and I saw my future laid out before me: I'd be overrun.

A silent, powerless statue, same as his mother. I wouldn't be saving anybody like that. Arianyte must be brought down, and Malakyte and Herkimer are going with it.

There's always a five-to-ten-minute gap where my door is unguarded when the SSPARROWs change shifts, so the moment the guards leave, I sneak out and execute step one in Project Sabotage: turn his right-hand lady against him.

Naresteé.

Her room isn't far from Malakyte's, so I shouldn't have any problems sliding Pacey's handwritten note under her door and scurrying back. I'm nearly there.

The letter is a double-sided mousetrap, using their weaknesses against them as they used ours against us. Pacey said in her letter that she wants to come to Naresteé, tired of living in squalor on the run. Her conditions? Free Ardelle and promise not to Recondition her again. Then? Pacey is hers again.

Our hope? Save Ardelle—which is unfortunately unlikely— but beyond that, if Naresteé believes that's the only barrier between getting Pacey back, she's going to pester Malakyte about it like crazy. When Malakyte ultimately refuses, this will hopefully drive a wedge between them, one I will continue to widen as we move along, possibly taking one of Malakyte's biggest pieces off the board.

This also keeps the horned bitch focused on Pacey, keeping her eyes off of me.

I peek around my shoulder, eyes bopping over the daytime quartz lights as my sneaky feet coast silently over the Honey-Gold-and-Onyx-flecked marble floor in only my socks, with the letter placed inside that little purse Malakyte insists I carry those strange syringes in.

It isn't long until I reach Naresteé's door, and as I approach it, opening the bag, my chest flutters. I insisted on being the one to do this, despite the risks. Gavrielle could have easily done it, but it has to be me. If others do, then I'm a passenger, and

I'm done letting other people make decisions for me. Plus, my convictions will waver, and Malakyte will suck me right back into his web of darkness and deceit.

I also need to prove to myself I can reach for the good and not the dark after everything I've done . . . I'll probably never forgive myself for what I did in those dungeons, but this is a start.

I bend down low, remove the letter, then slip it under the door.

Standing, I glance behind me and up to the camera in the wall, the seamless Gray Black square hardly noticeable as it lies flush with the sleek molding.

I smirk up at Pacey, knowing she's watching.

For better or worse, I've set this in motion . . . and there's no going back.

Not for me, for the others, or for the dark prince I love. The plan to take down Malakyte has begun, and I huff a cynical laugh at myself as I turn and head back to the room.

We're probably all going to die up here.

At least we'll go together again.

CHAPTER 44

"**G**ood, now, do that again," Gavrielle says seconds after I *almost* tripped him down to the floor of our dangerous training space. "But this time, put more force behind your attack to knock me to the ground. I felt your hesitation. Your opponent is going to laugh and know you don't have the confidence to follow through with an attack. Don't be afraid. The old you would've gotten me down. And don't count on the gravity going out again to save you like last time."

I smirk, the two of us circling each other in the dimly lit room, the only light some outdated lamp sitting tipped on its side in a corner, the entire space cluttered with the junkiest items strewn all about.

"Why'd you bring me to a section of the Azurite that has frequent gravity lapses?" I ask, feeling like myself for the first time in so long as Gavrielle and I spar together.

The sweat on my skin, the heat in my muscles, the rush of a fight. This is where I thrive.

But not even the blast of adrenaline can keep the darker thoughts and deeper sadness in my bones from creeping in.

Gav shrugs those massive, broad shoulders. "The perfect place to hide and train, love. Plus, we've only lost gravity once while being down here. Since we're in space, the gravity can disappear in a flash, and doing drills in zero-G is never a bad idea. You saw how easily Pacey shut down the gravity the other day when we coordinated that escape for you."

"Ennar screamed at me," I say, pretending to come at Gav. He doesn't fall for it. "Not sure if he believed I was there hiding the entire time because I was *scared*. Malakyte plans my days now, especially since the wedding is coming up. From my meals to my walks, to my exercise, even what I wear and how I do my hair. It's a lot."

Gav looks enraged. "It won't be for much longer, Kara, I promise. And at least Ennar believes you're sitting in the sauna right now reading a really spicy romance novel or something. Good job finding that emergency panel and tricking it to open by increasing the heat. Smart. Led you right into the servant's hall on the other side of the wall. Proud of you."

"Can we go back to the really spicy romance novel, please?"

I jab toward him, using my question as a distraction, pouncing fast, faking him out with my right hand as if I'm about to punch, but I duck and elbow him in the ribs instead. My back is to him, and he shoves me forward, my feet tripping.

"Rude!"

"Your opponent isn't going to play by any rules, guarantee it. Not when it comes to you."

Turning to him, I brace my back leg to push off as I come for him. He's mine.

"Too slow!" Gavrielle taunts, laughing at how pathetically I missed. "And I'm assuming this really spicy romance novel has an icy-haired Sky-Fae risking it all for the beautiful heroine?"

Gavrielle's there before I can blink and wraps his arms around me from behind, moving so fast I hadn't even had time to respond.

"Hey!" I cry, doing my best to get free as he lifts me up off the ground.

But let's be real, my best isn't shit anymore, and his arms . . . well, with his sleeves rolled up like this, the muscles in his forearms ripple as he holds me there as if I weigh nothing, thick veins threaded through all that muscle, his large hands just as beautiful as his face. With my back pressed tight against his hard chest, I'm painfully attuned to how close we are. His scent is so intoxicating, woodsy, with masculine ginger, and it sends me into a nosedive that tightens my lower core and makes me feel guilty simultaneously. But, stars, he smells so good.

"Being distracted is also another opening you allow your opponent to exploit."

His breath is warm on my ear as he whispers the words with a cocky little chuckle.

My feet dangle as I kick my heels against his shins, but that's about as effective as a mosquito bite, so I give up.

"I'm at the part in the really spicy romance novel I'm supposed to be reading where the beautiful lady is ignoring the icy-haired Sky-Fae because she knows she can't have him."

"You forgot *handsome*, icy-haired Sky-Fae," he adds, his laugh like a melody I've forgotten. "But who says she can't have him?"

Gav lets me down but doesn't make a move to strike again, and neither do I.

"Maybe she feels guilty," I say, voice unable to hold the joke. "She's supposed to love someone else, but her heart is . . . conflicted."

By two men . . . One I do love . . . the other I don't know—don't remember. And then there's Gavrielle.

When I turn to face Gav, looking up as the lamp's warm light illuminates him from behind, I say, "This place loses gravity, right? Ardelle should be here, training with us and making sure we don't float away . . . but he isn't, and I don't know how to help him. If I can just help him then it makes up for not loving him, which makes me feel like even more of a piece of shit because I *should* love him, right? That's what everyone keeps saying. Even Malakyte believes it so much that's why he wants him dead—because of me, because—"

"Kara. Breathe."

Oh . . . . right. I don't think I took a breath once in all that rambling. We breathe, and my guilt and fear take hold of Gavrielle's hand as he walks me off the ledge.

"Better?"

I nod, my cheeks reddening as I immediately change the subject because, Jupiter's Rings, that was embarrassing.

Wedging my sneaker behind his foot, I curl one leg around his knee, grab him by the shirt and twist my entire body, my momentum taking us both down.

Gav ensures he breaks our fall, but we land with my hips directly between his legs with him on his back. Our breaths hitch, and now it's apparent that he's also cognizant of where our bodies connect, my core ratcheting up as I resist the urge to grind on him, touch him, kiss him.

Damn, that image came to mind fast.

Instead, I cackle in victory, the sound echoing off the cluttered room full of long-forgotten items, discarded by the people who once loved them.

"See, all you need is a little bit of training, and you'll be kicking my ass again in no time. I knew that spunk hadn't left you."

"Not even erasing my memories can take away my fight," I tell him, the words sounding more confident than I feel.

I don't want to, but I slide off Gavrielle, sitting on the dirty ground as he heaves himself into a sitting position across from me. Space between us would be the most appropriate.

"I'm going to get your memories back, I promise."

"I know you will."

I believe it. I believe *him*.

"There's something I've been needing to tell you. I've never told you about it."

My eyes soften.

"Tell me what, Gav?"

He breathes in deep, one knee bending up as his elbow rests on it, his long hair falling to one side. "My parents were the rulers of my home-world. It's called planet Nyktos."

My brows rise. "Oh. Oh . . ."

He tries to smile, but it falls. "And I'm an only child."

Way to dance around the words, Gavrielle.

"Gav, you're a prince? And you never told me? Really?"

"It was too dangerous . . . for me and for you. And technically, I'm the king now. But I'm not. Once Malakyte took me and Naresteé erased my memories of you, he made me a deal. Twenty years of my life for my people's freedom. I took it. Once . . . *fuck, Kara* . . ." He rakes a hand down his face, his tongue dancing along one of his pointed canines as his eyes refuse to look at me, words faltering. "Please know that I didn't remember you. He said that if I could find you and bring you to him, he'd release me and planet Nyktos. My people's freedom. I said I would. So, I entered the Titan Games alongside you to do just that. It was only once I regained my memories of you that I completely changed course and I tried so hard to prevent you from coming up here. We fought, Kara. For real. And you kicked my ass. It was actually embarrassing how underprepared I was for you."

His voice shakes the entire time, as if he's twelve years old again, handing me a bouquet of dandelions.

I swallow, digesting the information. "Thanks for telling me, Gav. I get it . . . You didn't know. And I can be a little stubborn, so that tracks."

"A little?"

I play-punch him, and we laugh, but his nervous tension still lingers between us. "It's okay. I just hope we can keep your people safe, too. I'll do all that I can to protect them, Gav. Get you back home."

"You're my home."

 294

Our gazes clash, much like our bodies have these past forty minutes straight, but when Gavrielle's Purple Reign eyes look at me in a way that makes me feel strong and good and worthy, he's not only able to scale the wall built out of guilt and self-loathing but demolishes it. How could I ever judge him when he's accepted every horrible thing I've ever done? I can't, and I don't.

Gav's hand slides to my cheek, and he cups it so tenderly my skin prickles, leaning into his touch as if it could save me from this awful mess.

He's so strong, yet his gentleness is one of the most attractive things about him. A person shouldn't be both. Shouldn't have gone through something as awful as he did yet still find it in his heart to be kind and good. He was always those things, regardless of what Malakyte did to him. If he can survive Malakyte, so can I.

My eyes find that perfect mouth, and I heat somewhere deep, sparks grasping for a flame.

"Can I . . ." Stars, I don't know how to ask for what I want, and I awkwardly grab onto the hand holding my face, biting my bottom lip. "Can I . . . come sit closer to you?"

My heart flutters all the way to the moon when he gives me the widest, brightest smile, one I haven't seen since we were children. When Gavrielle Abraxas smiles like that, he's easily the most beautiful man I've ever seen.

Leaning into my ear, he says seductively, "You want a hug, love?"

His lips are so close to the shell of my ear I break out in goose bumps but not from the cold like I'm used to—from the *heat*.

I straddle Gav as he remains seated, and I fit right in as I curl myself around his warm, rock-hard body, legs around his waist, arms curled under his as my fingertips glide across his muscled back. My cheek nestles directly over his heart. It beats evenly, the beat strong. I nearly moan when he wraps his arms around me, pulling me in as tightly as he can.

Stars, I needed this.

"You're so warm," I say. "Never realized you ran so hot."

"I can think of a few other parts about me that are just as hot, if not hotter."

"Wow, Gav."

Gavrielle pats my head, my hair in a braided coronate. I guess I'll be wearing a real crown soon.

I break our hug, and it's easy to smile. Everything is easy with Gav.

He softly wipes stray hair behind my ears, eyes combing every part of my face as if he'll forget me any moment. Then those beautiful orbs trip on my lips, bouncing back to meet my eyes as if he stumbled upon a forbidden place.

So, we're playing this game for real, then?

His pupils dilate.

My core heats.

Pushing the boundaries between us, I let my gaze fall to his lips, too. Perfectly shaped, sharp yet soft *and warm.*

It isn't a terrible game to play, but one as dangerous as the ocean is deep.

My hands curl around his nape and tangle into his hair, catching a braid.

Gavrielle purrs and draws in, his lips grazing my cheekbone, leisurely traveling lower. Bypassing my lips, he stops at my chin. Both his hands cradle my head as he dips it backward, exposing my neck to him.

I lean back into it, closing my eyes, my legs tightening around his waist as my body aches for him to kiss me.

A dangerous game, indeed.

"Gav." I gasp when he gently presses his lips across my neck, instantly finding the spot that makes me go *wild.* There's only one single thing that could satisfy me now: that beautiful fucking mouth.

It's wrong, and I shouldn't do it. There are so many reasons and too many people between Gav and me, but when I step back from all of it—he's the only one that makes any amount of fucking sense.

I lick my lips, body growing hot and full of fire in Gavrielle's arms.

Let me feel good. Let me feel something other than the horror of what I've done.

Gav brings me forward, and my eyes flutter open, and for the life of me, I'd give anything to stay in this place. It feels like the rightest thing as his thumb softly caresses my bottom lip while his other hand still cradles the back of my head.

Again, Gav's eyes are trained on my mouth as if it's his sole salvation. Then they climb back up to meet my own, the expression all pleading desire, our gazes locked in as if we're the only two people in the universe.

Our lips finally crash together.

His are warm and soft and so different from Malakyte's chilly touch that it shocks me, but I recover fast and I'm all in—all consumed by his lips on mine, his hands on my body, all of it driving us harder and faster and deeper.

I know he feels the same in the passionate way he kisses me. All of his heart and his soul are poured into how his hands glide over my body as if he was determined to commit my curves to memory. As his tongue slides into my mouth, a little purr of *fuck yes* flashes inside my mind, my hips grinding into him on instinct alone, pressure tightening in my core by the second.

All my guilt dissolves into the dust of this doomed galaxy. I didn't know a kiss could feel like this, could feel so right and so like home and nostalgic that it's painful it isn't *mine*.

But nothing—not time or Malakyte or us forgetting the other was enough to keep us apart. We've both fought through Hell to find one another, and now we're here, in this moment.

Together.

Grinding into the very impressive hardness between his legs, I want more of him, but Gav breaks our kiss, eyes wild and ethereal and beautifully Sky-Fae. He looks at me in a way nobody ever has.

It nearly breaks my heart and heals it all at once, and I'm not sure which way it'll end.

We both take a deep breath, mine shaky and heart hammering.

It's the safest I've felt in a long, long time. And it's strange because Malakyte gives me a sense of safety, too, but they're different. With him, I'm untouchable from the outside, but with Gavrielle, I'm protected from the inside . . . He guards my heart.

A massive boom steals the moment as our head's whip in the direction of the door. It blasts open, not sliding on the tracks but *kicked off* the tracks.

The sexual tension is utterly doused in ice-cold water as it floods my veins, and instant fucking panic nearly blinds me as two figures stand in the doorway, backlit by the light from the hallway.

Ennar and Naresteé have found us, and they're *pissed*.

CHAPTER 45

YEAR 3, DAY 1,120: IN OUR CULTURE, WE WEAR THE KILLS WE MAKE IN THE NUMBER OF BRAIDS IN OUR HAIR. I EARNED MY FIRST BRAID TODAY, FATHER . . . AND I KNOW FOR A FACT YOU'D BE ASHAMED OF ME. I WENT AGAINST YOUR PRINCIPLES AND ALL THAT YOU STOOD FOR AND RAISED ME TO BELIEVE IN. I'VE RUINED OUR FAMILY NAME. WORST OF ALL, I KNOW I'VE BROKEN MOTHER'S HEART AFTER WHAT I DID TODAY. I'M TERRIFIED MALAKYTE HAS MADE ME A KILLER BECAUSE IT'S TOO LATE TO TAKE IT BACK.

GAVRIELLE ABRAXAS

Kara leaps off my lap, but it's too late.

Naresteé laughs bitterly. "Oh, this is rich." She shakes her head, horns and body a stark silhouette standing in the doorway.

Ennar's yellow accents glow bright on his suit, his form braced for battle.

Because there's no way he's leaving here alive, and he knows it.

Kara's body gets awkwardly stiff as we both stand, her brow pinched tight, body braced low, arms raised high, ready to defend herself. She's afraid, but it's the panic in her eyes that makes me feel the most helpless. Narestñé can Recondition her—and me—at any moment.

"I'm not going to let you take my memories again," Kara says.

I'm proud her voice is strong.

Narestñé laughs, stepping in and pulling a jewel-hilted dagger from her simple black pants. "I'm not going to Recondition you again, Kara. Think of it as a painful reeducation."

Ennar follows, reaching down to his outer thigh where his custom suit magnetically holds a long, intimidating dagger, twice the size of Deimos's. He pushes on the blade, and it pops out, the entire thing gray from hilt to sharp, flesh splitting tip. Arianyte steel. Like my swords. Which, again, aren't here.

I can kick his ass regardless.

"Come without a fuss, and things don't have to get ugly," Ennar says, but we all know that's not happening, especially as the two of them close in.

"No chance you'll forget the whole thing and walk away?" I try, chuckling like it's all but a done deal.

"You're a cocky bastard, Gavrielle," Ennar sneers, "and I like 'em feisty."

Ennar pounces for me, while Narestñé jumps for Kara.

And it's on.

They're both fast, and it's impossible for Kara and me to fight together as the two instantly separate us. I have to trust Kara can handle herself, but it's distracting as all hell.

Ennar is wickedly quick as his curved blade cuts the air right at my face, narrowly missing me—because I'm distracted.

Focus. Kara can handle this.

There's no reprieve as Ennar comes for me, that dagger a skilled extension of his body, his suit's mechanical whining as panels shift and bend under his demand. I hiss as he slices the flesh on my bicep, doing nothing but dodging. I need a weapon.

I reach into my pants, pretending like I'm pulling out a dagger of my own from the pocket there, but it doesn't exist—it's an illusion.

The green glow in my eyes is illusioned away, too.

Now, I'm the one attacking—pushing him back, forcing him to dodge. I drive the fake blade up under his arm where the armor breaks, and he lurches as if he's been stabbed. The mind believes what it sees—I've learned that from these people.

In the blink of time between my fake stabbing and Ennar realizing that it's an illusion, the suit's fans hum, the locking mechanisms click to allow more movement in the panels.

Then I bend my knees and jump, my right leg flying and kicking his dagger out of his hand, and it clanks ten feet away.

We both look in that direction, Kara and Naresteé in a war of their own, but Kara's holding my surrogate mother off.

Wasting no time, I somersault over to Ennar's dagger and risk turning my back to him for the briefest of seconds as I grab hold of it, his footsteps charging up from behind.

Swiveling up to a crouch, I face him, heart hammering, but now I hold two identical daggers, and he pauses.

Flaunting them both, I taunt, "Which one is the real one? Which one is the illusion?"

"You made me look like a fool in front of him," Ennar sneers, referring to the other day.

I pretend to yawn, and it takes everything in me not to turn when I hear Kara cry out in pain. *She's alright* . . .

"You think I didn't know what she's been up to?" he presses. "And rest assured, he's already aware of what I suspect. I'm going to drag her by the hair and let him ruin her. Especially after what we saw today. Bad idea, Gavrielle, to betray the man that gave you everything *like this.*"

Fuck . . . We weren't careful enough.

Ennar doesn't wait, coming at me fast and brutally. "And it's the one on the left!"

He's right.

As soon as he's in my space, a familiar sound whines through my ears, my gut plummeting through my feet as the lights flicker, Ennar pausing in confusion.

Well . . . shit.

Out of the corner of my eye, Kara kicks Naresteé off her—they've tumbled to the floor—Kara knows what's about to happen.

And so do I.

The gravity plummets off a cliff.

Ducking low, I charge, using my weight like a bull and the immediate loss of gravity to my advantage. I have barely one foot left to push off the ground, and we make contact as I knock the breath from his lungs as the two of us go flying into the air.

The gravity throws both Ennar and Naresteé off their games, Kara floating to the corner by grabbing onto stray wires hanging from the ceiling, swinging from one to the other like jungle vines.

Good job, love.

The air pressure is displaced, and the sensation makes my stomach flip in a similar way as Ennar and I spin. Items float everywhere, like we're stuck free-falling through a rainstorm of junk and forgotten memories mixed with dust and skin particles as we fumble through them, our bodies linked together by arms and legs. Something wet hits my face, and I know it's water from the lack of a smell likely from a broken pipe somewhere, but I ignore it all and squeeze the blade in my hand.

This is it.

My only shot.

It's either me and Kara or him. He isn't giving me another choice. He's right that if Malakyte discovers what we were caught doing, she's dead—I'm dead—everything we've sacrificed and fought for will be dead.

I know exactly where to strike, precisely how big the chink in his armor is, right along his collarbone, where the chest plate meets the helmet.

I reach up as high as I can.

"Gavrielle!" he hisses.

He *knows*.

His own blade dives to the hilt through his clavicle and straight down into his heart, and he's immediately choking on his own blood, the helmet allowing for zero reprieve.

I rip the blade out and shove him away, his dark-blue blood shooting out in strange, suspended blobs.

My heart cracks. A piece of my soul splinters. The monster they made has turned on them, as all evil creations eventually do to their masters.

The lights flicker again, and my stomach flips a second time as everything that's floating in the room drops at once. Everyone but Kara falls, too.

Ennar's suit whacks the floor with a metallic thud, and he's down for good.

"Ennar!" Naresteé calls, rushing over to him as he convulses on his back, choking on his own blood. I give him the respect of watching the horrors of what I've done—what I've become—but it doesn't mean it's easy to witness his death. He taught me what I know, and I cared about him, too.

She rips his helmet off, and I turn away the moment I see his sandy blond curls. I hate myself . . . but what choice did he give me?

I chuck his dagger to the floor with disgust, and it clanks, the sound bouncing off Naresteé's cries.

"Gavrielle!" she screams, so fucking enraged, tears streaking her cheeks, teeth bared.

Her hatred for me is mutual.

303 

She brings her attention back to him, reaching for something in her boot. When she pulls out a thin case and is about to open it, Ennar stills.

His heart rate was slow, but now, it's stopped.

He's dead.

The Silent Breath injection she holds—in that case—is useless now. It doesn't work on the dead.

Naresteé screams.

"What did you do?" she bellows at me, shoving the case back in her boot. "You both will fucking *suffer* for this."

"You attacked us!" Kara shouts, finally jumping down from the ceiling.

She looks fine, if not a bit tussled.

Breathing hard, Naresteé stands, and I reach for Ennar's dagger again, but this only makes her laugh. "Going to kill me next, Gavrielle?"

"If you're going to force me to, I won't have a choice, but you're not going to force anything, are you?"

She scoffs. "You're delusional. Nothing is stopping me from Reconditioning you both right here and now, or even if I don't, telling Malakyte exactly what you traitors are doing. You fucking each other, too?"

"You won't do any of those things," I say, and her brows rise in challenge.

Kara finishes my train of thought. "Not if you want Pacey back."

Naresteé's face snaps to Kara as she wipes blood from the corner of her mouth. "You *fucking little bitch*."

The rage seeping from her is palpable, oozing out of every pore.

I probably should've been the one to deliver that line.

Standing, I say, "Think about it, Naresteé. Recondition us, Pacey will know, and that's it for you, final nail in the coffin.

If you turn Kara in, tell Malakyte what you saw here today, I'll make sure you never see me or Pacey again. I swear it."

I hate the tears streaking her freckled face, I really do, but we have to convince her. Otherwise, we're fucked—Kara is fucked—and both my planet and the one below us is fucked. Eventually, she peels her eyes from mine and roars in frustration as she stands, passes Ennar without a glance, and stomps toward the door. Once at the threshold, she says, "Clean up your mess, Gavrielle, but don't expect me to be your fucking maid for long."

Then she's gone.

Kara releases a trembling breath, and we run to each other, slamming together like we've been apart for months.

I trace my hands over every inch of her body. "Are you alright?"

Is anything broken? Is she cut?

She mirrors me, eyes searching. "I'm fine, Gav. You're the one who's hurt." She evaluates the cut on my upper arm.

"My race has accelerated healing. It'll be fine. I'll have Ahren clean it later. For now, I need to get you back into that sauna. Act like nothing happened. I'll take care of this."

Kara's face goes from pale—to ghostly white.

"Will she really keep quiet?" she asks. "She hates me, Gavrielle. She had a clear shot to slit my throat, and if the gravity didn't kick off when it did, she would have."

I sigh heavily, the tension still coursing through my blood. "Despite everything, she loves me . . ."

"Well, she hates me."

"Shit. Yeah, that's true. Our timeline is now significantly compromised because of this. We can't wait when she can drop a bomb on us at any moment. We'll need to act soon."

Pulling her into a hug, I take in her scent and every detail about her that my senses can absorb—terrified this could be the last time I get the chance.

CHAPTER 46

ARIANYTE IS INTRODUCING REEDUCATION CAMPS
DESIGNED TO HELP REBEL DISSENTERS UNDERSTAND HOW
DETRIMENTAL A REBELLION WOULD BE FOR EARTH AND
THE TERRAN POPULATION.

MALAKYTE ARDEEN

"She's beautiful, isn't she?" Father asks, his mood pleasant.

Likely because he looks young and healthy again, but his high won't last, not like his excitement for the creature standing before us.

Deep within the Vivianite, Father and I look upon his newest creation as it breathes for the first time.

The room is dark, the monster casting a blueish light onto Father's skin, its pseudo heartbeat pulsating that light as if the machine truly had one. It completely lacks any semblance of a heart, but a weapon shouldn't feel or care or know what it is to love—it just makes you weak. Yet I can't help but contemplate what Karalevine would think of me if she knew of this creation of chaos.

"It is notably apocalyptic," I say.

"Your cock isn't going to ruin this for me again, will it?"

"I assure you, Father, my cock has nothing to do with it," I retort, knowing where this is going. "Karalevine knows nothing of this. Zariya destroyed it. Karalevine will not. I've put in hard work to ensure that she and this planet behave exactly as we intend them to, producing ample assets. It would be a moot point to destroy it."

"Hard work." He laughs. "You're a pampered prince. What do you know of hard work? This planet is bursting at the seams. You've lost control. Or am I out of bounds as I was in the throne room?"

He's let go of the notion that I killed Selenyte, but all that comes to mind is Karalevine's face in that moment when he snapped, how utterly shocked she was to witness the violence I've known for over two centuries. I had forgotten how bad it was. Father plays nice, but it won't last.

It never does.

If I am to inherit his crown, his power, I need him to be satisfied.

This weapon is the means to that end.

If I am to ensure Karalevine continues to love me, I need her people to survive the war she started.

I have a means to that end, too, but I'll be shattering one heart to prevent hers from breaking.

"How about we test it elsewhere first?" I compromise. "It would be a shame if it doesn't work as devised."

If worse comes to worst, I can stage an accident, and it'll be destroyed again. I won't allow Father to purge what's important to Karalevine. If this weapon does what it was designed, she will never forgive me.

It takes all my effort not to flinch when he clasps my shoulder. "See, you can be taught. Your idea, where to?"

We look back to the beast we created. An abomination made flesh—or, rather, a machine given life as close to flesh that can possibly be. Zariya had the right to destroy this.

I'm sorry, Gavrielle. You should have known better than to betray me by opting for the other side.

"Planet Nyktos," I say.

For her, it must be Planet Nyktos, so it isn't Planet Earth.

But to do so, Father's bloodlust must be satiated. I could likely get him to back down after the coronation, Mr. Dawson's death, and prevent the Terran people from the indubitable annihilation this weapon will unfurl across her world. I do not wish for that. There's still time to stop this—but not much.

Perhaps it is the guilt lingering in whatever sliver of a heart I possess.

It is unlike me to ponder such foolishness, yet Karalevine's light has changed something in me, something vital.

I don't like it.

She's gotten within my skin, dug herself deep inside my flesh, past bone and tendon and blood. Driving herself so far inside my heart that rooting her out would be a process I could not endure.

"It isn't going to be *you* who evicts her, big brother."

Selenyte's voice bursts through my thoughts like a wrecking ball.

I'm in the middle of securing my tie when my bedroom door shoots open, hurried footsteps pounding their way up the stairs.

Narestee's scent hits me before she makes it to the second-floor landing, and I turn around, her appearance disheveled.

"Frame someone else," Narestee spits, her eyes fiery and determined. "Blame another Terran. Who cares who it is. The brother has to live."

 308

I sigh, completing the final tug on my tie. "We already had this conversation, Naresteé, and it isn't the time to continue it. I'm meeting my parents and Karalevine for the engagement ball in twenty minutes."

"The coronation is in three days. There is no more time to talk about it."

"Father wants to make an example out of him."

Naresteé splays her arms wide, wrists flicking as if I'm being overtly obvious. "Right. Blame someone else."

I unroll my sleeves to button them at my wrists. "That's not possible. Father is barely convinced Mr. Dawson committed the murder because that cocky bastard won't confess, and Father already suspects me of doing it. Changing the perpetrator days before the coronation will lose all credibility for anyone we accuse anyway. Father wants what he wants."

Plus, now that I have the helmet safely stored where no one else can reach it, I feel assured he will never know the truth. Once I have a moment to breathe, it'll be destroyed, but for now, it's unreachable.

She approaches me, her eyes pleading in a way I haven't seen in decades. "After all I've done for you over all these years, I've never asked you for anything. The one time I do, you refuse me because, why, a little boy is a threat to your precious Star?"

"Watch it."

"*Fix this.*"

Naresteé doesn't back down an inch.

I turn my back to my second in command. "The letter is a ploy, Naresteé. She doesn't wish to return. You need to move on."

Naresteé doesn't skip a beat as I grab my cloak and head down the stairs. "You didn't move on after Zariya. You certainly as fuck didn't move on after Karalevine scarred your face and entered the games just to destroy you."

"I'm a powerful man, Naresteé," I say, throwing on my shoes as she stands over the railing looking down at me. "I don't have to."

Arabella K. Federico

"I'm a powerful man, Naresteé," I say, throwing on my shoes as she stands over the railing looking down at me. "I don't have to."

CHAPTER 47

ALL DISRUPTORS AND WEAPONS RATED CLASS A AND B ARE BANNED IN ALL ZONES WITH POPULATION LEVELS 1-4. ANY PERSON FOUND IN POSSESSION OF WEAPONS OUTLAWED BY TIE OCCUPATION WILL BE SUBJECT TO PROSECUTION.

KARALEVINE RUZZ

Step two of Project Sabotage almost didn't happen—it still may not.

I figured if Naresteé had ratted on Gavrielle and me, I wouldn't be dressed up like Malakyte's pretty little doll. The relief that floods my glitter-coated body is immeasurable, but now it's as if my head is in the guillotine and Naresteé will pull the lever at any moment.

Malakyte does one thing well—he sure knows how to dress himself.

He looks dashing in his black suit, the suede filigree pattern shiny against the smooth matte of the jacket. His hair is polished like glass, those high cheekbones sharp. We look like the dark king and queen in the making.

Too bad it's all a lie.

The ballroom is one of the bigger spaces on the ship, but what's striking is the vast, hundred-foot-tall windows separated by supporting pillars every thirty feet along the entire left wall. Outside, the stars glitter like the crystal chandeliers mounted on the high ceiling above the many guests as they mingle and drink, their smiles and aristocratic ploys so damned obvious I could puke. The Arianyte Council of Exstacé among them. The beautiful architecture is bloated, and anyone with eyes in their skull could see it's all a con.

The real Arianyte is evil. The real Arianyte hurts and conquers and kills. What was I thinking wanting to be queen of this place? And the others want me to rule this shit show? They're crazy. Where I once saw hope, I now see hate. In every angled archway, on all the pieces of fine art, to the rugs and the silks and the engraved "A" for Arianyte logo on fucking *everything*—it's disgusting.

Strange music plays softly in the background as we get bombarded immediately upon walking in. People congratulate Malakyte and me, nearly all strangers, and I stand by his side with a fake smile.

He holds my hand, icy and so different from how Gavrielle's hand felt just this afternoon . . . I was lucky enough to wash Gav's sent off me before changing back into this pretty packaged lie again.

The entire time, Malakyte parades me around, laughing and acting like there's no care in the world, all while lying through his sharp, wicked teeth.

We truly deserve each other, a pair of dirty, filthy liars.

"Are you alright?" Malakyte asks me once we finally get a break from these people. His mood is uncharacteristically upbeat. "You've been quiet all night."

"I'm fine."

My heart aches as his eyes get all soft and warm, as if this man made of ice can be thawed.

I look down, terrified he'll see the deception in my eyes.

His frosty hand grips my chin like he owns me, guiding me back up.

I can't be afraid of him.

My eyes are daggers as I pierce my stare straight into his soul. "I just want to make you proud. I'm afraid I won't be good enough for you."

None of it is a lie, and it doesn't register as one to him, either, because his smile is sympathetic.

I'm chilled as his hand moves from my chin to adjust a stray strand of my hair out of my face. His eyes soften further as he steps closer, his body a block of ice. "I promise you that I never would have chosen you if I didn't believe with everything that you were good enough for me. Never tell yourself that you aren't. You've freed yourself from pain and trauma. Now embrace your authentic self by my side." His hand falls to the jeweled necklace at my throat, shade Blackest Night. "The darkness looks stunning on you. Never hide it. Never from me."

Malakyte does something Gav can never do for me . . . and I doubt Ardelle did either, he makes me feel like my darkness isn't ugly—it's beautiful.

In front of everyone, he bends down and kisses me. His lips are strikingly cold against mine, a shocking sensation compared to Gavrielle's.

Yet my body bursts into flames. Hating myself, I kiss him back.

Ever the proper royal, he breaks our kiss rather quickly but holds my face in place. "You look perfect tonight if I didn't say it already."

I try to ignore the pit that opens in my gut because, although he's right that I do look beautiful, the process to get here was one hundred percent controlled by him. From my loosely curled hair, to the jewelry, to the dress—Malakyte chose it all. The Night-Sky blue gown accentuates my tattooed skin in a way that makes me feel like a goddess. The delicate A-line bust morphs into a corset with finely milled mica that glimmers under the nighttime quartz lights, but that's nothing compared to the voluminous, multi-layered skirt with thousands and thousands of tiny crystals hand-sewn into the fabric. For the first time, I feel like I own the title "the Star."

I smile. "Twice."

He grins, flashing both sets of his canines. "I'll spend the rest of my life telling you how perfect you are. Devote that time taking you out of dresses like this, night after night."

That heat grows to a roaring fire when his voice goes low, deep, and his free hand glides down my bare low back. He wants that future with me . . . yet he's done terrible things to ensure that he gets it.

"And how, exactly, would you do that?" I whisper bashfully, unable to avoid playing with him.

Unable to deny myself this rush that sweeps in and overtakes me when it comes to Malakyte. He's the quick burn of ice, not the slow burn of fire . . . and I don't know which one I truly want.

His eyes graze over my body, undressing and stripping me bare right here in front of his entire court. Malakyte's face is so ethereally beautiful, perfect, glowing that I can't look away as he takes me in. Then, grabbing my hands, he sways us to the soft beat of the music playing in the background.

"First, at the foot of our bed, I'd turn you around," he twirls me in the dance, and I spin away, our eyes locking for a split second before I spiral back. "Take one last look at you in this gorgeous gown, and then I'd slowly, *exceedingly slowly*, unzip the back of your dress for you."

Malakyte's voice purrs like the deepest velvet draped seductively down my skin in a caress that curls my toes. "Once I've unzipped you, I'll slip this fabric from your body, bend you over the bed, and help you step out of it. I'd keep your heels on."

I swallow, holding his stare and my breath. "And then?"

 314

"And then, Karalevine, I'd make sure to take all the time in the world looking at you in the lingerie set I had made specially for me. How foolish of me, I meant *for you*."

I roll my eyes. "Really?"

"You caught me. But can you blame me? So, then I'd take in my fill before ripping it off your body with my teeth."

Heat floods my cheeks at the image he's conjuring within my mind. Hot, forbidden, dangerous thoughts that seep into the spot between my thighs, making me all sorts of stupid.

"Once you're completely undressed, I'd get on my knees for you, for my queen, and I'd taste you, consume you, devour your pussy until you're screaming my name, exactly like last time. I'd edge you *for hours* until you're begging me to fuck you." He leans close to my ear so nobody in the room can hear the filthy words from his mouth. It's a quick, sharp whisper, a lashing to the tightness brewing between my thighs. "I'd want you insane with need, mad with it, every nerve in your body aching for me. Trembling, desperate *need*. That's when I'd fuck you, Karalevine. Fuck you slowly at first, just a modicum of what's to come with my cock buried inside you. And then . . . I'd fuck you hard, fuck all the tension out between us that I know you feel, too. I'd fuck you until you come so many times you can't take it anymore, ending it with my cum dripping down your thighs"

I lick my lips, hating that his words alone have left that pretty lingerie he was referring to completely soaked.

Who am I a traitor to more?

"Can't wait," I manage to choke out.

He chuckles as he stands to his full height, and an unfamiliar playfulness glitters in his eyes as he tells me, "We have all the time in the world to play. For me to teach you so many different ways to find pleasure together . . . different activities to explore."

"Even when I grow old and you stay as young and as strong as you are today? I don't live to be over two centuries old, Malakyte."

He doesn't seem concerned one bit.

"You'll remain this beautiful and young for centuries, as long as you're by my side."

I raise a brow, but before I can ask what the hell he means by that, Herkimer interrupts, completely dousing all the heat within me as if he had soaked me with a hose.

"Ah, our lovely couple."

His tone is joyous, relaxed, nothing like the cruel man who abused his son a week ago. He's also looking super young again, like when I first met him. How is this happening to him?

Zoisyte is gorgeous in a glittering gown I'd shade in the color Plum Tree. The smile on her face is genuine. However, her eyes are sad as she watches us together.

"If only Selenyte could've been here," Zoisyte says, looking around as if her daughter would part through the crowd and run up to give her a hug.

The pity I feel for this woman strikes me hard because she is me, just years—possibly centuries in the future if Malakyte is to be believed—and I almost fell into the exact same trap she did.

"I'm so sorry," I tell her, despite having been told Selenyte was out to kill me.

Zoisyte seems to be the only decent one of their entire family.

Malakyte fidgets by my side, his head snapping to the right as if someone had snuck up on him. We all look at him curiously, and it's as if it dawns on him we all caught whatever the hell that was.

Clearing his throat, visibly uncomfortable, Malakyte wraps an arm around his mother. "Selenyte would've loved Karalevine and been happy to—"

"Sir." A SSPARROW rushes up to us, panicked. Not just any SSPARROW, *Ennar*, who everyone believes is Ennar. His black armor, with its yellow-lit accents appears no different from how it did earlier, but now, Gavrielle is inside that uniform. "We have a sighting of one of the fugitives you've . . ." Gav hesitates, voice distorted, acting like he's unsure if I should be hearing this.

"Fugitives?" I ask—because why wouldn't I? "What's going on? Is it the rebels again?"

Ignoring me and turning to the fake Ennar, Malakyte instructs him to find Naresteé in the crowd and bring her to him promptly. My gut does an entire flip-flop at hearing her name. Then Malakyte turns to me. "I'll be back shortly. Enjoy yourself. Talk to people, Karalevine. It'll be good for you."

"You're leaving?"

"For a scant amount of time, yes. An incident has demanded my immediate attention."

His icy lips kiss my cheek as Gav arrives with Naresteé, and she shoots me a glower with all the force of a disruptor pistol that nearly drives me to my knees.

"I'll remain to guard the princess," Gavrielle says as Ennar.

Malakyte nods, giving me one last glance before turning and walking with Naresteé toward the main exit, her dress in her hands as they nearly dash out of here after I assume he told her who, precisely, was spotted.

Other SSPARROWs converge on them and then they're out of sight through the wide, triangle-shaped exit.

Pacey has been spotted.

They're coming for her.

Stage one of tonight's plan—complete.

That was almost too easy.

"I'm going to hit the little girl's room," I say to the emperor and empress, who are both eyeballing me as if I'm a piece of meat. "I'll take my bodyguard with me, of course. Well, not *with* with me. But you knew that. Okay . . . I'm going to just . . . go . . ." I turn and begin walking with Gav as Herkimer's eyes burn a hole in the back of my head.

Intentionally being awkward isn't a hard fake for me, but after witnessing Gavrielle killing my real bodyguard only a few hours earlier and fighting Naresteé to boot, the faking is only going to get harder and harder.

Step two in Project Sabotage has commenced.

hours earlier and fighting Naresteé to boot, the faking is only going to get harder and harder.

CHAPTER 48

Nobody notices me and Gav leaving the Azurite ballroom, as if, without Malakyte by my side, I'm nobody. Just a ghost haunting this ship.

As Gavrielle and I cross the exit, we trek down to initiate stage two of tonight's plan—getting undeniable evidence of Arianyte's crimes. From this point on, I wasn't involved in the planning, so I'm not exactly sure what to expect or what proof we're supposed to collect and how all that looks. Only that they said I had to see it for myself and that it's in the medical sector.

"Your performance is flawless, you know," Gav says through Ennar's mask, voice distorter on. "That kiss almost looked real."

I wince. "You want me to tell him no because his old prodigy is watching and wouldn't like what he sees?"

It's meant to be sarcastic, but my delivery comes off a lot harsher than I mean it to.

Gav shrugs, and it's hard to tell exactly what that's supposed to mean.

"I'm going to have to do a lot of things I'm not going to want to do. The night of the wedding, for starters. I don't know if I can give him what he wants. But he'll know something is wrong if I don't. I know everyone is thinking about it, including you. We don't need to beat around the bush. If it's what I have to do to atone for what I've done, I'll do it. But don't get mad at me for it when you and the others are forcing me into that situation."

Gav waits to reply as two strange-looking extras pass by. "We can find a way out of that for you. You shouldn't be forced to fuck him for this plan to work."

Even behind the SSPARROW mask, I can hear the indignation in his voice.

Kissing Gavrielle only complicated this entire thing.

I frown, biting my lip. "Do you think he'll force me?" I ask, trying to hide the trembling in my own voice.

It doesn't seem like Gav is going to respond, but he finally does. "No."

I blink, the distorted voice making him sound cold and distant, all emotion behind it stripped away by the alien tech.

"I can just tell him I'm not ready," I suggest, then shake my head. "He's perceptive, though. He knows when I'm lying most of the time."

"So, it's a lie that you're not ready?"

My cheeks instantly get hot.

Fucking stars.

More extras come within range, and I don't risk saying anything that could possibly get back to Malakyte.

"It's complicated, Gav," I say, voice sterner. "What's more important? What I want or what we're fighting for?"

"What *do* you want, Kara?"

I know what Gav is asking me, but I can't give it to him. My feelings are a mess, and juggling all this is just too much. I don't know what I want.

 320

"Slipping Narésteé a note was one thing," Gav says, shamelessly changing the subject. "Where we're trying to go next is a whole other planet in comparison. We're about to walk into a bad place. I need you to prepare for it, okay?"

He doesn't have to tell me twice.

The two of us slip inside the elevator, and the silence is an awkward third wheel as it takes us down.

The elevator descends into the deeper part of the ship, not as far down as the cells and the dragon's prison, but it's close. I silently hope Ardelle is still hanging on and that he knows we're coming for him.

Gav's Ringer magic pulls at my gut as he begins flaring it to life. His specific feeling is now a familiar tug inside my body I could never forget—even if Malakyte erased it a thousand times.

There will be no sneaking around this time, no elaborate distractions or hacking our way through anything. To get where we need to go, the only hand we have to play is one of pure deception.

I've never physically become one of Gav's illusions, and I don't know how it's going to look or feel from my perspective. There's no time to ask as the elevator doors whoosh open, and we're immediately met with five SSPARROW soldiers. They stand fifteen feet ahead at the entrance to the medical sector, their heads swinging our way.

I have to hold in my gasp when I hear Malakyte's voice from directly beside me.

Gav—dressed in Ennar's SSPARROW uniform—is completely gone and is now the spitting image of Malakyte. It's as if Malakyte himself is standing before me, dressed exactly as he was when we danced.

Gavrielle is *good*. No, flawless. He's got every part of Malakyte down. From his posture to his mannerisms and even the slow, deliberate way he speaks, it is spot on. I'm in awe.

"Your highness," a SSPARROW says, all the others bowing. "Naresteé."

To me, I look like me. My skin remains milky white, kissed with tattoos and dressed in my pretty gown. But to them, I'm the horned bitch Naresteé.

Gavrielle plays his role to perfection, and I will, too.

"I'm here to see the children," Gavrielle says, authority dripping from his voice.

Gav has come a long way from creating simple shadow monsters at the orphanage, that's for sure.

The soldier rises from his bow and says nothing as he and the other soldiers take us down unfamiliar halls. This floor of the Azurite is far different from the others. Where most of the ship is clad in dark walls, whose essence drips of mystery and longing, this place is just the opposite. The walls are Snowflake White like a sterile room utterly sanitized of anything good or warm, the lighting so bright no shadows can be found.

We pass room after room lined on the left side of the corridor. Behind glass-framed rooms, I see the true horrors of what Arianyte is capable of. He warned me . . .

This is a *bad place*.

People—likely human Tributes but who the fuck really knows?—are being tortured beyond my imagination.

Most are strapped to exam tables, and it looks to be a myriad of medical experiments being inflicted upon these poor people. Some don't even look like people anymore. They're distorted, animalistic, or zombie versions of what once was a human. Many are thrashing against bindings, glass prisons so similar to my nightmares I get nauseous. Some even battle against the doctors inflicting this cruelty.

It takes everything in me not to flinch from all the screaming.

This is wrong. This is sick. It's beyond fucked, and I've got to stop this.

Having a black hole in my memories is just . . . Stars, it's *agony*.

 322

I need to know what happened—I have to.

It's only going to get worse until I do.

We stop at a set of double doors, and I shove my revulsion down enough to focus on our goal.

Get inside that room.

Collect the evidence we need.

Share it with Trinity and the rebels on Earth.

Destroy what Malakyte holds dear: Arianyte's reputation.

We're going to be his death knell.

Although my gut drops to my ass when the SSPARROW says to Gav, "Your blood, your highness."

CHAPTER 49

PUBLIC EXECUTIONS OF REBEL DISSENTERS WILL TAKE PLACE AT NOON DAILY IN EACH ZONE, LOCATIONS OUTLINED BY TERRAN ZONE REPRESENTATIVES.

Heart thrashing, I act as if nothing is amiss as I watch Gavrielle's illusion roll up his sleeve and place his finger on the blood scanning device, the exact same one that locks Malakyte's little treasure trove.

No matter how good Gavrielle is, he can't make this machine think his blood is Malakyte's, but all I can do is watch what unfolds.

I'm impressed that the blood that flows up and into the analyzer is the same Nebula Navy shade as Malakyte's. Keeping my breathing even as his blood is scanned is an effort in self-control, the urge to bolt increasing with every heartbeat.

If we're caught . . . *Fuck* . . .

Perhaps I'm having a little PTSD from earlier today.

Gav isn't portraying anything amiss, so does that mean he anticipated this lock? Or is he flying by the seed of his pants like the hellion he is? Equally could be both.

I can't allow Gav to get taken. Be where Ardelle is or worse—likely much worse. He's too important to me. I need him.

A satisfying chime rings out, and the scanner seems to announce the blood was a match. Yet, when Gav goes to open the door, it remains locked.

Fake Malakyte turns to the soldiers with such animalistic fury that the rest snap to attention. "Why isn't the door opening?"

I scoff and cross my arms, as Narestȇȇ would do.

No shit the door isn't opening—because the real lock is being disguised by Gav's illusion magic, showing that it's all good to go, when, in fact, it's not.

Nice, Gav.

"I . . ." The SSPARROW shudders. "I have no idea. This has never happened before. Sir."

"Well, you better go about finding a solution to it. I don't have time to deal with your incompetence. Open this damn door. Now."

Gavrielle speaks smoothly, yet his voice drips with cruel authority.

Flailing around like a fish out of water, the soldier retrieves a Dezlar from his suit's panel—sort of like a pocket for the metal suit—and frantically taps on the screen. "The backup code is being generated now, sir."

"It better be."

"How much longer is this going to take?" I demand, hoping my voice comes off as Narestȇȇ's because, to me, I sound exactly like I normally do.

The SSPARROW looks around at the other soldiers as if they'll magically pull the code out of their asses until his Dezlar beeps and he rushes to the door's locking mechanism, punching in what appears to be one elaborate, complicated password. It takes him minutes to punch it in correctly, but once he does, the door slides open with a soft, smooth glide.

Darkness awaits us within.

"Leave us," Gavrielle demands, flicking a dismissive wave.

They do.

The door slides shut at our backs, and the two of us are sealed within a darkness that bridges beyond shade or shadow.

It's a darkness that permeates the soul with the foulness that lurks within it.

True Blue lights bounce off the machines that hold up each child as they're suspended, bodies hooked up to tubes, IVs, incubators, and other fucked-up shit I don't know what to name. Their little feet dangle, and I wonder why the occupation bothers to put socks on their feet when tubes are shoved down their throats and into their stomachs. The only mercy is that they're all asleep, soft lashes fluttering under closed lids as they dream of better places than this horrific, Arianyte-made Hell.

Behind each child is a small tank where various levels of a glowing blue liquid are collected to their left.

I've seen this liquid before, in the shade Sizzling Cyan.

I claw at my purse, hands trembling as I fumble with the clip, but I eventually unclasp it. When I rip out the case Malakyte had given me and open it, the two syringes glare back at me as if they know how complicit I am in their creation. Horror crawls over my skin as the beeping of machines hold the ghostly cries of the children.

"No . . ."

My voice cracks, throat so tight I can hardly get air through it as I look between the syringes and the liquid collecting from each child. They're identical. Down to the tone, saturation, level, lightness—*everything*.

Gav takes my free hand, and I hate the person I see looking back at me, his illusion still active. I do. I hate Malakyte. And the tears that fall are from sadness but also from something else, too.

Blinding fucking fury.

"What is this?" I ask, holding the case up to Gav.

 326

Clearing his throat, Gavrielle says in his own voice, "It's called the Silent Breath. This is where the serum is manufactured. There is another harvesting center on the Vivianite, too, as well as the many planets they occupy for themselves. They harvest cells from the young because they're freshest, and through their medical advancements, those cells are transferred and combined with a bio-absorbable injection. When you're injected, it quickly heals you or repairs damaged cells from aging or illness or injury. It's how they're all so old yet appear so young. It's because of *this*. They bleed the children dry until they inevitably pass away. But the Silent Breath isn't merely for the royals— it's a product they produce and sell and deliver galaxy wide. Well, for those who can afford it. The price is high. Only the top one-percent can afford it, but you better believe the Terran Officials have their claws in it. I know for a fact that they do. It's why their corruption has twisted their morals into indifference as they willingly turn the other way as children were ripped off the streets."

These are them . . . *the Hijacked.*

"Any one of these kids could've easily been us, Gav," I whisper, still shocked at what I'm seeing. "I'm going to kill him for this," I promise through gritted teeth, loathing the illusion of Malakyte I'm looking at.

I knew it was going to be bad, and I thought I had prepared myself to see it—but I wasn't prepared for this.

The only way I can tell it isn't Malakyte is through Gavrielle's warm hand anchoring me so that my sadness doesn't buckle my knees. If I fall now, I'll never get back up again.

I need to destroy this entire empire. Raise it to the stars and slam it down to the Earth, eradicating all that it is and does and stands for. My anger, a monster unleashed upon them, used against them just as they planned to use it against everything I loved and fought for.

And I was just kissing the man responsible for it all.

Each day, I find out more and more of the things Malakyte has done behind my back, and each day, I find it harder and harder to defend him.

Support him.

Love him.

He must really think I'm stupid, doesn't he? He knows—*he knows*—how I feel about the Hijacked.

And he doesn't care.

He thinks he's won—but he hasn't.

This game isn't over.

In fact, the queen is on the board now.

She's coming for *them all.*

CHAPTER 50

CONVICTED REBELS WILL BE SUBJECT TO EXECUTION BY FROZEN AIR. DEVELOPED BY ARIANYTE SCIENTISTS, FROZEN AIR IS AN EFFECTIVE METHOD THAT FREEZES THE AIR WITHIN THE LUNGS VIA A PRESSURED BLAST OF SUPER-COOLED VAPORS DELIVERED THROUGH A SEALED MASK. DEATH IS INSTANTANEOUS, PAINLESS, AND HUMANE.

It took two days for the footage we secured to be leaked to Planet Earth. I expected some disruption for me personally, but I did not expect this.

My security is so tight it's choking. I'm not allowed out of my room without Malakyte. No more gym, pool, or any other outings.

"It's all for your protection," he claimed this morning, trying to act like this bomb hadn't just been dropped. Trying to act like he doesn't suspect I had something to do with it. He does suspect me. I know it with every fiber of my being. Much like me, however, Malakyte wants to pretend that our illusion is still this dream world where the two of us are in love and nobody and nothing can interfere. He's committed, as I am in some ways, to our shared delusion.

He doesn't want me to see the leak. He wants me to remain ignorant. Take my Dezlar so I can't access the feeds. Keep me inside my room. There's no television to watch the news broadcasts from Earth. Make sure the servants and guards are careful with me, lest they slip, and I discover his filthy little secret. Since I'm supposed to be his ignorant, blushing bride, I don't fight him much, but I do push back some, if only to keep it realistic.

Naresteé still hasn't ratted on Gav and me, but it feels like that's another ticking time bomb waiting to blow the entire Azurite into the stars.

Gavrielle is still parading around as Ennar, but Malakyte has him doing stuff all over the Azurite to put out the fires of this blazing inferno we started. It's sort of perfect because as Malakyte orders him to check all the cameras for me and my movements, go through my Dezlar, and whatever else, Gavrielle is covering my ass while actively sabotaging as many things as he can without looking suspicious. He also has the most access to me he's ever had, which is lucky because they discovered the others were using the armored suits a while ago, and they do facial checks every single shift for all soldiers. They don't check their SSPARROW leader, since he's the one doing the checks. But with Naresteé aware of our ploy, any second can be our last, as Malakyte's suspicion of me intensifies to outright paranoia.

From what Gav has been able to whisper to me, Trinity took responsibility for the leak, and they made sure to say they collected the footage when they boarded the ship almost two weeks ago. Hopefully, keeping the heat off me. Doesn't seem to be working. I have no idea how the Terran people are reacting to this, and it's driving me up the wall.

As the day goes by, servants have been coming in and out of my room with nothing but nonsense about the wedding. The dress, how I want my hair, if my heels fit, what would Malakyte like, all the while I keep my ears open for whispers. And when the quartz lights switch to night, I'm a bundle of nerves.

Food comes in for dinner, and my table gets set for two.

Malakyte walks in a few moments later, looking . . . older. Tired. Stressed.

We exchange hellos and begin eating, no small talk. I can't even fake it anymore.

"You're quiet tonight," Malakyte says, the two of us sitting across from each other at my small table where the stars and moon shine brightly out the window next to us. "Also, why is your hair in a messy bun? You know I don't appreciate your hair being thrown up like that, Karalevine. It makes *you* look messy, which makes *me* look messy. We're better than that."

I stop chewing my food, afraid that even grabbing for my glass of wine will make him think less of me, its contents almost as dark as Malakyte's eyes as I force myself to look at him. Swallowing the bite as if it were made of ash, I take a sip, ignoring his comment and focusing instead on saying the words I've been rehearsing all day in my head.

"You expect me not to be quiet after what happened today?"

Something flashes across Malakyte's eyes, and he, too, reaches for his wine in the shade Bloody Cherry. His gaze never leaves mine as he drinks. I'm now under a microscope.

Play my role. Perform this dance of deception to perfection because it's not quite time to bow.

"Who told you?"

I practically laugh, setting my glass down. "Some of the maids thought I was sleeping, but I heard them gossiping about it. You know how I feel about the Hijacked . . . How when I was little, I was tormented by the thought of being taken. How I fought for those kids. You told me Deimos was responsible for taking them, but that was a lie, wasn't it? You fucking lied to me *again*."

There's no hiding the disgust in my voice, even as I recite my script.

"And to that end," I continue as he opens his mouth to talk, "why the hell didn't you tell me the tensions with the Terrans were so bad? War bad. Seriously? I'm supposed to be your wife tomorrow, and you can't even tell me the state of things? What the fuck?"

Malakyte sets his glass down, and his fork falls to his plate, the clank a heavy bomb dropping between us.

My heart races because I'm pissed. I want to hear his explanation, his apology, and his graveling.

He's done. Toast. There's no getting out of this.

"Karalevine." Malakyte's voice is deep and strong, as if he isn't guilty at all. Yet my name on his lips still makes my knees weak. I wonder if I was attracted to someone who I hated so much before he took away my memories. "The footage that was leaked was not what you think it was. Those children are ill. Sickened with diseases, both contagious and degenerative alike. What we're doing is merciful. We're trying to find a cure, so no other children suffer like they have. I'm trying to save them."

My laugh is bitter at best, completely bitchy at worst.

"That's rich."

"You think I'd lie to you?"

My mouth opens, and I almost stand from this chair and shout across the table that all he's done is fucking lied to me.

Don't let your rage ruin everything.

"You lied to me about how we're on the brink of war, my old mentor and a girl I saw as a sister being in the center of it," I say instead of what I truly want to say—instead of verbalizing the rage boiling in every drop of my blood that makes me want to leap across this table and strangle him. "About the other Starseeds and Ringers, about the rebels." I shrug in disgust, dropping my own fork to the plate with a clank.

"That's different," he claims. "I knew you'd feel responsible for Geonni and Trinity's actions despite their betrayal. Regarding the Starseeds and Ringers, I didn't want to burden you with having to choose between Arianyte and people you're magically shackled to. I wanted to give you peace, Karalevine. After everything you've been through, you deserve that."

I dig my nails into my thighs. "I don't believe you," I whisper.

Malakyte stands, the act frightening until he comes and bends down before me, turning my chair to face him. "You don't buy that my devotion to you causes me to omit details that I know will hurt you? That I don't wish to see you suffer over a circumstance you can't change or fix? Is it so far out of your realm of possibilities that I could love you to the point of not wanting to burden your heart with a war I know you'd feel responsible for? Sacrifice yourself for? Do anything and everything you could to prevent loss, even to your detriment? Damn me if you must—hate me even, if it makes you feel better—but I wasn't going to allow you to destroy yourself over these radicals that turned against you for loving me. I did this to protect you."

A disbelieving, irritated sound escapes my throat as I look down at him, but his reasoning seems so genuine that a conflicting tickle creeps over my mind like an insidious spider.

Malakyte takes my hands in his and places them over his Elendril mark—his heart. "I'd never do anything to ruin what we have, Karalevine. You don't know how much you mean to me; how hard I've fought for us to be together."

Oh, I know exactly what you've done for us to be together.

Feeling his heart beating beneath his chest, I wonder . . . is this the truth? Was he trying to protect me because he does love me? Is he sorry like I believed him to be earlier, or is this merely more of the same act? I see all of what he's done—I do . . . but despite that, he still makes my heart flutter when he says he loves me. Why does he make me feel like this? Why can't I just hate him and leave it at that?

I'm so fucking confused.

This wasn't how I expected this conversation to go. I was steadfast about bringing him down. Now I wonder how I can destroy a person who claims to love me this much. That's all I've ever wanted, and he's offering me the galaxy on a platter, with all the power I could want, and all I've got to do is take it.

Take his power.

Embrace my darkness.

It would be that easy . . .

Is my relationship with the others stronger than the one I've built with him? They claim it was, but I have no memory of that life. All I remember is him . . .

And Gavrielle.

I swear Dannanōk's voice creeps into my head once more, like he creeps in on these precipice moments to draw me back to the light. *"Zariya's sin doesn't have to be yours."*

"I don't know, Malakyte," I sigh, my apathetic feelings genuine. "I'm not sure if I can trust you."

All true.

Malakyte's expression darkens to that of a thundercloud, a coldness pouring off him as if *he* were the storm.

He releases my hands.

I let them fall away.

"I, too, wonder if I can trust you, Karalevine."

My stomach drops as he glares at me.

Eyes darken as the prince of Arianyte removes the mask and reveals his true face—including all those pointed teeth.

He knows . . .

CHAPTER 51

THE ARIANYTE EMPIRE DECREE #158

ALL PROTESTS AND RIOTS ARE ACTS OF REBELLION,
AND ANY PERSONS TAKING PART DOES SO KNOWINGLY
AGAINST ARIANYTE LAW AND WILL BE CONSIDERED
AN ACTIVE REBEL.

Malakyte brings me to the throne room immediately, and dread dampens my palms as the doors open and he nearly pushes me inside. I should have run when I had the chance.

Herkimer is sitting on the throne—looking as worse as I've ever seen him look—there's definitely something wrong with him. I think he's dying.

Yet the second person I see, I wholly don't expect.

Ardelle is strapped to a chair in the center, gagged and bound, his blond and Starry Midnight Sky hair caught in the gag. A thick, matte collar in the shade Void clanks around his neck, truly different than the others.

Our eyes clash immediately, so much fear on his bruised face—in various stages of healing.

"What is this?" I say, voice too weak as I look between emperor and prince.

"Your loyalty test, dear Karalevine."

ARABELLA K. FEDERICO

"What is this?" I say, voice too weak as I look between emperor and prince.

"Your loyalty test, dear Karalevine."

CHAPTER 52

THE ARIANYTE EMPIRE DECREE #162

TERRAN GOVERNMENT OFFICIALS ARE HEREBY
STRIPPED OF ZONE LEADERSHIP. ZONE AUTHORITY WILL
FALL TO ARIANYTE.

ARDELLE DAWSON

I'm scheduled to die the day after tomorrow, but it may very well be tonight.

That cold-blooded monster brings Thumbelina through the doors. I can't believe we're back here—in this room—all over again. It's obvious what's about to happen—but she's completely unaware, and it destroys me to see her shock as their ploy kicks off.

We're nothing but pawns.

She looks so different as Malakyte walks her toward the throne, his hands on her body so possessive that it makes me sick, and I grind my teeth on the gag. From the way she wears her hair to her clothes and her makeup, none of it is my Thumbelina. He erased her. I saw it in the prisons that day. Is she still that same, distrusting hand of Arianyte that

Malakyte turned her into? Or have the others managed to get her memories back by now?

The emperor stands from the throne, my head whipping in that direction. "Ignore the murderer for now."

Murderer. His son is the one who murdered his daughter, yet that son has muzzled me from saying so.

With a Dez pad in one hand, Herkimer grabs Thumbelina's upper arm in his other, and she recoils, straight into Malakyte's arms. "Oh, child, relax. I promised my son no violence, so there will be no violence. At least from me to you—I can't promise much else."

Violence? He hurt Thumbelina?

Herkimer practically drops the Dez pad in her hands.

She looks down at it. The transparent screen with two grips on either side is too far away for me to see any details, although I'm sure it's nothing good, knowing these sick people.

"What am I looking at? What do you mean loyalty test?" Thumbelina asks, looking more at Malakyte than his dad. "Malakyte, this isn't funny. Take me back to my room."

Malakyte moves to stand next to Herkimer as he nods toward the device. "It isn't complicated, Karalevine. The rebels mounted not one but two major attacks against Arianyte recently. If we are to trust that you're truly loyal to Arianyte, we need undeniable proof. This is the interface for one of our weapons systems, and it's currently set on the ten-block radius where the undersewers reside in Zarmenia. We have intelligence that pinpoints that area as a major rebel stronghold. As you're likely familiar with the Reptilians who reside in the undersewers, those blocks are deserted and free of any civilians. I want you to bomb them and prove to me you're not on the rebel's side."

Oh, Thumbelina.

He's such a manipulative, sneaky, dirty bastard. Her mother's grave is there . . . and he's right, the rebellion is there, too. Does she remember any of these things? Something must have happened for him to suspect her, but what? Not knowing what's going on is making me crazy.

Her eyes are wide as she looks at him in shock, her head subtly shaking no. Of course it is. Memories or not, Thumbelina isn't a monster. She isn't going to kill innocent people.

"And if I refuse?" she asks, eyes shifting back down to the Dez pad.

"Then, I'll have to assume you're working with the rebels and the wedding tomorrow is off."

Herkimer adds, "And the coronation."

"But I'm not, Malakyte. I swear. You know how important my people are to me. They'll get hurt."

"You don't have people anymore." Herkimer rounds on her. "You have Arianyte. And you're either with Arianyte, or you're an enemy of Arianyte. Like *him*." He points to me. "Now, choose your side. I'm not giving my throne up until I know for sure."

I swallow hard, locking eyes with Thumbelina as she looks over and silently begs me for help. I know those eyes . . . but I also *don't*.

I pull on my bindings—hard. Harder . . . harder . . . But, stars, the metal clasped around my wrists and ankles are too strong, as well as the collar, and I'm helpless. I can do nothing but watch as this is going to get much, much worse.

They want to take away what makes her a hero, what makes her good. Just as Malakyte had said he would do. Turn her dark, like him. But she isn't his darkness. She can't be.

"You'd only be hurting the guilty," Malakyte purrs, drawing her back into his black cloud, weaving a demented, calculative web around her where no answer is a good choice. "There are no innocents there. We've done several sweeps—I've ensured that because I want your conscious to be clean about this."

Thumbelina's chest is rising and falling rapidly, her breathing quickening.

The Dez pad trembles in her hands.

339 

Come on, Thumbelina. Say no, I beg her, hoping she'll look at me again and see it in my eyes.

I have zero context, no comprehension of what she's been through since we were last in this room together, when I was captured, thrown in a cell, and forced to fight night after night. We're likely two different people after what's happened . . . I know I am. What if . . . What if Thumbelina's truly gone? Did Malakyte corrupt her exactly as he promised?

"Decide, Karalevine. My patience is waning, and your hesitation makes me believe you've been lying to me."

"I haven't!"

"Then, send the message that the rebels don't fuck with our power."

"I—"

"Now or we're *done*."

Thumbelina's eyes turn glassy, face pale. She's not okay.

But she releases a shaky breath as she looks down at the pad, changing its position so she can hold it in one hand.

No . . .

She can't do this. He can't make her cross this line. She'll never forgive herself.

And the rebellion . . . it'll be decimated.

She looks back at Malakyte again, pleading with him, but there's no sympathy to be found. I can see her resolve wavering, her defiance dissolving down, down, down . . . every bit of her strength seeps out of her as her body fawns into itself. Her head shakes no, her chin quivers, but it's when she turns her body away from me completely that I guess what's about to happen.

My heart plummets when she pushes the button.

At first, there's only silence as I look away, and the heartbeat of a fly could be heard in the wake of her choices.

Herkimer laughs manically as the Dez pad clatters against the tiled floor. Thumbelina's tears are an added symphony to his cheers.

 340

"Are you fucking happy now?" she yells at Malakyte, and when I manage to look back up, Herkimer is at the window, likely waiting to watch the bomb drop like a grand fireworks show.

Thumbelina's complexion shifts to a pallid green, the lights in this place reflecting small beads of sweat on her temples. Our eyes lock for a split second, and my spine becomes a straight line because I see a glimmer of the old Thumbelina flash in her teary eyes, but she blinks them away, leaving behind only hard-edged misery.

We can't look at each other for long, and she peels her gaze away.

I slump back in my chair, wondering what's going to happen next.

If I'm here, it isn't going to be good. She's planning on marrying him tomorrow . . . That fact absolutely throws me. What is going on? Is she doing this as some kind of ploy—which they clearly suspect—or does she not remember a thing and she's genuinely about to marry this psychopath? I can't let it happen, but I don't know how to stop it, just like last time I saw this horrible room. I couldn't save her. She saved Pacey, and I couldn't save her.

"I'm leaving," Thumbelina announces, turning toward the door, but Malakyte catches her by the arm, the act enraging me.

"We're not finished here."

"I am!"

"You're not!"

The widening of her eyes and her brows hitting the ceiling shows that he scared her.

Your mask is slipping, buddy, and she sees it.

Malakyte leans in and whispers something in her ear. Then the two look directly at me.

My fingers curl around the chair's arms.

Herkimer shouts for her to come watch the missile.

Thumbelina and Malakyte ignore him as they continue to argue. I don't need to hear them to know what he's demanding she do next to prove her so-called loyalty.

My eyes close, and I bring up the memory that's kept me alive these last weeks, along with the person in the cell next to me, of course. But mostly, my memories with Thumbelina and Pacey and the others. I remember her as she was, a vibrant, beautiful, little-dog energy rebel who stole my heart and branded me with her love. I don't know if I'll get out of this room alive, but at least I had the time with her that I did . . . and that my sister is safe. Thumbelina could bomb the entire planet, and I'd still love her because she did that.

But this isn't her anymore . . . I know that because, the last time this bastard made her choose between us or the planet, she chose the people. That's the real Thumbelina, but I don't know if she'll ever come back.

It's just Kara now.

And I don't know her.

CHAPTER 53

KARALEVINE RUZZ

Malakyte's voice is a viper's hiss in my ears, and I want so badly for the drumming beat there to have caused me to miss-hear him when he said he wants me to kill Ardelle.

But I'm not that lucky.

"Don't make me do this."

Every word cracks through my clenched teeth. Sending the bomb onto what could be the entire fucking rebellion nearly ripped me to shreds, brought me to my knees, destroyed the last bit of goodness inside me, and I won't damage my soul for him any further.

And Trinity . . . Stars, what if she's there? What if she's dead?

Sacrificing a few for the many isn't worth it if I lose the Arianyte crown. If I do, we're all doomed. I need to go through with both the wedding and coronation to complete Project Sabotage and destroy him and his dad and Arianyte as a whole.

I need it to get my memories back.

Save the entire planet, not just a small chunk of one city.

But never has doing the wrong thing for the right reason felt so fucking terrible.

This power doesn't make me feel good anymore. I feel dirty.

Disgusting.

Ruined.

It isn't like when I killed my abuser. That was bad—dark and twisted and wrong—yet still, I relished it. As shameful as that is to admit. This, however . . . this is unforgivable. Which makes me unredeemable.

And I just want Gavrielle. I just want Gavrielle when I should be wanting the guy strapped to that chair.

Fuck . . . This is a fucking mess!

But I hold my composure. I'm fine, I'm calm, I'm not a rebel. *I don't know what the fuck I am anymore.*

Quelling the sickening, burning, agonizing fury that claws from my gut all the way to my heart, digging its claws in every inch on the way up, I straighten my spine and make sure my own mask does not slip again.

"I'm not a killer, and you're making me one, Malakyte," I warn. "*Stop.*"

"He killed my sister."

"Then, kill him yourself," I say, looking the prince dead in the eyes. The hand he has clasped around my arm loosens and nearly falls away entirely, but he remains there, caressing my skin like he's kissing away the grip of icy iron. "I just sent a bomb onto my city to prove my loyalty, and if that's not enough, then *I'm done.*"

I wrench my arm free to prove a point, but he also doesn't get to make his touch manipulative, too.

Malakyte sighs, eyes gliding over me, likely seeing every microexpression and hearing every beat of my heart. I must be calm. He knows the old me loves Ardelle, so I need to distance him and me, and a plan begins to form.

A deadly plan.

"Do it," I urge *him* now. "Kill him. You want revenge so badly?"

Fuck, this is a dumb idea, Kara.

I steal the device Malakyte is holding, the one he presented to me moments before. It's a little round controller with several buttons on it. It controls this new, advanced collar that's around Ardelle's throat. With one push of a button, Ardelle's head goes boom. It's also the key the others need to free him.

I walk toward Ardelle.

Our eyes lock, and I soften my gaze for the briefest of seconds. *I'm so sorry*, I plead. *Pray this works.*

Or you're fucking dead.

I know Malakyte and Herkimer well enough by now to make this bet, so I'm doubling down hard—feeling as if I'm completely outside my body.

I point the controller at Ardelle. "Do it!" Then I toss it back to Malakyte, throwing my arms up in the air like I don't give a shit. "Kill him now and be done with it. No waiting till the coronation where all those people can watch your sister's killer be punished. Who cares? Detonate the collar right here, *right now*."

Malakyte looks like he wants to kill me more than Ardelle.

Herkimer saunters back from the window with a look of curiosity pointed toward his son. "Now, wait just a moment. What are you two bitching about? You're not even married and you're fighting like a couple of old Grays."

"I'm not a killer," I quip before Malakyte can control the narrative. "I won't do it, so he can either be finished with our relationship or kill this guy himself with just you and me here to witness the Starseed's death."

Come on . . . take the bait.

Herkimer's eyes are the same dark, lifeless pits they've always been, but now they're framed by sagging, spotty skin as they shift between me and his son.

The emperor snatches the controller from Malakyte and tosses it over to the pillars. "I'm satisfied that she's loyal to Arianyte. We'll kill the Starseed bastard at the coronation. I want the Terrans to piss themselves when they know what's coming for them, those rebels most of all. I can't wait for the big reveal."

"Exactly," I echo, fearing what he means by *big reveal.* "Herkimer, I think we're finally on the same page."

Thank the fucking stars this egomaniac fell for it. I knew he wanted to make a spectacle of Ardelle's death because of his emotional ties to Selenyte, but I didn't know if it would work. It buys Ardelle at least another day and a half.

That doesn't give us long to save him, but for him to live, Project Sabotage has to survive, and I shredded my soul to ensure it does.

If dubious could become a man, it would be Malakyte, with his tilted head like a feline toying with its dinner, narrowed eyes full of suspicion, and tightly lined mouth that aches to rip into me. He won't go against Herkimer, not this close to the coronation.

"Let's go, Karalevine."

I leave the throne room without looking back at Ardelle and pray we can both stay alive before this all goes to hell, even if I know for certain that's where I'll end up after what I've just done.

I stand in my bathroom alone, still trembling from ruining my own soul less than an hour ago. Trinity has to be alive. No, she didn't get hurt. *I* haven't hurt her. The rebellion hasn't been demolished. I'm not a complete, utter *monster.*

Leaning over the sink, clenching the sides of the black granite vanity, I finally look up into my reflection, meeting myself eye to eye.

Malakyte's voice taunts me inside my head, repeating what he said to me moments after leaving the throne room. *That softness in you is a weakness*, he had told me. *I'm glad to see you're loyal to Arianyte, but these emotions you exude . . . they're too much. Father will exploit them. Our enemies will exploit them. You know how much pressure I'm under, and I can't think when you're acting this way. Don't ruin everything. You did so well with this before. Why was it different with the Starseed?*

He was unhappy with my vague answers until he finally stopped asking why I couldn't kill Ardelle. He dropped me off in my room, and that was it.

I did what Malakyte wanted tonight, proved my loyalty to a man I hate, and I likely would've gone so much further if he pushed me—and *that's* what scares me the most. What I'm capable of.

You're disgusting!

If it's protecting the people and the cause, then I can find a justification to kill innocence—*I just did.*

Because you're filthy and dirty and exactly like him.

I thought I was okay, thought after my abuser was dead, I could forget everything that happened. Thought after I made the right choice—to fight on the right side—that it would fix this erosion I felt eating away at my soul. It didn't fix me. I'm not better.

I'm worse.

I'm losing myself . . . I'm lost and alone and so afraid of the reflection staring back at me. Malakyte was supposed to prove I wasn't too broken, wasn't worthless, but instead, he's shown me that I'm not only all those things—*I'm more.*

I'm a villain.

Who could love someone like me? Only another villain.

What does this mean? Am I truly not ready for the fall, for the break, for the inevitable crash of betraying this man I love and hate in the same breath? The others told me the truth about Malakyte. They ripped me bare and stripped away my doubts, yet . . .

. . . Maybe the unvarnished truth lies right here in this mirror, where it's been all along. A villain is who I *really am*.

I'm not sure there's a way to climb back out of this.

Gavrielle promised me he wouldn't let me fall into the darkness . . . He's too late.

I've already plummeted.

CHAPTER 54

Today is my wedding day.

I want to puke.

Scream.

Rage.

Soon, I'll be granted a crown of darkness beside my equally wrathful lover. I'll either take it and embrace the shadow or fight for the light.

Rather than staring at myself in the full-length mirror they brought into my suite and admiring myself in my gown, my eyes never leave the two dozen black roses Malakyte had sent over this morning. The black roses are me, I realize. The dark, wicked thing Malakyte wants me to be. They're sitting on the table we ate dinner at last night, the note he sent with it crumbled nearby.

I'm sorry.

It was written in his handwriting. At least he did it himself rather than have one of his assistants do it.

Looks like Malakyte is also playing into the illusion that we're in love and happy on our wedding day. Maybe I should, too?

"You should smile more, Miss Ruzz . . ." a middle-aged attendant says, fussing with my dress alongside several other women whose faces I haven't cared to look at.

I stand atop a little dais they brought in before the ornate full-length mirror.

Dress on.

Hair styled.

Makeup perfect.

I look beautiful, probably as pretty as I've ever looked in my entire life.

Yet I can't manage to make myself smile. It's all a lie—I'm a lie.

A murderer.

A deceiver.

This wedding, this coronation, is nothing but a ruse. A power-grab for the most coveted seat in all the galaxy. Yet a part of me wishes it was still real . . . that this love I'm grieving in real time isn't fake but fated.

I force myself to smile at the servant in the mirror. "Just nerves, I guess."

Her smile is hesitant as she fluffs the train of my dress then stands, reaching to my head and adjusting the crown for the twentieth time.

"Mr. Ardeen will fall to his knees once he sees you like this," she says, sounding proud of herself.

My door slides open, and Ennar—*Gavrielle*—appears in the mirror behind me, his step tripping on his way to me.

"The prince wants me to discuss security protocols with the bride, and the information is sensitive. I must ask you all to step out while I brief her privately."

Once they're gone, the door locked, and he's standing beside my dais, Gavrielle's icy white hair spills out of his helmet, tied in a loose ponytail at his nape.

 350

"If this suit goes any further up my ass, I'm going to get pregnant. I've seen more room on an escape pod."

For the first time today, I laugh. "Gav!"

His eyes can't be contained as they lovingly glide up and down my body, as if he's scanning every inch of me into his memory. Stunned, bewildered, amazed, desire, hope—all flashing in his beautiful eyes, shade Petal Ink.

"You're the most beautiful thing I've ever seen, Kara."

The world narrows down to nothing but the two of us in this moment of time, where, in some fantasy world, I would be his bride instead. He'd be the one to bind himself to me in every way possible. And we'd be happy, fulfilled, able to leave all this darkness behind us.

A fantasy, indeed.

"Gavrielle," I say, my eyes watering, a terrible confession on my lips.

"Kara," he echoes, and I walk to the edge of this stupid little platform and hug his metal-clad body, unable to voice my sins.

"Zariya's sins," Dannanōk growls in my mind.

This dragon has to be genuinely speaking to me because I refuse to be crazy as well as a soon-to-be dark queen.

"It's nice not having to break my back to hug you for once," he jokes, the heaviness in the air dissipating. "You're almost the height of an actual grown-up standing on this thing in those heels."

"You know you love it," I say, breaking the hug. "I'd say if there was more room in that suit you stole you could just slip me into your pocket space and get us the hell outta here, but . . . you know."

The playfulness fades fast, and a blanket of doom chokes us both.

"It's all going to be alright, love. I promise. If you feel lost out there, just think of me. *I'm always with you.*"

I nod.

If he only knew how often I do exactly that.

"There's something we need you to do tonight, and it's extremely important."

"Okay . . ." I fiddle with the lace gloves all the way up my wrists. "What is it?"

He pushes a button on the interface of his suit's forearm, and a panel on his hip opens with a smooth whoosh. He fishes out a small opaque bag in the shade Blueberry Yogurt and hands it to me.

I open it cautiously.

"Is this a needle and vial?" I hold up the needle to the light and squint at it. It's isolated in a sterile bag.

Gav takes my hand, holding the needle in both of his. "We need you to get Malakyte's blood."

My eyes widen.

"Why?"

"That room you described to us, with the Elendril weapons and all of Malakyte's most coveted items, we need to get in there before the coronation tomorrow. It's crucial you do this and even more important that you don't get caught. If he catches you taking his blood, he'll immediately know what you're up to. It'll be catastrophic, love."

My mouth dries at the thought of having to do this.

"He'll feel it, Gav . . ."

I'm not sure this is a good idea.

"Ahren says it's a very small needle that's made for kids. Malakyte is a heavy sleeper, but I suggest staying up until he's been out for a couple hours. You don't need much. Once you get it, hide it in the freezer with this ice pack. Tomorrow morning, I'll find you before the coronation to collect it."

I take a deep breath, letting this all sink in.

Gav clears his throat. "One of the things we may be able to retrieve in Malakyte's treasure room is the key that turns on the memory machine. No pressure or anything."

 352

The hope he ignites within me is far from little.

"My memories could really come back?" I ask weakly, not quite believing it.

Gav nods. "That's our goal. You could have your memories back by tomorrow if things go right."

Tomorrow?

His words stoke embers that have nearly fizzled out. It feels both exciting and like I'm out of time all at once.

"You better get going," I say, taking his ponytail in my hand as I curl it around my fingers. "I don't want you to get caught."

He nods, going to pick up his helmet from where he left it.

"Time to get married…" he says, his lack of enthusiasm painful.

A pit in my stomach opens up ten miles deep.

"Here comes the bride," I playfully chant, throwing my arms up in the air and turning back toward the mirror.

I cringe.

Here comes the dark, wicked bride . . .

CHAPTER 55

I've waited nearly fifty years for this day.

Within the Azurite, one of my favorite places is the Observatory—perhaps because it was Zariya's favorite, too, and why I chose it as the location where she'll bind her soul to mine.

The three-hundred-sixty-degree dome view is unmatched on the Azurite as the vast beauty of space twinkles as if we were physically floating out amongst the stars. Earth and the moon bob in the background, the sun's rays filtering in as they hit the thousands of black roses decorated through the seats, statues, arches, pillars, and the aisle. The very archway I stand under, in fact, is illuminated by the sun's warm glow, a nice addition to the quartz lights as I adjusted them to shine in a soft pink tone for just us. Little birds fly, set free from the aviary, the air sweetly scented and the music soft and romantic. I hope she approves . . . Hope that, after last night, she can find happiness today. I pushed too hard, my paranoia getting the best of me.

The eldest council member stands next to me as the officiant of this ceremony. Her robes match her skin in the purest white shade. She nods her bald head to me, black lips curved in a viperous smile. They want this union, want to test my authority, see how far they can get once Father dies. One foot in his grave already.

Both sides of the aisle are packed, and there are an even number of people across each side. The Council of Exstacé and the Arianyte court are seated on the right. Father, Mother, and Naresteé sit in the very front, a seat left open for Selenyte . . . which looks empty to everyone else but me. To me, she sits all glammed up, posturing oh so facetiously. Her ghost even gives me a little wave.

Public officials and other spectators fill the left, but there is a special guest on the bride's side that I insisted be right in front.

Jance glowers in the seat closest to the aisle. After making a fool of me, I want him to watch, to know that his daughter is *mine*.

Around the edges of the dome is a heavy SSPARROW presence. An even number. Forty-four. The other Starseeds and Ringers will likely try to prevent this union from taking place, but we're prepared for anything.

My earpiece buzzes.

"The bride is walking."

Two, four, six, eight, ten, twelve, fourteen, sixteen, eighteen, twenty, twenty-two.

Thankfully, my black leather pants are hemmed to the perfect length. One sleeve of my suede jacket is hanging longer than the other, and I pull the shorter one down so they can match. My tie, thick and voluminous, looks a bit off-center, so I adjust that, too.

Stars, enough.

Shadows morph behind the frosted doors of the Observatory, and my spine snaps to attention.

The doors open in unison, and there she is.

Karalevine.

My Star.

A smile—a genuine one—slams onto my face at the sight of her like a hit to the skull. There's no preventing it.

The backs of my eyes sting at her beauty as our eyes catch with her in the doorway. She's too beautiful to be mine, but she is.

My little rebel isn't wearing all white, and why would she? I've trained her well because, instead, her gown is mostly black. My knees weaken at the top portion, cut into a beautifully soft A-line that perfectly cradles her breasts, pushed up by a tight corset. The corset is black and glitters like starlight, caged in by a body-hugging metallic filigree that reminds me of a serpent hugging its body around her perfect curves. There's so much to look at. Crystals, tulle, and gossamer, all flowing from black at the top, slithering down to ethereal, iridescent white fabric at the bottom.

The jewelry hugging her shoulders draws my attention next, earrings that dangle around her milky neck, an actual crown of black jewels nestled between the coronet of braids atop her head as my queen of darkness continues her journey toward me. Her hair should be down in curls, but I'll let it go this time.

Mine.

She's everything. There's no one better, not even Zariya was this perfect.

Mine.

I'll do anything to keep her with me.

Mine.

CHAPTER 56

I'm a walking lie, a beautiful illusion. The moment every little girl dreams of. I'm living it. My groom, handsome in all black, has a genuine smile as I approach. Can this castle in the sky love we share fix all that's broken around us?

Malakyte takes my hands, smiling at me lovingly, his cool skin soothing on my sweaty palms as I step up to stand under the archway of black flowers.

The white-skinned bald lady from their Council of Dipshits goes on about eternal love and commitment and all that, but I'm in my head, praying that my star doesn't light up during the middle of this ceremony.

Malakyte's thumb strokes my hand tenderly, as if to say, *It's okay, don't be nervous.*

He looks so handsome, so clean and beautiful. His hair is tied back, and his face . . . The scar isn't stark, and it gives him an air of rugged hotness I wish wouldn't curl my toes.

But look at what he did to you, I say back to myself as that stupid part of me tries to rationalize his behavior. *What he made you do last night . . .*

This entire situation fills me with despair, with heartache, and with fear. Maybe the rebels weren't hurt since they're underground? Or they were trapped there, suffocated.

"Now," the officiant says, her speech finally finished, "will the Groom present his left wrist to initiate the never-ending ring, as a symbol of true love and longevity?"

I have no idea what she's referring to as she grabs a small device shaped like some cosmic, futuristic doughnut, colored in Moon Ray White. She pushes a button and releases her hands, the device hovering.

Malakyte reaches out, suspending his wrist inside the ring, and a golden light appears all the way around, etching something onto his entire wrist simultaneously. A moment later, Malakyte removes his hand, and a new bracelet is tattooed there.

It's just like the ones I saw on his parents' wrist that first day I met them.

It's perfect execution-wise, the lines straight and even, no human error to be found. The lines are thick yet flow with beautiful masculine sweeps and edges. Somehow, it looks like him.

"Now, the bride's turn."

My eyes shoot up to Malakyte in a panic.

He smiles down at me, taking my hand in his. He unties the decorative lace around my left wrist, and now I understand why I was forced to wear the stupid thing. Some symbol of purity, no doubt. *That's hilarious.* Then he places my hand inside the strange doughnut tattooing machine.

My wrists are almost completely covered with my actual tattoos, but none of them done with any Arianyte tech. Geonni is dying all over again watching this from wherever he may be, his abhorrence for Arianyte tattoos never a secret.

I miss him. I hope I didn't kill his daughter with that bomb . . .

The light is hot as it sears into my flesh. It feels scorching and itchy, but it doesn't hurt as badly as a real tattoo. In less

 358

than thirty seconds, it's over, and I pull my wrist out far too quickly for it not to be noticeable.

Now, burned onto my body forever is my own symbol of commitment to Malakyte.

It's wholly different from his.

Mine is dainty, flowy, and feminine, the lines swirling around my wrist a bit too perfectly, intertwining within each other in a flawless design.

"Now, may the ring bearer present the couple their rings to honor our Bride's home-world traditions."

Another council member, the creepy one with the split face, appears from somewhere close, a golden box in his hands in the shade Crown glittering under the starlight.

The councilwoman takes the box and opens it slowly. "Bride," she says, eyes sharp with malicious daggers ready to strike, "place the ring on the groom's left ring finger."

It's obvious whose ring is whose, yet they both take my breath away.

Malakyte's ring is heavy as I pluck it from the little black pillow. Its color is the shade Black Eternal, the entire thing etched with little notches taken out of it. It looks like some strange, geometric pattern. It's subtle, not overwhelming or gaudy, but just right. True to his style.

I tremble like a newborn fawn as I slide the ring onto his finger, his hand like ice under mine. His thumb grazing the side of my hand keeps me together.

"Now, Groom, you can do the same."

With some apparent ease I could never possess, Malakyte plucks my ring from the box, takes my hand in his, and slowly slides it onto my ring finger.

The ring is the most beautiful piece of jewelry I've ever seen.

It screams *dark queen* as if it had a voice box to do it with. It's set in a polished Dark Silver gold, the jewel at the center is a twinkling, sharply cut pear-shaped beauty. Whatever jewel this is, I've never seen anything like it before. I'd shade it with a mix of Celestial Blue and Midnight, the pigment deep and saturated. Within it sits what looks like thousands of miniature stars, each twinkling as if the jewel was a universe all on its own. There are traditional diamonds on the upper and bottom setting that curve around my finger perfectly. On the sides, two diamond cut crescent moons sit opposing each other, seamlessly balancing out the large main stone in the center.

"It's beautiful," I whisper, hating that this ring is *me* in jewelry form.

He sees me.

"Malakyte Mallick Ardeen, crowned prince of Arianyte, do you take Karalevine Arriah Ruzz as your eternal bride till the end of your existence. Through any sickness and bountiful health. Through trials, wars, and hardship. Do you take this woman as your bride forever and until your heart stops beating?"

He doesn't hesitate. "I do."

The officiant turns to me and repeats the vow.

The tingling on my star shoots up to a solid burn as the entire room holds its collective breath.

But all I hear in my head is his voice repeating: *I'm always with you.*

Gavrielle's voice.

I'm a liar.

I'm a murderer.

I'm a villain.

"I do."

The relief on Malakyte's face tells me he genuinely feared I'd say no. I want to live in his illusion for a tiny bit longer while I can. Live in a place where I'm just a woman, standing beside the man she loves; the man who chooses her . . . That's what every little girl dreams her wedding day is.

Shouts erupt as our lips meet, heating up my core to the point of boiling, meeting him in a passionate kiss that's both sweet and hot all at once.

We break the kiss, both of us flushed, my lips tasting like him.

A taste I don't hate . . . despite everything he's done. Despite that voice in the back of my head screaming at me not to fall for it—not to fall for him—I don't know if I'm strong enough to resist Malakyte or the dark power he lays at my feet.

CHAPTER 57

After hours upon hours of wedding festivities, my feet absolutely ache as we sluggishly enter his suite, Malakyte holding my hand so tight as if trying to bend reality. That, just for tonight, he can pretend we're actually in love and that he hasn't ruined everything.

Maybe I want to pretend, too?

Malakyte was fun today, his personality bright and happy, a glimpse of the man he used to be. There was also no rebel intervention, and I'm sure that helped ease his anxiety.

The others remained silent, as planned.

I groan as I plop myself on his couch, instantly drowning in tulle and gossamer. "These heels," I whine, trying to reach them but am unsuccessful due to the corset. "Never make me wear these again. They're too hard to kick ass in."

He chuckles softly. "Whose ass do you plan on kicking on your wedding day, Mrs. Ardeen?"

My body tingles as he says the name. My eyes glance down to the bracelet tattoo and the gorgeous ring. "Anyone who may think about taking me away from you," I say, hoping it'll assuage any fears he may have of losing me.

He smiles, showing me those pointed teeth. "That's my girl."

Praise kink activated.

Malakyte sits on the armrest, affectionately patting my head. He's been touching me like this all day. Except it's less sweet and more . . . possessive.

His eyes—warm and soft and beautiful—look lovingly as we lock onto each other, not letting go.

Bending down, he kisses my forehead, those icy lips leaving a ghost of their touch behind. "Let me get you out of this." He swoops me up into his arms in one smooth motion.

Holding onto his neck, I cock a brow at him as he walks us to the stairs leading up to the bedroom. "I think you were supposed to do this at the threshold, tough guy."

He snickers again, and I feel it in his chest as he climbs the stairs. "When have you ever known me to follow the rules?"

Kissing his cheek, I'm about to whisper something ridiculously cheesy in his ear, but my attention is completely ripped away once we reach the top.

"Did you do this?" I crack a disbelieving sound mixed with a giggle.

The entire bedroom is covered in rose petals and fake candles, but they flicker like real ones. A little path of petals leads to the bed, where more are shaped into a giant heart against his black sheets. It's ridiculously cheesy, but more than anything, I know he didn't do it because the rose petals are *red*—Lipstick Red, specifically.

Laughing as well, Malakyte says, "It was likely one of the servants. I refuse to claim responsibility for this."

"Doesn't look like you, but you should have done *something*."

Side-eying me, he shoots me a look that says, *Just wait*.

I immediately get butterflies.

Malakyte sets me down before the full-length mirror, and I watch him stand behind me in the reflection.

The weight of this moment barrels down on me with the consistency of the flickering candlelight across our faces. The time to decide what I want is over, but the choice will define where I go from here . . .

Truthfully, it isn't about Malakyte at all, the darkness he wields and if I can find any goodness in his heart or not. It isn't even about Gavrielle. It's all about me.

What do *I* want?

What do *I* need to do to make a choice?

I spoke those vows as I stood on that altar. They didn't simply taste like acid on my tongue—they tasted like guzzling cheap paint. This love is *a lie*, but there's a horrible truth behind that lie. I don't want it to be fake. I want him to love me. I want this to be real like I once believed it was, and I want that love to fix this grade-A mess we've found ourselves in.

"You look troubled," Malakyte says, rubbing my shoulders. "You don't have to do anything you don't want to, Karalevine. I'm not going to make you sleep with me just because we got married today. We have time. Don't misunderstand me—I want to, but I'll never force you. You're safe with me."

Inhaling deeply, I relax as the pressure lifts off me like a fifty-pound weight. I can say no, and it'll all be fine. I wouldn't break Gavrielle's heart, wouldn't complicate our plans—it'll all be fine. But if I said no, then what he's done to me becomes real by the morning. The treachery, the violation, the war waging inside my heart. If I said yes, I'd get to be loved by him like he used to love me before this all fell apart.

Just love me like you once did, I silently beg as I glare at his reflection. *Love me like you promised. Forever.*

Out of every choice I've made thus far, this one is the most dangerous.

To sleep with him, to experience him like that . . . could be the very thing that shoves me over the edge from where there is no return.

No redemption.

No goodness.

 364

No Gavrielle.

No Ardelle.

No rebellion.

No saved Hijacked.

No Earth.

No dragons.

No Starseeds or Ringers.

No Jance . . . his secrets and all.

Just me and Malakyte and this dark empire against the galaxy.

That is what I'm risking by sleeping with him, by allowing him in so deeply his claws will be impossible to detach from my heart.

That's quite a risky gamble.

Everyone keeps telling me how I'm supposed to feel. Team Starseed claims I should hate Malakyte. Malakyte is adamant Team Starseed are corrupted rebels. Nobody has asked what I'm feeling, and honestly, the realest thing is my feelings for Malakyte. Gavrielle, too. I can have feelings for two people for different reasons, and I do.

"Your heart is racing," he says, eyes darkening.

I take a deep breath. "I'm nervous."

"It's alright," he says smoothly, his hands moving down my arms and to my waist. "We don't have to do a thing. We can lie in bed, I can hold you, and we can fall asleep. That's fine with me."

I don't want to fall asleep yet because, in the morning, what he's done becomes real. Tonight is all I have left . . . and I'm not ready for it to end.

CHAPTER 58

"**C**an I get you out of this gown?"

What a loaded question.

I nod, my eyes cemented on him so hard my will alone could miraculously make him appear as the man I had imagined he was. This mirror image of him, the man I once loved and will love for one last night.

"It's stunning, by the way," he tells me as he unties the bow at the top of my corset. "I nearly fell over when I saw you come through those doors. I don't deserve you."

He's right . . . He doesn't.

"You can choose who you want to be, Malakyte. You'll be crowned emperor tomorrow, and nobody will have any sway or hold over you anymore. You'll be free. Free to make better choices."

"Indeed."

I almost moan in pleasure as the tension from the corset releases and he pulls the ribbon through each slot. Once he finishes unlacing, he removes it from my waist and throws it on the little sitting chair near the closet.

The zipper of my dress opens to my lower back, and I feel the coolness of his body on my skin.

He hums, admiring the lingerie. "So appropriately bridal."

The lace lingerie is all white with very intricate beading and boning, just another annoying layer making it so I can't breathe.

It does look hot, though.

I don't realize how heavy the gown is until Malakyte slips it off my shoulders, the fabric pooling around my ankles.

He takes my hand, helps me step out of it, then tosses the dress next to the corset. Now, as I stand in my pretty white lingerie before him in the mirror, I'm entirely sure he can see me blush.

"I'm so naked compared to you," I say, hoping he'll get the hint.

His eyes haven't been able to look away, but he peels them off my breasts and hips to meet my gaze. "Indeed."

I laugh. "Do you know any other words, Mr. Vocabulary?"

Undoing his tie and jacket buttons, he smiles at me, so cocky. "Don't jest at the way I speak, Karalevine. I'll have to punish you for it." It's a joke, but it still makes me a little nervous. "I'm kidding. I can punish you another night. That's not what tonight is for."

"What's it for?" I whisper, my body getting hot as he reveals his bare chest to me.

He's thinner than Gavrielle, but his body is all muscle. I don't think I've ever seen abs so deeply chiseled like his before.

Hot.

So fucking hot.

If I want to bail, now is the time. But looking at Malakyte . . . I realize he's exactly like that god he claimed to be. The power he wields is too damn intoxicating not to be skin-to-skin with a monster trapped in cold, hard flesh.

How could anyone blame me for wanting to touch a god? To be the object of that god's attention, every single bit of it. On my body, on my breasts, between my thighs . . . I could search the galaxy, but Malakyte will always be the closest thing to a real god that I'll ever find. By the stars, just for tonight, while our love isn't tainted by betrayal or lies, *let me trespass* into his domain.

His throat rumbles as he hugs me from behind, arms curling under my own and back around to play with the front ribbons of my lingerie corset. *His*, he tells me with the possessive way his arms cage me to him. "It's for us to do whatever we want. What do you want, Karalevine?"

What do I want?

I swallow, not realizing how dry my mouth has become.

What do I want?

Malakyte nuzzles my neck, his icy tongue licking and his pointed teeth playfully dragging across my skin.

What do I want?

His hands move, slipping out and into the hollows of my waist, traveling around my curves, to my hips, to my thighs like he isn't about to get his crown and his power in a matter of hours—it's only me. It's always been only me for him.

"Tell me what you want, Karalevine."

"I . . ."

"Do you want this?"

His hand slowly moves between my thighs, fingertips featherlight as they graze the lace.

My heart beats steadily, the ache beneath his fingers blooming.

"Yes," I say, hating myself for wanting him.

Malakyte is my villain . . . *and I love my villain.* To my heart's detriment, to the crash that I know is inbound, against all my common sense and knowledge that every person I know will hate me for it . . . I love him. My divine mirror. I'm his wicked match, his dark queen, his villain, too. Tonight, I get to believe this love between us wasn't tainted by someone evil but rather by someone who loved me so hard he gave Death himself the middle finger and found my soul after my body had died.

He's stolen a piece of my heart, hidden it just as he did my memories, and I'm nothing but a slave to him now. Too weak to break free.

The perfect little trap.

 368

And I'm ensnared.

"Touch me," I say.

He kisses my neck, his sharp canines more prominent, their pointed tips digging into my flesh, shooting my temperature straight to boiling when he reaches the spot near my ear. All the protesting from my inner voice is silenced the moment his hand works the fabric of my underwear, his fingers teasing as they glide over me, lazily drawing circles that make my knees weak and core molten hot.

He's rock hard as he presses into my ass moments later, my body reacting to him as I watch him touch me in the mirror's reflection.

It's so fucking hot I could die.

He steals my eyes like he's stolen my sanity, a heady desire pooling in his own. "I love when you get wet for me," he purrs, nibbling on my ear without ever looking away. "And I want you soaked, babe."

Opening my legs with his knees a little, he slides past the fabric of my underwear and touches my bare skin—and I'm *liquid*. We moan as his finger meets the wettest part and sinks inside.

Malakyte pumps his finger in a skillful rhythm. This thumb caresses my clit in tandem, causing my spine to arch back, his breath in my ear.

He pulls out, robbing me of the pleasure far too quickly.

Malakyte sees my disappointment and returns it with a sly, cocky grin.

Without saying a word, he drops to his knees, curls his hands around my lacy underwear, and slowly pulls them down. Every inch they descend is followed by a kiss that's ghostly touch lingers on my skin long after Malakyte's lips have left. Soon, my underwear is around my ankles, and he lifts my feet—still adorned in my golden heels—out of them.

"On your knees."

My knees meet the granite floor.

"Good," he says, turning as he lies on his back.

"What are you doing?" I ask, Malakyte scooting his head up under me—facing up, the top of his head toward the mirror.

Like . . . damn near right under me.

I immediately retract to move away, but he pins my legs in place, my heart fluttering.

"You're fine," he says, my cheeks burning.

He inches toward the mirror even more, my legs his leverage, and I look down to meet his eyes *directly* under me.

They're absolutely glittering.

"Come down."

Oh. *Oh* . . .

Even though I can't see his mouth, I know he's grinning like a cat.

Adjusting his arms to wrap around my thighs, he gently pulls me down, my legs opening wider and wider the farther I sink until I can feel his cold breath on me.

He's really doing this.

I brace my arms against the mirror's thick frame, the reflection the most erotic thing I've ever seen, ever experienced. My heart gallops in anticipation.

"Ride my fucking face, Karalevine."

Fuck . . .

Malakyte closes that last inch between us, lifting his neck and the sound that escapes my lips when he licks all the way up my core to my clit is feral fucking bliss.

He only chuckles.

Then he does it again.

I grip the mirror's frame harder, my thighs trembling as all my nerves scream *Fuck yes.* Every cold kiss of his lips and lap of his tongue makes me gasp, the sensation so opposite of my own body it nearly short-circuits my brain.

His licks go from slow and teasing to a full-on feast, and I can't hold in my moans of pleasure as his tongue does unholy

 370

things to me that drive me insane. The skillful twirls and flicks and sucks have me doing exactly what he asked, riding his fucking face.

It's when his tongue plunges into me that I think I might die.

Malakyte's hands gripping onto my bare ass alone is cause for ecstasy, pulling my weight down as my legs tremble and give way to his mouth. With his angle, his tongue is so deep inside me it's unlike anything I've ever felt before, his upper lip curling around my clit, sucking and nipping and blowing every nerve ending to its max. My body shakes, and I can feel the bomb within me ticking closer and closer to its explosion. His mouth . . . *Fuck, his mouth.* I've never felt anything so good, so perfect, so intoxicating I damn near come right here on his face.

After everything he's done, he shouldn't be allowed to make me feel this good, and I'll forever be haunted by the ghost of this moment.

Sensing how close I am, he stops, and I almost scream at how cruel it is.

Again, he finds it amusing.

Giving me one last long, deliberate lick in all the perfect places, he comes out from under me and I lower myself fully, my thighs burning.

My husband licks his lips as if he just ate a delicious meal, while devouring me with his eyes.

Chest and cheeks flushed, I turn around and watch him, seeing the slight slickness left on his chin in the candlelight. "Why'd you stop?"

The look Malakyte gives me is pure wickedness.

He crawls to the bed, throws pillows and blankets down, and quickly makes us a little spot in front of the mirror. I definitely don't miss how he slides his leather pants off, either, leaving him only in his tight boxers.

In front of the mirror, Malakyte sits with his legs and arms open, beckoning me to him. "Lay against me, Karalevine."

Doing as he says, I crawl toward him, flip myself around so I'm facing the mirror again, and lean my back against his chest.

Malakyte wastes no time.

Using his legs, he opens mine, the mirror bearing me to him fully, albeit the dim lighting has me mostly in shadow.

He leans in and whispers, "Don't ever look away from your body, do you understand me? You're perfect, and I see you." Nibbling on my ear, he drags his hand across my hips and thighs, quickly finding my slick entrance once again.

His fingers are ice as he plunges two in at once as he goes deep, my head falling back into the crook of his shoulder. My heels hit the mirror's frame as he spreads my legs wider, giving him deeper access to me as his lips, tongue, and teeth bite at my neck more aggressively.

"Malakyte," I moan, his fingers pumping faster and faster, coiling me up into another frenzy.

His free hand comes around my neck, the squeeze he exerts is light, testing the waters along with my boundaries, but I like the choke, and he presses a little more. "You're close," he observes, increasing his pace. "I can feel it. But you get to come only when I say you can. Not until I know that you're mine and only mine."

"I'm yours," I lie, knowing my heart doesn't fully belong to him.

Someone else holds another piece of it, too, and it isn't the person who should.

Malakyte thrusts in so deep, pausing only when his fingers go in as far as they can, then he slides out, taking away the glorious pleasure nobody should ever have the ability to hold over me.

Locking eyes in the mirror, I promise to make him hate me as much as I hate him right now.

I slide my hands behind me, grabbing his cock through his boxers, back arching to get a good angle.

His breath hitches as I slide up and down that gorgeous, hard, throbbing length. Fighting against this cage as it begs to be free—begs to be inside me.

I turn so I can play more, tease him more, and I immediately glide his boxers down, freeing him and slipping them off.

"Now I'm the one who's wholly naked," he purrs, bringing his hands around to my back, pulling on the ribbon holding my lingerie together. "Let's fix that."

My hands find the smooth, velvet skin of his cock after he finally strips me naked, and I stroke his length as he gives me his sounds of approval.

Now you *moan for* me.

Now I make you *crazy.*

I dive to lick his head, a hiss sliding through his teeth as he watches me hungrily devouring him.

I do it again, twirling my tongue, only to retract it when it feels the best. I tease him like this, again and again, making sure he knows how it feels to get so close only to have it be taken away. I'm getting revenge in a million different ways for a million different things, taking too much pleasure in torturing him.

I dive, my mouth taking nearly half his length in one go as I grip his balls in my other hand, sucking and stroking him in a consistent rhythm until he's calling my name.

"You're so good, Karalevine," he whispers, hands on the crown tied in my hair as I take him on my knees. "I fucking love you."

I lock eyes with Malakyte, his own heavy with desire as he cups my chin, all of him still filling up my mouth.

Eye to eye.

Hungry.

Eager.

Consuming.

Desperate.

Pleading.

Broken.

The two of our fucked-up souls clashing together within this bubble that *will* burst.

Not yet.

"You're so good," he repeats, barely able to form the words.

After going some more, I feel him teetering on the edge, but because he didn't give it to me, I won't give it to him.

I release him, grinning.

Sitting knee-to-knee, I kiss him softly before retreating.

He watches me, thick black lashes framing assessing eyes as they travel along every curve of my breasts and angles of my hips.

The prince of Arianyte wants me just as badly as I want him, but is he thinking what I'm thinking? If I give him this access to my body, maybe it'll fix this mess? Maybe he could change, I could change, and our love could heal what's broken around us? Fuck, *please* let it fix everything. That's what society said love was capable of, right? Of fixing a broken world, fixing *him*, fixing *me*.

"What is it you want, Karalevine? Be succinct so there is no ambiguity."

"All of you."

Simple. Direct.

But I should say what I'm really asking for. *Love me like you used to before you shattered me to pieces.*

He smiles at me, one of those rare, genuine smiles that's so convincing I can genuinely believe he never broke my heart. "Who am I to say no to such a pretty, wicked thing?"

CHAPTER 59

He tosses the pillows in front of me, positioning my knees on top so I'm supported. "Face the mirror again."

I do it.

Malakyte presses up against me from behind, hard and ready. He pins my wrists to the mirror's frame, and I grab hold of it.

"Good girl," he whispers, voice dipping into that deep octave that drives me wild.

Fuck, this is real . . .

There's no going back from this. From the act itself and all the dominoes that will fall from it.

On both sides.

And I don't know who I'll be once it's over or on which side of this war I'm going to fall.

"Malakyte," I say his name as he touches me.

"Karalevine," he purrs, his breath glacial on the shell of my ear.

We lock eyes in the mirror.

Everything has been leading up to this one moment. From our first meeting that he stole to the fake ones he implanted in their place to right now.

Villain to villain.

Fuck me, my eyes plead. *Fuck me like I know you've been aching to for so long. Show me the real you behind the mask and let me* see.

The grin he gives me in return is all wicked teeth but also a promise.

He lines himself up from behind, and my chest fills with a heavy sensation, heart hammering.

The anticipation is so vision-blurring I can nearly taste it.

"It'll be cold at first," he warns. "Give your body a moment to adjust."

I feel the aura on my inner thighs first, then on the bare skin between them next.

He's right.

The second his tip meets my core, I gasp, the chill overwhelming.

Malakyte eases in slightly, then pulls out, gliding his head across my clit before slowly edging inside a little bit more. In and out, each time filling me deeper. *Fuck*. The ache, the pressure, the maddening *tease* fucking destroys me.

"You're so cold," I say, feeling it so much more profoundly the deeper he goes.

It's like pure ice—except it doesn't burn, thankfully.

My husband growls as he releases his grip on himself, leaning over me, his hands braced against the mirror above mine.

"And you're so fucking warm, Karalevine, *fuck*."

He pushes in farther as he says my name, pulling a cry from my throat as he fills me so completely, I can hardly hold myself up.

Arching backward into him, I draw him in deeper, using the mirror as leverage.

We both moan simultaneously, and I force myself to breathe. I quickly forget once he buries himself completely inside me. Goose bumps shoot over my entire body as my temperature plummets. It's the oddest sensation I've ever felt, like if I exhaled, I'd see my own breath.

"Do you know all the filthy thoughts I've had about fucking you? I've thought of every way I'd take you, but this way"—he motions to the mirror—"was always my favorite fantasy."

I can see why. Even in the candlelight, I see where we're joined. His body behind me, the two of us watching each other in the mirror, completely naked and ready to fuck out all this tension that's been building between us for longer than I can even recall, but I'm certain it exists.

I want it.

I need it.

I love it, and I hate it.

I'm repulsed and so deliriously hot for him.

We're both living in a fantasy world, and right now, I don't care if mine is real or not.

I push my ass into his hips. I do it again, telling him what I want without words.

He pumps into me at a steady pace, my bones quaking from the pleasure.

His hair pools over my shoulders and chest, bouncing off me as we find a sweet, perfect rhythm.

I'm louder than he is, my cries of pleasure soft but consistent.

He feels so fucking good. *He's everything.*

"Harder," I demand. "Fuck me, Malakyte."

I don't want sweet lovemaking. "Harder," I say again, his tempo not fast enough.

Then he finally obliges me, pounding into me, the mirror slamming against the wall as we beat into it, my vision turning to stars.

More, more, more. *Give me fucking more.*

I push against him, meeting his tempo, whimpering my approval as he fucks me.

It's everything I imagined it being—no, it's better.

His own growls increase, his body growing colder and colder, the iciness battling against the warmth of my body.

Our reflections glisten, flushed cheeks and chests and eyes burning with desire.

So fucking hot.

I'm close, and he better stop fucking edging me and *let me*. I'll fucking *hate him* if he doesn't.

As if reading my mind, he slows to a stop, and I growl. "Malakyte!"

"Easy," he chuckles, removing my hands from the mirror and sliding us both back a little bit.

"Let me," I snarl, not needing to clarify.

He knows.

"I will, babe. You'll come so hard, I promise."

I growl in annoyance.

He hums, pushing my upper body down to the floor where more pillows sit, arching my ass up. I go crazy from the stretch as he angles a good inch deeper. "The wait will be worth it, I promise."

My hands grip the corners of the pillows as he starts up again, immediately pounding into me hard and fast and slick. The heat builds within me again like a volcano. I'm putty. I'm *his*. I'm dancing inside his illusion, and I never want the song to end.

"Tell me you're mine, Karalevine," he demands, voice on the edge of madness himself. "Tell me no one will take you from me."

"I'm yours," I say, my body trembling and heart racing so fast my star lights up the pillows beneath me. "I'm all yours, Malakyte. Please, babe. Please."

I can't help but beg for the release he's cruelly denied me, and if he doesn't give it to me, I don't know if I can contain my crystal's power.

Reaching around me, his devious fingers tap my clit in a new tempo he's never used before, fast and hard as he pounds into me from behind.

"You want to come for me, Karalevine? Come right now. *Good girl*."

Like a rope being held too taut for too long, I snap. I explode. I lose all sense of myself. My body can no longer hold off my climax, and the friction on my clit tosses me over the edge of no return as it builds and builds and builds, my cries increasing as I come so hard it's impossible to contain it. He keeps going, fucking me harder and harder as I'm thrown into orgasm after orgasm, not knowing when one ends and another begins. It's just pure blinding fucking ecstasy. The reflection of us in the mirror only adds to it, the images so hot—it alone could make me come like this for days.

Malakyte's own release is close behind me as he trembles.

My clit is so sensitive I force his hand away, not being able to take it any longer, but he keeps doing it.

"Come again. Come for me again."

"I can't," I say, feeling exhausted—in more ways than one.

"You can," he orders, switching his technique to a slower, twirling motion, ratcheting up that coil between my legs.

He pulls back, slips out of me completely, then picks me up.

We're on the bed in a blink, my back bouncing once before he's on top of me, rose petals flying around us both.

There's a small hitch of my breath before he slams into me all the way inside in one powerful thrust.

I cry out, hating that it feels so fucking good—hating that he makes me crazy. It isn't enough. I need him to go harder.

The anger I have for him boils to the surface, and it doesn't feel good, reality creeping inside this illusion with every pound of his hips.

Positioned above, harder and harder, he ravages me, and I meet him blow for blow. I'm not his fragile victim or doe-eyed bride. I don't want him to be gentle. The two of us collide where our love and hate for each other ravage everything in its wake. This entire fucking mess is nothing but a casualty of our toxic love.

Gripping his shoulders, I dig my nails into his flesh and hold on. A painful hiss escapes his lips as I rake them down his back—drawing blood.

Good.

"You're such a bad girl, Karalevine," he says, the edge in his voice different. "I'm going to punish you for it."

"Do it," I challenge, meeting his eyes and considering just how good it would feel to take him down.

Let him be the one who is punished this time. To have his every move controlled, scheduled, watched—see how he fucking likes it. Take something vital from *him*. The thought gets me closer to another release, crashing this fantasy into shards that will cut us both.

He fucks me hard, a man so typically controlled now utterly undone inside of me. I am, as well, completely losing myself over to the ecstasy of this moment and the utter toxicity of our relationship. I don't know what's happening inside his head, but this is a fucking ride from body to soul, and there's nothing healthy about it.

We're both fucked up in so many ways, and it shows here, when all our walls our down—why we love each other so much when everyone, including us, knows we shouldn't. Nobody else could be us, and that isn't a good thing.

With my arms and legs wrapped around his body, I come up to that threshold of pleasure he loves to control. He knows I'm there again, knows I'm going to fragment into a million pieces.

"Malakyte," I gasp his name as I come again, this one harder than the others, sharper than the others, shattering me differently from the others.

This is the moment. The moment I feel it so profoundly I can't lie or delude myself for a single second more. Everything about this *is a lie*.

It feels so amazing and so horrible all at once. I'm insane from the maddening duality. From how good a lie can feel when I make myself believe it.

Then he slows, slows, slows . . . and I think he's finished—but he keeps going. A hand comes down to gently caress my face, and I flinch from the touch unintentionally. He finds my eyes, his own mystified, his walls fragmented to dust as he watches me with wild infatuation.

"I love you," he says, both of us moaning as he pushes in so fucking far, as if he could just get deep enough inside my body, it would keep me with him forever. "I love you so fucking much, Kara. Don't leave me, babe. I can't endure this life without you. *Don't leave me.*"

I close my eyes, my heart cracking. When I open them, I slam my lips into his, Malakyte's tongue sliding against mine as he glides in and out of me so tenderly it's *wild.* Who is this man all of a sudden? The gentle way he rolls his hips and cradles my body and caresses my face like I'm the most precious thing to him, damn near *ruins me.*

"I love you, too, Malakyte. I'm right here."

His tempo increases again, and I know he's close. I squeeze my inner walls tight, and that's what finally undoes my ice-cold prince, his body a trembling puddle above me as he comes, his last few thrusts hard and deep and all consuming.

He slows to a stop seconds later.

"Fuck," I gasp between breaths, not knowing how else to describe what I just experienced.

Malakyte inches down to kiss me in a way that's possessive in the placements of his hands and the way he curls around me, still inside.

Around and around, we go, the fate of my world—this entire galaxy—caught in the twisted crossfire of a game we call love.

Staring up at the skylight above the bed, I don't feel instant regret but rather the stark reality of choice.

Choose to stay inside the illusion or utterly decimate it?

I *have* to choose.

I'm out of time.

What I'm certain of is that I'm flirting with danger . . . such dark, beautiful danger.

CHAPTER 60

My moment of choice is now.

The hand with the small needle Gavrielle gave me trembles as it lines up with Malakyte's vein, thick and plump, protruding like dark nefarious snakes under skin kissed by the moonlight, shading him in heavenly Silver Cerulean. He lies beside me in bed, fast asleep after we shared a moment that truly gave me clarity.

Yet, needle in hand, I'm still undecided.

Sticking him is the most dangerous part of this. If he's going to wake up, it'll be the moment I pierce his skin. But I haven't done it—not yet.

Who am I going to fight for . . . and who am I going to fight against?

Good or bad?

Hero or villain?

Gavrielle or Malakyte?

Shit, throw Ardelle in there for kicks . . .

Decide if you're good and worthy or dark and irredeemable.

That's the real choice here . . .

Stay in the dream world or wake the fuck up from it.

The needle pulls back from Malakyte's vein without me having realized it, having not pierced his flawless skin. His breathing still steady and calm, such a contrast to the storm wreaking havoc within my heart.

My choice is made, and it's going to burn this galaxy asunder.

CHAPTER 61

YEAR 4, DAY 1,542: THE PRINCE DOESN'T SAY IT OUT LOUD,
BUT HE SEES ME AS HIS SON. NARESTEÉ SEES ME AS HER SON.
IT'S NOT A COVER STORY ANYMORE. HOW DO I SEE THEM?
YOU'VE BOTH BEEN GONE FOR SO LONG . . . AND I DON'T
WANT TO BE ALONE IN THIS WORLD ANY LONGER.

GAVRIELLE ABRAXAS

The future of planet Nyktos—my old home, and planet Earth—my new home, all rests on today.

On Kara.

We have limited time and too many eyes on us before the coronation, but as Ennar, I pretend to escort her to the atrium where the event is taking place. The moment we're alone, we dive into a supply closet so we can exchange Malakyte's blood.

Everything is contingent on that vial, and I'm hopeful as I close the door. The light of the closet flicks on automatically, but it's dim.

Like always, Kara looks beautiful. She's about to be crowned empress of Arianyte, so her gown is grand in a teal that matches the ends of her hair as it lays across her shoulders and back, her sword peeking out from behind her shoulder and a little purse around her waist. There are no words in my vocabulary to describe the emotions in my heart when I look at her dressed like this. My gorgeous, perfect mate.

You sent me such a striking woman, didn't you, Father?

I note the marriage brand along her wrist and the ring on her finger, but I say nothing about them. They don't mean anything . . . They're not real.

The helmet slides off my head, and I get a better view, my senses not so stifled in that thing, and I note how she's pulling on the lace sleeve of her gown, her eyes darting to the door behind me and the flush in her cheeks.

The weight of so much shouldn't fall on her shoulders. She shouldn't have to choose, but that's the position he—we—all of us—put her in.

It isn't fair.

Nothing about our lives has been fair.

I reach down to hug her when I catch it . . . Her scent is off . . . She smells like *him*. Between one heartbeat and the next, it dawns on me . . . and my spine straightens so fast my head whacks a bucket on the top shelf and it comes tumbling down.

A hollow thud bonks to the ground a second later.

She . . .

There's only one act that could change her scent that much, even after showering. I see red.

"Gav," she says, those large eyes looking up at me as beautiful as ever, but all I can hear is the thrashing in my skull.

My hand covers my mouth, and I drag it across my chin in disbelief.

Speechless.

"Gavrielle, I'm sorry. Let me explain."

I don't even have to say it as I gape.

She . . . she let him . . . she . . .

"What is there to explain?" I manage to say, hating the cruelty in my voice. "I can smell him all over you. It's not hard to put two and two together."

Kara bites her lip and looks away from me, and I hate that I make her eyes glisten with tears—*I hate it*.

Almost as much as I hate what's clearly happened. This is my mate—*my fucking mate*, and he . . . No. This was her choice. He didn't force her to do it. I had severely underestimated how deeply she felt for him, and it chills me to the bone.

"I had to," she claims, and I laugh bitterly. "What did you think was going to happen, Gav? Honestly? You guys told me to marry him. I wanted to just leave instead."

"I genuinely believed you'd say no. After everything he's done to you, to Ardelle, to all of us. I—"

I can't.

She sighs and sounds so sad it makes this all worse.

I was never conflicted about her—*ever*. And she knows that.

"I know he's a monster," she confesses, looking down and avoiding my eyes. "But I . . . I feel something for him, okay? I'm sorry. I knew it would hurt you, and I hate that it does, Gavrielle. *I'm so sorry*. I know you're mad at me, but . . ."

I laugh and look away, but the sound is like cyanide on my tongue. "Oh, I'm not mad."

"Gavrielle," she says gently, placing her hands on my shoulders. I have to detach my stare from a mop in the corner just to look at her. "I'm so sorry. If I didn't do this, I would never have been able to move forward without it eating me alive inside."

Those big, beautiful eyes are full of tears, and I'm surprised because it's obvious she doesn't care an ounce about how I feel.

I close my eyes with a pregnant sigh. He took her memories. She loved him—logically, I get all that, but . . . *she's my mate*. She's supposed to be with *me*. Mine . . . not in a possessive way, but in a way that makes sense. Like she's my star and I'm the Earth orbiting around her like a fucking moron, apparently.

But she isn't mine . . . she never was.

Do I even have a right to be this upset? I never explicitly told her how I felt or about the mate thing. In this mess of a situation, I couldn't dig up the audacity. I should have because I love her, and the thought of him touching her makes me want to rage and burn this entire ship down. Rip Malakyte to ribbons with my bare hands for getting her attention and love and her heart . . .

Stars, her heart . . .

My hands ball into fists by my side, my helmet stuck under my arm.

If she loves him, then . . .

Fuck!

I'm spiraling.

I thought I could accept it if this happened, but I genuinely didn't think it would.

I always lose what I love.

He always gets what he wants.

Kara finally says something after the two of us stand in tense silence.

"I came here to tell you the truth and that I've made up my mind about everything going forward. I knew I had to tell you to your face, Gav, you deserve that."

The pit in my stomach grows to the size of a black hole before she even finishes her sentence. I blink out the stinging in my eyes. I need to be a man about this, even though her words are going to shred me.

She sounds certain, positive that she's been convinced, her heart finally decided. If she can't love me the way I love her, I'll respect that. I won't be like him and will never force my love on her.

Finally meeting those eyes, I wonder if this is going to be the last place I'll see her. If we'll now, officially, be on opposite sides of this war.

Should I choose, too? Abandon the others, make peace with Malakyte so I can protect her from herself and try to rescue my people? Or do I stand strong to what I believe is right, fight her and him together, and let my mate fall into this darkness?

I promised her I wouldn't allow her to become my villain . . . but I failed her again, just as I did in that throne room. But even as my villain, she will still linger, still infiltrate every scar on my body, the cracks fissuring within my heart, along with the holes that have been perpetually leaking from within my soul since my family died. She belongs there, a place only my mate can reach, a dark and cold place where nothing good can grow . . . She is the flower that blooms in full color.

My dandelion.

The real Kara—the old one—she'd want me to stay. To protect the ones she loves. Who do I fight for? The old Kara or this new one? My ghost or the girl of flesh and blood who has my heart in her hands as she's about to crush it before my eyes.

It takes everything in me to open my mouth and set us both on the course that will change our relationship forever. "You didn't get his blood, did you?"

CHAPTER 62

THE ARIANYTE EMPIRE DECREE #166

THE POWER GRID WILL SHUT OFF AT NOON ZARMENIA TIME.

MALAKYTE ARDEEN

Everything has led up to this moment for me.

My crown.

My bride.

My Star.

And my power will be cemented, ruling over all. Even Father will fall to me.

Nothing prevents me from obtaining what I desire—*nothing*.

But Selenyte's ghost disagrees. "Not even your baby sister gets in your way, clearly."

Her voice is mocking as I stand poised to take the crown of Arianyte.

Unlike the dome-like structure of the Observatory, the Atrium looms over its subjects with high, magnificent ceilings clad in massive golden arches and hard-edged architecture that shoot up so high it seems like it goes on for eternity. I beam with pride at the glowing pillars, levitating platforms, and stained-glass windows providing an adequate representation of all the genius Arianyte is capable of.

I stand high above the accruing crowd of subjects gathering a few hundred feet below me as I survey them from the platform as it overhangs far into the air off the main ledge. Behind me, Karalevine, Father, Mother, they all wait by our thrones. The Council of Exstacé sits perched up in their own seats to my right, SSPARROWs en masse to my left. Naresteé—eyeing me with disdain over Mr. Dawson's impending execution—and Ennar, both stand by the exit looming behind them.

Decades of preparation. Countless deaths. Scheming, fighting, clawing for this power—my moment has arrived. Father doesn't want to surrender his empire, yet his body's destruction is giving him no other option.

That's a lucky break for me. Let's be honest, I've *earned this*.

Looks like playing the long game truly does work, after all, doesn't it, sister?

Beside me, Selenyte beams in all black, her stark-white hair a contrast to the shadows clinging around her, looking as real and alive as ever. "You've learned, big brother. Time to seize the power that should have been mine. I'll never let you forget it."

I stifle a laugh.

The power of the Star is mine.

The power of The Arianyte Empire will soon be mine.

And I will be unstoppable.

Father and Mother stand together on one levitating platform as it leisurely travels along its set path across the open space where the crowd stares up from the lower levels below, eyes glazed upwards in awe at our technology and power from which they owe their livelihoods. They'd have nothing without us.

Lifting one hand, Father quells the roaring crowd. Our subjects allowed in from the public sector shout their thunderous applause every time he speaks, but when he wishes to silence them, they heed.

They will obey me in the same way.

Karalevine and I stand on our own platform as it hovers alongside the overhang, but ours doesn't dance along the higher balconies or the black tapestries with the Arianyte "A" embroidered in red thread.

We wait.

I hold her hand as she wobbles, unsteady in her heels.

"Don't fall out there," I warn, trying to keep from nitpicking at her like an asshole. "It's only for the crowning. Then we'll stand on solid ground. Or, I should say sit, since our thrones are behind us."

Karalevine looks over her shoulder at where our thrones sit on the main overhang. "I'm surprised I have my own," she quips.

I throw her a wicked half-smile. "Why wouldn't you?" I ask, Father's speech continuing in the background. "You're my queen. I thought I made that perfectly clear last night that I plan on worshipping you like one for the rest of my existence."

Her heart flutters at my seductive tone. So easily flustered, it endears her to me. A smile flashes across her face as she looks up at me, quickly gripping my arm as the movement causes her to fumble again. *Dammit, Karalevine. Stand still.*

My focus slips back to Father as he addresses us, and I snap Karalevine's attention. "My last living child, my son, my heir . . . He will hold up the crown of darkness and rule Arianyte for the next millennium!"

The crowd erupts.

"Looks like they're happy to have you," Karalevine says.

"Us. They're happy to have *us*."

When my eyes peel away as Father and Mother's platform zips back our way, my Star is blushing.

"Ready to be empress?" I ask, taking hold of her waist to steady her as the platform below our feet vibrates and zips forward to meet them.

Karalevine takes a shaky breath, looking down at the adoring crowd below. Her grip frantically grasping at my arm as she sways *again*. "I've never been more ready for anything in my life, as long as I don't plummet to my death."

Our platforms meet twenty feet beyond the overhang, and Karalevine begins to tremble. Is it from the heights or merely nerves? Likely both.

"Malakyte," Father says, his face smooth, wrinkle and sickness free. "Do not destroy what I've built. Don't disappoint me. Don't make me regret this choice."

His eyes flash to Karalevine and flare, emphasizing his point.

He reaches up, hands plucking the three-pronged Arianyte crown from his head.

Karalevine must stand steady on her own, and I tell her as much with one last glance as I release her and drop to one knee. My hair falls forward as I bow my head, the crowd falling into a hushed silence pregnant with anticipation. This will be the last time I bow to him. I refuse to do it one more time after this moment. She gave me the strength to resist when I haven't in over two hundred years.

When nothing happens, I tentatively look up, my eyes slamming into Father's with the speed of a fighter jet.

He hesitates.

CHAPTER 63

KARALEVINE RUZZ

My pulse stops dead when Herkimer freezes, the Arianyte crown stuck in midair between his son and himself, much like we are suspended up on these little daises.

I say nothing—I wouldn't dare.

Malakyte looks up at his father, eyes expectant and full of a desperate, longing hope that literally makes my heart ache for him.

His father's acceptance, his father's pride and enthusiasm.

All Malakyte gets is resentment and malice.

Rejection.

Utter, cruel rejection.

It isn't fair. He doesn't deserve to be treated so badly. Herkimer is the problem, the reason Malakyte is so messed up. If we somehow manage to kill this man, Malakyte could be saved.

He could be good.

If he gets the crown, that is.

Is this not going to happen?

The crowd senses the tension, their mummers floating all the way up here. Herkimer's dark eyes break from his son's.

I nearly weep with relief as the emperor places his crown upon his son's head.

Emperor of Arianyte no more.

Malakyte stands, unable to witness the look in his father's eyes a moment longer, and the crowd erupts.

"We give you the new emperor of Arianyte!" Herkimer shouts at the crowd, their cheers of adoration and gratitude carrying all the way up the hundred-foot-high windows.

Herkimer's eyes catch mine as his son basks in the approval of his subjects.

I glare back, hating him.

Once the booming applause simmers down, I bow in the same way Malakyte had. Zoisyte's gown is Sunset Gold to match the room, but she still looks like a corpse. The crown she removes from her sleek, straight, Snow White hair is similar to the emperor's crown in the sense that it has the same three depthless black spikes in the shade Black Hole. But it's smaller, far more dainty and less imposing. They're accompanied by fat, elegantly cut black jewels in the shade Aurora Black. The metal workmanship around the band brings a beautifully elegant contrast to the dynamic spikes at the front.

Zoisyte's frail arms hold the crown at her sternum, her Forbidden Lake eyes assessing, pleading me to not make this choice.

To run.

My breath catches as she bends and softly places the crown atop my head.

It's heavier than I expected.

I don't react as Malakyte helps me stand, the applause growing, my ankles holding on for dear life to keep me upright as my body tingles with all this power, a seductive vise even more addictive than my crystal.

Holy fucking stars.

I'm Empress of Arianyte.

I wasn't sure how that power would feel once I obtained it, but it does feel good.

 394

Really, really fucking good.

Malakyte holds me by the hips and, without hesitation, kisses me deeply, pouring all of himself into this one act as he fearlessly shows the entire galaxy he loves me. I kiss him back with every single ounce of my heart and soul. Tasting him, remembering how his icy lips feel against mine and the tender way his hands cup my jaw. I take in all of Malakyte Ardeen because I know it's the very last time I'll be able to.

Power corrupts. Power begets power. And with my darkness, my selfish impulses are clearly subject to a temptation like this. I've been too victimized for too long to not let something like power corrupt me.

Just like it's corrupted Malakyte.

Just like Malakyte has, in turn, corrupted me.

An endless, toxic, vile cycle.

I have to end it, step out of his illusion for good.

Break it.

Shatter it.

And by making my choice, I will do just that.

The only way to do that is to become queen, only to sacrifice that power all at once.

Step three in Project Sabotage has begun.

CHAPTER 64

Malakyte and I, now crowned emperor and empress, sit together on thrones side by side on the semi-circle platform that reaches out beyond the other balconies.

My anxiety eats me alive as I wait for what's about to happen. But I have to let myself settle so Malakyte doesn't pick up on any erratic beats of my heart.

Ardelle's death looming near . . .

Gavrielle being pissed at me . . .

After giving Gav Malakyte's blood, I told him not only that I chose their side but that *I chose him.*

It's always been him. Since I was little, it's always been Gavrielle.

I choose him with my fucked-up, villainous heart, not that I had the guts to say *that* after his reaction.

I've never seen Gavrielle mad like that before. I told him that I found this point of clarity last night that I hadn't expected to find, and that clarity shattered Malakyte's illusion completely and utterly. The god? He's just a man. A man who's violated and broken me. A man I love—yes, I love Malakyte so much, but I didn't like how I felt last night. The sex was outstanding, and my body was on cloud nine, but my tattered heart? My hollowed soul? They knew better.

And I'm not conflicted anymore.

I'm all in.

As I sit on the Arianyte throne, Herkimer addresses the crowd below.

My blood crystalizes to ice.

"To commemorate their transfer of power, the former emperor is to bestow a gift to the new one, wishing them a bountiful rule," he says, looking back at us with a devious grin that prickles my skin. Like the air itself whispers of danger as it creeps nearby. "I had intended on only giving two gifts today, but a third unexpectedly dropped into my lap not mere moments ago, thanks to a loyal, long-term servant of Arianyte, Naresteé. The crown of Arianyte truly thanks you for your service."

Oh, shit . . . I knew she'd rat us out eventually. And now, of all times? And what second and third gifts is Herkimer referring to? Ardelle is likely one of those, his death a gift in their fucked-up minds, but that's all we prepared for . . .

Stay calm . . . It could be nothing but a bejeweled family heirloom or something.

"What's going on?" I ask, playing dumb.

Malakyte looks a bit confused, too.

"We all know of the Terran rebel scourge, do we not? These so-call *Starseeds*," Herkimer bellows, and the crowd instantly boos. I nervously tap my black acrylic nail on the throne's ornate arm, Malakyte side-eyeing me for it. "How they've scurried around this ship like rats, hiding within our walls, breaching them for the first time in three hundred years!"

Keep. Calm. He can hear your heart. Chill the fuck out. They're fine. Gav is fine. He's standing right behind you in Ennar's suit.

Herkimer's position changes to face Malakyte and me, his arm outstretched toward us. "To our new emperor and empress, the first gift I bestow to you are the rebels who have been terrorizing this ship! The very Starseed rebels who kidnapped our empress only weeks ago!"

I whip around so fast the throne nearly spins with me, and if I wasn't already seated, I'd fall over. The crowd's roar becomes muffled in my ears as I lock eyes with the last person I want to see.

Jance.

Then Saris.

Ahren.

Sylo.

Deimos—a blindfold around his eyes.

They're all dragged in by SSPARROWs, damn near ten of them. Malakyte's own SSPARROWs blanch, unsure of what's going on. Herkimer has his own guards, and Malakyte has his, and Gavrielle as Ennar looks visibly confused. My friends are bound, wrists and ankles, but there are no collars, possibly because there wasn't time, I'm not sure.

This is one-thousand-percent *not* part of the fucking plan!

Wait! Where is Pacey? Did she manage to get away, or does Naresteé have her? Herkimer said Naresteé helped him capture them, that it happened moments ago, so I'm betting the deal was the other Starseeds and Ringers in exchange for keeping Pacey. That's the only thing that makes sense given her motivation.

Naresteé, you fucking bitch.

I finally rip my eyes off my friends and over at her, but her face is drawn into a mask of complete apathy, but there's a slight curl to her lips.

Fuck, fuck, *fuck!*

What do I do?

Breathe . . .

Herkimer's laughter booms into the floating sphere microphone as the five Starseeds and Ringers are shoved to the edge of the balcony on their knees. This is bad. *Bad-bad.* "The capture just occurred. My SSPARROWs are the best in the galaxy, right, folks?" The crowd cheers. "Too bad I'm no longer your emperor, but I'm sure my son will eventually get the hang of what it takes to follow in my footsteps."

Asshole.

Herkimer chuckles deep as he grins at Malakyte, enjoying the dig. "Now! We'll keep them right there and get on to gift number two. Who wants to see gift number two?"

As expected, the crowd eagerly salivates for the surprise.

Malakyte is watching me like a fucking hawk.

Breathe, dammit, breathe.

One of those floating platforms descends from somewhere higher up than us, and I can't see who's on it at this angle, but Malakyte stiffens, eyes glued upward rather than on me.

"What is that?" I ask, eyes widening in horror.

"Death," Malakyte says, eyes sliding back to mine as I rip my scrutinizing gaze away from what I see dropping onto us. "It's death."

CHAPTER 65

The levitating dais comes to hover beside Herkimer, and standing on it is the most brutal looking humanoid machine I've ever seen. Closely resembling a SSPARROW soldier, but it's clear this creature has nothing living inside of it.

Malakyte is right—it's death.

This thing, it's completely—from head to terrifying toe—a monster made to look like a machine.

A nightmare.

In the shade Cold Black, the humanoid figure stands clear over six foot five, its body thin and sleek. It even appears as if it's breathing and exhaling pure poison from its artificial lungs. The crowd is hushed in awe as its body reflects the quartz lights. Its chest, abs, hips, and back all collectively come together in a patchwork that reveals a design that's as beautiful as it is haunting, but that's nothing compared to its face.

Or the lack of a face.

Similar to the traditional SSPARROW soldiers, this one is also faceless, but rather than a streak of light where the eyes should be, this monster's face is nothing but an ultra-reflective, black oval surface. Maybe there are red eyes glowing from deep inside, but I can't tell from here.

Herkimer's voice proudly erupts throughout the stunned room. "With these new and improved soldiers, there's no need for our living men and women to risk their lives in a dangerous rebellion." The crowd warms up to the idea. "These beautiful machines don't experience feeling, have no moral conundrums, nothing but one sole focus of thought programmed into them by the advanced artificial intelligence Arianyte engineers developed. From a secondary location, the AI orchestrates its program, and these new SSPARROWs move to execute it. In this case, they'll destroy the enemy rebels by any means necessary. As my gift to the new emperor, I have tens of thousands of these AI soldiers at the ready."

Tens of thousands?

I whirl on Malakyte.

He whips over at me. "Your people are fine, Karalevine. I've quelled his bloodlust. He's only posturing for the crowd."

My mouth opens to argue, but Herkimer keeps going. "Who wants a demonstration?"

The crowd is wild in its demands.

With a flick of his wrist, Herkimer signals the robot soldier, and I brace myself. With hardly a step backward, the machine leaps from its floating dais, soars all the way across the air, and lands on the balcony where a cluster of Malakyte's SSPARROWs stand at attention. It fluidly reaches towards a random soldier, a long dagger sliding free from a hidden compartment within its forearm, the blade catching the golden quartz lights right before it's buried into a SSPARROW's chest.

There's not even time to gasp.

The SSPARROW is too shocked to move as they stare at their torso, the blade driven all the way through.

Shouts of horror ring out as blood begins to gush all over the balcony floor.

I stand on instinct—shocked—but Malakyte snatches my wrist and yanks me back down to my seat. My eyes rake away from the soldiers to him, and he subtly shakes his head at me.

I laugh bitterly. "You're a fucking coward." I rip my forearm free of his cold grasp.

He growls at me, but I ignore him.

Turning back to this ridiculous spectacle, my concern for Team Starseed is growing more and more frantic by the second.

The SSPARROW soldier gasps when the one made of metal and code rips the blade from their chest, and he's down seconds later.

Dead.

Herkimer's laugh spreads like a virus across the high ceilings, completely ignoring the shock and fear reeking in the room. But a few people down there . . . they cackle, too. "We're not done yet, folks!"

Oh, fucking hell . . . what now?

Before anyone can even catch their breath, the AI soldier's chest opens up, and what appears to be dust pours out. Upon closer inspection, it's not dust at all but an organized cluster of tiny little spheres, all moving in tandem with each other like a hive mind. They've got to be nanobots or something. They fly around the high arches of the room as if they're a swarm of highly intelligent birds dancing among clouds and sunsets.

They dive, the swarm finding another normal SSPARROW, then zooms in for the attack, swallowing the soldier whole as he tries swatting at the nanobots like a horde of killer bees. The screams through the voice modulator are horrific, and the people are stunned into utter silence as they can do nothing but watch this madness unfold.

The nanobots eat through his metal uniform as if it were made of paper, and it's almost impossible to see beyond the swarm as it devours the person beneath.

This is *not* how today was supposed to go.

 402

"What the fuck have you done?" I whisper to Malakyte as I watch in shock, the shaking in my voice evident.

I can't even peel my eyes away from the raining blood.

Once it's done, having taken only seconds—the soldier literally gone—the little nanobots fly right back into the AI machine, the panel on its chest shutting them away.

Dead. Fucking. Silence.

"The Terrans won't destroy what Arianyte has built!" Herkimer shouts, sensing the crowd is turning on him.

But the more he eggs on their bloodlust and hate for my people, they start to come around. Like what they just saw didn't happen. How? After everything, how could they support this insanity? How can they cheer against their very own self-interests? Because it's Terrans now, but it can as easily be *them* next. Complicity is what allows tyrants to flourish—always.

"Kill the Terrans!" someone shouts from below, and my mouth falls open.

"Destroy them all!"

"Arianyte strong!"

More and more shouts of approval roar, as if I'm living in a topsy-turvy, fucked-up fun house in Hell.

This changes everything.

And we're not ready for it.

Herkimer silences the crowd to a pin drop. "Now, gift number three. The death of the Terran who killed our precious Selenyte. Bring out the bastard and let Arianyte's creation settle his debts once and for all!"

My heart claps like the crowd, and I whirl toward the door behind us.

Fuck . . . I've got to stop this. If I have to stand up and blast that AI monster with my crystal, I will. I'll . . .

Nothing happens.

Ardelle doesn't appear.

Seconds tick by, and I turn back to see impatience twisting Herkimer's cruel face. I look at Malakyte, but he's just as confused. Even Naresteé doesn't seem to know what's going on.

Finally, when it's clear Ardelle isn't being brought out, Gavrielle, dressed in Ennar's armor walks forward. He doesn't come out onto the overhang where Malakyte and I sit on our thrones but stands right behind the other Starseeds and Ringers at the main balcony ledge overlooking the Atrium.

There's no calming my body as the entire room waits on Gavrielle, the tension so thick I can nearly taste it. They all think it's Malakyte's head SSPARROW in there, only Ennar's suit has yellow lights that accent it.

I don't even breathe.

His hands come up to his face, and I almost release a bloodcurdling scream as he goes to remove his helmet.

What the fuck are you doing, Gav?

The crowd gasps as Pacey Dawson reveals her face, grinning like a fucking cat, her eyes pinned on the ex-emperor of Arianyte.

CHAPTER 66

YEAR 4, DAY 1,711: I DON'T WANT TO KILL ANYMORE,
MOTHER. EVERY TIME I DO IT, I SEE YOUR FACE. BUT EACH
TIME, A BIT MORE OF YOU SLIPS AWAY. I KNOW IT'S MY
PUNISHMENT FOR WHAT HE MAKES ME DO. SOON, I'LL
FORGET YOU COMPLETELY. BUT I'LL NEVER FORGET THOSE
BLACK AND TEAL FLOWERS YOU LOVED . . .

GAVRIELLE ABRAXAS

My breaths are all I can hear as I dash through the prison sector toward Ardelle's cell.

Saying we have no time is an understatement. *We have no time.*

The air turns bitterly cold, and that's how I know I'm getting close, Ennar's suit now with Pacey and the others. Are they alright? Shit, *yes*, they're fine. I need to trust they'll fulfill their part. Rescuing Ardelle is my job, so I focus on that as I jog along the endless dark.

Anxiety claws up my spine as I run, the halls growing tighter with every corner I round. *Please, please, Father, don't let me be too late.* If they've taken him to be executed . . .

I inhale sharply. There's a familiar sound of whirring and turning of micro-motors in the joints of a SSPARROW suit coming from up ahead. A humming of cooling fans and vents hisses as they dispel excess moisture.

A soldier.

Thank you, Father! If the guard is still there, Ardelle has to be, too.

I make myself invisible, becoming one with the shadows themselves, just as I had once the elevator door opened to the prisons. I walked past all dozen SSPARROWs keeping guard and snatched the keycard right off the desk, and they didn't even know I was there.

A silhouette comes into view fifty feet ahead and to the left.

The soldier turns in my direction, his SSPARROW suit whining, my pulse quickening like flame in the wind.

He hears my footsteps but doesn't see me. *Perfect.*

Distract.

Confuse.

Frighten.

I do all three as I body-slam into the soldier standing guard.

We hit the floor—me on top. I waste no time as I rip his helmet off and wrap my hands around his throat. He struggles, but he's out like a light within seconds. Messy, but it does the trick.

Ardelle's face is stunned from where he stands inside his clear cell.

"What are you do—"

"There's no time," I say, slapping the card on the outside panel, his cell finally unlocking.

A part of me hates that I have to be the one to free him . . . because, in doing so, I lose the woman I love.

And I do love her.

 406

Even . . . after what she did. She said she chose me, but when she remembers Ardelle . . .

Ardelle shakes his head and points to his throat. "The collar—"

I cut him off a second time by wiggling the small item in my hand.

"Please tell me that's what I think it is?" he asks, and I hear the desperation in his voice.

Poor guy looks like ass.

I grin, cocky as ever. "Let's get you out of here, friend."

Relief floods Ardelle's face as he exhales with a shuddered release as his shoulders slump and his eyes gloss over.

No . . . I'm glad it's me who's here. The others are too close to this Starseed. To see his body so bruised and broken and bloodied, to see him damaged like this, it would be too much for them. I can bear the weight of it instead. I owe them that.

I clasp Ardelle on the shoulder and cringe as he winces. "You're really getting out of here. But we're on a time crunch, so turn around."

He does, pulling his matted hair out of the way so I can see the green light beaming at the back of the collar. The key resembles a tiny remote, and I align it up to the locking mechanism.

"How'd you get it?" he asks as the magnetic component slides the key into place.

"Kara stole Malakyte's blood in order for us to gain access to his overly guarded junk drawer."

It beeps three times, the light turning blue, then snaps open at the hinges.

Ardelle's hands are slow as he reaches for it, like he doesn't believe this is real. "Does that mean we have her memories back?" he asks, the collar coming off. Once he turns, he already looks more invigorated.

"No, but we're going to. A lot has happened. I'll catch you up later. Let's go."

"Wait!" he calls before I can turn away. "We need to free someone else. In the cell next door. She's Pacey's Ringer."

My eyes widen, and I shake my head, dumbfounded. I waste no time as I step over to the cell in question and peer inside.

Ardelle is there in an instant, and confusion furrows his brow. "She's been quiet recently, but I figured it was because they've been taking her to the medical sector the last few days."

My gut twists.

I unlock the cell, and it is, in fact, empty.

"We have to go," I push, feeling time hounding down my neck as each second passes.

Reluctantly, Ardelle agrees, and we're off.

"Aren't we going in the wrong direction?" he asks as we continue going deeper into the dark and cold.

Looking over my shoulder, I toss him one of my signature mischievous grins. "We're right where we need to be."

We slow, and I squint, head whipping left and right. "Where are you . . . where are you . . ." I whisper to myself.

Ardelle stands beside me, looking at his hands like he's never seen them before.

I find what I've been searching for and heave the heavy metal door open, revealing the pitch-black airlock, the same one Kara, Deimos, and I accidentally got trapped in when we came to rescue Ardelle the first time.

Jumping within, I immediately feel for the handle Kara found. Stars, that feels like ages ago, but it was less than three weeks. She was so different then . . . She's come a long way. And I yelled at her today. . . All because I was a jealous prick.

My fingertips scrape the handle, and I grab hold of it, shoving hard with all my body weight. It opens, and I wave Ardelle through.

We go from a dark hallway to a green one, running toward the door that holds the dragons behind it. *Stars, Father, I need you again. Get me through this locked door.*

"How is she?" he asks, not looking at me as we run side by side. "When I saw her recently, she wasn't okay."

My brows furrow.

"When did you see her?"

"The day before yesterday," Ardelle says, the silver door coming into view a hundred feet ahead. "Malakyte and Herkimer gave her this cruel loyalty test. They were onto you guys, onto her."

Shit. Why hadn't she told me about this?

Ardelle continues. "She had to bomb the undersewers."

I stumble, feet staggering, and my neck nearly breaks as it whips in his direction.

She did what?

His face is pure agony. The bruises and his black eye and multiple cuts are brutally apparent in this harsh light.

"You didn't know," Ardelle guesses, and I nod. "Malakyte wanted her to kill me, too, but she played the situation off, and, well, I'm here, so . . . she saved me. I just got the sense that she's a lot different than who she used to be. I think we both are."

So many questions fly into my mind, but we'll have to deal with it later and hope the rebellion still exists once we're out of here.

We slow as we reach the door, breathing hard.

Before I try to unlock this thing, I turn to him. "Kara's still in there, and she's on our side. There was no way we would have been able to unlock that collar without the significant risk she took. She chose us, not him."

"But does she love him?"

I open my mouth to say no, but . . . "Yeah. Yeah, I think she does."

The words land between us with all the force of a missile, the silence piercing.

Turning to the door and pushing the reality of this fucking place out of my mind, I refocus.

Reaching into my pants pocket, I unzip it and grab the little chip we collected from a body in the morgue. Gruesome, but—well, he didn't need it anymore.

"This little chip can unlock most doors on the ship, although it's unlikely it could open this door specifically. But hopefully with your sister's reprogramming . . ."

I place it against the panel under my palm.

Please, Father . . .

One second.

Two seconds.

Three seconds.

It beeps, and the hydraulics whine as they move, one by one unlocking as dust falls to another below it, and so on.

Thank you.

The door opens a second later.

"I'd tell you to brace yourself, but . . ."

A massive growl shakes my bones, and a whoosh of hot air blows my hair back, my tiny braids flapping as if it were a windstorm.

"Holy stars!" Ardelle gasps, eyes wide with terror as his crystal spikes.

"It's alright," I say. "They're behind bars."

He looks paralyzed with fear as I walk in first, the dragons on either side of the giant space trapped along two sets of cells that sit opposite each other, exactly as before.

"I'm hearing a voice," Ardelle warns, eyes bopping around, feet staggering back and forward, still outside the doorway. "Why aren't you reacting to them?"

"It's because I can't hear them. It's your Elendril dragon, Ardelle. They can speak to the Starseeds telepathically but not the Ringers. You're fine, man. They're not going to hurt you."

I quickly give Ardelle the rundown of the dragons and their connection to Zariya, the crystals, all of it, and it's enough to get him to come inside.

"Why have you come without the Killer of Worlds?" Dannanōk asks, speaking aloud while poking his colossal head out of the hole in the bars like last time.

His neck twists like a serpent rising to strike, but I can't show my fear.

Getting close, I say, "I'm begging you, help us. We need to know the secret to the Elendril crystals. We want to destroy Arianyte, but we're outmatched and have no way to win."

They're lightning bottled in glass.

Pacing, tales whipping, teeth snapping, jaws clicking.

Growls shoot the hairs on my arms to attention, pungent sulfur thick and strong.

"Please," I say again. "I'm begging you."

Dannanōk's glowing golden eyes burn a hole into my soul, and I risk that very soul by stepping closer.

The others don't like that.

"What do I have to do? What do you want? I'll give it. I'll pay it. I'll take your place in this shit, just please help us. We won't make it out of this war alive if you don't."

Dannanōk growls, massive teeth bared.

Poor Ardelle gasps. He was right about one thing—he isn't the same.

"We do not require a trade in circumstances, Ringer."

"Then, what do you require?" I ask, voice echoing off the black metal walls stretching high.

Kara needs me. *We have to go.*

The dragon shakes his head. "The Killer of Worlds has not yet recognized that she is the reason we can't release the Elendril's secrets. Doing so would be as detrimental as revealing it to the Dark Starseed himself."

Not even I can come up with something to counter that, so I just speak from my heart. "She isn't evil. She's still in there, and I know that she's good because I see it in her eyes when she laughs in her determination to save her people. If she's so bad, she couldn't smile the way she does. You can't hope. And she still has hope despite her memories being ripped away from her and stuffed inside a fucking crystal against her will. Kara is *good*. I need you to believe in her like I believe in her and *help us*."

"Are you willing to bet your life on it, Gavrielle Abraxas, son of Andar Abraxas? The Universe itself and all the lives therein?"

"Yes."

There is no hesitation.

Dannanōk shakes his head, and it's obvious from that movement alone I didn't convince him.

Deimos was right . . . They're not going to help us. The realization hits me like a meteorite to the skull.

Tears prick my eyes, and I beg, "So, you're going to let her die again? Let us all die again while you do nothing and let history repeat itself? Have you truly learned nothing? We want you out of here. We want you to fight with us—please, help us so we can help you."

Dannanōk doesn't answer me, his judgmental eyes only watching as I all but slit myself open, spill my metaphorical guts onto this floor that's become their Hell.

We're wasting time down here, and this was clearly a mistake.

I wanted to give Kara the safest exit I could from Malakyte . . . since all of us know he isn't going to let her go simply because she wants out. Leaving an abusive relationship is the most dangerous, deadly time for the victim.

And it's going to get her killed. If anyone could help me save her, it would be these dragons.

I was wrong.

When I turn to leave, Dannanōk says, "We won't reveal the secrets of the Elendril crystals, but we can unveil the other thing you covet."

My footsteps falter, and I slow to a stop right before Ardelle, face-to-face. Without turning my head back to Dannanōk, I ask, "And what is this other thing that I desire so badly?"

 412

My voice comes off a bit cockier than I would have liked, and his growl says he agrees.

"The key to saving the woman you both love from herself and the utter annihilation she's bound to repeat."

CHAPTER 67

My jaw whacks the floor, same as everyone else's. Naresteé's voice slices the stunned silence. "Pacey?"

Pacey ignores her, pointing a metal finger toward Herkimer. "You want to execute my brother for murdering your daughter?"

The helmet bounces as Pacey adjusts it, needing both hands to do so. She flicks on some button on the inside, and the Lemonade strip of light where the eyes should be flickers from yellow to cyan, in the shade Celeste.

Malakyte shoots up from his throne, panic etched in every sculpted muscle of his taut body as he faces Pacey and the others to our left, his back to me.

Pacey holds the helmet up in front of herself, one handed, as it hovers over the balcony ledge.

Stars, don't drop it!

This must be it, the helmet both sides have been so obsessed with. They found it. They got it back!

Pacey's voice snaps the air in half. "Selenyte Ardeen's true killer has been right in front of you this whole time."

A projection fills up the entire Atrium above. The image is vivid, three dimensional in space, accompanied by sound.

Is that . . . the top of my head? It is—that's my star mark, and there's a dagger pressed up against it. Behind me is Alabaster hair, which I can only assume is Selenyte, and then way out in front of me ten feet away—dressed all in black—is Malakyte. It's a recording from someone's point of view from that day in the throne room. I recognize the surroundings.

This is the moment he had me Reconditioned—the moment he murdered his sister. It must be.

Beside me, Malakyte's coldness slaps me in the face as he can do nothing but watch his sins coming back to haunt him as the scene plays out in front of his parents and his entire court.

"Remove your hand from me, you cretin!" a female voice rings out from the recording.

A gasp in the Atrium follows. I turn to see Zoisyte standing near the balcony's ledge in front of the Council, hand over her mouth, eyes wide, body as rigid as ice.

In the recording, there's a struggle, and I'm sucked right back in. It looks like we're all trying to get free from each other, but none of us can. Then Malakyte's body moves quick—Sky-Fae quick—and we all fall over, the glass ceiling with stars behind it the only image for several long, nerve-wracking seconds.

In a scramble, I see my shocked expression, and there she is . . . the princess of Arianyte, lying there with a dark blade protruding from the center of her forehead, one single drop of Blue Charcoal blood dripping down her face, eyes wide and vacant.

The Universe itself holds its breath, the silence as suffocating as the void of space outside these bleeding, corrupt walls.

Zoisyte lets out a shriek that nearly slices the artificial gravity in two.

Pacey ends the recording, hand tipping as the helmet tumbles hundreds of feet down. It shatters on impact seconds later.

"You had the wrong guy, motherfucker!" she yells at Herkimer, his face seeming to have aged two decades in the last several minutes.

Before the ex-emperor can respond, there's a zipping sound from behind me—like the slicing of air. My body instinctively freezes, but there's no time as an arrow flies past Herkimer, through the empty space of the Atrium, across my eyes, and right into Malakyte's chest—center fucking mass.

Into his crystal!

He's down in a blink.

The crowd screeches as I leap on instinct, tripping over the throne's arm as I stumble for purchase, ducking for shelter. Then I notice the arrow—I remember it from Malakyte's treasure trove.

It's an Elendril arrow.

Ardelle.

If ever there was a cue, this would be it.

I fucking *bolt.*

CHAPTER 68

I've never known such chaos—at least—that I remember. I immediately rush to Pacey and the other Starseeds and Ringers as she attempts to untie them.

Naresteé intercepts me, and I duck, barely missing her right hook. Another arrow whizzes by inches from my face as it nearly slices the shell of my ear—but it hits home, buried in Naresteé's shoulder—the alien going down with a frustrated howl.

SSPARROWs are rushing everywhere, Ardelle's arrows flying like rain as Malakyte's and Herkimer's guards are getting nailed left and right. The AI SSPARROW remains motionless, and I don't care why, only that it is.

More screams from the crowd make the tiny hairs on the back of my neck rise, and I jolt to see what's happened, eyes darting in every direction when Herkimer wails on Malakyte in a murderous rage. He rips the arrow out and stabs him, blood spraying in a torrent.

I look away.

Once I finally approach the others, Deimos frees Ahren, and Pacey rescues Sylo. I go for Jance, but he yells, "Go! We're right behind you. Get to the meeting point. *Now, Kara!*"

Fuck!

I'm a trembling mess as I reluctantly race toward the door, skirts in hand, and I don't look back.

My heels clank against the sleek, reflective tiles, followed by heavy, leaded soldier boot steps.

"Empress, let us escort you to a safer locati—"

"Follow me or get lost!" I bark back.

I don't have time for them as I rush through the halls of the Azurite. I'm no longer blind like I was that day I saw that terrifying extra with the clipboard. It was telling me—hinting that something in this world was *wrong*. I was living in a dream-world. My reality was glitching, and I buried my head in the sand. I wish I had listened to my instincts.

I'm listening now.

It takes us ten minutes to reach Malakyte's door, and I enter without a word, sliding it shut on the soldiers before they can come in.

At any moment, the call is going to come in to grab me and not let me leave. Herkimer may have brutalized Malakyte, but . . . he can't die. And once he wakes up long enough to know that I've disappeared . . .

Fucking stars, he's going to *kill me.*

I just . . . vanished on him. He's probably losing his mind. He's alone. I left him alone.

But I've made my choice and can't go back on it.

I unclip my sword and throw it on a table along with my purse, with that unholy Silent Breath shit inside of it. Immediately, I change clothes, and I hardly get my pants over my ankles when I jump from the shouting at the door. Slams. Curses. A disruptor shot, and a thud follows shortly after.

I rush to the door, still half naked with only a bra and leggings on but not even caring and slam my wrist against the panel that opens it.

Six SSPARROWs look up at me, with an additional six SSPARROWs knocked out on the floor.

"For stars sake, Kiddo, put on some fucking clothes," a cocky, arrogant voice rings out, muffled by the suit's helmet with the modulator off.

Deimos.

That was fast.

The biggest figure jumps over the bodies and into the room, ordering the others to heave the unconscious soldiers into the suite, his accent thick and strong.

"Darling, you need to get dressed. We have to go right now. There's no time."

Jance.

I blink, unmoving.

This is happening.

I . . . I just left him. My lips echo with the cold reminder of him.

"Move, Kiddo!" Deimos snaps his fingers in front of my face.

"She's in shock," Jance says, grabbing me by the shoulders and walking me deeper into the room while the others drag the unconscious soldiers inside.

Jance picks up the shirt I had laid out for myself and maneuvers me into it. Then he sits me on the couch while he hastily slides my feet into my sneakers.

That last kiss I gave Malakyte . . . I knew it'd be the last one we'd share. This will be the last time I see this room . . . smell his scent, my life with him going up in flames. It's the right thing to do. For me, for Earth, for everyone, but I just . . .

I love him.

It was real, and that's why I couldn't let go of it last night—I still don't want to, even as our love is shattering right before my eyes. How can I abandon him, knowing I'm going to break his heart? But men like him . . . they can't truly love anyone because they don't love themselves.

This relationship is ending, and the stitching holding it together is ripping and fraying, finally giving way to the pull.

I zone back into what Jance is saying.

"The important thing now is that we get you to that room and get your memories back."

Right . . . my memories.

Finishing with my shoes, Jance pulls out something small from his suit's compartment, a chain dangling as it clanks against his metal forearm.

"This is the key to that memory machine," he says as cold metal meets the sweaty meat of my palms. "We found it in that room of Malakyte's you helped us access. We found a lot in there. You did so good, darling. This is almost over. Pacey was able to hack into some schematics about that machine, and it requires a key to initiate and use. This key should be all you need to implant the memories back inside your mind. Just keep that crystal shard safe at all costs."

Looking down at the key, I revel at how pretty it is, which is so at odds with the wickedness the machine represents. It resembles a fancier old-world skeleton key. The shaft of it is entirely made of crystal and shaved thin in the light-pink shade Blushing Bride. The tip of it is sharp and attached to the filigree bow is a thick chain that matches the key's Rose Gold coloring.

Jance's hands curl my fingers around it. Even though I can't see his face, I sense he's looking right at me. There's a pull to him, stronger than it should be, and it makes me ache to know what our relationship was like before everything went to shit and I forgot all the people I loved.

"Who are you to me?" I beg, *needing* to know.

The others hauled all the real SSPARROWs inside, the door now shut.

Jance places his free hand along my forearm, and I gaze down. His thumb is caressing those jagged scars I can barely stomach to look at. "You know who I am, baby. *You know.* I love you, and I'm never going to leave your side. You're *mine.* You will always be mine, no matter what happens. No matter how many times we get ripped apart, I will never stop fighting to bring us back together."

My body tingles and my cheeks get hot. For whatever reason, I feel compelled to look down at my arm at the letters carved there. As I look—really look—at these abhorrent scars. I don't remember anything, but a nauseating wave makes me dizzy, and a horrible pain in my head seems to crack my skull in two. J . . . F . . . J . . . F . . . Jance . . . F . . . F . . .

"We gotta go!" someone yells.

My head feels like it's going to explode. I'm so close but so far. Why won't he just *tell me*?

"Whatever happens once we leave this room . . ." Jance says, letting the moment fall away. Although with the voice modulator off the tone in his voice is dense with emotion. "You take this key, get into that machine, and get your memories back. No matter what happens, no matter what it takes, you do it. Understand me? Don't put anyone else before that. Not me, not Ardelle, or Gavrielle—and sure as fuck not Malakyte. Be selfish and do it. I promise it'll all be clear once you remember. I just need you to trust me a little while longer. I would never steer you in the wrong direction, Kara. You are everything to me. My entire world."

I clench the key, wrap the chain around my wrist, and nod to my Ringer.

"Shit's going down, we gotta go!" Deimos yells at the two of us. "We're on their comms. Malakyte has birds inbound. He knows you're compromised. Now!"

Jance picks me up and shuffles me out the door, but I stop him when I remember what we forgot.

"My sword!" I cry, trying to get past him and the others so I can go back for it.

Deimos growls at me through his mask. "There's no time! If he catches you, he'll kill you. It's your sword or your life, pick one!"

"Fuck," I hiss under my breath as I'm shoved out of the suite, tripping over SSPARROW bodies.

The Silent Breath syringes were left behind, too.

We're weaving in and out of empty hallways as fast as we possibly can, with me leading.

This is happening.

I'm finally going to get my memories back.

And as excitement, anticipation, and pure fucking joy flood through my blood as it pumps my ravenous heart toward hope, I'm also incredibly terrified.

Scared of who I'll love and who I'll hate once it's all set right.

What if the new me conflicts with the old me? What if what I want is different from what she wants? Gavrielle said it was like waking up from a dream, but what if I wake up from a nightmare?

There's an array of mistakes I'll have to own, wrongs I'll be forced to confront, a shield of ignorance no longer clouding them in obscurity.

Now, I will have to peer into the ugly, unequivocal mirror of truth and face what I had done prior to all this.

This entire situation is my fault, after all . . . I created this.

Knowing this will hit me, likely harder than I'm prepared to handle, trembles my bones as they carry me deeper into the Azurite. Each step closer I get to freedom, I'm more shackled to my selfish, destructive past. But then again, it isn't all darkness and terror. From what I've seen, the old me learned a lot about herself. Hopefully, once it all becomes clear, I can build off that progress.

I hope it works out that way and that I find some peace.

Jance grabs my hand, and I feel his words in his tight, reassuring grip.

You are not alone.

I use my wrist's implant chip to open the stairwell door, which reminds me that I'm going to need Ahren to remove it again.

The door opens at the pace of a snail, and I impatiently angle myself to slither through but then stop abruptly with a gasp.

Jance bumps me from behind as the others slam into him. He grabs for me as he tries to shove me behind him, but I swat at his arms while trying to make him look like any old soldier. That's the whole point of them being in the suits.

"You scared me," I say, mind reeling as my hand falls over my chest, palms beginning to sweat.

Herkimer stands in the stairwell a couple of steps down, hands resting on both sets of the handrails, face and royal garb bloodied, looking up at me with the grin of the Devil himself.

My mind spins for something to say, and I have to say it fast.

"Is everything okay?" I ask innocently. "I was scared. The soldiers are taking me to Malakyte."

I inconspicuously hide the key to the memory machine behind my back, hoping to the stars he hadn't seen it.

How the fuck did he get up here so fast?

The others remain silent, becoming the six guards who left the coronation room with me not even twenty minutes ago.

"Should we go find him, then?" I ask when he doesn't answer, the tension growing like a ticking time bomb, my heart the chaotic countdown to the implosion doomed for this place.

I step toward him despite all my instincts screaming at me to run. "I want to be with him. I don't feel safe here."

"Oh, Kara . . ." Herkimer finally says, peering down as he chuckles, bitter and cruel. The hair on the back of my neck rises.

When he looks up, his face turns to one of gleeful madness I recognize from the throne room when he attacked Malakyte and me.

I lift my arm and rest my hand on the doorway's threshold, blocking the others.

Herkimer licks his lips. "Is that the Memorantis key in your hand, girl?"

My heart drops to my heels. *Memorantis?* The memory machine?

Herkimer raises one hand, and I act.

Using the doorframe for leverage, I throw my entire weight back, ramming into Jance as my momentum knocks him backward. When he collides with the others, they all stagger on the other side of the door.

"Find the others and leave!" I say as I reach for the door's panel, which slides shut as they all yell their protests.

The last thing I hear is Jance calling my name.

I take a reserved shot at the door's panel with my crystal, frying its mechanism and leaving it incapable of opening again, the materials spraying sparks and zapping. I hope it doesn't start a fire, and I cough as the smoke fills the stairwell.

Herkimer approaches, and he slams me against the door, my face hitting it hard.

I fight as he wrenches the key from my grasp, but the scuffle doesn't last long.

"Tricky Little Thief," he whispers into my ear, cold breath so close.

I recoil against him. *It's all okay.*

Ardelle is free. Gav is alright. They can escape now. I've made so many bad choices lately—Gav hates me . . . but this time, I did the right thing.

Go, I silently beg them. *Please, just go.*

Because I'm officially dead.

"You want to play against real monsters, Little Thief?" Herkimer says, his icy breath coating my ear as I shiver against him, his weight still pinning me to the door. He dangles the key from its chain in front of my smushed face to tease me with how close I came to getting what I wanted most—my memories back. "Then, let's play."

CHAPTER 69

Herkimer drags me down the stairs, through the halls, and it doesn't take long for his SSPARROWs to meet us. By the time they haul me into the room within another, where this Memorantis is stored, I'm collared, and my magic is null and void.

It looks exactly as I remember.

The giant crystal in the center glows bright, illuminating the paneled walls in the purple shade Aurora. The other shards are there as well, their rainbow points glimmering with multiple hues as they sit on shelves labeled with names.

A lone crystal sits on the bottom shelf, the one with my name on it.

Herkimer manhandles me into a chair, and after a scuffle, my ass is firmly planted in it, his soldiers tying me down promptly. Then he scoots me so I'm sitting across from the treatment table that connects to the Memorantis.

I'm not going anywhere.

A SSPARROW hands Herkimer a black bag, and my eyes close, heart hammering as the soldiers leave me behind with the deadliest monster on this ship.

We're alone.

Herkimer wastes no time unloading the bag onto the long table connected to the Memorantis, organizing his items. I know what they're for.

It isn't until right now that I realize the reality of my situation that my body trembles in fear.

"You know," he begins, placing his items meticulously, "even though our powers are fairly similar, there's an innate distinction that yours has from mine. Your powers are legitimate antimatter that's impossible to recreate in quantities such as yours. I always imagined what an abundant amount could do. To a city, perhaps? A continent? An entire moon, Killer of Worlds? I don't often admit it, but the power I have is nothing compared to that amount of destruction. If we went head-to-head, I'm not sure who'd win, but you'd probably have the upper hand. And you know what that means, Little Thief? You can't exist."

I swallow. "So, you're a power-hungry, deranged supervillain? Creative."

He chuckles, the tone sounding exactly like Malakyte's. "To the contrary, Little Thief. I wanted power for my son so he could rule as I have. With multiple streams of magic that would keep him safe. You were one of those assets, but after you humiliated me and my family in front of my entire court, betrayed my son, and broke his heart, well . . ."

He tsks, turning to me, his grin causing my blood to run arctic. "I'm more of a vindictive, scorched-earth type of deranged supervillain. See, I have all the power I need. Sure, I could eat yours, but why bother when we have *almost* identical powers? I'd much rather open you up and see what that crystal looks like. But who knows? If you're delicious enough, I still might eat you alive."

"You're insane," I say, fear breaking out in a freezing yet sweltering sweat.

"I am. I've heard those words from so many rebels over the centuries. All of them formidable magic users. All of them

 426

powerful but refused to kneel. All of them idealistic . . . And all of them *devoured*."

Pain distorts time.

Minutes can feel like hours, hours like minutes.

Herkimer has been at it for a while now—maybe an hour, give or take—but I'm not good at telling time anymore.

There are only two constants in his Hell that's become my reality.

First, the pain. There's nothing else like it. It radiates from a central point—my right knee. Blood soaks into my Aquatic Turquoise sneaker, turning it an odd brownish-gray color I can't even name. Red and green are opposites on the color wheel . . . When combined, they don't mix well . . . *Focus on anything else but the pain.* But it licks up my thigh like a flame. The agony is bone deep as it creeps higher and higher, making me nearly insane from the sharp, throbbing ache drawing me to the brink of unconsciousness. I look for a way to distance myself from the maddening pressure, shoving it behind a door, closing it, locking it, boarding it up . . . It doesn't work super well.

The second constant is Herkimer's laughter. The pleasure he takes in my pain is humiliating.

And more than seeing me suffer, he wants something.

The other Starseeds and Ringers.

He wants them very, very badly.

But hopefully they listened to what I said and got the hell out of this place. And Gavrielle . . . After I broke his heart, yeah, I'd leave, too.

But he isn't the only person whose heart I've broken today.

I glance at the beautiful ring on my finger as my blood splatters on the big jewel, the wedding tattoo bracelet on my wrist . . . Whatever Herkimer does is nothing compared to the bigger confrontation looming over me.

Blood seeps from my nose, my lip, but mostly my knee. That's been Herkimer's favorite place to play. Punching me was fun for him, a rudimentary torture technique of prying information out of me about the others. Where they were, what were their plans, how they got the key to the Memorantis.

I give him nothing.

"I adore these little spears." He holds up a metal spike, and my eyes avert down, seeing the five embedded in my right knee. "Their ultra-thin design and sharp, pointed tips allow them to reach places in the body most blades can't—brutal, honestly. Sort of like you, wouldn't you say? Tiny yet so very lethal. You haven't screamed for me yet, Little Thief, but you will. Give me the others, and I'll stop this train. See, for me, I have all the time in the world to ride this out. I love taking the scenic route, stopping to sniff every single flower."

My chest rises and falls, heavy like there's an elephant sitting on it.

"But for you, this ride is turbulent, excruciating, and your time has a limit. I can end it all as soon as you talk. Otherwise, you and I are going to get very, very close over the course of the next few hours. I always love breaking pretty things."

His gentle caress of my swollen cheek makes me break out in goose bumps.

"Where are they? How have they been communicating with the rebels? What's their next move? I know they wanted you back. That's obvious. You're a powerful asset in war. My son wasn't completely brainless in that regard. But the rebel's bigger plan is still unknown, and I don't do well with that sort of mystery floating around."

I roll my eyes, panting. "Get fucked," I say through gritted teeth, my knee throbbing so badly I can hardly answer, let alone come up with a clever response.

His sigh blares with disappointment as it bounces off the shelves with the crystals and I swear they shiver in fear.

"We're getting nowhere, Kara." He rolls his sleeves up. A chime rings out, and Herkimer stalks over to the table, looking at his Dezlar, perhaps. His head snaps back to me, glee dancing in his eyes. "I just got some news that I think you'd be very interested in hearing."

My hands grip the chair's arms to prevent them from trembling. Sweat covers my body as I clench it so tightly every bone may snap.

He walks back over, leans down, and whispers, "I have your precious Starseeds and Ringers again. They won't escape me a second time."

My magic explodes within me, consuming my body from the inside out as his words infect me like a flesh-eating bacteria.

"You're lying," I say.

He has to be.

Herkimer's arm moves so quick that as another spike buries itself inside my knee, I don't even feel it for the first few seconds. Yet, when that pain hits—jostling all the other spikes around it—the agony is so intense I can't hold in the terror-filled shrill ripping my vocal cords to ribbons.

"Music to my ears. You sound lovely. That was the deepest one yet," he praises himself, straightening. "Guess I'll have to go that deep every time. So again, Kara, what are they planning with the rebels? Do they know about the plans for the Voidbringer?"

My head swims, and everything hurts, but I have to . . . *Focus.* What did he just say? Voidbringer? Is that what the AI SSPARROW is called?

Find out what his plans are! I order myself, but the pain is so fucking bad I can't think through it long enough to form any meaningful strategy.

He straddles me, another spike in hand as he holds up the pointed end an inch from my eye, and my breath hitches. His thigh knocks the metal spikes in my knee, and I almost puke on him. My vision goes black around the edges, his form blurring in and out of focus.

A cold hand holds my chin up, and another slaps my cheek. "Come on, wake up. There you go. Open those pretty eyes."

I hate him.

"Tell me now, or this one will really be brutal. And I'll make sure to do the same with each of your friends. But you can save them from ever knowing this misery. Just tell me what I want to know."

He kisses my cheek, his lips soft and icy just like Malakyte's.

I close my eyes and think of Gavrielle, the only anchor I can cling to.

Gavrielle.

Gavrielle.

Gavrielle.

Over and over and over, I always come back to Gav. Has he been taken, too? Are they hurting him right now, too?

You're doing so good, love, the version of him in my mind says. *You're so strong. It's almost done. Hold on a little longer. I'm coming for you.*

I need his strength more than oxygen.

As if his promise is real and not a figment of my imagination.

Herkimer slaps my face hard this time. The stinging in my cheekbone forces my eyes to open again, and I blink out tears.

I will not break.

I hold my chin up high. "Fuck you!"

He snarls at me, fangs bared. "Tell me what they're planning, or I'll make you really cry, Karalevine."

The rage glazing over his stare tells me he means it, but there's more in those Onyx depths. I've seen it before, the way he's always looked at me for too long. How his hands leave icy trails along my hips, my thighs—moving between them.

"Don't fucking touch me!" I snap.

 430

His laugh tells me that was a mistake.

Herkimer sniffs me, taking a long, deep breath in. "Naresteé let it slip what happened to you as a child. I can make your screams entirely different if I wanted to."

I refuse to respond to that.

"I smell my son all over you. You didn't mind it when he touched you, apparently."

My nose crinkles in disgust. "Who your son fucks shouldn't be your concern, yet here you are, creepiest dad of the fucking year!"

Just think of Gavrielle . . .

My lids close as I picture those beautiful eyes of his.

Gavrielle.

Gavrielle.

Gavrielle.

I go deeper and deeper into those eyes, listing all the shades I'd use to ink them. Into his beautiful, sculpted face, those muscled arms that have always made me feel like I was home, and his goodness not even Malakyte could erase.

Then a voice breaks through the walls I've cocooned around myself.

I know that voice.

My eyes snap open as steady footsteps come our way.

Malakyte has arrived, strolling in calmly, clothes clean and hair combed back. Yet, when he faces me, my relief gets dispelled like a bucket of ice water stoking embers. His eyes are ghostly, hollowed out versions of themselves. Even though his irises are dark, there was always something behind them, but now, the emptiness chills me to my very core.

He turns to survey me, Malakyte's expression unchanged as his eyes rake my bruised body, hardly sparing even a blink for my knee, leggings pulled up to reveal the bloodied, swollen, heap of a joint.

Herkimer slides off me and stands beside his son.

I'll probably never walk again, let alone fight. He knows that.

His freezing hand reaches for me, and I flinch—a terrified little cry escaping my lips. Only then does something flash behind his eyes, and he meets mine with unrecognizable rage.

My breaths come in fast, anxiety expanding my chest like a hot-air balloon, my head fuzzing. I've never seen him study me this way. He doesn't even resemble the same person. Murderous, fury, *darkness*. He's *become* pure ice. Cold, unrelenting, every emotion frozen.

There's no point in even trying to deny anything. He knows.

But so do I.

It looks as if both of us are going to be removing our masks today.

Herkimer clasps his son on the shoulder, but it's a play of dominance, Malakyte retreating back into nothingness. "I trust I've made myself exceptionally clear about what I expect of you going forward, boy. You take her side, you and I are *done*."

I roll my eyes incredulously.

Malakyte won't look away from me. We're locked in a battle, but there are no swords or weapons or words.

I know what you did! My soundless scream echoes between us.

I did it, he says with his eyes, glaring down at me so cruelly. *I fucking did it.*

My teeth clench so hard my jaw aches more than it did after the blows it took from Herkimer. But not even his torture had my heart rolling down a cliff and into a fucking stampede.

"Yes," Malakyte says coldly.

Without another word, he drops to his knees.

Get up! I scream at him in my head. *Stand up to him!*

"Now," Herkimer says, gripping Malakyte's face so hard it looks like his skull could crack, "I will continue to deliver the punishment for your sister's death, you traitorous filth. I strip you both of your crowns, of your power. You are emperor of Arianyte no longer, boy. But I will grant you one last opportunity to prove to me that you still have my blood in your veins. An opportunity to spare your worthless, pathetic life."

Silently, Malakyte stands as Midnight eyes crawl over every ravaged part of me, and he won't be my rescuer.

As the tension licks between us like flames, so does my temper because Malakyte looks at me as if I've done something wrong here. How dare *he* be mad at *me*?

Everything hits me at once, the violation, the lies, the manipulation—this unforgivable act—and the rage boils over, our love no longer holding the betrayal at bay.

"You took my memories!" I seethe, rage sharpening the words to daggers and I'm throwing hard. "You stole my choice, and you're a fucking coward."

Tears streak down my bloodied cheeks in a torrent, but I don't care.

He just stands there, watching me.

"Why?"

"Because I loved you."

His voice rings so hollow, so dead.

My eyes close, more tears sliding down my scorching cheeks.

"What are they planning, Karalevine? How long have you been scheming with them to deceive me? All for what? For *him*?"

My eyes snap open.

"Who?"

He laughs bitterly as if I'm being ridiculous. "The piece of filth you did all this to free!" he yells, his anger slipping its leash.

"Ardelle?" I laugh. "No, Malakyte. I did *all of this* because I wanted my fucking memories. I wanted to free my friends and save the Hijacked and my people from you *psychotic fucks*!" I scream the last two words. "You did this, you started this, you lied first. How dare you condemn me when you're the one who violated the deepest parts of me? You took away my choice! You did all this, you married me and made me your queen and told me you loved me all based on a horrific, violent, fucking lie! So, don't you dare come at me like I'm the one who did something wrong here. It was you. It's always been *you*!"

He doesn't even look remorseful. Where is the man I loved? Did he ever exist?

"We don't have to be enemies like this," I plead, trying in vain to bring that person I loved back to me. "I don't want that. I never did. I just wanted my memories. Please. If you ever loved me, put them back. I know you want to be better. This is your opportunity."

Snatching my cheeks with one hand, Malakyte forces my face forward. "Look at me." The hatred in his voice scares me to death, so I do it. "Do you love him?"

"Ardelle?"

Malakyte's brows crease in confusion.

"Why do you need to clarify who I meant . . ."

Horrifying recognition slackens his face, and he looks down to my forearm, where Gavrielle's dandelion tattoo rests forever branded into my flesh.

He laughs, and it's incredulously cruel. "Oh, that's rich, Karalevine. Gavrielle has always been a slippery bastard, but this . . ." His grip tightens and tightens, and I can see the gears in his eyes turning. "This, I did not see coming."

Malakyte looks genuinely taken aback.

"So, he's the one you love, then?" he asks bluntly, and I try not to scream as his grip becomes unbearable. "Were you about to leave me for him?"

My heart races, my antimatter building and building and burning and burning within my body, the collar preventing me from exuding any of that magic or pressure. Tears roll down my cheeks and across his icy fingertips, steaming as they make contact with his cold skin.

"I love you, too, Malakyte. But you took away my choice!"

He shoves my face away, turning his back on me.

I release a desperate, shaking breath as he stalks to the crystals sitting on the shelves, bends down, and plucks my shard off my shelf.

No, no, no!

"This is what you care so much about? This crystal was worth destroying all the love we had for one another? This is what you want so desperately you'd risk me, my crown, and everything that comes with it? I elevated you to greatness, and you sold me out. You set me up. For *this* and for *him*?"

"Yes," I confess, the single word shattering both our hearts. "Because I'm the only one who gets to choose who I love, not you . . ."

The words start off strong but end in a whisper.

The truth is a bomb shattering the last scrap of love between us.

"I have given you everything!" he roars, coming at me, and I think for a second he's going to strike me.

As I flinch, his eyes widen, and he immediately pulls back.

Straightening, Malakyte takes a deep breath, composing himself as his affect slithers back into the cool, calculated Malakyte that makes me shiver with terror.

I don't know this person.

"You're correct, Karalevine," he begins, voice calm again as he stares down at the crystal shard. "I did pilfer your memories. It was a diabolical ritual to witness, and it has haunted me ever since. You wouldn't have loved me as you were then, not after all that happened between us. I only wished for a fresh start for you and me. Can't you understand that I did this so we could be together? Were you not happy? Did I not give you every single thing you could have wanted? Did I not treat you well? My biggest adversary in nearly a century, given not a cell but a crown . . . and far more than that. If I'm so evil, then why did I hand you the galaxy on a silver platter? I brought you the man who hurt you and gave you vengeance. I gave you power—I gave you *everything*."

His free hand comes up to adjust loose strands of my hair. "I gravely hurt you that night. I knew that. Despite regretting it, I couldn't undo it. And you, so fervent in your hatred for me and Arianyte, would never pause your crusade to entertain the possibility of what we could become together. My only options were to lose you all over again or take away your memories. I chose."

"And did you choose wrongly, Malakyte?" I ask, hoping I can reach him. My hate coexisting with love as I pity the agony in his eyes.

Even as he confesses, I *still* feel bad for him.

How can a man claim he loves me yet break my heart again and again?

He ponders my question. "It gave me you."

My heart aches at the sincerity in his voice. It hurts more than my beaten, wrecked body ever could. No physical torture could be worse.

"It isn't too late," I beg, fresh tears overcoming all my anger.

It's pure heartbreak—I can't even find the rage anymore. I'm drowning in sorrow.

Malakyte sighs, looking at me as if I'm a pitiful, naïve child. "Karalevine, you misunderstand me," he says, voice deepening and eyes warming for the first time since walking into this room. Fear clamps my throat closed. "Reconditioning you was abhorrent, and it was a terrible thing I had done to you. But I'd do it a thousand times if it meant I could keep you with me."

And before I can even scream, Malakyte crushes my crystal with one strong clench of his fist.

CHAPTER 70

The cry that escapes my lips is the precise sound of a heart collapsing in on itself. Malakyte didn't just crush my crystal—he crushed my heart.

There's no difference.

As the shards and dust from the Memorantis crystal fall out of Malakyte's hands, his wedding bracelet stark against his pale wrist, I'm broken in a way I've never known—or remembered.

The pain is perpetuated by Herkimer's laughter and Malakyte's cold eyes.

How could he?

They told me . . . They all tried to tell me I loved a monster. I just couldn't believe them.

I thought our darkness matched, but they're different shades—different hues. Our darkness isn't the same, it never was.

I've fucked up.

Malakyte finally says something, but my ears are ringing, so I hardly hear him. "I'm going to retrieve Naresteé. Have her reset you. Be a good girl for me in the meantime, Karalevine. Your punishment for this farce will end here. This will all be like one bad dream."

"Why not just throw me in that machine and do it yourself?" I ask bitterly, hating I can't wipe the tears from my cheeks.

My crystal is going to kill me at this rate it's so bad. So severe I can't feel the pain in my knee anymore, only the fury inside my body that's about to implode.

"Along with a sedative to calm you down," he adds, shaking his head as he pats mine. I shake him off as best I can, disgusted. "But to answer your question, because that machine is for dumping sections of memory, you'd be nothing but a shell. I could potentially dump the last several weeks . . . However, Naresteé is more thorough and can create a new narrative. Plus, I want Gavrielle's memory erased this time as well."

"Stop it," I hiss. "Stop. This isn't you. You're just acting this way because he's here. I saw what he did to you in the Atrium, Malakyte. I saw what he did to you in the throne room. I see what he's done to you your whole life. *I see you*—the real you. You don't have to bow to him anymore. This isn't you."

"This has always been me, Karalevine."

I refuse to believe that. "No, it isn't. You can choose differently."

That flash of pity returns, and I loathe it.

Then he turns to walk away.

"I'll remember," I warn. "It doesn't matter if it's a month from now, a year, ten years, a hundred, I will eventually remember, and you'll be right here again. I dream of my old life. I knew something was off. My mind will show me the truth, even if you prevent the others from telling me. Stop the cycle of toxicity. You're a better man than this—I know you are. I've seen it. You're not *him*. You're not your father."

Silence rings between us, and his eyes soften at my words, the tiniest glimmer of hope flooding into my blood.

Herkimer answers for his son. "Of course he isn't me. He's a spineless, soft-hearted child who isn't man enough to rule my empire."

"He's never going to give it up to you," I tell Malakyte, ignoring Herkimer's bullshit. "He'll use any excuse to take his crown back."

"Watch it, Little Thief," Herkimer scoffs.

This is getting me nowhere.

I roll my eyes. Resigned to my fate, I sink into the chair with a frustrated exhale.

He doesn't want to listen, doesn't want to be better or be saved.

"I'm sorry, Karalevine." He kisses the top of my head and lingers there. "I've always wished I could be the man you believe me to be, but I'll never escape being your villain."

Then his coldness retreats as he walks back toward the doors, but not before threatening Herkimer to keep his hands off me. We'll see how long that lasts.

It isn't long before Herkimer's taunts jab me right where it hurts the most. "He never asked me not to hurt your friends. I'll make a recording of their screams as they beg for death, make sure you get very acquainted with the sound."

I glare at him with murder in my eyes. "Sucks Malakyte came in to ruin your fun, doesn't it?"

His eyes shift, cold as ice and cruel as Death himself.

Leaning against the Memorantis bed, Herkimer taunts, "Perhaps when he returns, I'll force him to watch as I make you scream and beg for him to make it stop? He'd deserve no less after what he's done. And you're going to pay for his crimes. If it wasn't for you, she'd still be here. I know he killed her for you."

"Selenyte was a psychotic bitch wh—"

Rapidly, so fast that I can hardly keep up with what's happening, Herkimer grabs another spike from the table, crosses the space between us, and plunges it into my knee.

My scream is bloodcurdling.

The star mark lights up, even through the collar, sparks of antimatter shocking Herkimer enough to make him edge back as they dance around my palms.

I force myself to breathe, but each breath trembles as it slides out through teeth clenched so damn tightly my jaw may snap.

It hurts *so bad* . . .

Coming back in, Herkimer says something, but I can't hear it through the pounding in my ears. Bullshit, no doubt.

Without thinking about it, I suck in a trembling breath, gathering spit from the depths of my throat and then—*ptoo!*—my loogie lands right on his face.

Gavrielle taught me how to spit like a guy, so my hidden talent finally came in handy.

"Fuck you, asshole," I smolder, death a promise as it glitters in my eyes.

I will kill him. I vow it to the stars themselves.

Herkimer laughs, wiping my spit from where it landed on his cheekbone.

He reaches for me again but hesitates as the door whooshes open, and he looks up. His eyes go wide, shock causing his expression to fall.

A familiar hiss slices through the air, sharp, loud, piercing, as an arrow whizzes past my cheek and impales Herkimer's eye.

Icy blood splatters onto my face, and my yelp is a mix of surprise and pure glee as the force blasts Herkimer backward, his neck snapping in two. The momentum drags him backwards and down, down, down, crystals wobbling on their shelves as he thumps onto the granite floor.

An Elendril arrow sticks straight up from his shocked, bloodied face, still vibrating from the impact. Herkimer is completely unmoving.

"Regenerate from that, prick!" a voice shouts from behind me.

Picking my jaw up off the floor, I crank my neck and see Ardelle rushing my way. He runs up to me, looking like hell, but he's here and alive, and I exhale in relief. But then I gasp, my eyes snapping to the man beside him.

"Gavrielle?" My chin trembles, the dam of my emotions finally breaking the moment I see his face. "You came back for me?"

I shamelessly ugly cry because *he came back for me.*

 440

Gavrielle seems shocked when he sees me, but he covers the slip quickly as he drops to his knees, takes my face in both his hands with such tenderness it nearly breaks me, presses his forehead up against mine, and says, "I'm always with you, love. If you're a monster, then I'm a monster, remember? We're never going to be separated again. I'd cross Hell itself to save you."

And I don't question it, not for one fucking second, because he already has. All of them have, and my abandonment issues couldn't be more nurtured—more healed—because of these people. Because of *him*.

I cry. I cry, and I cry, even as Ardelle slices the ropes eating into my skin. The moment my arms are free, I wrap them around Gavrielle.

Gavrielle wipes my tears, his thumbs caressing my broken, bruised skin. Finally, we break away.

Gavrielle looks over my wrecked knee. "Oh, Kara . . ."

His voice is the softest of whispers so low I can barely hear him.

The room goes graveyard quiet.

I glance at Ardelle to find him watching me with an anguished expression, his face beaten and bruised and cut in all stages of healing.

When our eyes meet, we nod.

But there's something a little bit off in his Deep Sapphire eyes I can't identify as our gazes rip away from each other.

Gavrielle says, "We need to get you to Ahren."

I straighten in the chair. "Herkimer said he caught them again! We have to—"

"It's okay, love, they're okay. We're on comms. Deimos got them out. It's alright."

I exhale a trembling breath as I sink into the chair, all my energy leaking from my body now that I know I'm safe. *They are, too. Everyone is safe.*

"Is he dead?" I ask, my head nodding to Herkimer.

Ardelle walks over and checks his pulse. "He's dead."

Relief tingles my body.

"Is there a collar key on that bed, Ardelle?" I ask, my body still a raging inferno.

"Yeah," Ardelle says, plucking one from the bed.

His hands are clammy as he removes the collar from my neck, my crystal mark soaring the moment the metal is free from my skin.

Gav doesn't inch away as my magic threatens to incinerate him. "You can hold it back, love. You got this."

We breathe together, easing my magic as it licks and snaps along my entire body, desperate to lash out.

Gav's fingers brush against my boiling skin, the sensation drawing my attention to how good he looks dressed in perfectly fitted leathers, his twin blades peeking out behind his broad, strong shoulders. The ginger scent of him anchors me, and, fuck, if my crystal doesn't purr at his touch, and it finally calms to a simmer.

"Good girl, love. No blowing up this ship. We don't have time for that this week."

I chuckle, but it helps.

Ardelle walks to Herkimer and pulls the Memorantis key from his pocket. Once he straightens, he looks over at Gavrielle and me. "Let's get these memories back." He beams, holding the key up by its chain.

Anxiety blooms inside of me.

Gavrielle smiles as he looks to where my name is on the shelves, only to find the space empty. Both their gazes dive to the shattered bits of crystal and dust littered across the floor.

The two go ghostly pale.

"Thumbelina."

Ardelle says the nickname with so much sadness I can hardly stand it. The silence that follows is heavy with a burden he doesn't know how to carry, Gavrielle's little circles on my wrists refusing to stop.

 442

"Bring me to the crystals," I ask Gav.

Although looking confused, he does.

It's agonizing coming out of this chair, gravity wrenching my knee downwards so far, I scream. Ardelle uses his gravity magic to keep my leg up until Gavrielle can get it into a better position, and together, they get me to the shelves.

"What happened to it?" Ardelle asks, voice solemn.

Sitting on Gavrielle's knee, I begin counting the many crystals on Malakyte's shelf. "Malakyte shattered it," I answer, and they both try to hide their reactions, but their anger is easy to spot. "But what he didn't realize was that, when Gav brought me in here that day, I switched my crystal with one of his."

Gav's audible gasp is a beautiful sound as I pluck the thirteenth crystal back—for the thirteen dandelions he picked for me that day.

"Is that?" Gav asks, Petal eyes wide as he focuses on the thing in my hand.

My energy soars as my fingers curl around the crystal.

Smiling, I peer at the two men who love me. "Yeah," I say, sniffling as I hold the shard to my chest like a baby bird. "*It's mine.*"

"You're a stars damned genius, Thumbelina." Ardelle uses his arms to hurl all of Herkimer's torture devices off the long bed. "Let's get those memories back, babe. Come on."

I look at Gav, silently questioning if he knows how.

He nods, confident.

We don't even need words to communicate. I hope that doesn't change when I wake up. I hope my feelings don't change. I want him—I want the wrong guy.

My heart pounds as I realize what's about to happen.

I'm about to relive all the trauma and pain and anger and fear and love all within a snap of my fingers.

I'm scared.

"It's okay," Gav says, sitting me on the bed. "You'll be okay."

There he goes, never missing a damn thing.

Ardelle nods confidently. Even beat to shit, dirty, and bloody, he smiles at me like he loves me, too. And this time, there's nothing missing in his eyes.

"Malakyte is coming back," I inform them, and they nod, assuming the risks.

Gav wastes no time getting me into the machine and lying me down on my back. My head slides into the half-dome contraption at the head of the table, the part attached to the giant crystal. The table is so long my feet don't come anywhere close to reaching the end.

The underside of the dome moves like an ocean of vivid colors swirling on a fluid, pixelated screen.

Gavrielle moves quickly around the machine, working the interface after he inserts the key and turns the thing on. Then he puts my crystal into a slot above my head.

Once done, he sits at the bedside.

Ardelle takes one hand, and Gav captures the other.

"Are you ready?" Gavrielle asks.

Chuckling uncomfortably, I say, "No."

What's going to become of me, my feelings—everything— once this is done? What of this darkness in me? Am I simply a rat in a cage morphed into a tiger, ready to spring forward and bloody everything in my wake?

There's no time left to contemplate or decide or waver. After all we've done to get here, after everything me and every single one of them have sacrificed, this is it. The moment has finally arrived. I'm getting my memories back—*right fucking now*.

"Do it," I tell Gav confidently, squeezing their hands.

They squeeze back.

"See you on the other side, Thumbelina."

A clicking whirs directly above my head, then immense heat zaps my face. Suddenly, the brightest, whitest light I've ever known completely envelopes my entire field of vision.

The last thing I remember is my startled shriek bouncing off the dome as the beam hits my eyes, and I'm immediately consumed by its flash.

And I'm gone.

CHAPTER 71

I've been here for so long.

My prison.

My Hell.

My punishment.

Ever since I became trapped within this cube inside my own mind, this is all I've known, wasting away in the dark void buried somewhere so deep nobody can reach me. I have no contact with the outside world. It's only me and the darkness.

I'm so afraid of the darkness now.

I've felt all the feelings. Fury broke my body against these transparent walls. Depression shattered my spirit. Now, nothingness claims my soul.

To the version of me who now rules my body and holds the light of my consciousness, I hope she hasn't gone as insane as I have, trapped within this darkness.

Where *he* put me.

After accepting my demise, I waited for death to claim me, but even Death is afraid to set foot here. Never hungry, never having to pee, never tired enough to find the oblivion of sleep to pass the time. I've been numb for what could be weeks, months, years . . . Time doesn't exist in this place.

In a corner, where the tiniest sliver of light shines the brightest, that is where I exist. Legs curled up tight, head bowed into my knees. I think I've been sitting like this for days, unmoving. Never aching, never needing to stretch. Just . . .

A tapping gently wakes up my ears, and I had forgotten I could hear. But it's nothing.

It taps again. It's annoying. When I look up, there's a figure standing outside the cube on the opposite side, mostly in shadow. I blink, and she remains. I've forgotten I could see.

"Who are you?" I croak.

I'd forgotten I could speak.

Then her silhouette comes into shape, her petite frame, long flowing hair, tattooed skin. "You know who I am. I came to get you out of here."

I laugh at this version of myself.

She's clean. She's pretty. She's glowing, and her eyes are bright. In comparison, I'm the complete opposite. My body is frail, beaten, and bloodied as it was the day I entered this place. Hair a mess. Still dressed in the raggedy, torn, grimy Titan Games uniform.

"Let's go home. They're waiting for us," she tells me, laying her palm flat against my clear little pocket of Hell.

I sigh, my head slumping back into my knees, so I no longer have to face my doppelganger. "You're not real."

"A lot has happened out there," she says. "If you don't come back, then I'll never remember what really happened. I won't remember them."

Them.

"Don't you see a problem with that theory, toots?" I mumble at this aggressively positive version of myself. "I can't get out."

"This old thing? This is nothing for you," she claims. I lift my head again. She appears to be more in the light somehow. "You're the Star. You're The Killer of Worlds who destroyed a moon. This is fucking child's play, *toots.*"

Ahh, going at yourself sure has its merits.

Little bitch is annoying. I can see why so many people find me irritating as all hell.

"Then, you bust me out of here." I bonk the back of my head against the cube for emphasis.

"I think it has to be you."

"Then, we're fucked, so, don't know what you want me to do. I've tried getting out, like a million fucking times."

"Try one more time."

"No."

"*Yes.*"

I grunt in annoyance and stand, kicking the stupid thing to make my point. "See? Not happening. It's a waste of time."

"You're being a fucking brat," she tells me, eyes on fire. "I know you've suffered—I have, too. But the others are waiting for us, and they're in danger. You have to pick yourself up and get the hell out of this cube. This isn't you. You're a fighter."

The others.

Jance, Ardelle. Gavrielle . . .

I look down at my forearm, the letters carved there, still bloody. J. F.

My father.

"Well, I don't want to fight anymore," I confess. "I can't face them. Not after what I've done. I'm at fault. I didn't learn my lesson soon enough. They warned me, and I *fucked up.*"

"They love you, Kara."

I shake my head. "I know that now, but I didn't realize it until it was too late. I didn't realize a lot until it was too late."

"They don't care. They just want you back, and so do I. Now, pull yourself together and *get out of here.*"

The silence on the other side of that demand rings out long and hollow in my ears, and it brings me to tears . . .

I do want to go home.

Break free, a voice deep within me says, a familiar feeling I haven't felt since the moment I was locked away in this dreadful place. *Break free, Killer of Worlds.*

That voice . . .

My crystal's voice.

I study the alternative version of myself. *She's just on the other side of these clear walls.*

I swallow, looking around the space, but it hasn't changed. There's never been anything here but me, the cube, and the darkness. So, if she's here, then maybe . . . Maybe they really did find a way to free me? Can that be?

"I don't know how to get out." Hot tears brim my eyes. I had forgotten I could cry. "I'm so lost in here. I can't break free of this prison or our past and all that pain and anger and everything that happened. *I don't know how!*"

This other version of me runs to my side of the cube, getting as close as possible. "I asked Gavrielle how we get past this, and you know what he said?"

Gavrielle?

My heart aches as she says his name. Gavrielle . . .

"He said we find a way to create meaning out of our suffering. Give it a purpose. Turn it around and make something good come from all this shit. And you know what? I think he was right about that. I think it can get better if we try. You just have to *try*."

I search her eyes—my eyes—as if they'll unlock the key to what I still need to learn about myself.

But I guess I can . . . *try*. I had forgotten that I could try.

"These walls are nothing but paper."

I nod and repeat her words to her—back to myself. I punch at the cube, and like always, nothing but a hollow thud follows, yet I do it again.

"You're not doing it with your heart. You have to break out of here with more than just your fists."

I slam my body against the cube, gritting my teeth with every crash to my shoulder.

These walls are nothing! They're fucking nothing! I'm stronger than this prison. I can get out. I can find a way to heal all this shit inside of me.

I heave my entire body against the cube's wall again, and this time, a crack the size of an insect appears. But it's still *a crack*.

Hope blooms. *Yes! I can do this!*

Another crack forms, spidering down a few inches.

My shoulder aches as I pound into the wall, but I don't stop.

"Yes, you're doing it! Keep going!"

I've made so many mistakes, all leading me right here, a culmination of my fuck-ups drawing the ones I love straight to their own Hells. Maybe that's why I was never able to break free. I couldn't accept that I hurt the people who loved me.

More cracks form as if the epiphany is making the cube weaker.

But they do love me. I'll never doubt that again.

"It's breaking. You're so close!" She jumps up and down, cheering me on.

I dash to the other side, gathering momentum as I crash into the wall with all my might.

Yes!

My skin prickles in anticipation. The final piece of the puzzle becomes clear, and she's standing on the other side of this cube.

The person I have to face most of all . . .

Is myself.

She welcomes me back with open arms.

My cheeks are soaked with tears as I rush to the opposite end, the wall in front of me bent and warped. I brace my body for one last hit, one last fight in this horrible, fucking place.

"I love you. It's time to come home, toots." She grins.

She understands. More than anyone else ever could.

"I love you, too," I say, never having said those words to myself, the foreign feeling coursing through my chest to the point where it might explode.

I cry for every part of me that's gone so unloved for so long—by me most of all.

And I'm sorry about that.

I have more work to do, but for now, I can face and forgive myself, for whatever awaits me on the other side.

As I charge toward the cube's wall, I know it's going to shatter.

I know I'm going home. Back to the people who love me.

With all the force I can muster, I charge forward. There's barely an ounce of resistance as the wall shatters.

And I'm wrapped in a massive, brilliant white light before my body hits the floor.

My own shouts of joy echo into the light, leaving the darkness behind.

CHAPTER 72

I awaken with a desperate gasp, a rainbow light hitting my eyes first, a strange heat warming my cheeks.

I mean to sit up, but strong hands hold me down.

Pain racks my body hard, so fucking hard.

In my head, my knee, my face . . .

. . . And then the pain becomes nothing as my memories flash one by one, again and again, another to another, all unstoppable and endless like a gushing dam.

The gunshot that killed Geonni. The cruel grin on Malakyte's face as he shot him in that room beneath the stadium during those first Titan Games. My intimate moments with Ardelle in the Mansion during the second Titan Games. Gavrielle being alive and our fight up in that dark, obsidian maze. Jance being. . . *Fuck*, this entire time, he was . . . He was . . .

Jance is my dad . . . And I had forgotten him.

The horrific scars on my arm are so clear now. Jance. Father. I tried to remind myself. The stinging pain of carving those letters into my flesh comes on strong and vivid. As I remember that I'm not alone in this world, that my parents didn't abandon me, I also remember that my mother, Astoria, was murdered the day I was born. That I bombed her grave merely two days ago. Love and pain. Salvation and sin.

The contraption over my face lifts, and two pairs of eyes meet my own.

Eyes of Lilac in Spring.

Another pair in Sapphire Sky.

Gavrielle and Ardelle.

I blink at them both . . . With so much information flooding into my mind at once, I can only stare dumbly at their faces.

"Give her some time," Gav says as he helps me sit up, the movement pulling on my knee as those shards rip every tightened tendon and muscle and bone.

Everything hurts.

"Am I really out of there?" I whisper, looking around at this strange room and how the purple light glows on the edges of their hair and faces. I've seen this room, I know where I am, but it *feels* so different somehow. They do, too.

"Yeah, love. You're out."

Tears turn Gavrielle's eyes glassy, and mine sting, too.

There's nothing but him and me for several heartbeats, and we slam into each other, embracing so tightly, tears intermixed with my disbelieving laughter.

I hold on to him for dear fucking life, my body a trembling mess as his long icy hair catches in my fingers. I take in his scent, allowing myself just one second to enjoy the hard strength of his chest and arms.

"It's okay," he whispers in my ear lovingly. "It's all okay. You're back now. I finally fulfilled my promise to you."

That memory of the unadulterated terror that ripped through me in the throne room. What Naresteé and Malakyte did to me . . . the Reconditioning.

"Malakyte . . ." His name burns like embers from a roaring fire. The love I feel for him raging within the inner recesses of my heart, while the hate that I remember sweeps in on an icy gust to smother those cinders to ash. "He's coming back."

We don't have long, but I have to address something first, and it can't wait another second.

I release Gavrielle and turn to Ardelle, my chest cracking into a thousand fucking pieces as all these recollections between us flood in like rapid fire, one after the other after the other. So much history . . . of us in that bookstore, in the pool at Jance's house, the moment we met on that rooftop when he first called me Thumbelina.

Malakyte's false memories of *him* being the one on the roof dissolve under the vivid reality.

I launch myself at him, sobbing—hating myself, linking my arms around familiar shoulders and tattooed skin I had completely forgotten about. I had forgotten him. He was alone down there for *so long*.

"Thumbelina," he murmurs, his hands soft as they lie on either side of my shoulders. "It's okay."

My neck arches to look up, and I place one hand on his beaten face, our eyes full of tears as I ache for what was stolen from us. "I'm so, so sorry, Ardelle."

I don't even know how to feel. I'm not the old me or even the one from minutes before—I'm someone new altogether. And there's so much flying through my brain my romantic feelings are a jumbled mess.

And I think . . . so are his. I can feel the canyon between us now, ever-growing.

"A lot has happened, hasn't it?" he says, and I nod, looking away in shame.

He knows . . . Somehow, he knows about Gavrielle and likely Malakyte, too.

I've been the worst to him.

Ardelle draws my eyes back to him. "But you finally found him, *didn't you?*"

We glance at Gavrielle, who's sitting patiently on the opposite side of the bed, looking just as torn up.

 454

When my eyes find Ardelle's again, my chin quivers as my feelings become more than apparent to me.

I nod, my emotions clasping my throat closed. I can't say it, can't betray the boy I used to love before this circumstance fucked it all up.

"Maybe we both found someone in this darkness, Thumbelina. In order to survive it, we had no choice. Things are different now—we're different now, but we'll talk about everything once we're out of here, okay? We'll talk. But know that I love you no matter what, and I'm always going to be right here."

I nod, agreeing. We have to go.

He hugs me one more time and says into my ear, "Thank you for saving Pacey, Kara. For that, I'll always love you."

Kara . . . He never calls me Kara.

"I love you, too."

The words spill out, a truth filled with emotion and raw honesty.

I just wonder if my feelings lean more towards Gavrielle now . . . Even Ardelle could see that it's always been about Gavrielle for me, and it likely forever will be.

Although that doesn't mean I can't feel love for Ardelle, it's just a different type of love now . . . for us both.

We collectively take a breath, and after a minute, Gavrielle gently picks me up.

The pain is damn near blinding.

Ardelle rips his arrow out of Herkimer's face. The gruesome image is haunting, but he honestly deserved worse.

They turn toward the door, but I stop them. "Ardelle, do something for me," I say, knowing we can't leave this place unscathed. "Destroy every single one of those crystals. And then demolish the Memorantis."

This will never happen to me or anyone else ever again.

CHAPTER 73

I don't want to be like my father. I don't want to be like my father.

It's what I say to myself as I stalk through the halls of my ship. No, I'm not Father—that's why he detests my veritable existence.

I *do* want to be the man Karalevine deserves and believes me to be. Nobody has ever seen the potential for any type of goodness in me, nobody except her.

This Karalevine—the woman I love, the woman I've killed and sacrificed and committed atrocities for—she's into me too deep. Her illuminating nature pinned down the darkness in my ruined soul, allowing some part of me to find its way up to the light.

To her light.

Is it too late to fix this? If I choose not to Recondition her again, could I keep her? Would she stay?

I stop and glance at the direction I came from, conflicted.

My anger throbs at the back of my skull, unaccustomed to such resistance as my logical rationale pushes against me, but . . .

I love her.

"Fuck," I curse, pacing in the hall as I debate my course of action.

Two, four, six, eight, ten, twelve, fourteen, sixteen, eighteen, twenty, twenty-two.

I'm the only one who gets to choose who I love, her voice sings within my mind, remembering how she looked when I crushed her memories in my hand.

I fucked up . . .

Perhaps I should let her decide? Allow her the free will she covets so vehemently. The thought feels a lot like the sensation I experience when dying.

I want to be the man who's worthy of her, so I shouldn't be such a damn coward.

Perhaps she'll see I can change for her and will come back to me?

"What will it be, big brother?" Selenyte's ghost chimes in from behind me, the voice chilling my body to literal ice. "You've lost all your power, your crown, and you're mere moments away from losing your Star, too. Who is the crown prince of Arianyte when pushed up against a wall? Do you choose her light or your darkness, Malakyte? You can only have one."

I choose her light.

CHAPTER 74

YEAR 5, DAY 1,999: THE PRINCE HAS ME FOLLOWING DEIMOS A LOT. HE'S OBSESSED. DEIMOS IS A MENACE—THAT'S NOT UP FOR DEBATE. HOWEVER, THERE'S SOMETHING STRANGE ABOUT HIS ACTIONS. HE'S HELPING KIDS, NOT HURTING OR KIDNAPPING THEM, WHICH IS CONTRARY TO THE PRINCE'S NARRATIVE THAT DEIMOS IS THE ONE TO BLAME FOR ALL THOSE MISSING CHILDREN. FROM WHAT I SEE, HE'S RESCUING THEM. FROM WHAT? FATHER, TELL ME HOW THAT MAKES SENSE? I'LL FIGURE OUT THE TRUTH. I PROMISE.

GAVRIELLE ABRAXAS

Every step I take is agony for Kara as she, Ardelle, and I race through the Azurite. I hold her as close to my chest as possible, but the faster we run, the harder it is to keep her still.

Hold on, love. I'm right here.

We need to get the fuck off this ship—and fast, but not all of us are free just yet. There's one more.

"Where are the others?" Kara asks.

We stealthily run through halls I've known since I was a child, passages that will keep eyes and tails off us, and thankfully, we haven't passed anyone yet. After what happened in the Atrium, I'm sure people are afraid to leave their rooms.

"Remember the medical sector where we found the Hijacked?" I ask, leading us around a corner as we enter the stairwell. "Well, Ardelle here was cellmates with Pacey's Ringer. They're holding her there. The others are meeting us so we can get her out, too."

"What, really?" She gasps, eyes moving from mine to Ardelle's as he runs beside us, his bow and arrow strapped to his back.

He smiles. "Her name is Ceplar. Arianyte has had her up here for three years." Ardelle says, his words dancing between breaths as we make it to the stairwell. "She's young, like us, not older like the other Ringers."

"Old my ass," I say, Ardelle throwing me a grin I chuck right back.

Punk.

But I have reasons to let my personality glimmer. I got her back. And the tension between her and Ardelle is . . . awkward. I'm a complete asshole for seeing that as a good thing. But I love her so much. And after what the dragons told me about saving her from herself . . . I'm unsure if he can emotionally handle the weight of carrying her through this forest and out the other side.

We reach the landing and fly through the door at the top of the stairs, running down another hallway on a different floor. There are people here, but we don't care. We run past them, and I have to yell at several to move so we don't collide. *Not with Kara in my arms.*

Malakyte will know where we are soon, if he hasn't already. We've got to go faster.

We approach the turn in the hallway that'll lead to the medical sector, the very same place Kara and I entered days ago. Our pace slows, eyes and ears on high alert.

Ardelle nocks an arrow, holding his bow taut as we round the corner and prepare for SSPARROWs.

We find them, but they're all down.

Ardelle releases tension on the bow, looking around and checking the pulses of the soldiers. There are no civilians, either.

"Still alive, just knocked out," he says, sliding his arrow into his quiver at his back. "They're probably inside."

We don't waste another second as we go in.

The white brightness in here is like the sun on a winter's day—blinding as all hell. We find multiple doctors sprawled on the pristine floor—unconscious—but I carry no pity for them. This is no place for healing but one of calculated suffering. The rooms are made of clear nanoglass filled with prisoners, who are sedated in their beds. It smells too sterile, like antiseptic is used on every smooth surface of this whitewashed Hell, but underneath it, something else lingers too long. It reeks of rotting flesh and hollowed souls.

This place is a maze, and we slither through many hallways that split into multiple forks of four to five different directions as we search for the others and the Ringer we're here to liberate. It doesn't help that each hallway is a nearly identical version of the previous one.

Our footsteps become prominent when Kara tenses in my arms, and my ears pick up on the reason.

"Someone's coming," I warn.

Ardelle gracefully reaches for and notches an arrow with the efficiency of a true master, aiming at the empty corridor.

A tall, metal-clad figure rounds the bend.

"Pace?" Ardelle asks, bow and arrow slacking.

Pacey's large eyes widen and mist the moment she sees us, the sickle blade arching long behind her head as she stands in Ennar's suit twenty feet away.

Ardelle is off, Pacey, too. They crash into each other, and it's so good to hear her crying happy tears for once.

He pats the back of her head, and they wipe each other's tears away. "Don't cry. I'm here. Are you okay? I've missed you so much."

Pacey nods, and the two talk for a couple minutes, then hug one last time before turning our way.

It's so touching I can't interrupt.

Kara has tears in her eyes as brother and sister come back to us. It's a bit awkward with Kara in my arms, but she leans over and hugs Pacey's shoulders as best she can.

"About time, Kara. I knew it was the old you the moment I saw your face. I told you we'd see each other again, didn't I? But look at what he did to you . . . Why did you close that door on us? Jance was *furious*. Don't do that again."

Kara chuckles. "Sorry I took so long to come back—and sorry about the door, too. Where's Jance? I really need to see him."

Pacey's eyes say everything as she winces. "They're all fine, but they're stuck hiding two levels up. I came to meet up with you guys here. But they're all fi—"

"I know it's important for all of us to reunite, but," I say, hating to be *that* guy, "Malakyte is going to rage when he finds his father dead and those memory crystals shattered, so let's get your Ringer and go from there."

Everyone agrees, and we move. Rounding several corners, pass three dozen cells at least, we reach a horrible sight.

"Are those . . . ?" Kara hesitates, looking up at me in shock.

She remembers them.

"The Terran Tributes that attacked us on the first challenge of the Titan Games?" I say grimly. "Yeah. Different people, obviously, but these are the same experiments that created those poor . . . creatures."

They're just as mad and crazy, too. They're clothed in nothing but a thin paper gown, the blood in their veins turned dark as night as if wicked worms have infested their bodies, the black deepening their mouths and nose. They scream at us, throwing themselves against the nanoglass of their prisons, the empty thuds they create as they whack it repeatedly becoming their anthem of madness.

"They look diseased," Pacey says.

Kara points downward and says, voice hollow, "So, what are we going to do with her . . ."

My eyes follow her line of sight, and my shoulders slump, my body weighted with sorrow. Sitting in the cell next to these poor souls is a young woman about our age. Her hair is orange-red, long but dirty, and her deep green orbs gaze up at us, heavy-lidded and hazy as she sits on the floor. Pacey's Elendril symbol is visible on her right hand.

She's the Ringer we came to rescue.

Ardelle rushes up to her, the walls made of the same material as their prisons.

Pacey unlocks the door with a keycard she must've taken off a doctor.

Ardelle rushes in and dives to his knees. "Hey, hey, it's me." He brushes the long, fiery hair away from her face.

The girl is just as beaten, bruised, and scarred as Ardelle is. What did they do to them in those cells? More importantly, why did Malakyte bring her here, next to these wild Tributes? And why now? I don't like it, and it reeks of that slippery bastard.

She doesn't answer him.

"Cep," Ardelle tries again, reaching behind her hair and unlatching the collar around her neck with the key he saved from the Memorantis room. "I'm here to take you home. I told you the others would come for us."

She doesn't look well. Her skin has the same grayish paleness the other Tributes have, and she appears exceptionally sick. Plus, her proximity to the Tributes concerns me.

"Did they inject you with anything? Expose you to those guys?" Ardelle asks.

She just blinks slowly.

"I . . . I was . . . I was good, like he wants . . ."

"Gav," Kara whispers so only I can hear.

I squeeze her tighter.

"If she's been exposed to whatever made them that way"—I nod to the Tributes trying to get to us in their frenzy—"she could slowly evolve into one of them. We need to get her to Ahren immediately."

Everyone nods.

"What did they do to her?" Kara asks.

"Turned her into my little Trojan horse, Karalevine."

The voice turns my blood to ice.

CHAPTER 75

Karalevine Ruzz

Gavrielle spins faster than light, my neck whipping around so fast the bones ache.

But I know that voice . . .

Malakyte stands a meager ten feet away, just as the turn in the hallway curves. He's a stark shadow of blackness against the bright Ghost White walls.

I tremble in Gavrielle's arms, and I can feel the color leaching from my face. Malakyte is a force, and he is absolutely seething.

Guess he found all those crushed crystals and a dead dad.

And all that malice is directed right at me.

But he isn't the only one enraged. Seeing his face after regaining my memories is like peeling back the mask completely. It's still his features, his strong jaw. The same scar is a deafening canyon across his brow and cheek, but he also looks entirely different, too.

How could I have ever loved him so much? How did I not see his mask so clearly secured as he performed for me day after day? I, the willing, naïve audience, watched and clapped at his fabulous performance.

Eating it up.

Fucking wow.

Yet my heart still aches for the man he could have been if only he tried. But none of it matters because he put me in that box.

And I suffered inside that box.

The people I loved suffered.

Sighing, Malakyte takes a step closer, and we all collectively take one back.

We're at the end of the ward. There's no way out other than through him.

"This has gone on long enough, Malakyte," Gavrielle says, the vibration in his chest deep as he speaks with authority to the man who raised him since he was twelve. "Kara made her choice, and so have I. Let us go."

Malakyte's dark glare slowly—as if being peeled away from my face by force—falls to Gavrielle.

"After everything, you betray me like this," he says, tone a mixture of anger and sadness yet composed. Malakyte doesn't slip his leash often, but when he does . . . he's terrifying. I remember that. "And you, Karalevine . . . You got even with me, didn't you? I found the crystals."

"I'd say we're even on that front, then."

I don't miss a beat.

He doesn't know I've regained my memories. He still thinks I'm the Kara I've been these last few months.

He scoffs, moving closer. "I came back because I realized that Reconditioning you isn't the appropriate decision. I chose the better path like you always wanted me to. You're correct—it was wrong to steal your choice and your memories. I'm sorry for that."

I expected him to comment about Herkimer, but whatever.

"Sorry isn't good enough anymore. You lied this entire time!"

"For you!" he yells, as if I'm the one being ridiculous. Then his voice goes quiet, like a desperate whisper of a lost ghost. "*For us*. I killed my sister for you. I lost my crown because of you. My father murdered me in front of my entire court and my mother because of you. How many people do I need to remove, how much of what I covet must I decimate to ash, for you to understand that I'd do anything to keep you with me? That's how much I love you."

Why does he always do this? I hate him one second and then he speaks, and it's like . . . he's able to suck me back in again and again. *Fuck!*

Remembering everything was going to fuck me up because the push and pull of this man, of Ardelle, of Gavrielle, and the mess I have made . . . seems like a knot of entangled chains I can't unravel, even if I had a hundred years.

Gavrielle squeezes me tighter, his body stiffening as he readies for an attack.

I sigh heavily as I say, "Malakyte, that isn't love. It's obsession. I'm not sure you even know what love is."

Now his anger withers to sadness, and the love I had for this beautifully lost man still wants to reach for him in hopes he could find the goodness I had, even in the dark.

"With you, I did," he murmurs.

It sounds genuine. Like the man I knew in the very beginning. The man I tried so hard to hold on to in that room last night.

His eyes are hard but sad as he reaches for me. "Come back with me, Karalevine. *Please.*"

He's never said please for anything in his entire fucking life I bet, but for me . . .

No . . . no! He can't do this. It's too late!

"I won't Recondition you again. I promise. If I was going to do it, Naresteé would be here with me."

My hands curl into fists, heart pounding and pounding, magic ebbing through my veins again, begging to be unleashed onto him—the utter unfairness of his demand.

Pacey's voice rings out into the tense silence. "Kara, don't. He's lying."

Malakyte's eyes flash to hers but come back to mine quicker than a serpent's strike. He steps forward again, pushing his hand closer to me for emphasis.

This is what I've wanted him to say, to do, and *be* this entire fucking time. Why now? Why does he finally get it *now*? Long before he ever Reconditioned me, I remember wishing he could be the person he was when we met. All I've wanted was for him to say these words, for him to mean them with his whole heart. I've always wanted to change him—*save him*—but I think I've known the painful truth and couldn't accept it.

There is no saving Malakyte Ardeen.

I never stood a chance.

Yet my heart . . . It loves him when I hate him. My heart and mind are two undecided forces, pulling and pushing and fighting against each other in a maddening battle for control.

And I have to make it stop.

"Gavrielle," I say, my voice cold and dead in my ears. "Let me down."

He squeezes me on instinct, as if his visceral reaction is to keep me close.

When I glance from Malakyte to Gavrielle, his eyes flare with fear and panic.

"Thumbelina," Ardelle whispers from beside us, as if he can't believe what I'm doing.

All their faces reflect this shock, but I *have to* do this.

"Gav," I press again, looking him dead in the eyes.

His chest pumps as he breathes deeply, holding back whatever words are flying through his head.

Then he lowers me to the floor gently as if I were a baby fawn about to walk for the first time.

I put all my weight on my good leg, and I nearly scream when my knee lowers due to gravity, the tiny spikes pulling at tendon and cartilage and bone as it tries to straighten despite me holding it at a bent angle. My vision blurs from the pain, and I can only lean on Gavrielle.

Then I hobble once, a cry of agony escaping my lips, but I force myself to keep walking toward Malakyte's outstretched hand.

Using the wall of transparent patient cells for support, I make it halfway to Malakyte before he rushes to meet me, and I collapse in his arms, bringing us both to the ground.

There's no way I can peer behind me, no way I can bear seeing the look on their faces.

The silence is only perpetuated by the slight humming of the Azurite, as if even the ship holds its breath.

I swallow, casually resting a hand over my hurt knee, fingers probing for what I need.

"Do you remember," I pant, the pain leaving me breathless, "when you offered to let me go after what your father did to us in the throne room?"

Malakyte's brows knit together, and I keep his gaze firmly on mine as my hand searches for what I need—unbeknownst to him.

"Yes."

I frown, an equally sorrowful sound escaping my lips. "Did you mean it?"

He searches my face, and the pure desperation in his eyes claws at the innermost walls of my heart, my love for him a shredded, bloodied mess.

"Yes."

I sigh heavily, tears brimming my eyes, and it feels like they'll never stop.

"You would have simply let me walk onto a transport ship and leave?"

He goes to open his mouth but shuts it promptly. Smart man. He knows I'm calling his bluff.

I curl my fingers around the longest protruding spike sticking out of my knee until I have a good grip on it. "See, I'm not sure if it came down to it, you would have ever let me off this ship."

"Karalevine—"

"This is my time to talk. I don't think you would have let me leave. And I get why. When your dad was torturing me, he said I was your weapon, not merely just your bride. And you know what else killed me about what he said? That he was trying to protect you, in his own sick, fucked-up way. I want you to know that. But there's one more thing I want you to know."

I kiss his frosty lips, distracting him, but the act is unfeeling, distant—I'm not sure he even moves when I do it. It takes everything in me not to scream as I pull the spike out inch by inch.

The kiss breaks, and we're so close, so connected, but the room is screaming with tense, unbearable silence.

I hold his face in one hand as I say sweetly, "I remember everything you've done." And between the breath of his gasp my voice turns, just like he's turned on me a million times from sweet to psycho—I do the same, parroting his words just so he knows for certain I remember *it all*. "You should know that you don't fuck with me and get away with it."

As fast as I can, I rip the spike out of my knee and, with all my might, plunge it into Malakyte's heart.

CHAPTER 76

Echoing Malakyte's own words back at him feels good, but stabbing him in the heart feels terrible.

I pierce his skin easily, all my strength pushing into this one—hopefully deadly—attack.

It shreds my heart to do this, but he left me with no choice. He will come after me and everyone I love if I don't end this here and now.

I've trusted his word again and again, and he's lied to me, gone back on his promises on too many occasions to count. If I were to leave with him, he'd have me Reconditioned before the quartz lights changed to nighttime.

The others would never leave this ship alive.

But as I push in to pierce his heart, his icy hand grips around my wrist, pulling the spike back out.

I shift to find better leverage, the two of us locked in a battle of push and pull, love and hate, but he's so much stronger than me. I'm weak, beaten, and in so much pain I can hardly think.

He's gaining the upper hand, pulling the spike from his chest inch by precious inch.

My blood from the spike mixes with his, Burnt Scarlett and Midnight Muse intertwining along the valleys of his chest muscles as the blood seeps into his black vest.

I bare my teeth at him, expecting to see shock and anger, but I'm the one surprised when I see something else.

Devastated heartbreak.

My eyes widen, and my body slackens a fraction from surprise.

Could he have meant what he said? Could his heart break like this if he was lying?

But as the wind turns, that heartache shifts to cold, furious rage right before my eyes, and it permeates into my gut as if it were a spear flying clean through me.

I remember that look.

Malakyte bares his fangs at me as he shoves me away—hard. He rips the spike from his chest.

Fuck!

As he chucks the spike down the hall, his cruel laughter penetrates my bones and freezes them, the sound deeply maniacal.

Move, you need to move! I remind myself, using my good leg to push back and slide down the hallway on my ass toward Gav and the others.

Gavrielle lunges for me, snatching me back to him and the others.

"We're done here," Gavrielle barks as he lifts me to a standing position.

"No, Gavrielle, we are far from being finished. Very far, in fact."

His words stop Gav cold.

That voice, that tone . . .

My mouth goes dry.

Malakyte stands but staggers into the now empty room Ceplar was in, which is sandwiched between the wild Tributes on either side It's identical to the others, a bed on the right, a built-in table with a sink and a cabinet mounted to the wall above it. The Tributes bash themselves against the clear walls that separate them from Malakyte, surrounded on both sides and more frantic with the smell of blood in the air.

"I trust that you haven't forgotten our arrangement, Gavrielle," Malakyte says as he opens a cabinet along the wall, digging for what I'm assuming are supplies. "The one about your people on planet Nyktos?"

Gavrielle stiffens beside me, going pale.

With his back to us, Malakyte finds what he's looking for, his Night Sky blood smearing all over the white packages as he unwraps what he needs, ripping off most of the buttons on his shirt for better access. "Well," he says with a bitter chuckle and undercurrent of amusement around the edges, "once you betrayed me, I considered our agreement null and void. I'm assuming you saw the AI SSPARROW demonstration at the coronation?"

None of us answer. Only the thrashing of raging Tributes and Malakyte ripping open medical supplies exists in the tense space between us.

He begins bandaging his chest, and my eyes dart around. We should run now while he's distracted, and I pull on Gavrielle's arm, but he's locked in on Malakyte, as unmovable as a mountain.

Malakyte says, "Father's bloodlust was set on the Terrans, and the only way to assuage that was to sacrifice one people to save the ones you hold so dear, Karalevine. I saved them *for you*"—he looks up at me, then looks directly into Gavrielle's eyes—"but Nyktos's fate was *because of you*. I thought you knew better than to play foolish games, Gavrielle."

I've never seen Gavrielle falter—he's as strong as a hover-tank, but we almost go down as his knees buckle and fresh tears flash in his eyes. Absolute devastation lingers on every inch of that flawless, handsome face. I can barely stand to watch his heart shatter.

"You didn't hurt them," Gavrielle seethes, as if by saying it, the words could make it true.

Malakyte laughs in his face, and I glare at him with disgust.

 472

"Nyktos faced the Voidbringer, and she leaves nothing alive. You should have known better than to take what you know is mine."

"I'm not yours, you son of a bitch!"

Malakyte's eyes narrow as he scowls vehemently. "That isn't what you said last night when you were *fucking me*."

Mother. Fucking. *Prick*.

I turn to Gav, knowing that's the last thing he needs to hear, and soften my voice. "Gavrielle." I shake his shoulders, trying to pull his rage-filled gaze away from Malakyte as his breathing becomes frantic, panicked, enraged.

His people . . . Stars . . . Is this Voidbringer thing—Herkimer mentioned it earlier—that powerful? Did it really destroy an entire planet full of people?

"I will kill you," Gavrielle swears through the haze of his rage, attempting to remove my hands so he can enact that revenge right here, right now.

"The Tribute serum is volatile, unpredictable." Malakyte switches subjects as he ignores Gavrielle's threats, taping gauze to his chest. "We've tested it on so many specimens. Sometimes, they come out of it completely normal, with three times their original strength. Some are twenty times stronger than they were previously, but their minds are frenzied and wild, uncontrollable. Others become monsters, like them."

We all look at the Tributes as their black blood smears on the clear nanoglass separating them from us. Other Tributes in our vicinity have awoken, all in the different stages Malakyte has described. Will Ceplar become one, too?

"I don't give a fuck. What did you do to my people?" Gavrielle yells, his voice a color of fury I've never seen from him.

He's barely holding it together. His skin is red, fangs exposed, fists tight—he's losing himself.

"Some can turn instantly. Others take time. Some turn out to be contagious through a bite, others, not at all. The complexities are . . . unpredictable."

Fuck, I don't like this . . .

My heart is a runaway hover-train, fear crawling up my spine, making the tips of my ears tingle with warning, my crystal searing. The power from when I was collared still taps on the surface of my control, ready to explode.

Malakyte turns his back to us and types a code into some locked cubby next to where he found his supplies, and he rummages through it.

Go now. Go!

"Gavrielle, I'm so sorry this happened, but we have to go!"

"Hey!" Ardelle yells in warning.

My attention snaps back to Malakyte, a huge syringe in my ex-lover's hands.

The liquid within resembles nighttime in the shade True Black.

We all lurch away collectively, Gavrielle dragging me back, as we're closest.

"We'll see what havoc Ceplar can unleash on my behalf," Malakyte says, waving the syringe.

He injected her.

"Malakyte, stop it." My voice is firm, strong. "You're acting like a fucking psycho again. Stop. It's over. Let me go."

He laughs and laughs, and the sound chases goose bumps along my entire body.

The black syringe twirls in his long fingers as he spins it nonchalantly, those eyes directed right at me as they glaze with vindictive fury.

This is the Malakyte I remember. How could he and the Malakyte I've spent all these weeks with be the same person?

"You're right, Karalevine. It is over. Which is why this will make it much easier for me to do what I've got to do."

I scream as Malakyte stabs himself in the thigh with the Tribute serum.

CHAPTER 77

My shriek echoes off the white walls of this horror show.

Ardelle's gravity magic soars, the memory of what it feels like coming back to me as he tries to prevent Malakyte's thumb from pushing the remaining quarter of the drug in.

The others try to stop me as I break free of Gavrielle's arms and hobble to Malakyte, using the wall for support. "Let me get it!"

It takes me way too long to get into the room, ignoring all my pain, and rip the syringe from his thigh and chuck it against the floor, shattering the glass.

But it's too late. The black spiders out through his veins like wildfire, clawing up to his chest and peeking out through his open shirt.

It's too fast . . .

Why is it happening *so fast?*

Red rims his irises, and my head slowly turns left and right, where the clear nanoglass walls trap me between wild Tributes on either side, but their red-rimmed eyes are here in the room with me.

"What have you done?" I whisper, leaning against the bed, the Tributes on that side of the wall hitting the nanoglass so hard that the bed trembles against their rage.

He tips his head back and laughs, but the motion throws his body into waves of convulsions, and I stand there, helpless to stop it as he staggers and slams into the table with the sink. Medical supplies go flying, and he whips his body a second time, but this time, it's toward me.

Using my good leg, I try to scoot myself away, but I can't dodge fast enough. His coldness hits me first and then I'm accosted by hard, frozen muscle. My nails dig into the fabric of his shirt as we fall.

My leg!

We slam to the ground, and the nausea hits me before the pain. My knee whacks the floor, and I scream, losing my vision entirely to bright stars bursting through my eyes as unadulterated agony floods into my body.

I believe I hear my name, but all that exists is my hammering pulse in my knee as it pulls me down, threatening unconsciousness.

Get up, get up, get up!

Malakyte's cold hands wake me up. I'm lying on my back somehow. Leaning over me, he grabs the collar of my shirt, and by the time I blink out the distortion in my vision, his red-rimmed eyes are filled with an insanity that isn't him.

None of what I'm seeing is him.

His black clothing rips at the seams, his muscles bulging the fine thread at his shoulders and biceps, but the fear shreds through me even more brutally.

"I loved you!" he roars. "And if I can't have you, nobody will. You want me to be your monster? That's exactly what I'll be."

"Stop it!" I shout back, grabbing his face with both hands, digging my nails in. "Tell me there's an antidote. You're not stupid enough to inject yourself with something crazy without knowing you could undo it. Where is it?"

I'm losing him second by second.

Then Malakyte flies off me, Ardelle's magic surging as he throws him across the room. Malakyte slams into the nanoglass and lands on the medical bed.

Gav is next to me instantly, helping me sit up.

"I have to fix this!" I cry.

I don't know if I'm saying it to Gav, the others, or myself.

Malakyte's crystal is shooting through the roof now, too. Its power hits me right in the gut as it soars, glowing beyond his bandage. The Tributes are going absolutely feral, all awakening to some collective madness that's getting out of fucking control—fast.

"I have to stop him!"

This isn't real. This isn't fucking happening.

Malakyte comes for us, and Gavrielle pounces, leaving my side and holding Malakyte back with brutally placed punches and kicks. There's no technique on Malakyte's part—it's simply uncontainable rage.

My eyes catch on the box Malakyte pulled the syringe from as it lays in a heap next to me, and I lean over, reaching for it. Once in hand, I dig through it frantically, looking for the antidote or a sedative—*something*.

There's nothing, but I freeze, my head snapping up as I hear it . . . a cracking . . . like a shattering of vertebrae. For the longest, most fearful seconds of my life while my back is turned, I wonder if Gavrielle is dead, if Malakyte, in his drug-filled rage, just killed him.

But when I follow the source of the sound, it isn't what I had thought.

The noise is of the two men snapping the clear nanoglass wall between us as Gav pins Malakyte against the wall.

They cracked it . . .

 478

Tributes on the other side slam against it, knocking Gav and Malakyte back as it bends.

I'm frozen.

The Tributes barrel through the wall, and I'm stunned at how they could be so strong. Gav and Malakyte pause, even Malakyte's poisoned mind sensing the danger in the room.

I . . . I can't move. All the sound is gone, replaced with a high-pitched ringing as the insanity around me unfolds like one of my nightmares.

But this isn't a nightmare. It's real. It's all real. This day—this stars awful day.

They're busting through . . .

"Kara! Get out of the way!"

I can't move.

They break through the nanoglass wall. Their hunger won't be satiated by freedom. They clearly want to feed and consume, and I'm right in their sights. They dive for me, mouths open wide and ravenous.

Malakyte leaps in front of me, taking the full brunt of one of the Tributes double his size as it chomps down on his shoulder, and they tumble hard into the opposite nanoglass wall, Tributes on that side coming undone as they become ravenous trying to get in here.

Cracking, breaking, snapping . . .

There's no time for me to react as the second Tribute flies at me. His body is triple my size and distorted in all the strangest places, long black nails outstretched for me and only me.

"Kara!" someone yells, and I think it's Gav, but I can't tell.

Everything in the world flips into slow motion. Each movement ripples down through time and space as I helplessly watch the horrors I unleashed play out before me, my nightmares now flesh and haunting bone.

Boom.

One shudder of my heartbeat claps down like thunder in my ears.

Boom.

My crystal surges.

Boom.

Another nanoglass wall cracks open.

Boom.

Tributes dive for me like zombies fueled by fever and madness.

Finally, my body reacts at the very last moment before Death can claim me as his own.

My crystal erupts and slams into the Tribute right before their teeth meet the flesh of my neck.

They go flying backward as my crystal's Antique Fuchsia light blasts into the entire corridor, blinding the space with my beam and antimatter bolts.

It's too much. The power far too pent up from the collar, and this is the result . . . I've lost complete control of it.

Stop! I scream at myself. *You'll kill us all. Stop!*

The Tributes aren't the only monsters in this place, but I manage to rein my antimatter in with all the control I can find.

From the second that my crystal fired, I felt no pain . . . but it sure as shit comes back in earnest.

Everything from today catches up to me, the release of my magic draining my strength as I'm suddenly so, so tired, the pain unbearable.

I'm tipping backward, falling unconscious before my back hits the floor.

The smell of my magic is the first thing I notice when I come to, and it's strong. I've hardly used the damn thing on this ship—I'm not used to it anymore.

Hands land on me . . . warm and strong.

Gavrielle's scent of crisp, warm, woodsy ginger pulls me back from this dark abyss.

Growls and feral snarls. Snapped wood, shattering glass, and the bending of metal . . .

That's what I wake up to as my eyes flutter open. I must've only been out for a few seconds. Gavrielle helps me sit upright, and I don't know where to look first.

Malakyte rips the Tributes into ribbons, and he's gone mad with a savage ire, unstoppable in his derangement—but at least he's attacking them, not us.

Then alarms scream, "Methane detected. Methane detected."

Gasping, I look up where my crystal shot.

A giant black hole is in the ceiling, torn wires sparking as a bunch of materials hang or fall, and I can't even tell how high the void goes. An odd rippling distorts the space around it, and the terrifying hissing that accompanies it causes me to break out into a cold sweat.

Oh, fuck . . .

"We've got to go! Now!" Ardelle yells, throwing the unconscious Ringer over his shoulder as he runs toward us. "Pacey, now! This place is going to blow!"

"I can try to use my magic to contain this if a fire breaks out," Pacey says, but her expression is grim as she looks up into the gushing wound I've inflicted on the Azurite.

If those sparks catch, then nothing can contain it, not even her crystal's power to control the elements. Stars, if they catch . . .

More Tributes come at us, and Malakyte dives for the ones closest.

He's protecting me.

Our eyes lock, and the person I love glimmers inside there.

"Run," Malakyte growls, the monster within him erupts. "Run!"

His clamoring roar shakes the Azurite, my bones quaking alongside it.

Gavrielle dodges another Tribute then scoops me up, the others making a mad dash through the hall toward the exit.

More alarms blare by the second.

They told me this would happen. Everyone said if I used my crystal on this ship, I would blow it up.

There's no way that would actually happen . . . They have containment protocols for accidents like this. I won't be responsible for the deaths of thousands.

"Wait!" I cry as Gavrielle runs us down the hall. "We can't just leave him down here alone!"

Gav grits his teeth as he hauls ass toward the others, not even looking back. "You better fucking believe we are!"

I can't even argue.

Malakyte is getting smothered by the other Tributes, his karma coming back to haunt him, and I can do nothing but watch over Gavrielle's shoulder as it happens. In the madness, we lock eyes one last time before Gav rounds the corner, and I don't know what I see there, but it pulls at a place so deep I can't resist.

Hand outstretched, I reach for Malakyte.

He does the same.

Then he's gone as Gavrielle turns the corner with me in his arms.

Gav runs like our lives depend on it.

Because they do.

CHAPTER 78

An explosion wracks the Azurite and hurls us to our knees.

No . . . no, stars, please. No.

"Shit!" Pacey cries as she's tossed down several steps in the stairwell. She falls back onto the landing, but Ennar's suit breaks her fall.

Ardelle shouts for her, barely catching himself on the railing while holding onto Ceplar.

Gavrielle is the only one who doesn't fumble too badly, dropping his weight back and sitting on a step.

"Are you alright?" Ardelle asks as he makes his way down a few steps to Pacey.

She stands, testing her body as she bounces her knees. "Yeah. Thanks for the suit, Gav."

Gavrielle gives her a cocky wink. "Don't mention it."

Another boom shakes the ship, and the lights flicker at the same time as the metal railings wobble. In the back of my heart, I hope Malakyte will be okay . . . He was knee-deep in the center of those explosions. But maybe it would be better if he doesn't survive because if he does . . . I can't even think about what war we'd be fighting, officially each other's villains once again.

"Where are the others?" I say, looking up as fine bits of debris fall from the ceiling. "We need to get off this ship."

What have I done?

"Let me get the others on comms," Pacey says, double tapping the tiny piece of tech in her ear.

"Team Starseed, this is Pacey, please respond. What's your location? We have a serious problem. If you can hear me, evacuate the Azurite. I repeat, get off the spaceship. It's going to blow. I repeat, the Azurite is going to ex—"

Another blast cuts her off, and this time, the lights in the ship go completely dark, smothering us in blackness so deep all I can do is hold on to Gavrielle for dear life.

"I'm right here, love."

Gavrielle's voice is my anchor, his strong arms tight around my body.

The lights struggle to return, but they manage to flicker back on.

Gav clears his throat. "While we wait for them to respond, we need a strategy on how to get out of here. There are emergency pods in the royal sector in Malakyte's room."

Pacey interjects, "Which is higher than we should probably go. Life-support ducts push airflow upward, and if the leak's in the system, it's pumping methane up there, too. Even a flick of a light switch could spark an entire new set of explosions. We risk methane displacement, too, meaning less breathable air. Although we're likely going to run out of oxygen, no matter what, if this ship is truly going down. And if we're forced to come back down? Bulkheads could close, floors could collapse, explosions cutting off every route. We'd be trapped in a matchbox with no escape."

Gavrielle looks as if he's pondering. "What will be our challenges if we break off at this floor and head east, toward the supply loading docks? We'd be staying on the same level, I believe." He stretches himself to see the door. "Yeah, this is level four. So, we could get to the loading bay from here, but we'd have to cross the entire length of the ship to get to the other side."

Pacey's eyes avert down, mind tinkering, then looks back up at Gav. "We'd be one floor above the initial explosion, and any subsequent explosions and fires are much closer. That means the floors, walls, doors, and just about anything else will be hot. Very hot."

"Hotter than me?" Gav jokes, and we all laugh.

"Yes, Gavrielle. Hotter than even you. That, and we could easily get trapped by fire without any way forward. The floors could collapse from fire or explosions or already be engulfed in flames at this point. The gases and smoke could suffocate us even if there's no flames. If we try to go across rather than up and we can't to the other side, we'd probably lose the valuable time we'd need to backtrack and head up. Both options suck, if I'm being honest."

Ardelle says, "You got this, Pace. Which option gives us the better chance to survive?"

Pacey nods. "Let's risk it and go up. I think that's our best shot."

"That seems like the obvious choice," Gav agrees.

I'm glad he does.

The Azurite sways, and boom after boom roars, the tremors wracking the metal giant.

A voice comes over the intercom. "Emergency protocol activated. Azurite Civilian will detach from Azurite Royal in ninety seconds. Evacuate immediately."

I seek Gav, my eyes wide. "They're splitting the two sectors?"

He nods grimly. "It was meant to protect the royal family, but in this instance, it's protecting all those lives on the other side. If they've initiated the separation, this ship is going down."

Fear. Fear I haven't felt since that night in the throne room permeates itself through all of us. This dread, it has a scent—a presence within this black-paneled stairwell.

It comes for us all.

I faintly hear Jance's voice buzz in Pacey's comms and nearly cry in relief.

Pacey gives a quick breakdown of our situation to them. "And what level are you on? Four? Where?" She pauses, listening. "Okay, go to the loading docks and get out. We'll meet you on the ground." Another pause. "Yes, she's here. Yes, she's got her memories back. I'll tell her. No, we can't meet you. We'll never make it across. Okay. Be safe, too." When she double taps her comms again, she looks right at me. "Jance says he loves you."

I bite down on my lip. I love him, too. He'll *be fine*. I was such a brat to him this whole time, and now he's on the opposite side of this ship where I can't reach him.

He'll be fine.

"Let's go. Lead the way, Pace," Ardelle says, smiling at his sister with all the pride in the world.

I was so awful to Ardelle, too, but as he holds Ceplar tenderly in his arms as we race up the stairs, I can tell something more happened between them, even in just an emotional way. I know him . . . He's connected to her. And she deserves every bit of his heart that's held on to me. They both do. He's right, we've both changed up here.

Pacey leads, her Elendril scythe bouncing as she takes the stairs two at a time.

"Is it me, or are we tilting?" I shout, smoke and gas filling the stairway, the blaring of alarms and our coughs becoming overwhelming.

"We're almost there, just a few more levels!" Pacey yells.

We keep going. Faster and faster.

"I'm getting you off this ship, Kara," Gavrielle vows, and only I can hear him. "No matter what, you're getting off."

"We're *all* getting off," I say.

I kiss the hot skin of his neck, tightening my grip around his shoulders.

 486

He nuzzles his face into my hair, kissing the top of my head. His pulse thunders beneath my lips—the warmth of him. He's alive. He's not cold or made of ice and granite.

"We're here!" Pacey shouts, using an unknown chip to open the door.

It zips open, and she flies through, but the moment she vanishes into the darkened hallway beyond, her panicked shrieks fill the Azurite.

CHAPTER 79

Gavrielle and I bring up the rear, so we can't see a thing as Pacey's scream brings us to a halt.

"Pacey?" Ardelle calls from inside the stairwell, his voice echoing off the metal walls and intermixing with the wailing of alarms.

No response.

"Something's wrong," I shout over the blaring.

And is the air up here a little thinner, too?

Ardelle doesn't waste another moment as he dashes up the last half of the stairs and through the open door, with Gav and me right behind him.

The voice I hear next increases the heartbeat in my knee as it throbs harder and faster.

Herkimer.

That motherfucker is supposed to be dead! Sure as shit, there he stands, his face sunken and wrinkled and aged as he holds Pacey by the neck in the crook of his arm. A sharp dagger at her throat glints in the emergency quartz lights as they flash in shade Blood Oath.

The entire wing is drenched in red.

The alarms aren't as loud in the hallway, so we hear him clearly as he says, "Whoever pulled the arrow out of my head was as dumb as the one who fired it," he gloats, that evil grin back in full force as he pins Ardelle with it. "You're going to die for what you did to me."

"Let my sister go," Ardelle growls, "and I'm all yours."

No!

"On your knees!" Herkimer yells, all amusement gone.

The three of us stare at each other, unsure of whether we should listen or attack.

Herkimer presses the dagger into Pacey's throat for emphasis, drawing blood. "Do it now, or I'll kill her where she stands. Use your tainted magic, and she's dead. Weapons down, or you know what happens. Now!"

Ardelle goes first, dropping to his knees as he sets Ceplar down. His bow and arrows slowly come off his back.

Gav follows, setting me down so I'm sitting, keeping the weight on my good side, my bad knee bent. He unhooks the blades at his back once his hands are free, never taking his eyes off Herkimer, his expression promising death.

I have to stop this.

"The ship is falling out of orbit. You need to get off," I suggest.

When those chilling dark eyes turn to me, all I see is rage.

"I'll take my chances. Especially when I've got, well, let's count . . . one, two, three. Yes, three of those Elendril crystals right here, ripe for me to pluck off the branch and savor. I think that should be enough for my son to, I don't know, get his head out of his ass and fucking rule like a man rather than a fucking pussy."

"Just because he isn't a cruel psychopath like you doesn't make him a pussy, asshole," I say. "And good fucking luck getting our crystals I'll fry your ass into oblivion before you can get one."

Herkimer laughs, rolling his head and pinning me down with eyes that promise vengeance. "Can you fry me before I slit her throat?"

I can't even scream as Herkimer moves to slash Pacey's throat, but his hand trembles as if he's pushing against a force. *Gravity.*

Ardelle's crystal mark glows red as his gravity holds the knife at bay, and Pacey takes her opportunity, elbowing Herkimer hard in the ribs, spinning, then kicking him down to the floor, rushing back toward us.

The ship tilts sharply. Side tables, fake plants, and wall decor all tumble down the hall, the emergency quartz lights flickering.

I'm not sure who starts screaming first when it hits us all at once, like a bat big enough to collectively crack our skulls.

The magic Herkimer was so fond of using on his son—the magic that brought Malakyte to his knees—finally comes out to play.

It's pure fucking torture.

My head splits, burns, screams. This isn't a migraine. This is . . . utter agony. I can't think, can't breathe, can't see or hear or fight it.

My star scorches my chest, and I feel Ardelle's, Pacey's, Gavrielle's, and even Ceplar's magic, all flare out of pure instinct.

Herkimer has all of us by the balls.

It's difficult to hear Herkimer over their screams and the alarms blaring from the stairwell, but he cackles with victory. *That sound!*

It. Isn't. Over. Yet.

Then his laughter abruptly stops, although our suffering does not.

"What? What have you fuckers done to my vision? Put it back now!"

Herkimer stumbles, slamming into the wall, crawling around as if he's suddenly blinded. His painful magic still has us all on our knees, but it isn't as intense.

Then an unfamiliar female voice strains to speak, slurred from drugs and misery, but her power soars. "Get out of here!"

Ceplar! Her Ringer magic has blinded him! Her eyes are blazing Divine Blue.

Ardelle leaps, taking the moment Ceplar gave us as he fights through the pain and hurls himself on top of Herkimer.

Ceplar passes out seconds after.

Herkimer's excruciating magic ratchets back up, and it's unbearable. The pain in my knee is nonexistent. It's only this endless torment.

Somehow, Ardelle can push past the pain, the outpouring of his Elendril magic such a familiar pull in my stomach—as powerful and strong as he is. His gravity pins Herkimer down, and he stands, needing the wall for support.

"Go!" Ardelle yells at all of us. "I can hold him. Go!"

"No!" Pacey cries, her cheeks slick with tears. "I'm not leaving you again! *No!*"

"You're all fucking dead!"

Herkimer's tone is fury incarnate.

We all hear the threat for what it is.

A promise.

Panic fuels me as Pacey and Ardelle argue. Everything hurts so bad I can't think!

All I know as I writhe on the floor is that we can't leave Ardelle again. I'm not sure we could even stand long enough *to* run.

There's a sickening charge in the air like aether, like lightning about to strike. I'm struggling to get enough air into my lungs, and the others are wheezing, too. The hair on my arms and the back of my neck stands stick-straight.

"Ardelle!" Pacey cries for her brother, who locks eyes with her as time slows, distorting around us.

Stars, no.

No . . .

Something's wrong.

Ardelle has Herkimer pinned with his gravity magic, the ex-emperor struggling as he tries to face him head on.

"You may have prevented me from moving, but you can't stop this!"

Herkimer has so many different types of magic at his disposal, and I can do nothing but watch as one of them is directed at Ardelle.

Pacey and I scream for him to get out of the way—to stop holding him there and *move*.

But Ardelle keeps pointing down the hall, shouting at us to leave him there and *go*.

We won't leave him.

I can only cover my mouth with my hand to muffle the bloodcurdling scream that crawls from my throat at what I see happening.

Ardelle's body begins to dematerialize right before my eyes, as if he's morphing into ash.

It's happening so fast.

It's the darkness causing me to see things. I'm not seeing this right now.

Pacey dashes for Ardelle, but Gavrielle jumps in at the last minute, saving her life as the two tumble to the ever-slanting floor.

His coloring turns from the color Flesh Pink of a living, healthy person, to a muted, harsh gray in the shade Spiderweb. From there, it's shade Endless Dark, bleeding into the shadows themselves. All so quick, so sudden, happening in a blink. Then he just . . . He just . . .

Crumbles away.

His body becomes like lost embers in the wind, completely dissolving as if he were nothing but dust being blown away by a single breath.

Snuffed out, becoming one with the very air itself, only tiny specks of him fall to the darkened Azurite floor, a floor I walked down a hundred times.

Gone.

 492

One second, he was there, alive and solid and here, and then the next he was just . . .

Gone . . .

Pacey's screams are the worst thing I've ever heard in my life, Gavrielle holding her back, trying to prevent her from being next.

I don't hear anything as my ears pop, hollowing out to nothingness.

The pain in my head skyrockets as every ounce of my being pushes and pushes and pushes against this reality.

This isn't real.

I'm in a nightmare. It's one of Gavrielle's illusions. It's anything but real.

But it isn't any of those things.

I can feel Ardelle, his essence, his soul . . . leaving this place. Leaving us . . .

Leaving me.

As if he touched my cheek as his soul departs this world, one last goodbye, one last *I love you* to assure me that he truly did *love me.*

His Elendril crystal is red. Red is a primary color. It's the base of so many others, and in the hierarchy of colors, there isn't one higher. The other colors can't exist if we don't have his red. I can't have my purple if I don't have his red. I can't be *me* if I don't have his red.

Shock wrenches itself up and into me, burrowing its way through my mouth, down my throat, and into my fractured soul. It comes inside, touching me in a place nothing else can. But Ardelle had gotten in. He was safe. He made me feel like I was a normal girl in a world that saw me as *other.*

For a moment in time, I was his and he was mine, and I loved him, and he loved me. He risked his life and suffered because he loved me. He stayed behind in that throne room because he *loved me.*

Our time together flashes before my eyes, and despite our romance being up in the air because we both changed due to the events on this ship, we still cared about and loved each other.

That never changed.

This moment finally reaches that part of me Ardelle found, that he fought to see and touch and love despite how much I kept him out. The part was reserved only for him, the boy with the raven tattoo he hid from the entire world.

But not from me.

It hits me, the pain ravaging me like a bullet impaling my heart. Shattering it, imploding it, destroying it. Herkimer's magic is nothing in comparison. Nothing.

My ears pop, and the ringing replaces everything.

Every conscious thought drops as fast as this ship plummets to the Earth's surface.

Red . . .

All I can see is *red.*

CHAPTER 80

Shoving off with my good leg, I fly at Herkimer, his laughter merging with the siren wails and my screams of fury.

All I feel is blinding rage.

Every bit of darkness built up inside of me my entire life is now untethered and loose, and all inhibitions are blasted away as quickly as Ardelle's body was obliterated before my eyes.

We collide, Herkimer on the floor, the slant even more prominent as the Azurite shudders beneath us. I land on top and straddle him, ignoring the pressure on my knee, ignoring the agony in my head—I can't even feel my body anymore.

"So feisty!" he mocks, cackling and high off his own murderous energy. "I can't wait to see how you'll be once I kill everyone you love!"

I snap.

Punching and slapping, scratching and hair pulling, but his laughter—it never ends.

As if Ardelle's life was nothing.

As if turning him to dust was the funniest, most satisfying thing he's done all year. My pain, his joy. My madness, his vitality.

I punch and I punch and I punch, screams of utter rage ripping my throat as I promise to kill him—*ruin him*—annihilate him, until my vocal cords tear and rip.

Herkimer won't stop laughing!

My punches aren't enough. Even though my knuckles bleed and feel like they're about to crack, I continue pummeling him.

"Kara!" Gav yells.

This isn't enough.

It isn't the justice Ardelle deserves.

I don't care what the consequences are when I pause my attack, pivot at my waist, and rip out another spike from my knee.

I feel nothing but uncontainable, thundering wrath.

There's no time wasted as I stab Herkimer right in the face. I stab him over and over and over again until those laughs finally give way to screams. He may come back from anything, but that doesn't mean he doesn't feel everything—and I'm going to make it fucking hurt!

I stab him in the neck, in the chest, in the face, in his arms as he tries to defend against me.

His painful magic finally ends. Good, but it's not enough.

"Kara, stop!"

I won't! It's not enough! He killed him! *He killed him!*

I don't stop when his dark blood splatters all over me.

In my nose, in my mouth, in my eyes—everywhere. It feels like ice cold water being shot right at me—drenching me.

Nothing else matters.

He has to die—I have to kill him. Otherwise, he'll just keep coming after everyone I love.

Using the spike, I slash his throat from ear to ear, watching blood gurgle and pool onto his chest from the canyon I created.

Strong arms—warm arms—wrap around my waist, lifting me up. "Kara, stop it! We've got to go! This ship is falling out of orbit!"

"No!" I scream, fighting him, trying to get back to Herkimer to finish him off.

"Love, stop!" Gav whips me around, anchoring me to his front as my heart fucking hammers so fast I fear it might explode.

Gav's voice goes soft. "You got him, love. He's done."

His thumb brushes blood off my lips, away from my eyes, the cold wetness on my face making my skin crawl as I stare back at him—breathless.

Ardelle is . . .

"Come back to me, Kara," he says, eyes stone cold as they pierce into mine. "Everything is going to be alright."

How could anything ever be alright after what just happened?

Gurgling erupts as Herkimer's wounds knit up so fast it's unreal. Before we can run, his eyes are open and focused again.

He's unkillable.

Gav picks me up, and we dash a few feet away, standing next to a shell-shocked Pacey and an unconscious Ceplar.

We're never getting out of this hallway alive if he can dust us in a matter of seconds without much more than a thought.

He's too powerful.

"Father, stop!"

My eyes widen as my head whips toward the voice coming from the stairwell. But it isn't Malakyte . . .

"Selenyte?" Herkimer gasps, and it's the first time I've seen him genuinely shocked. "You're . . . You're supposed to be dead."

I shake my head and blink, trying to understand what's happening. She *is* dead.

"Brother kept me locked in the cells. The explosions freed me. I'm so tired, Father."

"I saw you die on the recording," he whispers.

Her thin, ghostly frame steps forward, but it's still twenty feet down the hall. She looks disheveled and filthy, like she's indeed been in the cells this entire time.

"The Silent Breath saved me. I'm afraid. I don't want to die here."

Herkimer leaps to his knees, his injuries still bleeding but healing fast.

I look up at Gav, and it all falls into place. His eyes blaze green inside his pupils, showing me the illusion for what it is—a diversion.

"We need to get out of here," Selenyte's illusion says, turning away. "Come with me."

Then Selenyte's ghost dashes back into the stairwell, Herkimer calling after her to wait. He sees what he wants to see, head whipping to us, indecision distorting his bloodied face.

Gavrielle hides his glowing eyes from Herkimer as Selenyte's painful screams erupt from the stairwell, so realistic they even echo.

Herkimer can't resist. "Enjoy your final moments of life, Starseed trash. I'm confident the Azurite will execute you filth."

He runs off, chasing a literal ghost.

I nearly pass out in relief, but he can realize the con and return at any moment.

What happens next is like a waking dream.

Gavrielle sets me down and puts Ardelle's bow and arrows in my arms, leaving virtually no other trace of the man I loved left in this world. He then takes Ceplar and puts her in Pacey's arms, who, much like me, is a pale, ghostly shell, barely blinking as Gavrielle picks me up and gets us moving again.

Like zombies, we make our way down the royal sector, barely cognizant of what's happening. If not for Gav, I don't know if Pacey and I could get out of here.

This ship is going down, but I think we've already fallen. Fast and without a parachute, down and down and down.

And we're about to crash-land on a reality harder than the Earth itself.

CHAPTER 81

There are no other obstacles as we reach the suite I shared with Malakyte as we enter the room without issue.

It looks the same, but I'm not the same.

I'm still in shock as Gavrielle sets me on the couch, then dashes for the emergency escape pod.

Pacey silently sits beside me, her Ringer still in her arms, unconscious.

Her face is the color shade White Dove, a shell-shocked portrait of anguish and heartbreak. Her eyes are haunted, dead and dull and gone.

I can't even speak.

I can hardly breathe, either. The oxygen is too thin. The pain is too deep. The reality is too painful to accept.

Grabbing the blanket next to me, I wipe my face with it, the Night of Navy blood smearing off on the fluffy Ballerina-colored fabric. It smells like him . . . like Malakyte.

Loose items slide off countertops and shelves. Lighter furniture tumbles to one side of the room, my life with Malakyte personified in this moment.

Gavrielle comes running back, his face grave.

"We have a problem."

CHAPTER 82

YEAR 6, DAY 2,203: NARESTEÉ WAS ALMOST KILLED TODAY,
FATHER, AND IT MAKES ME RAGE. I WANT TO DESTROY
THE PERSON RESPONSIBLE, AND I DON'T CARE IF SHE'S
A STARSEED OR NOT, WHATEVER THAT EVEN MEANS. I
OVERHEARD THE TERM. MALAKYTE CALLED THIS PERSON
HIS "STAR." THE ONE HE'S BEEN OBSESSED WITH FOR YEARS, I
THINK. HER REAL NAME IS KARALEVINE, AND HE SUSPECTS
SHE'S A REBEL. I'LL FIGURE OUT ALL OF HER SECRETS.
SHE'S GOING DOWN.

GAVRIELLE ABRAXAS

"We have a problem," I tell the girls. "There is an escape vessel, and it appears to be functional. However, it isn't going to fit all four of us."

The fear in Kara's eyes is preferable to the lifeless, glazed look that's been there since I ripped her off Herkimer, but it's still crushing to see her spirit crack.

"Let me see," Kara says, voice barely audible over the sirens.

The room is darkening, the quartz lights dimming as I haul her into my arms, Pacey following silently. But all of us are struggling to breathe from the lack of oxygen.

The cylindrical escape pod is embedded in a hidden compartment in the floor near the big window. Once the panel retracts, the pod is visible below.

"It's down at our feet because it's primed to slide down an escape hatch built into the hall, using a magnetic launching mechanism that doesn't require power from the ship."

The hull of the pod is all black and reflective. Even the canopy—which I've lifted to reveal the two seats sitting back-to-back—is opaque black nanoglass. The engine rests in the rear, with the tip of the ship pointed like a missile.

"You're small," I tell Kara, my voice calm and steady. I have to be brave for her. "You can likely fit if you sit on Pacey's lap. It'll be really tight, but there's no other option. I can find another way off."

Nothing. No reaction. She just stares at the pod as the room trembles and shit goes flying.

"Love," I say, shaking her shoulders to snap her out of her shock. "I can make it off. There's likely another pod somewhere around here. I'll find one."

"There wasn't even one in my room," she tells me dully, her blinks heavy and exhausted.

I swallow.

She's right. There are escape pods all around the ship, but they're not as common as they should be. Arianyte's tech is relatively steady, while this utter failure is nearly unheard of. But I can't tell her what I know, that the likelihood of me getting off this ship is slim. She can't bear the weight.

"I'll get off and meet you on the surface. I'm always with you, remember? Get in the pod, Kara. Please. I'll find another way. You know that I will."

She shakes her head as I hold her in my arms, her eyes coming back to life, but it's pain and agony where all her vitality and brightness used to be.

"I can't lose you, too," she whispers, words desperate. "Don't leave me."

I'm not sure if she means in a metaphorical sense or in a literal sense, but I comfort her either way. "Even if I were to die today, Kara, I need you to hear me when I say this, I'm always with you. They can rip us apart again and again, but I will always feel that ache in my soul, rebelling against the cage of whatever body I inhabit because it doesn't know you. And you know what I'd do? Fight it. Beat the system that incarnates us and *find you again*. Time and space and a thousand lifetimes could separate us, but my soul will always find its way back to yours. Our memories can be wiped away, shattered and ruined, it doesn't matter. Young or old, alive or dead, *I'm always with you*. Nothing can separate us, love. Please, get in the pod."

Something electrical sparks in the room, and the tilt of the Azurite creeps toward forty-five degrees. We don't have time to argue about this. She's getting on that pod if I have to force her into it, even if she hates me for it.

"Let's go, Kara," Pacey says, although her voice is a zombified version of what it was before. "That spark is going to fire an explosion any minute. You can sit on me. Gavrielle will make it off, and he'll meet us on Earth with the others. We're running out of time."

I give her a look of immense gratitude as she runs back to the couch, heaves her Ringer into her arms, and returns to set her in the rear of the escape pod. She dashes to get her brother's bow and arrows, then sets them on top of the sleeping red-headed Earth girl, her veins having turned black beneath her porcelain skin.

Slipping into the front seat, Pacey looks up at Kara expectantly.

 502

I gently set Kara on the floor, who scoots forward, but her movements are slow and jerky.

Once I get her inside and that canopy comes down over them, she'll be safe, and I can release this coil in my chest. I need her to be safe, no matter what.

Get on, love. Get on.

Pacey and I help Kara down into the escape pod and onto Pacey's lap.

Good, it looks like they'll fit—barely.

Once closed, the ship will zoom down a pipeline and out of the Azurite, programmed to land in Zarmenia, where Malakyte designated it to go.

I type on the screen interface built into the wall, initiating the launch.

A robotic female voice chimes from the speakers in the room, although the failing electrics and power to the ship make it distorted and hard to understand.

"The emergency launch sequence will commence in sixty seconds. Keep all appendages within the unit. Canopy will close in fifty seconds."

When I look back, Kara's large, haunted eyes are watching me.

My chest tightens with an ache so familiar. It seems like I can't ever keep her for long. This knotted coil inside me won't loosen until she's in my arms again. Although a finality slices us in two.

This may be the last occasion we see each other in this lifetime. The final moment where these bodies of ours can stand in the same space, hearts beating and eyes open. Alive. Our mortality is a cruel, fragile reminder hanging in the thin air, a ghostly whisper that maybe we're destined to be kept apart.

I won't entertain any god, the stars, or even fate itself if that force aims to keep me from my mate.

I'm getting off this ship alive and coming back to you, Kara.

"The canopy will close in thirty seconds."

I can't look away from her. There's no self-control left in me as I memorize the beautiful soft curves of her cheeks, the lips I didn't get to kiss enough, eyes that have always brought me to my damn knees. Her adorable nose, the teal in her hair, her exaggerated expressions. I catalogue every tattoo. Any little detail I can catch, I shove it all in, using my senses to commit them to memory.

So, if I die today, she's the last thing I'll see.

My mate. My love . . .

She'll be safe, I tell myself. *That's all that matters.*

That's all that matters.

That's all that matters.

CHAPTER 83

"The canopy will close in twenty seconds."

My heart squeezes as I watch Gav, his eyes locked on mine as he stands above me waiting for the pod's roof to clamp down and take us off the Azurite and down to Earth.

Gavrielle will never get off this ship alive.

I feel it in my bones.

He'll be dead just like Ardelle is, and I'll never survive it.

Despite relief spreading out in his eyes, he reveals the anguish in the tight set of his jaw and the stiffness in his posture.

He knows.

He knows this is the last time we'll ever see each other, and he'll be gone—and I'll be alone without him all over again.

This is just history repeating itself. It's exactly like the orphanage all those years ago, where I leave him behind *again*.

My body tingles. The thought of abandoning Gavrielle here is unfathomable.

"The canopy will close in ten seconds."

Those gorgeous Lilac eyes never leave mine, not for one agonizing second as everything around me vanishes, and all I can see is him. The room where I bared my body and soul to Malakyte dissolves. It means nothing, and Malakyte means nothing. The ship imploding around us is of no consequence. It isn't urgent. Even what happened with Ardelle is too painful to hold, so I gently set it down for these few fleeting seconds and just see the man I love.

I love him . . . I hadn't realized it before my memories came back, but it's so fucking clear in this moment I don't know how I missed it. Choosing him was one thing, but loving him is another. *I love him.*

"The canopy will close in five seconds."

And I'll never desert him again.

I shove off Pacey and lunge for the floor—now above me. My good leg pushes against her thighs, and I leap.

They both shout in protest as I spring from the escape pod, my upper body whacking the floor as I heave myself up with my elbows. Pacey has her arms around my legs, but the canopy is lowering right on top of me, and her and Gavrielle have no choice but to give me what I want and haul me up.

I fall on top of Gav as the canopy shuts, locking closed, narrowly missing cutting off my ankle.

The intercom confirms the door is now locked and sealed as pressurization commences. Pacey is pounding on the thick, dark nanoglass canopy, screaming at Gav to cancel the launch.

But it's too late.

"The emergency launch sequence will commence in three . . . two . . . one . . ."

Pacey's cries vanish with her as the pod shoots down and out of sight.

"What did you do?" Gavrielle grabs my face, nearly shaking me as he sits me up, but the relief in his voice betrays his anger as his lungs ache for air.

I spill my heart to the man I love, the man I chose. "I'm always with you," I say, voice sure, even as I can't catch my breath and as fresh tears stream down my cheeks. "I had a choice back then when we were at the orphanage. I left you there, and it haunted me every single day. I'll never abandon you again, Gavrielle. If we die on this ship, then we're dying together. I don't care."

His face is an unambiguous fusion of anger, devastation, and utter relief—a look that shows me all of his heart.

Then he kisses me everywhere. On my damp cheeks, then my lips. "You're so reckless, love," he scolds between one kiss and the next, his own eyes glassy, his cheeks flaming red. He kisses my forehead, then the top of my head. "And such a fucking pain in my ass. Stars above."

I don't know whether to laugh or cry, but I just know that, as long as we're together, everything is going to be okay.

"I love you, Kara," he finally says, his breath hot on my lips. "And once we make it down, there's something important I need to tell you, but for now, I love you. I've always loved you."

My body tingles, but this time, it's a different type of feeling, and I release a whimper of relief as I fall into his arms, holding onto him for dear life. "I love you, too, Gavrielle. I've always loved you. I'm sorry about Malakyte. I'm sorry. It didn't mean what you thin—"

"It's okay." He lifts me into his arms and stands, footing uneven due to the slant. "We'll talk about it more once we're out of here. I just needed you to know how much you mean to me, how much I love you."

I nod, words unable to articulate my feelings. But my eyes say it all. And we allow ourselves five more seconds to communicate something unspoken yet so clear between the both of us: nothing is going to keep us apart.

Not this stars forsaken ship, not Malakyte, not this war, not even Death himself—nothing ever fucking again.

Yet we're in a nightmare where it's hard to breathe. Herkimer can be around any corner, and our options are basically get sucked out into the vacuum of space or burn to death.

"Where do we go now?" I ask, my mind spinning for a way out of here. "There aren't any other escape pods nearby, are there?"

Gavrielle shoots me a deadpan stare with a cocked eyebrow for emphasis, but that face is the last thing I see as we're plunged into darkness.

"Well, shit . . ." he mutters, his chest expanding as he takes a deep breath in. Or tries to, anyway.

Gav walks me across the room with his keen eyesight, not running into anything despite the space being nearly pitch black.

He stands me up against a wall when we reach the closet near the main door, and I hear him wrenching the handle open, followed by the rustling of him throwing our coats and sweaters aside and a sigh of relief.

"Thank the stars he still kept these," he says, voice muffled by the closet walls.

As suddenly as the quartz lights dwindled, they come back on but remain dim and flickering as Gav plucks out two spacesuits. They match, both in shade Dark Side of the Moon with Royal Orange piping, all sorts of textures and patterns within the paneling, making it sleek and as cool as a spacesuit could look. The helmets are even smaller than the bulbous, fish-bowl type spacesuits I've seen. These are shaped more like a head, solid black, except for the clear window in the face to see out of with peripheral vision in mind.

"Pacey was right. We're likely going to lose the atmosphere soon. Especially if the power is sputtering out," Gav says, examining the suits and breathing harder than ever. "The tech of these suits is fairly skintight, so let me get mine on first. Then I'll help you slip into yours. Take your shoes off in the meantime if you can."

Gav gets into his suit quickly, and the fabric forms to his broad shoulders and tall Sky-Fae physique. I'm unfamiliar with the material, but it looks strong enough to hold up to outer space, and that's all I care about. He leaves his helmet on the floor, then turns to me.

We get my uninjured leg in fine, but it's the other that quickly becomes the problem.

I bite down on my lip hard when he tries slipping it over my knee, but the scream crawls up my throat. Gav hisses and promptly skirts the fabric back, assessing it in the fading light.

"I think this one is the biggest hindrance." He points to one of the many spikes embedded in my swollen, wrecked knee—the one sticking out the farthest. "We can either push it in a bit more or rip it out. Take your pick, your highness?"

I throw my head back against the wall and groan. "Rip it out," I tell him, but my voice isn't confident. "But all my adrenaline has worn off, and I really fucked it up when I lost it on Herkimer. And it hurts like a bitch."

"I'll be gentle," he says, winking at me of all things.

Gav braces me against the wall, his body tightly pressed up to mine to keep me standing, I realize. With his own knee bent, he brings my bad leg up and over his thigh, holding all its weight as he manhandles me in a way that's tender yet weirdly hot. We're so close, in such an intimate position, and his scent distracts me as I try to focus on anything other than the impending pain.

Leaning in, our foreheads touch as he looks down at my leg. "Hey, you've been ripping these things out all day. You've got this."

I snort, rolling my eyes, but there's no keeping the slight smile from my lips. "Really not the time, Gav," I whisper, hands shaking as I brace them on his shoulders.

He chuckles, and I swear he sounds like an angel. "I know."

He examines my royally fucked-up knee. The suit has gloves attached, and his fingers come around the spoke. That's the problem child. His eyes flutter back up to meet mine, peering through silver-tipped lashes, all playfulness vanished.

"Eyes on me, okay? I've got you."

509 

"Wait!" I gasp, and his eyes flare in a panic.

Grabbing the back of his neck, I close the last inch between us. "I've been dying to do this all day."

Our lips collide, and I kiss Gavrielle like it's the last time. He meets me with just as much eagerness, just as much passion and desperation and love and desire, the spinning room having nothing to do with this ship falling. We kiss wildly with tongues and teeth as my blood heats to eleven. The tension is pulled so taut my back pushes against the wall to find more friction as our bodies grind together, desperate for there to only be skin between us. He's anchored me to this one finite moment in time, where it's just him and me. The world is literally crashing around us, but all I see is Gavrielle. He is my axis, my center of gravity, my fucking world.

I'm breathless when I break the kiss, lips swollen as my heavy-lidded gaze rakes over his beautiful fucking face. "Now you can go."

His chuckle is deep, and it quells the fear as his fingers curl around the spike. "Look at me," he says, and I sigh heavily, nudging my eyes up so they can meet his.

My center of gravity.

Gavrielle allows me one deep breath.

Then he rips the spike out, quickly and efficiently—but brutally.

Through my scream, I hear the metal spike clatter to the floor somewhere as one hand lies softly around my neck, thumb caressing my jawline. His body is as solid as the wall at my back as I push against him, the only thing I can do to ebb the pain.

He puts pressure on the wound he just ripped open, and I nearly pass out. "You're alright. I'm here. Just you and me. Breathe through it. There you go. Good girl."

My breaths come out shaky, my nails digging into his shoulders.

We never break eye contact.

I feel him. He's here. He gives me his strength. He's always done that.

Once he senses I've leveled out, he tries the suit again. It's tight and hurts like hell going over my knee and the other spikes, but we get it on. Once our helmets lock into place and the suits pressurize with fresh oxygen, Gav's face illuminates within the helmet, mine doing the same.

"Can you hear me?" he asks, his voice synced right into my helmet.

"Yeah, and you?"

He nods, and he's about to pick me up but first dashes into the room right as the lights go off again.

A huge, terrifying sound comes from somewhere below, the floor vibrating.

Gavrielle runs back, and I nearly cry at what I see in his hands.

"My sword," I gasp as he quickly straps it to my back.

He also clips that little bag around my waist Malakyte always ordered me to carry, full of Silent Breath syringes and other necessities.

If we're going to survive, we need a ride off this ship . . .

And then it hits me. Neither Gav nor I have wings, but we don't need them.

"I have an idea," I say, my voice echoing out into the helmet. "But it's batshit crazy."

Gav's laughter in my helmet is whipped frosting to my soul. "I'd honestly be disappointed if it wasn't."

I look Gavrielle dead in the eyes. "We're going to ride the dragons out of this motherfucker."

CHAPTER 84

The elevator is too risky as an option, so we take the stairs again, praying that we can get past the floor where the explosions began and then all the way down to the prisons and even farther below.

I couldn't look at the place where Ardelle was murdered. I just can't face it. Not yet . . . it can't be real yet.

We find trouble within ten minutes.

"Please tell me this raging ball of fire is your illusions playing a joke on me," I say, the two of us standing in the stairwell, trying not to melt like candle sticks.

"Not this time, love."

I sigh. "Didn't think so."

We could backtrack to the level above and risk the elevator shaft, but there's no power anymore. So, we'd be forced to climb down if they're not already full of fire.

Fuck, fuck, fuck.

I scour my memory bank, now full and vivid and bright, and gasp as an idea flashes through my mind. Ardelle may just save me again.

"Do you trust me?" I ask as the raging fire forces us back even farther.

"With my life."

My laugh is cynical as my crystal's power builds. "Good, because it's in my hands now."

My antimatter has never once hurt me. Not the case for anyone else, though. But we're a package deal, Gav and me, so my antimatter will cooperate.

Remembering the lesson Ardelle taught me in the library, remembering how I made that shield under the Titan Games arena when those veclear bombs went off, I attempt the shield again.

Gavrielle flinches as the antimatter bursts to life from my hands.

You won't hurt Gavrielle, I command it as it grows and grows.

I hold my breath as it crosses Gavrielle's suit, half-waiting for him to begin screaming, but he doesn't, and in less than a minute, we're encompassed in a bubble of pure antimatter.

Our shield.

"Kara . . ." Gavrielle's head swivels all around, disbelief leaving his jaw on the floor.

Sparkling, jagged bolts of lightning in saturated Fuchsia Seduction are beautiful and dangerous and destruction incarnate.

"Go," I say, voice strained.

He looks at me like I'm insane but takes a giant breath and flies down the stairs.

I hold the shield steady as flames engulf us.

We're completely blind. The steps themselves are holding up under the flame, but his unsteady footsteps tell me that they're not going to last long.

But, fuck, it's already getting sweltering in here, my body sweating inside this suit.

I tremble with the force of holding this slipping barrier. "Faster, Gav!"

Just when it feels like we're going to be stuck in this inferno for eternity, we break through, as my shield falters and blasts to pieces, denting the entire landing around us, the walls and hand railings warped.

"Holy shit," he howls, shaking his head like a dog shakes off water.

We have no time to be stunned, and he continues, the stairs unending. Gavrielle never falters, not for one step, and we finally reach the bottom stairwell and burst into the prison sector.

It's a straight shot toward the long, pitch-black set of stairs that leads to the dragons, and we find the door in less than a minute.

As we descend into the dark, my grip on Gavrielle tightens.

"I hate this place," I say, the light from our helmets the only bit of illumination.

A rumbling wracks the ship hard, and Gav stumbles.

"Gav!" I scream.

We're going to tumble all the way down.

"Hold on to me," he says, voice strained.

I do, wrapping my arms around his neck as our momentum tips forward.

His arms catch the walls, and I drop, literally choking him so I don't fall. He catches us before we completely tumble.

"This isn't how I wanted to introduce choking into our relationship, but since we're here…" he jokes as he heaves me back into his arms, clearing his throat with a light chuckle.

"Sorry I couldn't ease into it first," I quip back just as sarcastically, our breathing eclipsed by the groaning and pulling of the ship.

A robotic voice echoes out from the speakers like a phantom warning, dousing all humor. "Oxygen levels decreasing. Seek artificial sources immediately. Oxygen levels critical."

"Good call on the suits, Gav."

After nearly ten more minutes of him rushing down the steps, we make it to the bottom. Emergency lights illuminate the hallway beyond, once lit in the shade Jade, the lights shifting the space in the shade Blood.

The complex door that leads to the dragons is only about a hundred feet ahead.

We reach it quickly, but as we do, the ship groans, and there's a snapping boom before we're sent flying.

CHAPTER 85

"**K**ara!"

Ringing is deafening my ears, but there's a voice somewhere out there, too.

"Kara!"

I know that voice . . . It's the man I love. My friend. Gavrielle.

My eyes shoot open. Gav kneels over me, his voice muffled in my helmet. I'm on my back, with a hard surface beneath me.

"What happened?" I ask, disoriented.

"I think one of the thrusters blew. It's likely that Earth's gravity is going to rip us down to the surface. We're falling—fast. Can you get up?"

I groan as he lifts me up, my lungs aching.

There's no time to waste on pain.

We need to get through that door—now.

It doesn't take long for my Elendril crystal's power to swell to the surface again, and I blast the door wide open, the metal slab flying into the dragon's chamber and into the darkness beyond.

The Azurite shifts dramatically again, but Gav is there to catch me as I'm thrown off balance, my injured knee making it nearly impossible for me to stay upright on this topsy-turvy carnival ride from Hell.

A deep voice rumbles my bones from within the room, cruel and ancient and deadly.

"Have you finally come to terms with Zariya's sin, Killer of Worlds?"

CHAPTER 86

'm not even going to attempt to analyze what he means by that.

"I'm here to set you free," I call out, Gavrielle helping me get inside the giant room that's become their prison over the last forty years.

A multitude of growls and metal bending infiltrates past the alarms.

"Lies," one says.

Gav and I follow the long line of the cells, completely blind.

"Where are you, Dannanōk? I can't see down here, and if you can't tell, we don't have a lot of time."

For a second, I think my Elendril dragon is going to remain silent, but he blasts a small ball of fire down the hall between the two sets of huge cells holding him and his fellow dragons captive. It illuminates us in the shade Tiger Stripe.

Eyes of Harvest Gold glow alongside the firelight, and that's basically all I can see of him, but I'd know those eyes anywhere. I'd know his voice anywhere, too. It's haunted my steps within the Azurite these past weeks.

Leaning on Gav, my entire body trembles from fear, from anxiety, from pain. This was my plan, my idea, so I've got to sell it. "This ship is about to crash. It's going to land on the

Earth's surface, and once it does, what doesn't get obliterated by the atmosphere will explode on impact. You're all immortal beings or whatever, but you can still be killed, am I right in assuming that?"

His silence is my answer.

"We'll both die, too. So, how about lending your wings to help us survive the fall in exchange for your freedom. I'll let you go either way, but even when I do, you're still trapped on the Azurite."

"We are no pony ride service, Killer of Worlds," a female dragon from within Dannanōk's cell chastises, but my eyes remain fixed on Dannanōk himself.

A new siren booms from within the cells, that robotic voice coming across the airwaves again. "Warning. Warning. Artificial gravity systems at critical failure. Repeat, artificial gravity systems at critical failure."

I break my gaze to look over at Gav, his face lit by his helmet's light. We could really use Ardelle right about now, but then I remember with the most painful ache in my chest that he's never coming back. That he's fucking gone.

Gone.

I blink away the pain, the rage, and focus back on the situation at hand. Time is slipping.

"We don't have time to argue," I say, voice reflecting my anger. "Help us, or we all die here together."

Dannanōk asks, "How do you suggest you help us?"

Okay, progress, not perfection.

"I'll create an escape hatch with my magic, and you fly us out of here."

It sounded so much more logical in my head.

The same female in the cell with Dannanōk speaks up again. "We haven't flown in decades. Our wings are not as strong as they once were. We could get in the skies and plummet just as fast as this ship. Annara has never flown, period. She could easily die from your plan."

Their little baby dragon. I search for her, but she's hidden, probably terrified.

"She'll die for sure if you do nothing," I counter. "At least in the skies she—all of us—have a chance. But stuck on this ship, we're guaranteed death. Don't you want to live? Don't you want to fight against what he's done to you? I want that for you. Please help us."

I'm not above begging, not after everything.

Dannanōk's ancient eyes search my own, and whatever dragon voodoo they have that allows them to speak telepathically, his voice simmers through my mind, the textured sound dancing along its inner recesses. *We will ally with you, Killer of Worlds, but we won't relay what we know of the Elendril crystals despite any alliances. You have not earned our knowledge. You have not healed Zariya's sins.*

Zariya's sins . . . That phrase he keeps repeating.

"We don't care about the Elendril's secrets," I say aloud.

Although that information would be vital in the upcoming battle, but whatever. Later.

Then, the dragons will ally with you, Killer of Worlds.

I take a deep breath and nod to Gav. "We're a go."

Turning back to Dannanōk and the other dragons, my crystal begins to surge.

"First, I'm getting you out of these cells. Now, stand back."

The dragon's retreat as far back into their cells as possible, and I survey the space, mind whirling with how I can free them without wounding or killing them.

The glow of my crystal's antimatter illuminates the massive chamber as it zips in a condensed streak horizontally across the center of the bars, slicing them in half.

"Now, push through!" I shout over the increasing chaos, the ship's tilt getting steeper and steeper by the second.

The dragons obey, thrashing their massive bodies against the bars cut through the center.

The physical representation of their suffering—the bars—bends and cracks and snaps, the weight of their efforts finally freeing them after all this time.

Annara leaps out first, free for the first time in her life. She's barely ten feet long and six feet tall, her tail whipping frantically left and right. I can't tell exactly what color she is, but she's dark-scaled just like the rest of them.

Yes!

Her little mouth full of needle-like teeth latches onto one end of the bars, and she yanks, using all her weight.

A massive lurch in the ship throws me, Gav, and Annara up in the air five feet before we slam back down—hard. My knee pain is unbearable.

"We're hitting Earth's outer atmosphere. It's pulling us down!" Gavrielle shouts, and we hold on to each other for dear life.

The Azurite trembles like it's been thrown into a washing machine, shuddering and violently thrashing around.

My heart does the same.

Then there's a snap on one side of the room—opposite Dannanōk's cell. The entire structure of the cell's bars falls completely, clamoring to the floor with a boom and a dust cloud, which almost crushes Annara before she skitters out of the way.

I can only watch in awe at what emerges from those cells.

With dragonfire lighting it from behind, the first celestial dragon emerges from its prison of hate like a demon rising up from Hell. Its ancient wings extend up and out like a stretch that could reach the edge of the galaxy—the membrane damn near glowing Pumpkin Orange as its veins stand out stark against the leathery texture. A neck of scales and spikes lengthen higher and higher as the creature steps out completely. Firelight dancing behind a maw of long teeth as it opens its mouth and releases the loudest, ear-shattering roar of freedom that trembles me to my very core.

It nearly brings me to tears.

Beautiful, wicked creatures.

When I look over at Gavrielle, he's just as awe-struck.

A snapping sound to our left indicates Dannanōk's cell is broken down now, too.

The room becomes cramped rather quickly, not big enough for every dragon to extend their wings or tails, but that's the least of our problems, as there's a definite sensation of falling, the speed increasing faster and faster.

Then it happens.

The artificial gravity succumbs to the fall, and we're all thrown into a weightless tumble.

Gav keeps him and me locked together, holding onto anything that's still bolted down.

"Get on my back, Killer of Worlds, before you lose your shot!" Dannanōk yells within my head, and I pull at Gav, relaying what the dragon said.

The dragon is close, thank fuck, and Gav strains to float us over to him as we're thrown every which way, having no leverage in midair.

There's absolutely no control, no footing, nothing stable at all. Dannanōk's dragonfire is puttering out, and soon, we get confused in the darkness.

I don't know which way is up or down.

But Gavrielle has me, dragging me along foot by foot, inch by inch, with all his might, using the clipped bars on the ceiling to guide us until we reach Dannanōk.

Gav shoves me onto the dragon's back, his body so utterly foreign. His scales are thick, rough, and dry. We're sitting in front of his wings. Directly in front of my face is the last set of his many spikes that make up a deadly mane from his neck to his horns at his head. I grab both, one in each hand. I'm able to lay flat on my stomach against his back, but my fucking knee fires pain so sharp I nearly pass out. Dannanōk's girth is significantly too thick for either of us to grip our legs around and keep ahold of him.

Soon, Gavrielle's body flattens over mine, but the error in my plan begins to show itself the moment we're in position.

How are we going to hold on?

We're going to fly right off this dragon's hide the moment we hit the air.

Panic starts to build up inside me like a ticking bomb, even as a rush of cold air squeals into the chamber, an impossibly loud hissing accompanying it.

"Gav! We won't be able to hang on!" I yell.

He hauls his chest over my head, easily able to reach more of Dannanōk's spikes. "We will. Hold on to these spikes and use your legs as best you can."

One of those legs is fucking useless.

Then everyone slams down—*violently*. The shudder in the room near deafening.

Gravity seems to return . . . and in my delirium of fear and desperation, I think Ardelle has somehow lived and come to save us, but that isn't it. I want to scream because that isn't it.

It's Earth's gravity that's in this room now.

Not Ardelle's.

The Azurite has fallen enough that we're in breathable air—air the dragons can fly into—if they can even fly at all.

Which tells me one thing: it's time to finally get the fuck off this ship.

CHAPTER 87

We're near the bottom of the ship. That, I know for certain. I'll have to blast downwards to create a passageway. We're likely going to get sucked out fast.

"Wait to open the hall!" Dannanōk roars in my head. *"We're still too high. I'll tell you when it's time."*

With the gravity, Gav's weight on top of me is heavy as he braces both hands on Dannanōk's parallel spikes. I do the same.

"This was a dumb idea now that I think about it," I tell Gav, laughing a bit in my absolute panic.

"Nah," he says, voice so confident I'd love him for that alone. "It's going to be fun. Who gets the chance to fly on the back of a dragon? Sounds like a good time to me."

Dannanōk instructs Annara on how best to fly, her sweet little dragon face nodding and listening intently.

She doesn't look scared one bit.

This is her flight of freedom, after all.

Her instincts will take over, and she'll be okay. We'll all be okay.

It feels like we're falling incredibly quickly, and just as I wonder if it's time, Dannanōk yells back up my way with his voice so everyone can hear. "Prepare!"

Anxiety fills my chest at a level never experienced before. My body tingles from absolute fucking dread. My instincts scream, *No, no, no!* And I can nearly taste the terror on my tongue.

"You got this, love. I'm always with you. We're surviving this." Gavrielle's voice is strong, with not a hint of fear or doubt.

How can he be so calm?

For you. He's being calm for you.

My power builds, his voice my war song. My anthem.

The crystal sizzles along my skin, firing in my bones, rising like these dragons rose from their confinement.

"Soon," Dannanōk warns. "Hit down and to the left, at that angle. Everyone, brace for evacuation. Necks and wings in tight. It's going to be violent and loud and cold. Find the current and ease downwards, away from the crash site."

"It has been an honor flying with you," one dragon says to Dannanōk, and the others follow, each bowing their heads to him one by one.

My crystal's mark illuminates Dannanōk's scales, the power nipping at release.

Gav's chest presses down on my head as I'm nestled tight under his arm, tucking his chin as low as he can, his legs curled around mine. His heartbeat thrashes on my back.

My hand lets go of Dannanōk's spike, keeping the other clamped tight. I line up my shot as I tuck my head and take one last breath . . .

"I love you," Gavrielle says, a split second before I blast the Azurite as hard as I can.

There's no time for me to say it back.

CHAPTER 88

The boom quakes my bones to utter dust.

Metallic screeches as metal tears and rips, but it's the ear-bleeding whoosh of air sucking us out of the ship that nearly snaps mine and Gav's necks.

Gavrielle's arms and legs brace tight as Dannanōk is violently sucked downwards—along with all the other dragons—and I shriek at how fast it happens, barely getting my hand back onto his spike.

It's only darkness, sparks of light zipping by so fast they're like stars.

A loud, howling whistle is all I can hear, the force so strong I think Gav and I are screwed for sure and that, at any moment, we're going to be whipped off Dannanōk's back.

There's a moment of utter silence for a split second—*are we already dead?*

Then an immediate brightness of a clear Crystal Blue sky hits my eyes, so bright it burns them to tears.

The fact our necks alone aren't snapped by that exit is a fucking miracle.

It all happens so fast.

The roaring winds return as we succumb to the free fall, and it's an instant, uncontrollable tumble straight toward the surface.

Debris plummets all around us, from dark metal to balls of fire, and everything in between. It rains chaos and death, and we're caught in the middle of it.

Gav's weight lightens as Dannanōk somersaults, wings tucked tight. We're spinning so fast I don't know which direction is land. The only way I know which way is up or down is by Gav's shifting weight on my back, who's getting thrown around like a rag doll.

"Gav, don't let go!"

His loud grunts in my helmet tell me he's struggling to hold on—his hands slipping inch by inch.

And then he slams back down onto me, crushing me with his weight. He takes the opportunity to readjust his grip on Dannanōk's spikes when he's thrown up again, his weight leaving me completely this time.

"Gavrielle!" I scream, voice box shredding as I feel him slipping, his hands almost off the spikes entirely.

My howl is lodged in my throat as my stomach is shoved to my feet, lurching up again and Gav wallops back onto me, the pressure the most beautiful thing I've ever felt.

The sky is there one moment and gone the next. Sky, land, debris, sun, sky, a cluster of tiny fireballs, land, sky. Back and forth and up and down, so disorienting its nauseating.

We're cartwheeling down to Earth, and it's unstoppable.

Gav shouts as his entire body lifts off the dragon again, but this time I'm right behind him! My feet lift first as I slip and shriek—knowing I'm going to lose my grip. Gavrielle loses one hand, and the terror strikes me so hard I can't even scream.

"Dannanōk, we're slipping!" I bellow in my head.

Then Gavrielle slips off completely, shooting up instead of down. My own legs are nearly vertical as one hand barely holds onto the spike.

"Gavrielle!"

He's gone so fast, but I can still hear him in the suit as his breath gets lodged in his throat.

Dannanōk corrects somehow, and I whack back down, my helmet slamming onto his scales as his wings finally extend as he flips upright.

"Dannanōk!" I beg the dragon, hardly able to form a coherent thought. *"Gavrielle! Do something!"*

I frantically look for Gav. *I don't see him!*

Dannanōk bends straight into a dive and cranks his body just as Gavrielle comes zooming down directly beside us, the dragon pivoting upwards in the nick of time to catch Gav in his front claw.

I howl as Dannanōk straightens out, not even realizing how close I was to slipping off sideways, so I scoot myself back to center.

"Holy fuck!" Gavrielle yells, our helmets still synced. "Going to feel that one in the morning!"

I've never heard Gav's voice so shaky.

"Are you okay?" I cry.

Dannanōk evens out, and I can release a stars damned fucking breath, my body trembling so hard as my hands and wrists and knee ache, but I keep my grip for all I'm worth.

"Yeah . . ." he says, voice breathless as the sound of Dannanōk's wings flap through the air. "I think . . . *fuck.*"

I'm in shock, too . . . mind completely fried.

Dannanōk's wings beat, but it feels like he's caught some current of air, his unused wings stretching and shuddering against the Baby Blue of the sky in the sunlight, dodging falling debris skillfully.

Both our breaths are ragged and frantic in our helmets as Dannanōk soars much steadier now, and I don't want to get too hopeful, but it appears as if he's stabilized and leveled out, finally soaring on the wind like he was made to.

I'm comfortable enough to look around at my surroundings, at Zarmenia City in the distance, the mountains where Jance's house is straight ahead—thankfully miles away.

A massive light and near-deafening boom draws my attention to the left.

The Azurite crashes into the Earth in a giant, massive missile of fiery rage—the explosion is apocalyptic.

The moment the spaceship crashes in the woods on the outskirts of the city, a shockwave ripples like the hands of a god wiping out all the trees as their trunks and limbs bend back in a whoosh that I feel in my very core.

The explosion is at least six or seven stories high and spreads outwards thousands of feet along the Earth's surface, engulfed in a raging fireball.

As we soar closer to the ground, more debris shoots and flies in every direction. Metal, glass, insulation, electronic components, the jets—zipping out at the speed of a disruptor shot.

Could Malakyte truly survive something like this? How? He'd be incinerated—and so would Herkimer. I ignore the fear tugging at my gut at the thought of Herkimer, his AI freak soldiers, and hope to the stars the tech got destroyed in the fall. Yet a piece of my heart aches for Malakyte . . . and I'm truly unsure if I want him to be dead or alive. I'm sure Zariya thought he couldn't live through a moon explosion, and she was wrong.

Dannanōk banks to the right, avoiding the blast zone.

"Look below," Gav says. "There are people down there. That must be the survivors. Pacey and the others should be there, too."

I'm so stunned to see the Earth again. Summer is in full swing, my eyes still stinging from the sun, but stars, *the sun.*

It doesn't take long for Dannanōk to approach the surface, and he quite rudely throws Gavrielle a few feet before he lands with a jolt.

I groan as my knee knocks against the dragon's scales as his claws finally make contact with earth and soil. He seems to slide for dozens of feet, and my eyes squeeze shut. Once Dannanōk stops moving below me and I feel certain we've actually made it down to the surface, I tell myself it's safe to open my eyes and let go of his spikes. My fingers and wrists feel strange as it feels like I'm peeling them off one by one. Eventually, once I feel secure enough, my body goes limp as I do nothing but lie here like a beached whale.

That was . . . insanity.

With another grumble, I force myself to sit up as I take in my surroundings. Trees, survivors, dragons . . .

I remove my helmet, toss my sweat drenched hair over my shoulders, letting it fall wherever, and suck in the deepest, most precious breath of air I've taken in my entire life.

Fresh air.

I let the smells consume me, mostly of burning things, but I also smell grass and the bark of the trees and listen to the cicada's singing and the birds squawking in a panicked melody. The air is hot and dense as the summer sun beats on my face, and my eyes close, a tear threatening to fall free.

Ardelle . . . you were supposed to make it down here with me.

I open my misty eyes as I hear Gavrielle's voice, someone talking with him close by.

Dannanōk growls. "Get off me so I can find my offspring and mate."

There was no time to assess him flailing through the air, but Dannanōk isn't just a massive black dragon—he's *the* dragon. I see why he's the leader—he's the biggest. Twenty to thirty feet tall depending on his head—which has massive, curved horns with a ribbed textured face—those Honey Gold eyes come up to stare at me incredulously. *Get the fuck off, Killer of Worlds,* those eyes say.

But that isn't all. He's relieved. He's grateful we're alive. And so am I.

Yet there's one thing I notice about his scales. Yes, they're mostly black, but as the sun hits them, they nearly glow with a gorgeous Imperial Magenta color, shimmering iridescent purple in the sunlight.

Interesting coloring . . .

I'd bet catos to donuts the other dragon's scales shimmer a certain color, too.

"Told you we'd survive."

Gavrielle's chipper voice rings out from below, and he's standing to my right, hair a mess and that cocky ass smile on his face.

Damn, does he look good after nearly falling to his death. It's unfair. Stars damned Sky-Fae.

Gav's eyes widen from behind me, and I follow his gaze, a tiny shape flies through the air—albeit awkwardly as hell—making her way down to the surface.

Annara's landing is just as graceless as she tumbles down in a mix of dirt and Grape Juice scales, rolling several times until she stops on her back, talons stuck up in the air at all angles.

I chuckle. She's *purple*.

"Get off!" Dannanōk roars.

"Okay!"

More and more dragons land in various stages of aptitude, with only one having crashed completely, the others tending to it as Gav and I line up my dismount.

Terrans and extras are rushing all around, their shocked whispers and awe-struck gasps at dragons falling from the sky, never mind their home literally burning several hundred feet away. SSPARROWs walk about aimlessly, helmets off, unsure of what to do.

"Kara!"

My head snaps in the direction of the voice as Sylo runs up to us, arms waving.

I slide down Dannanōk, my knee erupting with agony even as Gav avoids touching it when he catches me. It's over double the size it should be.

Sylo reaches us, and it feels like I'm seeing him for the first time again. He looks so much older.

Does he know about Ardelle? Has Pacey found him and told him his best friend is now dead? I can't be the one to drop that bomb.

"It's Jance," he says, catching his breath. "You need to come now."

Something is very, very wrong, and the massive adrenaline rush from the fall surges back up to a ten.

Without thinking about it a second more, Gav readjusts me in his arms, and we follow Sylo through a small patch of trees.

"What's happened?" I ask, desperate for information.

"We were able to contact Trinity before we evacuated down, told her what was happening. So, when the ship crashed, we and the rebels were too close to the crash site, and once it hit, debris went flying like disruptor projectiles. A lot of people are injured by the explosion and the fall. Jance got hit with something. We don't even know what. He's in bad shape."

This can't happen.

Not after what I've lost today.

I can't lose him.

"But he's going to be okay, right?" I ask, desperate for Sylo to tell me what I want to hear—what I *need* to hear.

His silence is answer enough.

Jance is going to die.

CHAPTER 89

I'm not prepared for what I see.

Jance is lying on his back in the grass, Ahren and two other people I don't recognize hastily working on his injuries.

Trinity is here, along with rebels, more arriving every second, and I am so utterly relieved that she's alive—the rebels are alive—and that bomb they forced me to detonate didn't kill her.

Now I need a second miracle.

Deimos stands against a tree farther back, arms crossed, his permanent scowl softened as we lock eyes, his gaze full of pity.

Pacey and Saris stand a few feet back, holding each other, Pacey's eyes red and furious and so fucking sad I can't hold her stare.

Gav sets me down next to Jance, and I grab his hand, his eyes glossy and distant as he stares at the tree canopy, their strong warmth now dull and dying.

I didn't think after Ardelle that I could hurt anymore, his death leaving me so numb I couldn't feel, but that was a lie.

It was a disgusting, terrible fucking lie.

"Jance?" I say softly, my eyes grazing over the massive wound in his chest. His shirt is gone, and Ahren is doing something that isn't nearly enough to stop this gaping wound from bleeding out. There's so much blood, and it's so deep. "I'm here. I made it off the ship. You have to stay awake, okay?"

He squeezes my hand, my presence waking him a little.

Jance opens his mouth.

"Don't," I say softly. "You need to save your strength."

"Do you . . . remember me?" he asks, his voice like a foreign shore I remembered visiting ages ago.

Stubbornly, he didn't listen. No wonder I'm so thick headed.

I nod, tears filling my eyes. "I do. I remember you."

How he can smile at a time like this is beyond me.

"Good, I needed to bring you back to me. Take my ring. The others have it."

The ring he wore when he was married to my mother. I saw it in Malakyte's stupid treasure trove. Why didn't I take it? Why didn't I fucking remember my father? I need to make it right.

"You say that like you won't be able to give it to me yourself."

The way he looks at me shoots a spear through my heart.

I can't do this.

Turning to Ahren, I look at him exasperated—my body crashing, my sanity along with it. "Do something!"

Ahren's soft Blue Steel eyes reflect only helplessness.

"Ardelle is gone, Kara, my magic went with him. I can't heal anyone anymore, not like I did with you."

My body tingles, and I think I might pass out, a single tear falling to my cheeks.

When Gavrielle's hands rest on my shoulders, it unravels something inside me. Breaks me.

"No . . ."

I don't know who I'm saying it to, but no! "No!"

My screams echo out into the tiny valley of trees, the wind a grim reaper, swaying between branches and blades of grass while it waits to take another soul away from me.

Jance squeezes my hand as I scoot closer, not caring about how the spikes are digging deeper into my knee. "Baby, please don't cry."

I shake my head profusely. "I can't. I can't lose you, too. I need you. I can't do this without you."

Speaking is so hard for him, and it breaks every part of me to see him like this.

"You'll never be without me, because I'll never leave your side."

A cry breaks through my throat, and I can't contain it as I hunch over him, my emotions escalating to a point of hysteria.

Gavrielle collects my hair away from my face, patting my back because he knows. He knows I'm going to break, and I won't recover. Not after losing them both.

"There has to be something you can do!" I plead to Ahren, snapping back up.

Trinity says, "Our med bus should be here any minute. We have the best doctors and equipment at our base, but, Kara . . ."

She hesitates, her voice going soft. I know that tone . . . I remember she always used it when she was trying to soften a blow for me. Geonni spoke in the exact same cadence.

I shake my head, looking up into her Honey eyes, hoping she'll have an answer for me.

"There's likely nothing they can do for him," Ahren says, and I can tell it kills him to say it. "This type of wound . . ."

I can't hear it.

Jance's eyes flutter closed, and panic chokes me. I can't let this happen. *I can't!*

"I don't believe you," I whisper, my fear and anger and grief boiling over. "I don't accept that answer! There's Arianyte tech that's more advanced. There's got to be something. Some machine or some drug or . . ."

My eyes widen with realization—heart hammering in my ears as they hollow out with what I just remembered I had strapped to my waist.

I hysterically reach for the little pouch—the cursed gift Malakyte gave me—terrified I may have lost it in the fall or that it broke or something, but it's there.

My nails nearly rip the clasp off the purse when I open it and frantically snatch up the case that may save my father's life.

The sound that claws free from my throat as I open the case and see both syringes, good as new, is *feral*.

The Indigo liquid glitters in the sunlight. This brilliantly glowing substance is the key to my survival. Because, without Jance, I won't make it.

Nothing else matters.

I rip the protective covering off the syringe, squeeze out any remaining air in the needle, quickly reminding myself of exactly how Malakyte instructed me to do it. He told me to stick it in as deep as it can go. And it'll heal him. It'll save him!

My hand lifts back as I move to plunge the needle through his chest—

I stop, my mind catching up to my actions as I remember exactly what I'm holding.

The needle shakes—no, trembles—in my hand as it rests mere inches from Jance's chest and the wound currently bleeding life from him by the second.

A vial full of dead children . . .

This is the Silent Breath. The very fucking thing I've accosted and judged and raged against Malakyte for.

Everything I fight against.

Using this would make me more than a hypocrite.

I'd be exactly like him . . . more than I already am. More than merely the notion of a villain, but one that's worse. One that parades around like a hero.

I'd go against my ideals, my principles, what I've fought for—the Hijacked I've fought to save. I'd be disgracing them and their memory.

My chin quivers as I tilt my head away from Jance, tears rushing from my eyes as indecision throttles my conviction to save him at all costs.

A pin could drop, yet it's all their judgment that's as loud as the eavesdropping wind.

"Kara," Ahren says, voice low and seeking. "What is that?"

He knows what it is.

They all do.

But Jance is out of time, his breathing shallow and slow.

I have seconds to decide—if that.

"Another sin I'm going to pay for."

My iron will is steadfast as I drive the syringe downwards, the needle burying into his wound, my thumb the final hammer strike as it sinks the Silent Breath into his body.

Malakyte made me his little monster, alright . . .

Despite how selfish this makes me, how terrible of a person I am for it, if I lose Jance . . . I won't make it through this war. I won't save anybody if my father dies.

Once the syringe is empty, I slide the needle back out and wait with bated breath.

How long does it take to work? I wasn't too late, was I? Is the dosage not enough?

Panicking when I don't see any improvement immediately, I grab the second needle.

Too much can't hurt him, right? Malakyte never said too much would hurt.

I rip off the second protective covering with my teeth, spitting the plastic into the grass as I move to inject him again.

"Wait!" Ahren flings his hand coming over Jance's chest.

"You're not going to stop me," I hiss, teeth bared, but Ahren's eyes aren't judgmental, they're glinting with something else.

Hope.

He gently places his gloved hands over my trembling fists. "Let me get it into his veins. It may work better that way."

Before I decide, a doctor gasps and harshly whispers, "Stars, look at his chest. It's knitting up."

Just like that, my tears aren't ones of helpless agony but of wishful anticipation.

I give Ahren the second syringe, and he gets the needle into a vein, slowly dispersing the neon liquid into it.

"His pulse is strengthening," a female doctor says.

I have a vague sense of a hover pulling up, its brakes squeaking.

Ahren pulls the needle out when the Silent Breath is at the halfway point. "Let's wait to see if he requires more. This is a precious substance."

"If he needs it, he gets it," I say firmly, my eyes stuck on Ahren's. He nods.

"Ma'am," someone yells, and Trinity's head whips toward the voice. "We're here to transport the injured back to base."

"Get this man into surgery right now, him and that girl with him are the top priority. Nobody comes before them, got it? And I want him with Doctor Burter. Load him up now!"

The rebel medics lift Jance onto a stretcher and quickly load him into the hover-van, while Gavrielle brings me into the back with him.

Gav takes the remaining Silent Breath serum just in case Jance needs it, getting a fresh protective cover for it, but by the time the medical bus is moving, Jance's color already looks better, the gash shrinking.

Doctors and nurses tend to him, hooking him up to all sorts of machines. Some want to assess my knee, but I refuse their care, not wanting to take anyone away from Jance.

I don't know how long it is until we stop, ten minutes, maybe. I'm too frantic to notice time or much else as they unload and wheel Jance away through industrial doors down a gravel path and into a concrete base that looks like it stretches out for a mile. It's an entire ass complex.

All my attempts to join him are adamantly refused.

 538

Then he's gone, and it's out of my hands.

My father will either live . . . or he'll die, and there's nothing more I can do to save him.

I've already corrupted my soul, so what else is there to do?

CHAPTER 90

The pain medicine hits me like a baseball bat. Fast, rushing into me all at once, an overwhelming explosion that makes me feel light and heavy simultaneously.

After Jance was wheeled in, we're taken into a medical wing of this base littered with curtained off rooms and people rushing around like crazy, helping injured Terrans and extras alike. Gav got me to a bed in a seated position so my knee can stay bent. One rebel nurse got him all the medical supplies he asked for, and he cut away my leggings, got me set up with an IV, fluids. Now, the drugs sliding into my body are the sweetest, most numbing release I didn't know I needed.

Gavrielle sits in a chair with wheels at my side, patting my hair and pressing a kiss to my temple. He then wheels himself back to the front where my royally fucked-up knee waits, swollen and full of metal.

"I didn't know you had medical training," I tell him, the drugs slurring my words. "What else don't I know about you?"

Gav chuckles, and there's that fucking smirk again. "I'm sure there's a lot about me you're curious about. Certain body parts, perhaps?"

I snort, our little curtained-off room spinning. "You think so highly of yourself, don't you? You . . . *perv.*"

"Only about the parts of me that are extraordinary. Which is most of me," he quips, snapping on a fresh pair of black gloves.

His words are playful, but his face is grim. *I see what you're doing, Gavrielle.*

"Please, contain your ego for one second," I say, but words feel like so much effort.

"I have no idea what you mean, love."

I close my eyes. Just for a second.

"Stars, Kara . . ." he whispers.

My eyes pop back open.

He's finally taking a good long look at the horrible state of my body.

"I'm never going to walk again," I choke out, the certainty hitting me like a boulder to the head now that I'm looking at it. "He did it this way on purpose so I couldn't fight, even if I managed to escape. He wanted me crippled and powerless."

"We'll deal with that after we get these out."

Head falling back against the chair, I mutter, "I need him . . ."

"Need who, love?"

My throat gets so tight I hardly squeak out his name. "Jance." I sniff, sighing heavily. "I was so awful to him. And Ardelle . . . He was all alone. And he's . . ."

Gav moves in my peripheral, but I just stare up at the lights and let them continue burning my eyes for some reason. "Jance loves you, Kara. And if he could be here right now, you know he would be. And Ardelle . . . It wasn't your fault. Let's just get you feeling better, okay? You and I will do this together. I'll get you through this."

There's a long beat of silence before I glance back down and blink several times, hoping I'm not seeing what I think I'm seeing.

I stare wide-eyed at the huge needle in Gavrielle's hands, shaking my head. "That's not going in my knee, is it?"

Gavrielle's cringy smile is legitimately the worst.

"To numb you first."

Just look at his pretty eyes and his pretty face to distract yourself from the giant fucking needle he's going to stick in your knee.

I roll my head back and groan.

"I'll make it quick. Once I get the first one in, you won't feel the rest."

I can't watch.

"Okay, I'm right here. Try to stay still."

The needle goes in so deep I can't help but cry out, Gav's free hand holding my thigh down as it trembles uncontrollably against the chair.

"Gav," I cry, the pain like acid inside my knee.

"I know, love, it's okay. I'm right here. Almost there, just a little deeper."

Fuck, he's got to go deeper? The needle is scraping against bone.

I wrap my good leg around the dip in his waist. He moves so I can push against him—sturdy and immovable.

"I'm there, just pushing the anesthetic in. You won't feel much after this. You did so good babe. Just stay still. Almost done."

He's right. Soon, a deep numbing washes over my knee, and the pain goes with it. My body relaxes as Gavrielle works, numbing more portions of it until I can't feel much of anything.

"You know Malakyte and Herkimer are alive," I mumble, lids heavy.

Gav taps a spike, and the pressure makes the hair on my body shoot up, and he winces, apologizing. "Fuck them. It's just you and me right now."

I nod, the drugs giving me courage.

He takes a long, deep breath, eyes angled down at my ruined leg.

I tighten my good leg around Gav's waist and wish he could hold my hand.

He looks back up at me. *Beautiful fucking man.* "We'll go one by one. Are you ready?"

I nod, taking a deep breath.

 542

Jance and Ardelle would want me to be strong. So, I will be.

Gavrielle slides two fingers along both sides of the first spike, pressing down just a bit. With the speed only a Sky-Fae could possess, he rips the metal from my knee. Fast. Efficient. One and done.

I scream.

It's so much worse this time.

"You're okay. *You're okay.*"

I hate that I cry, that it hurts that much, and that I'm nothing but a fucking baby about it.

"Breathe, Kara. Look at me. Good girl. Just breathe . . . There you go. You're doing so good, love. I've got you."

Gavrielle won't let me break.

"Do you want me to try and go slower on the next one?"

I shake my head. "No. I need . . . more . . . drugs."

Slower would be worse.

"It may be too soon for more, love."

"No." I shake my head. "It isn't strong enough. I can still feel every single thing that I've done."

Gavrielle rakes his tongue across one of his pointed canines as his eyes look back down at my knee.

"There's no numbing that away."

He's right, of course. However, once he removes two more, I'm a blubbering, tearing mess, and he does, in fact, give me more medicine.

It helps, but my knee is so swollen, so tender, that it is utter agony no matter what Gavrielle does for me. Yet it still doesn't hurt as much as the emotional pain, and I know that will last far longer.

By the fifth one, I completely pass out from the pain.

The last thing I remember are the echoes of my own screams inside my mind, crying for my father who never comes.

CHAPTER 91

My eyes flutter open, heavy grogginess still in my head and my body, as if I weigh a thousand pounds.

I'm still sitting in the same medical bed, and the miss-matched curtains to my left and right are strung up by ridiculous means, but whatever gets the job done, I guess. The lights are dimmed, and it's quiet. The chaos from the fall has settled, and an eerie silence is left behind.

Gav is still sitting in the chair beside me, head and shoulders leaned over my lap, asleep.

He faces me, and I don't resist the urge to brush my fingers through the long silver hair that fell over his face, strands like spun spider's silk. I've never felt anything so weightlessly smooth, and even after the day we've had, his long mane of hair is knot-free. Even his little braids have no frizz as I roll one in between two fingers, mesmerized by the liquid-like texture.

I haven't seen him sleeping since we were little. The boy who was my best friend, a mischievous, clever little shithead. The hardness Malakyte honed into him softens while he sleeps, his hard angles looking much less lethal, and I tear up. That's the true Gavrielle, and he's mine.

With a heavy sigh, I glance down at my knee. It's wrapped neatly in white gauze, and surprisingly, the swelling has gone down a ton. It doesn't hurt as badly or look like a cantaloupe anymore, so that's something.

I unhook the fluids bag from my IV and slowly scoot my legs out from under Gav, doing my best not to wake him.

There's no grace as I hobble around the large room, which is empty except for those in the beds lined up on either side of mine. I peek into each of the little makeshift curtain rooms, but Jance isn't in any.

I have no idea where I am inside this rebel base, what time it is, or where the others are. It takes me almost fifteen minutes to find someone who notices me, and it takes that person another ten minutes to tell me if Jance is alive or dead.

"He's in one of the private rooms. This way," a doctor tells me.

I nearly collapse with relief. *He's alive. Thank you, Ardelle.*

While keeping pace with my slow gait as I hop after him, the doctor asks if I want a wheelchair, but I refuse. I just need to see Jance.

I'm irritatingly slow, but the doctor finally stops at a door, opening it quietly, the only light a dim table lamp.

Jance sleeps on his side facing away from me, which I find odd if he has a gaping chest wound.

"His injuries are nearly completely healed. Although I suspect he'll be rather sore for a while. Whatever Arianyte substance you injected sure did the trick. What was that, by the way?"

"I don't know what you're talking about," I say blandly. "Thanks for the help." I promptly shut the door on him.

The room is silent besides occasional beeps from the machines he's hooked up to, his breathing strong and even. I lean my back against the door, watching him sleep. Terrified those machines are going to scream and he'll code or have a seizure or a heart attack and I won't get to the door fast enough to get help and I'll lose him.

Nothing of the sort happens.

Maybe I'm just afraid . . . afraid that if I touch him, he'll dissolve just as Ardelle did. Any of them could be turned to dust in a second, and I'm powerless to prevent it.

Finally, I hop the ten feet from the door to the bed and sit on the edge, brushing my fingers through his Raven Feather hair, and I notice how healthy it feels. I immediately pull away when he moves, a cough rattling his lungs as he turns onto his back, his slanted, hazy eyes meeting mine.

I'm unprepared for what I see.

Jance is . . . *young*. He looks no older than twenty-two, if that. I gape at his face and see all the signs of his age completely smoothed away. Every line around his eyes, the stray gray hairs in his stubble, the rough texture of his skin that used to be there—are all gone. He glows with youth and health. It's him, but it isn't at the same time. Jance was always objectively handsome, especially before I knew he was my dad . . . But now, he's even more so, and it's weird.

This is how Malakyte, Selenyte, Herkimer, Zoisyte, and even Narresteé look so damn young. The Silent Breath reverts their bodies back to their prime, most healthy states. And so, it did with Jance as it healed his injuries.

"Hi," I whisper, trying to cover my slip.

He likely doesn't know what's happened or how he's alive.

He looks down at himself, then at me. Without saying a word, he shifts to his side, facing me, and scooches back to make room. I don't need him to speak to know what he's offering.

Carefully, I crawl into bed with him, burying my face in his chest, smelling his strong bergamot and coffee scent that I let myself forget. I wrap myself around him, as if he could be taken away from me at any second.

Jance holds me back just as fiercely, his arms strong and safe.

Exactly like they used to be.

I don't understand why I felt so much aversion to him when I didn't have my memories. How I could have treated him so

badly. I remember all the ways he tried to tell me something was wrong, how he was using his Ringer magic in the moments when I first woke up from a nightmare, trying to fix my fucked-up mind, and I missed it—I missed our connection. Even after carving "J" and "F" into my arm, for fuck's sake, I still couldn't piece it together! I understand why he never told me . . . especially after the first attempt to retrieve my memories failed and he was almost killed. If he had said he was my father, Malakyte would have known that I knew—it would have compromised everything. But in doing so, we lost our relationship.

And I almost lost him forever.

So much guilt riddles my heart. Guilt over how I saved him, guilt over how I couldn't save Ardelle . . . everything that happened with Malakyte . . . everything I've done. *Stars . . . look what I've done.*

I can't face it.

I might as well be back inside that stupid cube in the dark again, and I know I confronted this fear in there, and I know they love me, but I feel *so bad.*

His hand pats the back of my head, and I've forgotten how much I've missed his touch—his security. Jance fills a space inside of me I hadn't realized was a hollowed pit of darkness and pain, even before my memories were lost. His opinions of me, his approval, his love—is capable of breaking and shaping me, as father's do with their daughters. As they do with their sons, too . . . I don't miss the fact that this man fights with everything in him to ensure I grow into the best version of myself, and I wonder who I would be without his influence. Who would Malakyte be without Herkimer's?

And he's mine. Just like I'm his.

Behind these doors, when the world is asleep and everyone we know can't see, I finally let the wall I've constructed around myself shatter.

All the emotions flood out like a breaking dam, and the heavy tears are never ending, and soon, I can't stay silent as the emotions take me over.

I cry for my memories that were stolen, for everyone's suffering while they tried to swindle them back on my behalf even when I made it difficult. For Ardelle's isolation and torture and sorrow. For the girl in the cell next to him he cared for. I cry for his death, for the real love I had for him. I loved him. I still do. It doesn't matter that our romance was decimated—*I still love him.* I can't keep control. It snaps, and I wail in Jance's arms.

"It's okay, darling. It's just you and me here. Let it all out."

There's no keeping it in.

My sobbing echoes off the walls, my entire body shuttering under the collapse. I'm like the Azurite, imploding as I come crashing down to Earth. I don't know if I can physically bear this weight—this pain and guilt and fear—because the war isn't over.

Jance gives no mind to all the tears and snot drenching through his medical gown. He holds me tighter, his hands gently caressing me as I cry and cry and cry.

"I'm here," he tells me, his voice so soft it only makes me cry more because I don't deserve his gentleness. "I'm right here. We're together now. You came back to me—you saved me."

And I betrayed my principles to do it.

It becomes so much that I can't breathe. Nose stuffed, face and crystal searing hot—I'm a fucking mess.

"I love you," he says into my hair. "I love you *so much.*"

"But I'm a fucking monster," I claim. "Ardelle is fucking *dead!*"

How can anyone love someone like me?

"I don't give a fuck what he made you do up there, Kara. I'll go down to Hell if I have to, become a demon myself if I have to, just to pull you out of a dark place. It's okay. I promise *it'll be okay.* And Ardelle . . . Baby, he's still with us. His spirit is with us."

No . . . No, I can't accept that excuse. He's dead because of me.

I'm too upset, can't even respond, and after sobbing so hard for so long, a deep exhaustion sinks into my bones, pulling me down like a riptide. Sucking me into its depths again, where, in my father's arms, I feel safe enough to shut my eyes, finding the embrace of oblivion the moment they close.

CHAPTER 92

I cried myself to sleep.

Jance has fallen back asleep, too, and I slip out of his arms without waking him.

I need some air and a hit of a fucking smoke pen. It's unlikely I'll get one of those around here, but after asking an insomniac rebel or two, I'm lucky enough to find rolled nicotine in the form of a classic cigarette, so I take it.

The guy takes pity on me and gives me two.

After the day I've had, I've earned these.

Old habits and all.

With my two cigarettes and a light pen in hand, I limp out of the rebel base, guards' gazes following me as I barely make it down the steps and find a bench to sit on not far from the main door.

It's a warm night, the stars still twinkling like the world isn't about to end. Yet, without the other half of the Azurite up there glowing like I've known for all my life, the sky somehow feels . . . empty. The remaining civilian half is blacked out, and I can't even see the moon rays bouncing off its sleek remainder.

Where's Malakyte? I can feel him out there . . . his love for me curdling, becoming hate. We did love each other . . . but I can't help but wonder if he was speaking the truth about not

Reconditioning me again. I can't help but think of how our bodies were so close not so long ago, his eyes seeing me, his hands undressing me, his body taking me . . . And just like that, we're enemies. It feels like a lifetime ago. I got to touch that god I was so enamored with, got to live in his pretty illusion one last time. I was obsessed with the way he made me feel. And like a love-starved addict, I shot that shit into my veins every hour of the day. Let him dose me with his power and love, getting me high on it, leaving me dependent on it, love-bombing me into oblivion.

Soon, he was the dealer, and I was the junkie. I needed him for everything, including to confirm my own worthiness. If I could save *him*, then I could save *me*. Without him, I was nothing. Without his love, I was nothing. The moment he took his attention away, I would fall into withdrawal, becoming ever more dispirited, craving only him. He showed me these glimmers of a man worthy of me, but when I had a hold of him, he pulled back into this cruel stranger. His stonewalling, his retreat into that dark villainous mask he loves to wear—it's just another form of abuse. It's incredible how he could be two different people so seamlessly. Do I regret sleeping with him now that I remember everything he's done . . . No. Those feelings were real, like it or hate it. The only thing I regret is hurting Gavrielle.

Why the fuck do I even care about Malakyte anymore? After everything he did . . . Fuck, he destroyed Gavrielle's entire home-world. But with that one AI SSPARROW? This *Voidbringer?* That's a problem . . . but it's tomorrow's problem.

Tonight . . . Tonight, I hate him, even though his wedding ring is still on my finger.

Not wanting to give Malakyte one more moment of my energy, I look around and am grateful there's nobody out here that I have to forcibly converse with. Because I'm not in the mood. All I want to do is sit alone in my self-pity and smoke my cigarette in peace.

Tears brim my eyes as I light one, the heat of the flame warming my cheeks for a split second.

The tears fall a moment later.

I take a long, big drag, sucking the smoke into my lungs as deep as I can force it.

"Can't sleep either, huh, Kiddo?"

I roll my eyes as Deimos comes to sit next to me on the bench, forcing me over with his body. I don't face or greet him, and we sit in silence, the ash from my cigarette carried away on a summer night's breeze.

"You came back for me," I finally say, blowing out another deep drag.

I can tell by the angle of Deimos's head he's confused.

"During the race on the Sky Dais, when I barely made it over that crazy ramp and almost rolled on the way down, you said you couldn't go back up to the Azurite, but you did. You saved my life. Selenyte was going to kill me if you hadn't interfered. So, why? Why come back?"

Deimos huffs a laugh, and we both know how out of character that move was to begin with.

"Glad your memories have returned in such detail. You were a pretentious little shit the whole time, if you ask me. Even more than your normal self."

I snort. "The time on the Azurite hasn't changed you a bit, I see."

"Going to offer that other smoke, or you going to hold out on me?" He extends his hand, fingers beckoning.

Reluctantly, I relinquish my second smoke, taking another puff on mine, the cherry glowing bright against the starry night.

Deimos lights the cigarette up, puffs it, closes his eyes, and relishes the vice as much as I do. He opens his eyes. "At the time, I meant what I said up on the Sky Dais, that I couldn't return to

the Azurite. Once you fired that arrow, it was chaos, and I was able to sneak away relatively easily. If Malakyte intended to have me captured upon my descent from the platform, that all went out the window the moment you did what you did."

With another deep drag, he continues. "After I cleared the perimeter of the Mansion, I headed back to the rebel's base, expecting to link up with Trinity and the others. It wasn't until I got there and saw the place ransacked that I knew instantly something had gone wrong. Trinity, your Ringers, the other Starseed and Pretty Boy, all gone. Place looked like it had been trashed, too. To cover my ass, I checked the other bases covertly, but there was no sign of our group. I didn't dare expose myself, in case there was a rat in the ranks. Figured you were fucked at that point, and I watched the final round of the Titan Games. Once you won, I knew that would be my only opportunity to be able to stop whatever was about to happen. Since you idiots failed miserably, it was all up to me. Told you your idea was stupid. I knew they'd ship you up to the Azurite from the main loading docks, so I snuck into the flight hangars, knocked out a SSPARROW, stole his uniform, and followed you and my Ringer up to that wretched ship. I didn't want to go. I loathe that place. However, I couldn't let Malakyte win. Not after everything. Once I followed you to the throne room and saw what a mess you had created, I bided my time to reveal myself only when it was the most advantageous. Selenyte almost ripping that crystal out of your chest seemed like good timing. I still can't believe Malakyte killed her like that. It still haunts the shit out of me. You're lucky to have forgotten that night for a time."

"Nothing about what Malakyte and Narestée did to me was lucky, Deimos. But I'm sorry it still follows you around."

"More than you can know, Kiddo. That entire night fucked us all up real good."

I don't have words or the energy to reply. Remembering that moment . . . that primal, palpable terror of my memories melting away before my eyes makes me so nauseated I put out the cigarette on the gravel below my feet.

"I'm sorry about Pretty Boy. I really am."

Deimos says it with such sincerity—with no sarcasm or theatrics—and that's the worst part . . .

My eyesight blurs, and my throat tightens so much I can't respond.

Swallowing, I finally squeak out, "You were right. My plan was stupid. And if I'd just listened to you and the others, he wouldn't be dead—he wouldn't have suffered. None of this would've happened."

Deimos shakes his head. "Pretty Boy made his choice. He did it to protect his sister—to protect you—the two people he cared most about. He'd do it again, too, if given the chance. And again and again, no matter what idiotic choices you did or didn't make. I told Zariya that it was a good idea to merge with the Elendrils all those decades ago. I was adamant that we could trust Malakyte. Look where that led us. We all make mistakes. It's part of being alive."

It doesn't make me feel less shitty about it, though.

Deimos jumps up and moves to stand in front of me. I don't stop him as he snatches my face, his nails digging into my cheeks as he squeezes and looks me dead in my dark, fractured soul. "You listen to me Kiddo and listen good." His voice is sharp, brows knitted together in anger, the lit cigarette still sitting between the fingers in his other hand. "The moment you fall apart and let his death and your guilt destroy you, that's when his sacrifice amounts to nothing. He did it so you could go on and end this madness. So his sister could live a life of happiness and peace. If you lose your shit now, not only does Ardelle's sacrifice get pissed away, but ours does, too. Including Jance and Gavrielle's. Everyone. We stayed up there for you. Now, stop crying and get your head back in the game. Your memories have returned. The time for sitting back is over. Now, we *end this*."

I can't even hide the ugliness from my face, the tears that stream onto Deimos's fingers like a river cascading over rock. Even my chin quivers in his hand, for I'm nothing but a weak little girl, and he sees all of it. There's no hiding the truth from him. He's laid me bare.

"You are not acting like The Killer of Worlds that I know."

That fucking name.

"Don't call me that."

Deimos growls. "If you don't embrace who you are and bring that fire back into your heart, we're all going to die here, and you're going to be his puppet a second time, and I guarantee no matter how hard you beg him this time, none of your memories or your father or any of Gavrielle will remain. He will wipe you clean and remove anyone who could wake you back up again. Destroy the entire planet if necessary. Those AI monsters they created aren't meant as a sweet wedding gift. They're meant to obliterate this world. We already know Herkimer plans to destroy it, so this planet is a lost cause to Malakyte now. There's only one thing left here he wants, and wouldn't you guess what that is?"

Me. Malakyte only wants me. And he's going to destroy this world and all the people in it to get what he covets.

Deimos is right. About all of it.

He releases my face, but I can still feel his fingers lingering there like a phantom reminder that he sees me breaking—sees us losing this war because I'm breaking.

Sitting again, he takes a drag. "I think you did the right thing with your Ringer and the Silent Breath. Don't feel guilty about it. It's done. Those kids were already dead and gone."

I'm no better than Malakyte and his sick, cursed family.

"If you would've let him die there, knowing you could've saved his life . . ." He sighs, smoke pluming from his lips. "I know it would've broken you, and the world, these people you love so much, they need you. We need you."

I chuckle softly. "So unlike you, Deimos. I guess you have changed a bit, after all."

He rolls his eyes. "All of you sappy fucks have ruined my entire villain era. I'm pissed about it."

When I snort, I snatch the remaining half of his cigarette and puff on it. Deimos gives me a look that says, *I should end you.*

"Guess that makes you one of the good guys now," I say with a slight grin, trying to find a way out of this darkness.

He shrugs, shaking his head as if he hates the fact already. "Stars, help me."

CHAPTER 93

"She's waking up," a voice whispers.

My eyes sting as they open, and for a second, I still think I'm on the Azurite. But it isn't the quartz lights that blind me and not a cold body holding me as I lay in bed.

Then I remember everything, and the weight crashes down on me with the force of a missile to the face.

After talking with Deimos, he carried me back to Jance's room, the sweet asshole, and is now standing in the corner of the room which is currently cramped full. I lie in bed with Jance, who lies beside me with one arm around my shoulders, the other propping up his head.

All of Team Starseed and Trinity turn to me, but someone else is here too, and for the first time in what feels like months, my heart soars.

"Sadie!"

The once-street dog looks healthy, vibrant, and the husky-mix shakes as she bounces toward me, her miss-matched colored eyes sparkling, tail wagging, and nose wet. She smothers me in frantic kisses between whines of excitement, paws tapping eagerly at the bedside. I sit up on my elbows, barely noticing the ache in my knee as I pet her. She's okay. Thank the stars, she's okay.

Pulling my gaze away from Sadie, I look at each one of my loved ones' faces. The moment with Sadie is tender, but there's a ghost in this room. Gavrielle looks fresh and pristine—lucky Sky-Fae, but his eyes are haunted and hollow. Pacey's face is puffy, and I know she's been crying a lot. Sylo's eyes are dead, and Ahren resembles a ghost. Saris keeps watching Jance like he's going to die. Trinity looks ten years older, and Deimos can't even find the energy to look pissed off like usual, so, yeah, we've all been through Hell.

My eyes water again as I glance away, the silence in the room a choking reminder that our team is forever altered. Ardelle's absence is unbearable.

This should never have happened like this. He never should have died.

I take a deep breath, my voice shaky when I say, "I love you all so much. I know you went through Hell to get me back, and I—" My throat tightens, but I push through it. "I'll do everything I can to make it worth what you sacrificed for me. I'll stop Malakyte and Herkimer. They're not going to get away with this. In case anyone is worried." I take the ring on my finger and chuck it, the sound clanking on the tile. Gavrielle picks it up, looking at it like it's an interesting insect whose head he wants to rip off. "That's a nonissue. I choose each of you. I choose *you*, Gavrielle. Malakyte won't ever change. I understand that now."

"You still hold the Arianyte crown," Deimos says, like that makes what we all went through worth it or something.

I shake my head. "Herkimer pretty much undid all that when he was having his fun with me. I'm not sure with the fall of the Azurite it's been certified, but he'll likely undo Malakyte's coronation. So, I'm pretty sure that whole bit was for nothing." I turn to Trinity, Sadie bouncing between her and me. "Has Arianyte put out any sort of statement?"

She shakes her head, her brown-and-black braids now laced with Hot Pink hair. "Dead silent. The Azurite is still burning, too, but we've got control of it. We're questioning surviving SSPARROWs, all extras. Terran SSPARROW forces are dropping like flies, which is good for us. Those . . . dragons or whatever you flew down on, they're sorta loitering outside the base. We're not sure what to do with them. A rebel almost got fried to a crisp when we got too close."

Her voice is stunned and apprehensive. I still haven't forgotten her betrayal, which needs to be discussed before I can ever trust her again.

"Leave them alone for now. They're connected to all this stuff." I gesture to my star mark and sigh heavily, the sound defeated.

Pacey finally says something, her head angled down in defeat like a stray dog left out in the rain. "This is all my fault."

I furrow my brows. "Pacey, you're the last person who's responsible for this."

"No." She shakes her head, tears cascading. "You don't get it. When they had me up on the Azurite for all those months, they pushed and pushed for information on you, Kara. They wanted to know what would hurt you the most. They were trying to find a way inside and Recondition you so it would stick. It's how her magic works."

That's right . . . I remember how they faked that message where they abandoned me before the third game, so I'd be as wounded as possible for when we ultimately confronted Malakyte after the Titan Games. There was no time to consider how they knew to crawl through that particular wound inside of me, but my ears perk up as I listen.

Pacey continues, her red, anguished face finally turning my way. "And after so much time went by, I just . . . I just gave in, and I told them. I allowed this to happen."

She covers her face with her hands, cries booming through the room. Sylo pulls her into a hug, the girl falling to pieces. "If I hadn't done that, none of this would have happened, and he'd still be alive!"

I peer up at the ceiling, head shaking.

The light instantly burns my eyes. All the lights in this place are too fucking bright! Everything is shit, and everything hurts, and I'm so fucking lost.

Jance squeezes me tighter, and if he wasn't holding me, I think I'd completely fall to pieces.

"Pacey . . ." I say, clearing my throat when I finally pull up the nerve to look at her again. "They would have found a way if you had given them the ammunition or not. Ardelle would have sacrificed himself for you a million times over again." My eyes flicker to Deimos, parroting his words. "He isn't gone. He's right here with us. We know our souls live on. We know we're never truly apart."

She only cries harder. I can't blame her, can't be mad at her, not after what I've done. Plus, it's already happened.

Gav clears his throat. "I feel a lot of that weight, too, Pacey. I do. He . . . He killed my people with that weapon they created."

He can scarcely get the words out.

My chest cracks for Gavrielle, and I reach my hands out for him as I lay on my side in the bed; an elbow propping me up.

He comes over quickly, dropping to his knees, and I pull him as close as I can.

So much happened between Malakyte's horrific, cruel confession. Gav had no time to process any of it. He had to survive—had to get us off that ship alive—but he can't hold the pain inside any longer, and he breaks down, too. Quietly weeping with his head nestled in my chest, stripped down to that little boy I saw when he was sleeping. His people—his kingdom—wiped away. Just like that.

And planet Earth is next.

 560

CHAPTER 94

YEAR 6, DAY 2,204: FUCK, FATHER. FIRST, SHE'S A REBEL. FOUND THAT OUT IN NO TIME WHILE SEARCHING HER LOFT, BUT I'VE GOT A BIGGER PROBLEM . . . AND I CAN'T TELL THE PRINCE. I FOUND MULTIPLE DRAWINGS THIS KARA GIRL HAD DRAWN, AND THEY'RE OF ME. OF THE MARK ON MY HAND. HOW? WHY? THESE DRAWINGS TELL A STORY, ONE I NEED ANSWERS TO. ONLY ONE PERSON CAN CONCEIVABLY TELL IT TO ME IN ITS ENTIRETY: THE STAR.

GAVRIELLE ABRAXAS

"One bed," I say as I carry Kara into the room Trinity said we had to share due to space constraints. I clear my throat, an incredibly inappropriate joke coming to mind.

"At least it's a queen, but I suppose your balls will be blue for as long as we stay here," she says as I lay her feet to the concrete floor, assuring she doesn't lose her balance limping past the threshold.

She doesn't know what I did with her knee yet—but wait, did she just say she's going to give me blue balls? Kara couldn't be more perfect for me.

"Adore that you disguise all your pain with jokes and sarcasm, love, but is that a threat or a promise?"

Kara glances over her shoulder, a dark, perfectly arched brow lifting in challenge. Fuck, that little smirk, that fucking *mouth*, her gaze raking over my body like she wants to climb me like a tree. Then she hobbles into the bathroom without saying a word.

Fucking hell, she's already giving me blue balls.

Trying to forget about *that*, I shut the door. The room isn't much to look at, but it's an upgrade from where me and the other Starseeds and Ringers have been living on the Azurite. Beside the bed is a table and two chairs, which are likely to collapse the moment I set my full weight on those sticks they call legs. A dresser that only reminds me how we both need new clothes and no window, which we could both use.

Her voice echoes out from the bathroom. "Looks like there's only a toilet in here, so I need to head to the showers."

"I need one, too. I'll come with you."

A sexy little sound—suspicious as all hell—comes out of that mouth of hers as she exits the bathroom.

My hands fly up in a nonthreatening manner. "I'm sure there's more than one stall," I say, winking in hopes I can fluster her into a smile.

If we don't lighten this heaviness, we'll be crushed beneath it.

Those teal eyes take me in from booted feet all the way up to pointed ears, her plump bottom lip folding in as her teeth nibble down. The tension blows in like a summer's storm, lighting up her beautiful irises for the first time since we got her memories back. An ember of longing there pulls at my heart, the mating bond between us solidifying since she chose me. Like a switch of a light, her decision fuels this connection that was one-sided from the moment I regained my memories. I can practically feel what she's thinking . . . longing, lust, guilt, hatred, all of it hitting her—hitting me—wave after wave. Yet, underneath it all, I sense her love for me. Her need, her desire, her hope. She hasn't given up, and if she hasn't, then neither have I.

We find the showers, and I'm grateful they're empty, my ears not even detecting the dripping of water. There's a divided entrance for men and women, and we stand at the threshold awkwardly.

"My knee still hurts," she says, looking at my wrap job. "I may need your help."

I smirk. "Always here to oblige, my queen."

She throws me an expression that says, *Call me that again, and I'll cut your blue balls right off*, and my laugh echoes off the gray-tiled walls as we walk together into the woman's side.

I ensure to lock the door behind us.

Much like the rest of this place, it isn't much to look at, just some faded tiled walls and several stalls with questionably moldy curtains. But the farthest stall has a little bench built in, three water heads, and is triple the size of the others, so we choose that one.

"As hot as you can stand it," she says as I turn the water on after sitting her on the bench.

The streams hit her shins as she sits, steam beginning to fill up the stall.

Her heart is beating so fast. I must be making her nervous.

"You know, we're two people standing in a shower stall fully clothed," she deadpans.

It is a bit silly, I'll admit.

With streams of water slapping my back, I kneel before my mate.

It's so natural for me to bring my hands around her hurt knee, knowing I don't need to worry about the bandages getting wet.

"I need to confess something. A few things, actually."

"Yeah?" she says, voice soft.

I inhale, ripping my secrets off like a Band-Aid. "I used the remainder of the Silent Breath to save your knee. And I know that wasn't my call, that you never would have agreed, but you were right. You weren't ever going to walk again, let alone fight. We need you now more than ever for what's coming next. I didn't have a choice."

Her devastation is crushing, but more than anything, she just looks tired. "Gavrielle . . . we could have used it to help Ceplar. Trinity said the Tribute serum was making her so violent they had to sedate her."

"Ceplar isn't who's going to win this war for us," I argue. "You're more important, and more kids will die if you can't even walk into battle. She's in quarantine. The doctors are taking care of her."

Her sigh is heavy against the tiles, but she nods, acceptance washing over her face. "It did feel suspiciously better. I suspected you did it."

I massage her knee, and she moans as I knead the muscles and tendons. "You're my mate." I spill it out like a fucking coward, too afraid to even look at her.

"Mate?"

"I knew that night Naresteé came to the orphanage. My race, we . . . bond to certain people—for life. The mating bond is an unbreakable tether to another person. It's why I will also put you above my own life, my own needs and wants. It's biological and not something I can simply ignore. It's why I flipped when I found out about what you and Malakyte had done, I . . . I lost it. My instincts drove me insane because he took you for himself . . . You were his. And you were also Ardelle's. Yet, before anyone, Kara . . . you were mine. You had always been mine. I was just so young that I didn't realize what was happening. When my memories were stolen, I completely forgot. Now my life belongs to you. My swords and my heart and my soul are yours, Karalevine. They always have been. And I'd choose you a thousand times, in lifetime after lifetime, because you're my mate, and you've always been my mate, love. I know we're in a shit storm, and this is heavy and probably strange, but I can't keep this from you anymore." I look back up, tears welling in her eyes. "I love you."

Her mouth parts as she takes my words in, my pulse threading the needle of confident and crazy. I've never felt so vulnerable than now. She held me when I cried earlier, and I'm carving my heart from my chest and placing it directly in her hands where she could crush it. She could still love Malakyte. She could still love Ardelle and need to grieve and look at me, shoving this into her lap like a total asshole.

Without saying anything, she slides to the edge of the seat and wraps her arms and legs around me, pulling me in close. "I love you, too," she whispers in my ear, her words sending a jolt of relief through my nervous system. "I'm honored to be your mate, Gavrielle." Kara kisses my cheek.

I separate us, needing to see her face—her eyes. My emotions drop once more like they had earlier, ripping away my self-control. I can let my tears fall for her—and only her.

"I've turned into such a crybaby," I say as she wipes away my single tear.

"Me too."

I press my forehead against hers, sharing the same breath as the woman I love.

"I'm sorry about what I did with Malakyte," she says. "I just . . . felt it was the right choice at the time. But I'm so sorry that it hurt you."

"It's okay."

Her words are sad when she says, "I'm not sure it is, Gav. I don't deserve . . . *this.*"

I take her hands in mine. "We *both* deserve this. You don't think I felt the same way after my memories returned, and

I realized all the shit he made me do was Earth-shatteringly terrible? Like how he required me to hunt you down? Making me a deal to save my own people in exchange for bringing you to him? You don't think that I also hate myself for giving into his manipulation and turning me into a killer? If anyone knows how that man can get inside your head and twist you around until you're a completely different person, it's me. That's what is so insidious about Malakyte. The mask he wears is so convincing that you don't even realize he has you caged. *I understand.*"

"So, you're really okay with the fact that I slept with him, even though I ultimately wanted to be with you afterwards? Even I can see that makes me one giant fucked-up jerk."

I sigh, my head dropping as water droplets trickle off my nose and brow, my eyes trained on her delicate painted toenails. "I want to claw my stars damned eyes out at the imagery, but since my eyes are my best feature, I won't do that."

Kara snorts, but it's a delicate dance between amusement and bitterness.

"I wasn't okay with it," I say, still not looking up. "In actuality, I was pretty much resigned to the fact that I wasn't getting over it."

No need to look up to see the guilt in her eyes—I feel it flooding our bond. "But when you leaped off that escape pod, I knew that you loved me."

When I gaze up at her, the emotion on her face is a mix of awe and devastation.

"I'm never leaving you behind, again, Gavrielle. *Ever.*"

"I know. And that's a strike for your hero side, but more importantly, it's a strike for us. Risking your life was all the proof I needed to know that you meant what you said—that you chose me. That you love me, not him. If I get to have *you*, hold your heart, be the one who gets your love at the end of the day, then I can accept your choices if you made them willingly." I swallow, throat tightening as she watches me like I'm a ghost.

"We've never had time," I continue, "and I can't live another day, another hour, another *fucking minute* without loving you. Time has always been the one thing stolen from us, in one way or another, and I'm done waiting to love you. You're my mate. *You're. My. Mate.* In my culture, that puts you above everyone and everything. I know you may not understand it, but it's there, stronger than ever, glittering in your beautiful teal tapestry right on the edge of my consciousness."

Kara's eyes are wide and mesmerized. My hand rests on her chest, over her star. She wraps her small hand over mine, her grip strong. Exactly like she is. "I feel you, Gav. Through all the years we were separated, *I felt you.* Fuck, I was *lost* when I believed you were dead."

"Another strike for your good side," I say, leaning in even closer. "See, look at you, wracking the hero points like a total girl boss—or, wait, boss queen? That sounds weird. Shit, did I just fuck up a cute moment?"

Now I get a genuine laugh.

"There's that smile that I love so much."

My hand moves to cup her chin, and I toss all the love I feel for her through that bond, praying she can feel me, yearning for her to experience what I do—that I fucking *love her.* Good, bad, ugly—I love her.

Bewilderment shines in her glassy eyes, glimmering like a question she doesn't know how to ask.

"Those emotions, the lightning between us, it's me—it's *us.*" I hold her face, certain of it.

She shakes her head in disbelief. "How? How can I feel that mating bond when I'm not even the same species as you?"

"The crystals, maybe," I muse. "Even though I'm a Ringer, we're still connected. Like the dragons speak and the weapons whisper, we're all entangled in this web of cosmic magic. That's special."

Nodding, she sighs, but there's a lightness to her I haven't felt since I used to watch her from afar as Malakyte's spy—every. Single. Day.

We needed this conversation.

Her stare dips to my lips, then back to my eyes, that lightning striking, turning us to cinders.

"What are you doing looking at me like that?" I ask, my voice deepening as I watch her do it again. "Surely, you're not trying to give me blue balls?"

"One hundred percent trying to give you blue balls," she jokes, trying to brush off her grief and sorrow as best she can, but at least she's trying. We both are.

"Well, it's working," I confess.

Her head dips, and my hands fall away, our lips gravitating to only a feather's width apart.

"Prove it," she says, her top lip grazing mine with a touch so light it tickles.

I told her I was done waiting to love her, and I meant it with every fiber of my soul.

I slam my lips into hers, our collision cataclysmic.

Her lips are soft and full, and I take her deeply, pouring this love into her so she knows that, without a doubt, I'm the better choice.

She opens for me as I slide my tongue into her mouth, crashing together perfectly, as if we've ever kissed only each other. Her kiss is everything as all my senses dissolve to a single point in time and space. Her. Yes, I'm hard as a rock, but it isn't even about that. It's *her*. She is the gravity that's always held me to this planet. She's what gives me strength and keeps me fighting. Kara is who kept me sane when I was a lost prince orphaned on a foreign land. I had only her in this world, literally. She was my axis then, and she is *everything* now.

Kara's hands crawl into my wet hair, pulling the strands as I smile against her mouth.

 568

More, she tells me with her body. *More*, with every arch of her back, grinding into me. *More*, with each sexy little moan. *More*.

Fuck, I've dreamed of this.

I want her. My cock throbs for her, the yearning in my heart is a relentless drumming that beats only for her. My hands can't get close enough. These wet clothes of ours are too much of a barrier between us.

Whatever she wants, I'll give her. My body is hers as well as my heart and my entire soul if she asks for it. Strip me to my bones. Wreck me until I'm nameless. Use me until I have nothing left—that is what I'll sacrifice. But despite how much I want her right here, right now, finally able to claim her as my mate in the way my instincts demand, it may not be the best thing for her.

I break our kiss, her heady gaze looking at me with an aching desire I crave to satiate.

"We should stop."

Her disappointment crushes me.

I want nothing more than to do what she's asking. "You've been through a lot in the last few days." I'm serious as I try not to think of how blue my balls will be because of *honor and all that*. "I'd be taking advantage of you if we were to take this further. It's not the right time, love."

She looks devastated. "I need you."

"You need a distraction."

She laughs bitterly, her sigh giving way to defeat. "Well, don't you have me pegged? And not in the fun way . . ."

I shrug, smiling. "Trust me, it isn't that I don't want to. I just think when the time is right for me to fuck you, Kara, that you're not in a bad place. When I ruin all men for you, I want you mentally there for *all of it*."

She's giving me that look again . . . a look that tells me she wants us skin to skin, our flesh the only thing separating us. And I want that, too—my body *aches for it*—but not like this.

But there's more happening between us right now than she may even realize.

I stare back into her eyes, going deeper than these bodies of flesh ever could. Kara lets me in, in a way she hasn't up till this moment. The bond shudders as I'm allowed inside, and I can't help but reach to hold her face in my hands. Every part of her is behind those eyes, even with the sexual tension clawing at both of us, she's right here.

With me.

I see that girl I knew so long ago, see the fight within her and her playfulness and her strength. My friend . . . I see my friend.

Warmth floods my blood knowing she'd give me this level of access to her. She isn't merely offering me her body, but a much more guarded place no one else has seen before, and that means more.

Malakyte never reached this place. I know it with every part of my soul. That's enough for me to let go of my anger for what she did with him. He may have gotten her body, but I get her heart and soul, and that's far more valuable to me.

"Let me just take care of you right now," I whisper, "not by getting you off but by letting your body relax enough to know that you're safe. Because you are, love. You're safe now."

Kara curls herself around me as close as she can get, arms and legs melting in with mine, the water a constant patter against us both.

We sit like this for almost an hour, and there's no place I'd rather be.

CHAPTER 95

KARALEVINE RUZZ

We get an entire day to rest our bodies and minds, but that's all we're given.

I slept most of that day in the room with Gavrielle after we showered, and I feel good about where he and I are. I love him. More than assured in my choice, but Malakyte's ghost still lingers. In my heart, in my thoughts, and in the tattooed bracelet around my wrist I can't simply chuck off.

Jance and the others slept, too, and by the time we're all summoned to the war plan meeting, Jance and I are nearly completely healed, but none of us are used to his young appearance. I won't let the sacrifice of those children be in vain. I have to get my head back in the game. The time for licking our wounds is over.

We also get more info about our location. The base is about ten to twenty miles outside Zarmenia, with several entrances, all manned by armed rebels on the ground and roof. It also has a strategic advantage of being right on the Zarmenia River, which is good for us if Arianyte is going to mount an attack. Its main structure is concrete—in a Going Gray color—but it's colossal, giving the rebels access to living quarters, a kitchen and hall, training areas—including a shooting range—and garage and armory. It's clearly a military base from the old-world.

Dannanōk wants in on the team meeting, so the rebels erect a table and chairs for us near the river's edge, with Dannanōk's long head looming over us like some imperial snake lord.

I confirmed my suspicions about the dragon's black scales shimmering with different colors. Each Elendril crystal not only has a weapon but a celestial, ancient dragon, too. Except Malakyte, who killed his dragon to prove a point, according to them. The other dragons are Vex, a powerful male with a temper for days and shimmering red scales, Novara, the blue—Annara's mother and Dannanōk's mate—Solara, the orange, and Feena, the green.

Only Dannanōk is at the meeting as we begin.

Trinity stands at one head of the table, with me sitting on the other, the Reptilians, rebels, and Team Starseed between us.

Trinity clears her throat awkwardly. "Let's start with introductions since we'll all be allies in this war." With sharp eyes, she looks at me with an unspoken apology. She motions to her right, where her mother, Martha, sits. Martha looks similar to when I first saw her in the throne room. She's in her fifties, has cool-toned Umber skin, gray streaking through her black hair like bolts of lightning in a night's sky, but her cheeks have filled out and her eyes are sharp as she looks at me with guilt-ridden eyes. After quickly introducing her mom, Trinity then switches to a middle-aged, tawny-skinned man with long locs decorated with little jewelry and a cowboy hat in the shade Khaki. "Everyone, this is Hank. He was Pop's right-hand for a long time. Now he's mine. Hank, these are the people I told you about, with the magic."

"I like me some good, ass-kickin' magic. Welcome back to the ground," he says with a little twang before turning to me specifically and dipping his head, hand tapping his hat. "Kara."

I nod.

Finally sitting, Trinity points to Hank's right. "Shante, Terryn, you know everyone. Oh, except Gavrielle over there. He's Sky-Fae."

Shante's bald head turns toward Gav, her skull tribal tattoos as impressive as they were when we tried to fly up to the Azurite and rescue Pacey for the first time. Terryn has a long beard now, but his man-bun is still greasy.

I introduce all of Team Starseed one by one, Dannanōk chuffing when I forget to include him, his hot whoosh of air blowing everyone's hair back.

The Reptilian leader, Wey, is so mesmerized by Dannanōk he stands and bows, his scaly body shimmering Forest Leaves in the sunlight.

Trinity fills us in on how the Resistance and Earth have changed since my disappearance.

"Most of the rebels worldwide have come to Zarmenia to join with us before the Zone checkpoints were officially closed, but bigger Zones are mounting their own defenses, too. The final stand for Earth is going to happen here, in Zarmenia. Our numbers are strong. We have over twenty thousand members, Terran and extra alike, stationed around Zarmenia alone. I can't even count the number worldwide. You were that catalyst, Kara. The people rebelled once you disappeared. It was because of your sacrifice that we're in this position now."

My stomach tightens. Her betrayal led to *our* sacrifice.

"Where the Resistance is thriving, the civilian situation has completely collapsed," she says. "We have power on this base because it's got a protected generator, but the main grid is down, the Network is down, food has been off the shelves for weeks, no medical care. There's looting and assaults. Arianyte surveillance is suffocating. Drones, SSPARROWs, and cameras. A lot of Terran soldiers have defected, but not all, and Arianyte has been supplementing Terrans with alien soldiers. Which brings me to how our situation has gone from bad to worse."

Sylo butts in. "How can it get worse?"

"Our telescopes have spotted dozens of ships arriving in space. They're farther out in orbit than the remainder of the Azurite and the Vivianite, but we see them. More arrive every hour."

Gavrielle speaks up. "Those are reinforcements and battleships. Their crafts can also maneuver in space or in an oxygen-rich airspace. Are they big or small?"

Shante answers, and I remember all of a sudden that she's a pilot. "Both. Some are massive, not as big as the two motherships, but still large. I'd say half are medium, possibly two to four pilots needed. The other half are single or dual pilot crafts."

Gav doesn't miss a beat. "Those are battle fleets. They're preparing for war. They know Earth has weak aerial defenses, so it's a good weakness to exploit. I'd also expect thousands of extraterrestrial SSPARROW reinforcements to accompany them, as well."

The table collectively tinges green around the edges.

Trinity turns in her seat, Dannanōk standing stoic behind her as she looks vertically and says, "War is here. We need aerial support. The dragons could be the solution to that if you and your clan are open to fighting with us. I'd like you and a few of your best dragons to take up riders."

Dannanōk's Sunbound eyes slit, shimmering with a bit of fury. "I told her already," Dannanōk points to me with his nose. "We are no pony ride service."

Trinity chuckles, but that sound stops cold when Dannanōk bares his teeth at her.

"Dannanōk," I say, "let me ride. I've already been on your back anyway. My powers would be invaluable in the air. And maybe two more of us?"

If a dragon could look pissed, that would be Dannanōk. "One other," he counters, "and the dragon I choose must agree.

I also forbid Annara from flying. She is far too young for war. And only another Starseed."

"Agreed," I say, not waiting for Trinity to counter.

Deimos shoots up from his seat. "I'm the other rider," he proclaims. "I piloted back in the day, I can arrange our formations as well as use my magic to intercept any bigger creatures they're going to throw at us, like I did on the Sky Dais."

"You'd be better off on the ground," Gavrielle argues, but Deimos insists he flies with me.

Trinity says, "I'll get saddles created for you two right away. You should begin flying lessons, like, yesterday."

Fuck, am I really going to do this?

Dannanōk says into my mind, *"You're the Killer of Worlds, you can do anything."*

"Unlike you to be so kind."

"Do we know if that cunt bastard is alive or dead?" Deimos blurts, taking his seat again.

I snicker. "Which one."

Trinity stares down at her papers. "My whisper network is a lot quieter now, but in the last twenty-four hours, I've confirmed Malakyte was in bad shape, real bad, but he's alive and up walking around. The other one . . . radio silence on him. He hasn't been discovered. We've tried to search for bodies, but the Azurite is still burning."

"Probably incinerated in that explosion," Hank laughs.

"He's alive," I say. "I'd bet my life on it."

"Well," Trinity sighs, shuffling papers, "that's what my whisper network has reported. Let's assume he is alive. Did he get Ardelle's crystal? After what you described to us of his death, we need to know if he's got the power to manipulate gravity or not."

I hadn't considered that . . .

I'm about to speak before Dannanōk swivels his head over the table. "If the emperor acquired the crystal, he'd have to insert it. Vex has reported no new link since his Starseed transitioned. We always know when our Starseeds breathe for the first time and the last."

I guess that's a bit of good news . . . Ardelle's crystal doesn't belong to that evil son of a bitch. It stayed with his soul just like ours did when we died in our last lives.

"Herkimer's magical arsenal could be infinite," I say. "He's expressed how he specifically steals magic, so prepare for anything. I'll make a detailed list of the magic I've seen."

Trinity agrees. "One last topic of discussion. What the fuck destroyed your world, Gavrielle? We've been getting intel on a weapon being developed. That's why we breached the Azurite— in addition to the rescue mission. Do we know if the weapon was on the Azurite by chance?"

Gavrielle goes so pale. "I don't know how they did it, but Malakyte mentioned something called the Voidbringer."

"Herkimer said that name, too," I say. "That's got to be the AI that's controlling all those freaky new SSPARROWs. Remember they said something about that during the coronation?"

"What freaky new SSPARROWs?" Trinity asks, and we debrief her on the horrors that happened during the coronation. "So, this AI—aka the Voidbringer—is the program controlling these fully synthetic soldiers?"

We nod, and her face looks exactly like Geonni's used to as she thinks through something complex, biting her cuticles. "It's in Arianyte Tower."

"How do you know?" I ask.

"Because there's been wild activity over there since you were taken, so secretive I couldn't ever figure out why there was so much activity when the prince wasn't even there. And now, it's like a fortress. If Malakyte is on Earth and not on the Vivianite, that would make sense. They're protecting him, but what if they're protecting something else important, too? If their weapon is some planet-ending AI that initiates a program

 576

to those soldiers, wouldn't it make sense to store it on Earth rather than on the spaceships?"

"Remote code execution," Pacey says, voice dull. "That's what the AI is doing. But you're right. The AI wouldn't be able to connect from space to those robots. Arianyte satellites are still up, and I hacked those weeks ago. With the satellites in combination with some cyber-attacks I can likely pinpoint if something like that exists and its location, but I'll need equipment."

"I can get you that," Trinity confirms, then sighs heavily, looking at her mom. "Well, I think we're done, unless anyone else has anything to add?"

We're silent, and without a word, Dannanōk bolts into a run a breath later. His footsteps tremble the table before his massive wings beat, filling the air with mighty whooshes, the dragon taking off over the river in a graceful arc. He's magnificent . . . and he's *my dragon*.

I take a deep breath, and Gav is watching me with a grin that's the utter depiction of mischievousness.

"Flying lessons, huh?" he says, placing a hand on my upper thigh under the table, squeezing just enough to ensure he gets my attention.

Like I could ever fail to notice where this man touches me or that my skin flushes each time he does or that the thought of him inside me makes every nerve want to explode.

Until then, it's time for dragon-flying lessons.

CHAPTER 96

THE DEVOURING ACCORDS ARE HEREBY DISSOLVED. THE ARIANYTE EMPIRE WILL NO LONGER AID EARTH AS OUTLINED IN THE AGREEMENT, INCLUDING BUT NOT LIMITED TO SUPPORT THROUGHOUT THE AURORA SYSTEM OR ITS PLANETARY AND MOON BASES. ALL TERRANS REMAINING ON THESE BASES MUST FACILITATE THEIR OWN TRANSFER BACK TO PLANET EARTH. ALL OTHER ARIANYTE SERVICES ARE HEREBY PERMANENTLY DISMANTLED.

On our third night back on Earth, with the sky dark and stars bright, we say our official goodbyes to Ardelle.

Hundreds of rebels line up on two sides of a grassy aisle in the field adjacent to the base, a massive unlit pyre at one end, me and Team Starseed at the other. Every rebel holds a single candle, Terrans, Reptilians, other extras, and all six dragons have all gathered to honor Ardelle's life and sacrifice.

We wait for Trinity to give the signal as she stands by the logs thirty feet down from us.

There's no body to burn, of course, but Pacey wears his Elendril bow and arrows tied to her back, crossing over her scythe. We're all dressed in black, our Elendril weapons equipped in honor of our fellow warrior.

My lover.

My friend.

My teammate.

Trinity waves, and Pacey takes a deep breath, straightening her spine and steeling her face into a beautiful, stoic mask.

"You got this, babe," Sylo says, kissing the side of her head. "I love you."

With me on her other side, I take her free hand, an unlit torch in her other. She looks straight ahead, face drawn in a mask of fury and agony, from her tight jaw to her steeply furrowed brow.

Using her Elendril magic, Pacey lights all seven of our unlit torches, the fire bursting to life, illuminating the darkness around us like a halo of the angel we're about to say goodbye to.

With another deep breath, she takes her first step down the aisle, the torch burning like a beacon.

Ahren goes next, the man more of a wreck than I've ever seen him. Not sleeping, not eating, consumed with helping the other doctors and his patients. His Ringer symbol fading away from his hand, the link between the two completely severed. Like a tattoo poorly inked, the symbol is crumbling.

Gone.

I'm next. Pacey is just reaching the pyre.

I wait, giving her all the time she needs to say goodbye to the big brother who loved her so fiercely he died protecting her. She lifts the torch and spears it into the wood.

Then I force myself to walk, my knee virtually painless, but I'd take that physical ache over the pain that rolls through my chest in wave after wave with each step closer. Sadness and grief and anger are a raging inferno, mirroring the glowing embers before me.

I always thought because Zariya and Erodis—Ardelle's past life self—loved each other that it meant Ardelle and I were destined to be together, but what if we were destined to be constantly ripped apart? The profound tragedy of this leaves me deeply hollow.

The pyre is a massive, hot, bright beacon, and it isn't the heat burning my eyes that causes them to water. I almost reach my free hand into the flames because, between the flickering embers and the darkness behind them, I swear I see his handsome face. The life we had flashes between licking flames and sparks that reach for the glittering, star-filled sky. I see the way we laughed and the way we danced together before the Titan Games. Like a movie, I watch the tender way he loved me when I was so angry and afraid and broken, our love drawing us both that much closer to our real home. The tears fall and fall and fall, and I don't wipe them away, biting back the primal urge to scream till my throat is as raw as my heart, I do the only thing I know how to do.

They will die for this. I promise Ardelle. With everything in me, I vow they will die for this. And if Herkimer isn't dead, he will be the one I kill with my bare hands.

It almost feels like he's right here, wiping my tears away. Like he's standing right next to me, made of these roaring flames, smiling that beautiful smile with his natural blond hair, cut and styled and as alive as he's ever been. Our souls don't die. We know we don't simply disappear. I can feel him right here. His memory, our time together . . . He isn't gone.

He isn't gone.

I'll look after Pacey, I declare. *She will live through this. With my life, she'll live. I love you, Ardelle. I feel you, and I know you're watching over us. I know I will see you again someday. I will love you again. Fire an arrow for me when we win this thing.*

I angle my torch down, sticking it deep between the logs.

After watching it merge with the flames, I take the open seat in the front row next to Ahren, Pacey on his other side closest to the aisle.

 580

Sylo goes next, mourning his best friend in painful silence. After him, Saris walks, her expression stoic like always. Jance goes after her, moving like a man in his prime. Gavrielle follows, and I sense he's saying goodbye to his own people. Deimos is last, saluting the pyre before adding the final torch.

As Deimos takes his place in the front row with us, all the people stand, raising their candles.

To everyone's astonished gasps, Vex, Ardelle's dragon, approaches from the other side of the pyre. He isn't as big as Dannanōk, and in the dark, he nearly blends in as the moonlight shines off his massive wings and scales, the red sheen invisible. The glow that emits within his throat is the shade Heat Wave, and then he roars. Fire blasts from his mouth and onto Ardelle's funeral pyre, the dragonfire so intense the tears nearly evaporate from my cheeks.

The pyre burns like the sun, and I turn to look at the faces of all my loved ones who sacrificed so much to get us here. The blaze burns in their eyes, reflected in each of the glassy surfaces. Our collective love and fury is a presence all its own as we each clasp hands, lifting them into the sky at once in a silent vow. We won't let this stand. We won't give up. We won't forget.

He isn't gone.

CHAPTER 97

"**Y**our father is dead, Your Highness," my new lead SSPARROW says, flown in from nearly seven solar systems away.

He's in armor, but every day, I ask him to show me his face. I've forgotten what he looks like.

Naresteé and my lead SSPARROW discuss our current situation, and I must focus now that days have passed, and my body has healed, but doing so feels exorbitant.

The Council of Exstacé wants my throne after this royal fuck-up, the rebels are preparing their defenses. Terran SSPARROWs have fled, and the Azurite and all I held dear is gone, so I can't remain in bed.

Within Arianyte tower, I've been recuperating from the most painful death I've experienced since Zariya killed me on that moon. Suffering fourth- and, in some places, fifth-degree burns required full-body regeneration. That's rare. It's also exhausting and excruciating, especially when I can't even be medicated until my veins and skin grow back. I would have likely succumbed permanently had I not crawled out just in time for Naresteé to find me and drag my charred body out of the Azurite through an escape pod.

"I felt everyone's crystals going crazy, and I knew something went down," she told me when my eyes first opened again, but I was blind for the initial twelve hours as they regenerated.

I had no idea if Karalevine survived for the first several days. We did, however, find her and the other Starseeds and Ringers alive in Zarmenia.

Father, apparently, had not. But he's even more immune to death than myself. However, it's been nearly four days, so if he hasn't found his way here or back onto the Vivianite, then perhaps he did perish after all these centuries. Certainly, his declining health would make for a thorny escape—my ship is still in flames.

Selenyte's stark-white strands are harsh against the black bedsheets, curtains, and furniture of my bedroom as I stand, brushing my hair in front of a floor-length mirror. The hair is new and long like it was before it melted off, but this mirror . . .

"Father being dead would be such a lucky break for you, big brother. Having lost the crown and all. With him dead then . . . I suppose you get to keep it."

Indeed.

"At least that scar she gave you is gone now," she adds.

I meet my own eyes in the mirror.

It is gone . . . and so is *she*. Yet one piece of me remains broken, burned, and driven to insanity. Not from the Tribute serum I injected into myself—no, dying cured me of that blunder.

Karalevine didn't choose me.

She doesn't love me . . .

Two, four, six, eight, ten, twelve, fourteen, sixteen, eighteen, twenty, twenty-two.

She remembers what I've done, which is unfavorable. It's also puzzling, considering I shattered her memory crystal.

I'll admit my reaction to that was . . . well, I suppose I am just like Father, after all.

If she can't see the changes I made *for her*, then I revoke my pledge to be decent for her benefit. If Karalevine wants me to be her villain so desperately, I will give her everything she desires.

The sun shines bright and hot the next morning in Zarmenia as my SSPARROWs and I surround one of the many buildings we're purging. The others are being done all over Zarmenia and in all other zones across the globe. Soon, they'll all be mine.

"You can't take my boy!" a father screams, clutching his young son to his chest as my soldiers attempt to pull the boy away. "The Devouring Accords say explicitly that you can't take the children!"

I speak over the other parents as we drag them and their children out of their homes. "The Devouring Accords are null and void when Terrans took up arms against Arianyte."

The shouting of parents and children becomes chaotic.

Perfect.

Even more, we've turned the grid back on for this occasion, and the news reporters are scurrying over here right on time. Once the world gets wind of what I'm doing, it'll be the final push toward destruction.

Karalevine wants to choose Gavrielle of all fucking people? She'll regret the choice.

A woman screams as she's shoved through the building's front entrance. "You're not allowed to kidnap children! They're just little kids! You monster!"

I am a monster.

Because of Karalevine.

"I control this empire now." I lay claim to their dissent, every shout of theirs becoming my anthem of war. The crown upon my head is, indeed, heavy—although I bear the weight the same as I do my broken heart. The crown is one from Father's personal collection on the Vivianite. Thankfully, once we realized the room with my cherished possessions was compromised, I allowed Narestëe access to grab the most important items. But with the fall of my ship, most of my assets were lost. "The people of Earth have been warned time and again that I will no longer entertain dissent or rebellion. You have squandered all my patience, disrespected my mercy, and now, you will pay for your disobedience with what you value most. I saved this planet, and I can destroy it. That being said, I'm not wasteful."

The protests only intensify as my off-world SSPARROWs forcibly remove child after child from their parents, the cameras catch it all. I'm sure any remaining Terran soldiers will defect after this, but that's anticipated. I no longer need them.

I have something better.

Father's parting gift to me.

The tension snaps with the clap of a disruptor shot, not from a SSPARROW but from a civilian. The dad protecting his son still refuses to let him go. He will, eventually. Fathers always fail their sons.

The three AI soldiers stand obediently by my side, but with a nod, they move forward. They know exactly what they're supposed to do, and they do it without question or mercy.

There's no stopping them as they interject themselves into the situation. One rips the child away, disappearing him into the crowd and onto the transport-hover with the rest. He doesn't need to witness what happens next, but the world, they certainly do.

The consequences for pushing me.

The other two AI SSPARROW chest compartments shoot open with a zip, the nanobot technology viciously swarming the man as he instantly becomes a pool of blood on the concrete.

That's when the true screaming begins.

This is what you wanted, Karalevine. You'll watch as I truly break your heart this time.

CHAPTER 98

KARALEVINE RUZZ

By our fifth day on Earth, Malakyte finally makes his move, and I'm not prepared for it.

After a couple days of flying on the back of a dragon and retraining my crystal, I'm sore as hell, but that's nothing compared to the utter terror that floods my veins when I realize what Malakyte has done.

"You're not going to try and rescue them," Jance says bluntly as all of Team Starseed and Trinity's rebel inner circle stands inside the war room within the base itself. "It doesn't matter that he says he'll release them in exchange for you, you know damn well he will go back on his word the moment you're in his control again."

Not even Gavrielle's soothing touch against both shoulders as he massages them quells the nausea in my gut.

What Malakyte has done is over all the news feeds, which he turned back on for this twisted show, only to tell the Earth that, in exchange for me, he'll return the children. Not only that but that *his queen* has been kidnapped by the rebels, which is "an act of war against Arianyte."

That fucking jerk.

Pacey sits at the large table in the center of the room, littered with maps and devices. At her laptop, she types away, barely even blinking.

Trinity stands before the television, turning from it to me. "Girl, your dad is right. You can't go. I'll put out a rebel memo right away claiming you were forced to do this stuff. It'll be fine."

Deimos laughs. "The footage Malakyte played of their wedding doesn't make her look like a victim. And the footage of her, Gavrielle, and me fighting you, Trinity—the rebel leader—looks even worse. He's trying to turn the rebellion against her."

Deimos is right.

Calculated bastard.

Deimos continues by saying, "What I can't get past is how you bombed the undersewers, and you hid it from us until he ratted you out. Bad move, Kiddo. I get why you did it, that you felt you didn't have a choice, but the rebellion lost thousands because of that choice and they're not going to forgive you for it."

Trinity groans. Likely remembering how I was forced to confess my sins after Malakyte shared with the world what he forced me to do. The disappointment in Jance's eyes when I explained everything was enough to drown me in shame. My mother's grave . . .

I glance down at the tattooed bracelet, wishing I could rip it out of my skin.

"I'm sorry," I say for the hundredth time; it'll never be enough. "He knew this would hurt me the most, that's why he's doing this."

The room is cramped, and the muted news plays clips of Arianyte kidnapping Earth's children as footage from our wedding plays side by side. I didn't even know it was being recorded. The footage of me fighting the rebels on the Azurite is there, too. It looks *bad.*

"This is a message. He's punishing me."

Gavrielle's voice booms from behind me. "I agree with Jance. He won't keep his word and release them even if you arrive at Arianyte Tower by midnight tonight like he's demanding."

"And then we'll be right back at square one all over again," Jance adds, his voice the same even though his face is so different.

"I'm not going to go, okay?" I say, eyes rolling. "But we have to do something. We can't just let him take them and suck them dry for the Silent Breath."

They're right. I've learned my lesson with that one.

"Nobody is suggesting we do nothing." Trinity says, dark circles under her eyes.

Pacey gasps, shooting back from the laptop she's been glued to for a few days. Her eyes snap up to mine. "I've been using Arianyte satellites, figuring this AI would be emitting a crap-ton of heat, and I was right. Arianyte tower is lit up like the damn moon, bursting with thermal and infrared. I also just exploited the backdoor I found by using the encrypted satellite uplinks from the AI to the satellites, planted a virus into a system remotely connected to the Voidbringer, and retrieved the GPS metadata. You were right Trinity, it's in Arianyte Tower."

"Can you shut it down?" I ask, hopeful we can end this here and now.

A blaring sound comes from the laptop, drawing Pacey's attention back to the screen. Her face instantly sours, and so does my stomach. She grunts, pushing the laptop away. "It already booted me out! I was in for like five seconds. I've never seen anything like this AI. Shit . . ." She bites the tip of her thumb, glaring at the screen as if she were eye to eye with this Voidbringer. "But no, Kara, even if it didn't just kick me out of the tiny step I took inside of it, I wouldn't be able to do anything from here. I'd have to physically be there to deploy a full-scale shutdown."

A panicked knock comes at the door, and it quickly opens. The rebel's face is stricken with a cold sweat. "The emperor's right-hand horned bitch is here!"

Naresteé!

We all rush out the main doors of the western side, the late afternoon sun casting Naresteé's horns in Bloody Mahogony. She stands thirty feet in front of the steps, hands up in a defensive posture as the guards on the roof have their disruptor rifles trained right on her.

I stand at the top of the stairs, the others close behind, but Gav, Pacey, and Trinity push their way forward to stand at my side.

I yell up at the rebels on the roof, "If her eyes glow yellow, shoot her!"

Gav's head snaps my way. "Kara, please . . ."

"I'm not going to Recondition anyone, Kara, you can relax."

"How'd you know we were here?" I call back, not trusting her word for shit.

She shakes her head like it's obvious or something. "You really think he wouldn't find you in the rebel's not-so-secret base? The dragons caught on our drones were a bit of a clue, you idiots."

"Then, why are you here?" Pacey asks before I can reply with a snarky remark, voice far too kind for my liking, her eyes wide with conflicting emotions. I think this is the first time they've seen each other since the throne room.

Gavrielle is eying her lovingly, too. Yet I understand that internal divergence . . . profoundly.

Naresteé lowers her arms, and we all flinch backward. Fuck, we're way too jumpy. "Come back with me, Kara. Please. If you don't, the people we love are going to die."

I can feel everyone's eyes peel off Naresteé and stick to me like Velcro. "How about get fucked?"

Her mocking laughter really pisses me off.

"He didn't send me, if that's what you're thinking. I'm trying to save the people I love. That's it. Would it be so terrible for you to come back? To live in luxury and have everything you could ever want? You were happy—he made it so you were happy."

"It was a fucking lie!"

"A lie you relished living in," she argues, and I go to contest it, but I can't. She's right. "Come back, tell him you made a mistake, and we can convince him to let the kids go, leave this planet, and be done. Herkimer is gone. He didn't survive the crash. He was too ill. Malakyte isn't leashed to his psychotic rules anymore. We can leave."

He's dead?

"Why would I do that or believe a single word you say?"

She doesn't skip a beat. "Because if you don't everyone will die. Everyone. You, Gavrielle, your father—every living creature from Terrans to the tiniest microbe will be annihilated. Just like it was on planet Nyktos."

Gavrielle stiffens, and I take his hand, lacing our fingers.

Despite her hard exterior, Narestée's eyes soften when she looks at Gav. "I warned you this wouldn't end well for you, Gavrielle. Let her go. Don't allow two worlds to be destroyed because you're being selfish."

Is the Voidbringer truly capable of what she's saying? If it is . . . it doesn't matter what we do or if Herkimer is truly dead or not because Malakyte will decimate the entire fucking globe. His father may have abused him, and I hate that for him, but he's not this way because of Herkimer entirely but because that's who he is. He will never be capable of changing.

The weight of everyone I love and the rebels beside us feels like a thousand pounds pushing on me.

I look over my shoulder at Jance, who's subtly shaking his head. But . . .

I'm squeezing Gavrielle's hand so tight my knuckles have gone white and then I let it go.

This stuns him, but not more than my taking one step down.

 590

Gavrielle grabs me by the waist so fast. "No!" he snarls, fangs bared at her.

"Gavrielle," Naresteé says with impatient warning, a tone she's likely used a thousand times.

"She's my mate!" he calls back.

Naresteé's eyes widen in surprise but recover quickly. "So, you'll let the world burn for her?"

"I already have."

The realization hits me so hard that if he weren't holding me up, my knees would give way. Gavrielle didn't lose his planet and his people by some default revenge on Malakyte's end. They died because he chose me over them.

And he'll do it again.

There's nothing more romantically tragic than that . . . Gavrielle's love for me truly, unequivocally real.

Naresteé looks utterly disappointed.

"I don't want you both to die," she admits, talking about Gavrielle and Pacey as she steps closer.

This time, we do not balk.

Pacey clears her throat. "What does the Voidbringer do?"

When Naresteé's gaze lands on Pace, her face completely changes. She loves her. "Where's your brother?"

Pacey's lips curl back. "Herkimer murdered him, just like you all wanted!"

"Pacey, I'm so sorr—"

"Don't!" She breathes in deeply through her nose. "Don't even pretend that you care. What does the Voidbringer do?"

The wind blows Naresteé's hair, her heavy sigh as powerful as the breeze. "The Voidbringer commands the soldiers according to her program but also her discretion. They're a hive mind. The nanobots inside them are miniature piranhas. They shred anything in their path and can also act independently of the host soldier. Two weapons."

"Three weapons," Pacey whispers, so only we can hear.

"Through the mainframe, the Voidbringer sends a signal to all of the soldiers placed globally at specific points, deploying the nanobot technology like a net, planet wide. The shredding that they'll undergo will span thousands of miles in all directions per soldier, and there are tens of thousands of them. Herkimer has been working on this weapon for a long time. He almost had it completed when Zariya destroyed it all those decades ago. It's taken him this long to remake it. And you can't stop this. Pacey, you can't hack it—it's too sophisticated. We already know you tried. It alerted us and told us your location when you got into the satellites two days ago. The AI is more intelligent than any living creature, they created a monster. If you're on the planet after four tomorrow afternoon, you'll be killed."

A hush overwhelms the base, our very breath limited.

Naresteé lifts her hands again, palms forward as she backs up. "You have until midnight, Kara. He won't hurt you, fuck, I can even pretend to Recondition you if it'll just make you come back. Do whatever you want to Malakyte once we leave—kill him for all I care, just . . . come back so they don't have to die."

Then she bolts so fast it's unbelievable.

"Try to catch her but avoid eye contact!" Trinity yells.

Rebels take off, but I doubt they'll catch her.

The others said going back would be a stupid thing to do . . . but now, I'm not so sure.

CHAPTER 99

By the time Gav and I are back in our room later, I feel so incredibly defeated. Once word spread around the base of what Malakyte was claiming about me and all the footage he leaked, the rebels have been . . . prickly.

That's putting it nicely.

Sinking onto the edge of the bed, my head low and shoulders bent forward. "I don't know if I can stop this, Gav."

"Well, you don't do what he wants, for starters," he says, unclipping the sword harness on his chest, setting them on the little table next to the two chairs. He looks so damn good when he wears his swords. "Second, well, I'm not sure, but we'll figure it out. Try not to let the rebels get to you, either. We're all on the same side. They'll come around."

"I don't think I'm their *Star* anymore," I say with a bitter laugh and mocked pizzazz.

Deimos would be proud.

Gav chuckles as he comes to sit beside me on the bed. "Symbols of rebellion are overrated anyway."

"I disagree." Gav's brows rise. That fucking smirk makes him diabolically handsome. "Symbols are everything. The Star isn't about me, not really. It's about resistance and the people as a whole and standing up against insurmountable power. The Star can't fall. If it does, the entire rebellion crumbles."

"How about," Gav says, playing with loose strands of my hair, "we let all that heavy stuff stay outside this room just for tonight. Let everything that's happened wait for us tomorrow." He presses a kiss to the back of my hand, lips warm. "Just you and me."

There's no way I can't smile back.

"I like that idea."

"I'm as clever as I am handsome."

Our fingers lace together as I chuckle. "You're as cocky as you are tall, but I think you could use an extra inch or two because I'm not sure you're tall enough."

"Says the girl who barely comes up to my shins."

"Says the girl who can bite your ankles off in no time flat, then your height will really be in trouble."

His laugh curls my toes, the sound deep and masculine, but he really gets me going when he whispers, "I love that you flip me shit, you know that?"

"I love that you can take it," I say. "But on a more serious note, I wanted to somehow express how badly I feel for what happened with Malakyte."

He shakes his head. "You don't need to."

I completely ignore him. "I'm not good with words like you are, Gav," I begin, trying to express what I don't know how to say. "Art is the closest I've ever had to expressing my authentic feelings, the most vulnerable you'll ever find me. Because that's what you do when you're an artist. It's my job to crack myself open, unstitch every single wound the world doesn't see when they look at me, and throw it on an altar for everyone to judge. And so, that's how I can show my heart to you."

I stand and walk to the dresser across from the bed and rummage through the top drawer until I find the paper I hid there yesterday.

When I sit back on the bed beside him, I hand it to him.

"I needed to break my heart open after everything . . . So, I found paper and a few pencils and started sketching. I thought I saw the world in color before you came back, but truly, I didn't know color at all. Malakyte darkened my world, but you didn't just give it color, Gav, you *are* the color. You always have been."

On the paper is a messy portrait sketch of us in profile view, our foreheads together, that specific position important to his culture and his parents. His eyes are drawn in True Violet, and the ends of my hair are colored in Tempering Turquoise, the rest in pencil.

There's such a beautiful warmth flooding from him, and I know he's shooting it down that mysterious bond between us. I feel him.

"I had a good relationship with Ardelle," I begin, clearing my throat. "Yet there was always this small wall between us, even before . . . everything. We came from different worlds, but despite that we were happy. I was happy. But things changed up there. Him and I changed. I lost him, and I found you. Even if he were alive, Gavrielle, I would have chosen you."

Gav is silent for a long time.

"Can I keep this?" he asks, bewildered, eyes misty as he holds the sketch to his chest.

I smile softly. "Of course you can. It's for you."

He sets it on the bedside table, looking at it one last time before coming back to me. "It's beautiful, love. Thank you. I needed that."

"I know."

I rest my head onto his broad shoulder, his masculine scent intoxicating, but what truly sends tingles through me is when he finger-combs my loosely curled hair. I close my eyes and lean into his touch, immediately relaxed. "Don't stop," I say softly.

"Never," he says, going in with both hands.

I nearly purr like a cat.

595 

The moment Gavrielle touches me, I'm nothing but a hot wire, his hands setting me ablaze. The eye contact, the connection, the unbridled tension, it's all there, bubbling beneath my skin. My body responds to the memory of him, so fresh and so real and *mine*. A real memory, not a fabricated one. I don't simply ache for him to touch me. I crave it—crave the closeness I've been too afraid of until him.

Does he see that I'm ready? That I love him, that I choose him? Or does he only see what I did with Malakyte?

I lift my head, going out on a limb a second time and hoping he doesn't turn me away like he did in the showers. "Kiss me, Gavrielle."

His smile in return is gorgeous.

"I thought you'd never ask."

When his warm lips brush mine, he captures my mouth with the sweetest tenderness I could cry. Our tongues glide together as if they've never touched, never spoken this beautiful, wordless song they sing together. It's sweet and affectionate, my heart galloping toward him at an unstoppable pace.

The tension is electric as we claw at each other, touching and exploring and demanding our bodies get closer. I take his hand, placing it on my inner thigh—a clear signal of where I want this to go—and he breaks our kiss.

The fear of his possible rejection spikes through my blood. I'd deserve it, after what I did . . .

Gavrielle's eyes are probing, asking, but still warm with affection that I dare hope he'll want what I want.

My eyes fall to his mouth, then back to those gorgeous eyes, and his pupils flare with desire. I come in close to kiss him but pull away at the last second, and this gets a little chuckle out of him.

He dips his head, his lips peppering my neck from my collarbone, up, up, up, till our lips are so close it's nearly torture.

"Look at me," he says, but it isn't demanding. It's an ask. When I stare into Gavrielle's eyes, I know that I'm home.

My breath hitches as his hand slips between my thighs, touching me over my pants. It's the first time he's ever touched me like this, and my crystal flares in approval—my entire body flares in approval.

There's nowhere for me to hide or escape to with Gavrielle, but I don't want to do any of those things.

I close the gap between our lips, our tongues striking hard and hot, and I moan into his mouth; Gavrielle touching me as if he's known my body for decades.

I laugh and gasp when he picks me up and carries me to the little table on the other side of the bed.

He sets me down beside it, reaching around me to grab his swords, chucks them to the recliner, then kisses me on the cheek on his way back. He stands directly in front of me, wearing the most mischievous grin.

"Could you be any taller, though?"

The joke from moments ago slaps a stupid smile on both our faces. I do come up a bit higher than his shins but barely make it to his sternum.

Gavrielle's wicked grin only grows, his pointed canines coming out to play. "I'm confident I can find the perfect height," he says, his head at my collarbone.

"For what?" I ask, with a little laugh on my lips.

"You'll see."

He takes my hands in his, pressing a kiss into my palm as his eyes nearly glow in the shade Lost Amethyst.

I know that look. Attraction. Lust. Love. Desire. A pinch of madness.

Fuck yes.

My heart flutters as Gav lets go of my hand and throws his shirt over his head. Cruel Sky-Fae beauty. It's unfair. Every muscle is defined and rippling under Ivory skin—even the burns on the left side of his chest and shoulders are beautiful. He's sculpted, a honed machine, and his entire body is as hard as a rock. Hot as hell, and my mind is still blown that he's all mine.

He kisses my collarbone, my neck, my jaw, until finally those warm lips—that beautiful, taunting mouth—finds mine again. He takes the kiss slow, lazy as his tongue traces tiny laps around mine as if he has all the time in the world to torture me into insanity. Inside me, my core smolders, Gav's hands exploring every peak and valley of my body.

Until he finds the hem of my pants, lingering too long at the button. I nod to him before he even has the chance to ask. *Yes. Yes. A thousand times, yes.* He finally undoes them, the whizz of the zipper sliding down a promise of more. *Give me more, Gav.*

He slides the black fabric of my pants along my thighs, slowly and torturously, down to my ankles.

I step out and kick them away until I stand in nothing but my underwear and top, my hands splaying across Gav's bare shoulders.

Gav lingers along the hem of my underwear, snapping the elastic playfully. His hands tease my inner thighs, then grazes a touch so featherlight over my clit that I soak the fabric instantly.

Both his hands cup my ass, and he squeezes, lifting me up onto the table. I barely find my balance when his thumbs loop into the fabric of my underwear, tearing them to nothing but ribbons in one go.

I think he really likes doing that. The glitter in his eyes says enough.

Fuck, I love it, too. Like he can't even wait the two seconds it would take to just slide them off. He *needs* me. We're on the same page.

A shuddered gasp escapes my lips as Gavrielle reaches between my thighs, finally touching me skin to skin. His eyes glaze with pleasure, especially when I arch my back, his other hand supporting me so I can lean back and open wider for him.

"Gav," I cry his name as he slides a finger into me, giving me all of it in one, perfect stroke, keeping me locked into his eyes the entire time.

The intimacy is a little scary . . . but it's with Gavrielle, and I know I'm safe.

"You're so fucking tight," he growls, kissing my lips softly, tenderly, pumping inside me as I melt under his touch.

"Yes," I say.

I don't have any other words.

He pulls out, and it's way too soon, both hands coming to hold my face. He kisses my forehead.

Then drops to his knees.

Gav scoots me to the edge of the table, and I lean back, the heels of my palms holding me upright. I stare down as he opens my legs, his eyes dilating to pins as he gazes straight between them—my heart hammering.

With a cocky little smirk, he looks up at me and says, "Perfect height."

Then he feasts.

Gav goes straight for my clit, hands gripping my thighs as his tongue laps and sucks and flicks. I crumble, my legs falling over his shoulders, and I give up one of my supporting arms as I move a hand to spear into his hair, softly at first. But the more intense it gets, the harder I pull.

He takes it. He likes it. He spurs forward, fucking me with that perfect mouth until I'm molten inside, body trembling.

Fuck, he's *everything*. His tongue is so warm, so precise—how could I have ever wanted anyone else? It doesn't matter because, the second he glides a finger inside me again, I'm incapable of coherent thought. He pumps and sucks, and I moan, loving how he seems to know my body better than I do. Exactly how I like it, Gavrielle gives it.

I'm shooting past the point of no return, terrified he's going to stop it from happening, but he doesn't. Rather, he pushes another finger inside me, and the arms supporting me buckles. I fall back onto the table, his free hand finding one of mine as he latches on, and it's this—this connection to him that finally pushes me over the edge.

My vision goes spotty, and I'm instantly dizzy as I come so hard all I can do is moan through it. The crashing, the releasing, the pressure, the bond, all of it explodes as my star lights up bright, the magic—my power—strikes across my skin sending goose bumps down in a wave of pleasure that is Earth-shatteringly perfect. But Gav isn't done—no, he keeps pumping, keeps sucking, and I'm climbing the ladder to the stars again, immediately coming a second time that's somehow more dazzling than the first, the brightness of it is unmatched.

Finally, Gav stops, but he slowly, deeply continues to pump his fingers, making me crave more.

"Gav," I sigh between heavy breaths, "I need you."

He knows what I mean.

"Not because I'm trying to escape. I don't want to numb anything anymore."

I want to feel.

I hope he sees my heart is open and ready—because it genuinely is.

Gav pulls out, picks me up, and we're on the bed within seconds.

I'm not sure how he got his pants off so fast, but he does. And I practically rip my shirt and bra off, leaving our skin clashing against one another, Gav in nothing but his tight boxers and me completely naked.

My back hits the mattress, and this time, our mouths collide. We're ravenously hungry—no—starving for each other as Gav leans over me, fingers curling around my breasts, squeezing gently as his tongue moves from my lips to my collar bone, then my sternum, replacing a hand on my breast with his mouth.

Fuck. Yes.

 600

I bite my lip as he flicks my nipple with his tongue, sucking and worshiping, teasing and exploring, and I can't get past how warm he is—how different that feels.

My hands are greedy and curious as I reach down between his legs, needing to touch and know exactly what's waiting for me there. His moan is pure lust as I grab a hold of him through his boxers, my eyes widening.

"You've just been walking around with this the entire time, Gavrielle?" I laugh.

His chuckle rings in my ear as he comes up, and his sweet voice is a beautiful bell to my heart. "Oh, that little thing?" he says mischievously. "It's nothing."

No wonder he's such a cocky ass—because his cock is huge.

Heart hammering, I move from his length to the band of his tightly fitted boxers, pulling them down, down, until he slips out completely and I'm able to feel all of him in my hands.

Stars.

"Gav," I breathe, my mouth drying a bit.

He snickers, but it comes up short, his eyes closing as I stroke the long, thick, velvet length of him. I need him. I need him inside of me.

Without warning, Gavrielle flips us so I'm on top and he's lying on his back, and I get the full view.

Holy fucking Sky-Fae.

Gavrielle is a methodically sharpened blade crafted for the ugliest of duties, but when I gaze upon muscles so sculpted and strong, abs so defined, chest and arms and thighs so powerful, I don't see a dangerous weapon. He's an undeniable warrior, a man fighting for his people, his loved ones, *me*. This is how I've always seen him. Every single part of him is perfect. I'm officially claiming Gavrielle Abraxas as the most gorgeous man to ever exist.

And he's all mine.

This angle is a lot better, too, and after I completely pull his boxers off, I lean over so I can take him just like he took me moments before.

"Kara . . ." he moans.

I give his tip a long, unhurried lick, curling my tongue around his head in a quick lap before pulling away, my other hand stroking him softly.

Gav's hands run through my hair, over my shoulders and back as I slip him into my mouth, tongue swirling, my hand increasing its tempo along the remainder of his length. I *feel him* pulsing adoration down our bond. There's nothing better.

He's quiet until I take as much of him in my mouth as I can, my tongue dancing along his shaft.

"Fuck, love," he hisses through his teeth, his fingers coming to gently stroke the underside of my jaw.

His hushed sounds are satisfying, my tongue sliding along all that length. We go like this for several minutes until I'm aching for him to be inside me, and I stop.

When our eyes meet, his gaze glows with wild desire.

I know mine are, too.

Gav sits up, motioning for me to lay at the head of the bed, my back against the pillows. I listen.

Once he settles in front of me, he draws me close as he opens my thighs so he can squeeze in between them, the head of his cock near my entrance as a teasing reminder of where it isn't.

"I need to get you ready for me if this is what you want—but only if it's what *you* want."

His eyes penetrate me deeper than his body ever could, and Gavrielle is the safest place I can be.

I nod, the easiest choice I've ever made.

Leaning over me, he caresses my face before stopping his touch at my lips. Heat sizzles through me as he dips two fingers deep into my mouth, keeping eye contact with me. His free hand strokes the side of my head approvingly like a praise.

 602

Then Gavrielle slowly draws them out, moving to the aching spot between my legs, gently filling me with one finger.

Then two.

I lean my head back into the pillows, enjoying him. "I'm ready, Gav," I breathe, aching for him so much I can hardly stand the anticipation flooding my chest. "But first, I want a different position."

As I heave myself up, Gav sits, crossing his legs, and the sheets crinkle as I come to meet him. I scoot into his lap, my knees firmly planted on the mattress, one leg on either side of him. His hands find the hollows of my waist, his touch reassuring. I take his length in my hand, guiding his tip to my entrance as my heart flutters with expectation.

Once I have him at the right angle, I let him go, his head sliding into the perfect spot.

Gav gently takes my chin, drawing my face to meet him. Our eyes lock.

I'm fully in control, forcing myself to relax, even when my heart thrashes. His Violet Rush bedroom eyes are all I see as I slide him in, little by little by little.

Gav's hands quickly move to my ass, holding me as I slowly rock, easing him inside.

Fuck, his girth is insane.

One hand moves to glide over my clit, arousing me as I slowly, so fucking slowly, take him farther.

It's tight, and it's like I'm a virgin again, but Gav is patient, and he lets me take him exactly how I need to. The urge for him to just fuck me already is making me crazy.

He kisses my neck lovingly, licking and nibbling and raking his fingers through my hair, grabbing my ass, clawing up and down my back, worshipping every inch of me.

Gavrielle's hips drive up into me gently, taking control as he moves my body to better angles, slowly gliding himself deeper.

"Gav," I say, so desperate for all of him, this teasing agonizing.

"Yes, love?"

"I need all of you."

His growl is everything. "You're almost there. You're taking me so fucking good."

He pushes in a bit deeper on the last syllable of his words, dropping me onto him.

"I love you, Kara," he tells me, pulling out, then pushing in farther, ringing a moan from my throat, the pressure so fucking good.

"I love you, too, Gavrielle."

"I know, baby," he says, a pleasurable sound escaping his lips as he slides in, the both of us moaning together.

He's still not far enough, though, not yet hitting the tightest spot where he can truly get in deep.

"Trust me?" he asks.

I smile. "Always."

"If it's too much, tell me. I'll go slow."

Nodding, I feel him lift my weight, and he kisses me as he lowers me onto him, pushing up simultaneously so he slides past that tight threshold.

I gasp.

The stretch of him, the pressure, the fucking depths he can reach.

"I've got you," he says softly, breaking our kiss as he holds me steady.

Stars, it's a lot.

Yet my entrance adjusts to Gav's thickness, and it feels so good that, when I move on him after a minute of stillness, he slides in easier, my body finally stretching to take him all the fucking way. I lower onto him, slowly but steadily.

Gavrielle.

His eyes are heady with desire, our eye contact heavy, and he hugs me as close to him as our skin can get.

"Good fucking girl," he praises.

 604

A cry escapes my lips as he pushes up—even deeper.

I rock slowly, Gavrielle's hands exploring my body as he lets me set the pace I'm comfortable with. I have to begin slow—he's too big to go crazy from the start.

He's deep enough I can drop my weight and wrap my legs around his waist, but it's how my clit rubs against his hard abs that shatters the remaining bit of my patience.

He moans as my tempo increases, moving with me, and I can't hold in my cries of pleasure as he consumes me.

Our bond glitters like the sun's reflection bouncing off a meadow's pond. I feel every bit of that connection, every piece of Gavrielle. I love him, have always loved him. I ride this beautiful man like our bodies were made for each other, his arms cradling me in a safety net I never knew was possible. He feels so good. His cock feels so fucking good. This connection feels so good.

I'm slipping toward the edge, but it's too soon—this can't end yet.

"I want you in control now, Gav," I say breathlessly, eager to feel him fuck me—make me his.

He growls in approval, lowering me to my back without ever slipping out, and finds the angle that allows him to bury himself all the way.

I fucking love it.

I fucking love him.

"Fuck me, Gavrielle."

"I'm not just going to *fuck you*, Kara," he growls, increasing his tempo. "I'm going to claim you, consume you, conquer you. Because girls like you don't get fucked by guys like me. You get ruined. Ruined until the only words you can remember are 'please' and 'Gavrielle' and '*more*.'"

My nails dig into his shoulders, meeting his thrusts, our rhythm perfect—and, *stars,* he's right.

Give me fucking more.

Gavrielle does what he promised he'd do in the shower: ruin all other men for me.

Because he doesn't just fuck me but makes love to me, and it's otherworldly. Harder, faster, deeper. *So fucking deep.* He's present and knows how to use what was given to him as he pumps into me over and over, destroying me with every beautiful drive of his hips.

Fucking stars. He's built a space for me inside of him as he buries himself inside of me.

"You're my mate," he tells me, a fact. "And the way you're taking me, *you're so fucking hot . . .*"

"I'm your mate."

This undoes him, his thrusts deeper, harder, hands gripping mine firmer.

That coil inside me couldn't be wound tighter, but, fuck, this can't end. We haven't had enough time.

I close my eyes, trying to drive off my climax.

"Kara," he pushes, hand clasping around my throat gently, thumb brushing my lip. I open my eyes again "Let go. Don't think for one second that if you shattered to pieces, here with me, I wouldn't put you back together. You're safe. *Let go, love.*"

I moan, the pressure between my legs building to a crescendo, the edge so close all I can do is cry his name again and again.

Gav goes harder, faster.

I am safe here—*with him.*

My crystal lights up, my climax a surefire conclusion as he pushes me over the edge, the stretch of him so deep inside pulling me taut and shattering me all at once. I'm in pieces from him. Destroyed and then put back together. It feels so good, so hot, and he doesn't let me turn away as he watches me come, becoming an absolute puddle.

It's so fucking hot I can hardly breathe.

He slips out of me completely, flips me to my side, comes up behind me, then slides right back in, Gavrielle's lips stifling my cry.

One of his fingers twirls around my clit as he holds my top leg up with the other, hand under the back of my knee.

By the time I'm close to coming again, he's also there, his tempo fast and quick, and I can feel the shuddering in his chest.

"I love you," he says in my ear, his rhythm heart-shattering as he pounds into me from behind, his own release seconds away.

My entire body trembles, and my Elendril crystal cracks like a whip inside my chest and along my skin, burning me up from within.

"Gavrielle!"

The pressure shoots up so fast he's going to get me to come *again*.

"I'm right here," he whispers. "Come again, Kara. You're right there."

I am, and I whimper before the crash, my star's light exploding as I lose myself completely. My breathy cries can't be contained as Gavrielle takes me all the way to the edge again. The orgasm sizzles as it mixes with my magic—raw, unadulterated power zapping out from every nerve, tiny bolts of antimatter licking my skin, and I can smell the scent of magic in the air. If I don't tamp it down now, it'll shatter everything in this room, but it doesn't hurt Gavrielle.

My orgasm is still spiking through my body as Gavrielle quietly finds his release, hardly making a sound, but his chest purrs as he spills into me. He finally slows, our bodies shuddering as our heavy breathing rings throughout the room.

Gav kisses my cheek, finally letting my top leg down, pulling me as close to him as possible, remaining inside.

My hands grip his thick forearm as it wraps around my chest, his light kisses peppering my cheek. He sees me, all of me, and loves all my broken, darkened pieces.

"If you're a monster, then I'm a monster," I say, and his approval slides down that connected highway between us.

"If you're a monster, then I'm a monster."

Gav fell asleep a while ago, the two of us lying in bed with his arms around me from behind. He's so warm, so safe, and feels so right I don't understand how I could have been torn. It's always been Gavrielle.

However, my mind can't find any peace. I can't avoid what's waiting for us outside this room. Especially as the clock barrels closer toward midnight, Malakyte's deadline pressing in on me with a choking force that nearly breaks my resolve to stay put.

The old me would have gone. The old me would have snuck out of this room while Gavrielle slept, slipped out of this base unseen, and walked right into the hands of the enemy.

But I'm doing things differently this time. I'm staying with my team—my family—and we're going to face this down as one. Whether in this lifetime or the last—if we're all going to die tomorrow—then we're taking our second descent into death *together*.

CHAPTER 100

On our sixth day on Earth, Malakyte's deadline came and went, and Naresteé wasn't lying.

The war for Earth's survival is here.

The newly arrived Arianyte ships are now in low Earth orbit, moving closer every hour. We woke up this morning to a massive encampment of SSPARROW soldiers growing in the miles of fields outside Zarmenia. Maybe fifteen, twenty miles away from the rebel base. They haven't marched, but they're gathering and growing by the hour. And then there's the Voidbringer. Arianyte Tower is reported to be heavily guarded, something Gavrielle may have a solution to and has been training for.

By the late afternoon, we each finish strapping on all our weapons and armor, finalizing the plan. Time isn't on our side, and we're moments away from utter chaos and full-scale battle.

We got lucky, at least, that a majority of Terran SSPARROW soldiers defected and joined the rebellion. We have ten thousand more troops than we initially had. Even so, with the off-world SSPARROWs collecting not so far away, and the AI SSPARROWs dispersing globally, plus Arianyte's aerial fleet, we're still vastly outnumbered.

But we have a plan, and we're going to stick to it.

Together.

"I don't like this plan," Gavrielle says, as he, myself, and Team Starseed stand outside the rebel base waiting for orders to move out.

Trinity is here, too, along with others. The three other dragons wait downriver on the base side, Dannanōk and Feena loitering closest.

Gavrielle looks at me as he ties on his shin guards, looking as fine as I've ever seen him in sleek black fighting leathers, his dual swords strapped to his back, Silver Fox hair tied in a low ponytail.

Jance is also on Gav's side regarding the plan, but everyone else agrees with me.

Running up to the group, Shante comes with some good news for once. "We managed to steal thirty fighter jets from the airfield thanks to some Terran SSPARROWs," she says, dressed in a one-piece fighter suit in the color Army.

Trinity nods her approval, instructing Shante and her team to get ready and get on the dragon squad's comms.

My squad.

A squad neither Gavrielle nor Jance is on, which is why they're pissed.

Gavrielle helps me tie on my leather arm guards, which have the letters T.S.—Team Starseed—branded into the material. The attached armor set is thick black leather. The first piece goes over my shoulders and has attached dagger sheaths under my arms that are easily assessable. But the standout piece is the metal-lined leather corset tied around my torso with a dragon silhouette front and center. All the exterior leather pieces have dragon scales etched into them, along with hidden dagger compartments everywhere. The craftmanship is unparalleled. I've also caught Gav shamelessly checking out my ass in these leather pants, too.

Jance stalks up to me, Gav, and Trinity. "Put me in one of those jets," he says to her, which earns him a glare that would kill a lesser man.

But that isn't my father.

"Jance," she sighs, turning to him. "Kara's plan is solid, and we need you on the ground squad. You've got to let her go. She's a big girl. She'll be fine up there. Both of you have your places to be, and you know this."

She looks between Jance and Gav, and gears are whirring in her eyes.

I look between the two most important people in my life, knowing I'll be fighting without them.

"I'll be fine," I tell them for the hundredth time in the last few hours. "I'll have Deimos, the dragons, and the fighter jets with me. Plus, Gav, I don't trust anyone else with Pacey other than you. You're one of the strongest fighters we have, and getting her up to the top of Arianyte Tower alive is the most important part. If we fail there, and we're unable to stop the Voidbringer from hammering its lights-out final decree, then we're all dead anyway. And I know you'll lay down your life to protect her."

"Then, come with us," he argues, finishing tying my arm guards with a final tug at the strings.

I shake my head. "I can't, Gav." My voice is soft but still firm. "To keep him away from you, I've got to draw Malakyte away. Once he senses my crystal, he'll follow the pull. Plus, he and I have unfinished business to settle."

Trinity points up to the sky. "Their aerial army is huge, you guys. Kara's magic is the only thing that's going to put a dent in that. I don't want anything bad to happen to her, either. That's my girl." She slaps a hand on my shoulder, her braids tied back, Geonni's sunglasses sitting atop her head. Her eyes water, and mine widen. "I love her, always have. She's going to kill it up there. Pops would be proud."

The backs of my eyes sting.

"He'd be proud of us both," I agree. "And so pissed he's missing this, too."

She laughs.

"No double crossing us this time?"

"Thanks for ruining such a sweet moment, bitch," she chuckles again, the love between us unbreakable.

"Say your goodbyes," Trinity says, sliding back into leader mode, and I'm proud of her for what an amazing job she's done—what an amazing job we've both done. "We're saddling up in twenty. You've got this, girl. Give that cold-blooded bastard hell."

My smile and nod are my final reply to her as she turns, barking orders to the leaders of the remaining squads.

Dragon squad is me, Deimos, the dragons, and Shante's fighter jets.

Ground squad is Jance, Ahren, Saris, the Terran SSPARROWs, the Reptilian and rebel armies, hitting Arianyte's extraterrestrial SSPARROW forces, which are the most heavily armed.

Lastly is Tower squad, comprising of Gavrielle, Pacey, Sylo, and a small group of rebels and Reptilians as backup. Their sole goal is to get Pacey up to Arianyte tower so she can hack into the Voidbringer and stop the eradication of this planet.

If she even can.

Her chances are . . . slim.

According to Pace, the heat of the Voidbringer is still rising, and she projects that, within a few hours, it'll trigger its program, deploying the nanobots and taking every living thing out with it.

Gav, Jance, and I walk up to where Pacey, Sylo, Saris, Ahren, and Deimos are standing nearby, most finished readying their gear and armor.

"At least we look badass," Pacey says, her giant scythe strapped to her back. "I just . . . really wish he was here."

Her large eyes glisten with tears, the gorgeous Sapphire shade seeming to glow with emotion, matching the beautiful color of Ardelle's eyes.

She holds his bow and arrows, looking down at them as if they could be the answer to all her grief.

"Ardelle is with us," I tell her—tell them all. "I feel him in every moment. He's going to be watching over all of us. I believe that with my entire heart."

Pacey sniffles as she nods, wiping her nose with her sleeve, looking at Sylo as he stands beside her. He brings her in close, kissing her temple, their love bouncing between their eyes as they glance at each other.

"Here," Pacey says, handing me Ardelle's bow and arrows. My eyes widen, refusing to take them. "You'll have better use with these where you're heading than me. I'm not a very good shot, anyway. I know he taught you how to use them back when we were in the undersewers. Take them. He'd want you to have them if it meant protecting yourself."

I hesitate, not wanting to take something from her, but she insists, and so I have Gavrielle strap the quiver to my back, so they crisscross with my sword. We'll secure the bow to Dannanōk's saddle once it's time to go.

Jance opens his arms, sliding one along my shoulders, grabbing Saris on his other side. We mirror him, Gavrielle on my left as we interlace our arms and bodies to each other, making a circle, our heads bowed towards the center.

Toward each other.

"I have to say something," I blurt out, my throat tightening. "My entire life, all I've wanted was a family, a place where I belonged. I've been let down so many times that I never thought I'd find a home like that, and I had accepted it. I thought it was with the rebels, but they couldn't relate to the creature living inside me, not like you could. I didn't know what family meant until I found you guys. I was so afraid of losing you that I acted stupidly and recklessly and selfishly . . . I'm so sorry for that."

Pacey interjects. "Kara, you don't have to—"

"No, please, let me do this."

She nods.

"I haven't had the chance to tell each of you how much it meant to me that you not only stayed up on that ship but that you went through Hell to get me and my memories back. You didn't have to do that . . . I never would've known. You easily could've left me there, and you didn't. And I love you all for that."

Gav leans over and kisses the side of my head, my eyes closing as I lean into him.

"You guys mean more to me than you'll ever know. You're my family, and I'll do anything to make sure you're safe and to keep Ardelle's memory alive. We're not going to repeat the past. In this lifetime, we're not running from Malakyte—we're facing him head on, and we're going to win. Remember what we're fighting for. For each other, for Ardelle, for our family. For all those innocent children, for every Terran who once saw their freedom as some twisted patriotism but now sees the truth: Arianyte serves only themselves. We're the mirror, and we hold ourselves up to the people of this world, saying, 'Look. These are monsters. They don't care about you. They don't want to make your lives better. They simply want to enrich themselves while you're bled dry to keep them going.' Together, we can save this world—this galaxy—from this self-serving, corrupt, tyrannical machine that calls itself our leaders. It's been the honor of my life to do this with you all by my side, and I wouldn't have the guts to do it with anyone else. So, let's go out there and kick some alien ass. You with me?"

They each chuckle through teary eyes.

"You sure know how to give one hell of a rallying speech, Kiddo," Deimos says, eyes alight with the fire of a thousand suns. "Let's go get this motherfucker."

CHAPTER 101

Gav and Jance walk me to Dannanōk after I hug and wish the others goodbye and good luck, Deimos making his way to Feena twenty feet down the riverbank.

We stop near Dannanōk's leg, a pregnant silence falling between us.

"I'll get this bow tied to your saddle," Gav says, voice awkwardly stiff.

Jance picks up my long braid and moves it around Ardelle's arrows, so it sits better. There's so much happening behind those emotional Espresso eyes. The maturity and wisdom and love in them didn't change.

"You come back to me, you understand?" he says, gloved hands palming my cheeks.

"I will," I promise. "And you, too. I can't handle thinking I'm going to lose you again."

"I know, darling. I'll be safe. If you can't kill him, get out of there. Switch to my comms line, and we'll get off the planet somehow. We'll figure it out." Jance pulls me into his arms, hugging me tightly. "I love you, baby."

I hold on to him as hard as I can. "I love you, too."

"Malakyte is going to try and twist reality," he warns. "He's going to attempt to get in your head and make you believe his version of events. It's nothing but gaslighting. He doesn't define you, no matter what he had you believing or doing on that ship. That wasn't you."

"But what if it was, Jance?" I whisper, the truth so grueling to say aloud.

Jance squeezes me tighter. "I'll never accept that. I was there, Kara. I saw you pushing back against him, even if you slipped at times. You are mine, and I know your heart. I have complete faith that you'll make the right choices."

I close my eyes, my cheek against his chest. *I'm his. I can be worthy of his love.*

Sighing heavily, he releases me, kisses my forehead one last time, and heads off. "You protect my daughter with your life," he shouts back to Dannanōk.

The dragon chuffs as if he hasn't been eavesdropping.

When I turn to Gavrielle, he's leaning against Dannanōk's front leg, watching me with a cocky, mischievous grin, ankles crossed casually like we aren't about to rush into a war. If I didn't love him already, he'd make me fall head over heels from how good he looks.

It's honestly criminal.

The other dragons are taking flight, people, fighter jets, and hover-convoys flee the base, shouting that the Arianyte army has initiated its march.

Deimos is in my ear on comms, bitching at me to hurry up, but through all the chaos, there's only Gavrielle and me.

"Gav?"

"Yes, love?"

I smile as best I can when he calls me that. "Come kiss me like it's the last chance you'll ever get."

His teeth gleam—canines and all—pushing off the dragon, closing the space between us in a flash, grabbing hold of my face and slamming his lips onto mine.

Gavrielle kisses me exactly as I asked him to, hot and deep and lighting within me a fire that'll never cease to burn. Our tongues dance, as if knowing this truly could be the very last moment we get to hold each other, taste each other, be with each other. Our hands claw and demand ownership, memorizing every small detail our fingers can touch, my body surging with internal heat as this one kiss turns me on and lights that fire between my thighs.

The hard pressure growing beneath his fighting leathers says the same is true for him.

When we finally break the kiss, our foreheads touch, and we share each other's breath, stealing time between fearful heartbeats as the fate of the entire world rests on our shoulders.

"Come with me," he begs one last time, and I hear the desperation in his voice.

I almost cave . . .

"I love you so much, Gavrielle," I tell him, and I mean it with my entire, fucked-up heart. "And I'll see you when this is finally finished. We'll finally get that time together, okay?"

He looks into my eyes, piercing them straight to my core. "I've loved you long before I even knew what love was, Kara. I loved you when I didn't even remember who you were, yet my heart still knew, still remembered my love for you. Nothing can break that bond. You're my mate, and I'll lay my life down for you. Again and again, lifetime after lifetime, for eternity if I must. I'll find you, love. I'll always find you, and *I'm always with you.*"

I let Gavrielle feel how much his words mean to me, strengthening the bond between us and allowing all of him in as he does the same.

"One more thing," he says, voice rushed, but he straightens and turns to Dannanōk. "Your dragon has something important to tell you before going into this."

My brows knit in confusion as I look between them.

Dannanōk's Golden Regal eyes focus from me to Gavrielle, assessing us with the weight of a creature not of this world. "Zariya's sin, Killer of Worlds." My chest tightens. "Her sins are your shackles. If you wish to break free, you must heal the wound she inflicted upon your soul."

My eyes snap to Gavrielle for help—then back to the dragon. "I don't know what the fuck that even means. Speak in English."

Dannanōk looks away.

My mouth hangs open, Gav's expression sympathetic when I say to the dragon, "And I'm guessing you're still not going to tell us the crystal's secret, are you?"

A hot plume of steam shoots from his nostrils, and I'm glad he's turned away.

"I think it's about what she did," Gav says, checking my many daggers are secure in my armor. "I think you have to forgive her so you can forgive yourself, in a way. That, maybe, it all starts and ends with her, and for you to find your way out of the darkness, it's through her. I believe in your goodness, Kara. Just because he pushed you toward the dark doesn't mean you have no light."

Eves dropping Sky-Fae. But that's Gavrielle . . . He knows me better than I know myself.

"And you're telling me this now?" I say.

Deimos shouts from Feena's back.

"I'm ridiculously hot, love. I never said I was punctual."

I snort, climbing to my tiptoes as I wrap my arms around his neck. "I love you, and I'll be fighting for our future. I'll always reach for the light because that's where you are."

CHAPTER 102

Feena's wingbeats are powerful as she lifts us into the air, right over the Zarmenia River and into the skies, her scales glinting green from the sun's rays. I've flown fighter jets for years, so it's nothing new, but takeoff always adds a few hairs to my chest.

Turning in the saddle, I check to see if Kiddo makes it into the air alright. They're right behind us as we gain altitude, then glide into formation. I can't keep an eye on her like this for long. Soon, it'll become too hectic, and we'll be separated.

"Sounds like you care a lot about her," Feena says in my mind, her voice old and calm.

I snarl. "Stay out of my head!" I shout aloud, even though the wind whistles so loudly in my ears I can barely hear my own voice.

Kiddo is right there. She's fine. *She's fine*. Not sure how long that shit will last—damn kid has a knack for getting into stupid situations I've got to get her out of.

"If your Killer of Worlds can't mend the wound Zariya fashioned, allowing all that darkness to slip in, then all of you will lose this war."

I sigh, Dannanōk passing as he takes the lead. "I know."

I know.

CHAPTER 103

KARALEVINE RUZZ

Dannanōk shifts under me, feeling like a massive malleable tank as his muscles ripple beneath his dark, iridescent scales, gaining altitude fast as we cross the Zarmenia River, leaving the rebel base behind us and heading West, toward the outskirts of the city where the blots of dark shadows loom in the air.

Waiting.

Watching.

"Star, this is Shante, AKA Flying Fungi. You have my fleet. Ready to assume formation?"

"The fucking what?" Deimos asks.

I shake my head, my braid whipping in the wind. "Let's get into formation. The ships are straight ahead. Our goal is to keep Arianyte's aerial fleet from damaging Zarmenia and ground squad."

"Copy."

Shante's three dozen pilots fly seamlessly in with the five dragons, hanging back just slightly as we fly straight for the Arianyte warships.

They're close now, and I can make out more and more of their dark shapes as we continue to fly toward them.

Dannanōk's head scans the horizon, moving like a serpent, wings out long as he glides smoothly in the sticky, summer air. His spikey tail sways in and out of my peripheral as I sit strapped tight to the saddle.

Zarmenia looms to our left, the dark shapes of the buildings standing with bated breath.

I slide my goggles over my eyes, readying.

A guttural horn blasts into the tense air between Arianyte and us, and I look down to see where it's coming from. Malakyte's army marches East toward the rebels in the sprawling fields outside Zarmenia. Their hoard crawls with movement, Arianyte's side a mechanical military with towering alien tech that moves autonomously alongside SSPARROW soldiers in the tens of thousands.

With the majority of the AI SSPARROWs moving to coordinate the kill strike—according to Pacey—the ground army is mostly living beings inside those suits, but I'm sure AIs are there. Best believe every soldier is outfitted with high-powered disruptor rifles, grenades, and blades. Hover-cannons head straight for the much under-technologically equipped rebel army as they come into view from further out, marching towards Arianyte's army.

They're not defenseless, though. No, the rebel base had a massive stockpile of reserve weapons left over from the old-world, including rifles of all kinds, tanks, bombs, grenades, blades, javelins, and more shit I couldn't even name—not to mention all Geonni's engineered weapons he had been working on for decades, anticipating this moment. He's down there with Trinity and the others in spirit, and they've got this. Pacey even gave them a little EMP bomb that I know will be invaluable later.

Dannanōk's growl brings my attention back to the skies, where my blood runs cold. I have to strain my neck to look around his massive body, but I see exactly what we're going up against.

The Arianyte aerial horde is a sea of ships, the sun glinting off their black hauls, bouncing the light back into my eyes. They shine in the shade Blackout. Their warships are sleek as they hover motionless in midair, way too close to the city's outer blocks. Some are bigger—roughly the size of the dragons— and many are smaller, exactly as Shante described. A few giant ones pepper their outer and most inner ranks, their formation tight and precise.

"Deimos . . ." I say, my voice is a trembling mess.

"I see them," he says. He and Feena glide alongside us.

My head turns to him, our eyes locking across the skies.

"How many would you say?" I ask, hoping my quick count isn't accurate. I peer back toward the ships as they loom ever closer.

"I'd say enough to thoroughly kick our ass. A hundred, perhaps more. We're going to be busy."

"Great pep talk."

He laughs in my ear. "I'm not the warm and fuzzy type, Kiddo."

"The likelihood of our survival is slim, at best," Dannanōk says in my head.

Great, I feel so much better now.

Heart hammering, I say into comms, "I don't think we're going to be far enough out to avoid the city. We need to lead them farther away into the fields but not too far so that we hit the ground troops."

"Heard," Shante says.

"Did you get that Dannanōk?" I yell down.

He turns his head to glare at me. *"I can read your thoughts and do not require a play-by-play."*

I roll my eyes, but he doesn't appreciate that very much, and it so isn't the time, but I say back to him, *"What did you say to Gavrielle?"*

"You're right. It isn't the time, look."

Within the Arianyte formation, balls of lights pop up directly on both ends of the smaller ships in the shade Sizzling Cobalt.

"Oh, shit!"

Their crafts fire.

CHAPTER 104

"There's too many of them!"

A fearful knot forms in my stomach as Arianyte fire rains on us. Our forces want to scatter like rats to avoid getting hit as sizzling blue embers fly at our heads.

"Not for the dragons!" Dannanōk claims, pride fueling him as he dodges a missile with graceful speed.

My reaction? Not graceful. I'm going to barf.

"Stay in formation!" I call through comms, all of us dodging the first wave of firepower. "They're testing our resolve. This is an epic game of chicken, and we don't fucking flinch!"

The smallest Arianyte fighter jets are sleek and triangular, with sharp edges and long, aerodynamic cutouts in the wings. The cockpit, a shimmering oval-shaped canopy of dark glass, sits on top.

Our fleet seemed to dodge that first wave unharmed. Good. We got this, and even better, we slowly bob ourselves back into our formation like nothing happened.

I force a deep breath into my lungs.

A single beam of light in the shade Demon Red flashes through the sky, directly toward us—coming from one of the bigger vessels.

"Now!" I yell, and our three main sections sprawl away from each other as planned.

Shante left, Deimos right, and me in the middle.

The most dangerous spot.

The Arianyte ships charge forward, ours doing the same. The skies between our two sides closing fast as my heart races faster, faster, *faster!*

My crystal licks at the chance to escape—not yet—I soothe it. *Not yet.*

Dannanōk banks vertically, flying higher, and my stomach shoots straight to my ass, nothing else for me to do but hold on for dear life, squeezing my eyes shut as his powerful wings shred through the air like he commands the very skies themselves.

My eyes open when I hear animalistic roars and engines zipping through the air.

Several Arianyte jets are climbing with us—we're now in the fray.

Novara—Pacey's dragon—follows beside us, scales and metal barreling higher into the skies until she breathes massive flames straight through the Arianyte jet on our tail. The blaze is so hot the heat licks my back.

It's cinders in seconds.

Solara, Sylo's dragon, rips down three jets at once with a brilliant Ice Blue flame, then whips another into pieces with its massive, spiky tale. It happens right in front of me, the sun flashing a twinkle of Metallic Orange off his scales and into my eyes before flying away.

The remaining dragons around us roar, soaring into their formations as easily as breathing.

"Burn them all!"

Dannanōk's war cry bursts through my mind, but the dragons collectively roar in agreement. After being confined for so long, they're eager—no, thirsty—for flight and vengeance and death.

I know that feeling well, and I push Dannanōk forward with a squeeze of my thighs—still climbing.

Go!

He does.

The little ships aren't what Dannanōk and I are up here for—we want the bigger fish.

We hit a higher altitude and from there, the largest warships stick out like sore thumbs in the Crystalline skies, most of the chaotic skirmish happening below us.

Four times the size of the Arianyte fighter jets, these crafts look like three-pronged beasts. The matte-black metal is jagged and spiky, with wings that curve forward into points sharp enough to skewer any of the dragons. Tear their wings, crack their bones, rip through their bodies.

"Watch the fronts of those big ones, Dannanōk," I warn.

He growls, *"I have eyes!"*

"You ready?"

"Are you ready?" he asks with what I swear is a touch of sarcasm. *"Aww, you're learning, Dannanōk."*

My dragon charges the closest big jet head-on. He opens his mouth wide, teeth and fire ready to rip them into ribbons.

Same.

Dannanōk dips into a death dive, straight toward the closest gigantic craft. He pulls his wings in tight, and we spin into an aileron roll, going down, down, down.

I fucking scream.

Dizzy doesn't come close to describing the overwhelming nausea whirring through my insides as sky, city, and dragon fire blur into one another. Around and around until—*BAM!*—the dragon flies us directly *into* the ship's haul.

I blink, and we're through the ship in seconds, smoke and chunks of it bouncing off Dannanōk's spikey scales, narrowly missing taking my head off.

"Never do that again!" I scold, hardly able to keep my lunch down.

 626

"I asked if you were ready."

Fucking dragons.

He's already searching for the next giant vessel, finding it a few hundred feet to the right.

Now it's my turn.

I untie Ardelle's bow, pull an arrow from the quiver, and close my eyes, trusting Dannanōk while I center myself.

Stroking the feathers of the nocked arrow, I remember the sweet way Ardelle touched me the day he taught me how to shoot with his bow. My eyes sting with the memory of his beautiful smile, the utter agony that comes with knowing he's not here using the bow and arrows he adored so much.

I hear him in my mind. *"You got this, Thumbelina. I'm here."*

It's the first time I've allowed myself to remember the way his voice sounded. I can hear every bit of pride there. Every noble inclination and his endless strength. It's as if he's right next to me, so close I can smell his cinnamon-sage scent.

"You got this."

My eyes snap open, scanning every threat as Dannanōk weaves through the chaos.

I tighten my core and pull back on the bow. Ardelle is right beside me, and my power swells from within my chest, encompassing my entire body until it slithers from my hand to his arrow, exactly like it did during the Titan Games when I brought down that floating island of spectators.

I smirk, knowing I'm going to fuck Malakyte's shit up some more with these arrows.

And they're going to go *boom*.

I lock onto the larger vessel as it shoots a massive Candy Apple green missile straight for us.

Dannanōk twirls, narrowly avoiding it but throwing my aim out of whack.

With my hands unable to grip the saddle, my straps pull tight along my waist as Dannanōk flips and dives, yet I still hold Ardelle's arrow taut.

"You got this," I hear Ardelle say again, his love for me pushing me forward.

He's right.

I do.

Upside down, I see my opening.

There!

Guided by Ardelle's presence, I release the arrow. It flies fast—straight for the larger fighter jet, my antimatter coiling around it as it zips through the skies.

It hits dead on.

The explosion is bigger than I expected, and the heat sizzles on my uncovered arms as Dannanōk banks and heads up high again. The air is thick with burning fuel and magic.

The dragon steadies itself and floats calmly while I nock another arrow.

A strange dimness blankets the skies and pulls my attention toward the sun—the drastic dark spot I see causing a little hitch in my breath.

"A solar eclipse," I say to myself.

The moon is just beginning to cross in front of the sun, but it has energy to it, a whisper of ancient, brutal magic bursting at the seams to break free. Gorgeous, haunting, and I can't help but feel even the moon and sun are on our side.

But the city is still too close.

"Lead the ships toward the fields!" I yell over comms, realizing we haven't moved far enough.

The wind is so loud I can hardly hear their responses in my comms.

Collectively, the dragons and our ships move away from the city, allowing the Arianyte fleet to chase us.

Death beams and bombs follow, and we weave like mad to avoid getting hit. A few dragons suffer injuries, and Shante's fleet fires back with their onboard weapons protecting them.

There's a craft that I've seen twice now, hovering close, but it hasn't shot at us. It's colored Dark Silver, big enough for several people. I clock it but move my attention elsewhere.

Another beam of high-powered lasers comes at us like a three-hundred-foot sword, slashing the air and forcing the dragons and ships up or down to avoid it.

Dannanōk chooses to go up but nearly misses colliding with one of our ships, while Shante curses in my ear. Yet there's no time to apologize as more crafts fire. We can't ignore the smaller ones anymore.

Dannanōk and I battle the smaller Arianyte vessels as we try to pick out bigger ones where we can, dragon fire and antimatter arrows flying, colliding, shattering them to pieces.

My dragon blows up ship after ship, my arrows firing one after the other, Ardelle's soul guiding each one to their mark. I've fired ten and have only missed two.

That's not luck or skill. That's Ardelle—I feel it—I feel *him*.

This goes on and on, but soon, I'm down to only a few arrows. Dannanōk blasts through a bigger, more dangerous ship, my stomach flipping again.

Despite our wins, we're overwhelmed and losing ground fast.

The moon is a quarter way past the sun, and from all the smoke and bombs and fires from the air and below where the rebels fight the SSPARROW army, the skies are now full of clouds the color Forest Fire. It's an eerie, end-of-the-world orange, the sun a glowing orb sinking toward the horizon, the moon stealing its light bit by bit.

Exactly as these Arianyte ships are stealing our strength and numbers.

We can't go on like this.

I have to do something—and fast.

"Dannanōk, fly high!"

After blasting another smaller jet, Dannanōk's wings—now torn and ripped—fly straight up into the sky.

Throwing my arms out wide, I release a howl as Dannanōk rises higher and higher. Letting the wind whip across my body, I lean back, the saddle and buckles holding me as Dannanōk flies vertically, my hair whipping around, heart and crystal a cackling demon beneath my ribs.

I'm no longer scared because I'm not going to fall.

I'm not going to plummet to my death or be abandoned or ever be alone again.

Someone will catch me. The people I love *will catch me.*

I know that now.

I feel it in every fiber of my being.

For once, my crystal's power doesn't surge from anger or fear or vengeance but blasts through my body from love. It soothes my soul rather than ignite it. Fill me with nourishment, not numbing infinity.

Dannanōk levels out, hovering above all the warships and dragons, higher than ever.

My hands tremble as my arms stretch out before me, power jolting from inside my chest—star beaming—sliding down my skin like lava as two sizzling spheres hover over my palms like I'm a god. The Ultraviolet light is a bright contrast to the hazy Blood Orange skies.

The pleasure floods my brain, and now, the crystal is *my* god.

More, the beast within me roars—*more!*

After months of holding this magic inside on the Azurite, I unleash the monster within me.

I slam my arms downward, the balls transforming into jagged bolts of antimatter that aim directly for the Arianyte warships below, my view of them perfect.

Spears of purple antimatter in shade Burning Fuchsia streak across the sky, dancing beside ship and dragon alike. The crystal feels *sensational* as I throw my head back and relish in the glory of the power that utterly consumes my entire being. They hit their targets as power floods every pore, every nerve ending, down to my fucking bones. It's better than sex, better than any drug, better than any vice I've known.

Fuck, I've missed this!

Finally, the curse branded upon my chest and soul has a clear purpose—destroying Arianyte—destroying *him*.

Dozens of them go down at once, the cracking and booming and whistling of the wind in my ears is a symphony alongside my drumming heart.

I inhale with a deep gasp, my power ebbing, but there's no time for a break, and I bring it back up again, my arms flicking left with a *jolt*—I hit more! Then I aim right, and like booming thunderbolts, they fire from the sky—hitting more!

More, more, *more!*

Each wave knocks their ships away like they're nothing but gnats as I aim for the biggest collection of them.

One bolt hits a big ship, and it crashes into several more on its tailspin.

"Killer of Worlds!" Dannanōk cries, his roar shaking the entire Earth.

The enemy falls like rain.

Fuel catches fire, ships ram into their neighbors, burning parts damage the ships below them. It goes on and on in dozens of different ways until I'm scorched, my eyelids feeling like they're going to burn right off my face.

Not one Arianyte ship in this aerial battlefield is left unscathed—not one beam of antimatter touching our own forces.

Dannanōk is the thundercloud. I'm the lightning. Together, we rain down a storm of destruction on an apocalyptic level.

My arms fall limp at my sides, lungs wheezing. I can't keep going as my magic sputters out, the euphoria already creeping out of my veins.

Stars . . . Maybe that was too much, too fast.

My arms feel like they weigh a hundred pounds as I let them drop. I lift my goggles into my hair and let the air soothe my hot face, but it doesn't do much to soothe my feverish skin.

"Take a breath," Dannanōk says.

I don't argue.

We're high enough to rest, and what little of the Arianyte fleet that's left begins to retreat, likely needing to regroup. Yet one insidious silver ship hovers about one hundred feet back, as if it's watching me.

Is that him? Is Malakyte up here with us? We wanted to draw him out, so maybe it worked.

I press the back of my hand to my cheek—it's still too hot. I've only felt the burning of my insides when the collars are on, never from overuse. I do vaguely remember Ahren saying something could happen if I went overboard. Well, it's done, and I won't go crazy like that again.

Thankfully, the ships that have fallen do so into nothing but fields, just on the outskirts of the city.

I shift my gaze to the East, the two armies locked in battle, indistinguishable from one another.

Keep them safe, Ardelle.

Beads of water and sweat tickle my brow, the wind soothing on my skin as Dannanōk flies down toward the altitude of the others.

The moon is about halfway across the sun now, as if watching me as I carve my path of annihilation.

That same deep, Earth-shaking horn from earlier rings out through the skies a second time.

The war cry makes the hair on the back of my neck stand straight up, but it isn't the only thing that does.

A monster of a ship slowly materializes through the orangey haze as it hovers down from orbit, drawing out its descent longer than necessary, like it's trying to look ominous. It's all black and shaped almost like a pair of wings stretched out to full length, wider than it is tall. Etched into the metaphorical wings are thick lines glowing Blood Red as the color bursts at the slits in the metal frame, like Hell itself loomed inside, desperate to surge free.

Still several thousands of feet in the air above us, a circular door opens from its belly, the light seeping out of it like blood.

"Oh, fuck me . . ." Deimos rings out in my ear on comms.

A creature drops into the beam of bloodstained light and catches itself on massive wings made of slates of dark metal. It barrels toward us with a war cry screeching from its crafted maw of jagged blades for teeth.

It's a dragon . . . but unlike any type I could have ever conceptualized. A monster ten times the size of Dannanōk. Sleek and black and crafted by hands of a genius madman. If it's alive or being piloted or just an artificial intelligence—I can't even say. This is a massive— entirely mechanical—dragon, eyes a blaze of glory in the shade Crimson Neon.

It flies right for us.

My mouth has gone completely dry, and Dannanōk and I are frozen.

Deimos's voice comes through again, shaking me out of my stunned stupor. "Hope you saved some of that energy, Kiddo, because you're up. I can't control something that isn't alive."

I leave the horror creeping up my spine unspoken because he doesn't need to know.

There's a chance there could be more energy left in my crystal. Maybe my body reacted that way because it's been a long time since I pushed it. That's all. I didn't burn it all out in one shot.

But the sinking feeling in my gut says otherwise.

There's no fucking way I'm defeating this thing.

No way in Hell.

CHAPTER 105

YEAR 6, DAY 2,205: FATHER. I WAS WATCHING KARA FROM
ACROSS THE STREET, AND THE MOMENT I SAW HER FACE . . .
TIME ITSELF STOPPED. THE YEARNING I FEEL IS AN ACHE
THAT I CAN'T EXPEL FROM MY HEART. THE PRINCE VIEWS
HER AS HIS PROPERTY. HE'S CLAIMED HER, YET . . . I KNOW
IT'S CRAZY TO SAY, BUT I FEEL LIKE I KNOW HER SOMEHOW.
WHAT COULD THAT MEAN?

GAVRIELLE ABRAXAS

Getting into Arianyte Tower by making our entire group invisible with my illusions seemed like the most pragmatic strategy.

The courtyard is unrecognizable from the last time I strolled through it—a loyal soldier of the occupation. It stretches roughly three-hundred feet from the street to the main door of the massive skyscraper, deep in the heart of Zarmenia. Its entire perimeter is now militarized, blocked with hover-tanks and barbed wire and soldiers armed to the teeth with disruptors and explosives. With the eclipse pushing toward the halfway point, the sun and moon eerily loom over us all.

We've scouted fifty regular SSPARROW, and five AI SPPARROW. The AI are heavily fortifying the front door, the only entrance to the tower. Our group of thirteen have mapped out where every enemy force stands, our preparation for this attack taking us nearly an hour before stepping onto the tiled courtyard.

I've trained for days to push my illusion magic beyond myself, something I've never been able to accomplish before, but I had no other choice but to figure it out.

We creep across the stone courtyard—invisible—assuring the soles of our boots don't crackle against the concrete tiles. I barely breathe as we make it a quarter of the way. The three Reptilians are having the hardest time staying quiet, their metal armor on their hefty bodies clanking with every move. Irritation surges in Sylo's eyes. The remaining seven Terran rebels encircle Pacey, the only one here who truly needs to survive and make it to the top of this tower.

My palms sweat as I hold my dual blades in a white-knuckled grip, my power surging. *Shit!* I'm losing the edges of the illusion, the background warping and distorting just like I struggled with in practice.

Pacey and I lock eyes, her fearful expression telling me what I already know. We're not even halfway, and I'm slipping. I have to hold on to this illusion. If I don't, we're dead.

Alarms start blaring.

We freeze like prey.

My ears can hear every one of their heartbeats, and if I didn't know any better—they all nearly stopped beating, mine locked in terror. Is this because of me? Can Arianyte see us?

Every single living SSPARROW guarding the tower lifts their blue-lit disruptor rifles and takes aim. The five AI soldiers stand still by the door, watching and waiting.

"How are they seeing us?" Sylo says, voice a stressed whisper.

I double-check my edges. "The illusion is holding. Thermal sensors in their helmets, possibly?"

I'm betting they added that little feature specifically because of me.

I'm flattered.

"Oh, great, then we're fucked," a Reptilian hisses.

I push the others to the door, moving us the precious few feet closer we can get before this erupts into a shit show.

Sylo asks, "Why let us get this far if they could see us the entire time?"

"Because they wanted to trap us!" Pacey says.

My head whips left and right in a panic. The SSPARROWs are surrounding us, and now we're like animals, corralled in a pen with no way out.

"Pacey," I say, doing my best to keep my voice calm for them, "when I drop my illusion, I need you to strike with fire, lightning, whatever you can, but save the water strapped to your back."

"I need the elements there to work with first," she says, "and you're right, we need to save the water. Not much nature here but a couple landscaping bushes."

"The air from their lungs?" I suggest.

"With those helmets on . . . I can't . . ."

"I can't control any of them until they're dead either, so don't count on that," Sylo chimes in.

"Creepiest powers in the world, dude," I facetiously joke.

"We see you!" one SSPARROWs shouts. "Undo the invisibility, or we'll open fire!"

We all step backward to the point our backs touch, now unable to move in either direction.

Well . . . shit.

I sigh, a mad grin slipping onto my face.

We're here. So, we know what that means . . . We're going to do this.

 636

My illusion falls, and even though they knew we were here, the soldiers tense.

"Hands up, weapons down!" orders a SSPARROW Nest leader, his uniform clad in red light. "Drop them, or we shoot! Now!"

I slowly lower my dual blades. We're outnumbered but not outsmarted.

The AI SSPARROWs are still waiting to my left by the entrance, more than one hundred feet between us.

I'd say we're royally fucked.

"Pace . . ." Sylo whispers. "Charge your crystal now."

Pacey looks confused as she lowers her scythe but nods, trusting him as her pupils flare to a glowing blue.

Sylo holds his Elendril rifle as if he's going to drop it. Instead, he shoots straight ahead—but not at the soldiers.

We dive as SSPARROWs open fire on us. One of the rebels gets hit, but his screams are swallowed by the boom of an armored tank exploding as Sylo's bullet hits the flammable engine. The explosion knocks most of the SSPARROWs to their knees with a skin-peeling wave of heat. Because we're surrounded, only about a quarter of them are engulfed in the flames.

That's one damn powerful gun.

Pacey immediately understands, taking control of that inferno as she sculpts the feral fire into her own creation. Three giant firefoxes emerge from the carnage, and the soldiers scream in terror. Yet it really picks up once those same firefoxes charge directly at them.

I chuckle, pick up my swords, and sheathe them before helping the injured Terran rebel to his feet. "Let's go. This is our chance!"

Sylo snatches Pacey's scythe, and we dash toward the Arianyte Tower's main entrance.

The AI SSPARROWs wait for us, the living ones bolt to attack, and disruptor fire rains down.

Pacey's firefoxes attack all living SSPARROWs the moment we sprint toward the entrance. A disruptor shot slices my upper arm, but I barely feel it—it's just a flesh wound. One firefox guards our group as we make our way across the chaotic courtyard.

I thrust our injured companion to a female rebel as a SSPARROW leaps into the fray with a sinister short sword in hand. Unleashing my blades, I face him. My twin swords aren't separate entities—they move as one—move as *me*. I sidestep as the SSPARROW slices for my neck, then my heart—he's agile—but I'm faster. His black metal form dives for me, and I wait for the heartbeat it takes for him to get in close. He sees what he wants to, sees the illusion I've placed where I once stood, and he brings his blade up to strike but hits nothing but air, his body losing balance.

The soldier never even sees me materializing behind him, my swords ending his life before his head whacks the concrete.

Killing is as easy as breathing for me.

Malakyte made me this way.

I kill to protect my friends—my family.

I kill to keep this planet's people alive and free when I couldn't do the same for my own.

I kill to ensure my mate and I have a future.

Embers and blood rain down on us, and my heart beats to the anthem of screams and disruptor fire. I slice and hack and fight my way through this courtyard toward that entrance, my Starseed family beside me, the rebels and Reptilians fighting in earnest to get us through this melee. From close and afar, they're pummeling us, but we're holding.

Our group is scattered as three of our rebel comrades lie dead, several wounded. Two of Pacey's firefoxes engulf SSPARROW after SSPARROW as they run through them, rapidly reducing their numbers as they run literal circles around us. The acrid, burning flesh is nauseating, but we push through.

An opening in the SSPARROW hoard sits obstruction free to my left, the door to the tower unguarded.

Adrenaline is pumping like heroin in my veins.

"This is our chance. Move!" I shout.

We make the final thirty-foot dash to the door when my brain catches up to itself.

Fuck!

I'm in the lead but stop, Sylo and Pacey nailing into my back, while the remainder of our little group, three rebels, and two Reptilians freeze behind them.

Pacey's three firefoxes surround us, no more living SSPARROWs attacking, either with disruptors or hand-to-hand—they've been taken care of. But it's the things standing in front of us that's the big threat.

All five AI SSPARROWs stand between us and the door.

Naresteé's warning about how deadly these things are flashes through my mind, but I push it away.

We planned for this.

Without being prompted, Pacey swings the pack on her back around to her front, the water inside sloshing around as her thigh holds it up, her trembling hands unscrewing the cap.

One AI jumps for us—so fast we can't even scream or warn Pacey—and I brace my knees down, blades high, my body between them and it. But the mechanical soldier seems to burst into nanobots as they swarm from inside its chest, my eyes widening as Kara's face flashes through my mind.

For the first time in my life, I freeze, seeing my death as imminent as my next heartbeat.

Gallons of water crash into the nanobot swarm from the right, so close my face gets slapped with droplets. An eerie, violent cacophony of hissing, crackling, and zapping pierces my ears and angry tendrils of white-hot blue electricity scar the air itself with a snapping jolt that nearly puts me on my ass. The sound builds and intensifies until—*POP!*

We're blown backward, the suffocating scorched metal and some other scent burning my nose and eyes as all of us slam into the concrete courtyard, the nanobots tumbling right along with us.

Some water floats in the air like a warped bubble, sparkling from what remains of the sun as the moon passes in front.

"Come at us, motherfuckers!" Pacey calls, one of her firefoxes devouring the AI that lost its nanobots, the thing a charred husk.

But she isn't done.

"Do it now!" I shout, my head whipping back just as Pacey hits a command on the specially designed watch at her wrist, days of planning coming down to this single moment.

My head snaps back to the AI SSPARROWs, the remaining four charging for us on swift feet. We've got to get up. It didn't work!

I leap to my feet, heart hammering, watching as the AI approach but then one staggers, another jolts, its feet tripping and balance wobbling.

My blood soars.

Pacey howls.

Three out of four SSPARROWs tumble, completely immobilized, as if the AI piloting them was sucked right out of their metal bodies.

"I knew hacking their frequencies would work!" Pacey bellows, voice exhilarated. "Well, almost." She laughs.

"We still have one left!" I say. "Everyone on your feet. This isn't over."

Pacey's limited kill switch is only a temporary solution for a very specific situation. It won't work from this point on. Any other AI soldiers who approach us won't wait for her to take thirty minutes to hack their individual frequencies.

The AI that avoided Pacey's kill switch appears to look around at the situation, and bolts.

Great, so they're that intelligent?

"It's retreating inside!" Sylo yells.

It takes us thirty seconds to reach the door, and it's nearly pitch black inside the tower.

The AI SSPARROW is nowhere in sight.

"Hell yeah!" Sylo high fives Pacey, drawing her into a hug as he spins them both around. "Forcing a retreat is a win."

"Yeah," I agree, "until that thing pops out of a shadow at the worst time and grabs one of us by the balls."

Sylo stops their spinning, grabs Pacey's face, and slams their mouths together, kissing her as if they'll never get the chance again.

Initially, my instinct is to look away, but I watch Sylo embrace her, clocking the expression on Pacey's face as she closes her eyes, spearing her hands into his dark hair.

My heart aches but in a good way. She deserves a sliver of happiness after losing her brother. They both deserve this.

I think of Kara and how badly I miss her. How desperately I want to kiss her like this, too. Our time together last night is bright in my memory, and I need to finish this so we can have many more nights like it. So my mate can find the peace she deserves after this Hell. So that I can, too . . .

SSPARROW sirens ring out from outside, which means more will be coming for us—and soon. I clear my throat. "Guys."

They break their kiss and stare at each other as deeply as ever before finally separating.

Sylo hands Pacey her weapon, her firefoxes dispersed and water back in its half empty jug.

With our five remaining rebel and Reptilian companions, we dash up the long, treacherous stairs toward the top of Arianyte Tower before we're eaten alive.

CHAPTER 106

The mecha-dragon is a flying Armageddon.

It's a pestilence crafted from the depths of Hell. Its Midnight titanium frame shadows the city of Zarmenia in a cloak of death as it blackens the city streets and fields below as it arrives in our airspace. Its armor-plated wings, tail, and scales flash with what remains of the sun, each segment reinforced with an interweaving exoskeleton crafted to withstand any attack. The veins of Maximum Red energy thrum within it—especially within its wings—and . . . stars, its fucking eyes.

The illumination within this creature pulses and brightens, eyes bursting with the fury of a thousand stars. Its spikes—lined all the way from horns to tail—also thrum like a heinous heartbeat—with Bloodmoon light. With raw, unadulterated power.

As it rages toward us, opened maw with razor-sharp blades for teeth, its weaponry also comes into view, ionized cannon launchers, missiles, plasma shooters. But none of it matters as the mouth bellows a roar so loud that I cover my ears, certain this monstrosity is ripping open the skies themselves.

A radiant Bloody Scarlette glow erupts from within the mecha-dragon's throat, growing in luminosity as it smolders like the pits of Hell.

"That's dragonfire!" I yell into comms.

Dannanōk swoops away as the mecha-dragon fires a mouthful of plasma straight for us, the beam thousands of feet long as it slices the sky in two.

Dannanōk has no choice but to bank up so fast I'm whipped around, my neck feeling like it's going to be ripped right off my shoulders.

He roars as the beam hits his foot, blood splattering into the air as droplets hit my face.

"Dannanōk!"

Shouts from both Deimos and Shante ring in my ear, the beam from the mecha-dragon cleaves half our forces in one fell swoop, our fighter jets exploding like fiery popcorn before my eyes.

"I have to bail!" Shante screams, and moments later, she ejects herself from the jet as it goes spinning into the field in a ball of flames.

Shante's parachute bobs, and my stare darts above and around her, hoping debris doesn't tear her out of the air on her way down.

"Deimos?" I say into comms, panicked.

I can't see where he is. The only response is a high-pitched ringing in my ears.

"Deimos?"

"I'm here, Kiddo. Six o'clock high."

My neck aches as I look in that direction, he and Feena indeed flying up above.

There are maybe ten fighter jets hovering alongside us, and only the two of our dragons left in the sky.

"The other dragons are injured but alive," Dannanōk interjects, and relief floods through me that they'll live, but they're done, and we're out of reinforcements. *"You're lucky my mate survives."*

My heart sinks as I look back toward the mecha-dragon. The creature is so fucking gigantic it makes my heart pound, but my star mark sears hot.

I take a deep breath, my eyes drifting back to the sun as the eclipse hits the three-quarter mark. A glint of silver catches my eye far in the distance. I'm not sure what it is until I realize it's that silver fighter jet from earlier, hovering well out of range like a little coward. I'm convinced. It's Malakyte.

You want a show? I'll give you a show.

Sinking into the saddle, I know what I've got to do.

"Dannanōk," I say, the wind blowing my braid across my shoulders. "Fly me as close to the back of the dragon as possible. I'm going to destroy it, but to do that, I need to get on its back."

"Are you fucking mad?" Deimos says in my ear. "That's suicide. Don't be an idiot again."

"What other choice do we have?" I argue. "It's too big for me to just blast. I need to get closer. If I can blast it from the inside out, that'll pulverize it. I've got a plan."

A stupid plan.

Deimos doesn't hesitate when he says, "I know you feel responsible for all this, Kiddo, but you aren't. You don't have to throw your life away to atone for what happened."

There's no higher price I'm willing to pay, including my own self-destruction, to right my wrongs.

The mecha-dragon is powering up for another attack.

"Tell Jance and Gavrielle that I love them," I say, my voice low and somber. "And that I'm sorry. I have to do this."

"Kar—"

I rip the comms piece from my ear and toss it out in front of me.

Dannanōk dips his snout as he watches it go. *"You're a stupid human. But one I respect, Karalevine."*

"No more Killer of Worlds?"

He chuffs, steam blasting from his nostrils. *"I'll get you as close as I can."*

Then Dannanōk beats his wings once, twice, flying high and then banking left, cruising around the back end of the massive creature.

"You know," I begin, the wind flapping my braid as I put my goggles back on over my eyes, *"Arianyte is totally mocking you with that thing."*

"They can try!"

The Bloody Carmine light within its throat is brimming to life, the color even visible from its neck as Dannanōk brings me around behind it. But there are more glowing spots all the way down its back. They're roughly ten feet in diameter, going all the way from the neck to the base of its tail.

"Right there!" I point to the center of one Apple Red orb as it glows from within. *"Try to get me there, right on its back, between the wings."*

"You're crazy," he says but flies in that direction anyway. *"You'll die."*

"Just do it."

Reaching back, my hand grips the cold Rose Gold filigree of my Elendril sword's hilt, drawing it free in one smooth motion.

We're close. I grip Jance's ring as it hangs around my neck just as it had that night in the throne room. It will be my strength once more. I was wrong that day up on the Sky Dais in the maze, when I said my might didn't come from him . . . It had always come from him.

I love you, Jance.

The mecha-dragon spots us, flying our way with incredible speed.

Dannanōk blasts his fire as we narrowly avoid getting caught in its jaws, those teeth sharp as needles and easily ten feet long.

645

From out of nowhere, Deimos and Feena fly directly in the path of the mecha-dragon, drawing its attention from us to them.

"Now!" I yell in my mind. *"It's distracted!"*

The hesitation in Dannanōk's body is obvious, but he goes anyway, diving, swaying repeatedly from behind the mecha-dragon as it chases after Deimos and Feena.

Once Dannanōk gets low and I know he's not going to have to do any more crazy flight maneuvers, I unbuckle myself from the saddle.

The giant metal dragon is fast, but thankfully, it isn't as agile as Dannanōk or Feena, and my dragon is able to slide right between its wings, its attention fully on the others.

Throwing my right leg over Dannanōk, I hold the pommel with my right hand, sword in the other, leaning down.

He isn't as steady as I'd like, and for that matter, neither is the giant dragon. The drop is also significantly higher than I expected, probably fifteen or twenty feet down. The roaring winds don't help my cause, either.

I crank my neck back around, and my gaze clashes with Dannanōk's Gold Metal eyes, his wings shuddering to keep him in place.

I've got seconds.

Likely less.

For this one leap.

A leap of redemption.

A leap of victory.

A leap of madness.

I nod to the ancient dragon, fear latching itself around my heart and clenching tight.

Then I jump.

CHAPTER 107

Time stalls.

It's desolate—meaningless.

It doesn't exist as my feet shove off from Dannanōk, my body a weightless mass, hovering in the nothingness for that drawn-out heartbeat of time.

I grip my sword's hilt with hands high above my head, ready to stab this motherfucker deep. Spine arched in a backbend, knees bent and a battle cry that could summon a thousand armies reverberating from my throat. The crystal explodes from my body, the light bursting from me right into the blade as time resumes, and I fall for what feels like an eternity. The eclipse is nearly at totality beside me.

Dannanōk's war cry echoes around me as I fall, sword tip aimed right at the center of one of those glowing red circles.

I need to pierce the soft spot between the metal scales, or else I won't be deep enough.

As if Ardelle himself were here controlling the surrounding gravity, the blade stabs the mecha-dragon's metal hide as I crash into it, penetrating damn near to the hilt.

It screams.

It thrashes.

It fights.

I slip and slide, finding nothing to grip on to but my sword's hilt as I'm thrown around like a rag doll.

My hands and wrists ache as I completely lose all footing along the smooth surface of its metal scales, the dragon itself bucking and thrashing, trying to throw me off it.

No. Way. In. Hell.

Gritting my teeth, I hang on.

I push my crystal to its max, driving my power into my blade.

There's no burning out—not yet!

Living flesh or metal monstrosity, it doesn't matter. It will die either way.

Because I'm going to kill it!

Muscles rip as I heave myself up by my arms, finally gaining purchase by kicking my boot up under the scales.

My star is an absolute inferno as my antimatter surges inside the sword, light blasting in deeper, deeper, *deeper*—meeting the source of that pulsing red glow when—*BOOM!*—the two powers collide in an epic thunderous rumble that shakes my very bones.

Chunks of the mecha-dragon blow apart, explosions taking out its arm and half its wing in one ear-ringing blast.

Keep going!

I didn't damage it enough. I need to do more.

Without warning, the sky becomes the fields below me—the massive dragon is flipping sideways!

Barrel roll!

My magic instantly sputters as all my efforts go into hanging the fuck on.

The mecha-dragon rolls faster and faster with each tumble around, and with each flip upside down I barely manage to keep my grip and only because the sword is lodged in deep and my feet are tucked so far into its scale I can halfway hold on.

That only gets me so far.

 648

Not only do my hands creep farther from the hilt with each spin upside down, but the sword itself is coming *out*, inch by inch, roll after roll—my weight pulling it out as I lose the war to gravity. The more I hold on, the looser it becomes.

We're right side up, and I adjust my hold in the few precious seconds I have before gravity takes over again, but this will be the last time, the sword too loose.

We tilt, and I clench my eyes closed. *This is it.*

Dannanōk may catch me, but . . .

We're thousands of feet in the air. Anything can happen.

With little choice, I open my eyes and ratchet my power back up again, my body sliding down.

A jolt of black from directly below me steals my attention, and I look down.

My eyes widen.

Dannanōk!

He latches onto the mecha-dragon with his claws, barely twenty feet behind and below me, hooked onto its back, sitting right over one of those red dots. Our eyes meet once again, and the unspoken communication is as clear as day.

If I don't get off now, I'm dead.

Wrenching my sword from this awful creature, I slide down its artificial spine and scales—plummeting down— straight for Dannanōk

I hit his face first, feeling bad for stepping on his nose as I leap to his neck. His sharp spikes cut me as I roll across those pointy fuckers, his body arching to bounce me over them, the mecha-dragon nearly right side up again.

My body is jelly as I connect with Dannanōk's shoulder, falling toward the saddle thanks to the angle and gravity.

If I miss the saddle, I'm falling thousands of feet.

Dannanōk's claws barely hold their grip as the mecha-dragon tumbles and twirls, my braid thrashing and wind howling in my ears.

Reaching, my fingers make contact with the pommel of the saddle, and I hold on, my body whipping around precisely when Dannanōk leaps off the mechanical dragon's hide.

My ass slides into the saddle, fingers trembling as I strap myself back in, sword in its sheath a second later. We're flying off, level once again.

That sure as shit didn't go as planned, the mecha-dragon still as deadly as ever despite the damage I inflicted.

I only get a second to breathe as a flash of Deep Emerald steals my attention as it flies up from the left at such a high speed, I nearly miss it.

Deimos!

"What are you doing?" I scream, as if he can hear me.

He and Feena are going too fast, coming in too hot—straight for the mighty mechanical beast.

Fire in the shade Eternal Gravitas explodes from Feena's throat twenty feet before she crashes into the mecha-dragon's chest, the impact so rough I can nearly feel the collision.

Similar to Dannanōk's attacks with the bigger fighter jets, Deimos and Feena don't stop flying through, except this creature is twenty times the size of those other ships, and they don't have my antimatter to obliterate the debris and protect them from being hurt.

"Stop!" I cry, explosions booming one by one, compartments and panels collapsing.

Deimos and Feena are shredding themselves apart!

Dannanōk's roar of protest echoes my own throat-ripping screams, but neither of us can stop this.

Deimos and Feena burst from the other side of the mecha-dragon—Feena covered in blood and debris as she blasts up into the hazy skies, wings and scales ripped to shreds. The metal dragon goes limp as columns of sparks jut out in all directions. Its bloody lights sputter and flicker before it goes dark, body nearly sliced in two as it crumbles to the fields below.

 650

My eyes catch Deimos and Feena—they're falling!

Fast.

Too fast.

"Dannanōk!" I cry, the panic echoing out against my skull.

He doesn't hesitate to rush toward them, ravaged wings beating hysterically.

Please, please get there in time, I beg, heart thrashing and adrenaline bursting from every vein in my body.

Their plummet and our race toward them are at an impasse, and we're not going to connect.

Faster, faster, *faster!*

Deimos and Feena collide with the field in a massive, devastating crash that echoes through the earth, bones and hearts snapping.

Dannanōk swerves to avoid ramming into them and the ground, too. He slides to a stop, his claws digging trenches into the dirt, and even our landing is violent and rough as he finally skids to a stop.

Hardly waiting a breath, I unbuckle myself, rip the goggles off, grab Ardelle's bow, the four remaining arrows still strapped to my back, and leap from Dannanōk. I'm rushing toward them as soon as my feet hit the ground.

My ragged, crackly breaths are louder than my boots crunching over the freshly tilled wheat field as I rush toward them.

"Deimos!" I cry, utter panic in my voice. "Feena!"

Their names echo off the smoke from fallen ships peppered all over this field. The mecha-dragon landed far away, but I smell it burning in the air past the collection of trees to the left where the wheat begins.

Once I finally reach them, Feena is mannequin still. I see her neck twisted around, blood seeping out from snapped bones, her eyes completely hollow and vacant.

My hand covers my mouth, blood pressure and adrenaline plummeting.

The bow falls to the ground

She's dead.

"Oh, Feena . . ." I say, my voice hardly a whisper as the wind carries it away just as quickly, her soul with it. I unclip the quiver of arrows from my back and lay it beside the bow before I walk closer, terrified of what I'm seeing.

Her body is burned and cut all over, broken and battered from the fall, and my tears cascade down my cheeks for her sacrifice.

Moaning rips my tear-filled eyes away from the dragon, and I mad dash around her to find Deimos slumped over, still strapped into his saddle.

"I'm coming," I yell, reaching him a second later.

But the instant I see him, my mind knows what my heart can't accept.

He's covered in blood, the shade Deep Plum. His spine is snapped in half—that much is obvious from a quick glance at how he's hunched over in the saddle, but it's the piece of metal debris that's speared through his diaphragm that's my biggest concern.

"I've got you," I say, taking his weight with all my strength so he isn't being pulled, and I strain to reach and unbuckle him.

Deimos collapses on top of me as he comes loose, and I lower him, my knees buckling as he slumps on top of me.

"You're crazy as shit, Kiddo," he says, voice tired and full of pain.

I can see the agony in his eyes.

"Why did you do that?" I ask, my voice barely audible, my hands wiping the blood and dirt from his face.

He laughs, although it twists into a cough as he struggles to breathe, lungs grasping for any amount of air. "I know, so uncharacteristic of me, isn't it?"

I search for someone, a fallen pilot, Shante—*anybody*!

"Look at me." Deimos raises his arm high enough to hold my cheek in his bloodied, ruined hand.

 652

I look, rapidly blinking away my tears so my face doesn't give away what I'm slowly coming to realize.

Coughing more, he speaks again. "I'm sorry for hurting you that night at the carnival."

I'm silent, stunned, and needing to find words. "I don't care about that anymore," I say, shaking my head.

He smiles, rolling his eyes as if there's all the time in the world for his crap. "You were always such a piss-poor liar, Kiddo," he says, and I look away, eyes burning.

Clearing my tight throat, I look back down and say, "Well, I mean it, okay? So shut up and stop apologizing like you're not going to be here to make up for it."

The sadness finally cuts through the pain in his eyes.

"There's no Silent Breath for me."

I open my mouth to say that there's some back at the base, but Gav . . . Fuck, he used it on me.

"Well, I can go get some," I bargain. "There's got to be some inside Arianyte Tower . . . There is! I remember, I remember where Malakyte is hiding some, I can get Gav on the comms and tell him where it is and he'll bring it, and it'll fix you, and everything will be fine—"

He puts pressure on my face. "There's not enough time for that."

My body shakes as the realization hits me, and I can't hide it as I look around this empty field, nobody in sight to help me save him.

"Take this," he says, struggling with his free hand to unclip his Elendril dagger from its sheath at his belt. The ornate hilt is exactly like my sword. "I want you to have it. Take my crystal before he does. Don't let that bastard have it. You take it, you hear me?"

I shake my head profusely. "No," I say firmly. "No! I don't want your creepy ass puppet powers, okay? So, stop giving up and fight this. I can still save you."

Deimos's eyes close, and I think he's already left me, but they flutter back open, my sniffles too loud in this giant, empty place. The shadow of the eclipse is directly overhead, throwing the world into a dark, graveyard hush.

Shoving his dagger into my hands, he looks me dead in the eyes. "Take it." He means more than just the dagger. "Don't be a pussy."

I laugh, the first tear escaping, and I wipe it away quickly.

"I lied too," he admits, and my brows knit in confusion. "You're so much like her, and I felt her within you from that first night we spoke. You brought a piece of my Zariya back to me, and for that alone, I couldn't help but love you, Kara. I loved all of you insufferable, soft-hearted morons."

His admission throws me, but there's no denying the love he has for us—for me—his eyes slicking with tears.

I smile, realizing what I had never allowed myself to feel until just now. "We all loved you too, Deimos. It's okay. You can rest now. I'll finish this. You've avenged her."

I don't know how the words are making it out of my throat, as tight and burning as it is from holding the emotions back that want to rage out, but I can't break.

Not yet.

His eyes are becoming unfocused, his grip on my face faltering. He's close.

"Is it okay for me to come home, Zariya?"

Not yet.

My chin quivers, and I can't hold back my tears. Taking his hand as it slowly falls. He's talking to her . . . And even though I am—and am not Zariya, I answer as if I were her in this moment. As if I can give him this one thing that I know has haunted him for so many years.

"Of course it is," I tell him, my voice soft.

Not yet.

 654

Deimos's breaths falter, each one coming slower and slower, my grip on his hands tightening as his loosens. Something flashes in his eyes, and he smiles for the briefest of seconds.

"Ahh, I see . . ." he whispers as he looks straight ahead into the sky, as if I'm no longer here.

The ring of the full eclipse reflects in his dark eyes as it looms above.

As if the eclipse is calling him home, the light behind his eyes shifts. It flutters up somewhere far away, his body's last breath going with that light—with him.

I know the moment it happens, his body relaxing, everything about him going so unnaturally still.

Between his last heartbeat and a breath I can barely get into my lungs, my sobs overtake me.

The silent field detonates with the echoes of my heart shattering.

CHAPTER 108

YEAR 7, DAY 2,433: THE STARSEEDS AND RINGERS HAVE
RESURFACED SINCE THEY'VE FLED THE CITY AFTER THE
TITAN GAMES FINALE, AND I CAN FINALLY BREATHE AGAIN.
I WATCHED HER TAKE ON AND KNOCK OUT AN ENTIRE
NEST LAST NIGHT, FATHER. IT WAS INCREDIBLE. KARA IS
SPECTACULAR. ALL I COULD DO WAS WATCH IN AWE.
MALAKYTE WANTS ME TO FIND HER AND BRING HER IN, BUT
I CAN'T TELL HIM WHAT I KNOW. I JUST CAN'T GIVE HER UP
TO HIM. HE'LL RUIN HER, PRECISELY AS HE RUINED ME.

GAVRIELLE ABRAXAS

"**W**e're getting murdered down here!" Sylo's voice echoes from a flight down as he, a Terran rebel, and a Reptilian fight a hoard of living SSPARROW that quickly caught up to us a quarter way up the tower.

Pacey and I are caught in our own massive assault, along with the remaining two Terrans and single Reptilian.

We're also getting "murdered."

"Asshole!" Pacey cries, teeth bared in a hiss, bloodied hand clenching her other arm as she lifts one of her long legs and kicks a soldier hard in the chest, his metal body tumbling backward down the stairs.

"You alright?" I call back, narrowly ducking to avoid getting a haircut.

The stairwell is so damn dark it's hard for even me to see the black soldiers in their armor.

I can't imagine how hard it is for the others.

"All good," she says, swinging her giant scythe at another SSPARROW.

She's on the landing below me with a female rebel, and the Reptilian battles on the platform above me. I hold the stairs between them.

We're getting nailed from above and below.

Light surges up the stairwell in a massive whoosh of hot air, Sylo's Elendril rifle exploding as screams bounce off the dark metal walls.

"Could've just lit a candle, Sylo!" I yell, chuckling.

"Coming back up, asshole!" Sylo yells, my blades diving into the chest of a SSPARROW, this screaming and gagging a symphony I can't pity as I rip the blades free, his body sagging to the steps at my feet.

This is a bad spot.

"We need to get out of—"

My chest suddenly tightens, and I falter, my body plummeting so quickly I need to grab for the handrail to catch myself.

"Gav!" Sylo bellows, but he's too far away to help me as my knees give way.

What's happening?

The Terran rebel fighting alongside Pacey is closest, her cropped sandy-blonde hair damp as she charges toward me, a SSPARROW disruptor aimed right for my temple.

She collides with the SSPARROW, knocking his rifle to the stairs as it clanks down. They're in a brawl.

My lungs clench . . . I can't breathe.

Dread strikes through me like a spear, throughout bone and ligament, shredding them apart. My vision blurs, heart hammers. My entire body feels as if it's being minced by the nanobots.

Then my right hand is burning white hot—as if I'm being branded—a sensation I've never experienced.

My Ringer mark . . .

Ripping my fingerless glove off, I gasp as my mark glows green, which hasn't happened before.

The Terran female screams, a blade buried in her chest from the SSPARROW, and she goes down, eyes wide in disbelief.

Fuck!

I bare my fangs and try to stand, but my body is immobilized. *I can't fucking move!*

The SSPARROW returns with his rifle, determined to end me while I'm down. Sylo and Pacey are too far away to help, and right as the soldier braces the disruptor into the crook of his arm— taking aim—a second SSPARROW rushes him from behind. They both fall face first to the stairs, this new SSPARROW missing his helmet, revealing a dark-skinned extra, whose eyes are glowing orange. I remember him—because I killed him.

"I've got him in my grasp. Kill the other one!" Sylo shouts, his Starseed magic controlling the body of this dead soldier.

I do exactly that, grabbing the disruptor and shooting the soldier dead in the skull.

My body sags as the shot echoes within the stairwell, pulse still thrashing. The truth creeps closer and closer, but I can't accept it.

I shake my head. "No . . ."

I feel as if my own arm has been cleaved from me in one cruel swoop.

My Ringer mark glows, lighting me up in a wash of green against the firelight burning below. The mark flickers as if doused in water, then goes out completely.

It doesn't glow again.

In fact, it lacks the life and color it had before. Even with this dim red lighting, I can tell that it's different.

Deimos is dead . . .

I know it as certainly as I know my own heartbeat.

He's gone.

And so is my magic.

The magic I've known my entire life, the power that helps me wield my illusions, the one thing I've been connected to for as long as I can recall memory—has now quieted to a graveyard hush. I've lost so much that I've loved and held dear, but *this* . . . ? My constant, loyal companion can't be ripped away from me, too. It can't—my Starseed can't be taken from me. He's a prick, but he's *my* prick.

With my soul raw and empty . . . I understand now exactly why Ahren looked like a phantom dressed in flesh.

My bond with Kara is also painfully muted. I can hardly sense her.

A boom wracks the stairwell as the door to the landing straight ahead of me flies off its hinges, nailing a SSPARROW and flattening the soldier as the AI steps in.

The AI SSPARROW has come back for its kill, and it's got its sights pinned right on us.

CHAPTER 109

My bloodied fingers gently close Deimos's eyes, nothing but the wind comforting me between my sobs and sniffles.

He's gone.

Out of everyone, I'd never expect Deimos to sacrifice himself, for me or any of us.

Ever.

But he said it all in his last moments, something I never allowed myself to see.

His love for me.

For all of us.

It was there the entire time. I was just blind to it.

Blind to how much I cared about him, too.

Dannanōk's footsteps crunch over plowed wheat beneath his claws, Deimos's hand still clenched in mine, his dagger resting on his unmoving chest.

"I'm sorry," the dragon says with his voice, deep and somber.

"I'm sorry, too."

Finally peeling my eyes away from Deimos, I turn my head to face Dannanōk, even though the vertebrae in my neck ache in protest.

I pick up Deimos's Elendril dagger. It makes me feel closer to him. "His last wish was for me to take his crystal."

Fear creeps up my spine at the thought of what that looks like before, during, and after.

If I even want it.

"I heard," Dannanōk says, Medallion eyes heavy with grief.

"How . . . How do I get it out of him?" I ask, the thought of ripping open his chest twisting my face and stomach.

It's unfathomable.

I don't know if I can do this, Deimos . . .

Dannanōk steps closer, his long neck slithering down so his face nuzzles close to mine. He smells of sulfur. "You don't have to cut him." My shoulders sag as I exhale a desperate breath of relief. "The crystals always know when the host has perished. Call to it, and it will come."

My brows crease.

"Call to it how?"

"Extend a small amount of your magic into his heart, and it will come free."

"Won't that destroy it?" I ask.

Dannanōk shakes his horned head. "You can't destroy these artifacts. Remember what it is. The crystals are parasitic. They long for a home, a living, breathing, sentient heart. But you understand that, once you merge with it, you will never be able to remove it again. You will have two Elendril crystals, that'll likely put stress on your body and cleave your lifespan. They don't give without taking."

"The alternative is Malakyte possibly getting it, and he'd be unstoppable with powers like this," I say, reaching to unsnap the weathered leather holster at Deimos's waist. "I don't have a choice."

Dannanōk chuffs a reluctant agreement.

"Will it hurt?" I ask, a numbness taking over me as I mentally prepare myself.

Dannanōk hesitates.

A dragon—a fucking *dragon*—hesitates. Stars. There's my answer.

"How do I link my Ringer? Do I get to pick who it is, or is it someone random?"

"When you insert the crystal into your heart, it will insist upon a selection of your choosing before integration completes. Choose astutely, then repeat their name. Feel their essence, bring them into your being as brightly as you can."

Behind Dannanōk's wings, that silver Arianyte fighter jet appears in the skies several hundred feet away, heading straight for us.

No more questions. No more time. No more hesitation.

Laying Deimos on the ground, I hover one hand over his heart and check his pulse with the other, double-checking that he's truly gone.

He wants you to do this, I remind myself, shoving away my guilt for desecrating his body.

Gently, tenderly, I bring my power forward, thin wispy tendrils of antimatter slithering from my fingertips and into Deimos's unmoving chest.

There is no sound or screams of pain when my magic pierces through his flesh and into his heart, the Elendril power in me sensing the newly homeless crystal.

And it seizes it.

I feel a pull from within him, my antimatter latching onto his crystal and clenching it in its wicked, greedy claws like it just found the rarest of jewels.

"I'm sorry." I make a pulling motion with my fingers, and the crystal slides out much easier than I expected.

There's no resistance, hardly any blood, either. It simply . . . comes out.

The jagged Elendril crystal floats up to me, then plops softly in my palm.

 662

I release the shaky breath I've been holding.

I'm in awe of this . . . creature. Not an inanimate object, not even close.

This thing is *alive*.

It hums with an unseen heartbeat in the shade Green Inferno. Each one of its jagged points protrudes with an eerie purpose as the air around it radiates with otherworldly shimmers. My eyes are a pair of unblinking black holes, devouring every detail, down to the way the light refracts back against my skin in little speckles and how it feels both hot and cold as I balance it in my palm. Its color so bright, so saturated, so *green* it's unreal. This shade doesn't exist anywhere else, not in ink, not in paint, not inside a digital screen, only here—only *it*. I need this color. It has to be mine. I need to be one with its deep, stunning hue.

The resonance with this *creature* is instantaneous.

Be with me, it purrs, its seduction nearly complete—I need no convincing. I have no objections.

Mine.

Yes. It agrees. It wants to be with me, too.

Unable to resist it a moment longer, I bring the crystal toward my chest, my own mark flaring, as if in warning.

As if it's afraid.

Except there's no time to reconsider, and like a magnet, the crystal shoots toward my heart, colliding into my star mark with a whoosh of bright, Emerald light.

The heat hits me first, followed by the overwhelming pain flooding in second.

A cry escapes my lips, soft at first, but as the crystal literally melts into my chest, I can't hold it in.

I *scream.*

It sinks its claws into me and yanks. Burrowing into every nook and cranny entrenched within my being—farther than marrow and bone, deeper than heart and soul. I am it, and it is me, and we are one.

But it hurts so bad, *so fucking bad*—I can hardly remember I'm supposed to link my Ringer, but it's his face that brings me back enough to remind me.

Gavrielle, Gavrielle, Gavrielle!

Sweat drips down my body, the searing in my heart sharper, the muscle thundering like a hurricane, blasting the organ into cardiac arrest.

It's too much!

What if this was a mistake? What if one heart can't handle two crystals? What if it's going to kill me?

Get it out! You need to get it out!

But I can't, I can't . . .

Dannanōk places his head down close to me, the tip of his nose nuzzling my face. I think I hear him speak inside my mind, but I'm insane with pain.

My hands catch me as I fall forward, my screams and gasps for breath carrying across the field on the wind's lonely song.

Gavrielle, Gavrielle, Gavrielle! I think on repeat, imagining his face, his scent, his arms around me, those beautiful Violet eyes, the way he loves me.

Gavrielle, Gavrielle, Gavrielle!

I don't realize that I'm screaming his name aloud until the pain slowly starts to ebb, allowing my mind to find a grip hold to latch onto.

"You are alright," Dannanōk says in my mind, even as I wheeze through the agony.

My leathers are soaked through, the nape of my hair wet. My ragged breaths replace the shrieks in the wake of this merger as I hunch over my bent legs, lungs feeling like they're full of glass as I try to breathe.

I sit up and glance at my chest. I knew what was coming, but it's still shocking to see it there.

Two Elendril crystal marks.

My star, and Deimos's.

 664

One glowing Diamond Fuchsia, the other Treetop Green.

"Well, this isn't a twist I saw coming," Malakyte quips from behind me, voice vengefully cocky and dancing with amusement.

No matter how much pain I'm in, I'll never forget his voice.

Guess it was him in that ship, after all.

My eyes flash to my dragon in accusation.

"I told you that ship was landing," Dannanōk growls.

"I was a little fucking preoccupied."

Looking over my shoulder, he stands twenty feet away, two AI SSPARROWs looming like soulless bodyguards on either side of him as his hungry eyes devour me whole.

Malakyte is dressed from head to toe in sleek, malleable armor, shade Black Mist, with a sword strapped to his waist. His long hair is tied back, the dark ponytail blowing in the wind, a stark contrast to the pale wheat behind him. He looks healthy, strong, and handsome. The scar I put on his face is completely gone. In its place lingers a promise of death.

"Nice to see you again, *wife.*"

CHAPTER 110

A PASSAGE FROM THE CONFISCATED JOURNALS OF
GAVRIELLE ABRAXAS:

YEAR 7, DAY 2,449: MALAKYTE IS FUMING. I HAVEN'T
SEEN HIM THIS UPSET SINCE KARA SLASHED HIS FACE. IT'S
PROBABLY BECAUSE HIS SISTER IS HERE . . . BUT HIS STAR JUST
ONE-UPPED HIM, AND I CAN'T HELP BUT FEEL PROUD. SHE
JOINED THE TITAN GAMES, AND SOMEHOW, NONE OF THE
JUDGES REALIZED WHO SHE WAS. HE NOTICED, HOWEVER. I
KNEW, TOO . . .

GAVRIELLE ABRAXAS

"It's coming for the water!" Pacey shrieks as the AI SSPARROW slams into her, the backpack ripping as the machine grips it and tears it away like the straps are threaded with nothing but spider's silk.

"Pacey, duck!"

Sylo's voice booms off the stairwell walls, his rifle held high in both hands as he aims for the AI.

Pacey doesn't hesitate as she falls into a death drop precisely as Sylo shoots his Elendril rifle, the insane bullets plowing into the AI SSPARROW like a cannon, sending it flying as it smacks the wall fifteen feet high.

One of our Reptilian comrades fends off a living SSPARROW, one of only four left in this current Nest that we're battling.

Get up! I order myself. *These people are dying because you can't get up!*

I compel my joints to unlock, imposing my will onto my body as I take the knowledge of Deimos's death and compartmentalize it. Put him to the side where all my pain and grief lie, where my parents and my people go, locked behind walls because I'm not allowed to feel what I do. The world doesn't let me—*he* never let me.

Disruptor shots fire, the live ammo ricocheting off the railing or walls—I can't even tell in this chaos. Blades in hand, I leap down the six steps to the landing where Pacey, Sylo, and our remaining three rebels are.

The AI SSPARROW crawls back up. My boots land with a hollow thud, and I spin, both swords slicing the two living SSPARROWs at once.

They go down hard.

The rebels fight the remaining living SSPARROWs as we face the AI. The shot Sylo fired took out its left arm—currently hanging on by sparking wires. Its hip is also damaged, all bent upwards, but it stalks toward us.

Its chest compartment tries to open, allowing the nanobots to spring forward, but it's jammed.

Pacey holds the water suspended, but I can't feel her magic anymore.

The AI SSPARROW charges, its good arm becoming a blade as it stabs at Pacey's throat. She dodges, left, left, right, down. *Fuck!* This thing is fast as shit, and her scream rips through the smokey air as her side is slashed. How deep, I can't tell, but Sylo charges, completely losing his mind.

Her water bubble falls as she does, splashing to the floor.

Sylo takes her place, and I dive for Pacey. "I'm here. Let me see."

She cries as I check her leather armor, but I smell the blood. "I don't think it's deep, just hurts like a bitch."

"Stay here," I say, pivoting to face the AI. "Hey!" I call out, my voice a booming echo as I stand tall. "I'm the one with the blades." I smirk. "Come and get me you robot trash."

As if it has emotions, it eerily pauses. Then it turns, pushes past Sylo, and comes straight for me.

Two creatures of Malakyte's making going head-to-head.

The irony.

Our blades collide, mine taking the AI's arm—its sword—straight to the ground as my knee rises to nail it directly in its injured hip. It experiences no pain, but I feel the chink in its armor. Our blades twang as I release it, our positions flip-flopping.

Sylo drags Pacey back, the rebels behind them fighting the final living soldier on the steps going up. I'm about to charge the thing when an invisible force slams through my chest, exactly like before when Deimos died.

It takes my breath away, and the only thing that keeps me upright is my back crashing against the wall behind me.

"What's happening, Gav?" Pacey cries as the AI creeps toward me.

Gritting my teeth, it feels as if my entire body is burning up from the inside. "My hand again," I seethe through my tight jaw. "It's on fire."

Sylo raises his gun, but because the AI is between them and me, I can tell he can't get a clear shot without risking hitting me, too.

My blades tremble in my hands, my fingers threatening to abandon them. But under the glove of my right hand, a green beam burns bright, and not even the glove can suffocate its light.

That's the moment I feel her . . . She seeps into my body, my blood, my bones, and my being.

Kara.

 668

That magic that I've known since I was so young explodes through my veins again as if Kara herself were here shooting me up with heroin.

But unlike before, this magic is fueled, a jacked-up version of what I had. It's bright, it's vibrant, it's vivid, and alive with thrumming power. My power—her power.

"Your eyes, Gavrielle," Pacey says in awe. "They're glowing bright green!"

I have no time to relish in the potent power that floods into my veins because the AI is here, and its blade is coming right for my face. I raise my swords in an X defensive position, blocking its strike. I hardly expel any effort as I push through my legs, driving it back.

My swords come apart, and I twirl them each once to get a better grip, my left one coming up high, but it's a distraction. My right one swings low, arching upward to slide inside that little hole I felt with my knee moments before—the very wound Sylo gave it.

My sword plunges all the way up inside of its metal shell, the sensation is so different than I'm used to, but I feel it cutting wire and metal alike. When I twist the blade, I meet the creature eye to eye—figuratively because this thing doesn't have eyes—and rip my sword back out, sparks zapping and zipping as the metal soldier crumbles to the floor.

Sylo rushes up and kicks the damn thing down the stairs, its broken body bouncing all the way down.

It doesn't move.

I assess our surroundings quickly. All SSPARROWs are neutralized, although our remaining rebels look too injured to continue. Pacey's wound is bleeding, but if it were anything deeper than a flesh wound, we'd know by now. Sylo is unharmed besides cuts and bruises. And I'm . . .

"I can feel it coming back," I say, voice enthusiastic.

As I rip my glove off, we stare at my hand as if it was a living miracle. And it is—my mark glowing brighter than ever.

It feels incredible, the best sensation I've ever felt.

Her.

My mate.

She's my Starseed.

Although as elated as I am to not have lost my magic and to be so connected to the woman I love, I feel nothing but utter dread, pain, and terror coming from her end of our bond.

An unexpected sound shrieks from inside Pacey's backpack, and she turns to Sylo in a panic.

He rushes across the landing to grab the bag, handing it to Pacey as she pulls out a Dezlar, face turning grave.

The building's intercom system blares an alarm hauntingly similar to the one of the Azurite as it fell to the Earth's surface.

"What's happening, babe?" Sylo asks.

"The Voidbringer." She shakes her head. "It's counting down to launch."

"How much time do we have to stop this thing?" I say, strapping my glove back on.

Her face is white as a ghost, eyes locking onto mine with haunting certainty. "Twenty minutes before it destroys every living thing on the planet."

I take a deep breath in, my body feeling as if I could run a million miles and fight a thousand men, Kara's crystal reinvigorating me.

"I'm getting you up there, Pacey," I vow. "Let's run."

The three of us fly up the remaining stairs of the tower, finding no SSPARROWs the entire rest of the way to the top.

Once we reach the very last door, we burst through it.

Fifteen minutes left.

The hallway is dark as we enter, and the only direction we can go is to the right. Thirty feet to the end of the hall where the first turn is, there's a frantic pulsing of blue-purple light strobing from around the corner.

The Voidbringer.

I strain to listen for any signs of life, but all I hear is the zapping and popping from the doomsday machine. We can't see it, but that pulsing light is its haunting shadow cast by a demon made of wire and sinister, cold code.

"Eyes peeled, be ready," I say.

With bodies stiff and weapons high, we tiptoe through the darkness. The closer we get, the more light there is around us.

Pacey gasps when three figures casually walk out from behind the corner at the end of the hall, their bodies illuminated by the Voidbringer's insidious light as they come from its direction.

My chest tightens, and I brace down, readying my body to strike.

I'm just not sure who I'm supposed to pounce at first.

If I can pounce at all.

"I knew it would be you," Pacey snarls, eyes glued on the figure in the center, the same person my eyes can't peel away from.

The two AI SSPARROWs on either side of my surrogate mother stand motionless. We barely killed that last one, and in a space like this, with no natural resources for Pacey to utilize, I feel like we're beyond fucked with no time to fight our way through them.

Naresteé's haunting eyes shift from Pacey to me.

Pure disappointment.

"I told you this was pointless, I'm not sure what about that conversation we had convinced you that it would be a smart idea to try this," Naresteé says. "And look at you both, making it all the way up here to me. Now that you're here, I want you to come with me. I will ensure your protection. Karalevine's, too. Memories intact. That's what you care so much about, isn't it? *Her.*"

"She's lying," Sylo snarls.

Narestĕe hisses at him, the two AI taking a threatening step forward.

Perhaps her goal is to run down the clock, but she's still on the planet, so she'd be caught in the annihilation, too.

Something more is happening here.

"Shut off the Voidbringer, Narestĕe," I say, voice stern. "You're not a mass murderer. Don't make me have to fight you to save this planet—because I will."

The Voidbringer's light bounces off the side of her face and horns, and the look she gives me makes me feel so utterly small. "I thought you said you were ready to let it all burn."

I go to respond, but she continues. "He put me here to ensure it goes off." Her eyes turn to Pacey's. "I knew you'd come to try and disable it, so I didn't fight him on that. I'll shut it off if both of you come with me. I can't live without either of you."

"And if we don't?" I ask.

When her eyes shift back to mine, they're cold as ice.

"I'm sorry," she says, "I won't live without my son or the woman I love. And I don't want either of you to die. So just stop being stubborn children and come with me so I can get you off this planet in time."

"In time?" Sylo laughs bitterly. "You just said if they came with you, you'd shut it off. You're a liar. She'll just Recondition you both the moment you drop your guard. Babe, don't listen to her."

Sylo takes Pacey's free hand, but her face isn't as sure as Sylo's resolve.

Pacey steps toward Narestĕe—my surrogate mother's face lighting up, but Sylo doesn't let Pacey's hand go. I move to stop her myself, all six of us moving in tandem until Narestĕe hisses, and we all freeze.

We don't have time for this.

"Did you ever love me?" Pacey asks.

For the first time, Narestĕe's eyes soften.

Pacey may not understand the truth in that gaze, but I sure as hell do.

Naresteé extends her hands out to Pacey. "Come with me. You're the only one I've ever loved. I betrayed him for you."

The frantic beeping in Pacey's bag rings out into the tense room, a constant, blaring reminder of all that's at stake.

One love or billions of lives.

I hate that I'd choose Kara over this planet, over my own, over a thousand planets if I had to. So, I can't judge Pacey for her hesitation, but their connection was based entirely on a lie, on manipulation. Love born out of the deepest violation.

Just like it was for me . . . but the years of real love that formed from that lie—that was genuine. That's what keeps me chained. It must be keeping Pacey locked in this Hell, too. And Kara . . . Stars, I hope she's strong enough to break free, as well. We're all caught up in this web of deceit spun by these people.

Ripping her hand free from Sylo, Pacey closes the gap between us and them, my eyes widening and Sylo rushing to stop her.

I prevent him from grabbing her, one AI SSPARROW stepping in front of Pacey and Naresteé, the two arm-in-arm.

"Gavrielle," Naresteé beckons, saying my name in the exact same cadence as she used to when I was in trouble.

I was always in trouble.

As Pacey stands in the Voidbringer's light. I wonder exactly what sort of game she's playing.

If I want to play, too.

Or if I'm the only player at all.

I shove Sylo off me, and he trips several feet backward, with a look of utter betrayal.

"Kara comes with us," I say. "And I want Malakyte dead."

Naresteé's smile is as wicked as I've always known it to be.

"Fine. She's yours."

"The Voidbringer?" I ask, sliding my blades into their sheaths at my back.

She shrugs. "I can't shut it down. We need to go now. There's a ship on the roof. Only he can shut it off. He's too smart to allow me access to something like this. If you want Kara, we need to go get her now before this machine enters its final phase. I'm sure we can come up with a way to trap Malakyte on the planet, let him go down with his ship. Not even he can survive the Voidbringer."

"You guys are fucking crazy for believing her and letting all these people die! Pacey!"

"Shut up, Sylo!" she yells, agony in her eyes.

"This isn't you. Either of you." He pleads with us, but we don't listen.

We can't.

Not if we want to be with the ones we love.

"I'm just like Kara, Sylo . . ." she says, voice soft. "Once I came back, I was never the same. This is what my brother would want. For me to survive and find a way to be happy. If you run, maybe you can get to the others and find a safe place underground. That's your only chance." She turns to me, her eyes steeled in a way I've never seen. "But I'm going. Gavrielle and I both are."

He turns to me, face looking as if he's drowning in sorrow and disbelief. "Have you been lying and spying on us exactly like they raised you to do? All that time together running around the Azurite, it was all a lie, wasn't it? Were you two in on this together the entire time?" What else could explain this?

My grin is cruel as I shrug.

Naresteé answers for me. "He's always been such a good boy. Well trained. I didn't even have to ask him to bring you to me. He just does it. Malakyte may have ordered him around, but he learned everything from me. I'm the one he's loyal to. I'm the one with the brains behind this empire, and I'm sick of being number two. I served that bastard for nearly two hundred years, never asking for as much of a damn thing, but the moment I

 674

do, he refuses me. He betrayed me. Now that Herkimer is dead, this empire can be ours." She squeezes Pacey for emphasis.

"Arianyte strong," I say, eyes gliding to Naresteé's.

My mother's eyes beam with pride as the clock to the Voidbringer clicks down.

CHAPTER III

My villain.

My enemy.

My lover.

Dannanōk growls as Malakyte approaches, and I force my wobbly knees to stand, tying Deimos's dagger belt to my waist quickly.

I inhale deeply. "I want a divorce!"

My words fall flat.

He keeps coming, so I palm a throwing dagger strapped to my leathers and chuck it at his heart. It spears through the air with a hiss, and it's right on target when one of the AI soldiers steps in front of him, the knife bouncing off its sleek metal frame, landing ten feet away.

"Why is your first instinct to be so violent?" Malakyte mocks.

"Why is your first instinct to like it so fucking much?" I quip back.

His grin is only perpetuated by his cocky, arrogant chuckle. *I hate him.*

Dannanōk growls as the AI SSPARROWs brace down, ready to fight. "I will destroy these monstrosities."

Malakyte's crunching footsteps stop ten feet away.

"You think you can, old friend?"

"I think I can burn you to a husk, Dark Starseed."

Malakyte is the picture of arrogance as he waves his gloved hand, the AI SSPARROWs pouncing, closing the distance between us in a blink.

Dannanōk roars, his mouth opens wide as fire explodes from his throat with little more than a flicker of flame to warn me.

I jump and somersault away, the AI SSPARROWs bouncing around with agility that defies gravity. There's only four, equivalent to, like, twenty normal soldiers.

When I look back, I find Malakyte gone.

Fuck.

I move around Feena's body, my back to her.

Dannanōk charges across the field, chasing two AI, the other two following. He's going to be busy with them, and I have an emperor to kill.

But where the fuck is he? How do you lose a person in a giant field?

"Your heart's beating so fast."

His cold breath tickles my neck, and I jump.

Fuck! He's right there, half a foot behind me.

I reach for another dagger at my rib cage, but his ice-cold grasp snatches my wrist, and we struggle for a heartbeat before he yanks that arm forward, slamming our bodies flush together as his coldness wraps around me like a dangerous shadow— possessing what he views as his.

My breathing is still labored, my lungs still clattering as his dark Onyx eyes tilt down at my chest, at the two symbols there.

"He's finally dead," he chuckles. "About time."

"You're a heartless prick," I spit, trying to get free.

He still doesn't look me in the eye as silence expands between us, Dannanōk's war cries the only sound.

When Malakyte opens his mouth, he still refuses to meet my eyes. "You broke my heart."

His voice is soft, sad . . . devastated. As if I did, indeed, shatter something I didn't think he had in the first place.

"I loved you," I say, my voice as cold as the ice in his veins. "Even after all the fucked-up shit you did to me and the people I love. I thought you took that awful thing in me and almost healed it. For a while, it appeared as if you fixed me, but truthfully, you brought out the worst in me.

"Then I found out it was all a lie. I should've seen that coming, but I wanted to believe in you. I wanted to believe in *us*. I wanted to be whole—not *this* anymore. I wanted to fix you, too. I wanted to believe you weren't your father. And that was my biggest mistake, believing you were better than him. Believing I could fix you in the way I thought you had fixed me, but we couldn't do either of those things for each other. You made me believe you could change, and that meant I could, too. That I wasn't too much or too fucked up or too dark because if you weren't, then neither was I. Making me believe all that, Malakyte, is far worse than your lies, than you taking my memories, than any of it. You made me think I was better, that the darkness in me was *good*. That I wasn't fundamentally broken. But it was a trap . . . So, you think I broke *your heart*?" I laugh, and it's bitter and cruel, and I know he hears every ounce of pain in my voice. "You did far worse to me."

Now, our eyes meet, and there's no hiding for either of us.

"You aren't broken, Karalevine. You're perfect."

"Then, why do you want to keep changing me?" I snap.

"Because you wouldn't love me otherwise!" he booms across the field.

Pain, anguish, even fear—he lets me see it all. But there's love, too, and I fucking hate that there's love.

"Stop looking at me like that," I say, my eyes burning.

"Like what?" he asks, voice calm again. "Like how I looked at you that night? When you made love to me, then betrayed me the very next day?"

 678

"You betrayed me first when you took my memories. Your actions have consequences, Malakyte, and those were it. I wanted to be with you that night. I loved you. Your illusion was shattering, and I wanted to hold on to you as long as I could. Yes, it was selfish. I already know that. I'm the worst, okay? I hurt everyone with that choice, yet I still made it because I desperately wanted one night with you, where you were the very best version of yourself, the version I knew you could become. Just one night."

"You never loved me," he argues, fangs bared. "You knew what you were doing and systematically plotted to ruin me—to destroy my crown and crush my heart in one fell swoop. My fucking Azurite is a smoldering heap on the Earth's surface as my father lies dead within it. My entire court is in chaos, and thousands of my workforce has died. Those blood sucking council members are moments away from seizing my throne, and I'm in a full-scale war with Earth. Was this what you yearned for? Are you satisfied, Karalevine, at your revenge against me? Your rebel agenda executed to utter perfection. I hope you're exultant—because your consequences have repercussions, as well. You remember how that works, don't you?"

So, Herkimer really is dead, then . . .

"I remember the vile, disgusting thing you did to me in that throne room. How you violated me, shattered me, trapped me away and nearly made me go insane."

"Do you also remember how good we were together?"

I grit my teeth, but he continues before I can quip back.

"How I took care of you? Showered you with everything and anything you could have wanted. How I loved you?"

I stand on my toes just to prove my point. "You don't get to twist the narrative to escape culpability for what you did to me. You will *never* escape it. I didn't just forget. I was trapped in the dark. You trapped me in the dark!"

My marks are sweltering, voice shaking, but I have to get this out—I have to.

"You destroyed me. In every way a person can be broken . . . you shattered me."

Malakyte shakes his head like I'm telling lies. "You were happy until they began to poison you against me."

"*You* poisoned me against you!" I shout. "You chipped away at who I was. My hair, how I dressed, my posture, my makeup, what I thought and felt and loved. You took and took and took! You don't love me. You love Zariya, and I'm just the closest thing to her you can get. You don't even know who I am. You erased my memories just so I could stand to be in the same room with you without wanting to kill you. This is all because of you, Malakyte. I won't take responsibility for you wanting a relationship so badly with someone who hates you."

I know my words wound him, but it's the ugly truth.

"I never wanted this," I say, unable to stop a tear falling to my cheek. He's nothing but a broken man I can't save from himself.

Yet Malakyte shakes his head vehemently. "Oh, no, you did."

"I wanted to find the friend you took as a child and Reconditioned, making him your slave and assassin. You tried to turn him into you, but his heart is good. He'll never be like you, no matter what you forced him to do, just so he'll feel loved by you."

"Is that what Gavrielle told you I did? Is that why you fucked him, to get back at me? I can smell him all over you so don't even deny it. All this time, my eyes were firmly planted on Ardelle." Malakyte chuckles, as if this is all some ironic joke. Or maybe he's laughing because Ardelle is dead. "But Gavrielle has always been clever—how he knew exactly how to evade my sight and come for what I loved most is facetiously ironic. My own son, stealing my bride right from under my nose. Poetic if it wasn't so absurdly *disgusting*."

"He loves me," I challenge, and I regret saying it the second the words leave my mouth.

My breath hitches sharply as his hands cup my cheeks, his cold skin pushing through his leather gloves. "Not like I do, he doesn't." Malakyte leans in, and I think he's going to kiss me, but he stops short. "He'll never see you for who you truly are. You'll have to change for him, suppress, dull yourself to be on his level. I know him, and he can't give you what you truly need. I have power, influence—I have everything, and he has nothing. With me, you'll own the power I know you covet. By my side, you would be a god amongst peasants, untamed. Gavrielle can give you none of it. But me? I can give you a galaxy that will bend its knee for you and all your darkness."

His breath is cold on my face, smelling like citrus and the masculine shadows I'm so attracted to. Releasing one hand from my cheek, he reaches behind, pulling something from the strap around his waist.

A black rose.

"I told you," he says, eyes dancing from me to the rose— the insidious thing almost pricking my fingers with its thorns as my fingers wrap around its stem. "You've always been my *violent*, dark lady."

His hands come back to caress my cheeks like I'm still the same girl I was on the Azurite. Yet make no mistake, we're in battle, and this rose is his weapon. This black rose flies at me just like a dagger would—straight into my heart. I see it for what it truly represents. I also see *him* for who he really is. It's Gavrielle's love that's finally shown me the difference between love that is healthy and good and love that is toxic and bad for me.

I finally understand.

"That isn't going to work anymore." I breathe deep, lifting my free hand to cup his cold, sharply angled face. "Love isn't about any of that—it's not transactional. Love isn't what you get from someone, Malakyte. Truly loving someone is selfless, giving everything you have to that person without expecting anything in return. You don't love to *take*, you stupid prince, you love to *give*."

I drop the rose, its petals falling in a silent quake.

Malakyte looks at me as if I slashed his face again.

He has no concept of love because he's never experienced it.

And a man who doesn't know love, who feels rejected and wronged, who has power and strength and an immortality I can't defeat, is a dangerous man, indeed.

CHAPTER 112

She is my lover no longer.

Neither of us are willing to budge or relinquish our hard-fought positions.

This battle will end in death.

Either hers or mine.

My Star . . . my enemy once again.

For not having a heart at all, it sure feels as if mine is shattering.

Karalevine's words flash into my mind. *Stupid prince.*

But I've given her everything. I gave her my body, my heart, the keys to my kingdom. I did more than *give*. Fuck, I crossed the galaxy looking for her. I changed my unyielding position for her. I *killed* for her.

Don't I deserve something after all this fucking nonsense she's put me through?

She fights me as she tries to free herself, stepping on the rose I brought for her. I place my other hand back on her cheek, both my hands tightening their grip on her face, and she stops her protests.

As my grip intensifies, fear crawls into her lovely eyes.

Eyes that will never look upon me with love again.

The others have ruined that for me, and in return, I'll ruin everything for them. Ruin their world as they have decimated mine.

Until there's no one and nothing left but her and me.

"You're hurting me," she says, and I suppose I am—I hear it in her voice. I see it in those beautiful eyes.

Selenyte's ghost appears next to us, and she mockingly coos, "That's all you've ever done to her, isn't it? Hurt her, hurt me, hurt Gavrielle, Father and Mother, Naresteé, and Ennar . . . Who don't you hurt, Malakyte?"

No wonder Karalevine hates me so much. I'd hate me, too.

I *do* hate myself.

Karalevine grips my wrists as she attempts to rip my hands away, but I only squeeze tighter.

The sounds that escape her lips cleaves my heart. Stars, I'm hurting her, and it makes me sick, but I can't stop myself. Perhaps I hate her as much as I hate myself now.

It's the only way I can stomach doing what comes next . . . The only way I can conceive of us being together after this.

Karalevine knees me straight in the groin, and I release her, a reflex I'm not quick enough to dispel.

She twirls away, but those eyes stay trained on me. Eyes I'll never forget, even long after her body has died.

Haunting me for eternity.

"I have to end your life, Karalevine." When it happens, I want her to know why. "We'll never stop warring with each other. Not now, not in the next life, and not in the one after that. The love we shared was a fallacy, a dream I held onto from the time Zariya lived. I've realized that. But your crystal—what connects us—that can remain with me till the end of my days. We can be together then. Forever."

"You've lost your fucking mind," she says, reaching for her Elendril sword.

Mine lies in a burned husk where the Azurite sits demolished. She took that from me, too. All the things I held dear, she pilfered and destroyed.

"Perhaps," I agree, drawing my own sword against her. "But your crystal is the only piece of you I can have now."

"Well, you're not going to get it."

I smile at her challenge, but my grief weighs the corners down. "I always get what I want, Karalevine. Always. You should know that by now."

CHAPTER 113

We circle each other, the wheat crunching underfoot with every unwavering step. Both of us committed to our positions, neither of us willing to budge, the love between us unrecognizable.

My legs tremble as we move beyond where Feena and Deimos fell.

Deimos's magic would have been helpful, but it's useless without training.

Except it isn't the only crystal I have.

Or the only weapon.

Thing is, I'm burnt out. If I want to use my crystal to kill him, I need to reserve its power until the very moment I intend to make my kill strike, but even then . . .

Malakyte spins his own sword tauntingly, the promise of death in his eyes is gut wrenching.

"Come and get me, then. Or are you not man enough to do your own dirty work this time?"

He chuckles, twirling the eerie Steel Gray sword. The sun peeks out from behind the moon to reveal little etchings down the center of it. "We both know that I'm more than man enough to do anything that I please, Karalevine, including ending your life. It wasn't that long ago that my so-called dirty work had you screaming my name."

"Fuck you." I raise my sword up in a defensive position.

He grins exactly like his father. "Oh, I think you'll find the way I fight is a lot like the way I fuck. I'll take your breath away here, too."

I bite the inside of my cheek.

He can't know that his words are getting to me.

We edge near the tree line that borders the field, our circling coming to an end as Malakyte strikes—and strikes hard.

My bones vibrate with the force of his hit as our swords slam against each other. Once—faster! Twice—higher.

I have to raise my sword high to block his aggressive attacks, but I hold my ground. The crunching foliage beneath our feet offers a manic tempo for our swords' clanging symphony.

Malakyte is strong.

But so am I.

Our fight pushes us inside the small forest bordering the open field. It will be easier for his larger reach to get caught in the branches, giving me the advantage if I can keep my footing.

I duck, his slash aimed for my throat, but his sword strikes a tree with lethal force, sending bark flying.

Wrenching his blade free, I find an opening and nick his thigh before he dodges behind another trunk.

"You're right." A cry claws from my throat as he pounces aggressively, his blade slicing open my bicep as blood spills across my tattoos. "You do fight like you fuck. What about me?"

His chuckle is like bells to my fucked-up, tragic heart. "More or less. Although I prefer the sound you make when you come rather than when you cry."

"Then, stop."

A twig snaps, and he strikes. Our blades crash together. They tremble with raw, unadulterated fury.

For a flash, he almost looks torn, but his iron-cold resolve returns in earnest.

The blades shift and slide as Malakyte uses his weight to push me down.

Fucking hate being short!

Remembering my fight with Selenyte, I know I'll be fucked if I get locked in a back-bending struggle for control against him, and I shove against it with all I've got.

Our swords pivot down, a dramatic twang singing through the forest as our blades veer downward in a wide arc before separating. I back away, but he doesn't give me an inch and barrels his weight into me, causing my feet to patter backward, backward, backward . . .

My back slams into the rough bark of a tree, pieces splintering exposed skin as he uses his body to overpower me. Our swords slide flush with our chests with nowhere to go as he hurtles into me. Skin as cold as winter ice consumes me like an avalanche, besieging my sweltering core.

I dig my back into the tree so I can push against him, but his knee arches up to gain all the leverage over me.

"You've forgotten," he whispers in my ear, the coldness of his breath pure ice against my hot, sweaty cheeks, "that I know you. Know how you move, how you fight, how you sound when I'm buried inside you. Don't think that I can't anticipate your every move."

His free hand moves to my throat, and he squeezes. No easing into it, no hesitation—he violently begins to strangle me. I struggle beneath him, trying to slide my sword out. It's stuck between us.

"I told you I'd take your breath away." He tightens his grip.

I kick and push and claw and scratch and pull his hair, but he takes it all and holds me even firmer. All I have is my one free hand, his body weight like an anchor against mine.

Spots appear in my vision, his wickedly gorgeous face becoming fuzzy as my attacks lose their vigor.

He's going to fucking kill me if I don't do something now.

I reach for my crystal's power, and . . .

I can't latch onto it.

It's not there, it's not there, *it's not there!*

My blood runs arctic, unstoppable terror gripping me internally in a vise as tight as Malakyte has my throat this very moment.

Where has it gone?

My fingers are speared through his hair as I nearly rip it from his scalp, but without air, that tug becomes nothing but a pathetic pull. My hand releases, catching on his armor as it falls.

My vision is so black I can't even see him, but I do feel him adjust his body, moving one hand all over me while taking even more air from my lungs as he prepares to end my life right here—right now.

I can't breathe . . .

My fingers glide across something smooth . . . the long hilt of Deimos's dagger. It's nearly trapped between us, but I manage to slip it out.

With my last remainder of strength, I pull the dagger free and plunge it into Malakyte's side.

To the fucking hilt.

His cursing transitions from muffled to clear, agonizing bouts of rage as oxygen seeps back into my blood, my vision returning.

Ripping the dagger free, I shove him off and engulf a mouthful of air so precious I almost cry, although my coughing makes it difficult to enjoy.

I sheathe Deimos's dagger and rub my neck, realizing he stripped me of all others. That must've been what he was reaching for a second ago.

My throat is already bruised and swollen, and I'm shocked at his brutality against me.

I shouldn't be . . . but I just can't fathom how we went from loving each other to this violence.

Low laughter reverberates from where he's leaning up against a tree.

"What's so fucking funny?"

His dark armor absorbs the color of his equally dark blood, but I can see wetness around his abdomen and side. He sticks a hand into his armor's pocket, which didn't do him much good against an Elendril weapon. And I have two.

Malakyte reveals a small syringe and grins with delight.

The Silent Breath.

"And there's plenty more where that came from." He stabs himself with it in the same way he stabbed himself with that Tribute drug.

My mind shifts back to that awful day.

His cheeks are blooming to life in the shade Ocean Deep as he tosses the empty needle. "You can't win this fight, Karalevine, so just give up now so I don't have to continue hurting you. It doesn't bring me pleasure."

"If you want this crystal, you're going to have to work for it."

He smiles, showing off all his pointed teeth. "You know I love it when you fight back."

We rush toward each other, two sets of vicious battle cries ripping from our throats as we strike and fight and kick and swing our blades in a death dance of love and vengeance.

It's because I love him that I have to kill him—I'm sure he'd agree. Nobody else has the right to end our lives but us. We've always been twisted. It's why we're drawn to each other.

We stumble out of the miniature forest, the wheat cracking under our feet once again.

"You're looking at this through a cracked mirror, Malakyte," I say between sword strikes and kicks, trying to guide us back to those trees where I have more of the advantage.

He nails my shoulder with his fist and dodges my downward strike. "And how should I be looking at the downfall of my empire thanks to you? With my family dead and empire in ruins, the woman I love responsible for it all . . . tell me, how should I react?"

"Ardelle is dead!" I yell, my fury ripping from my lips with no thought to how it'll piss him off. "My father almost died. Deimos is dead. You've kidnapped Earth's children a—"

I freeze, the gasp that escapes my lips unveils a hush as my death flashes before my eyes.

The tip of his blade is less than an inch from the center of my throat.

We lock gazes, and his eyes flare with victory.

Terror and betrayal lock me in ice.

My crystal still doesn't come when called. The new one doesn't either.

My heart thrashes against my rib cage, and my blood pressure plummets.

He's got me.

CHAPTER 114

YEAR 7, DAY 2,455: I'LL FINALLY BE ABLE TO GET CLOSE
ENOUGH TO SPEAK TO KARA. AFTER ALL THIS TIME, MY
FREEDOM IS IN SIGHT. WITH THIS ONE ACT, I CAN SECURE
PLANET NYKTOS'S SOVEREIGNTY. ALL I HAVE TO DO IS
ENTER THE TITAN GAMES, MAKE SURE KARA WINS, AND
THEN TURN HER OVER TO HIM. WHY DOES THAT FEEL LIKE
BETRAYING MY OWN HEART? SHE CAN'T EVER KNOW THAT
I'M GOING TO DO THIS . . . SHE CAN'T KNOW THAT I'LL DO
ANYTHING TO KEEP MY PEOPLE SAFE.

GAVRIELLE ABRAXAS

"Don't make me hurt you," I tell Sylo.

He points his rifle at us—five against one.

I wedge my body between Pacey and Naresteé just enough to not be noticeable.

"I'll do it, you traitorous piece of squid shit," Sylo growls.

"And are you ready to shoot her?" I ask, nodding toward Pacey.

Hesitating, Sylo looks between Pacey and me, his uncertainty obvious.

Recognition plays across the Starseed's face, and he lowers his Elendril weapon.

"Good boy," Naresteé coos. "Now, let's go."

She and the AI SSPARROW turn their backs on me, and I have this one solitary heartbeat to make my move.

I shove Pacey in the direction of the Voidbringer, the light dancing across the dark walls as it sits inside a room right around the corner. Her eyes go wide as another version of her appears directly in her place.

Relief floods her expression, followed by clear understanding, and she darts around the corner and out of sight.

Yes, go. Stop this insanity.

A similar expression of relief flickers in Sylo's eyes, but he holds his brow furrowed in a now-pretend rage.

Dude was probably about to shit his pants.

Thank the stars my assumption that Pacey was acting paid off—because I was, too.

It doesn't look like Naresteé or the AI soldiers saw. Pacey's fake form stands more vivid and realistic than my older illusions—which were damn convincing as is. I hide the glow in my eyes, too, obviously.

"Gavrielle," Naresteé says softly as me, and the fake Pacey walks behind her and the SSPARROWs, finally rounding the corner. The Voidbringer's light is bursting through a set of double doors twenty feet away. "Malakyte may not be privy to when you use your magic around him, but a Ringer can always feel another Ringer."

Well . . . shit!

Sylo shoots his Elendril rifle at the AI SSPARROW closest to Naresteé, its black body flying into the wall. He fires the second round, but the AI dodges and leaps for him. It comes in so hot that Sylo has no choice but to use his rifle as a shield when the AI's hand becomes one of those long, wicked blades aimed at his head.

I grab Naresteé and wrestle her to the floor, but she knows what I'm doing, of course, and prevents me from pinning her by headbutting me with her horns.

As I tousle with Naresteé, I don't see the other AI SSPARROW rush up behind me—but I hear it. I look up to see its foot rising above my head, barreling down fast. I'm too slow as I'm nailed in the temple. Pain erupts as my vision spots, but thankfully, I don't need to see to use every weapon in my arsenal.

"Gavrielle!" Naresteé rages, grabbing the leathers at my chest and shaking me. "What are you doing?"

The two AI SSPARROWs stop fighting because the entire hallway is now filled with dozens of duplicates of me, Sylo, and Naresteé.

They can't tell who is who, as I illusioned each with a heat signature, as well, something I never could have done with Deimos as my Starseed. *Kara, my powerful, beautiful mate. You saved me again.*

Shoving Naresteé away, I swivel my body and trip the AI that curb stomped me a minute ago. Reaching for the blades at my back is second nature as I free them and stab the machine with both my swords all the way to the hilt, making sure I hit the compartment with the nanobots inside.

"I'm stopping you," I say, teeth clenched tight as I rip my blades free, the robot beneath me twitching, sparking nanobots spilling to the floor.

Sylo's rifle booms out once, twice, three times—the AI SSPARROW he's fighting blown to bits. He hits mine two times, just in case.

Double tap!

Blood trickles down the side of my face, and I'm dizzy as I sit on the floor next to Naresteé, who's looking at me like I'm a monster, the betrayal in her eyes similar to what I'd assume a wrathful god would look like when you tell it you don't want to be friends anymore.

An eerily female voice booms out from the speakers before either of us can move toward the other. "Protection Protocol initiated. Mother network attack imminent. Divert all local assets for Protection Protocol, stage one."

"What does that mean?" I growl at Naresteé, her face torn between triumph and panic.

"The AI is sophisticated, and these robots are her loyal soldiers and protectors." She throws her hair back, so it doesn't tangle in her horns. "Pacey's hacking is a threat to the Voidbringer, and she knows it. She's sending all the AI SSPARROWs in the city or nearby Zones to defend her since she doesn't have a way to physically defend herself. I tried warning you this idea would get you both killed."

"All of them?" Sylo blurts as the walls vibrate with thuds from all directions, floors, and doors. As if Arianyte Tower is trembling from the weight of all the AI robots barreling into it at once. "How many of them are in the city?"

Naresteé scoffs softly, our eyes clashing despite the danger I know exists there. "Hundreds."

Hundreds . . . heading here . . .

Directly for Pacey.

CHAPTER 115

If Malakyte wants me dead so badly, I'm going to force him to watch every single violent, visceral moment of it until he can no longer stomach his own soul. He doesn't get to look away. He's going to suffer the weight of it for the rest of his miserable existence—I'll guarantee it.

Even at the peak of my distress, both my and Deimos's crystals are completely out of reach. Why? I don't know, but it doesn't matter because I'll be dead soon.

Maybe Malakyte is right. He does always win.

Except instead of stabbing his blade into my throat, he grabs me by my leathers, wraps his hand around my waist, and pulls me flush against his front—then kisses me full on the mouth. His cold lips are a shock to my system.

Maybe it's the relief flooding in that he didn't just kill me or our toxic love, but I don't automatically shove him away. I despise how my body reacts to him.

I break the kiss as it leaves me breathless, looking up into those eyes in the shade After Dark. "I hate you," I say, body trembling against his.

Brushing a loose strand of my hair behind my ear, he gives me a sad smile. "I know."

Emotions overcome me, and I wrap my arms around him, hot tears betraying my cold façade. "Stop," I beg, holding onto this man as I bury my face in his chest. "Please, just stop. I don't want this."

Because how am I supposed to kill someone that I love, even when I fervently hate him?

He can't do it, either—he just proved it.

Malakyte's sigh is deep, long, and so fucking sad.

"You don't have to be like him anymore," I push, lifting my head up to him, shameless tears streaking down my cheeks. "He's dead, Malakyte. This entire time, you've been telling me how you see the darkness in me and how it's okay for me to embrace who I am, but I'm telling you this now. I see the light in you, and it's okay for you to be good."

"I'm not good, Karalevine."

I stab my sword into the dirt at our feet, so it sticks straight up, then I take his face in my hands. "But you can be. I've seen the good in you, Malakyte. You don't have to be like him. *He's gone*. He can't hurt you anymore."

He looks away.

"I'm asking you to end this. I know you don't want to kill a planet full of people—that isn't you. Let the kids go, stop the Voidbringer, and leave Earth. Heal. I saw what he did to you. *I see you, Malakyte*. You deserve to find peace. But you have to let me go. If you truly love me, you'll let me go."

"To be with him? The boy I raised as my own son?"

Bitterness laces every single word.

The urge to argue with that statement is maddening, but I soften it instead, praying I can convince him. "Gavrielle and I were connected as children, long before you ever found us. He loves me. He loves you, despite everything between the two of you. I'll tell you exactly what you've always told me. Stop denying who you are because you don't like how it would look. You're not defined by that man anymore."

This whole war is Herkimer at its core.

"The Voidbringer is going to execute its program soon, Karalevine. We don't have long to settle this."

I almost laugh. "Then, do it. Kill me." Sliding Deimos's dagger from the sheath at my belt, I slam the heavy blade into Malakyte's hands.

Calling his bluff.

"I'm not going to let you destroy my world or take those kids. If neither of us will budge, then one of us will die in this field today. Or the Voidbringer will take us both out. Maybe that's what you want in the end. Repeat what happened with Zariya, relive that awful fucking trauma—because isn't that what this is? History repeating itself? But you don't want to come after my soul again once I reincarnate, though, right? You just want to lock me away inside your heart so I'll never leave you, is that what you think it'll be like if you take my crystal? Because that's not what happens, and you know it."

His long fingers curl around Deimos's dagger, the mention of her name turning his eyes to ice; or maybe it's me calling him on his insane bullshit, I can't tell.

Whichever it is, my death whispers on the wind's breeze like a warning as it sways our hair around our shoulders. I can feel Malakyte's edge returning to his energy, just as the breeze shifts.

No matter how much I love the wind, I can't tame the way in which it blows or its deadly nature.

Maybe giving him the dagger was a massive mistake.

Acting on instinct, I reach for the blade, but he's quick and holds it high above. Looking up, Malakyte examines Deimos's dagger with the intensity of a burning flame. "This blade almost ended your life once, and now it's yours. I find it interesting how circumstances can change so drastically. How a person can go from someone you love to someone you hate in a blink of an eye."

The finality of my situation hits me as I stand here, feeling empty, as if I'm in that cube again, surrounded by the dark void where he trapped me for what felt like an eternity.

But you did break free, a voice reminds me.

I did.

Except, this time, my prison is made up of him, and his edges cut and slash and cause me to bleed all over everything else I touch.

I can no longer meet his eyes.

My heart races, searching for my magic.

My power, Deimos's power—any fucking power.

Perhaps I can't have both crystals . . . Deimos's magic replacing the Star's power? If that's the case, then . . .

Then, I have to find that new magic.

Fast.

Malakyte sticks his sword into the dirt beside mine, pulling me into his chest tighter as his arms wrap firmly around my back. That dagger is lined up right above my heart from behind.

Giving him the dagger was royally stupid. I genuinely didn't think he would do it . . .

Why stop himself one moment only to do it the next?

I try to break free, but his grip is like frozen iron.

Fear shoots through my blood. True fight-or-flight fear.

I get my arms in between Malakyte and me. Our power struggle is no longer subtle. I push against his chest, trying to separate our bodies, but his grip is so strong, and I grunt as I try to shove myself free of him.

I'll never be free of him.

I kick between his feet, using our weight to fumble us to the dirt. We hit the ground hard, tousling, punching, and scratching the entire way down as I try to regain control. In the scuffle, I manage to get on top, but I shriek as the dagger flies right for my chest—a kill strike!

My forearm takes the blow instead, successfully blocking it from my heart, but the blade has gone all the way through the meat of it—leather cuff and all.

Our eyes go wide as he realizes what he's done, my blood spilling out all over him.

That would have killed me . . .

Malakyte wraps his legs around my waist and twists his hips to the side, taking me down to the dirt hard. Before I know it, he's on top of me, my screams bloodcurdling as he rips the blade from my arm.

His eyes are glassy, and I know that whatever prevented him from killing me the first time has assuaged itself within his heart because this time the guilt is written all over his face—he's going to do it. The tears in his eyes tell me he's going to do it.

Malakyte's weight pins me, and he's got me on my back, the dagger in both his hands as the blade comes down, down, down toward my chest—my heart.

"Malakyte!"

I gasp his name like a prayer.

But the man I love doesn't answer.

He isn't here.

Ignoring the pain in my arm and the blood pouring down it, I catch his wrists on his downward plunge. But Malakyte has the high ground, and I'm losing, inch by inch.

"Stop," I plead, tears welling up in my eyes. As a last-ditch effort, I say the words I think he wants to hear. "I love you."

I'll say anything. If only love were enough to fix a man who doesn't want to change.

"I can't," he seethes through clenched teeth, tears of his own falling to my chest as they roll down the front of my leathers.

Once the blade pierces my skin, I know there's no going back.

Betrayal feels like a vicious, feral animal. Something inhuman and incapable of empathy, wanting nothing but carnage. That is what I feel at this moment as Malakyte is trying to end my life.

 700

There's only one way to save myself now.

I reach and reach for my magic, remembering the way Deimos felt when he used his magic on the Azurite. Remembering how it felt when he slithered into my mind and took control.

The sensation of this crystal is so different from the one I've always known, but as my adrenaline spikes, I finally touch it, grasping my metaphorical hands around it with panicked speed.

Deimos's crystal!

My crystal.

Perhaps, I'm being delirious from fear and blood loss, but I swear I feel Malakyte's body pulling back at the very last second—but it's too late.

Anguish is what I see in Malakyte's eyes, and it feels as if I'm being sucked right into his head as my magic links to him, the sensation leaving me gasping.

Every emotion that Malakyte feels—they come crashing into me. No buffer to hide the overwhelming, heart-shattering pain inside him. His love, his fear, his devotion—the obsession he clings to, and the absurd rationale of his unhealthy mind that houses this pain and sorrow and brokenness. Every shade of gray, every fried ribbon that morphs in and out of his wrecked soul—I feel Malakyte Ardeen in his entirety.

Malakyte freezes in my grip, his eyes glowing green, a green glow I know is in my eyes. Jade Green. Deimos's dagger has cut pretty deep, but I command Malakyte to stop, to release the pressure—and he does.

Now, I've got him.

We share the surprise of how I did this, and his body trembles against my hold. Who knows how long I can keep him suspended like this.

I crawl out from under him and reach for the dagger but then stop.

You have to kill him, I tell myself. *He was seconds away from murdering you.*

I know! I argue back. *But it's a little hard to do that when I feel every single emotion inside him. I didn't even know he could feel this much. And it felt like he was going to stop like he had last time. What if he was going to stop? What if I'm the one who goes through with this awful act? What if* I'm *the terrible one?*

His surprise shifts to regret then back again. I feel his anger for faltering, the relentless heartbreak that I've caused him, even the shame for what he felt was necessary to do to me. He must *hate* himself for hurting me.

I can't read his mind, I can only feel what he feels. And in all that regret, there's malice for me, too.

My resolve wraps around my throat like a noose, choking the air from me. I have no choice—he's leaving me *no fucking choice.*

I feel his fear as I make him turn the dagger on himself. I feel his struggle as I make him line it up with his heart.

There's nothing more heartbreaking in this world than yearning for poison. To him, it feels like I'm his deadly elixir, his poison pill, his dagger to the heart . . . How ironic. That he hungers to be with someone who hurts him so badly. I don't need Deimos's magic to know what that feels like, because I, too, ache for what dooms me.

With just a thought, I allow Malakyte to speak, desperate to hear his beautiful voice one last time.

"Do you hate me now?" I ask, unable to look at him.

Fucking coward. Fucking murderer.

"It's the love I have for you that's at the root of the issues between us, Karalevine. It's that I ache to hold what isn't meant to be mine, that makes us war like this. The true problem is that you're the tide to my sandcastle . . . my destruction all but guaranteed."

"Then why do you keep trying to rebuild something destined to crumble?" I ask, my voice hollow and desperate. What's this part of me that still hopes he'll say it's because he loves me?

"It's the love I have for you that's at the root of the issues between us, Karalevine."

Around and around we go.

My head dips low. If I want to live, if I want this planet to live, he has to die. Otherwise, we'll just continue in this cycle of toxicity and savagery until every single thing around us is decimated and ruined.

Even though I may be willing to crumble underneath the weight of Malakyte, I won't condemn the others to it anymore.

Looking back up, I hold his eyes when I say, "I truly did love you."

These words seem to tamp down his fear, but they also expose me, too.

I'm in love with a man who hurts me, abuses me, and can't see the error in his ways enough to change and want to be better, even for himself.

Love shouldn't ever be this painful. This destructive.

We've brought an entire planet—a world of people— to their knees.

A toxic, fucked-up romantic gesture if I've ever seen one.

A blaring sound comes from somewhere deep within the city, a massive bright light shooting a giant beam into the sky, the shade Periwinkle exploding up through the haze and into the clouds.

The Voidbringer.

Gavrielle.

I'm running out of time.

I scooch myself close, and my forehead leans up against his, holding onto him as the both of us tremble underneath the weight of where our love has led us.

He thrashes against the magic that's binding him. He knows I'm going to force him to kill himself with that dagger.

Murderer. Murderer. Murderer.

I close my eyes. "I'm sorry," I whisper into his ear, barely able to get the words out.

I force Malakyte to extend his arms, the dagger's tip pointed at the center of his chest, and with brutal efficiency, he stabs himself straight in the heart. The long Elendril blade slices through skin and ligament and bone, shredding his heart muscle as quickly as I can make it. I don't want him to suffer. He doesn't cry out, although I feel the overwhelming torment inside him. I can't bear his feelings anymore, and I release my magical vise.

He slumps forward, and I catch his body as it sags into mine. A sob escapes my lips, and it feels like a dam breaking. My tears fall onto his black armor, his form blurring. "I'm sorry. I'm so sorry."

A minute ago, this man nearly killed me, but that doesn't stop my heart from shredding layer by layer, slice by slice, piece by piece, till I can't feel a thing anymore.

Love and hate are nearly identical when you get to a place like this . . .

Malakyte opens his mouth, trying to talk but struggling to breathe.

I interlace my fingers through his hand, squeezing tightly.

"Kara." One tear slides down his high cheekbone.

"I'm here," I say. "It's going to be okay."

Liar.

I'm crumbling, the pain in my heart a desperate thing that wants him to live and be the man I saw glimpses of up on that spaceship. It hurts so much because I can't allow him to come back . . . because he will never be that man I had manufactured in my mind.

That man was a lie. A beautiful, twisted lie.

That doesn't mean this is easy . . . Watching Deimos die was horrible. Helpless to prevent it as Ardelle drifted away into nothing was pure agony. Watching a man I love die by my own hand . . . is a different type of Hell.

Thinking I could do this easily was fucking delusional.

"That night . . ." he manages to say, blood leaking from the corner of his mouth. "That night, when I tried to set you free . . ." His words are slow, his dark eyes unfocused, but he comes back to me, forcing himself to hold on. "I would have let you go."

The words bleed into the screaming silence, and his wrath doused in love pins me to his eyes as they shift with a flicker, an unfathomable distance crawling inside them. His essence flutters away, kissing my cheek as it goes like a haunting breeze. A ghost promising to haunt me for all eternity. It's I who won't forget this moment for all my days, not him.

"Malakyte?"

He doesn't answer me, doesn't move.

I shake him. "Malakyte?"

I bite my lip to keep the howl inside my body, but it doesn't work for long. I rest my face against him and, unable to contain myself, rip my throat apart. My tears replace where my antimatter should be, with so much pressure I could die from it. Yet nothing emerges as I cry and curse and *scream*.

It isn't fucking fair! Why does he have to be this way? Why couldn't he just find his way out of the darkness like I had? I would have walked him out, but he wouldn't take my hand.

Should I let his crystal revive him? I said I wouldn't, but . . . *I don't fucking want this!*

There has to be some other way, some agreement we can make.

But when I look up and see the light from the Voidbringer, I know it isn't possible, and the agony replaces that little piece of hope I desperately cling to.

We'll go right back to where we started.

Forever at odds.

Forever hero and villain.

This was always where our story was going to end.

I lean over and close his eyes, kiss his lips, brush his hair.

"I'm sorry," I tell him again. "Please, find your peace, Malakyte."

Once I remove the dagger, I'll have to act quickly and get his crystal out before it can revive him.

As for inserting it, once it's in my hands . . . I won't. I don't care how alluring it may be. I don't want it. It feels too much like Malakyte. Like he would be with me for the rest of my life, his ghost on my shoulder, taunting me, drawing me to the darkness, punishing me for what I've done to him.

Never.

I guess his logic about feeling like these ancient crystals hold our essence wasn't so far off, after all . . . I get it now. He wanted a piece of me with him forever, and I want nothing more than to be free of the man who nearly destroyed me.

Stealing my resolve, I grip the dagger's hilt and take a deep breath.

It's time for Malakyte to die for real.

CHAPTER 116

Their heavy, frantic footsteps clang against the walls of Arianyte Tower as every AI soldier in the city rushes toward us. It sounds nearly identical to the SSPARROW boot steps from the orphanage that very first night this all began, except now, the soldiers are here to kill.

Sylo's face is grim and pale.

"When they come, we're all dead. I'll protect her for as long as I can."

Then he's gone, disappearing around the corner and into the room where Pacey and the Voidbringer are.

My eyes slide to Naresteé, who has the sense to look concerned.

"Come with me before you get yourself killed. I'm begging you. Throw Pacey over those big shoulders of yours and let's go before it's too late. Please, Gavrielle. *Please.*"

Smashing glass erupts from lower levels. I hear doors bashing off their tracks and hinges. As they come careening up the stairs, their boot steps the thunder of an inevitable storm.

The Starseeds are in danger.

My friends.

My family.

A family who doesn't lie or manipulate me or turn me into their mindless soldier who kills for them. A "good boy," Naresteé called me . . .

"I'm not some dog the two of you trained, and I'm not going to come when called anymore." I raise my hand to her cheek, hoping my point is clear. "Goodbye, Naresteé."

Her eyes flash with pain as I turn around and dart for the Voidbringer—for the others.

Are we utterly fucked? Yeah.

Our only hope is Pacey hacking the Voidbringer before we get completely slaughtered.

I round the corner and burst through the double doors to the room housing this doomsday device, and I find the Voidbringer sitting upon a flat platform forty feet back.

The room drones with a horrible, high-pitched buzzing that charges the air with a crackling, insidious sizzle that feels so charged the oxygen itself could catch fire. This artificial intelligence towers like some mechanical god, an immovable beast of Arianyte steel and interwoven veins of cabling that pulse with the pilfered lifeblood of Zarmenia's power grid. Wires slither down from the ceiling through a bulbous core that shelters a grotesque, glass-like oval vessel that's filled with zapping light as it fluctuates like contained lightning. The sparks swim violently with bright shards of blue and fragments of purple, pulsing with the radiance of a living thing. The color morphs and swells as if it sees me looking at it somehow.

Holding up what could only be described as the Voidbringer's brain is a metal base that curves around it like an intricate stand. Servers with struggling fans attempt to cool her insatiable appetite. Built-in modems glow around it like vigilant eyes eager to execute her lethal demands. Attachments and lights and screens and keypads and sensors are built into the stand. It isn't computing but rather consuming, and she wants to take the sentiment of the Devouring Accords literally and swallow this planet whole.

Pacey leans against the console that's attached to the Voidbringer's base, implementing her hack as blood drips at her feet.

Her brow is covered in sweat as it creases down, face zoned in and focused with the attention of a microscope.

Sylo stands near, guarding her back for the incoming attack.

"The AI SSPARROWs are here!" I roar, hearing them bursting onto this floor.

Dashing back to the doors, I slam them closed, grabbing up a random broom from the corner and wedging it between the double doors.

That will last about . . . three seconds maximum.

Kara would totally give you shit for this one.

Moving like the wind, I snatch anything that isn't nailed down and either toss or roll it toward the door, wedging the items in so they'll squeeze tighter when pushed. It's not perfect, but it'll hold slightly longer than if it wasn't there.

Even five seconds could make the difference between this entire world living or dying.

Once finished, I take a deep breath, closing my eyes.

I won't fail. I won't fail this planet or the people I love. If I die saving them, then I die doing my race—my true parents— proud. If it's my fate to die in the same battle they gave their life for—to finally bring this tyranny to an end—then I can accept that.

I'm just unsure if Kara can.

There's a large booming sound near the double doors, my makeshift barricade about to fail as the hoard of AI SSPARROWs come to utterly decimate it.

Sylo rushes up to my side, only the two of us here to stop nearly one hundred of these things from getting to Pacey and tearing her to ribbons.

They've already got the door wedged open.

Several slip through, but what's terrifying isn't that they're not getting inside due to my barrier but are struggling to get inside because there's so many attempting to squeeze through the tiny space at once.

The Voidbringer's voice cracks through the electrified air. Her voice is a fractured echo of something long since stripped of all its mercy and humanity. Her declaration cold and absolute.

"Project Oblivion will execute in three minutes."

Several AIs gain their footing, their lethal attention pinned on Pacey and Pacey alone. They don't even see Sylo and me.

I wasn't built to stand here motionless.

I was bred to kill.

So, now, I will kill.

"Can you stop it in time?" Sylo shouts back at Pacey as he shoots at one, blasting it into the wall.

The two of us dance across the room, putting our bodies between Pacey and the door. We have about thirty feet to work inside of, but when a hundred AI SSPARROWs get in here, that's going to get tight fast.

Pacey types faster than I've ever seen anyone slash keys. "I don't know, guys."

The panic in her voice shoots terror through my bones.

"No fucking way, babe!" Sylo fires his rifle again, but the soldier ducks, and the ionized bullet hits the wall, sparks and other debris flying everywhere. "You can do this. You're Pacey fucking Dawson, you hear me? Your brother is in this room with you right now, and he's going to give you what you need to destroy this bitch!"

The door shudders with a boom, and all of the crap I stacked against it shifts.

Fucking perfect.

Pacey's face hardens into stone before I draw my blades. She has her job, and I have mine.

An AI finally reaches me, and I swing, swords flying, slashing, destroying. Aiming for the weak point in their design—those nanobots can't be allowed to escape through those hatches. But I only have two arms—two blades—and with the four AI that have gotten in so far, one is deploying the nanobots.

They come for Sylo and me, a vicious swarm that blasts through the glowing light of the Voidbringer and straight for us.

I charge at the closest one, drop my blades, grab it under the arms, and check it right into the nanobots swarm, and the mechanical horde eats it alive.

Several more AIs squeeze inside.

The female voice of the Voidbringer calls, "Project Oblivion will execute in two minutes."

Pacey slams her fists against the console. "Come on! You fucking bitch!"

"Language!" Sylo calls, and I shake my head only because I didn't think of it first.

"You can do this, Pacey," I yell, the AIs waltzing up to us with those cold, blank, mirror shimmered faces pinned on Pacey's head, the rest beating down the door.

"Gav, I— "

"We all believe in you. Your brother believes in you. Sylo is right. He's right here, and now it's time to dig deep and find a way. You can do this!"

I don't wait to hear her response as nanobots fly through the sizzling air, the AI that deployed them on my ass.

It takes all my speed to duck and dodge the horde, but I manage to get in close to the AI and plunge one blade deep into the soldier's hollow abdomen. We're as close as any two living things can be, my chest pressed up against its beautifully crafted torso. Then I step back, rapidly shifting my weight as my other sword cleaves its head right off.

The head slides across the smooth floor, its neck sparking and sputtering, a red light in its face blooming red hot until it fizzles out completely. The swarm of nanobots this specific AI deployed also cascade to the floor, as useless as little marbles.

Well, isn't that interesting.

"Sylo!" I roar, "I think if you cut off the heads, the nanobots are useless! The head must be some kind of receiver."

When I don't hear an answer back, my gaze whips around the room. The light of the Voidbringer casts such dark shadows. Too many bodies, too many AIs.

Where the fuck is he? Panic rushes through my blood.

There!

An AI has him pinned by the neck up against the wall, his Elendril rifle on the floor, the AI's blade hand arched back, ready to slice right through his throat.

Not if I get there first!

My thighs burn as I rush across the room. The random items of my barricade fly across the floor as I dodge SSPARROW after SSPARROW. Chairs, desks, straight debris, I dart past them all.

Sylo screams, and I hear Pacey do the same—*focus.*

With my angle and distance, I can't stop the AI's attack. If I don't dramatically change my current trajectory, I won't make it to him in time.

Without thinking, I spring onto a desk sitting close to Sylo and the AI, using the adjacent wall as leverage to push off and leap towards them. Once I'm in the air, my body spins—and I'm right there! Blades slice air, then metal, then wire, the weapons I earned through blood slicing the neck of this soulless creature right off its shoulders.

It's completely decapitated before my feet hit the ground, its headless body falling onto Sylo as he pushes it off him in disgust.

Sagging in relief, Sylo meets my eyes with wide-eyed shock. "Holy shit, dude," he says. "If I wasn't straight, I'd have one hell of a hard-on for you right now."

I laugh. "You're welcome." I wink. "Go for the heads!"

 712

"It's always cutting off the head," he says in faux irritation as he picks his gun up off the floor and takes aim.

I crack my neck, roll my shoulders, and face the doors. About a dozen AI arms and legs squeeze themselves into the gap of the doorway.

They'll break through any second now.

"Project Oblivion will execute in one minute."

The tower trembles again, the light from the Voidbringer brightening and shuddering, the AIs outside becoming even more frantic to get in.

Sylo and I lock eyes.

"You look like ass," I tell him with a bigger grin than before.

He throws me an unbothered smirk. "Fine, pristine, top tier ass."

"Top fucking tier," I echo proudly. "You're a good dude, Sylo."

I can't tell if it's the flickering light from the Voidbringer, but it seems as if his eyes are a little glassy. "You too, man."

The doors blast open as the remaining items go flying. I bring my attention forward, brace my body low, swords out in front, heart hammering its death song.

Before it's too late, I push my words, my feelings, my love for Kara down that connection between us that magic and love has created. Our bond that's always been there, even as children. *I love you, Kara. I love you so fucking much.*

Then Sylo and I rush toward the AIs, toward death.

CHAPTER 117

"**B**ehind you!" I shout.

Sylo turns in time to shoot one of many AIs, its metal body flying across the room.

I call out, "We're getting absolutely *railed* here—and not in a good way!"

"Perfect!" Sylo says, kicking and firing, then kicking again. "I absolutely *love* getting gangbanged by robot dongs. A dream come fucking true, man!"

"Will you two shut the fuck up?" Pacey yells.

Right. Bad time for a conversation like this, but I can't help but grin ear to ear as I slash off another head, one of the dozens of AI SSPARROWs bursting into the room.

We're not going to last much longer, especially as the AI are driving us farther and farther toward Pacey. One positive? The room is so cramped their nanobots are mincing them up, too, so they've stopped using them against us. They don't need them. Their numbers are enough.

One crawls up the wall on all fours, its head spinning around at insane angles like a devil-possessed doll—attention locked in on Pacey. She's too focused on the Voidbringer's console, completely oblivious to the AI hurdling toward her at the speed of a fighter jet.

The AI leaps from the wall with its arms outstretched for her throat.

I'm too far away!

I thrust my arm and chuck one sword as hard as I can, aiming it directly for the back of Pacey's head.

It flies in slow motion, the light from the Voidbringer glinting off the blade with every lengthy rotation—a deadly, deliberate, precise shooting star.

Time finally catches up, the AI's outstretched fingers morphing into ten deadly claws, reaching and reaching and—

The blade buries itself directly in the neck of the AI precisely as it reaches Pacey, the force knocking it to the Voidbringer's metal base as it crumples to her feet.

I jump over SSPARROW bodies and slash the head off this SSPARROW before it gets back up. "You got to hurry, Pacey," I growl.

Her fingers fly across the keys as panic etches into her furrowed, sweaty brow. "Gav," she says, "we're not going to—"

I jump for another attacking SSPARROW.

A sharp pain slices my thigh, and an AI rips its sword-arm through muscle and flesh, sending my blood splattering to the floor.

We'll add that to my never-ending list of injuries.

Sylo tries to get closer to us, but he can't move an inch, let alone ten feet, the SSPARROWs surrounding him completely.

My body, drenched in sweat, blood, and panic, rages against me the harder I fight, fueled only by soul crushing fear and the drive to protect what I love at all costs. It's what keeps me battling, keeps me slicing head after head.

"Project Oblivion will execute in thirty seconds."

More light generates from the ceiling, casting the room and an eerie blue glow that makes for the perfect graveyard.

Sylo's cry rings out into the air. He falls to one knee but shoots back, his rifle going off again and again, taking as many heads as he can.

They're an unstoppable swarm.

I'm breathing hard as I knock another soldier from Pacey's back. My movements are becoming sluggish, my decapitations less clean.

But there is no rest for me. Only fighting and killing and fighting and killing, what he bred me to do. And if I stop now, I not only lose my home-world but this one, too. If I'm to get past this discrepancy in my character and find a way to move forward, I have no other choice but to accept it. I'm efficient at ending life, and that is nothing to be proud of, but the very thing I hate about myself is giving Pacey more time to save us. To save the world.

That isn't an evil thing, I realize.

What I do have control over is using my curse to kill for good and only good. Malakyte may have taught me the art of murder, but I get to choose when and who I kill. My choice is no longer made for me.

Yet I'm not sure if my skills are enough to get us to the finish line.

"Project Oblivion will execute in twenty seconds."

"Pacey!"

Sylo's cry for haste is all wrapped up in the way he calls her name.

I blink rapidly as a bright orange light burns my eyes.

Jupiter's rings!

Naresteé is standing outside the doorway, a flamethrower in hand as she blasts the AI hoard, keeping the remaining soldiers from entering. I can't help but feel love swell in my chest. She didn't leave us.

"Project Oblivion will execute in fifteen seconds."

"Turn the fucking thing off!" Naresteé screams.

 716

I'm distracted as an AI kicks my lower back from behind. My weight slides forward, and its arm wraps around my neck as it brings me to my knees.

Another marches forward, directly in front of me.

Great, I'm getting tag teamed now—and not in a good way. *Way to make light of your death, big guy.*

"Project Oblivion will be executed in ten . . ."

The Voidbringer's voice swoops the entire room into nothing but muffles as a high-pitched ringing spears into my ears, time slowing down to the rate of my pounding heart.

"Nine . . ."

The AI in front of me jerks its arm, and it becomes a sword as the other holds me on my knees from behind.

"Eight . . ."

I see my own reflection in the AI's face as it draws its arm back, readying to strike.

"Seven . . ."

Kara's face flashes before my eyes.

"Six . . ."

Sylo screams for Pacey again, panic ripping his vocal cords.

"Five . . ."

A sword-arm plunges toward my chest, and I drop my blades to catch it, gloves and skin tearing.

"Four . . ."

More swarm closer, like they can't wait to taste the bloodshed.

"Three . . ."

Many reflective faces stare down at me with malice and hate, showing me how powerless I am at Arianyte's feet.

"Two . . ."

I close my eyes to give myself one last moment to see her face. Knowing for certain we'll be together soon.

"One . . ."

CHAPTER 118

I keep my eyes clenched, braced for death, hoping it'll be quick.

Something hard hits my face, and my eyes snap open.

The AI SSPARROW has fallen on me, slumped over my shoulder, stiff and lifeless. The one holding its arm around my neck also slackens behind me.

One by one, each metal body collapses, as if their puppet strings have been severed.

The light of the Voidbringer fades down, down, down, the room darkening by the second as the thrumming sound of the core distorts and warps, ultimately leaving us in a hollowed silence.

"Oh, my fucking stars . . ." Pacey half cries, half laughs, her chest heaving as if she just ran a marathon. She falls to her knees, covering her face, her sobs mingling in the air, with Sylo and me panting like dogs.

Sylo runs to Pacey, tiptoeing around the bodies of the SSPARROWs until he makes it to her. He sinks to the floor, grabbing hold of her with everything he has. "I knew you could do it, Pace." He kisses her temple, her forehead, her cheeks, her lips. He takes her face in his hands. "I'm so fucking proud of you! Ardelle is so fucking proud of you."

Relief unlike anything I've ever felt floods into me, and I start to laugh—cry—maybe both, I don't know. It doesn't really matter. We're alive.

Earth is alive.

We did it.

Pacey did it.

Down to the last stars damned second, but *we did it*.

Naresteé has fled. Stars know where she's run off to. She saved us, though. Her love for Pacey and me was too strong for her to stay away. I'd like to think that, anyway. Like to think that I mattered to her in some way, despite how our relationship had to end.

"I really didn't think I was going to make it in time," Pacey says, looking as exhausted as Sylo and me. "There were two paths I could have taken, and I had seconds to decide which one and I just felt Ardelle guiding me through it the entire time. I know that sounds crazy, but . . . I felt him. I was going to go the other way, but his voice was in my heart, telling me not to. The moment I did, I found the way through and was able to shut her down."

"You shut that bitch down, alright," Sylo says with the brightest, proudest smile.

"You saved us, Pacey," I say, voice soft, the weight of her victory interlaced between each word.

She shakes her head. "There's no way I could have done it without you both. I saw how hard you were fighting to keep those things off me. If you weren't here, I'd have been killed ten times over again. *We* saved us. We're a team. A family."

A family.

"Team motherfuckin' Starseed!" I beam, and they do, too.

"I'm still waiting on the T-shirts," Sylo laughs, and I'll wear mine proudly.

From my biological family to one made from lies and manipulation, to this beautiful melting of stars and time and magic bringing these old souls back together again, it's been a long time coming.

I can't let it slip through my fingers. "This battle isn't over." I stand on uncharacteristically shaky legs. "You don't have to come with me, but I'm going to help Kara."

"Are you kidding?" Sylo says, standing as he reaches to help Pacey. "We're for sure coming."

That will mean so much to her.

"Let's go get our empress," I say, throwing them a smirk.

We make a mad dash out of Arianyte Tower, the building such a hollowed husk of what it once was. Our surviving rebel comrades are nowhere to be seen. I hope they made it out alive.

Once we reach the courtyard, the sun is no longer hidden by the moon's shadow, and it beats hot against my face. It's silent except for our footsteps and still smells like fire and burnt bodies as the regular SSPARROWs lay dead, nothing but metal husks.

We're almost to the street when footsteps rush up to my left, feet so light and quick there's not even time for my pulse to spike when I'm nailed in the temple with the force of a meteor strike.

Everything goes black.

CHAPTER 119

The battlefield isn't what we expected, Pops.

It smells like war, and war is death, fear, and desperation. Ash, smoke, scorched wheat, overheated wires, and ionized air all mixed in with gunpowder and piss and shit. What reeks the most isn't the bodily fluids or the Arianyte-made machines that shred us to ribbons—it's the fear.

The complete fucking terror that comes with being on the losing side of an unwinnable war.

But you didn't raise a quitter—nah, you raised a fucking queen.

Standing half inside the roof in an old-world tank, I point to the Arianyte army, but we're so intermingled we're all one cacophony of fuckery.

"Snipers!" I roar through comms. "Hit that left flank harder! They're kicking our asses."

Our snipers are in the tiny forest to our right that separates the fields where I saw one of the dragons go down, but I don't think it was Kara's.

Girl, your little ass better be alright, or I'm going to kill you myself.

My eyes scan the battlefield. At least the sun is back out—*stupid eclipse*—and we have more light. Metal and rebel soldiers frantically battle within this swarm of madness, but I search each one for the adult Ringers. Even in this chaos, I've been keeping my eye on them, but I haven't seen either in a minute. Maybe more, I don't know. It's been a grade-A circus around here, and those aren't my stars damned monkeys, but still, I do it for my girl.

Where are you people?

I say into comms, "Terryn, Mom, Hank, have any of you seen the Ringers? I don't have eyes on them."

I suddenly duck as an Arianyte bullet whizzes so close I feel its heat on the right side of my face.

Shit!

Assholes.

I'm so done with these fucking squids!

"Haven't seen 'em in twenty—could even be longer than that!" Terryn says.

It sounds like he's busy, so I don't push. I peek my head back up, wondering why I don't have protection for this face. Mom and Hank don't answer, but I've got eyes on them, too, and they're also a bit preoccupied with a bunch of cock-sucking sky-rats.

I scan the field again. It's massive, so it's possible they're just off somewhere that I can't see, but it's odd I can't find them, and we specifically agreed they'd stay close. I switch my comms to the med squad at the very back of our ranks.

"Hey, it's Trinity. You got eyes on that new doctor—the pretty blond one?"

An explosion draws my attention, and I scream at a bunch of soldiers to take that Arianyte cannon launcher down.

A voice answers in my ear. "Trinity, he hasn't been here for a while. He ran off to help someone and never came back."

Oh, fuck me.

Each body I scan is either the enemy or one of us, but none are the Ringers. I put a call out comms-wide, to all squads except the dragon squad, asking for the Ringers.

Nobody's seen them for a hot minute.

 722

Fuck, if anything happens to them, Kara is going to fry my ass for breakfast. She's just started trusting me again, and if they get killed—if her father gets killed after what I did—*fuck!*

I don't know what's going on, Pops, but I've got a bad feeling about this.

CHAPTER 120

KARALEVINE RUZZ

I'm not sure which hurts more, killing Malakyte or loving him. Like both sides of the moon, light and dark coexisting in a void of chaos. It can't be helped. Girls like me love boys like him, boys that make us think they can be saved if only we love them hard enough.

"*I'm flying back to you, Killer of Worlds,*" Dannanōk says. "*The Dark Starseed's metallic soldiers have all shut down. I believe the Voidbringer has been neutralized.*"

I glance toward the city, and that bright column of light from Arianyte Tower is gone. *Pacey, you did it. You beautiful genius.* I always believed in her, and I feel Gavrielle is alive, as well. Now it's time for me to end this, no matter how much it may shred my heart to pieces.

I can keep my promise to Deimos and end this. Then we can all go home . . .

With the dagger firmly in my grasp, I bring my magic forward—only feeling uncontrollable tendrils of Deimos's crystal, mine still nowhere to be found, but it's got to be enough. I'll remove the dagger, then the crystal immediately afterward, so there's no time for him to revive.

I get the dagger halfway out when my right shoulder is violently jerked back—yanking my hand from the dagger's hilt as it damn near gets ripped out entirely.

A vehement wave of pain wrenches a cry from my ravaged throat as I find one of Ardelle's Elendril arrows sticking out of my right shoulder.

Mocking laughter follows, and my blood runs the frigid cold of a cloudless, moon-chilled night.

Herkimer stands tall twenty feet away, Ardelle's bow and arrows in hand.

He grins the most repulsive, wicked smile I've ever seen. "Long live the emperor."

Herkimer wears regal armor, his face young and healthy and whole as the wind blows his short black hair across his prominent brow.

No…No, he's supposed to be dead! Malakyte said he was dead!

"I'd do this all over again if it meant I could see the look on your face right now." He laughs—his favorite weapon.

It grinds of my last fucking nerve. Not more than seeing Ardelle's bow in his cold, cruel hands. I dropped it by Feena and Deimos like an idiot.

"Hurry, Dannanōk," I say. *"Herkimer is here!"*

"I'm close!"

Mine and Malakyte's swords are too far away from my spot. The only weapon within my reach is Deimos's dagger, barely hanging out of Malakyte's heart. If I remove it, then Malakyte's crystal will revive him, and I'll be forced to fight them both at once, and even with Dannanōk, a battle against two immortals surely doesn't bode well for my odds.

Especially with an arrow shot clean through my shoulder, the pain creeping in alongside all the rest. My other arm is still bleeding from where Malakyte stabbed me.

And my most powerful crystal is a total no-show. This couldn't get any worse.

An unexpected sound has my head whipping to the left, expecting it to be Dannanōk, but that isn't flapping wingbeats that I hear—it's the revving of a ground-hover.

Panic turns that arctic ice within my blood into a raging inferno.

Herkimer laughs like he's already won as my friends and family are dragged out of the hover by living SSPARROWs, who I'm assuming are savagely trained extras who have been on the Vivianite, loyal to Herkimer and Herkimer alone. They'd have to be good—lethal, in fact—to have caught each one, including Gavrielle, Jance, Pacey—everyone.

Gavrielle and I lock eyes, the side of his head gushing with blood. He's collared, beaten to shit—just like all the others. And Jance . . . His neck has a big gash in it, and he's breathing really hard.

Herkimer can dust them at any moment. It happens so quickly, so abruptly. There's no time, no goodbyes, no saving them—no fucking nothing! I can't watch this happen again. *I can't.*

Six of us. Ten of them plus Herkimer.

One of me.

One of me.

One of me . . .

A calming rush floods over my body, and the confusion snaps me out of my panic when I realize it's coming from *Gavrielle.* He's flooding our bond, so bright and intense now that we're Starseed and Ringer, his angelic Violet Rush tendrils gently brushing up against the edges of my mind, comforting my soul like a soothing caress. *"I'm always with you."*

"Now," Herkimer says, walking closer to the others, who are all dragged to the wheat field, arranged side by side on their knees. "In case any of you even think about wanting to try me."

The SSPARROWs mimic this, standing directly behind the others, holding them hostage at disruptor-point execution style. I'm thirty feet away, watching Herkimer cross the space between him and them.

 726

He waves at the nearest SSPARROW soldiers, who, despite their certain loyalty, becomes instant dust with the blink of an eye. Within three seconds, the man who was once standing beside Herkimer is gray dust, the wind literally blowing him away.

Panic seizes my insides. It closes my throat. It locks every joint.

Herkimer laughs, the other soldiers standing motionless, as if their comrade didn't just fucking die. "I can ash them at any moment, and there's so much more where that came from. I want them to watch what I do to you before I end them. You may have stopped my Voidbringer, you may have slain my son, but I'm the true threat here, and I always have been. I'm in control, you understand me?"

None of us dare speak.

His dark eyes narrow at Gavrielle once he comes to stand next to them. "Don't think I don't know about the little trick you pulled with Selenyte back on the Azurite. I've got something ultra special reserved for you, boy."

"Get fucked, prick."

Stars, Gavrielle . . . can you not act like a cocky ass for once in your life?

A roar sounds from the skies, and I desperately peer up, Dannanōk's wings coming into view, as if this dragon can be the salvation I need to keep my loved ones alive.

"Ah, the dragon!" Herkimer coos, throwing his arms up in the air. "Just in time."

Dannanōk lands with an earth-shaking rumble, his black scales simmering off the sun in the shade Purple Mountain Majesty. He bends his head low, lips snarling back to reveal rows of needle-like teeth in a clear posture that indicates he's about to scorch this entire field up like a matchbox left in Hell.

"Burn me all you'd like, dragon, it won't work." Herkimer is right. It won't. Nothing will. He's invincible. "But now that you're here, it's the perfect time for you to reveal the coveted secrets you've kept so close to the chest all these long decades—or should I say, close to the 'scales'? It really doesn't matter.

What does matter is that, each minute you make me wait, I kill one of your precious Starseeds and Ringers. Tell me the secrets to the Elendril crystals, or I ash them all."

"No!" I blurt, trying to stand, when I fall back to my knees. Even exhaling feels impossible with this fucking arrow in my body. "Why do you even care? You hate the crystals."

When Herkimer turns back to me, his eyes are no longer dancing with triumphant amusement. They're dark, and they send a spindle up my spine. Without saying a word, he fishes into his pocket and pulls out the exact dragon figurine that was sitting on my coffee table in my room on the Azurite.

The others look confused as Herkimer holds the little golden statue out to me, his grin all teeth and arrogance, but I know . . .

I shake my head, the movement pulling the arrow embedded in my shoulder. "You planted the dragon in my room," I say, trying to fill in the others so they can understand exactly how we got here. "And it was you who first mentioned the dragons in the first place."

"Why not use the dragons to break the suspect?" he had said.

Fuckin hell . . .

There he goes again—laughing. No wonder Malakyte had gone insane, having lived over two hundred years with this madman.

"You walked right into it. I almost thought you caught on to me and were doing it on purpose, but no, you're just that easily manipulated. It couldn't have played out more perfectly for me. You found the dragons, and in your desperate situation, there was a good chance those pretentious lizards would give you their secrets just to make up for their utter failure the last time."

"Well, your plan failed because they never told us shit." I give a cocky chuckle of my own, knowing how much he hates it. I think back to our conversation in the Memorantis room. "And for what? To help Malakyte?"

"Of course it was for *him*!" With Ardelle's bow in his hand and voice bitter, he points to Malakyte. "Because he's weak!

 728

Spineless! The only halfway decent thing he ever did was choose someone powerful to stand by his side. Since he couldn't keep you on your leash, I had to come up with a plan to ensure this empire survived once I had gone—to make him another version of me to ensure this empire continued to thrive."

Nobody should have the crystal's secret power. I don't care what it is, but Malakyte specifically? Bad fucking idea. Herkimer really set all of this up just to get me to wrangle the secret out of Dannanōk?

"Malakyte is dead, Herkimer. He isn't going to come back."

"Oh, Little Thief, you misunderstand my motivations." My brows furrow, blood pressure dropping fast. "Assisting my son *was* my goal in the beginning, but then you all pulled the wool from my eyes. I've said from the very start Selenyte's killer will die by my hands if it's the last thing I do. It just so happens that my son's crystal is also my salvation. It's a win-win. That scar on his face disappearing is proof of that. When I regenerate, if I have a scar, I reform that same scar. My disease comes back with me, no matter how many times I regenerate. My son's crystal will heal what plagues me. I will conquer death itself, and not you or these dragons or this fucking planet can stop me. Those crystals will be mine, and I'm going to learn their secrets, especially if they're going to be a part of me now."

My eyes fall to Deimos's dagger, which slipped out even more as Malakyte lies on his side. "So, you're totally fine killing your own son just so you can keep living?"

"You did my dirty work for me," he says. "Like you said, he's dead, and he's not coming back. You didn't take the crystal for yourself like a smart person would have. How unstoppable you would have been. But I'm here now, and I will ensure my true heir gets her vengeance."

"Don't go off into a evil fucking monologue, *please.*"

His smile falls. "Come on, Little Thief, you know how I like to play. Who will it be first? Ringers, right? We don't really need them to keep the crystals in play, if I'm understanding this overly complicated magic system correctly. So, who's first? Oh, yes, the bastard that made me believe my daughter was still alive."

Herkimer chucks Ardelle's bow and arrows and rips Gavrielle out of line by his metal collar.

Gav fights, but with two SSPARROW assisting him, Herkimer and the soldiers have Gavrielle on his knees in front of the others, facing me.

Our eyes collide, and my crystals burn, they fucking *burn*, but I still can't find my antimatter.

All I find is the memory seared into my mind of Ardelle turning gray and fading into nothing. If Gav . . .

I won't let this happen! My antimatter crystal may not be working, but Deimos's is.

Feeling that magic surge within me, I lock onto Herkimer's eyes, waiting to feel that connection link into place, but . . .

"Oh, eerie eyes." He itches the side of his head and smirks down at me. "But I'm impervious to mind tricks like that. Narestee's, too. Must be some random power I've collected over the years. I see the new symbol, so you did take another crystal, after all. I thought one of you was missing . . . Where's the crystal you used to slice off my hand? You would have used it on me already if you had the ability. Performance anxiety? Burnout from blowing all those ships to pieces? Or maybe you're so traumatized from our time together you can't get it up? Regardless, you're out of tricks, Little Thief, so what will you do now? Who's The Killer of Worlds when her back is against the wall?"

You've got to be fucking kidding me . . . *Really?*

"Dannanōk, tell him!" I beg the dragon. *"Please!"*

"I can't, Killer of Worlds."

"Why the fuck not?"

"If he unlocks this power, it will be the end of everything."

 730

"If I lose Gavrielle, I will be the end of everything! Killer of fucking Worlds, remember?"

"The power can't be given. It must be earned," he growls.

What the fuck does that even mean?

My attention is drawn back to Gavrielle as he struggles against their hold, but he doesn't break eye contact with me. He never will.

Herkimer cocks his head toward Dannanōk. "Tell me the secret."

Dannanōk's deep, guttural growl gives me goose bumps, sulfur thick in the air.

"I love you." Gavrielle pushes down the bond.

I hear him as clearly as if he spoke the words.

"Don't you say your goodbyes to me!"

Not yet. *Not yet!*

I claw at the door to my antimatter's power. *All my life, all you've done is explode and destroy, but now when I need you most, you're going to disappear? I need you!*

Breaking eye contact with Gavrielle, I stare down at my own chest as if I could meet that creature inside me eye to eye and beg it to come back. The way Deimos's symbol sits within my Star looks so foreign and strange, but I don't stop shoving my hope down that highway between it and me that it'll return.

As if a weight had suddenly been chained to my ankles, that familiar sensation takes me over, just like it did all those months ago when I first experienced a vision by looking at these Elendril symbols.

No, no, not now . . . This can't happen now!

But I can't stop the blackness wrapping its sweet numbing arms around me, wrenching me down into its embrace.

There's nothing but darkness for several long, disastrous heartbeats until a brilliant white light materializes in its place, and I try to blink out the stinging in my eyes.

The transition is nauseatingly abrupt—quicker than usual—but my consciousness is no longer in the field outside Zarmenia. I'm somewhere else entirely.

A beautiful scenery takes shape, a place where the sky is rich with Blueberry Parfait, Orange Popsicle, and Ballerina-colored clouds mixed with glowing stars that twinkle like glitter.

I'm standing on a long white marble walkway stretching endlessly in either direction, surrounded by still water that reflects the sky above. In front of me is a stunning rotunda with filigree stonework etched into every white pillar and archway, looking like a palace for a god.

I lift my hands, expecting Zariya's greenish skin tones, but instead I see my own, finger tattoos and all.

This isn't one of her memories, and it certainly isn't one of mine.

Am I . . . dead? This doesn't feel like one of the Elendril's visions. Did Herkimer dust me?

A figure appears from between the pillars forty feet ahead, and she casually strolls toward me.

Her long hair blows in a warm, pleasant breeze—the entire place exuding an overwhelming feeling of peace.

The closer the figure gets to me, I pick up more of her features.

Her extremely large ears poke out between wisps of long, stark white hair in the shade Winter. She's dressed in alien leather, Treebark Brown and weathered, a contrast to her Wasabi skin color, smooth and glowing and beautiful. But her skin is nothing compared to her face, which shines with a radiance of pure peace—gorgeous and haunting and unique. Big, round, tranquil eyes in an interesting, green-flecked brown I could only match with Dark Moss Green, but they bring out the freckles stamped across her nose.

When she stops, the two of us are a few feet apart.

I know her instantly, her tall frame towering over me, but I can only blink out the tears forming in my eyes as she smiles warmly at me.

"It's about time we had a conversation, Karalevine."

"Zariya . . . ?" I whisper.

CHAPTER 121

Zariya's face is so much like Deimos's it's freaky, not only because she's so unbelievably lovely but because I see so much of him in her.

Alien in every sense of the word, yet eerily familiar.

We stand face to face.

Me and the true Killer of Worlds.

The woman Malakyte loved with every bit of his blackened heart. The person responsible for the deaths of every person she loved besides her father, only cursing him with four decades of living with the trauma of having to watch his daughter burn. I vaguely remember thinking on the Azurite how what she did sort of wrecked my soul. Killing everyone you love will leave a scar—a nasty fissure within—and she didn't have to pay for that—*I did*.

Zariya's sin.

"Am I dead?" I ask.

"No." She chuckles, examining me. "You're probably wondering why your crystal isn't working."

"Is it gone?"

The panic in my voice is evident.

Zariya shakes her head, and her hair floats on a phantom wind. "Of course not. I had to get you here somehow."

Relief floods through me that I haven't lost it, but anger sizzles it away. "Gavrielle is about to die! I don't have time for this. I need to get back there."

Zariya reaches for my braid, the hair loose and wind-blown. "You don't need to worry about any of that right now."

"You're wrong," I say. "There's tons I've got to worry about right now. Everyone I care about is about to die."

"We've been watching."

"Who's we?"

"Do you want the secret to defeating someone like Herkimer?"

"What?"

"The key, the secret, the unstoppable power that not even a power-heavy immortal like Herkimer Ardeen can withstand. Do you want it?"

I open my mouth to say hell fucking yes, but my gut twists as the words form on my tongue. I look at Zariya, really look at her. This is weird.

"What's the catch?"

"You'll have to become the next Killer of Worlds. It's the only way. Take the power and win, or don't, and die."

Power. Power to save Gavrielle and Jance and all the people I love. Power to stop Herkimer, keep Malakyte in the grave, save the Hijacked he stole away, and save the world.

Yes. I want that power.

I've always wanted that power.

"Will it help me save them?"

I'll sacrifice anything to protect them, but it's more than that . . . I want this power, always have. There's no point in trying to hide from myself. Zariya knows me—she *is* me.

"Didn't you ever wonder why I was able to blow up that moon and you couldn't get anywhere close to doing something so big? It wasn't me alone, wasn't just the crystal. It was a moment exactly like this. I took the power offered to me, and I chose to do what I did with it. What you choose is up to you, but just know that, by saving them, you may also be sacrificing them. Power always comes at a cost. I didn't quite understand that until it was too late."

"So, Dannanōk told you the secret, after all?"

"The Elendril crystals have many secrets."

I didn't expect this, I . . . I just want to save the people that I love from a madman. We're so close. We stopped the Voidbringer. Malakyte is down. I'm sure the rebels are kicking ass on the front lines. There's just Herkimer left and then Arianyte is finished.

If I take what Zariya is offering me . . . then I can beat him.

Then we can all go home . . . That's all I want.

The power to save them is at my fingertips.

Take it!

The darkness inside me whispers. It speaks to me in Malakyte's voice. It wears his face.

Take it!

Take it!

Take it!

I'm powerless against Herkimer. He's invincible. If I don't take it, we'll all die. Those kids will be bled dry, Earth destroyed—surely, he can reprogram the Voidbringer. Do I honestly have a choice?

"Give it to me."

My voice doesn't even sound like my own.

Zariya lifts her hands to my chest—long, pointed nails and all—but something in me recoils from her touch, a visceral, full body shriek.

"Wait!" I cry, my voice trembling, and Zariya looks down on me with expectant eyes. I blink a few times. "Tell me something first."

This is all happening too fast. It's too weird.

She nods, hand not moving an inch as it hovers above my heart.

"Why did you do it?" We don't need to specify what I mean. "Through all of this, I've been compared to you. By Malakyte, by Deimos, by everyone who knew what you did . . . but you weren't the one who paid for that act. It was *me*. I'm the way I am because of you. You ruined me. By killing them all, you cracked something fundamental inside me. And the darkness just . . . crept in. It ate me alive, Zariya. It still is. I always think I'm finding a way to fix myself, but I don't. *I'll never be better.*"

Zariya looks devastated by my words, and I'm taken aback when she pulls me into a tight embrace.

"I'm so sorry for that," she says. "I thought I was saving them. I thought I was protecting the greater good. I thought I was stopping evil and liberating the galaxy like some sort of tragic hero. Malakyte was going to hurt them so badly. So, so badly . . . There are fates worse than death, Karalevine. And in my insanity, in my desperate, selfish longing to save them, I took their lives to make sure they'd never know the evil that was planned for them. It was an atrocity that I committed. Not only against them but against myself."

Against me.

She separates us, and the anguish, the guilt, the regret is written all over her pretty face. And for the first time, I understand Zariya's unfathomable choice. I've hated her for the decision she made that day, hating her for putting me in the situation to suffer for it when I didn't make that choice—*she did!*

Except being with her now, hearing her explain it . . . I can, at the very least, understand *why*.

But can I forgive her?

Take the power! You will never hurt again, the darkness with Malakyte's voice whispers, reminding me how close I am to obtaining it.

Something else feels more important, some stronger thread pulling me toward the woman standing before me now.

Take the power! No one will make you their victim ever again.

If I can't forgive Zariya for her choice, for fracturing our soul, then how am I supposed to expect the others to forgive me for my mistakes? Forgive me for embracing the darkness Malakyte exploited?

You want the power. This will give you the ability to do what Zariya could not—save the ones you love.

How can I forgive *myself* if I can't forgive *her?*

My darkness has a point, and the more I ignore it, the more it fights to be heard. The more powerless I become, the more power it covets.

I release a tense breath, knowing what must be done but also knowing I've doomed us all.

"Keep the power you're offering me, Zariya. I don't want it. But I do want to tell you that it's alright. I understand you now. I forgive you for what you did . . . You brought me Gavrielle. And Jance and Ardelle and all of them. And I love them so much. *I just want to save them.*"

Tears well up in my eyes because, without this power, I don't know how to save them, but I'm not willing to sacrifice them, either. I won't. I won't repeat her mistakes or my own.

When Zariya smiles, she's the most beautiful woman I've ever seen. "Congratulations, Karalevine. You passed the dragon's test. I'm proud of you."

I blink away my tears, confusion pulling them back into my eyes. "What?"

"Thumbelina."

Gasping, I whip around and nearly collapse when I see Ardelle standing a couple of feet behind me on the marble walkway. And he isn't alone. Deimos stands next to Ardelle, and Geonni beside him, sunglasses and all, and . . .

Oh . . .

I know her instantly. She's the smallest, her Stormy Blue hair long and loosely curled around her chest. Her teal eyes are large, petite frame familiar. I understand what Jance meant

738

when he said he recognized me that very first night we met because staring at my mother Astoria is like looking in a mirror.

They're all here, standing side by side. They look so good, so healthy, so radiant and young.

Those tears return to my eyes when I look at my mother and say, "You came to see me?"

It feels like she only takes a single step and she's directly in front of me, the others, too.

When she cups my face, her hands feel as real and as warm as a living person's. Her eyes—my eyes—wash over me with a love I didn't realize existed.

"My strong, brave girl. I've always been with you."

There's no holding in the raw emotion as I slam into her small frame and hold on to her with everything I have, my tears uncontrollable. The hug I get in return nearly brings me to my knees. She's so small, but her arms are strong, and she hugs me so fiercely, profoundly, patting the back of my head in a gentle contrast. I could stay here *forever*.

But there's an insistent prodding against the back of my mind, and I know time is winding down for me in this place.

It takes everything in me to separate from her, and once she assures me she won't disappear, I find myself jumping into Ardelle's arms next, his body solid and exactly as I remember it, all the way down to the cinnamon and sage smell I loved so much.

"Are you real?" I whisper, taking in every inch of his handsome face, no longer bruised and cut, his body whole again.

"As real as I've ever been, Thumbelina. We're in a sort of in-between world. I'm waiting to cross until everything is over. I've never left."

"I've felt you with me," I confirm through my tears. "I'm so sorry, Ardelle."

He shakes his head, his blond hair styled exactly as I remember. "It was my time. I don't regret my choice. Tell Pacey that I love her and that I'm okay. It isn't her fault."

I nod, but there's one more thing I need to say.

"I love you."

His eyes soften, and his smile both lifts and sinks my heart all at once. "I love you, too, Kara."

Swallowing the tightness from my throat and wiping my tears, I look around. "I'm confused, Ardelle. What's going on?"

Zariya speaks from behind me. "Back then, when I had the choice to take the same power that was offered to you just now, I failed the dragon's test . . . I got a sliver of power and became The Killer of Worlds because of it. The true power has to be *earned*, Karalevine."

Dannanōk had said something about that right before I came here.

From either side of me, the two dragons that have passed on approach from the water surrounding us, Feena and Xyphos—whose name I remember from Dannanōk, Malakyte's Elendril dragon.

Feena's giant head dips down to meet me face-to-face, eye-to-eye, my soul stripped bare before her celestial, ancient eyes. "Have you healed Zariya's sin, Karalevine Ruzz?"

Have I? Have I forgiven Zariya?

"Yes."

Feena bows her head to me, and so does Xyphos before she says, "You have earned our knowledge, Karalevine. We do not grant you power, only the knowledge of how to obtain it. It's up to you what you do with it, but we trust you to make the right decision. The only way to gain this power is through your fellow Starseeds, through their willing sacrifice. The secret to unlocking the Elendril crystals is to reform them back into one. Before they were severed, they were one silver crystal."

Ardelle places a hand over my heart—over my Elendril symbols, and I immediately feel a burning sensation filling up my chest.

"I'm sharing a kernel of my crystal's power to you, Thumbelina." I feel it—I feel *him*—entering my being. "It's only a little bit, but you'll have it forever. If the others give up a small piece of their crystal to you, together their sacrifice will reform a version of the silver crystal for you. Separate, the crystals are powerful, but together, we're invincible."

My eyes are wide, my body is searing hot as I look back at Ardelle, his form fading, exactly like this world around us is fading.

Frantically, I grab hold of him, reaching for my mom and pulling her in. Geonni comes in behind me, whispering silly shit in my ear. And then Deimos, and finally Zariya.

"Can't I just stay here with you?" I bargain, looking up at Ardelle.

He smiles tenderly but also shakes his head. "You have to go back, Thumbelina. There are people back there who love you."

My chin quivers as I shake my head. I know he means Gavrielle. "I did love *you*, too. I just . . ."

"I love you, too," he echoes, but it's laced with a painful acceptance that neither of us can change, just like I can't change how the world around me is quickly falling away. "And I will cherish the time we had together. It simply wasn't meant to last forever this time, but that doesn't mean it wasn't real. I will see you again. *I will love you again.*"

The words I said to him at his funeral . . .

This is all happening too fast.

I hold on to him tighter, begging for one more minute— one more second—I'll take anything—*anything*. Not yet. I have more questions! I need more time!

"I don't want to go," I beg. "I'm not ready. Don't leave me."

This world melts away, becoming that white void of nothing once more. The black is coming next, but I hold on *so tightly*.

As if their voices have melted into one, they collectively say, "*We are* always *with you.*"

The blackness is rushing over me, pulling me back, back, back . . .

CHAPTER 122

I inhale the biggest, most desperate gasp that's ever passed through my lips, as if I've been underwater for minutes and my lungs finally touched air.

I'm back in the field . . . forever changed, a single tear falling down my battle-stained cheek.

Everyone's head snaps toward me, including Herkimer's.

"Her chest!" Pacey calls, and I know exactly what she's seeing because I feel it coming to life as it burns like a wildfire.

Ardelle's mark appears over my heart, the little circles aligning precisely with the corners of my star, just like in the tattoo I gave him where we laid the symbols over each other. The only difference between his mark and my two others is the lack of transparency. I don't have Ardelle's crystal, just a portion of it. Therefore, his symbol is much more faded than my other two, but it's there and it's all I'll need if I can get the others to give me a piece of theirs. If I can get all six, I can stop Herkimer.

Crunching footsteps grow closer as Herkimer stalks over to me, and I don't have much time, so I rip the arrow from my shoulder, but it's agonizing, and my hands tremble as I try to hold in my screams. Jance tries to get up, but he's slammed to the ground by a SSPARROW.

When Herkimer reaches me, he easily yanks the arrow from my hand and chucks it.

He squats before me, and we're eye to eye, the coldness of his body rather soothing to my flushed skin. "Keep looking at me like that, Little Thief. It won't save you." His eyes go from the wound in my shoulder to the symbol on my chest. "Now, what is that?"

I'm silent.

Almost bored, he leans over to Malakyte, who still lays dead beside me. Herkimer snatches his son's face. He turns his head a couple of times and tsks. "Such a fucking disappointment, but at least not all of him will be a total waste. Once his crystal is mine, I'll suffer this plague no more, both the sickness that ravages me and the son who did nothing but fail me."

He shoves Malakyte away like he's disgusting, the dagger slipping out even more.

Ever the one to be impatient, Herkimer seizes my face next, his grip icy and ironclad. "What is that new mark? Why does it look different than the others? You didn't have it two seconds ago."

His tone is far more irritated and much less amused.

"You fucked up," I say softly, the wind drying the tear left untouched on my cheek. "When you killed Ardelle, you lost your one shot to gain the power you fought so hard to discover. I know the secret now, and you'll never obtain the power of the silver crystal."

He scoffs, but I can see the wheels turning in those eyes, shade Black Weapon. "There is no silver crystal, you stupid girl!"

I laugh, taunting *him* now.

"Oh, I see," he says, letting go of my face as he leans back on his heels. "You think just because you suddenly discovered the secret you said five seconds ago you didn't know that I'll believe you? It's nothing but a ploy to try and save your friends.

But you're powerless here, Little Thief. I'm the one in control. And you know what?"

He leans even closer, so near his cold face bites against my searing cheeks. "I've thought a lot about how I want our time to look like once all this is over. Make no mistake, I'm leaving you alive. Once all the people you love are dead, their crystals mine, my traitorous son strung up for the galaxy to see, my health restored, and Selenyte avenged, you and I will have our fun. I see what I'm going to do to you extremely *vividly*.

"See, I think I know how to take your crystals out while keeping you alive. Intravenous Silent Breath has been studied thoroughly on the Vivianite, and I'm almost certain it could heal any damage the crystal inflicts upon removal. Maybe you'd die, but I'd do my very best to keep your heart beating. For what you've done to my empire and my family, Karalevine, I will make your existence an absolute living hell. Imagine this with me. You'll have your own room on the Vivianite, and each night, I'll make your dream of being Empress of Arianyte come true—because that's what you wanted so badly with my son, wasn't it? Well, you'll get that experience. You and I will be emperor and empress every . . . single . . . night. I can already taste how much you'd hate me, loathe me, fight me, but you'll come to realize I'm the one in charge, and you'll learn your fucking place very quickly, I assure you. Then—and this will be my favorite part, mind you—I'll make your body betray you repeatedly, even though we both know you'll try *so hard* not to give into me. I love to fuck warm-bloods, you know. Now, does that sound like the future you want, Little Thief?"

His icy tongue licks all the way up my cheek, and it takes every ounce of control I have not to rage against him the way Jance and Gavrielle are yelling and cursing at him right now. Herkimer made sure they all heard. Rape isn't about sex—it's about power. Herkimer has been obsessed with me from day one, and I genuinely think it's more about how Malakyte has something he'll never get—someone who loves him—and that fundamentally challenges Herkimer's world view. He doesn't know love and never has. It threatens him, and by me loving Malakyte, it strips his control over his son. I won't give him the fight he wants because he gets off on it.

That future he's thought long and hard about, it'll never happen.

A live ammo shot rings out into the field—echoing for miles. For a moment, I think it's one of Herkimer's SSPARROWs. But then several rounds fire, and I realize from the booming shockwave that those aren't disruptor pistols—they're old-world rifles, and they're coming from the trees nearby as a flock of birds spear into the smoky skies.

Snipers!

Four SSPARROWs go down behind us, and Herkimer's head whips around, his back to them. The other Starseeds and Ringers react, fighting for control.

Herkimer is distracted!

There's no time to think about what I'm doing, and I reach for the dagger in Malakyte's chest as several more rounds burst from the trees.

A voice from hundreds of yards away shouts, "Kill that motherfucking squid!"

Trinity!

I yank the dagger the rest of the way free, and without hesitation, I ram the blade straight into Herkimer's neck.

It goes all the way fucking through.

His eyes bulge as they meet mine, his blue blood gushing as he gurgles and chokes, but I'm not done yet. I've learned my lesson with this family. I leap onto him, my weight causing him to tip backward onto his ass, and I brace my legs on either side of him, gripping both hands on the dagger's hilt as I turn the blade more and more and more. I use all my strength and don't look away as I twist the dagger through flesh, through tendon, through fucking bone and vertebrae—*I relish in it.* Blood spurts in a torrent all down his front, all over my arms and chest and legs, but I don't stop. The gruesome sights and sounds are only tolerable because of the image he put into my mind only a minute ago. His eyes nearly pop out of his head when I whisper sweetly, "The only future I'm going to have is the one where you're fucking dead."

Malakyte's gasp of life erupts through the air on the cusp of a few more gunshots, and he is revived at the precise moment I cleave his father's head from his body.

Herkimer's head thuds to the ground right next to Malakyte's legs, Malakyte staring at it in complete shock.

There's no time.

"Dannanōk!" I cry, the dragon's head shifting in different directions like a snake. I spare a glance at the others, and it seems like they're alright. All the SSPARROWs are down. "Burn him!"

Dannanōk braces down, the glow of fire already swelling in his throat—no hesitation.

I sheath Deimos's bloody dagger at my waist and grab the stunned Malakyte under his arms, and I drag him off.

"Fuck, you weigh a ton," I grit out as I heave him through the field, staggering backward until we're a safe distance away.

Things have changed, and I need him alive now. I need a piece of his crystal if this doesn't kill Herkimer. I won't live with his crystal inside of me for the rest of my life—I refuse to be taunted by the very thing that represents him. If that means he lives, then I'll deal with that later.

Malakyte doesn't speak as Dannanōk blasts Herkimer with a massive burst of dragonfire, the flames so hot they burn my eyes, and the force knocks me over.

Malakyte lands on top of me but finally shows a little sign of life, and he . . . protects me with his body?

Why bother?

Finally, the initial blast of dragonfire eases up, and I cough from the smoke.

 746

"Kara!"

Gavrielle's voice rings out somewhere close, but I can't see him through the plumes.

"Gavrielle! I'm here!"

Gav reaches us, and he quickly pulls me out from under Malakyte, and we embrace each other the moment I'm on my feet. Gavrielle kisses me, not giving a fuck Malakyte is watching, and I kiss him back. I choose Gavrielle—I'll always choose Gavrielle.

I put a hand on his face. "I don't think this is over."

CHAPTER 123

Turns out, I'm right to worry.

Herkimer is already beginning to regenerate, even as a smoldering husk. We've moved about forty or fifty feet away to avoid the smoke.

Sylo blanches. "Does this guy ever fucking die?"

After we unfasten them and unlock their collars—thanks to the SSPARROW's key—I explain what happened in my vision and how I got a piece of Ardelle's magic. They're all shocked, and as I hear my name being called from down the field, I let them digest it.

"Kara!" Trinity rushes up to us, her mom and Shante on her heels.

"Trinity!" We embrace each other tightly. "You saved our asses, but you really shouldn't be here. It's too dangerous. He's going to regenerate, and I know he's going to be pissed."

"Well, I sorta owed you all a save, and Hank is in command over there."

"Uhh, guys!" Sylo shouts.

We all follow his finger as Herkimer's charred body begins moving. Wiggling is more accurate, but, stars.

I turn to each of them as we stand close together. "It's your choice," I say, taking in a deep breath, even though it's thick with smoke. "I'll be permanently taking some of your magic, so it'll weaken you. I don't know how much. Ardelle said it was a kernel of power, but that could mean different things to each of you. Also, I'm unsure if it's the right move to give it to me at all. That kind of power could . . ."

Gavrielle shakes his head. "You won't lose yourself, Kara. We trust you."

But should they?

"I'll do it," Pacey says, no hesitation. "Tell me how."

"Me too." Sylo looks at Pacey lovingly, and they smile at each other.

Malakyte, who's still sitting on the ground in a posture that's irritatingly casual, is watching me when I look down at him.

"Your psychotic dad is planning on killing you," I tell Malakyte, even though it'll hurt him. "He wants your crystal to cure his illness. He *will kill you*."

Malakyte doesn't say a word. He just glares at me; the expectations of the others is a hammer that he withstands with no apparent pressure.

Herkimer begins moaning. Guess his head is growing back.

Stars, he's going to be pissing mad when he comes to. But if I don't have all the crystals, then . . .

My head whips to Dannanōk. "Can I gain some power if we have five instead of six?"

Jance interrupts. "Malakyte, give her the power she needs. Your father wants you dead."

As before, Malakyte doesn't speak. Not to me, not to any of them. It's only his dark eyes that follow me around.

This man is maddening!

"He's a useless coward, Jance. Forget him," I say. "Dannanōk, will it work with only five? I don't want to take their power if it won't do anything."

Dannanōk says, "The crystals are raw power. You won't reform it into the silver crystal, but you'll gain something."

"Something is better than nothing," Pacey surmises. "Tell us how, Kara. We want to."

There's a bit more life in her eyes since I told her what Ardelle said. The proof of his soul's existence branded right here on my chest.

Gavrielle is a steady force at my back, but he keeps looking over at Herkimer. Fuck, he's regenerating so fast.

"Put your hand over the marks, and I think you just push a bit of your magic into it. That's how Ardelle did it."

Pacey goes first, her fingers dancing before she places her palm flat on my chest. Our eyes lock in tight, and I see her brother's eyes in hers, see our love for each other, the fear and the hope and the devastation. Her eyes glow Azure, and I gasp, Gavrielle's grip on my shoulders tightening.

Pacey's power surges into me like gunfire, my chest heating to molten hot levels and the marks smolder. Feeling like a brand, but coming through my skin like before, Pacey's symbol begins to materialize but still lacks the transparency of my two. It's the smallest of them all, curling right in the center of Deimos's perfectly. The geometric design of these marks is really starting to make sense.

They used to be one.

They used to be silver.

By the time Sylo goes next, Herkimer's skin is coming back.

His is even more intense, and the rush of power almost brings me to my knees. I feel like I might just die from the power zapping its way along my skin, the rush glorious as it begs to be set free.

"You're right, Dannanōk, I feel their power."

"It won't be enough." All our heads snap to Malakyte, an elbow propped up on one bent knee.

"You're lucky we don't kill your ass, you fucking squid," Sylo says, sneering down at him with hatred. "Look at what you've done! The least you can do is help her get rid of this psychopath. Kara, just use Deimos's crystal and make him give up his share."

Malakyte locks eyes with me—daring me to do it.

But Dannanōk interjects, "That won't work. It must be freely given."

Herkimer's cruel laughter stops Sylo from responding. Somehow, Herkimer's armor is coming back, too. I don't even want to understand how that's possible, but he's already climbing up to his knees.

We're out of time.

Gavrielle tries to put himself in front of me, but I squirrel around him. "You need to go!" I shout. "He can dust you all, please. You're a distraction for me by staying here. Take my father and the others and go!"

I look at Trinity. "If you care about me at all, you will get them out of here!"

Dannanōk's growl thrusts my head around, and my eyes widen as Herkimer is on two feet again, but that isn't why the dragon is freaking out.

Herkimer has brought his hands together, and that same blinding Ultramarine light from all those weeks ago in the Azurite throne room bursts into existence. The ball of destructive light is damn near blinding as it grows bigger and bigger.

"I told you all not to fucking try me," Herkimer calls over, but he's speaking directly to me. "Now, it'll be me who becomes The Killer of Worlds. This planet is *done for*. I'll crack it in half just like Zariya did to that moon. Poetic, don't you think?"

Spitting fucking mad. Got it.

"Go!" I yell, but Jance is being as difficult as Gavrielle, even when Saris and Ahren rip him back.

"I'm not leaving you alone with him!" Jance fights, but not even he can overpower Dannanōk's body as the dragon nudges him in the opposite direction with his nose.

"I love you," I yell, "and I'm not alone."

751 

The others are with me. My family is with me.

His eyes turn glassy as the others shove him away, even though he fights them. Pacey, Sylo, and Trinity are trying to thrust Gavrielle back, but he's an immovable tank.

"No!" he bellows, physically shoving the other three off him.

"I won't lose you like I lost Ardelle, and he will use you against me. Now, *go*! If you love me, you'll go!"

I'm stronger now, and when I shove Gavrielle, he moves. His expression is wounded, but I don't care.

The others take advantage of the momentum and physically haul Gavrielle toward the trees, kicking and screaming as they follow Dannanōk and the others.

I throw up an antimatter shield around both groups as they dart toward the tree line, assuring Gavrielle can't maneuver his way back.

I can smell ether in the air, the burning of some twisted magic that erupts from within Herkimer's corrupted soul.

"Running won't help your friends, Little Thief! Or you, for that matter."

I turn to face Herkimer, and the warm breeze blows my loose braid to the side. "Oh, I'm not planning on running."

The setting sun illuminates one side of Herkimer's face in a warm Golden Nugget color, and on the other side his ball of Sparkling Azure offers a stark-blue contrast.

My power sings, the antimatter so easily accessed as it floods my blood, star mark lighting up and burning, burning, *burning*.

This power . . . I shake from it, from the pleasure flooding my blood like heroin. *They shouldn't have given me this* . . .

"Destroy the planet and you'll lose all the crystals, dumbass," I call out, our powers snapping and lashing out through the air as we charge up.

Yet if I can still stop this, no matter how slim my chances, I've got to try.

He smirks. "I've done this enough times to know how it works. I'll rip out those crystals once your bodies are charred and make it out with plenty of time to spare."

"All of them?"

Malakyte still sits around here . . . somewhere. Oh, no. He's gone. He's fucking *gone*. My head whips left and right, but he's nowhere to be found.

Herkimer notices what I do and hollers with gleeful laughter that's both mocking and triumphant. "Told you he was a fucking coward! I'll find him sooner or later and rip that crystal out, too."

Guess I should have let him get hit with the dragonfire.

With nothing but my bare hands and the magic of my fellow Starseeds flowing through my veins, I brace my knees as I build my attack to match Herkimer's.

He's ahead of me, his ball of energy nearly three feet in diameter.

My crystal grows fast. The antimatter accumulates in front of me, but it doesn't have a distinct shape, the colors Electric Purple dancing with Strawberry Slush. Long streaks of white-hot lightning extend out, reaching and snapping forward as it itches to take on Herkimer.

We're roughly fifty feet apart. Should I move closer? Is it better or worse, or should I stay here?

There's no time to decide.

Herkimer moves his arms in a fluid manner around his ball of energy, and steps forward, the ball coming right for me.

Shit, he's actually throwing that thing at me! But he's not chucking it like a beach ball—he's powering it from behind.

This. Is. It.

I have to propel my antimatter out in a similar way. Otherwise, it'll give Herkimer all the high ground.

This is where The Killer of Worlds is made—or unmade.

Ignoring all the pain in my body and the blood I'm losing, I throw my arms out straight ahead as I shoot my antimatter toward Herkimer's beam of Rich Blue, mimicking his attack style.

Both magics collide, and the entire solar system quakes from the impact, me included. The energy, the power—*it erupts.*

For a heartbeat, everything stops. The world and all that resides within it withers down to nothing but the raging thunder in my ears and the slight hitching of my breath. Time takes an oath just for me, promising to delay my inevitable death a precious moment longer.

The blast rips the earth and knocks me off balance, but I keep my footing, the wind whipping around me like a hurricane.

Our magic clashes and morphs and bleeds together at the halfway point between us, the energy so bright it makes my eyes water. Purple Fire fighting against Slate Blue, sucking in and destroying anything not secured. A chunk of earth flies past my head, nearly taking it off.

Herkimer howls my way, "Yes, keep fighting! That's how I like it! Till your last breath!"

His magic nearly engulfs mine, the blue overtaking the fuchsia. This blue force literally devours mine. His magic is overconsumption at its core, gobbling up my antimatter. The light around me is becoming more and more blue by the minute. Soon, it'll overtake the pinkish-purple of my antimatter completely.

No! I grind my teeth, diving into that well of magic that is deep, and I wrench it up from the dark depths so it can finally touch the sun. The others gave me a piece of their own magic to boost mine. This is because of them. They're here with me—I feel them. I won't let them down.

More! I order my crystal, electric power flashing through my veins in a white-hot snap that completely shatters any previous ceiling.

Yet even the glorious rush—the fucking ecstasy that comes with this boost in power—doesn't quell the nausea, the molten curdling within my stomach or the volcano in my chest.

It's working. My magic is shoving his back!

The roar of the moment is so splitting that a trickle of blood drips from my ears. That's just from the sound.

That's all.

The force of this attack makes everything ache, my purple light becoming a giant, unfocused ball as the world tips sideways.

Stay upright!

Blinking rapidly, I right myself, gritting my teeth as my chest burns internally. Too much. It's already too much. He's so strong, and I'm not strong enough.

Icy arms latch onto me from behind, and it's like frostbite kissing a flame as Malakyte's arms wrap around my boiling chest, his subzero body sending a jolting gasp through me that echoes out into infinity.

"You and I have unfinished business, Karalevine."

CHAPTER 124

Caged in Malakyte's arms from behind, I freeze.

My antimatter continues to rage, to increase even, but terror straightens my spine. Malakyte brought my sword with him, and he stabs it into the ground beside us.

Herkimer howls, "Yes, son! Kill that fucking bitch! Reclaim your place at my side!"

"This is your chance to get even," I say to Malakyte, not sure he can hear me through the roaring winds. "Make Herkimer happy. I'm done playing these games."

Malakyte bends and says into my ear, "We have unfinished business, but I'm not here for my revenge. We can settle the war between us once we destroy *him*."

My eyes widen, the gusts whipping our now unbound hair together.

"Please, Karalevine. Set me free."

I crank my neck to the side and look at Malakyte—really look at him—and he doesn't need to speak to beg me to kill his father.

His eyes say it all.

It's the same look he had that night Herkimer first attacked us, Malakyte Ardeen stripped down not to the man who's lived over two hundred years but rather the little boy trapped inside, so unloved and abused by the one person who was supposed to do right by him.

"Why?" I ask.

Stupid, I know. Bad timing—but after everything, *why?*

"I was your phantom once I was gone, but I watched everything play out. When he vowed to hurt you that way, I knew he'd enact every sick bit of it, and I couldn't bear that for you. I saw the contrast between him and I—what I had nearly become in my rage and insanity—*him.* Then I returned, and I knew I had to make things right for both you and I," he says, and I can barely breathe—stunned into silence. "Death brings clarity, Karalevine. And so does living."

Before I can reply, Malakyte palms his hand over the glowing marks on my chest, his eyes blazing a brilliant Sunflower Yellow as a dash of his magic rushes into me. The power of all the Elendril crystals forges something altogether new inside me as his symbol appears on my chest alongside all the others.

I'm not prepared.

Malakyte catches me as I cry in a wave of pleasure and pain, all the marks on my chest shifting before our eyes. They're *scorching.*

The marks glow in succession, each of their colors fading into a sparkling silver in the shade Big Bang.

The silver crystal.

Instantly, my purple antimatter is transformed into a pale silver color as it erupts against Herkimer, pushing his magic back as if it were nothing.

This is a mistake—it feels *too fucking good.*

The silver crystal hits me like a tsunami crashing through every pore, every follicle—every nerve ending goes supernova with pleasure that shouldn't exist. Like a body-wide orgasm that cascades up and down through every part of me. It's in my hair, my teeth, my nails, my lashes. The darkest fractures where I hide my truest self, the silver crystal finds its way through— consuming me body and soul.

Fuck—I've never been whole until this moment.

All the colors are saturated. The world trembles under my fingertips as if it fears I'm going to crack the sky. Fracture light itself. Break sound. Command the stars to dim and the oceans to scream.

Killer of Worlds!

This isn't power—this is me trespassing into the land of the fucking gods, and that power has clawed its way deep inside, greedy for hit after hit, and I'm the junky desperate for every last drop.

This is why villains sell their souls.

My lungs seize, my knees buckle, and I almost lose the flow of magic completely to this soul shattering high as the silver crystal remakes me into the monster I feared I would always become. But there's no way I'm ever letting this go. *Ever.*

"Stay with me, babe." A voice pulls me back, shaking me as he holds me up. "Karalevine!"

He . . . Who is he?

I blink out wetness from my lashes, not realizing I was crying. His voice . . . That's right . . . I'll never forget his voice.

Malakyte!

My mind catches up to the power it now wields, and I come back to myself. What had I nearly done? Was I moments away from losing control and destroying *everything?*

Malakyte literally keeps me upright by tucking his arms right under mine, so I'm supported by him as my weight falters. His hands grasp my forearms, holding them up as they threaten to fall from the magic pouring out of them. My back pushes against his chest as I find my knees again, his body solid and unmoving.

We're pushing Herkimer back!

"Your eyes," Malakyte says, staring down at me in awe. "They're glowing silver."

And silver is taking over my soul. Silver is destroying my body. Silver has too much power for me to contain. I'm collapsing under its weight—it's killing me.

Herkimer shouts at us, but I hear the fear in his voice as my Celestial colored antimatter overtakes him. "I'll fucking kill you, boy!"

"Get fucked, asshole!" I snarl, but I don't think he hears me.

Malakyte does, and he adjusts his hold on me.

We're there, we're right there!

Malakyte's body suddenly begins to thrash, almost like he's having a seizure, hands squeezing my arms like a vise. Something's wrong!

No . . .

No, no, no!

It hits me a second later.

I've only known this pain one time, flashbacks to when Herkimer used his dark power on us when the Azurite fell and Ardelle died. If the silver crystal was pleasure on an unimaginable scale, Herkimer is pain. Unadulterated suffering.

It's as if someone took a red-hot power tool directly to my brain. It's deep inside my skull. A sensation so horrendous we both nearly collapse, my magic ebbing and Herkimer's taking over.

His laughter . . . Jupiter's rings, his fucking laughter!

"Hurts like a cunt, doesn't it? A fitting end for the two of you!"

Malakyte is the only reason I'm still standing, but he's in agony alongside me.

"*Breathe*," he says directly in my ear. "I know it hurts. Breathe through it. Keep pushing!"

I'm losing my power. The magic slipping away—*I'm* slipping away.

"Hold your arms up," Malakyte says, letting my arms go. It takes all my strength to keep them up and keep that magic flowing towards Herkimer.

Malakyte's frigid body loses its sturdiness as I push my back into him. He's grabbing something in his pocket, but even that's a struggle.

With smooth efficiency, he stabs me in the thigh with a needle.

"What are you doing—"

The pain is already diminishing.

He injects himself next. "The Silent Breath won't hold it back for long, but if you push hard enough, you'll annihilate him. Now, *push*!"

Even with the silver crystal's power, Herkimer's painful magic is staunching its strength. I can't give more—it's already eating me alive in every way that it can. If I push one ounce more—I'll die.

Blood drips from my nose and ears again, my arms sinking as the wind carries Herkimer's laughter over to us. It's not long before his destructive magic overtakes mine.

"You're doing so good, Karalevine," Malakyte says, voice ardent, "but if you want to beat him, you have to be strong."

It's so unlike him to comfort me, but I cling to him because he's my only lifeline.

"I can't!"

"*You will!* I'll make sure of it. For once I'm going to be the man you deserve, the man who will stay and fight this Hell with you instead of creating it. It's what I should have done from the very first moment I found you again. I've got you. I'm right here. You can beat him—*you will beat him*!"

I look down, feeling myself slipping more and more as the Silent Breath wears off, Herkimer's pain shooting back into my skull with a vengeance. Sweat drips down my entire body. I'm boiling from the inside. Not even Malakyte's skin feels cold anymore. Everything blurs from the pain in my head. My lungs wheeze as my balance sways, and there's a strange popping in my ears.

The light of my brilliant antimatter flickers off the dark Amethyst blade of my sword as it sticks up from the ground, solid and unmoving in this chaos.

"You're done, Killer of Worlds, I feel you slipping!" Herkimer calls. "Two more minutes of me, and both your skulls will crack."

He's right.

Malakyte and I are about to die. I can't keep going. The power is going to snap any second.

"Malakyte, *I can't!*"

A flash of movement from my left catches my eye right as I say the words, and something thin and fast shoots directly for Herkimer. An angry shrill spears through the roaring wind a split second later. His magic sputters, precisely as my own reaches a limit that I can't bear for one single second longer. My silver antimatter fizzles, but it's not alone. Herkimer's stops, too, as does his horrendous head-splitting magic. Both destructive magics sizzle through the air as they evaporate within the space between us, the earth utterly demolished. Streaks of lightning dance around us like we're in a thundercloud, whipping and crackling as if the air itself were charged. These little ghosts are lingering in places where they should know better.

Nausea wraps itself around my stomach, and I hurl. I immediately try to hold it in with my hand, but the blood that spews up gushes out through the spaces between my fingers before I ultimately give up and blood splatters everywhere.

Malakyte curses, and I know by his tone of voice that it's bad.

"It looks like someone shot an arrow at his neck, it came from the direction of the others," Malakyte says hurriedly, reaching inside his pocket again for what I'm assuming is another dose of Silent Breath for us.

Breathing hard, I look over at Herkimer and see him fumbling for one of Ardelle's arrows that's currently protruding out of his neck. He'll get it out soon, and when he does . . . he'll be healed within seconds.

My pulse pounds, every part of my body aches, but I hear the words screaming against my skull. *Now! Go now, this is your one and only chance!*

I don't think, just act. There's no time for the Silent Breath. Herkimer heals too quickly. If I don't move *right now*, he'll kill us all.

I engulf the charged air that reeks with magic, lungs crackling like a campfire, rip my sword from its place sticking out of the ground and push myself up into a run straight towards Herkimer.

"Karalevine!" Malakyte yells after me, but he can't catch up.

The silver crystal hasn't merely boosted my antimatter. It's enhanced every single one of my senses and physical abilities, including my speed.

What lays before me is a field cracked in a hundred places. The ground is destroyed, pitted, scorched, and on fire as I cross the space between Herkimer and me. Forty feet—maybe fifty. The world around me is a blur of burnt earth and color, falling rocks that were blown up into the air along with other debris fly by me in a dizzying array of colors. I'm zoned in on one thing—the emperor of Arianyte.

And his death.

Herkimer grabs the arrow and wrenches it from his throat, dark blood a gushing torrent down his side as he grins at me in a confident challenge, arrow in hand.

I rush up on him, having crossed the space between us in seconds.

This is it!

I'm on him in a second, sword at the ready, but he dodges my first strike. I turn and try again, but he slithers away a second time.

Faster!

Herkimer spits blood directly into my eyes as his neck wound knits up completely, laughter following shortly after.

Motherfucker!

I cry, wiping it from my burning vision as I step back, dodging his attack by a hair as he thrusts Ardelle's arrow downwards—straight for my heart.

Gasping, I pivot just in time to dodge but not fast enough to prevent the bloody arrow from raking all the way down my arm.

We both parry, expecting the other to attack, and that's when it happens—I see my opening.

My hair whips forward as I bend my knees and dive low to his left—but it's a fake! He falls for it, and with every ounce of energy I have left, I turn in the opposite direction—fast and brutal—my sword driving up and straight through the center of Herkimer's chest.

Right in the heart.

There's no stopping me until I see the blade pierce all the way through, our breaths and blood intermingling as I come in close, the act disturbingly intimate.

My power is already surging into the sword, a sweet release that promises god-level ecstasy, and it comes on quick, so ready to destroy and consume. Exactly like what I did with the mecha-dragon, I'll do the same here, and this time, it'll work.

It has to!

It has to!

My antimatter detonates into the blade and into my body and soul, and we're both consumed by it.

The power hits me with a thunderous jolt, funneling from my hands, swirling down into the sword and right into Herkimer's body, exploding him from the inside out. The silver crystal lights up the blade with symbols in a white-hot, silver color that burns my eyes.

It's beautiful.

I've seen the world in color for so long but never realized gray could be the prettiest shade of them all.

That's me.

Karalevine Ruzz, in the shade Morally Gray.

Would I want to be shining Bubblegum Pink like Pacey? Yes. Would I like to be a strong Navy Steel like Jance? Absolutely. Would I wish I was the bright, mischievous Violet Storm of Gavrielle? I'd give anything . . .

But that isn't who I am.

I've been existing in shades of gray for as long as I can remember, hating that I couldn't purge the black from my soul, but maybe that isn't the point?

Grays can be just as worthy as all the other colors, too, shading the world in the duality of triumphs and mistakes, wins and losses.

I don't need to be perfectly white to be worthy. I only need to be true to myself and my heart and trust that it's enough.

As the silver antimatter bursts into Herkimer, he tries to fight me with his brain-splitting magic as one last-ditch effort of survival, intensifying it to a near blackout, but I refuse to stop now, even though it feels like I'm being eaten alive by my magic and his.

I'm too close to give up now! *I will end this!*

Then Herkimer's pain sputters . . .

He can't use his magic anymore. I'm overpowering him!

I ignore the blood pouring from my nose and ears as it drips down my neck and chest. Ignore the blinding nausea as it sears my stomach. Pain slices through every inch of my body, through muscle and bone and organ and soul. My heart has never surged so fast.

None of that matters.

"This is for Ardelle!" I hiss in his ear, teeth bared, but I still manage a wicked little grin just for him.

For everyone who's given their lives for me, for this mission. For the people of Earth, the Hijacked. For all those around me whom I love and who love me. For everyone we've lost. For Malakyte and the man he could've been if only he were

 764

loved the way he deserved to be. This empire dies today. All that Herkimer represents will die here today, right here. I'm ending this war of attrition—*right now!*

The light continues to blaze from the sword as I stand eye-to-eye with this immortal nightmare, a future me I will never succumb to.

Despite his eyes bulging with genuine terror, Herkimer laughs. He laughs, and laughs, howling into the screaming wind even as the antimatter disintegrates his body from his center outwards.

The sound is insanity personified.

It's only when the world behind him comes into view through his torso that his mad cackling shifts to shrills of being shredded apart—the sound a blood-chilling curse.

Finally, after all these centuries of eating people like me, consuming powers and planets and entire worlds, he's the one who gets *devoured!*

I won't stop until every single particle of him is erased.

It'll take everything I have, and I won't be coming back. The certainty of death isn't a punishment but a promise.

This is the right thing for the right reason . . . *for them.*

Herkimer's feral screams finally fade into a soul-shattering echo that cracks the setting skies in two as the silver light annihilates him—every atom of this monster shredding, fragmenting, disappearing.

Until not a single shred of the emperor of Arianyte is left in existence.

Let it go, I tell myself, not believing it's real. *You can let it go. It's over. He's gone for good this time.*

I've craved power like this for so long, but I easily let it fall away. Not one ounce of me is afraid to set it free.

Gavrielle's face flashes in my mind, a bright white light surrounding the man I love. The faces of everyone I love surge through my mind and heart, too.

I was never alone.

For the first time in my life, I'm not ashamed of who I am. The pride surging in my heart is every bit the beautiful thing I always dreamed it would be.

That warm light welcomes the darkness in me with open arms, and I don't run away as I close my eyes and fall into it.

CHAPTER 125

There's a brutal cost for my arrogance.

Her silver magic dissipates, echoes of sparks zapping throughout the air, the scent of magic overpowering the smell of smoke that chokes this battlefield.

Someone has finally done it. Someone has finally killed my father. Not just someone . . . My Star has done the impossible. The relief nearly brings me to my knees.

He'll never return. Not this time. Not after Karalevine.

Although, her magic abruptly fades to a screaming halt . . . I don't feel it anymore.

It's hard to see her through the smoke and dust. Has she fallen?

Anxiety begins to build inside me. True, unadulterated fear.

I leap into a run, crossing the broken earth in a panic. I never should have let her go over to him alone.

Through the dust and debris, I search for her as dread eats its way through blood and bone—it's too quiet.

She's there. Slumped on her back, appearing so small. So still. *This is your fault.*

I shove down the alarm bells going off inside me and close the remaining space between her and me.

My knees hit the dirt.

I take her in my arms, shaking her. "Karalevine!"

Her heartbeat is no longer a delicate rhythm in my ears.

This is your fault!

I was between life and death when Father was taunting her earlier, and I heard him promising her suffering. My visceral reaction was such a profound disgust that I realized something in that moment: I wanted the opposite. The opposite of his plans, the opposite of *him*. His chains would never allow such dualities to exist. Only power, only strength, only cruelty. I don't want that anymore.

Now, because of Karalevine, I am, indeed, *free*.

My Star freed me.

I wanted her dead less than an hour ago, certain that I could endure it. I wonder how I could lie to myself for long enough to convince my twisted mind that I could take the life of the most precious thing in this galaxy to me. She was right. I had gone insane.

Rushed footsteps grow closer as they pound against charred dirt, and I don't need to look to know it's Gavrielle. He shoves me off her, threatening me with an animalistic growl that says far more than any words could.

But his attention whips from me to her in a flash as he sees exactly what I've painfully realized.

"Kara . . ."

His voice is a ghostly whisper as the silence screams what we both can hear.

Nothing.

No breathing. No heartbeat. No life.

That hesitation lasts only a moment. However, when he drops to his knees, he checks her neck for a pulse no longer there and starts compressions on her chest.

"Come on, love," he begs, his rhythmic downward thrusts the perfect technique, but her body does nothing but patter along with his efforts, her beautiful eyes unfocused and empty of that fire that made her—her.

He breathes into her mouth, then starts compressions again.

Gavrielle presses down so hard her ribs crack like forest twigs, tears falling as he desperately tries to revive her.

"Come back to me, baby. Please. *Please, Kara.* You can't leave me here alone."

This . . . This is not what I thought I wanted. This feels like every fire in the galaxy exploding within me. Ripping and tearing and devouring all the good in me she planted there. The rage is a creature, a demon that wails and ungodly roar so vicious the Devil himself hides in fear.

Dannanōk's thunderous bellow echoes what Gavrielle, and I already know . . . she's gone. Jance has collapsed, the man too broken to even make it several yards past the trees.

"This is your fault!" Gavrielle seethes, his compressions finally coming to their inevitable end. He shifts my direction, seizes the collar of my armor, and violently jostles me.

Tension ripples along his jawline, brows sharply furrowed, eyes drenched in tears—enraged yet *pleading.* Through all Gavrielle's rage, he's reduced to the young, orphaned boy demanding that I make this better. I had always done that for him in the past—at least I thought I had. I thought I had been better to him than Father was to me, but given his shift in loyalty, it seems as though I was continuing a legacy of violence and abuse that I inevitably perpetuated against Karalevine.

Gavrielle is right. This is your fault.

"You killed her!"

This is when the strength in my heart pulverizes.

I raised my son strong. He doesn't cry. Yet Gavrielle looks at me with nothing less than utter animosity and sorrow. His head dips, and he sobs into my chest, fingers curling around the fabric beneath my armor.

It's uncomfortable for me, but I'm compelled to console him, and I raise one hand to the back of his head, hesitating, knowing I'm the cause of his grief. Reluctantly, I bring him closer, trying to give him what I never got but always needed.

That's what love is, right, Karalevine? You told me so yourself. "You don't love to take, you stupid prince. You love to give."

I believe I understand what she meant now. The turmoil within me tempers down slightly as hope glimmers across the blackened heart of mine she loved so fiercely.

It's like lighting a candle when someone is lost in the dark, giving that light freely and solely because you want to. That's what she was trying to tell me love was. I couldn't understand that until now. I couldn't see she was that light for me. I've never known such things.

My entire life, I was bred to be one thing: merciless, believing only the cruel survive. Strength and power came hand in hand, and that meant taking what I wanted, controlling what I wanted, shattering what I wanted.

Father seared that truth into me over two long centuries, his evil like a brand upon my soul—I could never flinch, never show an ounce of mercy even when I wanted to. Otherwise, I would be the one *devoured.* Love can't exist. Weakness can't exist. Only power and supremacy could thrive.

But it was all a trap because power is a prison. This crown is a prison.

Then a star lit up all that darkness in my life. My fucked-up, excruciating life. I unintentionally wanted to dim her, draw out every ounce of darkness I saw in her heart, destroy anything virtuous I could find—because I saw what I would never deserve, or be, or have. Freedom. Light. Goodness. I tried to extinguish that star. Fuck, I nearly had.

"I loved her, too," I say softly.

"What you felt wasn't love," Gavrielle claims, separating himself from me. "You were possessive and controlling, and

 770

you wanted her to be *just like you*—a fucking monster! Exactly as you made me and everyone else around you, your psychotic little puppets."

There's no point in arguing, not as I comb her hair away from her face with my fingers, closing those gorgeous eyes.

Selenyte's ghost appears next to me. "With all your piles of regrets, big brother, I'm pretty sure this one will sting even worse than Zariya. I suppose after all you've done, after trying to kill her today, this is your ultimate punishment. *This is what you deserve.*"

There's no sense in arguing with Selenyte, either.

Gavrielle breaks down, burying his face into her chest as he weeps.

I want to cry like that, too, but if I lose my composure now, I'll never be able to be that light in the dark for her.

There's only one way for me to make this right.

I wipe the blood from beneath her nose, clean up her face as best I can, untangle pieces of her hair. Despite my best efforts to draw the darkness from her, she always looked at me with those eyes . . . eyes that said I could be *more*. More than this sanctimonious, cruel, controlling bastard that I am. Even when she hated me, even when she killed me, she still found some kernel of decency in me that I'd never been allowed to dream of existing. I didn't have to be my father's son. I could make my own choices despite the shackles that melted into my skin over so many years of being locked in chains. Karalevine choosing Gavrielle made removing those manacles nearly impossible, but that's when it all made sense to me. I couldn't remove them *for her*. I had to unlock them *for myself*.

Now, here I sit—at the very end. I've died so many times, and I don't know why this time would be any different. Perhaps because there will be no glory waiting on the other side. No throne, no power, no redemption. Only the choice I'm proud to make. They won't remember me as a hero—stars, even thinking that sounds boisterously pretentious. I'd rather my reputation remain as it was, stay the villain in their eyes if that makes it easier. She'll live. That's enough for me.

This won't bring me forgiveness for all I've done to her. There's nothing I deserve less. That's not why . . . I'm doing it because, for the first time in my life, it feels good to choose someone over myself.

That's the true freedom she's given me—a choice.

I place my hand on Gavrielle's shoulder, and he snaps up, eyes searching my own.

The air is thick with smoke and death and magic as I take it all in. The setting sun, my city beyond the tree line, Karalevine's gorgeous face, the wedding bracelet tattooed into her wrist. I could stare at her for ages, but there's no more time.

"I can trust no one else with this," I say, feeling the searing pain swell beneath my ribcage.

Gavrielle's eyes widen as he desperately tries to hang on to me. "What are you doing?" he demands, voice laced with dangerous hope. He angrily wipes the tears from his face, yet all that does is smear the dirt there.

He's got to be better at keeping his face clean—hadn't I always told him that?

My answer to him is as clear as I can make it. "What nobody ever did for me."

"What? Wait, what does that mean?"

I'm stiff as I turn to Gavrielle and grip him roughly by the back of the neck, pulling him close. "Insert it immediately. She's already been under too long. Don't wait. Take care of my Star."

His jaw slackens as he finally understands.

Yet there's one last thing I need to tell him.

"I'm sorry for all of it, Gavrielle."

Gavrielle shakes his head, his tears rolling in earnest.

But I couldn't stop this now even if I wanted to.

This time, I have a chance to do what I couldn't for Zariya.

 772

Say that I'm sorry.

Show that I'm sorry.

Beyond an apology, a vow. I'm a wicked, cursed prince who found a way to love with the sliver of a heart that survived this life. With it, with my brief taste of freedom, I'll do something courageous.

My fingers curl as I feel my crystal disentangle from my flesh—pulling the creature free. The wicked being residing there is resistant to move after all these many years, yet I evict it with force. Through muscle and bone and icy blood, it ravages my body beyond all repair, true dark closing in around me.

Yet the darkness within me had a star. A twinkling ray of light that blankets me in all her burning brilliance, my shadows wrapping around her so she could blaze as brightly as she dared.

CHAPTER 126

I'm in that in between place from before. I recognize the tranquil, color-melted sky as my eyes flutter open, and it's the first thing I see.

It's so warm and peaceful as I lie on my back, my head in someone's lap. He's blurry, but his long dark hair tickles my cheeks as I try to focus on Malakyte's face.

He catches my hand when I reach up to touch him.

His skin is so warm . . . How odd.

"Did we die?" I ask, my eyelids heavy as weights. "Where's . . . everyone else?"

"They're right here."

"I'm so tired."

"I know," he says, "but you did so well. Thank you for setting me free. It's over now. You don't need to fight anymore, Karalevine. It's all going to be alright."

I can't get a clear lock on his face, no matter how many times I blink.

Malakyte's fingers glide through my hair, and his touch feels so familiar.

He did this every single night on the Azurite. "I love you," he whispers—and it sounds like he means it with his entire heart. "I'm sorry for all the pain I've caused you. I did what I thought was right."

I sigh loudly. "Me too. When you go back, don't make Gavrielle kill anymore. That's how you can make it right with me."

It's hard to care anymore. Not when I know what's happened to me and why I'm here. But I want Gavrielle to live a long and happy life.

Even though he's blurry, I can still see him smile, it was always his most beautiful mask.

"I'm not the one going back, Karalevine."

"Hmmm?"

My eyes close shut, and no force can open them again.

I don't know what he means.

"I love you, Karalevine. I'm sorry."

I try to say his name, but I feel like I'm being pulled away from him, falling downward through the floor as I grasp for purchase, but finding nothing but air between my fingers as I'm being pulled, pulled, pulled . . .

The pain brings me back—a fire from which I'm reborn, Death himself pissed he didn't get to claim my soul.

My eyes snap open with a gasp of life that shoots through my lungs, my vision temporarily blinded with nothing but a glorious white light.

Malakyte's basic shape—an after image—flashes for a moment in time, fading away into the world before me.

I'm lying on my back in the field outside Zarmenia, several figures standing over me, but I can't focus on anything other than the intense burning sizzle on my chest as I blink in confusion. The sensation is identical to when I merged with Deimos's crystal . . . And the moment I think it, the newest crystal speaks to me in a psychic, telepathic way, as if it knows what's happened more than I do.

Ringer . . . it speaks. It wants a Ringer—it demands one.

Trinity is the first person I see, and without being able to stop it from happening, I intuitively feel her becoming my new, linked Ringer.

She begins hissing as she holds her hand up, the others jump up in confusion. "My hand!"

Ahren rushes to help her, a few others, too . . . Shante, maybe?

I release a trembling breath, and Gavrielle takes my hands in his, pressing them to his face, his cheeks wet with tears.

"Herkimer . . . ?" I say weakly, everything hurts.

"He's gone," Gav says, immense pride radiating off him as he looks down at me, his eyes red.

Oh, Gavrielle.

I feel our bond wrap around me, warm and solid and safe, as if it had been cut somehow. His Violet Sky color floods me, enveloping me as if he had been missing. *Gavrielle.*

Jance steals my attention from Gav as he leans over me on my other side. "You did it, darling. You did so good," he says, his voice drenched in emotion and pride and love.

I take one of my hands from Gavrielle and give it to my father.

He takes it quickly, bringing it to his lips as tears stream down his face.

"Jance," I say, looking up into his young face, a bit confused.

"It's okay, baby. I'm right here."

Something happened . . . but my mind is fuzzy . . . I don't remember.

I'm in a daze, the pain is still searing hot on my chest, and it's as if I was hit by a hover-bus.

Ahren comes back to take my vitals, and Pacey cries silently on Sylo's shoulder. But . . .

I gasp, suddenly remembering where I was right before my eyes opened. "Where is he?" I ask, looking around for him as I realize he's missing. "Where's Malakyte?"

They all go so very silent.

 776

My heart is thrashing all of a sudden. I try to go back to that place I was right before this. But the memory is collapsing like a dream does when you wake up. All the details and words he spoke to me flutter around my memory, but I can't grasp them. It was only a dream, right?

Wait . . . Didn't I just merge with another crystal? Whose?

"Gav . . ." I say, not seeing Malakyte anywhere.

But Gavrielle's face softens, looking almost guilty when his eyes flicker down.

I follow his gaze to my chest and nearly scream. All six symbols are there, but where there are three transparent marks that look faded, there are also three very solid, very dense ones, as well. My star, Deimos's, and . . . and . . .

Malakyte's crystal . . .

Malakyte's crystal.

Malakyte's crystal!

No . . . I don't want this! "Take it out!" Nausea comes on quick. "I don't want it, Gavrielle! He'll . . . He'll never let me go now!"

I sit up in a panic, both feeling the incredible urge to run and freeze and fight simultaneously.

"Love," Gav says, his face close as Jance pulls my loose hair out of my face. "His crystal was the only way to save you. He gave up his life . . . for you. You were dead."

Dead?

I vaguely remember blasting Herkimer into bits, but that's all I recall. Just lying in that strange world where I met Zariya and my mom and Ardelle, but I didn't see them that time. I only saw Malakyte.

I look at Gavrielle. "He's going to taunt me for the rest of my life. It's like he's inside of me now."

"Darling . . ." Jance says, rubbing my back. "He's not inside you. He was just a man. He's gone."

"Where is he?"

He isn't far, but they moved him so I wouldn't wake and see his dead body beside me.

Gav carries me to Malakyte, and everyone follows. His body lies as still as ice. Eyes closed, dark hair lackluster as it splays across the charred wheat. He's really gone. He's not coming back. He saved me in the end, and now he's just . . . *gone.*

Is this how it ends between us? With him sacrificing his long, arduous life . . . for mine?

I've lost Malakyte once today, but that small thread of hope still existed that I could revive him if I wanted to.

There's no reviving him now.

"What . . . how? I don't . . ."

I can't even form a sentence.

Gavrielle tries to make sense of this for me. "I was there, Kara. He didn't do this to taunt you. I genuinely think, in the end, it was an act of love. For the very first time in his life, he understood what it meant to love someone else. He wanted to save you because it was the right thing. Because he loved you."

A sob escapes my lips, and I clasp my hand over my mouth. The guilt that I feel for crying over him after all that he's done is shameful. Because I loved him, too. Despite how flawed he was, despite what he did, I loved him.

"I wouldn't have beaten Herkimer without him. He . . . he kept me going."

"We watched," Gav says. "We weren't sure what caused him to come around, but something did."

Malakyte saw the contrast in his father, saw his hate and didn't want to be that mirror another moment longer. Maybe he just wanted that cruel bastard dead? *To be set free,* as he had said. Or maybe he really did understand what love meant in the end.

I wanted that for him. Stars, I wanted to *save him.*

Yet, somehow, he saved himself . . . by saving *me.*

There's an echo of his voice inside my mind, like a memory slipping in and out of my consciousness. *"I love you, Karalevine. I'm sorry."*

I never doubted his love for me, but I did doubt his perception of what love was.

Not anymore.

He understood exactly what it means to love . . . and I'm alive because of it.

From villain to hero.

From darkness to light.

Freeing me from the guilt that my love for him wasn't so misplaced, after all. I didn't love a monster—I loved someone like me.

At the end of the day, the shades that make up him are the same shades that make up me . . .

"Who shot the arrow?" I ask dully, looking around at each of them in turn, but they appear confused.

Gavrielle asks, "What arrow?"

I think back to right before I killed Herkimer, wondering if I'm remembering what happened correctly, and I'm sure that I am. I explain to everyone what transpired in those final moments.

They look at each other, brows furrowed in uncertainty.

Sylo says, "His bow is around here somewhere, but we didn't have it. Nobody fired an arrow."

I open my mouth to argue, but I can't find the words.

"It was him," Pacey says before anyone else speaks, her voice confident. "It was Ardelle. I know it. I don't know how, but I do. The arrow you pulled from your shoulder, Kara, had to be the same one that got picked up by the wind your battle created. It hit home. Ardelle made sure it hit home."

I release a shaky breath, holding back my tears because I feel the truth as it seeps through my bones. There's no way that's some random coincidence. "We all would have died if it didn't."

The silence says it all. Without Ardelle's spirit guiding that arrow to where it needed to go, none of us would be alive right now, and Earth would be on the brink of full destruction.

Pacey nods, tears welling up in her eyes.

None of us say it, but I think the truth lands on target for all of us as we sit with the information presented. Ardelle's death was no accident.

His sacrifice was no coincidence, and I know for certain that one day, we will see him again.

We will love him again.

CHAPTER 127

THE ARIANYTE EMPIRE DECREE #168

EARTH IS A FREE PLANET ONCE MORE.

In no uncertain terms, Earth won the war against Arianyte. Team Starseed and I are with Trinity and her people at our new headquarters in Arianyte Tower two days later.

"Dammit, Kara!" Trinity says, slamming her fist onto the table as her eyes bop all around the sleek office, avoiding making eye contact with anyone. Her Honeycomb eyes are full of anger and color—the yellow glow flashes for several seconds before it flickers out again. "I can't control this new magic you forced onto me *and* get the entire planet back online at the same time. You could have made the pretty blond doctor another Ringer instead of me."

I lock eyes with Ahren, giving him a sympathetic smile. Turning back to Trinity, I say, "I saw your pretty face first."

She curses under her breath. "Girl . . ."

"At least we got the grid back on planet-wide," I say, trying to dispel the tension.

She's mad about being a Ringer? Well, I'm mad that Malakyte is essentially under my skin now, the crystal a physical representation of him *within me* for the rest of my life. His ghost has been haunting my dreams every single time I close my eyes. We won the war, the bad guys are dead, but all of us are forever changed.

Some of us lost our lives entirely.

Even the room we're in reeks of him. It isn't his office—only because I refused to set foot inside of it and made them move everything Malakyte used into a different room—but it has his fingerprints all over it. His sleek, dark taste, his look, his scent—*his everything.*

I can't even come to terms with the power they've given me, let alone confess how close I came to letting it consume me and everything else. Dannanōk said he'd help me control it, him and the dragons choosing to stay on Earth. After everything Malakyte put them through, they deserve peace.

Gavrielle points to the television as he stands close to me, where the photos of Malakyte's body have been disseminated to prove that the Arianyte leader is dead. I've seen the pictures. I can't look at them again.

"We got all the children Malakyte took back off the Vivianite, along with complete control of the vessel. Malakyte's body was a good bargaining chip and was the final piece of resistance we needed to demolish. Not having to storm that ship and take it by force is a huge win for us. Cheer up, Trinity. We're making good progress. And you'll get a hold on those abilities. I can help you."

Trinity glances up from one of the many Dezlar devices strewn across the table and throws Gav a smile, which lasts all of two seconds.

But Gav is right. Getting the Vivianite was a damn miracle.

Surprisingly, the last living member of the Ardeen family came to us.

Yesterday, after the news of Malakyte's death went public, Zoisyte sent word that she wanted to negotiate, and so we went.

We took control of the ship within minutes. There was no resistance.

With my Starseeds, Ringers, and the high rankers of the Resistance by my side, I got the final call on what to do with the ex-Empress of Arianyte.

"Where's the Council of Exstacé?" I asked her once all of us had collected in the throne room that reminded me of the color Gilded Cage.

Nobody sat on the throne yesterday, and only Zoisyte's personal SSPARROWs remained by her side, her handmaidens as well. Soldiers unmasked, her staff pale, and Malakyte's mother seemingly ready to accept what she believed to be her imminent death.

"They've fled," she said matter-of-factly, her affect dull considering the circumstances, but I can't judge her.

I vividly remember the words I said next.

"Since my husband, the crowned emperor of Arianyte is now deceased, along with the former emperor, I'm legally empress of this empire."

I feared Herkimer would have done some official nonsense to dethrone Malakyte, but there wasn't time. With the Council gone, only Zoisyte was left to challenge my authority.

Zoisyte's words were calm and melancholy when she said, "I will step out of your way without resistance—on two conditions."

"Which are?"

"Allow me, my staff, and guards to live and freely exit the Aurora System entirely. I have private land elsewhere that I can settle. I assure you I have no desire for power or ruling."

"And the other?" I asked.

"Allow me to bring my son with me so I can bury him where I settle. He deserves a proper burial."

Her requests were reasonable, but I still didn't like either of them. The thought of her taking Malakyte terrified me—it still does, as if she'll find some mysterious alien voodoo to bring him back to life again. But his autopsy was completed before we flew up to the mothership.

I agreed, telling Malakyte in my mind, *"We're even now. My life debt is paid."*

I've been talking to him a lot like this since I woke up in that field. Like he's now a part of me in a way that I'll never be able to detangle from.

Zoisyte said one final thing before we escorted her off the Vivianite. "I will instruct all my subordinates who run this ship to obey their new empress with all the loyalty they did for us. Karalevine Ardeen, you rule the stars."

The prospect is absolutely fucking terrifying to me, and as I peer out the window of Arianyte Tower, I question if I'm capable of handling all of this.

"About Ceplar . . ." Pacey says, sitting at the table typing on a laptop, then stops to explain Ceplar's medical situation.

Ahren's face falls flat. "The Tribute drug they injected her with has eaten away at her organ function, leaving her on the brink of death, if I'm being frank. She's not going to make it if we don't intervene. Even advanced Arianyte medicine isn't effective. Her body is rejecting any treatment. The only thing that's likely to save her is the Silent Breath."

I sigh heavily. "Gav and I confiscated what reserves of Silent Breath that were already manufactured and hid them, so no one else but me and him know where they are."

"Also," Jance interjects, "if we give it out for one person, then we'll be expected to do so continuously. I know that's hypocritical of me to say. However, the public knows about it now, so we have to walk this line carefully and ethically."

"If we use it frivolously like they did, we're no better than them," I say, feeling so much guilt for using what I have. "But she's one of us, and we can't let her die. We'll get her a dose, but unless one of us is also on the verge of death, it's a no-go. We're going to do things differently from Malakyte. So, don't ask me when you start getting wrinkles."

Jance is right. We're being hypocrites.

"So, you mean, I'm stuck with having it appear like I'm his sugar momma?" Saris motions to Jance, and the entire room looks at her like she sprouted three heads.

"Saris," Sylo says, voice overly surprised, "did you just tell . . . *a joke?*"

Jance chuckles, the sound deep and healthy as his eyes beam when he looks at her. "She did. And don't complain, Saris, you know you *like it.*"

Gross.

Trinity goes over some other stuff, like shipping off the extraterrestrial SSPARROWs, how we're going to establish order, dismantling all the insane decrees Malakyte put out when we were on the Azurite. We spent a long time—days—going over all this shit.

But ultimately, the way Arianyte was going to run was . . . up to me. We connected Zone leaders from around the globe who we felt weren't corrupt and who also wanted a democratic way forward. As for Terran officials like Pacey's parents, they weren't getting their positions back. For them, though, Ardelle's death seemed to damper all their thirst for power, and if Pacey feels safe and can assert healthy boundaries, then I'm supportive. We need to do better this time, pick better people to rule this world as a collective, not an empire.

That is what I want for the world. Freedom. Choice. A democracy where I don't rule over the world but where the world rules over itself. Malakyte got his freedom, and the people of Earth deserve theirs.

Many very qualified people are stepping up to help me—and by me, I mean us, Team Starseed and Trinity—because no way in fuck am I doing this alone. And these people are helping me understand how to go from rebel to empress. There's a lot to work out.

I'm not alone in this. My family is right here beside me.

ARABELLA K. FEDERICO

me understand how to go from rebel to empress. There's a lot to work out.

I'm not alone in this. My family is right here beside me.

CHAPTER 128

Gavrielle and I walk hand-in-hand across a field that's both familiar yet foreign, the grass and weeds nearly up to my waist as our footsteps crunch and bugs zip through the air on this sticky summer's breeze as the day shifts toward twilight. Several weeks have passed since the war ended, and we've done a lot to be proud of, but we both agreed there is one final task to be done before we can both put the past behind us.

Where it belongs.

The abandoned Naresteé Orphanage looms several hundred feet away as we trek closer to it, the sun setting behind those dilapidated walls that still seem to cry with the pain of the night they burned. The hole I blew in the side of the building is a gaping maw; nature having wrapped herself around its teeth.

"Are you sure you're okay with letting Naresteé go?" Gavrielle asks as I swat away a bug.

I shrug, still not happy about that decision, given everything we learned about her involvement in my mother's death. Jance and I were right. Malakyte had ordered Naresteé to kill my mother and take me. Naresteé confessed she planned on killing me that night. I think she wanted Malakyte for herself, but she wouldn't admit to that. When Naresteé couldn't make the kill, she dropped me off at a church. She then threatened the coroner to tell Jance that I was dead inside my mother—he had no idea that I was alive. The conversation was too dark to ask follow-up questions. Jance and I want Astoria to be at peace. Her grave, mercifully, did not get destroyed in the bombing of the undersewers.

"She doesn't have her Ringer powers anymore, so she's not as much of a threat. Plus, you and Pacey both wanted her to live, and she did save your asses up in Arianyte Tower, so respecting your wishes was more important to me than getting even with her."

"So mature of you, love."

I roll my eyes and bump into him playfully. "Oh, shut up, I'd still wish she'd crawl off and die."

We laugh together, but before long, we're standing at the main entrance to the orphanage, the wind gently blowing our hair, the cicadas singing exactly like I remember them doing every summer.

"It looks the same," I whisper, nostalgia hitting me like a rogue wave at sea. "It even smells the same."

Like musk and dust and wildflowers.

"It does, doesn't it?"

We stand in the entrance for a long, long time.

Gav asks, "You ready?"

"Not yet," I blurt, my heart pattering quicker, the sound reminiscing of the way the SSPARROWs boots sounded that late afternoon, on an early night exactly like this one.

He squeezes my hand tightly, then finally, we step past the main entrance and into Naresteé Orphanage.

We each feel a bit like ghosts as we walk through the place we first met, where we lived before everything changed.

Plates left abandoned on tables as light leaks in from the dirty windows, spearing over onto shoes and toys and books that lie covered in years of dust. The entire space is frozen in that moment Arianyte came for the two of us, those long tables now old, decrepit and eaten away by rodents and bugs and time.

Once we reach the top floor boys' room, where I blew the roof off, we're both really quiet.

"Do you think he meant for all this to happen when he gave Naresteé the order to come get us that night?" I ask, looking around at all the overturned beds, their frames bent and mangled, most of the bedding blackened or covered in moss and greenery. The building still bears evidence of the fire I created that night, despite most of it being covered in the plant life that found a home here.

Gavrielle contemplates my question. "I don't think he ever anticipated this outcome, his ego and arrogance so all-consuming that he couldn't have fathomed not getting everything he wanted. But you showed him from the very first night that you weren't going to bow to him. Even someone as powerful as Malakyte Ardeen, Prince of the Arianyte Empire, never stood a chance against you. My beautiful, strong, courageous mate."

It's strange that I can smile with such happiness and sadness simultaneously.

"Are you still having nightmares about him?" he asks, his hand coming up to graze my cheek.

I often wake up in the middle of the night due to Malakyte's constant haunts. Recently, however, if I don't immediately wake up Gavrielle with cries or dangerous power slips, I go to Jance instead. Saris hates it, even though she doesn't complain, but he kicks her out of their room for me, and it's the only time I can get any peaceful sleep at all. I feel bad but . . . I just need my father right now. I often fall asleep with Gav and wake up with Jance.

"A little," I say, not wanting to worry him. "Do you think it's him or just my mind screwing with me?"

"I think he'd want you to be happy after everything," Gav muses, having known Malakyte the longest. "I don't think he'd want to torture you like this from his grave. If anything, he learned his lesson, and that's why he gave his life for you. It's your subconscious that has to reconcile him being both your villain and your hero. A lot happened between you two, and it's only been a few weeks. Give it time, love. You'll find peace, I promise. Malakyte can't hurt either of us anymore."

I step into Gavrielle's arms, and as I turn my head, I see the pillar I hid inside that night, the loose panel broken into pieces on the floor. I nearly missed it entirely under dust and vines. Everything changed inside that pillar.

I changed inside that pillar.

"He did all this—caused a war all—so he could be with me . . . And in the end, he just . . . died."

Gavrielle shrugs. "I don't know. It seems like he got what he wanted most." I raise a suspicious brow at him, and he clarifies, "To be with you. In a strange way, he got exactly that. Didn't you say you feel like he *is* the crystal in some way? That, when he tried to kill you in the fields, he said something similar about your crystal, which is how he justified wanting to kill you?"

Pointing his head toward my marks, I realize he's exactly right.

Malakyte did get what he wanted in the end, didn't he? For us to be together forever.

"Do you think Deimos is lingering around inside me, too?" I ask, my soft laughter lightening the heaviness.

Gav laughs, too. "Man, I miss that cranky old bastard." He takes a deep breath in as the sun moves in, peeking in through the hole in the ceiling as if Deimos himself has popped in to give us the middle finger. "But, no, I don't think so."

"I agree," I say. "I think Deimos has finally allowed himself to rest."

"Me too."

We stand there, simply holding onto each other, taking in the moment, taking the time, taking the goodbye for what it is.

The end to this painful, yet strangely beautiful, chapter in our lives.

"Close your eyes," he says after a while.

I peek up at him curiously.

I'm suspicious, but I love how we play together, and after a few unspoken little jabs at each other through our bond, I finally do as he asks and close my eyes, hearing him rummaging through all the junk and foliage.

His footsteps crunch on his return, and I feel his strong body standing in front of me. "Open your eyes, love."

My lashes flutter open, and I gasp, the sound bouncing off the dusty cracked walls of this long-forgotten place.

Gavrielle holds a single dandelion in one hand, offering it to me just as he did that day.

No illusions this time, only the wish-ready dandelion in all its fluffy, perfect glory.

My eyes sting immediately, and I try to blink the tears away but don't succeed.

Gav clears his throat. "I saw it sitting over in the corner. The light was hitting it perfectly, as if someone up there was shining a spotlight right on it. I had to grab it for you. Just think . . . if you hadn't blown this roof off, it never would have found its way up here."

"Hmmm."

Gavrielle brings the dandelion up to my lips, his Violet Reign eyes dancing with cunning mischief.

The Gav I've always known and loved.

"Make a wish, Kara."

My hand gently rests on top of his as he holds the fuzzy stem, but I meet his eyes past the white fluff.

"All of mine have already come true."

"Oh, all this time I thought you were going to wish for a devilishly handsome, Sky-Fae male to be your sworn sex slave, but I guess I was wrong."

I snort. "You really know how to ruin a moment, you know that?" Shaking my head, my eyes dance across his cocky, smiling face.

"No way this moment is ruined. It's perfect."

"You got me there, but I actually do have a wish now."

"Oh?"

"I wish that Gavrielle Abraxas—who's my sex slave and all—takes me into the woods out back, presses me against one of those trees out there, and does devious, wicked things to my body until I'm screaming his name so loud the birds fly away."

Then I blow on the dandelion so the seeds fly onto his hair and into the air, gently floating to their new little homes.

"You know, I think that wish may just come true . . . but only if you're a good girl and ask nicely. Sex slave or no."

"I've always been a bad girl, Gavrielle—you know that."

His smirk is full of lustful, devious cunning as he presses me hard into his front, our bodies flush. "*My favorite.*"

I grin right back.

We take each other's hands and quietly walk out of the orphanage, finally able to leave this place behind. There's a sort of beauty in ending in the same place that something began . . .

As we exit, we do so far differently than we did the last time we left this place.

Together.

EPILOGUE

10 YEARS LATER

"I can't believe we're finally leaving Earth after all this time," I say, looking up into the sunset sky, the Vivianite floating in orbit as our farewell party at the house—which has remained Jance's—really gets going.

All our friends and family collected here to wish us goodbye and good luck on our ventures through the stars. Some of them are coming with us, some of them are staying here.

It's time.

Our search parties have found survivors of the Voidbringer on Gavrielle's home-world, so we're heading there first.

Jance, Gavrielle, and I sit on the swing seat in the backyard as their long legs gently push it back and forth. The two most important men in my life on either side of me.

Jance yawns. "Trinity still refusing to come?"

I snort. "Yeah, she's not coming, but leaving Earth in her hands seems like a good plan. We've got to leave one adult in the room, I suppose. Everyone else is coming, though. Besides the dragons. Dannanōk says they don't want to go back into space. I don't blame them."

A high-pitched voice breaks us out of our conversation as that little head of icy hair in the shade Snowflake runs up to us.

"Momma!"

"Oh!" I laugh as she leaps directly on the three of us, the four-year-old as fearless as her father and as stubborn as her mother. Not that she looks like me, though. *Damn Sky-Fae genes.* Although she does look so lovely with Gavrielle's stunning Lilac Petal eyes.

Adélla snuggles up in Jance's arms, one of her favorite people. He's just happy he gets to raise her with Gavrielle and me, having missed all those precious milestones when I was young. I'm happy she has him, too.

"Adélla," Jance asks, "are you excited to live in space for a little while? Or are you *scared?*"

She proudly proclaims that she is, in fact, already an astronaut and not scared of shit. Which tracks.

"And I'm going to fight all the space monsters with the space dragons and fight all the bad guys."

"We've been training a little too much, I think," Gavrielle chuckles, voice pretending to be serious.

For those two, there's no such thing.

Pacey shouts from somewhere in the yard, two practice swords in her hands, while Ceplar shakes her head beside her Starseed, twirling a third one. "Where is my niece, and why aren't we fighting? There's been no proclamation of victory, young lady! If you want to learn how to use that gravity magic, you've got to start young. Now get your butt back over here, or I'll put you through hacking drills again."

"Auntie Pacey is scary sometimes," she confesses, but I smirk anyway.

"She just wants you to grow up big and strong. You're a Starseed, you know. That comes with a lot of responsibilities."

Adélla looks down at her chest curiously, so innocently unaware of how precious she is to all of us. Ardelle's mark sits upon her tiny chest, his soul back where it belongs.

Back home, with us.

To say we were all stunned when she came out with his mark was an understatement. Ahren, who delivered her, instantly became a Ringer again the moment she drew breath. He was so shocked we all thought something was wrong, and that's when we found out. Right then and there. My love for Ardelle transformed into something so deep and profound, but he was his own person, just as Adélla is hers. Like I'm me, and Zariya is Zariya. We may share the same soul, but we're different people. Ardelle will live in all our hearts as Ardelle, and I'll forever love him for who he was and how he loved me and saved me in so many ways.

I will love you again, we had said to each other, and we were right.

Without looking back, she hops off the swing and charges toward Pacey, calling for Gavrielle to follow. He gives me an *If I could stop her, I would, but you know I can't so* . . . look and then he's gone.

I watch as they run into the yard, my heart full and happy.

Jance wraps his arm around my shoulders, drawing me close.

I rest my cheek against his shoulder, listening to everyone around us with a permanent smile on my face. Jance gently pats my head like he always does. We've made up for our lost time, and he's lived up to his promises to love me unconditionally in the way I desperately needed. I sometimes wonder how I could've ever doubted his love for me. Seems silly, in retrospect. But I've also grown to love myself now that I'm older and have a better perspective on life and love and what it means to be a part of a family.

"It's been a wild ride, hasn't it?" he asks.

I curl my legs up and snuggle deeper into him, his arms wrapping up around me as I allow myself to close my eyes and listen to the beautiful symphony of my life.

"It has," I agree. "I know I still struggle sometimes. Malakyte still haunts me on my bad days. But I'd go through it all over again if it meant we'd end up in this place at the end. I always thought I'd be that selfish girl who ruined every positive thing in her own life, but you and Gav and everyone else showed me that I could be more. Shit, even Malakyte showed me I could be more, in his own way. I'm grateful for that."

One eye cracks open, and I peek down at the wedding band tattoo still inked on my wrist. I couldn't bring myself to tattoo over it. Gavrielle's wedding ring sits on my finger where Malakyte's ring once was for an entire day, if I'm remembering correctly.

"I always had faith in you, kid."

I smile, believing him with my entire heart. Jance has restored my faith that a man can be good, and consistent, and gentle.

"I love you, Daddy."

He squeezes me tighter, pressing a kiss to the top of my head. "I love you too, baby. I always will."

When I open my eyes fully, I see a world that I fought so hard for flourishing and thriving, planet Earth an unrecognizable jewel of freedom with rights and choices. Now, ready to stand on its own as I go forth to do the same across the galaxy, planet by planet. Helping girls like me who are lost, hurting, alone, girls who need someone to see past their sharp, prickly edges to the beautiful queens underneath.

I'll do it until my dying breath, with my Starseed family by my side. Together, we can do anything.

The kicker is, I was capable of doing it all along. I just needed someone there to show me the way.

To show me I was worthy of being saved and loved and *seen*—by myself most of all.

You can't erase the parts of you that are ugly, dangerous, or dark, but you can carry them. Own them. Become the person who can hold both light and dark inside them and still shine anyway. I didn't destroy the world with my power like I feared I would. I allowed it to blossom.

A girl from the streets became a queen of a cursed empire, almost becoming the villain herself along the way. Finding my

way back was only due to my family's unwavering belief in my own goodness, strength, and worthiness. Without them, I know without a doubt that girl I saw in the mirror that day on the Azurite is exactly who I would have become. They, by far, are the most precious gift this journey gave me, because I saw what a person can become when they don't have love behind them.

I'll never forget it.

And I'll never forget the prince who loved me during the darkest, weakest, and most selfish days of my life, showing me that even darkness can be beautiful if I'm brave enough to love who and what I am at my core.

Never shying away from my many shades of Morally Gray.

THE END

Support

If you or someone you know is experiencing abuse, assault, or violence, you are not alone, and support is available.

U.S. Domestic Violence Hotline: Text BEGIN to 88788, or call the National Domestic Violence Hotline at 1-800-799-SAFE (7233) for 24/7 confidential help. Visit their website at www. TheHotline.org
U.S. Sexual Assault / Rape Crisis Hotline (RAINN): Call 1-800-656-HOPE (4673) or visit www.rainn.org to connect with trained support.

International Support
Discover local help for domestic or sexual violence through the NO MORE Global Directory or the HotPeachPages International Directory, both offering global, language-diverse resources.
In Europe? The WAVE Network provides access to national helplines across 46 countries.

You deserve to feel safe, to be heard, to be held. Reaching out is not weakness; it's the most potent kind of courage.

MORE BY ARABELLA

Did you love *The Mark of Shadows and Starlight* and the entire Mark of Creation Chronicles series? Consider leaving a review or simple rating on Amazon, Goodreads, or wherever you like to leave reviews. Also consider making a post on social media to share this series with other readers.

So, now that the series is complete, what's next? The audiobook for *The Mark of Shadows and Starlight* will be starting production immediately following publication and will be released early 2026. Also coming in 2026 is Arabella's next book, A Life Too Immortal. This medieval, gothic, vampire series promises a deadly tournament, a female villain, and one hot demon book boyfriend. Add A Life Too Immortal to your Goodreads TBR and stay tuned for the spicy, unique, celestial fantasy that you've come to love from Arabella.

If you're still stuck in The Mark of Creation Chronicles, there's one last piece of this amazing story that I saved specifically for you! A deleted, spicy scene from Gavrielle's perspective is available by clicking the link below! It's an extended scene of chapter 94 that was ultimately cut—but not forgotten! Click it and get you some Gav!

Links to all your favorite review platforms are included in the QR code's link below.

Acknowledgments

The Mark of Shadows and Starlight has been a long time coming. When I wrote *The Mark of Dreams and Darkness*, that book poured out of me and it was the easiest book I've written. That being said, *The Mark of Shadows and Starlight* was by far the most difficult. There were many plot elements that made it tough on a technical level. Did I truly have the skill set to pull this book off? I remember believing that I didn't. That, this is the story I should have attempted on my seventh or eighth book, not my third. But here I was, with nothing but a couple plot points, vibes, and one hell of a cliffhanger.

I've never shed so many tears on a book, either. When they say authors, "bleed on the page", I cried on the page—literally. Yet, through all these challenges the bigger picture eventually became clear. This book's theme touches on darker topics, but I think the obvious one is the discussion on toxic, abusive relationships. This topic specifically is one I took so incredibly seriously.

Victims of this type of violence are often stigmatized, misunderstood, dismissed, forgotten, overlooked, not believed, and underrepresented in media and books. I wanted to change that. There's many things in this book that I never personally experienced; Kara's story is fictional. However, this particular situation is familiar to me. This is why I felt it necessary to depict domestic violence not only in its entirety, but authenticity, as well.

Despite running the risk that it would make Kara unlikable Women are often harshly judged for not simply "leaving" their abusive partners or situations. This is why Kara made the choices she did, in the way she did. It was 100% intentional. That's how this stuff happens in the real world, and I wasn't going to sensationalize or throw rose-colored glasses onto this book for the sake of Kara's likability. She's never been particularly loved, let's just say, but she's real . . . and that's what matters the most to me. I hope Kara made you proud by the end of her journey. I hope this series concluded in a way that brought you joy, comfort, connection, hope, but most importantly, I wanted it to make you feel something. That's who I am as an author. It's important for me to say the things others are too afraid to speak out loud. I'll challenge you to see the world outside your lived experience. And if you're one of those few that understand Kara in ways you can't speak of, whose real-world life rubs up against the darker corners this book discusses, then I'll say to you: you're not alone. You've never been alone. I will be your voice, and I will do my very, very best to honor your strength as a survivor.

I never would have finished this series so strong if it wasn't for the amazing work from all the talented editors at Writer Therapy. Tanner Parks, you had such a massive manuscript to untangle, and you unraveled the core of this story and gave me a roadmap to follow so I could tell the story that was in my heart. I felt a little lost for a lot of this book, but after I got the manuscript back from you, I finally saw the path to the vision I had, and I'm so grateful for all the hard work you put in with the developmental edit you did. It was feat, so props to the amazing job you did. Everyone at Writer Therapy pitched in, including Chersti Nieveen, Andraea Jones, and Ben Stapley. I'll say that nobody in the industry understands story like you guys. Storytelling is such a deep, complex web of technique, art, science, and the human condition, and I'd be utterly lost without this team at my back. Editors can and do, in my opinion, make or break a book's success. This entire series has been edited by this team, and I know its success is because of your knowledge, skill, attention, and dedication to this series. Beginning and ending my debut series with you all has been an honor, and I have learned so much since we first met back in 2021, when I was just starting my journey. I am by far a better author, better storyteller, and better businesswoman because of your dedication and guidance over the years. Thank you for believing in me, in Kara's story, and this series. I think I've said in every one of these acknowledgements, that I couldn't do it without you, and that's even more true with this book than ever.

I'd like to thank Samantha Pico at The Goth Editor for your hard and dedicated work on the line and copy edits for this book, the proofreading, and formatting. You, too, have been with me since *The Mark of Chaos and Creation*, and my books would never have that final polish without you. I know you have my back and I am so happy to have you on my team.

Next, a big shout-out to Stefanie Saw with Seventhstar Art who did my beautiful covers. Another member of my team who has been with me from the start, your attention to detail and work ethic is unmatched. I'd also like to thank Florian Cavenel at Modefact Art, who made each of the beautiful custom weapons on the covers. I can't even count how many times I've sold this book because of these covers. The eye-catching, bright, colorful beauty of these book covers is unmatched. The story of how we came to work together still gives me chills, and I can't thank you enough for getting me in at the last minute and taking me as your client. It was meant to be, and I'll forever be grateful for your hard work and dedication.

To my audiobook narrators, who will begin production on *Shadows and Starlight* shortly after the print publication, I thank you in advance for the hard work I know you'll do with this book. Nikki Grey, Connor Brannigan, and Jon Vertullo did an amazing job on the *Dreams and Darkness* audiobook. Together, we paved a new path, redefining the very expectations of the industry by creating a hybrid of dual and duet narration. I was so happy with how it came together, and so were the listeners. I have no doubt that *Shadows and Starlight* will carry the same dynamic, epic, unique flare as *Dreams and Darkness* did. Nikki, you make Kara come alive, you embody her so perfectly, and I wouldn't choose anyone else to play her. I hope her story stays with you and inspires you long after the final page is turned. Connor, you humanize Malakyte in ways that make him so hauntingly relatable, I can't wait to hear how you finish his story. Jon, all of Gavrielle's spirit and charm comes alive because of you. I'm excited for all the jokes and sarcasm to come. A book like this one requires talent to execute and bring to life, especially with such heavy subject matter and complex characters. I know each of you work so hard to bring these characters to life. Making the audiobooks is beyond a highlight for me, it's one of my favorite things about being an author—especially having all three of you. It's cool and I admire each of your individual talents, and I appreciate you walking down this uncharted path with me to make my vision a reality.

To all of Arabella's Army, my readers, social media followers, and those I've met at events who come back year after year—from the bottom on my heart—thank you. I know how long you waited for this book, and it's my hope that the wait was worth it for you and that Shadow and Starlight ended in a way you felt profoundly—because it did for me. The tears that I've shed over this manuscript were unlike anything else I've ever experienced writing a book before. I'm not sure if that's normal or not, but what I do hope is that you felt it. That it translated to the page. We've always said how truly underrated this series is, and I hope now that it's finally complete, it'll get the love, attention, and success it deserves. All in all, the book and this series would be nothing with you. Your positive reviews, your posts on social media, your recommendations, your shares, likes, and comments—they all matter and they all push the needle forward. This series is special, it's unique, it's unlike anything else out there, and with you, my beautiful army, it will succeed. Of this, I have no doubt.

To my friends, I thank you for supporting me. I hadn't realized how many people in my real life actually picked up my books. We're taught as authors that our friends can't be our core readership, but I was still pleasantly surprised by your support. I also want to shout out all my fellow authors in the industry. My stars, do I love you guys. Keep kicking ass, and we'll take over the world together.

Big thanks to my mom, who supports me, my dreams, and is my biggest fan. I'll always strive to keep dreaming bigger.

There's one last person I want to thank for making this series happen, and that's myself. Publishing *The Mark of Chaos and Creation* was one of the scariest things I've ever done. Art of any kind is a terrifying endeavor. It isn't safe, it isn't secure, it isn't easy. However, along the way, I found that my heart was pushing me towards a greater purpose, and that purpose is these books. Writing is my destiny . . . and even though I'll always have things to improve upon, telling stories is what I'm meant to be doing in this life and living my dreams is a gift that I've given myself. I didn't let life get in the way, I didn't let my fear or excuses, or anything stop me like it had in the past. It's scary to live your dreams, but I have full faith that these crazy books of mine will find the people who need them most. People who will see them and love them and cherish them. I'm proud of myself that I finished them. I'm so grateful I took that leap of faith for myself. I'm so happy that I did it even though I was afraid. Even though I, too, am made of up blacks and whites and shades of gray, but that's exactly the very thing that needs to be shared, and for that—thank you for being brave.

#SaveKaraSaga
#TheMarkofCreationChronicles
#TheMarkofChaosandCreation
#TheMarkofDreamsandDarkness
#ArabellasArmy
#ArabellaK.Federico

About The Author

Arabella is a loving dog mom who enjoys art, roller skating, good TV shows and movies, and all things fantasy and supernatural. When she isn't writing she's often drawing character portraits for herself and other authors, making content on her social media accounts, and helping other aspiring writers realize the dream of becoming a published author. Arabella loves to inspire and teach the craft of writing to others and finds fulfillment in sharing her knowledge with the world in hopes she can give back to those who taught her along the way.

You can find Arabella on social media by searching Arabella K. Federico or by
visiting https://www.ArabellaKFederico.com. Arabella has a reader's only private Facebook group where there's special artwork and one-on-one access to Arabella all throughout the year. You can find the Facebook group by searching Arabella's Army on Facebook.